The Rogue Mage

The Sundered Web Book 2

Alex Thornbury

Shadow Lore
PUBLISHING

Shadow Lore
PUBLISHING

To Steve and Aileen. Long ago, you helped me cross the bridge to magic and to the future I never would have had. Thank you, from the depths of my heart.

SERAMIGHT
Salt Marshes
Wild Barrens
The Great Rift
Hunter's Forest
Maysea Islands
Springlands
Mountains of Fire
WINDHAL
Black Quarry
Al-Terren
Dac-Terren

Glossary of Terms from El'Sandria's Language

Amena, fia neda Arala Dia'Neka	You are not Arala the Daughter of Neka
Morta neda veria la fia	Blood does not lie for you
Aleaya	Daughter of the gods
Seeya neda veria	Speak no lies
Isa shamorg deiri fia si	'Tis shadow's heart you seek
Morna frya deari	Still the fire in your heart
Fia mana	You are mine
Afaya te mia	Dream of me
Ima lesa mana nera elesa, Aleyala	I gift you my dark soul, Aleyala
Afaya mana	Mine dream
Fenri nada mana elesa	Fear not my soul
Ledan nada mana deari	Shy not from my heart
Ima lesi mana elesa	I gifted her my soul

CHAPTER ONE

Al-Terren

"We remember the day, We, the many, became one ... one creature inside this body. It was the day we awoke in the world of Seramight, the world from our dreams. We remember seeing through the strange eyes of a man. Seeing much that was wondrous ... and yet not seeing what must be there. Seramight is not beautiful as Alafraysia is beautiful. It is not as magnificent or dazzling. And we grew uncertain. Then we, or rather the man who sheltered us, took a breath and touched his face and we Felt. *We felt the smooth, warm skin beneath our fingers, we felt the air rush into our chest ... we smelt it in his nose. Upon it, we smelt the odor of the man and felt disgusted. Aye, we* felt *that emotion, so alien to us. We heard the sounds of the world that we so long desired to live in. A world made of true stone and earth, water and air, and life. A solid, unchanging world which is more than a mere dream ... Then we saw our Tsarin Reval standing before us, fire and being as one. 'Your task, Bluelight is to write the history of our combined realms. It is to be a gift for my beloved Arala. 'Tis why I brought you to this world.'"*

The History of Alafraysia and Seramight,
By Mageguard Bluelight

They said all stories began and ended at the Bridge to Magic. The wise priests who knew such things, men who had listened to the tales of their forefathers, and old women who told them to their children.

But they were wrong. Stories *ended* at the Bridge. And then began anew. At least for those, like her, who had survived the crossing.

Elika crouched down and brushed the shimmering water as the old sea rolled over her shoes and retreated again. Cold. Icy cold for it was winter. She brought her fingertip to her lips. Salty. Just as Bill Fisher had told her. He was ancient and had seen the great sea that had once covered half of Seramight. That was before Syn'Moreg had sundered their world.

Her gaze ran over the sparkling water towards the dark chasm, and then beyond it, to the grey silhouette of the city she had left behind. Only this morning, she had stood on the other side of that dividing dark scar, gazing across at the vast, empty plains of rock and dust of the Deadlands. All her life, she had stared at them from across the chasm and wondered.

She was the last to cross the bridge before it unraveled, the last to walk towards that lifeless landscape. But magic was treacherous, and it had lied to them all. Instead of the deadlands, she was greeted by a vibrant world of color and life and men's voices. And a frightening feeling crept up on her; perhaps it was she who had lived in the deadlands all her life whilst life went on here, across the rift.

Her city was now a broken rubble—dull, lifeless, abandoned. All the lands beyond it had been destroyed by the Blight. Death reigned there now instead of man. There was no sea on that side. It had drained away long ago into the rift, leaving behind endless salt marshes and mud plains bestrewn with carcasses of ancient ships.

Yet here, on this side of the divide, the sea ran up to the chasm and stopped abruptly, held back from spilling over the edge by some force … by magic. The thought wormed its way into her. Magic. She was in the land to where it had been exiled, the land ruled by that untamed force, with no way back home. The bridge that had brought her here was gone. She had stabbed it and destroyed it. Some secret knowledge deep in her soul suspected she might have made a terrible mistake.

Voices cut through the crisp air, shouts and calls of alarm. She turned and faced the towering city wall of the other half of Terren. For six hundred years, men believed this half of their city had perished in the great cataclysm. Yet, here it was, built from the same silver-veined grey stone, only larger and fiercer than before. The streets, which once joined with those on the other side, ran to the edge of the fissure. The houses, which had once stood across Rift Street, were a mirror of those she had left behind. But that was where the similarity ended.

Here, the residents had built an enormous outer wall between their city and the chasm, capped with towers and battlements, as if against a giant enemy threatening them from the Abyss. The wall encircling the city had sprung up behind abandoned old buildings and ran into the sea on one side, and along the coast on the other. Even from here, she could see enough to know that this Terren had grown and grown whilst her world had been shrinking.

In front of a circular stone courtyard was a squat city gate, tall enough for a horse and rider to go through. The portcullis was raised but seemed unwelcoming. It faced the chasm across the courtyard. There, she saw the upturned cobbles and the gouges in the ground where the roots of the bridge had once held firm.

She beheld the empty courtyard. Turned to take in the empty beach and the old cobbled road along the other half of Rift Street. Turned again, and an ache rose in her chest. No one was waiting for her. Neither Mite, nor Penny, nor her parents. Her parents had died crossing the bridge. Penny likely thought her dead by now. And Mite … he had left her behind to find a new life for himself. Did she truly expect him to be standing here waiting for her?

Aye, you did, a voice inside her mocked. *Foolish that you are.*

Bells began to ring.

"Dae-Terren!" Men shouted from atop the city wall, and the guards rushed to the parapet to stare and point at the city on the other side of the rift.

Folk emerged from the gate into the empty courtyard. They were clad in loose clothes made of strange, brightly colored cloth. Some wore shimmering garb and plaited their hair with silver lace. No one was looking at her. The ruinous city from where she had come transfixed them, as if they had never seen it before.

"'Tis Dae-Terren … it's real," said a boy in wonder, as he came to stand beside her.

"'Course it's real, you fool," replied an old woman next to him. "Where do you think all them damned Daes came from?"

They spoke in the common tongue of men, but with a soft accent unfamiliar to Elika's ears.

"Where did the fog go, Nan? Do you think it's Ilikan who's up to no good again?"

"Now, how am I to know that? Besides, it's Reval who controls the clouds, and fog is like clouds, ain't it?"

More folk came to stand on the beach. "Hey, you, Dae, did you just cross?"

Elika felt eyes on her and turned.

"You, boy, aye. Did you just cross?" The man who spoke was staring straight at her.

She shook her head and walked into the crowd, away from his suspicious frown.

More and more folk piled out of the squat gate, and she shoved past them towards the city.

"Where's the bridge?" she heard someone ask.

"What happened to the mist?"

Aye, there was an impenetrable mist when she crossed, but it disappeared soon after the bridge fell into the Abyss.

The crowd grew thicker. The guards joined them, too, scrutinizing the newly uncovered old street and crumbling houses. She needed to get away before more of them realized she did not belong. She had to find a quiet place to think.

Out of nowhere, a dark shadow fell over them, as if a thunderous cloud had blocked the sun. Elika looked up … and gaped in horror. Up in the sky, a mountainous island of rock and gardens floated towards them. It spun and turned, as if it did not know which way was up or down. A crystalline palace lay in its though her dress seemed plain compared to the man's gold-leafed coat.

"Been here a while," Elika lied. She could tell from their faces that they did not believe her. In her rough spun trousers and shirt, she must look like a beggar to them.

"Mummy, is that a barbarian from the other side?" the boy whispered to the woman.

"Aye, dear, 'tis one of them. He's from Dae-Terren."

"Where magic-haters live," he breathed, eyeing her with wonder.

"Shush. The old race has not been civilized like us."

"Pa says they're invaders come to destroy our world, like they destroyed their own."

"Your pa's not wrong, boy," scoffed the man in the suit. "Get the guards before this one causes trouble."

Elika noted that he did not step closer to her himself.

"Might be the guards are too busy cleaning up the mess," she snapped and pushed past them. The woman gripped the boy as if she thought this barbarian might kill him.

None of them followed her outside.

In the street, the destruction left by the vortex was reminiscent of a war. Men and women lay lifeless on the ground, like broken dolls in pretty dresses. Others were walking around, dazed. Roofs had been ripped off and buildings lay in ruins. None of it seemed real. Elika hugged herself and walked in the opposite direction to the folk rushing to help the injured. She needed to find a place where the eyes of these people did not follow her.

This was Terren, her home, yet she did not recognize any part of it. The unfamiliar streets and unknown faces disorientated her senses. Everything was brighter, the colors more vivid. The blue sky itself seemed wrong, whilst the air was thick with some vital force. She felt it deep in her bones. Reach out and she might touch it. Even the familiar grey buildings of old Terren were more vibrant somehow. And she felt as if she had awoken from a dream into a stark and frightening reality.

She turned into a quiet, dead-end alley and ducked behind a large plant pot with a small tree growing from it. She crouched against the wall next to a closed door and tried to gather her scattered thoughts.

She had crossed the bridge—almost died crossing it. Instead of the Deadlands, she had found herself here in Terren … the other half of Terren they had thought destroyed. The folk here had not died six hundred years ago when Syn'Moreg sundered their world, but lived on. These were the descendants of those who had long ago vanished. They must have known there was another world across the chasm. Many had crossed from it. The incomers from her world must have carried tales of another Terren. But why did no one cross from this one into hers? Might be because these descendants believed her kind to be uncivilized barbarians, she thought with rising bitterness.

Magic-hater, the man had called her. His scorn-filled words did not sit easily in her mind.

Scarcely a moment ago, magic had torn the city apart and killed those poor fools who got in its way. Only in tales of long ago, when the tsaren still lived in their world, had she heard of such dire things.

A terrible realization finally struck her. The tsaren, the enemies of mankind, the ones who had started the Sundering War—were here. They had not vanished or died, only crossed the bridge long ago. She had not merely stepped into another world, but another time which her own people had long ago resigned to history.

Was there a human king here also?

The cutting cold from the stone at her back pushed that thought aside. Winter chill had crept into her body, numbing her hands and feet. Overhead, clouds had gathered, threatening snow. She had lost her cloak and would not survive the night if she continued with these useless musings about kings and tsaren, instead of finding shelter.

She caught sight of her trousers—ragged, dusty and torn. Her clothes betrayed her as a Dae and drew attention to her. She needed new garb to blend in with the locals. Might be she'd find a gang of orphans to join, or an abandoned building for shelter. Either way, she could not hide here all day.

She rose and examined the iron-studded door beside her. The lock was unlike any she had ever picked. Instead of a hole for the key, there was a brass insert for a medallion. She could not pick it and steal inside. Neither could she see an easy path to the roofs. So she emerged from the alley and chose a direction to follow.

The old, grey bones of this city reminded her of home. This was Terren. She knew this city, knew how to survive on its streets. She just needed to relearn the streets all over again, that was all. Surely its people could not have changed that much. They were human, after all, and spoke in the same common tongue.

The clouds grew darker and darker, and dropped their snow— thick, heavy flakes, the size of a babe's hand, larger than she had ever seen before. Unnaturally so, she thought grimly and hugged herself against the biting cold.

Everything was different here, but she refused to allow fear any sway over her heart. She had been raised on the streets, lived on them most of her life. This was no different. Search for the familiar; that was how they had taught the new orphans to survive the unknown.

She forced herself to look more closely, but try as she might, the differences were too many and overshadowed the familiar. The houses might have been built of the same grey brick, but the windows were fashioned of colorful glass—red, blue, yellow, green and too many other colors to name. The folk were human, but their clothes were far too fine, regardless of whether they were gentry strolling by or washerwomen with baskets of laundry by the wells. Chickens had strangely colored feathers. Horses had their manes plaited with red and gold lace, and the carts rolling past were brightly painted.

With every step, she had to remind herself that she was still in the Realm of Seramight. This was merely the other half of her world. This was still Terren, its folk the descendants of her kind. She was glad they had not perished, glad the city lived on.

Suddenly, a building moved beside her and black branches tangled in her hair. She cried out and leapt back in fright, leaving behind a clump of her hair. The strange house, woven from magic, stood side by side with those built of stone. It reminded her starkly of the bridge she had crossed into this world. The black walls were a matted web of slick, slithering tendrils. There were silvery windows you could not see through, and no door she could discern. No one around her paid the monstrous house any mind. Instead, *she* was the one they regarded with unhidden disdain.

"Bloody Dae magic-haters," someone sneered in passing.

Elika quickly walked on, trying to appear unafraid.

And in that instant, as if her eyes were suddenly opened, she saw another, even less familiar city. This Terren, unlike her own, was infused with magic. It lurked everywhere. A barrel walked past on spindly black legs. Elika jumped out of its way and watched it walk down the stairs into the cellar of a tavern. Further ahead, the street widened around a thick limbed tree with branches twisted and plaited towards the ground. There was a blue obelisk made of water in the center of a courtyard. Children darted through it and laughed when they came out dry.

Find the familiar, she reminded herself. But the prevalent sense of magic would not allow her to forget that she was far from home. Much farther than the span of the chasm she had crossed to reach this place.

As if on instinct, her feet turned in the direction which would have taken her towards Riftside, and back towards the Hide. She wanted nothing more than to go home. Penny was here somewhere. Walk back to the Hide and see Penny and her pack …

Elika shook her head to clear it. Her mind was wandering. The day was fading, and her fingers and toes were numb from the cold. The snow had been melting on her, and her clothes and hair were damp and icy. Panic set its claws into her. She had to find shelter, or else steal a warm blanket before her mind wandered its way into oblivion.

She looked around frantically. A man caught her eye. Like her, he stood out from the others on the street like a goat amid the doves. He was clad in a drab garb made of fabric she recognized as being from her world. It was more than the clothes that marked him as one of her kind. His hands were buried deep in his pockets, and his shoulders were hunched as he regarded the magic around him with deep suspicion. He was subdued and edgy, like a thief caught in another man's home. He gave a magic-woven building a wide berth and was still startled when the branches moved.

Excited to find another person from her world, she crossed the road towards him.

He slanted his gaze her way, seeming neither surprised nor interested to see her. Around his neck, he wore a silver band stamped with a mark of three faces and a small hook where a chain might be fastened.

"You're … one of us," she whispered when she caught up to him.

"What do you want, kid?" he said and lengthened his stride.

His abruptness took her aback. "I … I'm looking for someone … a friend. We were separated when we crossed the bridge."

"Leave me alone before they think we're conspiring against them." He glanced around as if afraid to draw attention. "I don't fancy ending up in the back of one of them prison wagons headed for the temple."

"If you'd just tell me where to find our kind …"

He sighed with impatience and stopped. "One of the last ones to get here, hey? Look. This is how it is. Your friend's likely in one of the many workshops they put us all in when we arrive. At least those of us who can't buy our own freedom. Do you see any beggars or street urchins here?" He waved his hand at the street.

She had not thought about it. But now she realized that there were no orphans on the street, no sign of gangs, not a single beggar huddled in some corner, who she could speak with. Worse still, there were no ruined or abandoned buildings to hide in.

"Not a bad thing either, if you ask me," he continued. "Your kind used to rob me of my last pair of shoes in Dae-Terren."

"My kind?" she echoed, confounded by his hostility.

"Aye, damned street brats, thugs and gangs. Well, they don't tolerate thievery here. So be on your way. If you've half a penny worth of sense, you'll find a kindly master to offer yourself to before the mages get hold of you. You dress like a boy, but I suspect there's tits beneath that shirt. The mages won't be fooled by your disguise, brat. They have a lust on them somewhat fierce." With that, he crossed the street as if he could not be rid of her fast enough.

Her heart sank. There was no help from her own kind either, it seemed. She noticed more and more Daes, all wearing metal collars around their necks. None of them paid her any mind, or each other, for that matter.

Out of nowhere, someone grabbed her arm. She looked up in fright into the stern face of a fat pouch in fine silks with a jeweled brooch on his scarf. "Who is your master, Dae?" he asked in a soft accent.

"My master …?" she stuttered.

His grip tightened. "It's a crime to be a beggar. Come with me."

She tried to yank her arm back. "I'm not a beggar."

The folk on the street watched them with shaking heads. She imagined how she must look in their eyes, dressed in foreign clothes, scruffy and lost.

"If you've no money, then you're a beggar," the man hissed. "You certainly dress like one. No self-respecting master would send out his servants dressed like that. And where's your collar?"

"I don't have a master," she objected.

"Then where's your freeman's mark?" He showed her the back of his other hand, with a small gold tattoo of a circular rune marking his skin.

In one smooth motion, she snatched her knife, cut his hand, broke free, and ran. Women jumped aside with a screech. Men tried to grab her. She searched for somewhere to hide but saw only pretty stalls and neat shops, and she cursed her carelessness. Somehow, she had blindly stumbled into a wealthy quarter of the city, where she looked like a beggar in truth.

She turned a corner and ran into two guards. One grabbed her arm with a crushing, iron grip. "Another Othersider without a master," he said with the local accent. He had a ponytail tied with a long piece of leather strap. "No mark on him either."

"We'll take him to the magistrate," said the other with a healing cut on his lip and a bruised jaw. "Must have crossed recently."

With a wash of relief, she realized he spoke with the familiar tongue of her people. She gazed up at him pleadingly. "I stole nothing … I've done nothing wrong."

Pity touched his eyes. "Not like home, hey, kid?" He smiled kindly. "There are no orphans running the streets here. But don't be afraid. You won't be harmed. They'll just find you a master. Everyone earns their keep. No begging's allowed."

Elika had never had a master. The idea frightened her more than finding herself alone on the streets at night in this snowstorm. She imagined being locked in a pitch-dark cellar, having been beaten and worse.

She wriggled in the other guard's solid grip, then reached for her knife too late. Manacles snapped around her wrists.

"Stop struggling, or we'll have to knock you out, too," said the guard with the ponytail. The threat, though mildly spoken, had steely authority behind it.

Elika stilled. She was no use to herself unconscious.

They did not lead her far. The magistrate's office was in a house beneath an arched wall spanning a wide road. Along the road, tall statues of winged animals rose between each doorway. Archers patrolled the wall above the street. They were not watching the streets, however, but the sky and the floating island hovering menacingly over the city whilst rolling this way and that.

The guard yanked her arm towards the house under the arched wall. Inside, a fat, officious man was writing in a ledger at his long desk. Thick books of different colors lay in a pile in front of him. He wore a fat gold chain with a heavy medallion hanging of it.

When he looked up at her, it was with bored disinterest. "Another Dae," he drawled, and his jowls wobbled. He put aside his quill, pushed away the ledger he was writing in, took a great big blue tome from the stack of them and opened it. "When will it end, I ask you?" he complained to himself and dipped his quill into the inkpot. "Othersider, are you? Recently arrived. Damned mess this is. An invasion is what we thought it. Well, out with your name, girl."

"Girl?" the guard with a cut lip whispered to the other, and they stifled a snorting laugh.

"I'm … Lika," she said.

The magistrate wrote it dutifully in his ledger. "Parents," he said without raising his face from the page.

"Don't know them. They're dead."

"Age."

"Sixteen … I'm told."

"Alone or with family here?"

"I'm alone." The words choked her, and the cold reality of that seeped deep into her bones. She was alone in a world where nothing was like it should be. Mite was not waiting for her as he had promised. And she did not know where Penny might be. Everything here was alien and wrong. The people, the way they spoke and dressed, their laws, and the way they regarded her with a mix of disgust and pity, as if she was a wounded wild beast.

"How many more of you are left there?" he asked dully.

One of the guards cleared his throat. "It seems there won't be any more coming. The bridge is gone."

"Gone?" The jowls wobbled. "Where has it gone to?"

The Dae guard shrugged. "Just not there anymore. Only the chasm with no way to cross it."

The magistrate's surprise dissolved into relief. He made another note in his ledger, finished writing, picked up a magnifying glass in a silver frame and peered at her through it. Immediately, he recoiled, lowered the glass to look at her, then raised it again. The glass distorted and enlarged his surprised eye. It blinked.

"Hmm," he said and placed the eyeglass on the table. "Strange, but who am I to argue with magic? If it shows me a spider, a spider she is."

Elika's heart stuttered. How could the glass know she was Eli Spider? That had been her street name. What else did the treacherous magic know about her?

"Take her to Mage Aeon-Rah in Yarn Row. Seems magic wants her to weave. She is his property now. He'll know where to place her." The fat magistrate waved them away and turned his attention to the next guard who came in, holding a prisoner in chains.

"Caught this one stealing," said the guard.

Elika started as a greasy, unshaven prisoner was led inside. Blood Dog. He saw her too and laughed roaringly. "Well, well, look who's here, a little cunny from the past."

Elika ducked her head as she walked past him.

His guard yanked him towards the magistrate. "A Dae, claims to be a freeman, but got no mark to prove it."

The magistrate sighed. "All Daes claim to be freemen. Want something for nothing, they do. You have to buy your freedom, you worthless vermin. Same as you buy a horse or a rug."

Blood Dog spat on the ground. "I was born free, and I'll cut the throat of any man who says otherwise."

Their voices faded as Elika was led outside. The snow was still falling thickly, and she shivered violently. One of the guards whistled and waved a horse-drawn carriage forward from a line of them. As it drew closer, she saw that it was not a carriage, but a prison wagon. They pushed her in the back and closed the gate behind her. Slowly, understanding of the magistrate's decree seeped into her cold-numbed mind. She was to be taken to a mage as a prisoner ... as his property. The horror of all that meant cut through her.

The prison wagon lurched and drove onward. She strained against the numbing cold to remember everything she had ever heard of the vile mages. They had existed long ago, and each tale of them she recalled was more terrible than the last. Men hated and feared them for their cruelty and spite, or so the stories told. Mages in turn hated men. She had to escape. But the guards at the back of the wagon were watching her closely.

Never before had she been caught by the guards. But others had. Few returned unmolested, unbeaten or with their fingers intact. The cutting cold was making it hard to think, to plot. No one was coming for her, she had to think sharply to survive. Her knife was still tucked in her belt. And she had her own magic to draw on. *Fight and run*, whispered her frightened heart.

Aye, she could run ... but where?

The wagon rolled through unfamiliar streets. The light was fading fast, her wet sleeves were growing frost crystals and her body was numb. She doubted her fingers could grip the knife even if she could reach it.

The wagon came to a stop outside a house woven of water and seaweed, with small fish swimming in its walls. It looked like an absurdity wedged between the grey-stone human homes. The door was made of beaten copper with an engraving of a wave encircling a sewing needle.

Coherent thought fled her. "What will the mage do to me?"

The young guard from her world unlocked the cage door and helped her down. "'Tis not so bad as you think. He'll just place you with a master so you can earn your keep. No more stealing and begging for you."

As the cold invaded her body and her stomach tightened with hunger, being placed with a master suddenly did not seem so bad. She would gladly work for a warm bed and a bowl of hot goat stew. Might be it was time she earnt honest coin.

The guards approached the strange house without fear, and she borrowed her own bravery from them.

Inside, a human servant told them to wait in the hall whilst Mage Aeon-Rah was notified of their arrival. As they waited, Elika's gaze roamed over everything in sight. There was nothing here that looked like it was made by human hands—mirrors, vases, urns and even flowers all belonged to a different world. There was also an odd hollowness to everything she saw, as if it was a reflection, or a drawing come to life. Edges seemed to merge with air, and colors shifted as if undecided what they should be. She had a strong urge to touch the urn close by to see if it was real.

A large figure appeared above the stairs, and her every thought faded and died. None of Bill's stories of mages could have prepared her for their reality. The man, if he could be called that, was dressed in night robes as if he had been pulled from his bed. He came down the stairs, inelegantly, awkwardly, clutching the bannister as if he had never mastered the proper use of his legs. A deep sense of repulsion shook her. Mage Aeon-Rah was grim-faced, ugly and foul, though she could not grasp the essence of the foulness that hung about him. He was pallid, wan and oddly waxen. As he drew closer, she caught a faint stench of death and decay, masked by a thick layer of sweet perfume. Instinctively, she recoiled and took a step back, bumping into one of the guards behind her.

The mage regarded her with equal disdain. His eyes were bleached of color. With a fumbling movement, he produced an eyeglass, akin to the magistrate's one, and peered at her through it. There was neither surprise, nor interest in his face.

"The spider and the princess." His voice was as vile and strange as he. It sounded as though two men spoke at once, each one echoing what the other said, but not exactly. "*The princess and the spider,*" echoed another voice from deep in his throat, though his lips did not move this time. "How ... quaint," he said before that other voice stopped speaking. He lowered the eyeglass. "We can make no sense of this. But aye, she must be a weaver. Mistress Oblana had another ungrateful wretch run away. Perhaps magic sends this one to replace her. Take this she-human to Yarn Row." He waved dismissively in her direction. "We will send the finder's fee to the magistrate in the morning."

The guards bowed as if the king himself addressed them. "As your eminence commands."

Ire rose in her at their deference. *When had men begun to bow to magic?*

The mage turned away.

"How long am I to serve this woman?" Elika asked.

His back stiffened. Slowly, he turned. "Insolent she-human," he hissed. "*She-human,*" hissed another voice inside him. "You do not address us until we demand it."

"Am I a prisoner?" she persisted. "I committed no crime."

"This is Al-Terren, Dae. You are a bonded servant from the day you come into this world, no matter the manner of your entry. The cost of freedom is fifty sherrings, as set by the laws of Archmage Tridamor. Do you have wealthy parents or perhaps a freeman lover who might purchase your freedom from us?" When she did not reply, he huffed. "Then you must work until you have the coin to buy it yourself."

"Is the same true for you, too, mage?" she asked before she could stop herself.

"Watch your tongue, she-human, before we decide to remove it."

Black tendrils of magic appeared from nowhere, crawling over her face and prying their way into her mouth. She cried out and tried to claw them away.

"*Remove her tongue,*" an echo added beneath his horrid voice. "*Rip it out.*"

Then the strands vanished. Her tongue was still there. She staggered back from the mage in horror.

A hand fell on her shoulder and squeezed. "No more questions," the Dae guard said to her. "Forgive her, master. She's recently arrived and hasn't yet learned our ways."

Elika lowered her gaze, feeling grateful to the guard for saving her from her stupidity.

The mage huffed and turned away. "Then she'd better learn quickly," he threw over his shoulder and began to climb the stairs in the same awkward way, as if his feet could not decide which one should go first or where they should step when they did.

Distracted with watching him, Elika did not notice a servant approach until it was too late. A silver choker snapped shut around her throat. She gripped the metal collar and tried to rip it off, but there were no clasps or seals she could feel. Her fingers ran over a smooth metal band.

"Too tight," she gasped and tugged.

The guard stopped her. "It's not tight. Breathe calmly. You'll be used to it soon enough. It won't strangle you … unless your mage master wills it." He said the last as a quiet warning, giving her a meaningful look.

She fought to steady her breathing. "How is it you're not wearing one of these?"

"Only freemen can join the city guard, so the captain paid for my freedom. There's coin in each legion's war chest. It's twenty years of service to pay it back."

"Do they take girls as guards?" she asked almost hopefully.

The guard laughed and ruffled her hair.

In the mirror, she caught sight of an engraving in her collar of a wave encircling a sewing needle. The same mark was etched into the seamless collars of Mage Aeon-Rah's servants. The collars that could strangle them. That thought churned and churned in her head as they led her away.

It was dark by the time she was brought to stand before another house three streets along. It was a shop with lavish fabrics displayed in the windows. Around them, the streets had grown quiet and shops locked their doors. Fresh snow covered the road and paths, cleansing them of signs of men's passage.

The guards took her along a side path. They removed her manacles and led her into the house through the back door. The heat hit her immediately, dizzying her with the pleasure of it. She was in the kitchen, where a large stove and cooking fire took up most of one wall.

A plump woman with her sleeves rolled above her elbows was working dough. The first thing Elika noticed about her, was that she was a freewoman, who did not belong to a mage. She scowled at them from under her sweaty hair. "What's this then? Another Dae? Ain't there any nice girls left in this city save for these magic-haters who take their fill of our food then run away?"

"Ask Mage Aeon-Rah, woman, or hold your tongue," answered the guard.

The cook wiped her hands on a cloth. "I'll tell the mistress then, since there's no other servant left in the house. And I dare say the mistress will be sending me away soon, too. Had one customer in three days. How are we to feed another worthless mouth, you tell me?" She disappeared through the open door.

They did not wait long before a prim, stern Mistress Oblana appeared in the doorway of the kitchen. "An Othersider?" she said with uncontained annoyance. "I asked for a local, Alterrian girl. Why did you bring me this useless wretch?"

The cook returned to rolling the dough. "It's what I said to them. She'd do better for the mills."

"Mage Aeon-Rah sends her," said the Dae guard as he warmed his gloved hands by the cooking fire. "He says she's to weave. Our job is only to deliver."

"The last girl he sent was useless," said the mistress. "In the end, I was glad when she run away. Even gladder when they caught the wretch and sent her to the mines." The woman came forward, looked down her pointy nose into Elika's face and regarded her as she might a maggot climbing up her boot. "Which workshop have you come from?"

"Arrived recently," replied the guard for her. "You are her first master. Ahem … mistress, that is."

"Well, at least that's something," said Mistress Oblana. "I hate it when they bring bad habits from indulgent masters. Meena!" she yelled.

Immediately, a young woman with an unkind face appeared. She wore a plain frock. Three golden plaits fell down her back. When she saw Elika, instant dislike lit her eyes. Meena did not wear a metal collar. But on her wrists, she wore two gold bands etched with the mark of a bird carrying a piece of yarn in its beak.

"Take this girl to Tikka's old room," the mistress instructed. "Tomorrow morning, she will begin work." She scrutinized Elika's collar. "And make sure she is stamped with the mark of my workshop. I do not want her getting lost or thinking she can run away. And I'll be damned if anyone tries to steal another of my girls."

"As you say, mistress," Meena said politely and smiled at Elika in a way that promised some cruelty to come.

After the guards left, Meena led her to the uppermost room, under a low sloping roof. She was a head taller than Elika and carried herself with airs befitting the daughter of a lord.

"Sit there," she pointed at the chair beside the table.

Elika did as she was told. Meena sat across from her, and with the tip of a thick needle began to engrave. The needle appeared to be made of similar metal to the magical collar. There was a faint blue hue to the silver. Whilst Elika waited, she noticed in the mirror that Meena was engraving the mark of a bird with a yarn in its beak.

Without warning, the needle pressed deep into her skin. Elika gasped in pain and surprise. She grabbed Meena's hand to stop the needle from digging deeper.

The girl's icy eyes were hard. "I know your kind, Dae. I hate the barbaric sound of your voice. And I wish you'd never come into our city but stayed where you were in your barbaric world."

Elika made not a sound, shocked by her viciousness. The shock quickly cooled to anger. She was Eli Spider, no one threatened her. At least no scrap of a whelp like this chit.

But the foolish girl did not know this. "In this house, I'm your mistress," she continued blithely. "And you'll do as I say. One mistake and I'll beat you. You're here to work, and if you don't earn the money for my mistress, you don't eat."

In one quick move, Elika pushed away Meena's hand, grabbed the girl's hair and slammed her face into the table. The girl screeched, covered her bloodied nose and ran out, dripping blood through her fingers as she went. That was the way they dealt with mindless bullies in her pack.

Then Elika waited.

Shortly, Mistress Oblana came up, stiff but composed, holding a skinny long cane. "Turn around, girl."

Elika did, unafraid, shaking only with anger. The mistress hit her with the cane, once, twice, thrice until an inadvertent groan escaped her.

Then she grabbed Elika's neck and pushed her to her knees in front of an ugly, misshapen, black stone statue. It was decorated with the bones of small animals and dried flowers.

"This is the shrine to magic. You will pray for its favor each night before you go to bed. If magic favors you, you will be a good weaver. If not, you will be sent to the mills." She leant in closer to Elika's face. "Magic hates vicious little rats like you. So watch your manners."

Abruptly she was released. The door closed. The lock turned.

Once the footsteps had retreated on the stairs, Elika rose to her feet. Her back was throbbing and her shirt stuck to her bleeding wounds. She strode to the window, unlatched it and flung it open. Relief flooded her. The roofs were her escape. They had always been her freedom. Without thought, she climbed out.

Icy air hit her like another sharp cane. The snow continued to fall, the skies were heavy with clouds. The floating island was lit up against the night sky as if swathed in sunshine.

Elika hugged herself and looked around, seeking a path, a place to go, and her heart froze at the city's enormous expanse. In six hundred years, this half of Terren, had grown far larger than the one she'd come from. In the light of the torches, she could make out the old wall. Al-Terren now extended beyond that long-forgotten boundary, and two more dividing walls had been erected. A great black outer wall with many towers like fangs along it surrounded the outer reaches of the city, as if straining to contain its swell.

The cold grew sharp and piercing, but at her back, warmth crept from her small attic room, treacherously enticing. She did not need to run, at least not yet. The cage had a secret escape after all. She climbed back inside, closed the window and sat on the bed.

Was it only that morning she had found the courage to cross the bridge? Only that morning she had plunged into the chasm? Just a few vague hours ago that she had been certain only the barren Deadlands awaited her here?

She blew out the candle and curled on her bed, wishing only for sleep. Might be when she awoke, she would be back home with her pack, and Penny cooking by the fire. Her eyes would not close, however. In the dark, the ugly shrine grew more menacing, and the curved stone became a monstrous face watching her.

Eventually, she must have fallen asleep, for deep in the night, dark chanting invaded her dreams. The incomprehensible chanting grew louder until it called forth the giant spider with yellow eyes who hunted her from its shimmering web.

CHAPTER TWO

The Mage and The Spider

"Sometimes we ponder the price we pay to walk upon solid ground. To see and feel and breathe and know the unfamiliar comfort of unchanging landscapes. Seramight is as different to our realm as rock to water. Humans are rocks. Each one is unalike, each one is alone. Each can be broken and cast aside. The Laifae are water; we ... or rather 'I' are a drop from that stream. I am one and many. Yet why do we envy the lonely rock its aloneness, its solidity, its harsh shape and unique thought?"

The History of Alafraysia and Seramight,
By Mageguard Bluelight

In the dark, she was falling and falling. She opened her mouth to scream, but only the howling winds of the Abyss emerged. Something prodded her hard on the shoulder ...

Elika sat upright, shaking with the lingering echoes of terror. She was not trapped in the eternal Abyss but sitting in a narrow bed in a darkened, cold room, her body coated in sweat. Her back hurt. Everything around her was unfamiliar. She raked her mind for some sense of where she was and the events of the previous day rushed in to fill the void. The bridge ... falling through the chasm ... then ... *Terren*. She was in Terren. Her hands flew to the imprisoning choker around her throat, firmly sealed and unyielding.

A dark shape appeared in the corner of her eye. "Put this on." Meena threw a grey dress onto the bed. Her nose was bruised, her icy gaze murderous. "You'll keep yourself clean and tidy. You'll fetch water from the well each morning and use some of it to wash yourself." In her fist, she gripped a cane. "You'll scrub sheets and clothes at the end of every second day. There is a pile of them in the laundry cupboard beside the kitchen."

Elika rubbed her face, trying to rouse her sluggish mind. Above her, a desperate breath of daylight fought its way through the thick snow covering the window. A yearning for home grew heavy in her chest. Before it smothered her, she threw aside the blanket and grabbed the dress.

Meena jumped back, her cane raised and ready to strike.

Elika stilled. "You don't touch me, and I won't touch you." Her voice was hoarse from the screaming she'd done the day before when she had plunged into the Abyss.

Meena's glare turned venomous. "You touch me, and I'll give you to the mages to touch." Her lips parted into a sly smile. "I did that once to a repulsive Dae like you. After they finished with her, she knew her place. Kissed my feet when I told her to, worked when I told her to, and best of all, learned how to keep her tongue silent."

Elika began to dress. She had been threatened more times in her life than she could count. Such was the way of the streets. The ones you had to fear, however, were not those who used threats to frighten you, but the silent, watchful types. Those who came at you with intent and resolve when you least expected it. But whether you feared them or not, you never, ever let them think they had any power to scare you.

"Look, it might be best if you simply keep out of my way and I out of yours. Then you won't get hurt again," Elika suggested, as she buttoned the dress at the front.

Meena's cane twitched.

"See, I just don't scare easily," Elika continued. "Seen bigger, scarier toughs than you. Stabbed a few of them, too. There was one I got with his own spoon. Rammed the end of it into his ear so deep, it took two men to pull it out. He couldn't hear on that side of his head again. And you can hit me with that cane. But then I'll snatch it from you and ram it in your eye before you can blink."

Meena's hand stilled, and her expression clouded with a tinge of uncertainty.

Elika struggled to hold back a smile. She could talk tough with the best of them. It was how the boys tried to scare each other in the Hide—a game they played to see who could talk meaner and scarier. They particularly enjoyed playing it with the new arrivals to the gang.

"Or else," she continued. "I might sneak up on you in the middle of the night and cut off your ear. 'Cause you see, ear's easy to cut. A quick slash and it's gone before you wake up. It takes longer to cut off a finger or a hand. Need a bigger, sharper knife for that, too, and all that effort wriggling it through the bone. You might think you could lock the door to keep me out. But then there you are, walking about, and I jump out at you and cut your throat before you remember to scream." She sat on the bed and slowly pulled on her boots. "You see, I know toughs. They taught me how to take a beating, and then give back thrice what you receive. You give me a bruise, I bleed you. You stab me, I cut off a piece of your flesh. See?" She sprang to her feet and smiled in a friendly way, just like a tough would before he stuck you with a knife.

Meena's stony expression did not change, but her eyes betrayed her fear. "You don't scare me, Dae. Work hard and do as you're told and I won't set Mage Aeon-Rah on you."

"As you wish," Elika replied with a nod. "I'll work, and you keep away from me with that cane of yours. So, lead the way."

Meena began to move, then stuttered. "You don't tell me what to do."

Elika nodded again. "As you say. You tell *me* what to do."

Meena narrowed her eyes, trying to work out if she was being mocked. "Follow me," she barked and marched ahead down the wide, winding staircase.

The house was deceptively large. On the candlelit landing below the attic room, doors led to six small bedrooms. Another level down was entirely Mistress Oblana's personal chambers. The double doors were open to a lounge with polished furniture, plush rugs, and a fireplace on the far wall. Despite the apparent lavishness, Elika caught signs of impoverishment—the dust, the fading polish, the sun-bleached curtains and frayed lace runners.

The paint was peeling where the damp had got in, and the steps creaked and popped.

The stairs led down further, into the workshop above the shop itself. It was an open landing that spanned the entire floor. The timber floors had lost most of their polish and were grey and worn. Tall windows faced both the front and the back of the house. They would have allowed in plenty of light, save that they too were buried in snow along with the whole street. Even so, the room was warm and grew warmer beside the chimney rising from the kitchen below.

The workshop was filled with many different looms, barrels stuffed with matted piles of white wool and buckets with dyes. There were chairs for half a dozen workers, though only one girl was working at the spinning wheel by the light of a candle.

Elika's gaze snagged on her. It was hard not to stare. The girl wore the same grey frock as her, but it was trimmed with lace and decorated with fabric flowers in pretty patterns. Dried flowers also adorned her straw-colored plait, which fell over her shoulder and down her body. A wreath of dried vine leaves crowned her head. The girl looked like a bride ready to be wed in a spring meadow. Her freckled face peered shyly from behind the wheel, while she spun into a thread the fine strands of silk emerging from a barrel with crawling worms inside it.

There was a rack with hanging yarns of silk that dripped dye into a trough. And on a long table against one wall lay rolls and rolls of finished bright cloth.

"This is where you'll work each day, dawn till dusk," said Meena. "You'll weave the yarn into cloth."

Elika blinked at the strange machine with many parts and levers. "I don't know how."

"Another stupid Dae. Here, I'll show you. There's nothing to it." Expertly, Meena arranged the thread on the loom. Her fingers moved nimbly and too fast for Elika to catch the subtleties of those movements. "Pass this shuttle through here … then here …"

Meena spoke impatiently, as she explained the workings of the loom. Before Elika could understand half of it, she was left alone to do it herself.

As soon as Meena's steps faded downstairs, the bride-girl stopped working and stretched her back with a glance at the snow-covered window. "I don't know why the mistress is wasting candles she can ill afford. The snow has sealed us in." She spoke with the familiar accent of home. "The whole street is buried to the roofs."

"You are from the other side," Elika said with some relief.

The girl smiled shyly. "Me and my brother crossed last summer. Smiley Sam they called him." She pulled on the thread in the barrel. "They used to call me Sleepy Liffy." She chuckled. "'Cause I liked sleeping late into the day. And often, my brother would find me sleeping under our orchard trees, instead of picking the fruit." The pleasant expression on her face faltered. "I miss home and our farm and the apple trees in bloom. Father said that apples were Arala's favorite fruit. He's dead now, for he refused to leave his orchards when the Blight came."

Elika wrapped her arms around herself against the rising chill and stared at the window. She had never seen snow bury a house to the roof, not in Terren. That only happened in the mountains. "I hate magic," she mumbled.

Liffy started at that. "You must not say that." Her gaze darted with fright to the corner of the room.

Only then did Elika notice another dark shrine to magic. There were flowers, pebbles and leafy branches neatly arranged around the deformed, twisting shape. It reminded her of some gnarled creature trying to find its earthly form.

"We must win magic's favor," Liffy whispered, as if afraid something might overhear them. "To do that, you must love it." She knotted her fingers together, as if pleading for mercy, and chanted:

> *"Gentle magic, grant me power,*
> *Let me serve you how I can.*
> *Sweetest magic, grant me grace,*
> *Let me show you beauty's face."*

When she finished, she resumed spinning the wheel and pulling silk threads from the barrel with worms.

"'Tis the gods you should be praying to," Elika said harshly and gritted her teeth against saying more. Since when do men pray to magic?

"Oh, no, not here. It's not the gods who grant us favor, but magic that rules this land."

"Might be I don't want its favor."

"You do," Liffy said, nodding keenly. "Everyone does. And to get it, you must pray to it many times a day and give it offerings. Magic loves beauty, which is why I make myself beautiful for it." She adjusted the wreath on her head.

"You love magic?" Elika asked, doubtfully. One simply could not abandon a lifelong fear and hate of something so easily.

Even now, though she knew men had unwittingly caused the Blight that destroyed half of Seramight, she still blamed magic for it. Might be if it was not so wicked and destructive, men would not have got it into their heads to burn it in blood-salt fires.

Liffy gave her a wobbly smile. "I'm trying to love it, but it's hard," she said quietly, with another sidelong glance at the shrine. "But don't let the mistress see you not working. If she thinks you're lazy, she'll not feed you. Or worse … she'll send for Mage Aeon-Rah." Her hand absent-mindedly rose to her collar, before she abruptly resumed spinning the thread.

Elika sat at the loom and tried to recall what Meena had shown her. She had made it seem easy, but Elika's fingers kept losing the thread or tangled it altogether. The silk weave was loose or too tight and had to be redone. Whilst on the rack nearby, more yarn rolls were waiting to be woven into fabric.

Downstairs, she heard Mistress Oblana pacing and complaining to Meena about the snow keeping her customers away. "Go out there and sweep the path, girl."

"But the snow will bury me if I open the door," Meena cried.

"The mages have melted a path through the streets with their fire, so the horses can pass. But even they can't keep up with this wretched weather. Cook's cleared the back door, but it'll be buried in no time unless you pick up the shovel and help her, instead of buzzing around me like a pestilent fly. I have a headache again. I must lie down. Bring me tea after you finish."

Shortly afterwards, the mistress mounted the stairs past their workshop, up to her rooms.

Elika gazed at the windows thickly buried in snow. "Why is Reval doing this?"

"He's mad, that's why," Liffy replied as she strung the thread through various loops and holes. "It's best not to pay him or the other tsaren any mind. Everyone says so."

She might as well have said to pay no mind to the fire encircling you, thought Elika. "Might be I could, if they paid *us* no mind," she said aloud.

"Oh, they don't. I dare say they barely notice us," Liffy replied without taking her eyes off the spinning wheel. "They just sit in their palaces and war with each other. It's the mages we've got to worry about." Her face grew haunted as she said that. "Though one day, I won't have to worry about them at all," she added quietly, and there was hard certainty in her face.

Elika's hands froze on the loom. "You won't?"

Liffy glanced at the shrine and shook her head. "When me and my brother buy our freedom and save enough for the passage on a trade ship, we are going to Wavestar. It's the only free city in the realm, where magic may not enter and mages have no sway. But first, I have to win magic's favor," she whispered in confidence.

Elika's heart sped up at the thought of a free city with no mages in it. "How is that possible? Syn'Moreg gave this half of Seramight to magic."

"They say that long ago, the old Duke Firestorm made some secret, wicked deal with the Lord of the Abyss. No one knows what was traded, only that neither the tsaren nor the mages go near his city."

This did not sit right with Elika. A city beholden to Syn'Moreg could never be truly free. Despite that, the possibility that there were other cities beyond Terren filled her with a sense of longing. Until now, they were unreachable places in stories from long ago. Some had been destroyed in the Sundering Wars, others by the

Blight. Elika knew little of those cities, save that each was different, with its own folk and ways of living.

Something must have shown in her face for Liffy added, "You have to be a freeman to travel without a master. And there're tolls to enter every city, too."

After that Liffy fell thoughtfully silent, and for a while, they worked without speaking. In that silent void, Elika's mind drifted back to the chasm, where the winds wailed their death song. It took her to the bridge, the plunging into darkness, the piercing sound of her terror. And once again, her heart raced with unexplained panic. Her chest grew tight. She wanted to erase the terrifying memory. She felt changed by it somehow. Always, she had feared the dark and eternal, the edge of the Abyss which cut through their world. Touching that Abyss had altered her, made her tremble when there was no cause to be afraid. The ground no longer felt as solid, and any moment it would open beneath her feet …

She stopped that thought before it swallowed her whole, took a deep breath and reached for the soft sound of Liffy's spinning wheel, a faint thread that pulled her back into the light. She focused on the movement of her fingers until they grew lithe and quick and found their way with the wooden shuttle and the strands of silk. And as the stream of smooth, green cloth grew from her loom, the emerging pride kept her from slipping back into that chasm. It was hard not to feel pleased with herself. The silk she wove looked as fine as the finished rolls on the table.

Without warning, light flooded the room. Elika stared at the windows and the shuttle slipped from her hands. The snow had vanished. It did not melt, did not leave behind puddles and streams of water, but simply vanished. One instant it was dark, the next, sunlight flooded their workshop. She rushed to the window and was joined there by the equally stunned Liffy.

The workshop overlooked the row of similar buildings across the road, all selling yarn and cloth, all bearing the mark of Mage Aeon-Rah above the door. The ground was frosty, but nothing remained of the snow, as if it had never been there at all. People began to emerge onto the streets, scratching their heads, gazing up at the sky as if the answer to the mystery lay there. Then carts and riders on horseback appeared and went about their business as if nothing unusual had happened.

"But it was real … the snow …" Liffy said breathlessly. "I felt it melt on my hand."

Elika was speechless. How could she live in a world where nothing was certain? Where reality was as cutting as a sword and yet as waning as a dream?

"Get back to work, before I take a cane to you," said Mistress Oblana's stern voice behind them.

Liffy raced to her seat. Now that the street was cleared and the skies were bright, Elika wanted nothing more than to explore the city. Instead, with an inward sigh, she returned to her loom.

"I will not have laziness in my workshop," the mistress added and rubbed her temples.

"It's only that the magic surprised us," Liffy said hastily.

The mistress was not an old woman. But there was a haggardness to her, a bitter set to her lips as if life—that glorious, shining champion of her heart—had failed her again and again.

"There's nothing to be surprised about. Tsaren's magic never stays for long."

The door to her shop opened and closed, and the mistress rushed downstairs.

Shortly, a man's raised voice carried up. "This silk is not fit for a beggar. How am I to sell to it the ladies of the court?"

"I sold three rolls to Seamstress Rowla only yesterday."

"Seamstress Rowla sews dresses for the impoverished clerks' wives. I do not know why I continue to come here." A moment later, the door slammed shut.

"Damn that wretch. He wants to rob us," Mistress Oblana cursed.

"That's Merchant Grandin," Liffy whispered unhappily. "He always complains so that Mistress Oblana lowers her prices. He'll be back again tomorrow. And the mistress will give him the lowest price for the best silk she has, to keep him from complaining to Mage Aeon-Rah. Then she'll blame us for the poor quality of our silks, and we'll not be given dinner."

Throughout the morning, customers came and went. Merchant Grandin was not the only one who found cause to complain about the diminished quality of Mistress Oblana's silks. The customers called them common, unremarkable, and fit for a peasant. Elika could not understand it. The silks were as fine as any she had seen a lady wear.

When she said this to Liffy, the girl shook her head sadly. "It's not the silk they want but a touch of magic in it. Else it's just plain cloth. Tikka had magic's favor. At least for a time. And the mistress sold the best silk on Yarn Row. Now she can barely afford rent, and Mage Aeon-Rah has threatened to throw her out and give this workshop to another merchant."

The little flame of pride in Elika's chest dimmed and died. For the rest of the morning, whilst the silk rolled and rolled from her loom, she pondered what Liffy had said. As she grew hungry, the thought of missing dinner daunted her. What manner of magic did their customers want?

At midday, they grabbed a potato pie each from the bowl the cook left out in the kitchen. Then Liffy led them outside through the back door into a small courtyard surrounded by grey buildings, and archways leading to the streets beyond. There was a well beside which women scrubbed sheets and hung them in the sunshine. Young children clung to their skirts or played nearby. With a sense of rising horror, Elika saw that even the youngest wore collars of ownership.

Under a leafless vine, there were benches arranged in a circle where a dozen workers ate their luncheon. Elika sat amongst them next to Liffy. There were old men and young alongside women and children. Most were Alterrians, though there were enough Daes here that Elika did not feel ill at ease. Many of them wore metal collars stamped with a mark of the workshop to which they belonged. When she saw old Alterrians wearing the enslaving collar, her heart stuttered with unvoiced dread, but she refused to indulge it, and stifled the suspicion lurking deep beneath.

The floating island in the sky had vanished with the snow, leaving behind only a few playful clouds. Tsarin Reval's sudden appearance and the chaos he had caused were the main talk in the courtyard. Everyone had their say on the matter. Most agreed that in that grief-addled head of his, Reval had been thinking that Arala would return one day. But now, with the bridge gone, it seemed her death had been irreversible after all.

"She's half goddess," said an old Dae man whom the others called Sticks, no doubt for his long skinny limbs. "And gods can't die. 'Tis likely she's gone to the celestial realm."

"But the gods *can* die," said a local youth with dye-stained hands. "Ever since Gorgeran, God of Youth and Health, was killed by Moreg. That's what brought death and sickness into the three realms. Now everything grows old and dies."

Elika ate her pie and listened, as they argued about which gods had died since Gorgeran fell afoul of the God of Death. There were many. Though unlike Gorgeran, none were true gods but their half-breed children, like Arala herself.

"You girl." An old woman pointed at Elika. "Are you a Sachi?" Her bony fingers played with a Sachi ward of the moon dangling on the string around her neck.

All eyes turned to Elika and lit with curiosity.

She swallowed the mouthful of her pie and shrugged. "Might be I am. No one can tell me." In truth, she did not know. She had their look, but the Sachi always denied she was one of them.

"Then you can hear the gods?" asked the man with a long grey beard and shaved head.

"If I can, then they are staying silent and not speaking to me."

"Maybe you're not listening right."

A young woman named Daila, with a babe in her belly, chuckled. "Leave her be, Pen. You might scare her with that mean glare of yours." There was a kindness in her face which was largely masked by the wry set to her lips.

"I'm only wondering why she's here and not at the temple if she's a Sachi. They'd buy her freedom, they would, if she was one of them."

"Might be she's on a mission from the gods," said the old woman with the moon ward. "Well, are ye, girl?"

"No," Elika replied and having finished her pie, wiped her fingers on her dress.

"See this ward?" Pen pulled out a wooden carving of an ear through his grey beard. "It means that the gods might listen to what I have to say. And what I have to tell 'em is that they need to get Reval healed." He spoke loudly into the wooden ear as he said the last. "'Tis not much to ask. Neka can heal a broken soul, she can."

"Perhaps if you keep nagging them, they'll give you what you want," Daila said with another chuckle.

"That's what I was thinking, meself," he said and tucked away his ward.

Elika stuck her hand in her pocket and took out the wooden bird she carried. The Sachi would say it had brought her here, showed her a path to follow. Odd how the ward now seemed hollow, as if it had spent its power and was nothing more than an empty vessel. Though she always carried some ward or another, she never truly believed in their power. Yet in this land of magic, she suddenly felt as if anything was possible.

All too soon, Elika followed Liffy back to their workshop and worked until dusk. Mistress Oblana hated to waste candles, and after the sun had set, she sent them to their rooms without dinner, for she had not sold a single roll of silk that day.

Sullenly, Liffy retreated to her chamber. As Elika mounted the stairs past it, she heard Liffy reciting a prayer to magic behind the closed door.

The attic room was cold, made chillier still by the oppressive presence of the black shrine. *This is my room not yours*, she imagined it saying. *I know you hate me, and I don't want you here either.* She wanted to throw the vile thing from the roof.

Her stomach rumbled from hunger. She opened the window and climbed out into the crisp winter night, if only to get away from the menacing shrine. She sat on the frozen tiles and stared out over the rooftops of the city and the forest of smoke rising from the chimneys.

For a time, she wondered what had happened to Penny, Anten and the children. Then she thought of Mite. This city was so vast, it would take her a lifetime to find them. Right now, though, she was tired and at her back, the soft bed beckoned. She climbed inside, fell on her bed and had just enough strength to ponder vaguely whether this was to be the rest of her life before sleep stole the answer from her. That night, once again, dark chanting invaded her dreams. And she was falling and falling, all the while watched by the spider in the web.

~

After that first day, each one that followed merged with the other. Elika's new life smoothly replaced the shreds of her past, like fresh skin growing over old scars. The choker around her throat soon felt as if it had always been there. Her increasingly nimble fingers wove silk as if they had done it all her life, and Mistress Oblana found little reason to reprimand her.

When the mistress had sold one of the silk rolls, Elika received a penny for it and could not suppress a ridiculous tingle of pride. But then the mistress instantly took the penny back as payment for food and lodgings ... and her debt. When Elika objected about the debt she could not have incurred, the mistress had calmly taken her upstairs to a small study. There, she sat at the desk, opened a ledger, and spun it round. "Here is the sum of what you owe me." She stuck her finger in the journal.

Elika stepped forward and stared at the jumble of letters and numbers she could not read. "It seems a lot," she said uncertainly, staring at the many, many lines of them.

The mistress' finger moved to the top of the page. "Day one. The dress you wear and a spare frock in your wardrobe, bedding, breakfast, lunch ... hmm, no dinner. The daily rent of your room. That unsellable first silk roll which you wove so dreadfully. Day two. Breakfast, lunch, a bar of soap, dinner, and the daily rental of the room. Day three ..." As she recited, she moved her finger down the lines. "The rental of your room. An extra pie at lunch— a theft, for which there is a penalty of three extra pennies ..." And so she went on, giving a thorough account of the debt Elika had incurred. Finally, she came to the end of the third page and looked up. "Twenty-three coppers and eight pennies. You have so far earnt a penny against this debt."

Elika's stood there in speechless horror and the creeping realization that she would forever be indentured as the property of Mage Aeon-Rah.

You'll never be free, unless you free yourself, taunted that niggling voice which knew the streets and the greed lurking in men's hearts. And the collar around her neck grew tighter, the mark of ownership stamped on it became a burning brand.

After that, she worked even harder and faster, hoping her silks would earn her another penny. And they did. On some days, she even earnt two. She never took more food than was allowed and was careful not to use too much soap. But the debt grew and grew regardless.

Then winter began to retreat, and the days grew longer, as did the hours she spent weaving. There were times when she missed life on the street. She pondered how much simpler and quicker it would be to steal what was needed. A morning of filching and pickpocketing, and her debt would be no more. But then the mistress would ask where she had got all that coin, and Elika would have no answer that would not send her straight to a grimy gaol.

Neither did it help that Liffy often spoke of that mythical time when she would be free, living in Wavestar with her brother, Sam. She'd have no master who might hurt her, and she would make apple pies to sell in the market as her ma used to do. And every penny she earnt would be her own. Elika hated those musings. Liffy would die of old age, like her, in this cursed workshop. The fifty sherrings she had to earn might as well be a king's chest of gold.

Another day had arrived, and at dawn, Elika raced to the kitchen to wash and grab whatever breakfast the cook had left out the night before. Liffy was already there, wearing a new adornment in her hair to impress magic. She must have worked late last night, adding fresh strands of green lace to the sleeves of her grey dress. Matching lace was braided through her plait. She had picked small daisies that grew between cobblestones in the courtyard and added them to her wreath.

She smiled warmly when Elika came in. "The mistress is abed with a headache this morning, so Meena will be too busy to trouble us today. She rushed upstairs not a moment ago with a pot of chamomile tea."

"Meena is never too busy for malice," Elika said as she made her way to the back of the kitchen.

There was a slyness about Meena that never ebbed. She berated Liffy and hit her with a cane when there was little cause for it, saying, "Magic must truly despise you for it to ignore you so."

Once Meena sabotaged her spinning wheel when no one was around to see it. Liffy had been in tears, for she was certain it was magic that had broken it. Elika was not so easily fooled. Meena fed on another's misery.

Elika washed quickly in the wet pantry using the water which Liffy brought from the well earlier. Tomorrow morning was her turn to do that. She then snatched some sweet rolls and they rushed upstairs, before Meena returned and chased them away with threats of beatings.

At her spinning wheel, Liffy dutifully recited a prayer before starting work. Today, she had a new one, for none of her previous prayers had enticed magic to look her way.

> *"Wondrous magic, hear my heart,*
> *With love, it's filled, and love I grant ..."*

Elika cringed inside. It was as silly a prayer as any she had heard from her.

Those who could do things better than others were said to have *magic's favor*. Liffy said it was like a blessing the gods bestowed on men. Daila from the courtyard said it was merely that magic worked through you. Elika thought some people were simply better at doing things than others. That was all there was to that.

"Why do you keep praying to it?" she asked. "Magic serves no one but itself."

"Without magic's favor, you'll be working a hundred years to save enough pennies for your freedom," Liffy said as she spun her wheel. "I don't know anyone who's bought their own freedom. Daila's father paid for hers when she was still a babe. But he was a silk merchant. Daila's husband isn't a wealthy man, so they both have to work to save fifty sherrings for her babe's freedom."

"Might be you'd do better to ask magic to spin gold for you," Elika said a little moodily, and pondered again whether life on the streets was better than this.

Liffy grew wistful. "That's what I'm praying for. Tikka would produce the finest, shimmering silk from the same thread I'm spinning. It shimmered like gems. The mistress gave her a copper for the roll of it, and more food than she could eat. Meena was pale with jealousy, for the mistress doted on Tikka as if she was her own daughter. Then magic abandoned her for stabbing a mage. See how your silk is … common. It doesn't catch the light the same way. It doesn't shimmer and shine like water."

Elika considered the blue material in her hands and recalled the man with a strange shimmering cloth in the shop that first day she arrived. "The mistress will give me a copper if I weave silk that shimmers?"

"Aye. And if you have magic's favor, another master might offer to buy your freedom … if you agree to work for him and no one else. Or a mage might give you your own workshop, so you'd have no master at all."

"Might be I'll make up a prayer, after all," Elika mumbled without conviction.

Liffy looked doubtful. "Magic won't be fooled by your secret contempt. The love has to come from the heart. Magic hates liars. Everyone says so."

"Liars hate liars," Elika said. "Like thieves hating thieves."

"Once, I hated magic, too. But we're here now. We can't hold on to the old ways. Magic destroyed half our world. Maybe it's time we made peace with it. Else you'll be wearing that collar into your grave. And you'll never be allowed to go anywhere without our mistress's permission."

Elika's choker seemed to grow heavier. She wanted her freedom. If the only way to get it was to use a little magic, then might be she'd swallow her pride and call on the thing inside her to help weave those blasted shimmering silks. As she passed the shuttle through the threads, she wished as hard as she could for the light to stick to it. In her mind, she fixed the image of the shimmering cloth the rich pouch had been wearing.

Nothing happened. The creature inside her did not stir.

Elika closed her eyes and reached out further, seeking some essence of the power she had felt from the moment she had arrived in Al-Terren.

There it was, the sticky presence of some vital force, something intangible and yet strong. If she could pull it …

She opened her eyes. There was a briefest, faintest flash of light … Or had she imagined it? She wished for it again, pulling on that essence which hummed around her as she passed the shuttle back and forth. Then she saw it, the light coating the thread. And the fabric emerging from her loom changed from the dull blue silk into another material that shimmered like blue gems.

Liffy gasped and stared at it with mouth ajar. "I … I do not understand. You hate magic," she said on a choked breath. Then her lips firmed and trembled, and tears glistened in her eyes.

At that moment, Meena came up for more silk rolls. "Why aren't you working, lazy wretch?" she snapped at Liffy, then followed her gaze towards Elika's newly woven cloth falling away from the loom. Her eyes widened. "Mistress!" she shrieked. "Mistress!"

Mistress Oblana strode upstairs. "Stop your screeching, girl, before I …" She stopped and gaped at the shimmering silk. A slow smile spread across her face. "At last! Magic grants us its favor, once again."

"But she never prays to it!" Liffy cried. "She hates magic. She always says so. It should have been me. I did this, not her. I made it bestow favor on us. *My* prayers did that."

"Quiet girl. Dress as you like and pray all you want, but you can't fool magic with your worthless ploys." Almost reverently, the mistress lifted the shining fabric and felt its texture. "Very fine indeed. Now that we have regained magic's favor, we'll need the special dye for this cloth. The nobles pay richly for those silks."

"But only Tikka knew how to use the mage's dye," Meena objected.

"Tikka was useless," Mistress Oblana snapped. "Magic had abandoned her long before she ran away. And she spilt the last of the dye, the clumsy rat. The beating was too good for her."

"She did not spill it but poured it away," Meena said. "After she tried to stab Maj-Dun'Flower."

Elika knew that no common weapon could kill the mages. Stabbing them was useless.

"I've saved enough gold for another jug of Dun'Flower's dye," said the mistress. "Tomorrow, you'll fetch it from him."

For the first time, Elika saw Meena's eyes fill with fear. "No … I mean … it would be best to send Lika. She's the one with magic's favor, and the mage will be more generous to her if he knows it."

"Hmm. I hadn't thought of that. You are right, of course. Lika will fetch it tomorrow."

From Liffy's relieved expression and Meena's sly glance, Elika knew that something was amiss. Still, it was hard to think beyond the possibility that she might yet earn her freedom.

~

Magic lies. That lesson went deep into her bones with her first step onto the soil of this wondrous and terrible world.

So, when Elika gazed into the mummer's mirror, her reflection did not frighten her. Instead, it chilled her. Before she crossed the Bridge to Magic, she was known as Eli Spider. The magical mirror must know this.

She ignored the sneers and laughter of the crowd and turned her head. The white spider in the mirror followed, turning its ugly head and giant fangs. On its round back was the inky mark of a burning butterfly, like the one on her lower back, hidden by her clothes. She raised her arm, and the spider followed, lifting one of its hairy legs. The spider even wore the same dress as her. She looked down at her muddied skirt and muddy boots, and the spider in the mirror did the same. More ridiculous still, atop the spider's head sat a golden circlet of leaves and flowers. It was a frightening and comical sight, so she did not begrudge the laughter of the gathered folk.

The mummer had pulled Elika out of the crowd and placed her before the mirror, showing neither surprise nor alarm at the reflection. His reflection was that of a horned man with hoofed feet and a tail.

He danced towards the mirror and spun it on its twisted legs. "Behold she who gazes at the truth and does not shy away."

The mirror spun and spun, and the spider faded.

"A penny for the glimpse of truth," the mummer called out. "A penny for your soul's reflection."

A young woman shoved Elika aside. "Let me see," she demanded, and after giving the mummer a penny placed herself before the mirror.

When the mirror stopped, a different reflection awaited; a whore in green lace and a heavily painted face.

The crowd jeered.

The young woman gasped and reddened. "It's naught but lies. Give me back my penny."

The mummer showed her his empty hands. "'Tis but a small price to pay for the glimpse of your soul, my *lady*," he said and danced aside when she tried to hit him with her basket.

"'Tis wickedness I tell you," she cried, chasing him around the other mummer, who started to play a fiddle.

"If it's a wickedness to show what magic sees, then truth itself must be wicked."

As the crowd laughed, a man stepped out, grabbed the incensed woman by her waist and dragged her back. "Enough of your foolishness, wench. Let another have their turn."

A skinny lad, whose clothing hung loosely on him, paid to peer at himself in the mirror that lied. The mirror showed him a fat, brightly garbed merchant with gemmed rings on his fingers. The lad put his hands on the hips and turned this way and that to better examine his reflection. "Aye, it's the truth that I have just become Merchant Silkfair's apprentice. The mirror shows me my future."

More pushed forward to take a peek at themselves.

Elika continued on her way through Peddler's Market. She had not a penny to spend and knew she risked a beating by taking a different route to the mage's shop to the one Mistress Oblana had instructed she take, so as not to be late in returning. But Liffy had spoken so often of this market and the marvelous items it sold, Elika had to see it for herself.

There were talking birds, and lanterns which caught the sunlight and released it again at night. She stopped by a map-maker's stall to study the map of their world. As she did, a hessian bag with rolls of maps stacked inside it, rose on fluttering wings and flew around her until she fled.

"Pardon him," the mapmaker called after her. "He's not usually so misbehaved."

An old herb-witch sold glass vials of steaming potions that she swore would cure any sickness and turn even the feeblest body to a warrior's brawn. "A potion to make him love you." She thrust a red vial towards Elika. "Ten pennies is all I ask for love eternal."

"I've not one to give you for any kind of love," Elika replied.

Magical items had all been destroyed in her half of the world after the Sundering War, and a part of her never wanted to believe such frightening things had existed. But all Bill Fisher's tales had been true. He had lamented the loss of magic, even as men cheered its demise. And she wished he was here to see this wondrous place for himself.

Daylight was fading, and lamplighters made their rounds through the streets. Bemoaning the short days of early spring, Elika increased her pace. She had lingered too long in the market.

Before she left the shop, Mistress Oblana had threatened her with all manner of evils were she to run away. Elika had no wish to run away. The winter still held them in its thrall, and as the night encroached, her breath steamed. She had a warm bed, food and work to pay for it. Yet, finding herself out in the streets again, her fingers itched for their old life. It would be easy to pick some pockets. Rich pouches in Al-Terren strode about unguardedly, their pockets large and easy to filch. She ignored the temptation. That life held nothing but strife and fear, and she had discovered that earning honest coin was its own reward.

She turned into a quiet alley. Charms and wards were everywhere, hanging from beams, on the walls and windows. There were gaudy crystals that warded off mischievous magic, and charms made of feathers and sticks which kept bad luck away. And it was in this dark silence that she sensed the magic of this world most acutely.

If she focused on it, she could feel the palpable presence of some invisible force. It was the same power she had drawn on when she merged the light with the silk thread. It was not the same as the magic living inside her, but vast and ancient, and it permeated the air and stone and even the ground she walked on.

Ahead, she saw the three-headed stone statue of the serpent she had been instructed to seek. It marked the mage's abode. Upon reaching it, she found herself before a long cove of black branches with a single door at the end, exactly how the mistress had described it, and just as menacing as Elika had imagined.

The branches formed a low ceiling cavern. They moved and slid despite there being no wind. The doorway of the cove—for she could not rightly call it a house—was a crisscrossing of slick, black tendrils. She eyed them with trepidation.

There was no natural beauty about magic when it manifested itself in their realm. It did not belong. It invaded their world from another, and she had a strong sensation that it liked men no better than men liked it.

As she walked towards the mage's home, the branches brushed her face and snagged on her hair. She swiped them aside and ducked to avoid their grasp, fighting the urge to take out her knife and cut them. It would only anger the mage within. Mistress Oblana had spent her last coin on the precious supply of the magical dye for her yarns, and Elika could not return without it.

Through the gaps in the webbing of the walls, she spied Maj-Dun'Flower inside, mixing powders and muttering a chant:

> *"Spider, spider in the web*
> *Grant me strength*
> *And lend me magic.*
> *Spider, spider in the web*
> *Show me light*
> *And send me magic."*

The mage must have sensed her, for he raised his dreadful face and his unnatural cloudy eyes fixed on her. The eyebrows and eyelashes were missing. Black veins ran under his skin like poison. His human features were misshapen as if he were wearing an ill-fitting skin. Once he had been human, now he was two beings merged into one body—a repulsive aberration.

Every mage she had seen was just as vile. She watched them in the streets, striding along as if this was their realm and men were pestilence to brush aside or made to serve them. They leered unashamedly at beautiful women regardless of whether they were whores or fine ladies, and beat boys who were not quick enough to jump out of their way. But it would not do to show him her contempt, so she adjusted her face into a meek, respectful expression.

The branches of the wall parted to make a doorway for her to enter. When she did, they wound behind her again.

There was a faint odor of death about the house, which chilled her blood and warned her to tread lightly. Before her face betrayed her disgust, she bowed as the mistress had instructed her to do. There was no sense in annoying the mage. She'd simply take the dye and leave.

He tilted his head in interest. There was a curious glint in his eyes, as if he was seeing her and not understanding what it was he was seeing. "Who is your master, Dae?" As with all mages, his croaky voice was echoing as if two men spoke at once. Maj-Dun'Flower was a merging of magic and man, and she wondered which of them spoke now.

"Mistress Oblana sends me to collect the dye of Sky and Air for her thread," she replied and placed a pouch with coins on the table.

He titled his head as if something about her alarmed and excited him at once. "You look familiar as from a dream. Have we seen you before?"

Elika shook her head.

He shuffled closer. One of his legs dragged. "Magic knows you. Why does it know you?"

She lowered her gaze. "I'm Mistress Oblana's servant, I've not been long in your city."

"Where is that whimpering girl she usually sends? The one who thinks a knife can kill us?"

"She ran away."

"So Oblana sends you to us instead?" His lips stretched into a smile, akin to a beast baring its teeth in a parody of appeasement. "Then she shall have more cloud for her yarn."

A chilling sensation of threat ran over her skin. There was an awfulness about every mage she had ever seen, a malignant glint beneath their politeness.

The mage hobbled to the back of his sanctum, awkward, ungainly, as if he'd only just learned how to walk. His arms moved strangely, too. When he took a jug from its hook and dipped it into his steaming caldron, it put her in mind of a puppet on strings.

Maj-Dun'Flower covered the jug with a lid and brought it to her. "Tell your mistress that we are pleased with you." His fingers reached out to touch her.

Elika snatched the jug from his hands and stepped away with a bow. Despite steam rising from the jug, it was cold in her hands.

A dark tendril emerged from the mage and wound around her waist. It began probing her body, running along her neck, towards the laces of her dress, pulling on them.

Quicker than she could think, she drew her small knife and slashed the tendril. "Don't touch me."

The mage cried out in pain and released her. "Vicious little beast," he hissed, cradling his arm. "Magic-hater, are you? Like all Othersiders. We will enjoy teaching you not to defy your masters, human she-child."

Elika stepped back and lowered her face. "I'm but a servant, not worthy of your notice. Mistress Oblana eagerly awaits the die for her yarn. I must deliver this without delay or she will beat me."

He turned away and stiffly scribbled a note on his table. He sealed it, stamped it with wax, then thrust it to her. "Give this to your mistress. The next time you come here, you will kneel before us." *Kneel before us*, echoed another voice. "Now, go. Get out."

Elika fled, trembling with rage. Meena had gleefully warned her this would happen. Any mage could have you as long as your master agreed. And no one in this city would refuse a mage what he wanted. It was best to let them do what they would, Meena had said. If you fought, they would punish you.

When Elika was out of sight of the serpentine statue marking the entrance to the mage's abode, she stopped and leant on the stone wall. She was glad rage masked her fear, for fear made you weak. She looked at the note in her hand. Though she could not read, she could guess well enough what it contained within. Later tonight she would be beaten and sent back to him with instructions to do what he demanded.

She scrunched the note in her fist and wished with all her might to burn it. When she opened her hand again, the note was ashes in her palm. A gust of wind blew them away.

Her fear vanished. She was Eli Spider of Bad Penny's pack and not a helpless street urchin. Might be it was time she remembered that.

But then, fierce hunger struck her, as it always did when she used her magic.

CHAPTER THREE

The Silvery Web

"Human's do not understand magic. To them magic is everything beyond the rock they sit on, for they cannot see the power that flows over them and binds them to the Great Web. When by chance they touch that light, they call it a favor bestowed upon them by 'magic'. Three wells of power there are, Ethereal Essence, Celestial Spirit and Elemental of the Earthly. Most of the lesser beings like pure-blooded humans drink from one well. Others, like the glorious tsaren, the illustrious gods or the greedy human kings of the Sacred Crown drink from two. But there is another being, foretold but never found, who can drink from all three: a trika. We must hope this creature remains a prophesy, never reality, for even the gods fear its arrival."

The History of Alafraysia and Seramight,
By Mageguard Bluelight

"Insolent girl, how dare you return so late?"

Elika's hand flew to her cheek where the mistress' slap stung fiercely. "I lost my way," she said calmly, though her blood heated with outrage.

"I had half the guards in the city looking for you."

Elika doubted that was true. City guards cared little for chasing runaways. The magic in the collar drew mage trackers well enough all on its own. There were always whispers amongst the Dae about runways. Most were caught within days. But there were some who had vanished, never to be found again. Liffy thought it was because they were dead.

"Give me that dye, you wretch." Mistress Oblana snatched the jug from Elika's hand. "Go to your room and pray to magic. If you lose its favor, I'll be selling your worthless hide to the mills."

Upstairs, Elika closed the door of her chamber and leant on it. Her cheek still burned. Even so, it was hard to hold onto her anger, for beneath the mistress' fury, she heard a note of fear. The food in their house had grown plainer. The cook now only came every other day. And the mistress suffered more and more from headaches. Her brows were always furrowed with tension, and the creases of pain and worry were now deeply engrained into her skin.

Overhead, the window was a terrible temptation. Aye, she could run from this house, but she could not run from the collar. Only a mage could remove it. But there was another way—earn the coin by using her magic and buy back her freedom.

The shrine watched her darkly. *Ask and I might help*, she imagined a sly voice whispering to her.

Elika straightened and crossed her arms over her chest. "You want a prayer? Well here it is.

> *Vile magic, grant me power,*
> *Serve me now or let me rest.*
> *Ugly magic, grant me grace,*
> *Else show me not your foul face."*

She grinned and felt better for it. Mockery and laughter were the only way to dispel fear from your heart, Penny always said.

But the shrine remained grim and forbidding.

Her smile fell away. How was she to make peace with this creature she hated? Aye, she hated it still, despite now knowing the terrible truth, the cruel reason for the Blight. The world could not exist without magic. It was why Dae-Terren was now a tomb.

The room became stifling. She strode to the window, climbed out onto the roof and breathed deeply the fresh air. The city was lit up with countless street lanterns that fought off the night. Torches burned along the city walls. Overhead, the stars lit up the sky, and in the distance the sea glistened in the golden moonrise. A perfect night for roaming.

To the east, the mountains, cleaved by the chasm, were dark against the moonlit sky. Dae men and women were often sent there as slaves for the coal mines, and she wondered whether Mite was amongst them, sleeping in a camp. No, she mused, Mite would never be so foolish as to get caught and be enslaved like her.

With everything that had happened, her mind remained restless, and no doubt would keep her awake late into the night. Having enjoyed the brief taste of freedom that day, she was not ready to give it up as yet. A reckless sense of adventure took hold of her. She examined the outline of surrounding roofs, noting the arrangement of three chimney stacks and other markers to lead her back home. She then chose a direction that led deeper into the city and began to walk.

To survive on the streets, you had to know the streets. The roofs were the best place to learn them. From up here, she studied the flow of the roads, the crossings, the intersections and dead-end alleys. A map formed in her head of the roads around Yarn Row. As she made her way through the woodland of chimneys, it occurred to her how empty this landscape was, how barren. In Dae-Terren, the roofs were always busy with watchers, thieves and orphans. Here, only stray wisps of firewood smoke roamed the skyline with her.

A gust of icy wind stirred her hair, and on it, she heard a deep, incomprehensible sound. She stopped in her tracks, for she recognized the dreaded chanting that turned her dreams to nightmares and called forth a giant spider. She slid on her belly to the edge of the roof and peered down at the streets. There she saw robed, hooded figures walking in pairs, chanting and waving smoke lanterns. Though she did not understand the alien language, she felt the dark meaning of the words they spoke.

Unmask the terror and it will hold no power over you, she thought, and on whisper-quiet feet, followed them from high on the roof. When she reached the end of the row of houses, she climbed down the gutter pipe onto the street and peeked around the corner at the menacing figures.

The chanting grew louder, a grim drone that put her in mind of nearing death.

She stepped into a sunken doorway and hid from sight.

Two men came into view. Beneath their hoods, they wore black masks with round eyeholes and spider fangs protruding from the jawline. After they had passed, Elika followed, darting from doorway to doorway, and from alley to alley. Though she need not have feared them catching sight of her. They never looked back, never turned their heads, staring only ahead. She could walk two paces behind them and they'd not see her.

As they went from street to street, others joined them, converging into a growing procession of masked figures filling the streets with their ominous humming and sinister smoke. They came to a circular courtyard where a dark stair led to an underground pit. One by one, the hooded figures descended into it. When the courtyard was once again empty, she darted after them.

The stairs circled down, deep below the street, towards bronze doors flickering in the torchlight. No one stood guard there.

Keeping her back against the wall, she crept towards the murmurs. As she drew closer, they became an incantation, the sound reminiscent of prayer.

She poked her head around the corner and faced an underground temple, a Sachi temple. It was like no Sachi prayer house she had ever seen. They were always humble, welcoming places. This one was an underground palace, lined with marble columns.

Emboldened, she stepped inside and found herself under the looming shadow of the statue guarding the door—a hooded man with spider limbs. It was the god Moreg. In his hands, he held a web. The Sachi believed that at the beginning of time, the God of Death bound the three spheres of life with the web he had spun. It was a courting gift to Neka, the Goddess of Life. Their union was brief, for Moreg was ever unfaithful. Before Elika could examine his form more closely, another, more frightening creature drew her gaze, and the very depths of her soul froze with recognition.

In the center of the hall, chanting and humming like a hive of bees, hooded priests knelt on the ground before another grand statue—the spider that haunted her dreams. It had those unmistakable spines along its back, like curved daggers as tall as a man. There were silver markings on its body, akin to runes. And it gazed at her through many eyes of yellow gems that flickered in the light of the torches.

Elika did not believe that dreams led men to another realm; did not heed the old Sachi superstitions that spoke of such things. Yet seeing this creature from her dreams, brought forth those unquenchable doubts.

The chanting intensified and grew into an ululation, and an answering darkness stirred in her soul. The air intensified with power and she wanted to throw her head back and release the creature within her into the world to answer their summons. It tried to claw its way out, and she fought to hold it back. The voices rose again, and the creature in her would be contained no longer …

She fell to her knees, felt something rip from inside her and push its way out of her skin … pain ripped through her body … then stopped abruptly.

The hall was silent. Her eyes refocused on the marble floor. She crawled behind the statue as a deep voice boomed. "Bow, all here, to the Lord of the Abyss."

As one, the hooded figures fell to their knees and bowed their heads, chanting again in a subdued whisper.

Elika peered from around the statue and her gaze snapped to the stone spider, its yellow eyes trained on her.

Lord of the Abyss? She thought as panic struck its first bell against her chest.

On the dais, beside the spider, stood an old Sachi, with long grey hair falling over his shoulders and down the length of his black robe. The priest's eyes were fathomless black pits of age and wisdom. In his hand, he held the dark mask. "Hear our prayer, Son of Moreg." His arms rose in the air.

"Syn'Moreg," she whispered, yet the name resounded hard through her. *Syn'Moreg is a spider?* She had always imagined the demigod who had sundered their world to be a man-shaped being, like the gods and tsaren and the mages.

The Sachi priest lifted his face. "Send us a message and guide us in your service."

Suddenly, from above her came a raucous caw, and her head snapped up. There, high on the beam, perched a white-tipped crow she recognized.

"You," she whispered.

The bird cocked its head at her. It had flown across the bridge and Elika half-thought she had imagined the damned bird that stalked her.

Then the bird flew towards her and over her head. It opened its beak and a croaking voice came out:

> *"To Gods I sing*
> *To Gods I crow*
> *A child's prayer on my brow*
> *She seeks to wound*
> *She seeks to strike*
> *A child's wrath upon your might*
> *Destruction, death*
> *And vengeance right*
> *Beware the anger of her spite.*
>
> *Where there was one,*
> *There shall be two,*
> *A goddess comes for all of you,*
> *Beware her wrath,*
> *Beware her spite*
> *Beware the hot blade of her might."*

Hooded figures spun their heads towards her, looking at her through the slits of their faceless masks.

"*Aleyala shi miyana?*" There was surprise in the old priest's question.

Slowly, she backed away, measuring the distance past them to the door. "I do not speak your tongue."

Two faceless figures rose from their knees and advanced on her.

"It is not our tongue but yours we speak, Aleyala," said the loud voice of the old priest. "Come here, child." He beckoned her towards the spider from her nightmares.

The other robed figures had risen to their feet and silently moved aside to create a path for her towards him. She looked behind her and saw that others moved to block her escape.

"I didn't mean to intrude," she said.

"Our prayer has drawn you to us," said the old priest, his dark eyes roaming over her face.

"She speaks like a Dae," said one man in a mask. "She is not Aleyala."

"The messenger has spoken," he said as the crow landed on his shoulder. "This child is Aleyala. You have answered our prayer, now hear our words and carry them to the Lord of the Abyss, guardian of the great web. Tell him we honor him. The night belongs to him and in the dark we seek him."

More men rose to their feet, seeking to block her escape. Elika moved before too many of them were between her and the door. She flung out strands of her magic, knocked the two guards blocking her way off their feet, dashed for the temple door, ran up the stairs and into the street. And as she ran, she felt as if the dark Abyss itself was chasing her.

~

The bright hues of dawn tainted the horizon at the edges of the distant sea. With just the meagre remnants of the night, Elika saw no sense in trying to snatch an unsatisfying morsel of sleep. So she sat on the edge of the dewy roof, waiting for the light of day to dispel the nightmares of the night and with them her terrors. She dared not close her eyes, no matter that she had not slept, for in her dreams lurked the spider. For so long it had haunted her, and tonight she had learned its terrible name.

"Syn'Moreg," she whispered, trying to make herself believe it. He was here, in this world, the shadow that had sundered Seramight, looming large and fraying the edges of her courage. He was inside her thoughts and dreams and she knew not why. Might be she'd heard the tales of the terrifying spider as a child, which she now forgot. Bill had many such frightening tales he was eager to share on a cold night by the burning fire.

Overhead, clouds drifted by, but not as they might under the guidance of a natural wind. They floated in different directions, as if the mind that controlled them knew not what purpose to send them on. They morphed and changed shape into all manner of strange patters, stretched thin, then fat, taking on the shape of a bird whose wings beat, a horse galloping across the sky, its wispy cloud legs moving. A fickle power controlled those shapes, carelessly casting its own will into the clouds. Aye, there was a wonderous beauty to the childish spectacle, yet her heart could find no joy in the power which could so easily turn beauty to terror.

A subtle threat lurked in those shapes. *See what I can do, see how easily I wield the unwieldable*, it said. *Obey me. Obey me, or else my daydream will turn to your nightmare.*

She might have sat there all day, but work beckoned. She climbed back through her window and went downstairs.

Liffy was already at her spinning wheel, looking miserable. When she saw Elika, her misery turned to sullenness.

Elika yawned and sat at her loom. "You're up early."

"The mistress says my yarn is too coarse. She says it's because magic hates me. And because of you, she made me work all night, so you'd have enough thread for the magic dye. She wants it to be perfect for the web."

"The web?" Elika asked, and her mind conjured up the stone spider with yellow eyes.

"The web," the mistress repeated, as she strode in with Meena in tow. "Maj-Dun'Flower's dye is for weaving webs. Not common cloths." She held up a fabric spun from strands as fine as a gossamer, opening wide and taut, yet the fabric did not tear. The pattern was too intricate and too elaborate for a human hand to have woven it. Worse still, the pattern was not repeating itself, but evolving smoothly, imperceptibly as it went. No two places on the web were the same, and yet it seamlessly merged into a natural pattern of a greater whole, like the branches of a tree.

"This is Silian's Web. It is priceless, for so few can weave it, besides Mage Silian himself of Ilikan's court. And when I say priceless, there is, of course, a price on it that will change our fortunes. And you will weave it, Dae Lika."

Elika could only gape in disbelief. She had only just learned how to weave common fabrics. The mistress was asking the impossible. "But the shimmering silks …?"

"If we have indeed regained magic's favor, then we will weave webs such as this one and not silk. Meena will explain to you how it is done. Each web must be unique. No pattern must be repeated. The magical dye is not to be wasted on common patterns. The webs are for the most illustrious noble houses, for the wives and daughters of dukes to wear, and the courtesans in the courts of the tsaren. If you waste the dye, you will work for the mage until you pay it off. Meena, show her what to do." She refolded the web and left them.

Meena looked as if she had swallowed a poisonous sewer beetle. "Bring me the dye." She pointed at Maj-Dun'Flower's silver jug on the table.

Elika uncorked it and peered inside. The pale liquid looked like a blue sky with swirling clouds. Cool steam rose from it. The smell put her in mind of sparkling streams in the blue sky, and gardens floating upside down. She reached out to touch the clouds and felt herself floating up.

"It's … beautiful," she said, feeling like a cloud.

"Don't sniff it," snapped Meena. "Else it will send your mind into the realm of dreams."

Elika shook her head and held the jug at arm's length. "What do I do with it?"

"It's like any other dye. Except you use it as you weave the web. There's nothing to it. Just pour a little into that jar strapped to the loom."

Elika did as she was told.

Meena then dipped a long, silver needle into the dye, and passed the silk thread through its eye. The needle was a wick that drew the dye towards the thread.

"You make the web by joining the strands with this hook, rather than the shuttle," Meena explained abruptly. "The machine merely guides them in a pattern you choose yourself. If magic truly favors you, it shouldn't be hard. Otherwise, it's impossible."

And that was that. Meena marched out, leaving Elika no better able to spin the web than she could raise a mountain.

"Meena doesn't know how to do it," Liffy said, whilst battling to hide a resentful expression behind a tense smile. "None of us do. That's why the mistress was so angry when Tikka ran away."

"Then how am I to weave them?" she asked, bewildered, for Meena had shown her nothing but how to tangle the thread.

Liffy's wavering smile gave up the battle and vanished. "You are the one with magic's favor. Maybe you should ask it."

The transformation in Liffy's demeanor was so stark, Elika thought she faced a stranger. Yet she could not bring herself to be angry with the girl dressed like an unwanted bride. If Elika could give her the magic, she would.

Liffy twined her fingers together and began to recite a new prayer:

> *"Magic of wind and air and clouds*
> *Still thou rage and wild thoughts*
> *Humbly I kneel before your fires …*
> *And …"*

"And wish only to serve your fickle desires," Elika finished for her and smiled. She had hoped to cheer the girl, but it only made Liffy's jaw clench harder.

"You stole my magic," she said bitterly.

"How can I steal what you don't have?"

"I don't know how, but you did. Why else would it grant its favor to a magic-hater like you?"

"Might be it's trying to win *my* favor?" Elika suggested with a note of humor.

Liffy glared at her, then returned to her work and remained broodily silent.

Elika pulled the thread through the needle's eye, and the dye coated it in a silvery blue hue. Then the dye on the thread touched her hands and she dropped it with a gasp. The magic was cold, damp, and left behind an odd tingling in her fingers.

She examined her hands. The tips of her fingers were stained with blue sky and clouds. She wiped them on her apron, then carefully took the cool thread. The dye not only changed the color but the feel of the yarn, too. The silk was finer than before, light and airy as a cloud. Elika could almost believe she was touching the sky itself.

But the dye was a trick. It was magic, pretending to be sky and clouds. She could feel it crawling over her fingers, could sense its life force. She looped the thread over itself using the hook and tried to find a pattern to repeat. But the emerging web looked like it was being spun by five different spiders, all with their own ideas.

She heard Liffy sigh in frustration. "Tikka once told me she only needed to imagine the web and her fingers did the rest. She said it was like falling into a dream. You do not move your fingers but allow magic to move them, for it's the magic on the yarn which spins itself. She never made the same web twice because she never *imagined* the same pattern. It's why the ladies of the court love them so much. No two are the same."

The advice was offered grudgingly. Still, Elika was grateful for it.

Let the magic guide your fingers. She became aware then that as her fingers wove, they felt laden, as if two minds were pulling them in different directions. The sensation was both subtle and deeply unsettling. Elika stilled her hands, if only to prove that one mind controlled her body.

But then, her fingers began to move again, driven not by magic, but by some arcane knowledge buried in the forgotten depths of her soul. Her fingers moved, because they needed to weave, as surely as she needed to breathe. She stopped and stared at her hands as if they were alien objects. But the sensation that spread through her body was akin to holding her breath. The ache in her hands intensified until she returned to her task.

She could sense the magic clinging to her fingers from the yarn. It wanted to weave a different web to the one she was spinning. Yet it obeyed her wish, wanted to please her. Magic was not controlling her, but she was controlling it, making it obey *her* wishes.

The web flowed smoothly from within her, as if she had waited all her life to spin it. The pattern felt right, as the gossamer cloth grew and grew.

Sounds became distant—the roll of cartwheels on the cobbles of Yarn Row, doves cooing on the windowsill, distant chatter and laughter, the clip-clopping of horses as they carried riders past their window. And those sounds became living patterns in her web, the doves and horses and pretty swirls of laughter …

"How did you do that?" Liffy whispered with breathless wonder.

Elika's fingers came to an abrupt halt, and her mind snapped back, as from a dream. The skin of her fingers was raw and tingling.

In her lap lay a web, softer than a gossamer, lighter than a breath, and cool as spring. But it was the color of it that froze her in wonder. It was the sky itself, with clouds moving through the silvery blue abyss, and she was sinking, falling into that sky where horses galloped and doves flew.

"Magic," she uttered under her breath.

"But that's not how it's meant to be," Liffy cried.

Elika frowned in puzzlement. "How's it meant to be?"

"Tikka used to spin with this dye, and it always came out blue with white markings, not actual clouds that moved. And yours has a silvery sheen to it, too."

Mistress Oblana stormed upstairs. "Why are you screeching, you useless —" She stopped abruptly as she caught sight of the web in Elika's hands and her face changed into utter disbelief. "What is that thing? What have you done, girl?" she demanded in a high-pitched voice.

"Only what you asked me," Elika replied. "It's a web … I'll do better next time," she rushed to add.

Mistress Oblana's eyes widened. Reverently, she took the gossamer cloth as if it was a precious babe and spread it out in front of her face. "You made this?" she uttered in wonder. "It is … magnificent. How is that possible?" Then once again her demeanor hardened. "Get back to work. I want another one like it by the end of the day." She strode out, taking the material with her.

The rest of the day was miserable. It rained outside somewhat fiercely. The muddy courtyard was empty as everyone remained inside their kitchens, and there was no escape from Liffy's sulkiness and pointed silences. These were only broken by her stilted efforts at light chatter about her brother, followed by barbed silences. Elika was glad to return to work, if only to escape Liffy's moods.

As the sun dipped towards the sea, and Elika's eyes were drooping sleepily out of her head, they heard the door of the shop open below. "I fetched him, mistress," Meena announced loudly.

"Where is the girl?" asked an echoing voice that sent shudders of disgust through Elika.

Her stomach lurched with dread, as she remembered Maj-Dun'Flower's demand and the note she had destroyed.

"Upstairs in the workshop," said Mistress Oblana.

Liffy also stopped spinning. There was stark fright in her face.

Footsteps grew louder on the stairs, then a misshapen, ugly face appeared in the doorway. To Elika's relief, it was not Maj-Dun'Flower. Her relief was quickly replaced with weariness, as Mage Aeon-Rah's pale eyes fixed on her and the web in her hand.

He strode forward. The ever-shrouding whiff of death preceded him, and Elika turned away before revulsion showed in her face.

A tendril emerged from his body, gripped her jaw and turned her face towards him. "We remember you, insolent girl. Have you learned to love magic?"

Her hand tightened into a fist around the weaving hook. Only a flash of sense breaking through her disgust held her back from stabbing the hook into his tendril.

"I live to serve magic," she said as dully as she could manage. The lie tasted vile on her tongue.

Seemingly pleased with her answer, he released her and took the web from her hand.

"You were right to send for us, Oblana," he said as he examined it. "Strange is this vision before us. A dream woven into a cloth. But it cannot be, for even we cannot spin such dreams into cloth." His deathly pale eyes settled on Elika. "'Tis not our magic that favors her, but another."

She dared not breathe. Only the mages and the tsaren could command magic. What would become of her if Mage Aeon-Rah discovered that it was not magic that acted through her, but she who commanded it to carry out her will?

"I do not understand," said the mistress. "What other magic is there?"

"'Tis not for your small human mind to understand, imprisoned as it is in the crude confines of your flesh."

"Then you don't know either," Elika said before she could stop herself. She knew a liar when she saw one. This mage was as puzzled as the rest of them.

"Hold your tongue, she-human. Three wells of power we drink from. Seems the one meant for our glorious tsaren has taken a liking to you." Again, his eyes roamed over her, perplexed. "Old magic favors you strongly. Do you carry out all the rituals each night and honor us?"

"Mistress Oblana would have it no other way," she said, carefully avoiding another outright lie.

He narrowed his eyes. "And what prayer do you say each night?"

She did not pray to magic. It went against everything she had been raised to believe. She had come from a world where being infected with magic was a crime, for which you would be burned alive in blood-salt fires.

"Tell us your prayer, girl," the mage said with rising impatience.

Elika hated the way he regarded her with such contempt and disgust as if it were she who stank of death. Some self-destructive urge took hold of her and she lifted her chin, looked the mage in the eyes and recited:

> *"Vile magic, grant me power,*
> *Serve me now or let me rest.*
> *Ugly magic, grant me grace,*
> *Else show me not your foul face."*

Silence.

Elika tensed, ready all at once to jump, to fight, to flee.

Silence.

Liffy paled, her mouth hanging open. Mistress Oblana's face turned red.

Elika flinched inside but refused to show it as she stared back at the mage.

Silence.

Then the mage threw his head back and laughed—hoarsely, coughing as he did so, as if he had inhaled smoke. "We like your human humor. It is … peculiar and stony … aye, stony, that is what it is. A hard rock that breaks the water and sends ripples of foolishness along the surface. It seems your amusing prayer has served you well. Continue to serve magic faithfully, lest it abandons you." He faced Mistress Oblana. "As long as you have our favor, we will make certain you never run out of Laifae's dye."

"You are too generous, your eminence. We will serve you well," Mistress Oblana said with a bow.

"Be sure that you do, and perhaps at the Spring Parade we will whisper to the archmage of your loyal service. Give the girl and the magic inside her three small wishes that are in your power to grant. A token from us."

"I will do as you say."

When he left, Mistress Oblana eyed her with a greedy glint. "In this world, those who are favored by magic rise to great heights. You will spin webs for me, Dae Lika, and you shall want for nothing."

Three wishes … Aeon-Rah's words echoed in Elika's mind. She glanced down, as if in submission. "I'll be pleased to do as you ask."

The mistress began to turn away.

"Only …" Elika stopped her. "The mage said I might have three wishes."

Mistress Oblana's lips parted in a feral smile. "I give you food and bed and the clothes you wear. What more do you need?"

My freedom, she wanted to say. "I ask only three coppers for each web I weave."

There were fifty coppers in a sherring. She'd earn her freedom in no time.

Mistress Oblana's smile grew strained. "And why do you need so many coppers? What do you lack?"

"Only a little diversion in the markets," she said quickly. She'd save every penny and buy her freedom, and she'd do it honestly too, without stealing. "If you would also grant me permission to go to markets."

"Very well. You may have what's left of your coppers to spend on trinkets … *once* your board and debt have been settled."

"And perhaps … I could have the seventh day to myself …"

Mistress Oblana's smile died on her lips. "A day of laziness and idleness."

"Oh, no, mistress. I shall use the time to go to the temple to pray and ask magic for its continuing favor." Elika smiled as innocently as she could. "So that I may continue to serve you well, of course."

"I suppose there is sense in that. It's best not to let this gift slip away. Once lost, it never returns. So heed my words, Lika, if you lose your gift, I'll make certain there is nothing left for you in this life to cling to." She turned on her heel and stormed off.

After the mistress left, Liffy frowned. "The gift of three wishes is so rare and yet you squandered them. You could have asked for Meena's banishment."

Elika picked up the thread and resumed her work, smiling inside. "I don't care about Meena. I got the wish I wanted."

"You got three," Liffy pointed out with a deepening frown.

Elika did not reply. She asked for three but wished for just one—her freedom. And now she had a way to gain it.

CHAPTER FOUR

The Dae Resistance

"Alafraysia is a realm of dreams and wishes, where anything and everything a mind can conceive is brought to life. Men visit our world through the portal of dreams. They pollute its beauty with their malformed, pestilent desires, and reshape our world in ways we despise. How is it, then, that these intruders resent our answering presence in their world?"

The History of Alafraysia and Seramight,
By Mageguard Bluelight

Elika put another copper into her secret box—a rusty tin someone had thrown out in the back alley—and counted her precious glimmering pieces of hope. Three coppers she was given for every web she spun. Yet she was barely left with one to hide away and a few pennies to spend. The mistress was ruthless when it came to lodging costs. And of course, there was the debt to repay.

Everything had changed in the days since she wove that first web. The mistress had replaced the curtains in her rooms, and a carpenter had come to polish the stairs. The cook was here every day, baking delicious pies filled with meat, and pastries stuffed with stewed apples. On some days, they even had seasoned fish and boiled potatoes. Each evening, when Elika retreated to her room, there was a tray waiting for her, with a generous portion of bread, cheese and dried fruit. Magic needed feeding as much as a human body, the mistress said. It must be kept strong. Yet no matter that Elika was given enough food to fill two stomachs, her hunger never ebbed.

The mistress was never generous. She took coin for every extra mouthful. When Elika was given new clothes she did not need, this, too, was taken from her coppers. There was no giving back the dresses. "Now that you are blessed with magic's favor, you cannot dress like a beggar," the mistress insisted.

She instructed Liffy to tidy Elika's hair and decorate the prayer shrine in her room. "No cost is to be spared," the mistress announced. And it was not. Two coppers-worth of useless trinkets were placed around the shrine in Elika's room, with the cost of them deducted from her earnings.

The mistress then demanded that Elika pray each morning and night to thank magic for its continuing favor. "If you lose it, I will send you to the mills."

Liffy would always shrink under that threat. When she first crossed the bridge, she was taken to work in a cloth mill in the Daetown district of the city. With a haunted look on her face, she spoke of daily beatings, hunger, and girls disappearing in the night.

Elika silently refused the demand to pray to that which she detested. Though, now and then, there was no help for it. During the expected prayer times, she would sometimes hear Meena's clumsy feet tiptoeing on creaking steps towards the door. Elika would then recite her usual prayer loud enough for Meena to hear.

"Vile magic, grant me power,
Serve me now or let me rest ..."

It was during one of these false prayers that Elika discovered the shrine's sole usefulness. Underneath it, there was a hollow large enough to hide her box. She was not naïve enough to believe the mistress would allow her to buy her own freedom. Indeed, each day another ingenious way was devised to strip more and more from Elika's pay. So to keep any suspicions from taking root, she had another "secret" place to hide her coppers. A place where everyone always searched—under the bed. She made a cloth pouch, placed some coins into it, and hid it behind the chamber pot for Meena to find.

Elika now counted five coppers and eighteen pennies. This was the first day she was allowed to spend entirely by herself, and she was eager to explore the markets. If she returned empty-handed, the mistress might suspect she was hoarding her coins. She took all her pennies and replaced the tin box inside the shrine. She then grabbed her cloak and raced downstairs. It was still early, but Meena was waiting for her at the bottom of the stairs, a sly glint in her eyes.

"What do you want?" Elika asked her wearily.

A cruel smile spread over those plush, red lips. Elika had never before met a beautiful woman with such an ugly smile. "Mistress Oblana wants you to fetch more dye from Maj–Dun'Flower."

Elika's insides jolted sickeningly. They were running low on the dye, but somehow, she had hoped to be spared this task. "We have enough for a few more days."

"As this is your free day, you can fetch it *today*. The mistress hates idleness. Besides, a note came from Maj-Dun'Flower. He says if she does not send you back for more dye, he might make magic shun you as he did with Tikka."

Elika frowned. "He can't do that …"

"He's a mage, he can do *anything* he wishes." Her gaze darted to Elika's collar. "Seen one strangle a lazy magic-hater once. Slowly, slowly, tighter and tighter, till her lips turned blue. Took a long time watching her die, touching her as she did."

Never show them fear, thought Elika and shrugged nonchalantly. "If the mistress wishes it, I'll fetch it."

Meena's eyes narrowed. "You must not upset him or he might refuse to give you the dye."

"As you say. Bring back more dye and don't upset him. Now I must go before the best wares in the market are gone." Elika strode past, refusing to show how rattled she was. She'd deal with Maj-Dun'Flower, and she would return with the dye.

As soon as she was outside and out of Meena's view, the tension went out of her shoulders. The clouds parted and the sun's warmth hit her face. Her irritation evaporated, and she dismissed the errand from her thoughts. Spring was here. The briny scent of the sea hung on the air and she followed it towards the harbor.

It took her through the market of the Winged Folk. Everything they sold was adorned with colorful feathers—jewelry, robes, hide, clothes and even knives and axes. Being here, it was hard not to think of Rosy Rose and her blue feather, hard not to wonder whether she and Penny were enslaved like her, perhaps working for a cruel master. Surely Anten would never allow it. He was a fat-pouch, after all, who had lived in the Silver Circle. But then, they had five freedoms to buy. An intense urge to find them struck her.

To what need? she wondered bitterly. *To free them, when she could not free herself?*

A hand holding a red feather appeared in front of her. "A gift from Aila." The arm belonged to a woman with red and yellow feathers in her black hair. A bright bird with the same exotic plumage was perched on her shoulder.

The woman pointed at the bird. "Aila is molting. The tail feather bring you luck," she said in the thick accent of her folk. "Eight pennies, for the luck I offer."

Elika crossed her arms. "It's bad luck to give away all I have for a feather, no matter how pretty. Besides, I've plenty of luck already. I'll give you one penny."

The woman laughed. "Ah, me like a clever girl. I'd give it to you for that, but Aila would leave me if I sell her precious feathers so cheap."

She scratched the bird's chin. It opened its wings wide and released a note so pure and wistful, it drew gazes from across the market.

"See, she is offended. Is she not beautiful enough? she asks. It cannot be less than five pennies for her feather."

Elika rubbed her chin as if considering it. "She's a fine beauty, I agree. Still, it's only early spring, and this is her winter plumage. The best feathers are only just beginning to grow. And everyone knows luck from the winter plumage of a bird lasts only until mid-spring, then it fades. Might be I'll wait until summer to get one of the luckier feathers." She turned to go.

"Wait, clever Dae girl. I see you know much about the ways of my people."

Elika turned back, putting on a curious expression.

"Three pennies. But only since you speak truth; luck will fade with spring. You have time to make use of it still."

Elika dipped her hand into her skirt and traded the coins for the feather. Only fools shunned luck when it was offered.

That morning, she spent most of her pennies; too many of them on silly ritual tokens for the ugly shrine in her room, if only to keep her mistress happy. She bought a string of wooden beads, a brass flower, and a silk ribbon, which she meant to give to Liffy. Might be a gift would thaw her dour mood.

When Elika passed a girl with a basket of steaming sweet pies, she couldn't help spending another coin. She ate the pie as she perused the curious wares on offer.

There was a sudden crack of the whip and a loud curse. The scars on her back tightened at a flash of memory of another whip used to drive magic from inside her. The crowds parted as a prison wagon went past. Wretched, grimy faces stared miserably out of it—all Othersiders from Dae-Terren. They were clad in the heavy fabrics from her world. Fabrics that had been patched a hundred times. The prisoners wore no collars, for they had no master. Only one fate awaited them now. It was no secret. The wagon was stamped with the flourished silver butterfly, the mark of Archmage Tridamor. They were being taken to his temple, to be merged with magic.

"Magic-haters," voices grumbled on the street as the wagon passed.

Someone threw a stone at the bars, hitting one man on the shoulder. He covered his head with his chained hands as horse dung was thrown at the cage.

"Magic-haters!" the crowd shouted.

It was said men gave themselves to the service of magic freely. There was honor and pride to be had in being chosen as its host. The desolate faces of these prisoners made a lie of that assertion. There was no pride in their expression, only resignation to their coming fate. These men would wake up tomorrow as mages.

One prisoner caught her eye, an unshaven thug with a crooked nose, a cut to his brow and thick-knuckled hands. He wore a mismatched suit and boots, reminiscent of Peter Pocket's men. The suit was torn in places. Someone spat at him, and he leapt to his feet and grabbed the bars. "Bloody magic-lovers," he shouted. "One Eye will kill every one of ye damned human vermin. Each one of you traitors will be burned alongside the mages …"

A stone hit his head and knocked him back into his seat.

He staggered to his feet, bleeding from the cut, and gripped the bars again. "The Blight will come for ye, too, ye bloody traitors! Hear me, Daes, wake up and rise against these bastards. Terren is ours, not theirs. Our forefathers built this city. Don't let them take it from ye."

A whip rang out, and he staggered back. Blood ran down his cheek.

"Shut your mouth," said the guard.

Someone bumped into Elika. "Watch where you're walking, Dae."

A hand grabbed her arm. "Look here, a Dae whore…"

She snatched the knife from her belt, slashed at the hand to free herself and ducked into the crowd whilst the man cursed and bled.

Across the street, a fight broke out between Dae youths and soft-faced Alterrians. She quickened her pace, as the fight drew in more men and caught the attention of the guards. Before the guards reached the scuffle, Daes fled in all directions, blood dripping from their knives whilst the Alterrians were moaning and groaning on the ground.

Elika lowered her head and kept walking, blindly turning into alleys and streets, as the echoes of the prisoner's words chased her. Everywhere she looked, she saw Daes with their eyes downcast and metal chokers tight around their throats. Alterrians made a stark contrast. Few were indentured. Those who were, walked with their heads held high, as if servitude to magic was the sole purpose of their wretched lives. They bowed to mages whilst glaring with disdain at their own kind, the invaders from the other side of the dividing chasm. *Othersiders. Magic-haters. Dae pigs. Barbarians.* Every barbed insult, every hate-laced word struck her, and it grew harder and harder to close her ears to them.

Then there was silence, and angry voices grew distant. She stopped, as she recognized the courtyard with the stairs spiraling underground into Syn'Moreg's temple.

Turn around and walk away, she thought. But the prisoner's words stirred darkness inside her. And towards darkness, it drew her.

The priests of the Abyss, they called his worshipers. Each night, their dark chants haunted her peace as their smoke found its way into her room. Each night, they called forth the spider to invade her dreams.

In daylight, the temple did not seem so menacing. No one was about. Feeling bold and foolish in equal measure, she descended the stair slowly, keeping her ears sharp as she went.

Silence came from below. The doors were wide open, and the prayer hall was empty save for the stone spider in its heart. Torches lit up the underground cavern, and they shimmered in its yellow-gemmed eyes. Drawn to the dark demigod, she walked towards it. There was a dark beauty about him, a certain elegance of form.

"What do you want from me, beast?" she asked, hating this creature of nightmares.

Penny once told her that dreams were but shadows of one's past, and echoes of one's hopes. But the Sachi believed dreams to be gateways to another realm. Might be they were. Then why did the spider stalk her there?

On the marble dais by the spider's legs, lay rows of golden bowls holding finely carved prayer tokens. The Sachi priests spent their days carving them from wood and stone. In this temple, they also fashioned them from metal. But these were not like any wards she had seen before. The Sachi prayer tokens always resembled wishes, hopes and dreams that folk asked the gods to grant. But these tokens were of dark things—skulls, weapons, strangling vines and angry beasts, animal organs, severed heads, claws, teeth and blind eyes. Nothing a sane man would pray for.

Elika took out the wooden bird from her pocket, needing to hold onto something pure.

"Rage shines in your eyes, Aleyala. Has the old god offended you?" said a deep, familiar voice.

She turned towards it. The old, black-robed Sachi priest stood serenely beside an entryway which led deeper into the underground temple.

"Name's Eli," she said. "And 'tis evil you pray to."

"Evil? There is no good or evil amongst the gods, only justice and might."

"The Lord of the Abyss has broken our world."

"And he must mend it," the priest replied. "All we can do is pray to him and wait for his answer."

The spider's eyes gleamed overhead, as if he was listening to them and laughing. And she gazed back at the demigod who had rent their realm, giving half to men and half to magic. Except, the half he had given to men was always doomed to die. It was a lie, or a cruel lesson, perhaps.

"Seems he cares not for your prayers or our realm. Destruction is all he knows."

"Question not the judgment of the gods. Judge not their actions, nor seek reason for them," he replied with that unwavering worldly patience of the Sachi priests.

"Blind are those who do not seek the truth." She repeated what another Sachi priest once told her.

"Yet those who find the truth may also not see it. Another blindness of sorts. Perhaps our prayer has not reached him, but it brought you to us. 'Tis for us to ponder on this."

There was nothing to ponder, she thought. She believed in chance and coincidence as firmly as the Sachi refuted it. Their lives revolved around that untouchable power called Fate. Its whims and purpose to be analyzed with every rising of the sun and every wail of a babe.

"Tell me, priest, can the gods be killed?"

"All that is born can be killed," he replied with his usual unflappable grace. "But the gods are not our enemies."

"Neither are they our friends."

"And yet you are here, seeking their guidance. Has the prayer token in your hand served its purpose? For I can see you are ready to exchange it."

She tore her gaze from the spider, remembering the wooden bird she was still holding. It was meant to guide the lost home. It had guided her here, to this world. "Aye," she said and gave the priest a small smile. Always she found strange comfort in the perceptive wisdom of the Sachi. "Which token should I take, priest, since you see so much?"

"The choice must always be yours. This temple honors the darker gods, death and the shadows that live in our hearts. For they, too, must be acknowledged. Search deep inside yourself and find what is it you fear. Then take a token to ward yourself against it."

She regarded the golden bowls with many dark and terrible tokens. Only one drew her, an impulse she could not resist. She bent down and took the stone spider, before placing the bird in its place amid the teeth-baring beasts.

"From the web of light, we weave life," said the Sachi priest. "From the shadow's pool, we weave death. If your heart is true, the token will help you quench your fears and lead you into the light. But if you feed on darkness, it will lead you instead to the Abyss and the god of judgement. Seek not his mercy then, only swift death."

She closed her hand over the spider and shoved it into her pocket. "What does Aleyala mean in the tongue you speak?"

"Daughter of the gods," he replied sagely and bowed.

~

The sea's whisper filled her mind, an ancient language speaking secrets she could not grasp. The briny air was fresh, for it had rained early that morning. She sat on the harbor wall, eating a creamy pie stuffed with fish and potatoes, whilst her feet dangled over the water. What magic drove it to run up to her feet and then retreat, she did not know. In her other hand, she toyed with the spider as she watched the dead city across the chasm. *Home.*

There it was, the other half of Wharf Street, with its abandoned stone cottages and rotting fishermen's huts. The endless mudflats, with Bill's blue boat still there, and the crumbling buildings on Rift Street. Streets she had walked all her life, forever now beyond her reach.

Behind her, the Wharf Street of Al-Terren was a thriving hive of warehouses and bustling taverns. There were stalls with fresh fish and crabs. Seagulls eyed them from the roofs, whilst screeching for their next plunder. One seller had waved the same bird away thrice already. It did him little good. The bird remained intent on stealing a fish from his salt crates.

Traders with exotic faces and clothes had arrived on a ship from the southern lands. Next to them milled dark Islanders, adorned with pearl necklaces and bracelets and cloths fashioned from fish scales.

The harbor's magistrate and his officials inspected every cargo and logged arrivals into a ledger. Every ship, every traveler and every crate of fish had to be accounted for. Seas, lakes and rivers, and everything living in their waters, belonged to Tsarin Ilikan, which meant there was a tax to be paid to him for their use.

He must have been very wealthy indeed, for the harbor was teeming with ships. Most were small fishing boats that looked like bobbing toys beside large sailing ships anchored at the dock. A long line of sailors carried boxes aboard one, as a fat merchant buzzed around them anxiously. A small group of richly clad passengers awaited their turn to embark, whilst the captain stood at the gangplank, perusing his manifest. On the deck and up masts, sailors raced like busy squirrels readying the ship for departure. As she watched them, Elika nursed a temptation to sail away from this alien Terren and the ever-present sight of her past. Would that the fog returned to hide the haunting vision of her old city in ruins and the stark reminder of countless lives lost.

"Hey, you want fresh cockles?" said a voice next to her.

She turned to the Dae boy. His hair was roughly cropped and his face was muddy and crusty from where he had smeared his runny nose. His ears were too large for his head and curled like dried leaves at the tips. He scratched the inside of his ear with dirty fingernails and stuck out the basket of shells for her to examine. "Picked them this morning meself."

"Don't have use for cockles. The cook hates anything taken from inside a shell. Thinks it's where Ilikan hides his curses. But I'll give you a lucky feather for some answers." She showed him the bright red feather no kid could resist.

It caught his attention, just as she expected. "Oh, you are one of us." He wiped his nose with the back of his hand. "You dress as one of *them*."

She shrugged. "I wear what my mistress tells me to wear."

He eyed her collar. "My master is also one of us. He crossed six years ago and worked hard for his master. Bought himself freedom and got himself a boat. That's the yellow one over there with the drying nets. Says I could do the same if I work hard. He takes me out before dawn to fish out there." He nodded at the sea. "Threw up all my guts for a whole sennight, before I got used to going up and down them waves."

"When did you cross?"

"Last summer, when they started burning the folk. My ma got caught for being an Echo and burned on a pyre. But Pa died on the bridge. I made it though. Not so bad here. At least they're not burning anyone anymore. Though I hate the mages. One chipped my ear when he thought I was stealing from him. See?" He bent the ear to show her it was cleaved at the tip. "I wasn't, though. Just wasn't looking where I was going. No one here's standing up to them. Though they should."

"Aye, they should," she agreed quietly.

"But blood-salt's forbidden. So, how are we to fight them?"

She had no answer to that. Blood-salt fires and the burning of the magic was what brought forth the Blight. But how else were men to fight that which no other weapon could vanquish?

She gave him the red feather. "Know of any Dae gangs about?"

The boy's face shuttered, and her suspicions were confirmed. If she knew her own folk, they would not sit idly by and be enslaved by magic. Penny would not allow that to happen to her or her own. Neither would Mite.

"Ever heard of Bad Penny?" she asked him after he clamped his mouth shut and refused to speak.

"Aye, and Peter Pockets, and Rimley, too," he said, brightening again.

"Well, I was one of Penny's pack, in the old city."

His eyes widened. "Gor, that's something. You don't look tough, though."

Faster than he could blink, she had a knife in her hand, startling him. He took a step back.

"I carry this for protection." She held it out to him and he came closer again. "You got one yourself?"

He shook his head.

"Then here, take it." Buried in her boot was her favorite knife, which was far sharper than this one. She had found this one in the old shed at the back of their workshop, where many forgotten tools were rusting.

"It's got blood on it."

"'Tis the blood of a man who tried to grab me earlier."

His caution crumpled. He took the knife. There was not much to it, a rough wooden handle and a crooked blade, but he stared at it as if it was made of gold. Then he tucked it under his shirt and pocketed the feather. "They say Pockets is dead," he said.

"Aye, I saw him die myself," she said.

"Heard nothing of Bad Penny. But Rollers says that Rimley made it over with some of his thugs. But as soon as they crossed, they got caught and sent to the mines, and Rimley's now a mage. Or so say those who know him. There are dog-gangs about in Daetown. But they don't do much but steal, drink and whore, or try to set a mage's house on fire."

She'd heard of Daetown. Many who had crossed settled there, keeping close to their own kind. They used to have troubles with Daes there until they replaced the mage overlord of the district with Lord Snowstorm, whose father was a nobleman from Dae-Terren. The Othersiders grumbled but accepted the human overlord and had quietened down since then.

"It's One Eye you've got to watch for," the boy continued. "He's been quietly taking the streets since last summer and driving off rival leaders one by one. So now half the toughs answer to him. They say he's the one who's been making them mages go missing and setting the Dae slaves free."

Her heart did a flip of hope as her hand rose to her neck. "What about the collars?"

He shrugged. "They say he's found a way to remove them. I'm not allowed to speak of it. But since you're one of us, I don't think my master will mind."

"Did he remove your collar, too?"

He readjusted the strap of his basket on his shoulder. "Never had one. My master says no one has the right to enslave an honest man. So, when I crossed and the guards grabbed me, he was on his boat and saw me. Raced over to help and paid the magistrate for my freedom. He said I could stay with him, seeing as his sons were dead. Name's Bobquick, in case you were wondering. But everyone just calls me Quick. 'Cause no one's faster than me, see?"

Her attention was caught by a large ship with blue sails and a big, gilded fish at the bow, gliding into the harbor. The ship moved as if driven by magic and not wind.

Bobquick followed her gaze and whistled. "That's even bigger than the last one to come from Maysea Islands. Tsarin Ilikan's ships are the biggest you'll ever see. My master's worked on one of them, and he's been to Maramer. Said the whole city was made of water, even the houses and streets. And the fish were flying around like birds."

"Sounds like a foolish city to me," she said and grinned at the image it conjured.

The air was suddenly rent with a violent roar and boom and Ilikan's blue-sailed ship was engulfed by a ferocious fire.

The boy staggered back in surprise. "Gor, look at that. It just burst into flames."

"Why did it do that?" Her voice came out oddly high-pitched.

The boy looked about, then pointed at the sky, where Reval's island floated upside down amongst the clouds. "Reval hates Ilikan, and Ilikan hates him. So they attack each other with magic. They always war. And we're caught between them."

Bells rang as smoke rose and spread, and memories of another life invaded. Those awful bells tolling *Blight!* The red smoke and the screams of burning folk as the mob raged through the streets. Another ball of fire came from the sky and struck the mast, dragging her back to the present.

Shouts came from the city wall, and guards ran towards the wharf. Men from every ship rushed to the boats to launch them into the water.

The fire spread along the sails and masts of the great ship. Sailors jumped over the side, though many could not swim. Others tried to fight the spreading flames with buckets filled with seawater, as rowboats raced to reach them.

Screams rose above the roar of flames. They were coming from fine ladies and lords gathered by the railing of the ship, fearful of jumping overboard where bodies were floating face down. Then flames pushed a woman in a voluptuous dress into the water. Elika rose to her feet, helplessly watching the battling arms and legs fight the swirling green silk as the woman sank. A rowboat got there just as the last of her silks merged with the dark depths.

The tsaren were fighting, but it was the humans who were dying, Elika thought grimly as the sky darkened with smoke. And all the while, with the sails ablaze, the ship continued to advance on the harbor.

"It's going to run into the other ships," Bobquick said with mesmerized wonder.

Without warning, her heart jolted painfully, as if a hand reached inside her chest and squeezed. It took her a moment to realize its cause. Amidst the guards and workers racing to the boats, a single shape caught her eye.

Mite.

Suddenly nothing else existed in her world but Mite. Neither the fire nor smoke. Neither the drowning nor the screaming. He was there, dressed as a city guard, in blue and black, a freeman. Her heart resumed its beat, fast and furious. She took an instinctive step towards him … and stopped. Another man with red hair grabbed his arm to pull him away from the water's edge. Mite shook him off, his attention on the burning ship.

He looked larger, broader. He had grown since she had last seen him. And as ever, he was there, in the midst of it all, eager to help, shouting commands to men around him … Except, he had not helped their pack when they had needed him most. He had left them to face their fate without him. And face it they did. Most of them were dead now, slaughtered, burned in the blood-salt pyres or thrown into the chasm.

She hardened her heart against the pain of grief.

To see him was to see again all the horrors they had lived through without him. He had vanished into the Deadlands, and she had believed she would never see him again. Certain that he was dead or lost forever, she had even stopped being angry with him.

Seeing him now, alive and as gallant as ever, the forgotten hurt and anger rose afresh. *I'll wait for you on the other side*, he had promised. A child's promise, she thought with a bittersweet turn of her lips. Many a lonely night, she had imagined looking for him in Al-Terren. But there he was and she could not bring herself to walk towards him. Did he still think of their old pack … of her?

Fool, she chided herself. *Of course, he did not.* He'd more likely think of his ladyloves he used to bed and leave. He had not been waiting for her. She had sensed him before she had seen him. Yet, even now, he saw her not. Mite, who never missed a detail around him, never missed an enemy or friend within his sight.

More guards rushed to his side—his comrades, companions, friends. No doubt he had lovers scattered across the city, too. He had his own life, now, one she had no claim to. He had left their pack … and her.

Despite the pain in her chest, she could not look away. He shouted commands, which the other guards rushed to obey. The red-haired man raced to tie down the rowboat which carried wounded sailors. Many had burns to their flesh. They helped them to shore, whilst Mite threw off his leather armor and greaves. He pulled off his boots, and clad in only his shirt and trousers, jumped into the same boat. Two guards took the oars and rowed as fast as the strength in their arms allowed, headed towards the ship as it glided towards them, unmanned and afire. Closer and closer it drew to the wooden harbor and other ships anchored there.

With strangled breath, she watched Mite jump overboard, and emerge again to climb a rope onto the burning ship. He raced to the front, past the flames and the smoke to drop the anchor. His shirt began to burn, then his hair. Her feet moved of their own accord, running to get closer wanting to save him, certain he was dead …

He dived back into the water. She halted again. He was swimming towards the waiting boat. The red-haired man helped him climb out, as men cheered from the shore.

The ship came to a jarring stop, close to another in the harbor, and the flames leapt the divide between them, setting on fire the sails of the other ship. Sailors threw water as more boats rowed out with men rushing to help fight the flames.

Then Ilikan's ship did something more frightening than anything she had seen in this world so far. The gilded fish at the bow, grew watery tentacles, ripped a burning mast and sail from the deck and threw it at the city. The burning beam landed on the roof of a warehouse and set it ablaze. The tentacles then ripped off another mast and threw that too at the buildings along Wharf Street. Elika ducked as it flew overhead, the searing heat from the flame brushed past her.

The buildings exploded into flame as the fish threw more and more of the burning debris, barrels, beams and planks. As it slowly sank, it ripped parts of the burning deck and hurled them at Terren. A large piece of fiery deck flew over the wall and into the city itself. Smoke thickened. More screams rose from behind the wall.

Beside her, Bobquick was taking it all in with his mouth hanging open. "Gor, look at that. Never seen anything like that before."

Elika was speechless. Hatred of magic was burning as fiercely in her chest as the surrounding buildings. She wanted to stop this senseless destruction, but what could she do against so much magic?

Bobquick grabbed her arm and yanked. "We must go, quick. The mageguards are here."

She turned to where he was pointing. Mages in red robes galloped on horseback through the crowds, heedless of whom they trampled. They swung their whips and loosed them on anyone within reach, their gazes fixed on the sinking ship hurling burning debris at the city. These were not like the mages she had seen. They looked much more human, their movements smooth not awkward.

Bobquick frantically tugged on her arm. "Come, we must leave before they take it into their heads to blame the Daes for this. They always blame us, even when they know it's not us."

But she couldn't move. In the distance, Mite was being helped out of the boat by his red-haired companion. One of his sleeves had been burned off, and much of his hair on one side of his head. He should have been burned to a crisp, like the wet sailors who followed him to shore. But the skin of his face and arm was only slightly flushed. How could that be?

The boy was tugging on her arm as he hastily closed his basket and strapped it to his back. "Come. More mages will be here soon, and they'll be asking questions. You don't want to be here when they do, 'cause they don't stop asking till you give them the right answer."

From the corner of her eye, she saw the mage pull on his reins and turn his horse. "You two. Stop."

With an effort, she let Mite go. He was alive and free, and he was not alone. That was enough for her to know. "This way. Run!" She grabbed the boy by the hand and darted for the nearest alley stacked with crates and barrels.

Hoofs resounded in pursuit.

Elika pushed over an empty crate and as they rounded a corner, she glimpsed the horse swerve to avoid it. As it did, it reared before it trampled a barrel strolling along on creepy, black legs. That slowed the mage enough for her to push Bobquick up over a wall into a garden and climb behind him. They ran through a gate into an adjoining street, then down it. To her surprise, the boy was keeping pace with her on shorter legs despite the basket bouncing on his back.

The hoofs grew loud again. Then fire burst in front of them, blocking their path.

"This way!" He pulled her into another street, then turned abruptly to dart under an archway and press himself against the door. She hid behind a column of the doorway, listening as the galloping hoofs went past. When the sound faded, Bobquick bent over, breathing heavily. "Told you … I was … fast," he panted and straightened. "Come … let's go back to Daetown."

It was late in the day, and the light was fading, but Elika was not ready for her freedom to end, so she followed the boy. They did not have far to go. Daetown bordered the eastern harbor and took up much of the eastern quarter of Terren. Its boundary was marked by an inner-city wall encircling the district. Many such district walls ran into and over each other, proclaiming the boundaries of some mage overlord's domain. Guards patrolled them back and forth, and residents used them as occasional overhead walkways.

In Daetown, many of the streets were taken up with large workhouses and the notorious mills with tall, fat chimneys and grotesque metal gates. The streets were grimy, alleys stank of piss, and skinny chickens ran underfoot. She saw beggars, though they took care to keep out of sight. Old tinkers sat on benches, mending whatever folk brought them. And here and there she saw roaming packs of children chasing stray cats and filching careless pockets. A pang of nostalgia hit her, for nowhere else in this city reminded her as much of home.

Bobquick turned into a tavern with a sign of an eagle's feather above the green door. "Come, you can meet the rest of us. Everyone in Daetown knows *Eagle's Feather*. Innkeeper Tipps doesn't serve Alterrians. He hates magic-lovers. Says they are not people like us, but magic disguised as men. Else they are possessed by it and can't be trusted."

Inside, the tavern was narrow and long. Only two frosted windows on either side of the door let in any light. Oil lanterns in sconces burned along the wooden pillars. Three long tables ran the length of the room. From somewhere in a darkened corner came a tune filled with wordless sorrow. Everyone here was dressed in the common garb of folk from her old city. And with a pang of ache, she thought she was finally home.

Then everyone turned to stare at her.

"What rat 'ave you brought in here, Quick?" A weather-beaten man in a leather seafarer's coat called out from one of the long tables.

"Aye, take it outside and stamp on it," another shouted from a different table.

"She's one of us, Tom," he called back to the man in the leather coat and walked towards him. "Just got a master who dresses her like a doll."

Laughter rang out.

Elika strode forward, undaunted. She was home and she knew these folk as well as herself. "Might be she dresses me, but she doesn't make me love magic any better."

"That so? Then be welcome, girl," said the man called Tom. His skin was tanned and leathery. His beard was unkempt and tangled. But there was a trusty glint of laughter in his eyes. "There's too many of them and not enough of us in this city."

She liked Tom instantly. Beneath that weathered rough, she saw a good-natured man who looked at Bobquick with an undisguised affection and pride of a father. Never mind that the boy was not his.

Bobquick sat next to him at the table, placing his basket of cockles on the floor. "I sold half. Would've sold them all, but then the ship burst into flames and started to hurl burning barrels at the city, and a red-robe chased us …"

"Ho, there boy. What did I tell ye about babbling? Start at the beginning. A bloody mageguard chased ye?" Tom sounded affronted by it.

Elika joined them at the table. Men moved aside to give her room, whilst listening intently to Quick tell them about the burning ship. Some moved closer to listen and ask questions about every fine detail Elika thought unimportant, yet they found interesting. What had the main mageguard worn? Did he have the flame medallion or the butterfly?

Elika played with an empty mug someone had left behind as she listened and learned the faces of the men and the names they gave each other.

"Didn't get a chance to look closely, now did we," said Bobquick defensively.

"Well next time look, will ye?" Tom said.

"Why does it matter, anyway?" asked the boy, and Elika wondered the same.

"'Cause we want to know which mageguard faction came to look. Reval's or archmage's or Arala's," said the man with the look and smell of a tanner, whom the others called Skinner. The skin of his hands was dry, cracked and peeling.

"Since the bridge has gone and vanished, Arala's mageguards been prowling the streets, asking odd questions," Tom explained with more patience. "Asking about the bridge and its unravelling and who it was that stabbed it."

Elika stared intently at the empty mug, turning it in her hands, keeping her face expressionless. Then a mug of foaming ale appeared in front of her, and the empty one was plucked from her fingers.

She looked up into the tavern keeper's round face. "Got nothing left on me, but ribbons and trinkets," she told him.

"Pay me next time, then," he said as he wiped the table with a cloth, before flinging it over his shoulder. The tavern keeper was a burly man, who'd not struggle to carry a barrel full of ale under each arm. He was gruff like most others here, and she got the impression that he, too, was listening closely to what was being said.

Bobquick kept answering a barrage of questions, most of them with the same answer, "Dunno, now do I? Didn't stay long to find out."

"I'd say Reval's taking revenge for Sabreshore," said Tom, and laughter dimmed in his eyes. "Poor bastards. They made the best smoked herring in the realm. Generations of fishermen and their kids, all gone." He shook his head and looked into his ale.

There was no one in Terren who'd not heard of the coastal village washed away by a rogue wave. Ilikan had sent it in the middle of the night, when the folk were sleeping. It dragged every villager and animal into the ocean, leaving nothing behind but stone chimneys.

"Why'd he do that?" Bobquick asked.

"'Cause the fools replaced the shrine to Ilikan with Reval's," said Tom. "Ilikan claims any village that touches the seashore. But Reval says that anything not touched by the water at high tide is his."

The innkeeper left and shortly returned with more ale for their table.

"Why don't the tsaren just kill each other?" asked Bobquick with sulky anger.

No one had the answer to that.

"We need Prince Southfire to side with us," Bobquick said miserably. "He's an heir to the Sacred Crowns, and he'd be our king."

"I said it before and I say it again, Southfire is Reval's puppet," said Tom. "'Tis the archmage's arse that warms Terren's seat of power, and Southfire is a sniveling coward. There's no help there, boy."

"We need more blood-salt is what we need," said Skinner and was instantly shushed with stern looks from the others and pointed glances darting her way.

She pretended not to notice, whilst flinching inside at his words. So, they did have blood-salt, she thought with a sinking heart. Still, none of what they said about the tsaren fighting over man's realm like dogs over a kill, sat well with her. "I say that anything in Seramight is ours," she said and everyone nodded in eager agreement.

"That's what we say too," Bobquick replied, brightening again. "It's why we've formed the Dae rebellion. We are the resistance, see?"

Tom cuffed him. "Don't go blurting that to strangers. The lass might be a spy for them."

"For whom?" asked Elika. Having finished her ale, she was back to toying with her empty mug.

"Alterrians, mages, you know, *them*."

"I'm not."

"See?" Bobquick said as if that should be good enough for them.

"Spare me from the fools," said a gruff voice Elika recognized. "You and your bloody resistance. All ye do is talk about how much you hate them whilst you drink your ale and scratch your arses. Half of ye are stamped like cattle, with your masters telling you when to eat, when to piss and when to screw."

Elika's hair rose on the back of her neck as the ruffian at the next table turned around. Blood Dog.

He raised a mug to her with a sly smile. "Hey, little mouse. Seems you can't keep away from me. You sure I can't tempt you with a prune?"

She frowned. He wore no collar. Yet last she saw him, he was a prisoner in chains like her, brought before the magistrate. "How did you get free?"

He spat and leant back with his elbows on the table. "I got free 'cause I ain't a little mouse like you who'll let myself be chained like a dog. So I killed them. Then I carved out their insides and spread them around the magistrate's chambers."

Tom crossed his arms. "Seems to me you're the only one around here barking, Blood Dog. You and your wild tales. Yet you're the first to slink away whenever a mageguard comes snooping around. So laugh all you want, but we've got spies all over the city, and loyal men ready to rise when the time's right."

Elika was not certain Tom had taken the right measure of Blood Dog. She half expected the greasy tough to jump over the table and cut the fisherman's throat.

But he only laughed instead. "Ye're nothing but a pack of bickering women. The mages will turn you all into their whores when the time's right."

"If you are the resistance, then who's your leader?" Elika asked.

Blood Dog barked another laugh. "Go ahead, tell her." He waved his mug at her.

Tom scratched his beard. "Well, I am … that is until we get someone else. Thought Dog over there might be a good man to ask, but he's …"

"Sick to the death of listening to you, fish breath."

"Pah!" Tom waved his hand at him and turned back to her. "You gotta pardon our caution, but we need to know who drinks beside us. Where you're from, girl?"

Before Elika could answer, Bobquick blurted out, "She's one of Bad Penny's pack."

"Is that so?" Tom said with clear surprise. Others, too, turned to regard her, some with respect, some with disbelief.

Blood Dog seemed to take interest in that, too. "Bad Penny, hey?" he said, assessing her as if seeing her in a different light.

There was no use denying it that she could see. "Aye, I was."

"Then why are you still wearing that blasted ring around your neck," Blood Dog asked. "One Eye can have it off ye, if you don't have the wits to get it off yourself."

"'Cause it serves me well enough for now to wear it."

Blood Dog waved that away and turned back to his companions.

A creeping sensation on her skin made her turn her head and follow the guidance of those inner instincts that had kept her alive on the streets.

In the darker corner of the bar, a minstrel was testing the strings of his lute, whilst staring at her with undisguised curiosity. He was a giant of a man and bizarrely wide. She could not judge his age. Though he was full-grown, there was a boyishness about him, as if the world was still fresh and wondrous. He sat with his legs up on the chair, his large fingers caressing the strings of the lute. By all rights, those fingers should have broken the fine strings, but the soft music that emerged might have been played by the wings of a butterfly.

There was an odd quality to him that set her on edge, as if he was a dream that did not belong in the waking world. The thought made no sense, yet neither did he, though there was nothing obviously amiss about him. For an instant, she imagined she alone could see him, so vague was he to her senses. It was as if he was vanishing between blinks. Bill Fisher had been like that too, silent to her senses, as if he was not quite there. Always, he would appear without her awareness of him.

She must have stared too long, for the giant smiled broadly, tested a few notes on his lute and began to sing.

> *"I heard a crow not long ago,*
> *Fly through the fog and screech*
> *"Beware! Anon!*
> *There comes a foe*
> *Far more than you can see."*
> *The white tips flashed,*
> *And men looked up,*
> *And still it screeched at me,*
> *A song I shall tell thee ...*

> *"To Gods I sing*
> *To Gods I crow*
> *A child's prayer on my brow*
> *She seeks to wound*
> *She seeks to strike*
> *A child's wrath upon your might*
> *Destruction, death*
> *And vengeance right*
> *Beware the anger of her spite.*

> *Where there was one,*
> *There shall be two,*
> *A goddess comes for all of you,*
> *Beware her wrath,*
> *Beware her spite*
> *Beware the hot blade of her might."*

As the crow's words flowed from the minstrel's mouth, he kept looking at her with a laughing glint in his eyes. After he sang the last verse, he swung his feet off the chair and strode towards them, lute in hand. He straddled the bench across the table from her.

Bobquick instantly straightened. "Pebble, you should have seen the ship throw burning planks at us. You'd have made a great song of it. I can tell you all about it so you still can."

"Who is your friend, Quick?" he asked in a gravelly voice.

"That's ..." The boy stumbled. "Um. I forgot to ask her name."

That earnt him another cuff behind the head from Tom. "You didn't even ask her name before you brought her here?"

"Lika ... name's Lika," she said as Bobquick rubbed the back of his head.

"Pebble, they call me." The minstrel gave her a flourished bow, which seemed only half mocking.

"You look more like a rock than a pebble," she said, though in truth he looked more like a boulder.

"I gave myself that name to annoy Father. He hates embarrassment even more than he hates me."

She turned accusingly to Bobquick. "I thought you told me Alterrians weren't welcome here."

"Oh, Pebble isn't one of them, but one of us. He's a *tane*." Bobquick leant in and added in a whisper. "He's two hundred years old."

The broad-faced minstrel gave her that boyish grin of his. "Bastard son of Draygan," he said with an exaggerated incline of his head. "Father has many, as you may have heard. And he hates every one of us. But he loves human wenches."

Tanes were half-breed bastard children of the tsaren, and none seemed to have more of them than Draygan, if what was said of him was to be believed.

Elika's weariness increased. The two tanes she had known were ancient, and they had both tried to convince her she was a tsarina.

As if he read her thoughts, he said, "It's a wonder how you managed to remain such a delicious secret for so long, princess."

"I am neither a secret nor a princess."

His smile widened, showing big teeth, which she was certain could chew stones. "As you say, thus it shall be."

Bobquick looked from Pebble to her and back again. "What secret is she keeping?"

"I told ye she was a spy," said Tom with frustration.

Elika gave the minstrel her meanest, most threatening scowl. "I'm keeping no secrets. Everyone knows the tanes are mad and come out with all manner of nonsense."

He smiled cockily and played some notes on his lute. "But we all keep secrets, do we not?"

"Are you a spy for the mages, girl?" Tom demanded.

"I spy for no one."

"How do we know that?" asked Peters, a thick-armed man sitting next to her. It was the only thing he'd said all evening. He had lost most of his voice, and his throat strained to rasp his words.

Tom and Bobquick waited for her reply in anticipation, as if everything depended on her answer.

Elika sighed. "'Cause I hate mages."

"If she hates mages, then she hates magic, see?" Bobquick insisted, determined to defend her.

"Well, do you, princess, hate magic?" Pebble asked whilst tweaking the stings of his lute.

"I don't like *you*," she snapped at him.

He laughed.

Tom and the others seemed to relax at that. "Oh, aye, this one's a magic-hater, alright. Hates even the sight of a tane."

"Of course, she hates me." Pebble said it so quietly, Elika thought she was the only one who heard him. He raised his eyes to her, challenging her to deny it.

That grated. She knew what he was alluding to. Bill had told her that the tsaren hated the tanes, and magic, too, rejected them. She did not want to give Pebble the satisfaction of correcting him on her account.

"I thought tanes loved magic," she said mulishly to him.

"It is hard to love that which hates you," he replied and played a few more notes.

"Aye, 'tis true," Tom said. "Saw it myself, a mage beating near half to death a young tane girl in the street for nothing more than being a tane, and there was nothing anyone could do."

Pebble stretched his thick legs in front of him. "What did you think of my latest song, princess?"

Bobquick replied before she could. "Never heard you sing it before. Where did you find it?" He turned back to her. "Pebble goes to all kinds of strange places, looking for songs. He says they are flying all around us, but he wants to catch only the best."

"Oh, I had a wonderful adventure some nights ago. It was filled with darkness and chanting …"

"The priests of the Abyss?" the boy said breathlessly.

"Aye, them who walk the streets at night, calling the shadow. And a shadow did follow them that night," Pebble said in a hushed voice, and the table fell silent, as men leant forward to listen. "The priests were foolish, you see. They thought they could bid the shadow to carry out their will, but then, it unleashed its power …"

"And killed the priests?" Bobquick finished in a whisper.

Grimly, Pebble nodded.

"Ha!" cried Elika, outraged. "Minstrels spin tales out of the empty air they breathe."

"I was there, you know," he said mildly. "Seeking songs, as Quick here says. I was drawn by the unfamiliar essence of a mysterious new power. So I followed it, and it led me to the temple. And when I saw you … just now, of course, I had to sing you this song."

Elika's skin crawled. She knew not whether he was friend or foe, but his tales were dangerous and the gleam in his eyes was as challenging as it was curious.

"Why her?" Quick frowned.

"He's mad, that's why," Elika replied.

"Is it a prophecy?" asked Tom.

"They say crows only speak when there is a prophecy to be told," Bobquick added.

"Well, is it, princess?" Pebble asked innocently as if she alone knew the answer.

"Sounds like a song you made up," she said with a shrug.

Tom and Bobquick looked disappointed.

Pebble put aside his lute. "'Tis a tragic thing to be a minstrel. No one believes me, even when I sing the truth."

Thankfully Pebble spoke no more of the matter, and Elika studiously ignored him the rest of the night, choosing to listen rather than speak, and to learn what was what in this world as these men saw it.

It was late when she left the tavern where Daes dreamt of purging mages from Terren and claiming the city for their own.

True to Blood Dog's words, they drank ale and talked of plans that would never come to pass. For on the morrow, they had to fix the boat, check the crab pots and dig for more cockles. They had to finish tanning a pile of hide for the armorer and bake enough bread for the early merchants passing through. Tomorrow Peters would drive his wagon to the mills and bring back crates of clay pots for his wife to fill with her delicious jam for selling at the markets. Aye, Blood Dog was not wrong to laugh. Still, a spark of hope tickled her heart, for where there was the smoke of discontent and anger, the fires of battle could be lit.

Bobquick was fast asleep at the table when she left, whilst Tom was yawning and arguing with Skinner about whether black crab or red had more flesh on it. Either way, both agreed that black crab tasted sweeter.

Outside, Elika faced the dark, sleepy street and braced herself for her last task of the day. She had avoided it long enough.

The door opened and closed behind her. And her skin chilled and prickled, for she was still alone. No one was behind her. No one was around her. No eyes were on her. She could always sense eyes on her. There was silence out here, beneath the muffled voices leaking from inside. Slowly she turned.

Pebble loomed above her like a thick tree, so close she should have sensed him, his heat, his scent. Their vagueness chilled her. It was absurd. For there he was, his size truly formidable.

She took a step back, unsettled, and eyed him wearily. "Don't be thinking of following me again," she warned him, though she didn't know what she'd do to stop him. Run, she supposed.

His face was solemn. "I mean you no harm."

"Then why did you say those things to them?"

"She seeks to wound, she seeks to strike," he said quietly. "We are not blind like the mages. I know what you are, what you can do. The crow warns us, so I warn these men, for I care for them. You will bring grief to their door." His lips quirked up boyishly. "But it will make for a great, eternal ballad, will it not?"

She could not hold back a small smile. "You have me all wrong, Pebble."

"You hate them," he said with a curious tilt of his head.

"Whom?" she frowned.

"*Them.*" He waved his hands dramatically in the air. "The tsaren, the mages. You pity the humans. Perhaps I am wrong and you can help this sad pack calling itself resistance."

"If they suspected I had magic in me, they'd skin me alive, then burn me in blood-salt fire."

"I would not let them." He seemed truly horrified by the idea. "I can help you, tsarina."

She looked aside at the warmly lit windows of the tavern, wearied by him, by what he was and what he thought he saw in her.

"Help *them*," she said with a nod towards the tavern and strode off, bracing herself for another meeting with Maj-Dun'Flower.

CHAPTER FIVE

Maj-Dun Flower

"The ceremony of our birth, the merging of Laifae with man's body, is a secret known only to the tsaren and Archmage Tridamor. No other mageguard can bring our kind into the realm of Seramight. He was given this gift by Arala, for he was the arch of her mageguard and most loyal advisor. And because of this gift, Reval bestowed upon him Terren's Seat of Power and entrusted him with keeping the peace in the realm, until Arala returned."
The History of Alafraysia and Seramight,
By Mageguard Bluelight

The moon was high, and the night could hide no secrets in its shadows. The trading houses and workshops had closed. Market stalls stood empty. Faint candlelight burned in the windows. The streets were silent, peaceful, and the world was hers and hers alone.

The bell tower chimed the late hour. When the sound faded, the peace did not return. In the distance, the bone-chilling droning of the Priests of Syn'Moreg haunted the night. Their smoke lingered on the air long after they had passed. Their prayer, chanted in an alien tongue, pulled on some deeper essence of her, just as it had done in the temple. It called to her in a way she could not understand. Nor did she want to. So she avoided them and walked the other way until she could no longer hear their voices. Only then, the restless creature inside her—eager to answer them—stilled.

Even then, with each step closer to Maj-Dun'Flower's home, her footsteps grew leaden, her reluctance increased, and she found herself taking a longer route where there was no cause for it. Save that she did not want to confront the foul mage again.

When she came to the cavern woven of black branches, her steps faltered altogether, along with her slippery courage. Sick dread settled in her stomach. She knew what Maj-Dun'Flower would demand for his jug of dye. It would be easy to run, hide and seek the notorious One Eye to remove her collar. But she knew better than that. She was not a child anymore. Fears unconquered would always turn you into their lowly wretch. There was no hiding from the cruelties of the world, no escaping the vices of men. If she gave in to fear now, she would be hiding and running all her life.

She pulled her favorite knife from her boot and stuck it into the pocket of her dress. Her fingers wrapped around the hilt and lingered there until her fear retreated into the depths where her magic resided. She reached for that ball of power and found it alert and ready.

Face your fears. She had learned that lesson well when she finally crossed the frightful bridge to come to this world. Often, the fears were worse than the battle itself.

With a deep, determined breath, she took an assertive step forward. The black branches of the cavern shifted like lazy snakes and pulled apart to allow her inside. Then tangled again behind her.

Maj-Dun'Flower was hunched over his steaming cauldron, stirring the dye he was brewing. "So, you are back," he hissed over his crooked shoulder.

Elika bowed, hoping to keep his anger at bay. "Mistress Oblana sent me to fetch more dye."

"This late in the day?" He turned his ugly face towards her.

Elika cursed herself as a thousand types of fool. Days and nights held little meaning to a thief. Only that her old pack would save the most unsavory tasks for the darker hours. It did not occur to her how he might perceive her appearance at this hour.

She scrambled to find a believable lie. "Forgive the unusual hour. The mistress had a customer who demanded his web by morning. Unfortunately, we ran out of the dye before I could finish it."

The mage's face contorted with menace. He straightened into a larger, taller creature than she thought him to be. She saw now that he was younger than he appeared, despite his stooping and jittery movements reminiscent of an old man whose body no longer obeyed him.

"She never replied to the letter we gave you to deliver," he said in his awful voice. "*Insolent wench*," hissed the other voice inside him.

"She has been busy of late. And she suffers terrible headaches that make her forget."

Maj-Dun'Flower poured a ladle of the dye from the cauldron into a jug, sealed it with a cork and placed it on the table between them.

"The she-human lies to us. Aeon-Rah came to see us and tells us we must give you as much dye as you need. He also tells us that an errand boy will come and collect it. The boy came earlier."

Her stomach jolted. Meena's malicious smile flashed in her mind. A trick … a trap. Meena had sent her here on a false errand, knowing what the mage would do. Once, Elika could read people better than anyone—knew when they were lying. Yet somehow, this morning, she forgot to listen to those instincts.

"Then the mistress made a mistake in sending me. As I said, she is forgetful." Elika turned to leave, but the branches remained firmly twined across her path.

"She sent you to us," said Maj-Dun'Flower behind her. "A gift."

"No!" She spun to face him. "You can't touch me, mage. I've magic's favor."

He cackled. "*We* bestow favor on you, and you keep it by bestowing your favor on us in return. We recall telling you the next time you came here, you would kneel before us."

Elika's body began to tremble of its own accord, and for an instant she considered dropping to her knees and begging for mercy. Then Mite's face flashed before her eyes. She remembered him climbing up the burning ship. She remembered the laws of their pack. No one went to their death meekly. No one was to cower and cry. Come what may, death or mercy, you must fight for your place in this life.

Her trembling stopped. "Let me go," she said darkly and this time she did not keep her expression meek.

"You dare disobey us, human she-child?" he hissed and tried to grab her.

She ducked and stepped out of his reach. "I won't let you touch me." She pulled out her knife. "Faced bigger toughs than you, mage."

"We will have you whipped for disobedience. You have not faced our power, she-human. That knife is naught but a nuisance to us." A black tendril shot out and struck her across the face.

She stumbled in a daze, and suddenly he was atop her, pushing her against the table, hiking up her skirts.

"We will teach you respect, girl," he hissed into her ear.

Elika could not breathe. He was crushing her, yanking her hair back.

"No!" She twisted in his grip, elbowed him hard in the stomach and yanked her head away.

When she staggered away from him, he was left gripping a black clutch of her hair.

More tendrils raced at her.

She ducked and skipped aside and sliced them with her knife, putting all her rage into the strike. He cried out and recoiled in surprise. "She-human cut us." He stared in confusion at the deep, bleeding gash. "*Impossible*," hissed the other voice. "It … hurts."

Outrage twisted his face into a mask of fury. Black tendrils came at her from everywhere at once, too many to cut or avoid. One wound itself around her throat, the other around her hand that held the knife.

Help me! She frantically called to her own magic.

It replied at once. Her own tendrils emerged and would around the mage. She lifted him off the ground.

His eyes grew wide with fear and surprise. "What are you?" he hissed. "A she-mage?"

Elika did not know—only that she could command magic … Could she command *his* magic?

"Hold!" She pushed that command at him. The vibrant force of this world thickened around her, and in it she felt *his* essence. She grabbed it.

He cried out and squirmed in her grasp, as his tendrils retreated back into his body.

A sense of power surged through her. His magic was under her control. She was in command. And with that power, her ire intensified. This vile creature thought to use her for his own gratification. The tendril around his throat tightened. She wanted to kill him as he would have killed her. But as the tendril tightened around his neck, she realized it had no effect on him. No cry of pain, no change in the color of his face, no sign of discomfort. Then she saw that he was not breathing, was not choking either, only dangling there like a frightened goose, his arms flapping by his sides.

What was this creature? she wondered. That question was mirrored in his face as he stared at her with the same bewilderment.

"You are of the Black River," he rasped. "*One of us*," hissed the voices inside him.

Elika ignored them. "Who made you, mage?"

He squirmed yet seemed compelled to speak. "We are Maj-Dun'Flower. Archmage Tridamor brought us here. We belong to him. If you hurt us, our master will not forgive it."

"You speak of *we*, but I see one man."

"Why do you ask these strange things of us? We are Laifae. We are of the river, like you."

"You were once human …"

"It is the greatest honor to be merged with magic. We are one now." There was frightened tension in his voice, and she heard the lie in it.

"Who am I speaking with, magic or man?"

Again, he wriggled in her grasp. "How do you command us? These human eyes are worthless. We gaze through the blind eyes of man and see not what stands before us. Tell us what you are?

For no mage can command us save the one who gave us this form."

"Are you magic or man?" she asked again, shaking him where he dangled. "Speak truth, or I'll know the lie and curse you."

"The man to whom this body once belonged is dead. It was his sacrifice to free me."

"Free you?"

"Free me from unending dreams and the realm spun of lies. Long have I waited to breathe and touch and taste and feel the silk from which human flesh is spun."

Disgust filled her. "You killed a man to take his body for your own."

"We are not like the tsaren who can fashion their own form. We have no voice, no power beyond the fleeting. Ever men seek to destroy us without hearing our cause. Why do they seek to kill us?"

"You seek to enslave them. You invaded our realm."

"Our worlds are one now. Neither can exist without the other. To unravel one is to unravel the other."

Elika knew he spoke the truth. She had seen the Blight caused by the destruction of magic. Still, this creature was vile. He had killed a man and stolen his body to walk amongst men as if he was one of them. She could not release him to abuse another, nor to carry tales to Aeon-Rah of her powers. But the only way to kill a mage, to kill magic, was with blood-salt fire. She had none of that on her. Then what was she to do with him?

"Release us," he said, seeing her indecision. "We will not touch you. We touch only humans."

His admission, so casually said, sent shards of fury through her.

Bill Fisher once told her that a tsarin could undo a mage. Could she return him to his own realm? Might be she could sunder this vile merging of man and magic and free the human from its grip.

"You should never have been," she said, though more to herself than him. "The archmage killed a man to make you."

"No ... he gave himself freely," he whimpered, and she knew it to be another lie.

A sudden sense of knowing came to her, some innate understanding. Like his home, the cavern and the door, he too was made from those dark tendrils of magic. The Black River, he called it. She recalled Bill telling her of the flailing threads of the web and balls of rolled-up magic. That was the mage's true form, a thread that could be unraveled. It was the vibrant essence she now held in her grasp. If she focused on it, she could sense it, see it with her mind's eye. She pulled upon that thread.

The mage screamed. "Spare us, mistress. We want to feel ... we want to live."

Elika pulled harder, watching without emotion as his eyes grew vacant, as the black tendrils faded away. Then she released him, and the body of a man, stripped of its invader, fell to the floor.

For long moments, she stared at the lifeless body, human and very young ... a Drasdane, one of the mountain folk, with pale hair and blue eyes. Signs of decay were showing in his skin, and the stench of death was strong about him. Even so, she could tell he was once a handsome man. When had he died? How long had it been since his life and body were stolen from him?

She looked at her hands. They were steady. She had unraveled a mage. She had the power to end them. Everything in her stilled, reordered. With striking clarity, she understood her fate, her reason for being. Might be the Sachi were right after all about such things. Syn'Moreg gave this world to magic. She would take it back and restore it to men. She would send every mage, the being calling itself the Laifae, back to his realm.

She picked up her knife, wiped the dark blood from it, sheathed it in her boot and left Maj-Dun'Flower's house. The doorway was just an empty wooden frame, the walls were common stone, and the cavern of branches outside was gone.

CHAPTER SIX

The Rogue Mage

"Those who claim that Alafraysia is a peaceful place of dreams, speak false. We have known many wars. Before the tsaren brought order to our world, we of the Black River flowed in many different branches. Each branch dreamt different dreams, each wanted to shape the world to its own designs. This created ripples and currents and anger. Some branches sought to unify into a river that always flowed the same way. A worthy cause, save that each wanted others to flow where it went. We warred without end, conquering and absorbing lesser branches. Then the tsaren came and gave us another world, one which they said was no different to man's domain. For a long time, we believed them, and this dream gave us peace. But then, the tsaren started to war with each other. It began with Arala's arrival."

The History of Alafraysia and Seramight,
By Mageguard Bluelight

She could unravel the mages, destroy them, and undo the horror the tsaren and the archmage had inflicted upon man's realm. The thought was intoxicating, and her soul vibrated with purpose, whilst in her hands, the silken web took shape. Elika wanted to throw it aside and march out into the city to find another mage to destroy. Only her aching hunger and Liffy's voice kept her anchored. "Sacred magic, glorious magic, gift me grace, and lend me wisdom ..."

Her voice was filled with pleading devotion as she recited another worthless prayer, and it was a sharp scrape against Elika's senses.

"You don't know what it is you are praying to," she said as the image of the young man's rotting corpse swam before her eyes; murdered so that the vile creature from another realm could possess his body.

Liffy ignored her outburst. "Sam came to see me yesterday." She twirled the green lace in her hair which Elika had given her that morning as an offering of peace. "By summer he'll have enough sherrings to buy his freedom, and then he'll find a way to buy mine and take me to Wavestar." She resumed spinning her wheel.

Liffy often spoke of her brother visiting. Elika was yet to meet Sam, though she knew much about him already. She knew of his flesh-rotting illness in the old city, when Liffy had nursed him back to health. It left deep scars on his body. They had lived on the street for a time, after their apple farm was destroyed by the Blight. He was kind and brave and saved Liffy from the lecherous guards. He held her hand as they crossed the bridge and made her unafraid. Now, he worked as a smith and was the best in Terren, so it was only a matter of time before he bought their freedoms. Whilst Liffy spoke of all the wonderful things they'd do in Wavestar, her voice became a wordless hum in Elika's ears.

Her mind drifted to the night before, to that rush of heady power as she ripped the strands of the mage's essence out of the stolen body. The power had left her breathless with the fear of it, with wonder … and with insatiable want.

This world was rich with an essence she could grasp and make it obey, that vibrant essence pulsing with life. And now that she had touched it, she was touched by it in turn. She pulled upon it now, and it quivered under her command. Her head swam, and she grew drunk and giddy on all that this power promised.

The sound of hurried horse hoofs clip-clopping on stone brought her back to Liffy's voice. "There must be another runway," she was saying from beside the window whilst looking down at the street. "I've never seen so many mageguards about."

"Question every servant and master. Search every workshop." A cackling, broken voice carried up to them from outside.

Elika's fingers stilled with premonition. She had killed a mage, had done what no man could do. Still, she had not expected the mages to track her here so soon.

She joined Liffy at the window. A contingent of red-robed mages on horses was riding through Yarn Row, trailed by human guards. The mages seemed agitated. Their eyes roamed the street, as if seeking a hidden enemy.

Rage shook her afresh, for Elika now knew what they were; vile creatures, dead men possessed.

They split up along the street and the riders dismounted. Two mageguards stood beneath her window.

"Question everyone in this street," commanded the one wearing the black medallion in the shape of a butterfly over his chest. From the talk in the *Eagle's Feather* last night, she knew it meant he was one of Arala's mageguards, who now belonged to the archmage. He was different to the others, in that he could easily be mistaken for a human. His skin was not as grey, his movements supple and natural. Only his horrid, unnatural voice betrayed him. He watched from atop his horse as the mages and guards dispersed through the streets, striding into shops, banging on locked doors.

"Who do you think they're looking for?" Liffy asked with apprehension.

A man was dragged out of the house across the street. "I know nothing of Dun'Flower's murder. I saw him only briefly yesterday," he cried as they herded him into a waiting prison wagon.

Liffy gasped with fright. "Maj-Dun'Flower's dead? But where will we find more dye?"

The door to their shop below opened and closed.

Elika's mind raced. She had only a moment to run, but if she did, they'd know her guilt. *Think, Eli, do not panic*, she chided herself and put a wall between her fearful heart and reason. They could not know it was her, else they would not be searching.

"Maj-Dun'Flower is dead!" Meena's voice was shrill. Then it dipped to a murmur.

Elika well suspected what it was that Meena was saying.

They cannot know, she repeated to herself, before her feet decided to bolt of their own accord.

The mage poked his head out the door below and said something to the mageguard on horseback. He looked up at their window.

Liffy jumped back, and Elika followed. She composed herself and strode calmly to her loom to resume her work.

Heavy footfalls sounded on the stairs.

Elika braced herself and continued to weave. Liffy shrank where she sat, her eyes wide and panicked.

"It was her." Meena pointed a finger at Elika.

Her insides jolted, and the thread tangled in her fingers. She fought another urge to flee, lifted her face with a puzzled expression, then looked behind her as if uncertain at who the finger pointed.

The mageguard stepped forward, his eyes dark and sharp. "You girl, stand up."

Elika did as he bade her, keeping her face lowered.

He stepped closer, peering at her in confusion. "You are … different. Why? Magic knows you."

"Magic favors her, your eminence," said the mistress from the stair, with a tremor of anxiety in her voice.

"I work hard to serve it," Elika added.

"This she-human you call Meena tells us you went to see Maj-Dun'Flower last night, to get more dye for your yarns."

"She must be mistaken," Mistress Oblana replied instead. "I sent Toby, the errand boy, to fetch it for me yesterday."

"Well, girl, did you go to see him yesterday?" the mage demanded, ignoring the mistress.

"Aye," Elika said slowly, feigning confusion. Mite once taught her the trick to lying convincingly to the city guards, if ever she was caught, was to tell the truth for the most part. "I did as Meena instructed, and went to fetch more dye," Elika said and was gratified when the mistress started in surprise and then slowly turned to glare at Meena in a way that promised a cane to come.

Meena wrung her hands, looked down at the ground. "I … I didn't realize the mistress had sent a boy already," she lied.

The mistress must have known it too, for her lips firmed and thinned.

"And then what happened?" the mage demanded impatiently.

"Well, when I saw him," Elika continued. "He had none left. Told me the boy had already been to collect it and sent me away so that I didn't bother him. I'll go again today to ask him for more if you wish."

"Maj-Dun'Flower is … gone. Dead, as you humans call it. His presence is … missing, from your realm and our own."

"I don't understand, master," Elika said, and it was true.

"Of course, you don't, ignorant she-human."

"You will address him as your eminence, girl," the mistress snapped. "Forgive the child. She is simple, like all Daes."

"She's lying," Meena objected. "She's not as meek as she pretends. I say she did it."

"Hold your tongue, stupid girl." The mistress scowled at her.

"Did what?" Elika asked as innocently as she could.

"Killed him."

Elika made her jaw drop in surprise. "Kill a mage? Is that possible?"

"You know it is. You're a Dae," Meena persisted. "And everyone knows Daes are magic-haters. Didn't you burn it and the mages in blood-salt fires?"

"I didn't burn Maj-Dun'Flower," Elika said with unfeigned outrage. "How would I start the fire… and where would I get the blood-salt? Besides, he's bigger than me. And stronger. And he can kill me with his magic."

"Enough!" the mage roared. "Maj-Dun'Flower was not burned but *undone*."

"Undone?" That was Meena now, blinking in confusion.

"See, not burned." Elika crossed her arms. "I told you I didn't burn him."

"Quiet! Stupid she-humans," the mage hissed. "Did you see anyone else there?" he demanded of Elika.

She shook her head, then scratched it furiously, as if she had lice that were biting. "No … well, aye, there was another mage and a slave girl walking past his home. I saw a cart go past, too, with sacks of grain for the mill. And a couple of city guards were strolling about … perhaps a few drunks —"

"Was Maj-Dun'Flower frightened, agitated … unusual?" the mage interrupted her impatiently.

Elika pretended to think. "He was angry at me for disturbing him. He told me to go away, and I did …" she trailed off thoughtfully. "How *does* one unravel a mage?" she asked musingly.

His face contorted in disgust. "One can't!" he snapped. "It can't be done. At least not by you humans."

Elika shrugged. "Then I'd best get back to work before I upset the magic that bestowed its favor on me. I think it likes it when I work hard."

The mageguard spun on his heel. "We are wasting time here," he said to the other mage behind him. "These fools know nothing."

"Perhaps it was Reval … or one of his mageguards."

"Reval cares only for his own grief," the mage replied as they walked downstairs. "Besides, why Dun'Flower? They were nothing but small drops in the river."

On her way out, Meena hissed at Elika, "I know you know something, Dae."

But Elika was giddy with relief and it took great effort not to smile back smugly. The mages did not know who or what they were searching for. No one would suspect an indentured girl of killing a mage. There was no better place in the city than this workshop to hide her power from them. Power to unravel the mages and free men. In this world, filled with magic, she was not at its mercy, but magic was at hers.

She resumed her work, as the fires of purpose burned hot in her chest. The night could not come fast enough.

~

Floor creaked outside, as steps crept closer to her door. They were not sly, but proud, so she could tell it was Mistress Oblana come to check on her nightly prayers.

Elika silently lowered herself to her knees before the shrine.

> *"Vile magic, grant me power,*
> *Serve me now or let me rest.*
> *Ugly magic, grant me grace,*
> *Else show me not your foul face."*

She lowered her voice and mumbled, "Dreadful magic, thus I swear, I will do all that I dare. Grant me power to continue, in my toil to destroy you."

The steps lingered, waited.

Elika finished her recital, rose to her feet noisily, blew out the candle and lay down with a plop on her straw bed. She adjusted the blanket and stilled.

The steps retreated. A door closed below. The house grew silent.

For a little longer, she stared at the shadows on the sloping ceiling of the roof. When no sound came from the slumbering house for some time, she rolled silently off the bed onto her feet.

Taking care to step on the boards that did not creak, she snuck to the window and climbed out. She closed the window and flicked the latch on the inside with a pin, in case Meena or the mistress came to her room and found her missing. They must not suspect the window as her escape. She always took care to keep it unlocked and slightly ajar when she was inside her room, and locked when she was out.

The air was crisp. The moon was high, a perfect night for prowling. From behind the warm chimney, she pulled out a bundle of clothes and changed into trousers and a shirt, threw on her cloak and hid her face under a hood. She hid her nightdress behind the same chimney, and strode along the ridge of the roof, her way bathed in silver light, her purpose clear.

Her stomach growled, but she ignored it. Ravenous hunger was a constant hum inside her, which she could never abate no matter how much food she ate. Whenever she used magic, it took flesh from her bones as payment. A price she'd happily pay to unravel every mage in the city.

She found a shadowy corner, far from any street lantern, and slid down the gutter pipe, landing softly on the ground. As soon as she straightened, a big shadow came around the corner and blocked her path. She recognized him instantly, with his ridiculously broad face. His size alone would have betrayed him even in pitch dark.

"Are you following me?" she asked the giant minstrel.

Pebble smiled and nodded as if proud of it. His face was wide, and when he smiled, it gave him the look of a flattened rock with eyes and mouth and thick teeth.

"I'd rather you didn't."

"I'll stop if you can convince a moth not to fly towards the moon," he replied with a dramatic flair and a flourished wave of his hand at the moon. "Oh fair mistress, I see adventure in your eyes, and songs are spinning nigh around you."

"What do you want, Pebble?" she asked with a sigh.

He handed her a handkerchief wrapped around a pie. "Here, for you."

She thought about refusing, but her hunger stomped on her pride. She took it unashamedly. As soon as it hit her mouth, her hunger became another type of beast, one that would not be appeased. She barely chewed the bite before swallowing.

He leant on the wall as he watched her. "Why did you undo him, tsarina? You had him at your mercy, yet you showed none."

Elika lowered her pie. "Undid who?"

"Maj-Dun'Flower," he said flatly.

"What makes you think it was me?" she asked and bit into her pie again.

"I watched you do it."

"You followed me last night ..." It annoyed her that he could do so without her realizing. Still, he had not betrayed her to the mageguard. So she saw no reason not to tell him. "They kill men and steal their bodies."

"How else are they to live in your world?" He sounded genuinely puzzled.

"They shouldn't! They have their own realm ..." A realization stopped her. "You knew they did this ... you know what they are." Unable to look at him anymore, she began to walk.

He adjusted the leather straps of his lute hanging over his shoulder and fell in step with her. "You truly hate the Laifae?" he asked, surprised. "But you are —"

"The majren are abominations." She interrupted him before he finished that thought.

"I am often called that, too. Yet you look at me and do not recoil. How is it you do not loathe and revile me on sight?"

"Why would I revile you?"

Tanes look like men, and aye, there was a strangeness about them she could not quite grasp. But they never gave anyone cause to hate them. They had no powers of any type, and their only crime seemed to be their exceedingly long lives and meddling in other people's affairs.

"Because you are one of them, tsarina," he replied.

She cringed, hating being called that. "Well if I am, it's not by choice and to my great shame."

"How strange you are, being what you are," he mused aloud.

She waved the last piece of her pie at the city. "You must know the city well, being as old as you are?"

Suspicion entered his face, followed by a frown. "What is it you're asking?"

She chewed and swallowed the last bite. "I need you to give me a name ... a mage who likes to hurt. Maybe someone important."

Pebble shook his head. "'Tis folly what you are thinking."

She stopped and turned on him. "What do you seek, tane? Your father's attention? I can give you that. You'll have the best song in all the lands. A street urchin ending mages."

"I fear that is not the ballad I'm destined to write, but rather the one about your gallant if tragically misguided quest, the inevitable capture and untimely, sad end."

"I fear not their reprisal. They murder men, steal their bodies. They must be stopped. You wanted me to help Tom's resistance ..."

"Not by waging a war against the archmage."

"How, then?"

He threw his arms into the air. "By revealing who you are. By claiming your place amongst the tsaren. Up there ..." He pointed at the sky. "In the glorious courts of the great powers, where all you command shall come to pass."

He gave that boyish grin, and she thought him absurdly naïve, for a two-hundred-year-old minstrel. Would that the wars and hatred could be stopped with a single command.

"My place is here," she said firmly. "You wanted to help me, this is what I ask. Help me strike into the very heart of the mages' power. I don't know who they are, but you do."

He did not look convinced. "I cannot ..."

"Must I command you?" She said it in jest, with a small smile playing on her lips.

But his face was grim, as he considered it. "She comes to wound, she comes to strike ..."

Her smile fell away. "I'm jesting, Pebble. I command nothing, merely ask for a name."

It seemed he reached some decision. A wide, sad smile stretched his cheeks. "If you must reshape the world in your vision, who am I to oppose your will or the prophecy sung by the gods' messenger? Besides, nothing makes the songs more interesting than stirring a nest of serpents."

"Give me a name."

He sighed. "Aeon-Greengrass. He is an acquirer of votaries for the archmage. Mostly prisoners when they have them, any man who offends a mage, thieves, or magic-hating Daes. Destroy the archmage's procurer and you'll disrupt his supply of bodies. At least until another takes his place. But the Laifae are always slow to restore order amidst the chaos. Too many voices all wanting to be heard, you see."

"Where do I find him?"

He looked down the long street, to where fog was rolling in from the sea. "His house is woven from grass and tree on Waverock Alley. I'll take you there."

Dark chanting reached her ears, growing louder, closer. "I'll go by the roofs."

He glanced up uncertainly. "Never was one for heights."

"I thought the tanes didn't feel pain, so if you fall —"

"We can still break bones," he finished for her. "It is a rather unpleasant sensation."

"You don't need to follow. Just meet me here tomorrow with another name."

He looked relieved to be left behind. "We'll meet on Trapdoor Road near here. Best not to be seen in the same place twice."

After they parted ways, she climbed to the roofs, using a sturdy rainwater pipe and decorative cornerstone pieces.

Aeon-Greengrass' house was easy to find, illuminated as it was with moonlight. The chimney was a weave of branches, and grass grew from the walls. She peered down from the edge of the roof to a small balcony, and silently lowered herself onto it. The tree branches stirred under her feet, then stilled. Instead of a window, an airy opening, with black webbing barred her way inside.

"Open," she commanded in a whisper, pushing her will into the surrounding essence, and felt the answering quiver.

The black strands parted, and she strode inside into a darkened lounge. Had she come here to rob, she would have needed ten sacks for all the loot.

Every surface was crowded with silver ornaments in strange shapes and flowing forms that resembled nothing you'd find in nature. She was drawn to a figurine that resembled a twisting, spiraling shape of a man, as if his body was made from water. Another figurine was of a dog, his earthly form also looped and stretched around itself, a grotesque torment of the natural order. There were trees and flowers and animals, all twisted and bent. Yet there was an odd beauty in the grotesqueness that tugged at her primal heart. Was this how they saw her world? Strange that these ugly beings searched for beauty and crafted it in their own appalling way.

What do you want from our world? she pondered. *Surely your own is of much greater splendor, abounding as it is with magic and wonder.*

Dangerous musings, she thought, and abruptly turned away before her resolve wavered.

Inside the house, there were no doors, only archways in the walls made of branches with strange, whimsical fruit sprouting from their tips. No fruit was the same, and when she touched one, it felt hollow and light as if spun from dust and wishes. Under her feet, there was a carpet of grass. In it grew small flowers, akin to those a child might draw with a stick in the mud, both extravagant and clumsy in their form. The petals were of different sizes and irregular in shape. Everything gave an impression of simultaneous worship and corruption of nature, as if the Laifae did not understand how it all fitted together.

At the end of the hall, she came to a doorway. A black web barred her way. Beyond it, she felt his essence, the creature who gave this house its form. She focused on that essence, placed a hand on the webbing and whispered, "Do not resist me."

Warm, slick strands trembled under her fingers and parted before her, allowing her entry into the majren's bedchamber. A light glowed in a lantern beside his bed, illuminating the youthful face of the sleeping mage. He was a youth ... no, the *body* he had stolen belonged to a youth whose limbs had not yet developed the bulk of a full-grown man. It was an absurdly wrong body for the man who held such an important position in the archmage's dominion. Curled on his side, he looked like a child in peaceful slumber.

The child is dead, she reminded herself, willing the anger to grow.

Still, she could not look at him and do what must be done. She sent a black tendril to extinguish the flame in his lantern, and the room was plunged into darkness.

Aeon-Greengrass startled awake and sat up.

"Who's there?" He moved his face searchingly, back and forth, past where she stood.

She froze, realizing that he was blind in the dark of night. His ears were sharp, however, and he must have heard her intake of breath, or perhaps the frantic beating of her heart.

"Guards! Guards!" he shouted from inside the dead man's chest, a sound akin to a strangled roar.

Without further thought, she grasped the threads of his essence and pulled.

"No! Spare me. I have gold and riches."

"Riches you earnt by selling the lives of men."

"Who are you, mistress?" he gasped.

In reply, she pulled harder upon the threads. He groaned and writhed and finally fell lifeless back onto his bed.

"A life for a life." She uttered the mantra from long ago, which they had lived by on the streets. And something inside her grew cold and dark.

A crack under her feet … She plunged through the floor and hit the lower level with a rough thud.

She groaned, rolled, noting that nothing was broken, and looked up. But of course, she thought, with the Laifae gone, so was his magic. The grass floor morphed to rotting wood, decayed and barely holding the house together. The walls of the house were wilting and vanishing, and the stones which had been held firm by black webbing began to crumble and crash around her.

Elika scrambled to her feet, raced to the window and jumped out. Behind her, the house fell to rubble and dust chased her down the street. Shouts and calls came from the folk as they emerged to gape at the rubble she had left behind. When she was out of their sight, she slowed to a walk.

A wind brushed her hood.

She stopped, and her heart raced with recognition and fear.

The wind blew again, stronger this time.

She knew that cutting wind. Knew it as well as her own breath. She had lived beside the dark chasm most of her life, had listened to the shrill screams upon it. But she was far from the chasm, and the wind of the Abyss did not travel far past it. Yet here it was, filled with biting rage, swirling around her. And on it, she felt a dark presence. Something followed her that was not a man.

She spun around and probed the deep, lurking shadows of the night, straining her ears to listen to the silence hidden by the wailing wind. A terrible power drew near. She felt its approach in the depths of her bones. The very essence of the world bent and trembled beneath it. It charged the air with its rage. A pulse of that rage went past, and a tremor shook the ground beneath her feet. She staggered but managed not to fall, turned again, and tried to see where the approaching storm was coming from.

It stilled, as if it, too, was listening. Then, as though it caught her scent, the terror charged towards her.

She darted for the closest rainwater pipe and, in an instant, scrambled up it to the roof, lay flat on her stomach and peered over the edge. No one was there. No sound, no movement in the faintly lit street. Even so, the sense of danger prickling her skin was a physical sensation she could not ignore. Something was there, seeking her, scanning the roofs where she had climbed. Aye, there were eyes searching for her, brushing past her.

Darkness moved, and she saw it, a large shadow darker than the night untouched by moonlight. It moved and vanished. And the winds of the Abyss grew still.

She rolled away from the edge, stared up at the moon, and waited until she was certain the shadow had left. Then she rose and ran home.

CHAPTER SEVEN

The hunt

"Eternity is but a restless wind, which traverses the Abyss between three spheres. The Great Web binds these spheres and holds them from drifting apart. It is the source of all magic that permeates our world, and the source of the essence of life. All of us, the Laifae, gods and even barbaric, apish humans are bound to the web. Destroy the web, and you destroy us all. Destroy us and you destroy the web. Gods guard the web and punish those who threaten it."

The History of Alafraysia and Seramight,
By Mageguard Bluelight

Power was a compelling and demanding beast. It was food to starved vanity, fuel for ambition. It was glorious and all-consuming. The nights could not come fast enough, and Elika barely noticed the passing of days. When not bemoaning lack of sleep, her thoughts were taken with reliving her hunts and anticipating her next strike against the mages. She lived and breathed for the darker hours. And she nursed every victory in the darkening depths of her soul. She dared not probe those depths, lest she shone light upon the horrors lurking there … and wavered. She dared not think beyond what needed to be done.

Night after night, she went out to unravel the mages, whose names Pebble whispered to her—with a disapproving shake of his head. Always, he spoke of doom and her inevitable capture. And each day, it had grown easier to destroy the Laifae, until one name was no longer enough. So she demanded two then three from Pebble, which he surrendered with a sigh.

"You are growing drunk on your power," he would scold her.

Aye, she was growing greedy. But she could not stop. Not when each day, no matter how many she unraveled, she watched mage after mage pass under the windows of their workshop. The majren were as rife in the city as rats. It would take a lifetime to unravel them one at a time. So she would not return home until she unraveled three. Then four. Last night, she had unraveled five. Still, the immensity of the task grew only more daunting with each hunt.

The days became a vague haze of weaving and Liffy's chatter, of Meena's scorn and Mistress Oblana's cooing praises of the silken webs Elika spun. The door of the shop opened and closed with ever greater urgency, and she could not weave fast enough to satisfy the growing demands from noble houses with daughters to adorn. Especially since Prince Southfire, the uncrowned heir of the Sacred Crowns, had got it into his head to find a bride to give him more uncrowned heirs. So the mistress was now buying baskets of candles, insisting that Elika work long past sunset.

"You look sleepy, again." Liffy's voice cut through the creaking of her spinning wheel.

"I've been praying late." Elika mumbled her usual lie.

Liffy adjusted the thread. "Well, whilst you were napping during our luncheon, Sticks was saying that the Blight has leapt over the chasm and come to this side."

Not eight days ago, rumors had raced through the city of wilted crops to the south and animals lying dead in the paddocks with no obvious cause. Daes blamed the mages. Alterrians blamed the Daes. The mageguards rode out to investigate and returned blaming the Rogue.

"It's not the Blight," Elika replied over a yawn. "I've heard the dead fields have re-sprouted. Nothing the Blight ever touched came back to life."

A city crier went past, as he did each day, ringing his bell. "Hear! Hear! One hundred gold pieces for the Rogue Mage! One hundred gold for the one slaying crops and beasts alike with magic. One hundred gold for the murderer of majren."

Elika's hands stilled. It did not surprise her that the mages rushed to blame the Rogue for the deaths of cattle and crops, and indeed every evil to befall Seramight these days. Not when their own grip on power grew slippery. Too many on the streets were singing Pebble's ballads of the Rogue Mage. Too many cheered the demise of the majren, and not all of them were Daes. From Pebble, she had learned that half the Alterrian nobles were secretly toasting the Rogue. Since the sundering wars, they had lost cities and lands to the mages' rule. Many of them still hungered for the old ways and dreamt of the return of the old order where mages bowed to the human kings.

"I hope they catch him soon," Liffy said fiercely.

Elika's head snapped up. "Why? He's the only one standing up to the mages."

Liffy readjusted her newly braided crown of fresh flowers and lace. "Because he'll make it worse for the rest of us. And mages always blame the Daes for the troubles. They already say the Rogue is a Dae. And now they say he's the one killing the crops and the cattle. And the mageguards are snatching any Dae who looks at them the wrong way. They are punishing the whole city because of him."

Elika smothered any guilt before it took root. "Might be the city needs to be punished for men to wake up and realize they have to fight for their freedom. That's the true price of freedom, Liffy, not coin but blood. Do you wish to live in fear all your life, and wear that collar around your neck?"

"My brother will buy my —"

"You will never be free!" Elika exclaimed, tired of the lies they told themselves. "Not until the city is freed from mages. They are the ones who put these chains around the throats of honest folk."

Liffy's face grew petulant. "I hate it when you talk like that. Do you know what the mages would do to you if they heard you, and to me for listening?" She slapped her hands over her ears. "Sacred magic, hear my love, I pledge to you my life. Sacred magic, hear my song, I pledge to you my very soul. Sacred magic ..."

Elika could take it no longer. She had to make Liffy see the truth. She marched up to her and pulled her hands from her ears. Liffy squealed with fright.

Blood throbbed in Elika's temple as she lowered her face and said, "They kill men to possess their bodies, Liffy. They strip men of their souls and put their own essence into the dead."

Liffy shook her head. "No. You lie. You are a liar." She snatched back her hands and began to weep. "I hate you, and I hate the Rogue Mage. I just want to go to Wavestar. I want my brother." She sobbed into her skirt, her crown of flowers hanging limply from her plaited hair. "I want my brother back," she sobbed, repeating it again and again.

Elika could make no sense of those tears. She stepped away, feeling wretched and cruel. "I'm sorry," she said abruptly. "You are right. Your brother will take you to Wavestar, as you said. He'll come to see you again soon. Might be I'll finally meet him."

Liffy only sobbed harder.

Hating herself, Elika returned to her loom, and for a long time, they worked in silence.

It was still early in the day when the sky darkened as a menacing shadow passed overhead and blocked out the sun. Reval's Island. It had returned again. Usually, it hovered high above, but today, it was so low, Elika thought she might just touch the jagged rock were she to reach out the window. As it passed above their street, both she and Liffy held their breaths, fearing it would crush them were it to drift any lower.

Through the window, Elika saw a dark flock of birds emerge from the island … No, not birds but men, descending upon Terren on small, floating clouds. An army of mageguards dressed in silver armor with an emblem of burning fire on their chests. The fire burned with a real flame, though they did not seem to notice. A group of four landed below her window. The clouds vanished, and the mageguards began to walk and … sing?

"ARALA!" boomed the thunder overhead, shaking the city with its power, and shattering weaker glass in the windows. "I AM COMING FOR YOU. RETURN TO ME, MY LOVE."

~

Elika placed the stone spider on the bed beside her.

Walk, she thought.

The spider remained still.

Ever so gently, she pushed the essence of magic from inside her into the lifeless spider. Like a ripple, her magic disturbed that strange ethos of their world, the invisible, vital force that always hummed around her, were she but to listen.

The stone limbs moved, and the spider walked.

Burn, she thought more harshly, and the spider burst into flames. Her blanket caught fire. She jumped to her feet, cursed and smothered the flame with her cloak. When she lifted the cloak, the spider was whole and uncharred, as if the flame had never touched it. Yet she had felt the heat. There was a hole in her blanket, too, though no charring at the edges, as if a large moth instead of a fire had eaten it.

She rubbed her eyes. She knew nothing of magic and wanted to learn. But there was no one to ask. At least no one she might trust.

So far, she had discovered there were three types of magic she could call upon. One was linked to that ball of power inside her, black tendrils she could cast out like the majren. The tendrils emerged from the floor and the walls, table and chair, or from anywhere else she wished. They felt like an extension of her body, a spare limb she could use. She wanted them to wrap around the shrine and lift it, and so they did. Or rather ... *she* did. She could even feel the weight of the shrine.

Then there was magic linked to her wishes. She did not truly understand it, for nothing seemed beyond possibility. She wanted water to fly from the jug into the air, and so it did. She willed a chair to dance, and so it did. She wished for the stone spider to burn, and it did. Like the snow Reval conjured, the flame was real, hot and bright, until it vanished ... but not always. Sometimes, it was cool, faint and lifeless, as if it was just a dream. Sometimes a new chair appeared, identical to the one in her room. It danced and felt real to the touch, and then it vanished. This too, she did not understand. This magic was as baffling as it was dangerous, and it drew more from her than she was willing to give. Even conjuring a small flame made her famished and cramped her muscles with weakness.

But the one she understood the least, was the magic she used to unravel the majren. The essence permeating this world, which she could grasp and break, was the same essence that made the spider move and the flame burn brighter. And through the disturbance in that ethos, she always felt the hunter approach.

Each time she unraveled a mage, the hunter drew near, searching for her, stalking her. She knew not what drew him to her, only that like a god of death he was always there the instant the mages perished. So far, she had evaded him, and with each victory, she grew more reckless. Aye, she knew the signs of being drunk on victories, the dangerous sense of invincibility. She had seen it many a time in the streets and the dire end that followed. And each night, she would return from her hunts, shaking with the thrill of it, with doubts and above all else, with ravening hunger.

She was hungry now, though she had eaten plenty. The house had grown quiet, and the air chilled. With a sigh, she forced herself to climb out the window into the cold night. She wanted nothing more than the comfort of her bed and a long, restful sleep. But a deeper craving needed sating. She needed to unravel more mages, free more of their slaves, save another human from fear and torment. No matter that she was tired, hungry or sleepy. As darkness returned, her purpose grew bright. One by one, she would drive the invaders from Terren. It was a far more palatable use of her power than dressing noble ladies in fine cloth.

Outside, she changed into dark trousers and cloak, and with an oddly unsettled heart, went to meet Pebble on Wharf Street.

For most of the way there, she kept to the roofs. Prince Southfire had increased the number of guards patrolling the streets. The archmage had also sent his own army of mageguards to find the Rogue. They rode on horseback under the light of torches. From the roofs, she watched the leader bark commands from atop his horse whilst nervously panning around. Might be her vanity was truly starved, for she took pleasure in their fear. She, Eli Spider, was their fear. She was the terror that haunted their nights. No longer were men helpless against their cruelty. No longer were mages indestructible.

And with that all-pervasive knowledge, a subtle change had come upon the city. She had noticed it in the days after she had destroyed Aeon-Greengrass. On the streets, the Daes held their heads a little higher, and the fighting glint had reignited in their eyes. She gave them that; she gave them hope.

When she reached Wharf Street, Pebble was waiting for her. He stood there with his arms crossed, kicking dirt with his boot, unable to meet her gaze. With each of her hunts, he had been growing more and more agitated. "Whatever you are doing, you must stop," he said as she approached.

He was asking the impossible.

"How many majren are there in this city, Pebble?" she countered.

"Thousands. Too many for you to unravel."

"Then I must keep going until I unravel enough that the rest leave of their own accord."

He handed her a jam-filled bun, rather grudgingly she noted. "Have you seen yourself, tsarina? You are fading. You are not feeding your magic. Even I can see that. In unravelling them all, I fear you might unravel yourself as well. You are … frail-looking."

Elika was too tired tonight to argue. "Let's get this done, so I can return to my bed. I need sleep and plenty of it."

"Then go and sleep. Abandon this madness. The archmage is tearing the city apart searching for you. And now, seeing as only a tsarin can do what you do, Reval has sent his mageguard to find …" He drifted off, looking aside, absently kicking dirt with the tip of his boot.

"I'm not Arala," she said firmly.

He shrugged without looking at her.

Elika hugged herself. Pebble was right, she was weak, faint, a hollow shell of herself. "I cannot stop now. Men need me. Give me another name."

"Another field grew fallow today in Mageswell, a small village south of here."

"It will re-sprout. They always do. And as a minstrel, you should know better than to go about believing every rumor you hear. I had nothing to do with that."

The set of his lips told her he did not believe her. "You are doing something that's causing death beyond the walls of Terren. It is getting worse with each mage you unravel."

She refused to believe that, for if it were true, they were surely all doomed. "Not every unexplained death is my doing. Nor are the endless rains that swell the rivers. That's Reval, I am told. And the mountain shaking itself apart is Draygan. And might be bad things happen in the world that are not caused by magic. Nor did I poison the wells in Daetown. I dare say that'll be the Alterrians."

"Who blame the Rogue for the fear and unrest on the streets," he said smugly, as if that proved something.

"I need names, Pebble."

He shook his head firmly. "No more."

"Then I'll unravel any and all who come across my path. There are enough Laifae around for me to simply find them."

"Not all of them deserve your wrath," he boomed. "Not all of them are wicked."

Her temples began to throb. They'd had this argument many times before. "They are all invaders in our realm."

Aye, the task was cruel, but so were the slave collars around the necks of babes.

"Dark are the songs you spin, tsarina. Cruel is your purpose. I cannot help you kill any more of them, for 'tis far crueler than you realize." With those cutting words he stalked off.

So be it. She did not need him. Every mage had to be purged from Seramight. She was not burning them in blood-salt fires. Nor was she destroying magic, merely unravelling and sending the invaders back to whatever dark realm they had come from. Yet, even as she thought that, her heart grew heavy, as it did each night when she began her hunt.

~

Elika sent out wisps of her magic. Fine, black strands crawled over the floor, up the table and the candles, gently extinguishing the flame. The room fell into darkness.

"Copperpiece …"

"We are here."

"We see nothing … the light is out."

The other majren groped beside him for … something, anything perhaps. "Grassroot, we are afraid."

There were four of them sleeping in one big bed. From the shadows, Elika watched them fumble blindly for the lantern, which she had placed on the floor beyond their reach. For her sake, if not for theirs. She could tell they had not been long in this world, for their movements were as clumsy as a babe's.

"Petaldrop, why are you so silent?"

The one they called Petaldrop would never awake again. He was the first she had unraveled before the others awoke.

"Is somebody here?"

Elika imagined the web and the yarn linking the majren to it. In her mind, she grabbed the thread and pulled. They cried out as one.

"Stop …"

"Someone is here …"

"Who are you? Show yourself."

Elika yanked harder, tearing the yarn from the web. The mages fell back on the bed. Four bodies lay there with their eyes open, mouths frozen on a plea, their life extinguished. It was hard to look, even in the dark, but she did regardless.

You killed them, whispered her heart.

No, she did not kill those men. They were already dead. She simply returned their bodies to the rightful owners. Their families could now grieve them in peace, rather than wonder and hope for their eventual return.

There was a disturbance in the air, and the winds screeched outside. Perversely, she had begun to wait for it, to even look forward to it. The shadow that hunted her charged towards her, wild and angry. Suddenly, the room was no longer in darkness as light strands raced through the walls and the floor. Before she could understand what was happening, they wound around her feet and held her firmly in place. She panicked, pulled out her knife as the threads of sticky light raced up her legs, and severed the strands. She felt the presence start, as if what she had done was unexpected. Without another thought, she sprinted up the stairs to the attic she had used to steal into the house and crawled out onto the roof.

The presence vanished from her senses, which always meant that he had lost her, too. Emboldened, she made her way to another majren's house. They were easy to find from up high. The roofs of their homes were never made of tile, but a strange mix of natural and unnatural—stone, branches, grass, black tendrils, feathers and sea shells, and anything else a mind might conjure.

The next house was formed from merging tree branches, intertwined in the most unnatural, messy way. Here and there, they sprouted leaves. Elika climbed down from the roof along the woody branches of the walls, until she reached a window. Silently, she pried it open and stepped into a room with a narrow bed in one corner. The mage was asleep, and it took but a moment to rip the Laifae's invading essence from the human body. She knew not this majren's name. It did not matter … and yet somehow it did. She quenched a pang of guilt, again growing angry with herself and Pebble for putting doubts into her head.

Once again, the dark power was there, closer this time, moving faster than before, racing towards her. Some reckless, wicked thrill made her want to taunt him, mock him. So she stood there a moment longer, daring him to get closer, before calmly climbing out the window to the roof. Once there, she ran. The hunter gave chase, she was certain, though she saw no one behind her.

Again, light exploded all around, and the glowing webbing chased her from all sides—more strands than she could fight and cut with her knife. She jumped to the nearest drain pipe and slid to the ground. The sticky strands of light followed her down, racing faster than she could run.

"Fire," she whispered and imagined it behind her. The street exploded with flames that rose up and up to the roofs, setting houses afire.

Elika stopped and gaped. She could not have done that … her flames were always small. Yet these were as she had imagined, big columns of flame rising high. Overhead, the threads of light chasing her recoiled and vanished.

She wished for the flame to vanish, and it did. Leaving behind a burned roof and charred walls. She turned and fled, cornered sharply, keeping her balance. Ahead, she saw a busy tavern. She burst through the door, and without taking in the scene, raced through to the kitchen, pushing patrons aside. She ran out again through the back door.

Cries of alarm came from the tavern, as something followed in her wake. Elika slipped into the nearest house through an unlatched window and ran through it until she sensed the presence chasing her fade. Still, she kept running, using every trick she knew to lose her pursuer; jumping over fences, changing alleys often until she was certain no one followed.

Then she leant on the wall, panting and puffing. He had almost caught her. She had felt his murderous rage, his strength, his determination. He wanted to kill her. Yet she was still alive. Once again, she had outwitted and outrun him. The usual thrill did not follow that thought. She hugged herself to stop the trembling. She was being reckless. Penny would cuff her. She had to be smarter than that, else she'd be dead before spring's end. Whatever he was, he got close enough tonight to use his magic against her. Next time, she'd be more careful, she thought as made herself the same promise she had broken again and again.

~

"To the Rogue Mage!" Tom shouted and every mug in *Eagle's Feather* was raised into the air with a cheer.

Elika lifted her own tankard with them, intoxicated on ale and praise. And the mugs banged on the table in tune to Pebble's song:

High up above, hope spreads its wings
And sends the Rogue to earth.
God's judgment comes for tyrant's rot
For those who seek to rob.
Strike hard and fly, a fiend to foe
The Rogue will bring you hope.

As his gravelly voice rose above the boisterous fervor, she grinned from ear to ear, until her cheeks were sore. *She* was the one who had put the fight back into their hearts. The mages were not invincible, they could be killed. It mattered not that these folk didn't know she was the Rogue. Pebble knew and he smiled mischievously at her as he sang. He had shrugged off their argument from the day before, but still refused to give her anymore names.

Tom sat at the central table, surrounded by Daes who had been arriving in their droves from across the city to join his resistance. Bobquick was sitting proudly beside him, singing and banging his mug on the table. There were many new faces. The tavern was crowded with men and women who had been freed when their masters had perished, for upon the death of a mage, the magical collar fell away. Many of the newly freed fled before they could be caught and given to another master. They came here, to Daetown, pledging their strength and service to the growing rebellion and the ever more notorious One Eye.

Talk at their table was of the archmage's latest decree that only coin could buy freedom and not the death of a master. It mattered little that the council of human dukes argued in favor of the old laws of the Sacred Crown, which allowed slaves to be freed upon their master's death. As long as they had no part in his death. But then, in this world, archmage's laws unseated any human ones. And Prince Southfire, as ever, bowed to the wishes of the archmage. Elika, however, cared little for the affairs of the courts. Those were beyond her power to affect. Instead, she listened with one ear to Tom and the others, whilst soaking in the joy of the folk around her, allowing it to soothe her increasingly burdened heart. It was to be a short reprieve, for soon, she was to face another night of hunting.

Bobquick took a big gulp of his foamy ale. "Never seen anything funnier than them mages all hiding like frightened mice in their homes. I'd give anything to know who …" He hiccupped. "… he is."

"It's got to be One Eye," said Tom. "This morning, when I was fishing on me boat, I saw his men throw a mage's body into the sea. The same one who was fished out again today by the mageguards."

"I saw them, too," Bobquick piped in proudly. "'Twas me who pointed them out, remember?"

"I don't think it's One Eye," said a fair-haired Drasdane woman with big shoulders and big hips who had taken a brazen liking to Tom. "I heard this mage's body was all cut up and drenched in blood-salt. But the Rogue kills them clean, with no blood."

Tom shifted uncomfortably, eyeing the woman who was staring boldly at him, then scratched his head. "'Tis what bothers me, too. Maybe there's more than one of 'im."

One Eye's men were also in the crowd, drinking their fill. Many were tattooed with a cross over one eye, others had an eye tattooed on their hands. Word on the street was that One Eye proclaimed himself the overlord of Daetown. Elika supposed Lord Snowstorm would have some say on the matter, seeing as he was the overlord of the district.

A rough hand fell on her shoulder. She looked up into Blood Dog's menacing face. He jerked his head. "Gotta talk to ye. In private."

She shrugged off his hand. "Say what you want to say here. I'm not the fool you think me, to be caught alone with you."

"Aye, ye are, seeing as you probably don't want them to hear what I gotta say to you. Look, I'm not gonna play ye, just want to talk."

"Go ahead, girl, I'll keep an eye on ye," Tom said and scowled at Blood Dog.

He scowled back. "If I wanted her harm, you'd be the last person who could stop me, fish breath."

Elika rose and followed him to a table in the corner occupied by three youths.

"How's about you soft-bellied crabs scram and let mousy and me have a quiet drink at this table," Blood Dog growled.

The youths took him in, ignoring her altogether, exchanged glances, then left, grumbling and taking their mugs with them.

Blood Dog took a seat, threw his feet up on the table and kicked off an empty mug to the floor. "Listen, Mousy. I know ye don't like me and I don't care, but I have this bizarre wish to warn you anyhow."

She sat across from him, keeping her distance. "About what?"

"One Eye's looking for you, and not in a friendly way either, going about asking about ye in every tavern and whorehouse."

"After me?"

"I say it's you, seeing as the description he passes around reminds me of what you were back in Dae-Terren when I first saw ye in the temple with them damned priestesses."

She shrugged. "There's many who look like me."

"Someone who goes by the name of El, or Eli Spider of Bad Penny's pack?"

Elika stilled, keeping her face unchanged. "Name's Lika ..."

He waved that aside as if bored. "Spare me your squeaking lies, mousy. I know it's you. Ye told Bobquick rather stupidly you were of Bad Penny's gang, and it's only a matter of time before the idiots over there ..." He jerked his head towards Tom's table. "... remember that and tell One Eye's jesters over there ..." He flicked his head towards the table with suited, tattooed roughs. "... that you used to be one of them bad pennies. Anyhow, seeing as One Eye is offering a juicy reward for bringing you to him, I'm rather tempted."

"Then why haven't you already?"

His grin was slow and sly, and it was as if his eyes sharpened and became something else entirely. *He* had become something else ... or rather someone else. Aye, how had she not seen it before? There was shrewdness in his eyes, and mocking contempt too, as if the whole world was a joke for him to laugh at.

"Scratch me head, but I don't know," he said in his usual mocking way, and she did not believe him. "There's a fight about ye. And I like a good fighter. Or might be I've got a soft spleen for skinny, brave lasses. Especially those with secrets to hide and faces which remind me of a long-ago past. Or maybe I'm beginning to see something you don't want me to see." Again, his eyes grew sharp and piercing, as if he was looking into her very soul. "Aye, there it is," he spoke with quiet mockery. "An icy, murderous glint in your fair eyes. Truly chilling. Seen that look before, you know. Long ago, in another life, and in the face of another woman who thought she could challenge the Fates without the Fates extracting their price."

Elika looked aside, unsettled, drank her ale and shook her head. "Look, I don't know this One Eye …" Words died on her tongue as her mind raced back.

"Aye, you do. Long face, skinny."

Rory.

It could not be.

"He's raging mad at you, and I got a feeling he won't be nice to you either. Just so ye know."

If it was him, then he might be rightfully mad. She suspected it had something to do with Chelik, One-Eyed Rory's son who she was meant to protect.

That put her in mind of another boy. "What happened to young Tix who crossed with you?" she asked if only to stop Blood Dog from looking at her so intently.

His face instantly soured. "Rich bloody pouches, they're all the same. As soon as we crossed, he threw out his name to the guards who accosted us. Lord Redwrath, he called himself. Next thing I know, both of us are being hauled before a magistrate, and a doting father and mother take him into their bejeweled arms. They look at me as if I'm a slimy leech stuck to their precious son's arse. So they whisk him away and I get a collar around my neck."

"How did you lose it, then?"

His grin widened, sly and secretive. "Curious mouse. You have your secrets and I have …"

The door burst open with a crash, and the tavern fell silent.

A group of mageguards in red robes strode in, followed by city guards.

"Stay where you are, Daes. We are seeking the Rogue Mage. We hear that you are harboring him."

No one moved.

Blood Dog spat. "Then ye hear wrong. No one here but honest working men."

"Silence magic-hater," the mageguard hissed. "Take them all for questioning. Arrest those without a collar or a freeman's mark. There's a bounty on catching runaways."

Everything slowed and moved at once. Chairs crashed to the floor and tables overturned. Weapons were drawn. Elika did not know who was slain first, or where the wail of pain came from. A woman screamed. Another was grabbed by two guards, chained and dragged outside into the waiting prison wagons. More human guards charged at the patrons as black strands of Laifae magic crawled over the floors and tables and pinned men to the walls. Elika saw Tom wrestled to the ground by two guards. She darted towards him and stabbed one. Tom turned and threw his fist into the face of the other. One Eye's men fought in the midst of it, killing guards and … wounding mageguards. How was that possible? It was then that she saw a flash of red coating their weapons that was not the blood of their assailants. Blood-salt.

More and more mages and guards piled into the overcrowded tavern. Tom ran at them with a knife, Tipps the brawny tavern keeper was beside him, roaring and throwing punches. Elika turned and got a glimpse of Bobquick darting through the back door. Those who could, leapt out the window. Others raced upstairs.

Mages sent out tendrils that wrapped around whom they could and dragged them to the waiting prison wagons.

Someone grabbed her arm. "Move, you bloody fool," Blood Dog growled.

Elika dashed for the bar. She knew there was a door to the cellar behind it. She was abruptly yanked back by the hair and promptly released with a curse. She turned to see Blood Dog pull his dagger out of the guard's throat. The man fell to the floor, bleeding and gasping. A hard glint shone in Blood Dog's dark eyes. But more terrifyingly, there was no fury, no fear, no panic, not even surprise. He was calmly taking in the scene with a sharp, impassive gaze, as if he had seen such things countless times before.

Then she saw no more as a fat, black tendril came at her. She ducked to avoid it, rolled and jumped behind the bar. A trail of spilt ale was draining between the floorboards. She clawed at them, found a fingerhold, and pulled open the trapdoor ... and was shoved into the dark hole. She rolled down the stairs, tangling with a larger body.

When they came to a stop, Blood Dog groaned. "Damn, you are a bony one to land on." He rolled off her, and the movement send shooting pain through her bruised body.

They were in complete darkness. From above came shouts, cries and crashes of thrown chairs and overturned tables, breaking glass and falling bodies.

Elika rose to her feet slowly, testing that nothing was broken. Her head throbbed where she had banged it on the floor. She looked around and saw a faint light above another stair leading out of the cellar into the street.

"There," she pointed to the hatch door. She could hear Blood Dog breathing close beside her, could smell the stench of his old sweat.

"Aye, I see it." He went ahead. After listening at the hatch for a few moments, he broke the lock, unbolted the door and peered outside. "We'll have to make a run for it. The front door's around the corner." He held there a moment longer, waiting, watching. "Bloody fools, so much for their damned rebellion. Fools, the lot of them. 'Tis not how you fight the bastards."

Elika could not find it in her to disagree. She could hear the cries and the battle above. These men were not warriors but dreamers. They were bakers, tanners, millers, blacksmiths, honest men who knew nothing of war, and she had brought this disaster to their door, just as Pebble forewarned.

"We have to help them."

"And how do ye think to help them?"

Magic, she thought but dared not utter.

"See them mageguards holding back at a distance?" he said.

She squeezed next to him to see Reval's fiery mageguards, hovering above the houses on small clouds, watching the battle but not taking part.

"They are not like the other mages," he continued. "They wield Reval's power. You can't fight them, mousy, not without barrels of blood-salt and fire or the very power of the gods. And I bloody well hope the Rogue doesn't try to intervene here," he added and she noted a warning in his voice as if he *knew*. "'Cause they will contain his magic if he does. See those shimmering chains hanging off their belts?"

"Aye," she said with a frown.

"They bind magic of any mage, tsarin or demigod."

"How do you know this?" she asked.

"Save your questions for the priests, mousy. Got no time for them." More mageguards raced past towards the tavern. After they turned the corner, Blood Dog threw open the trap door. "Now, don't you look back. It's over. There's nothing to be done for them." With that, he tore in the opposite direction to the guards, and she followed.

Blood Dog cursed and swore as he ran.

Around them, the biting wind screeched and screeched, and the shadows grew darker.

~

"ARALA! RETURN TO ME!" A thunderous cry rose from above the green storm clouds gathering over the city, and the monstrous clouds unleashed a river of rain.

Elika watched from the window of the workshop as folk caught out on the street fought to get to shelter. Streets turned to rivers, sweeping away everything that was not tethered—carts, boxes, horses and men.

"Mistress, the water is coming in!" Meena screeched downstairs.

"Get it out, girl, get it out," the mistress shrieked back.

But there was no escape from Reval's madness, his endless cries for Arala, his wild moods that brought disaster upon Terren. Elika could only grimly watch on.

For days the rain did not abate, flooding every house, every street and cellar, and kept folk confined to their homes. Elika, too, was trapped inside, nursing dark thoughts. The rain turned rooftops into waterfalls, and water seeped through her window and pooled on the floor. Soon every cloth in the house was wet.

On the fifth day, the rain ceased as abruptly as it arrived, and the green, churning clouds vanished as if they had never been. Within moments the streets and homes were dry, as if they had merely dreamt the rain. Only, they had not. There were overturned carts and drowned animals, and men lying dead face down in the street.

Elika's thoughts turned darker than the Abyss. *Damn Reval and his mindless destruction.*

~

"Where is everyone, Tipps?" Elika asked the innkeeper as she walked through a door askew on its hinges.

There was no sign of Tom, Bobquick or Blood Dog, or any of the regulars for that matter. She had expected the worst. Now she faced it.

Only a few grim, downcast patrons sat at the tables. The innkeeper still nursed a bruised eye and a broken arm. He was limping to and fro, picking up mugs and broken pieces of tables and chairs from the attack five nights ago. Reval's rains had added their own mark to the destruction.

Tipps righted a table with his beefy arm. "Dead or being questioned," he replied stonily. "Haven't seen anyone today, except those who got away. But more might turn up, now that the rains have stopped."

It was her seventh day, that precious day of freedom, and forgoing breakfast Elika had left the house before anyone was awake. It was also the first time she had been able to venture outside since the night of the attack, seeing that Reval had half-drowned the city these past days.

"I was lucky a guard tried to grab me and not a mageguard," the innkeeper continued. "Magic-loving scum. I stuck him deep in the gut with a knife. Bloody traitor." He spat and righted a chair. "They'll get what's coming to them. One Eye sent his men to speak with me. Gave me a purse of sherrings to help fix this mess. Said they'll find the Daetown guards who sided with the mages and will make sure they never side with them again. It's time we reminded them what we do with traitors."

"Aye," said one of the men at the table. "Let the Rogue take care of the mages. We'll take care of our own bastards."

Mugs banged in agreement.

Tipps eyed her collar. "One Eye can take it off you, girl. He can free you. Just ask one of his men."

"Might be I will one day," she replied. "Right now, my mistress treats me well enough, gives me bed and food and pays me coin I can spend."

"Suit yourself." He shrugged and returned to picking up broken pieces of his livelihood off the floor.

For the rest of the morning, Elika helped Tipps set his tavern to rights; gathering broken glass, sweeping and scrubbing blood off the timber floorboards and walls. For that, he gave her a mug of ale and a large bowl of his hearty vegetable stew. She sat with the other patrons as she ate, their silent anger feeding her own.

Neither Bobquick nor Tom returned. She went to the harbor to search for them. Tom's yellow boat was still there. An old fisherman salting his catch in barrels told her it had not moved in five days. "I've not seen Tom or his wee scrap either," he added.

She greeted that dreaded news with a numbness that might have frightened her were she to allow herself to feel. Tom never missed a morning of fishing, save when the storms turned the sea to froth.

After that, she returned to Daetown, icy determination pumping through her veins as she waited for the night to fall. For a while, she perused the wares of Salve Row, where you could buy anything and everything for a fraction of the price elsewhere in the city. Mostly it was either broken or stolen, but everything here was crafted by human hands and untouched by magic.

She stepped out of the way of three barrels walking by. They turned into a house made of grass and mushrooms, and the sign of a cask with limbs above the door. Maj-Brittlesticks' name was well known in Terren. He fashioned barrels, crates, tubs and kegs that walked. Though most merchants could rarely afford them.

Three doors along, she strolled past the house built from colorful glass beads. It was the home of Maj-Sunfire, who sold magical charms and wish-beads. You need only whisper a wish and the magic inside the bead would grant it. Though from what folk said, those wishes were rarely what the purchaser intended. And whatever you wished for would eventually vanish.

When she passed a cobbler's shop, she became aware that her shoes were rubbing. She walked in and was met by a lanky youth with slumping shoulders as if he was afraid of hitting his head on the low ceiling.

"Master's out buying more leather," he said in a Dae accent. He wore a collar like her. "Come back later."

"Just need boots that fit me." She stuck out her foot. "Nothing fancy, something old would do. Don't have much coin, so anything you've got will be good enough."

"Might have an old pair out the back in my shed that might fit you. Just don't tell my master. I'm not supposed to sell anything without his permission. Thinks I'll rob him."

"I won't," she said.

At the back of the shop was a small garden, and a stone tool shed where the youth slept. She hovered in the doorway whilst he strode inside. There was a hoard of broken things, pots and pans, buttons and dented shovels. It was a tinker's treasure cave full of adventure and possibilities.

"All this is yours?" she asked with unhidden interest.

"Tinker Tan they used to call me, in the old city," he said as he rummaged through a polished and freshly oiled wooden box. "I used to scavenge and mend things and earnt more than my master does selling shoes. But I'm a tinker no more," he added with a wry twist of his lips and scratched the back of his neck. "They put me with a shoemaker 'cause a piece of glass told them to do it. Trouble is, I hate making shoes." He pulled out a pair of old boots made of supple leather. "Magic doesn't lie, they tell me."

Elika huffed. "It lied about the Deadlands."

"It's what I told them. But you can't convince Alterrians of anything when it comes to their precious magic. Here." He held out the boots. "They're not much, but they won't leak."

She examined them. There was fresh stitching at the edges, and the leather was polished and oiled to a shine. Tinker Tan had even added pretty iron clips to the side and a holder for a knife.

"Looks to me like you'd be buying your freedom sooner as a tinker than working for your master." She reached into her pocket for the last of her coins.

"Not here I won't. There are tinkers around who make items more beautiful than I ever could, 'cause they use magic. My master keeps talking of magic's favor and how I should ask for it from a lump of rock in his workshop. He was once a Dae. Crossed fifty years ago, and never looked back. Likes it here. I'm not so sure, meself. He promised to help buy my freedom from the bastard mage who owns this street." His face darkened with constrained anger.

"The mage is cruel, is he?" Elika asked conversationally and held out the last of her pennies to him. "That's all I've got. But you can have my old boots, too."

Tan pocketed the coins without looking down to count them. "He's worse than cruel. Aeon-Blackrain is a rabid murderer. I'd put him down meself if I could. Likes to hurt. Uses the choker to hurt his slaves when the mood takes him." He tapped on his collar. "Mostly girls though. Strangled one to death only last night. Heard her screaming and pleading. No one could do anything to help her, though we tried. Lives at the end of the street, so everyone heard what he did to her." He rubbed his eyes as if to cleanse them of the memory.

"Might be he'll get what's coming to him," she said as she took off her old boots and pulled on her new ones. They were comfortable, the leather supple. "Don't care about magic things myself." She tested out her new shoes. They were more comfortable than any pair she'd had before. "I'd say us Daes would sooner buy from an honest tinker than one who dabbles in magic."

He said nothing for a moment, glanced at her collar and spoke quietly, as if afraid to be overheard. "It's what One Eye's men told me. They came to see me before the rains, waited till my master was gone, and said men are born free and One Eye is promising freedom to anyone who's not afraid to work. Don't matter whether you are young or old, man or woman. Says Daetown belongs to Daes, and we don't need magic, mages or masters. Not even human ones. They say he found a way to remove the collars."

"Maybe you should think upon their offer."

"And you," he said.

"Tan! Where the blast are ye?" shouted a cranky voice from the shop. "You'd better not be tinkering again."

"You'd better go," Tan said to her and ushered her out the garden gate.

A moment later she was back on the street, her mood dark as she watched a mage amble along with a servant close behind, her eyes downcast, her face expressionless, her life stolen by the vile creature who now owned her.

When the light left the day and the city quietened, Elika strode along the dimly lit streets of Daetown, renewed purpose burning in her chest. Tonight, she would hunt as many as she could find. She would avenge *Eagle's Feather* and the men who had not returned. And she would start with Aeon-Blackrain, she decided as she strode past the cobbler's darkened shop, towards the house made of leaves, stones and feathers and towards the mage who liked to hurt.

~

In the dark of night, Reval's personal mageguards were easy to avoid. The fools wore fiery armor, whose glow could be seen two streets away. Elika hid behind a garden wall and watched them march past. They had the form of humans, but they moved like painted clay figurines. Their skin was smooth with no marks or blemishes, or even stubble. It was the type of perfection that was ugly. They were long, slender and far too alike in face. They looked nothing like the majren. As they walked, they threw flowers to the ground and sang in smooth, lyrical voices:

> *"Arala my fair queen,*
> *Hear my love upon these winds.*
> *Fair your beauty, fair your grace,*
> *Love I sing to you in peace,*
> *Fear not my love for you,*
> *Return to me, it shall be true."*

On and on they sang as they strolled through the streets, casting flowers as they went.

After they had passed, she emerged from behind the archway and headed for Maj-Brittlesticks' house of grass and mushrooms. The windows were made of thick glass, and light poured out of them onto the street. Now and then, his shadow moved in front of the light. He was humming a childish tune:

> *"Apple and roses, petals and sweets*
> *Make my love linger upon those fair cheeks.*
> *Peaches and honey, sleep little one,*
> *Fear not the darkness for light won't let it come."*

He continued to hum wordlessly as he moved about, whilst the other voices inside him joined in.

Elika surveyed the nearby houses and alleys until she found an easy path to the roofs. She crept silently on tiles, carefully placing each foot until she reached the mage's roof. The street below was empty. She lowered herself to the window ledge and peered into the room next to the one he was working in. She took out a pin, wedged it through a tiny gap and flicked up the latch on the other side. Then she swung inside and landed lightly on her feet. A faint smell of death accosted her, masked by musty sweet perfume and talcum powder.

The room appeared to be used as storage, with many small and large barrels aimlessly walking around, lining and reordering themselves against the wall, jumping one on top of the other and then back again. Some sat atop shelves, dangling and kicking their black, spindly legs.

As soon as she took a careful step forward, the barrels surrounded her, bouncing lightly on their feet like children asking for treats. She took out her knife, but the barrels appeared neither afraid nor hostile. She decided to ignore them and pressed her ear to the door. The mage's humming drifted away down the corridor, then stopped.

She waited.

When no sound reached her for some time, she pried open the door and tiptoed along the corridor.

The barrels followed, skipping and bouncing after her. She turned to shoo them away, but they only bounced excitedly around her. Giving up, she continued to creep towards the majren's bedchamber.

Inside, he was deeply asleep, snoring softly. A soft humming also emerged from his throat, as if another creature in him remained awake. The barrels nudged her, and one squeezed past to peer into the mage's room. And as she watched him, safe and content in his bed, the hard shell inside her cracked, letting in an unpleasant trickle of pity. She'd never heard a bad word spoken of him. This majren kept to himself and never uttered a cruel word. Or so it was said of him.

Angrily, she shook off those creeping doubts and thought instead of the empty, yellow boat that had not sailed in days, and of the men and women who had not returned to *Eagle's Feather*, Bobquick amongst them. For them, she would be a monster's monster. She would be this monster's terror in the night. She would be death come for them. She forced herself to look more closely at the body Maj-Brittlesticks inhabited——a short, stout man with a kind face lined with creases caused by frequent smiling ... whose life had been stolen by this creature. Aye, her pity was hollow, for she was not looking at a man. He was already dead. The creature possessing his body did not belong in their world.

Before her resolve wavered again, she closed her eyes and pulled on the threads of his essence. The creature cried out, pleaded—they always did—and she closed her ears to his terror. Then he fell back in his bed, a silent, decaying body returned to the realm of the dead.

Around her there was stillness. The barrels who had followed her lay on their sides, their legs gone, nothing more than wood now. She stifled another pang of regret and quenched the echoes of emerging horror. Seramight belonged to men, she reminded herself harshly, and to men she would return it.

She leant her head against the wooden door frame, feeling worn, weak and hungry ... and faint, as if she, too, were slowly unravelling. There was that familiar disturbance in the fabric of their world. She had expected it. The hunter. He was there after she had undone Aeon-Blackrain and Maj-Whitebranch and another mage whose name she did not know. And he was here now, charging towards her, fury preceding him. She did not move. For a brief despondent moment, she wanted to be found, wanted to be stopped. Her soul was wearied, as if each time she destroyed one of them, they took away a piece of her. Might be this was justice racing towards her.

In her mind's eye, she saw mugs raised in the air, and the Rogue Mage's name upon the cheer. For them, she would become the monster to chase away their monsters.

She pushed away from the wall and her feet spurred into motion. Once again, those fine threads of light surrounded her, forming a web to trap her. Without further thought, she jumped out the window, climbed to the roof and ran. She glanced behind. A dark shadow, cloaked and hooded, watched her. He knelt and placed his gloved hand on the slate tile. Tendrils of light emerged from his fingers and raced towards her. Before they reached her, she swung from the roof onto the balcony below. From there she hopped down to the street, ran, turned into an alley and came to a staggering halt.

A menacing shadow blocked her path. He was cloaked, dark and terrifyingly large. A glowing sword appeared in his hand, nearly as long as she. With both hands around the hilt, he struck the tip into the ground. There was a deep boom, the ground shuddered, and something struck her in the chest. She knew a moment of weightlessness, of everything racing past, and then her back and head struck the hard cobbles.

With a groan, she rolled to her knees, winded and dazed. Her hands were suddenly chained by the glowing webbing that pinned her to the cobbles. She looked up at the cloaked figure advancing on her—calm, certain, deadly. His face was hidden inside the shadow of the hood; his faintly glowing yellow eyes were fixed on her.

Fire, she thought and pushed it out through her hands at the imprisoning webbing. Abruptly, it released her, and she scrambled to her feet. But the hunter was almost upon her. She threw out her arms and pushed out the strands of her own magic to block his advance. Tendrils emerged from the walls of the buildings and the ground, rapidly twining a web as black as night in front of him. He raised his sword and slashed it.

The pain was sharp, piercing, and burned through her like a lightning strike. Elika cried out and staggered back. Her legs gave way beneath her and she fell to her knees, breathing harshly. Her hands clutched her stomach, trying to stem the flow of blood … except … there was no wetness.

She looked down at her hands … no blood. She probed where her body was cut in two. But there was no cut to her flesh or her clothes. Her head snapped up, and the screeching wind ripped her hood from her head. The cut strands of her magic web were bleeding, the dark red blood pooling on the ground.

Horror and confusion choked her. She could feel the pain, knew that it was *her* blood on that ground, felt it flow out of her body. Yet it came not from her body but the black web she had spun.

The hunter raised his sword again to slice the path through it to reach her.

A cry of fear emerged from her throat, and she raised her hand against the fall of his giant sword. She braced herself for more pain, whilst desperately trying to pull together the shreds of her pain-muddied mind. She tried to rise, but fell again, as if her limbs were broken, as if her body knew not how to stand against the wound he'd dealt. But the strike never came. She raised her head, met those glowing angry eyes condemning her, and waited for the sword to fall.

Again, he pulled it back to do just that … and hesitated, looking at her, his fury a potent force between them. He took a step forward, his sword twitched. He raised it higher … But once again his hands stilled.

Then slowly, inexplicably, the sword lowered and his hooded head appeared in the bloodied gap of her web, his face still hidden in shadow. The blood of her magic pooled at his feet. The faintly glowing eyes grew intent, and she thought she saw puzzlement in them. She stared back, unable to look away, her arm still stretched out in defensive horror. More strands of light came at her along the ground. She backed away and cast small flames to keep the light from reaching her. But her mind was muddled with pain, and small spots of flames erupted on the cobbles and her trousers both. She patted the fire out on her clothes, burning her hand as she did so.

Why do you just stare? She wanted to yell at him, for his study of her was more terrible than his anger. A cat watching a mouse.

She pulled out the knife from her boot; the movement wrenched a groan from her throat. But he just stood there in curious silence, as if pondering his next attack, whilst those relentless strands of light tried to find their way around the flames she conjured. She sliced at the glowing threads with her knife, and they recoiled. His head tilted ever so slightly, and she realized that he was testing her magic, seeing what she could do, what she *would* do.

Then another giant shape charged at her from around the corner. It came to an abrupt halt, and she almost wept with relief when she recognized Pebble. But his horrified face was looking past her at the shadow beyond her pitiful web of magic. "Shoran," he said on a breath, so quietly, she might not have heard him were she not sitting at his feet.

The shadow's eyes released her from their grip and captured Pebble.

The wind picked up, and it was the wind of the Abyss. It ripped at her hair, at Pebble's clothes.

"Stonewald, son of Draygan," said a grim, rumbling voice that sounded like the night and all the terrors that lurked in the dark. A voice that wrapped you with fathomless dread. A voice that invaded your body and filled your blood with quiet terror. "Are you a party to this mischief?" He spoke slowly, deliberately, as if eternity was at his command. "We will speak of this, you and I."

Pebble cursed, fell on one knee, and bowed his head to the shadow. "Forgive me, my lord, and grant mercy." He then rose just as abruptly, grabbed Elika and yanked her to her feet.

She moaned as pain lanced through her. Again, the shadow tilted his head quizzically.

"Run!" Pebble said in a strangled whisper.

She half ran, half limped, with Pebble supporting her as they went.

When she glanced back, the shadow still stood there, behind the web, sword in hand, watching them flee. And somehow, it did not seem like mercy keeping him where he was, watching his prey flee.

CHAPTER EIGHT

The Arch Mage's Parade

"We have been to Tridamor's Spring Parade, and it is with pleasure that we watched the human dukes bow low to the Arch of the Laifae. And no one grovels more than the heir of their worthless Sacred Crown, Prince Southfire. Him, we despise above all else, for in him we see the weakness of humanity. They are servants; we are masters. Tsarin Reval tells us they were not always so weak, that once, long ago, the Sacred Crowns were demigods who chose the realm of men as their domain. But they took human women as their queens, and over many centuries the blood of the gods faded until their descendants could no longer drink from the wells of power, nor command the elemental magic of the earthly realm."

The History of Alafraysia and Seramight,
By Mageguard Bluelight

Pebble was visibly shaking as he paced back and forth. He ran his hands through his hair. "We are doomed."

Elika rested on the ground, leaning back against a tree in an empty courtyard, waiting for the pain to fade. Though there was not a mark on her, she felt deeply wounded.

"I told you to stop. I warned you …" Again, he dragged his fingers through his hair, his eyes wild. "I fear you are in more trouble than you realize, princess."

But even his agitation could rouse no feeling in her, beyond an intense wish to sleep. "Who is he?" she asked, whilst fighting to keep her eyes from drifting closed.

Pebble stopped and spun around. "You don't know who Shoran is?" He all but shouted his incredulity. "Syn'Moreg's voice, the enforcer of his will. It is through him the Lord of the Abyss demands his wishes be heeded. Through him he metes out his godly justice. And you have drawn his wrath ..." He froze and stared at her with open-mouthed disbelief. "You're alive."

"Barely," she grumbled, feeling as if she'd been trampled by a horse.

"He didn't kill you ..." Pebble blinked at her in sudden dumbfounded confusion. "He looked like he wanted to. Badly. Slowly. Very slowly. And fill the night with your screams of anguish."

She shifted uncomfortably. "He's been following me from the day I killed Aeon-Greengrass. Somehow, he always knows when I unravel a mage, knows where to find me."

He threw his arms into the air. "You never told me this."

"Didn't want to worry you. You do nothing but complain as it is."

He spread his arms dramatically. "With good reason. You have prodded Syn'Moreg who can end a tsarin quicker than you can blink. He can kill you." He said it as if it was quite a feat to do that.

"I'm not as hard to kill as I look." She chuckled and pain shot through her insides. "Ow!" She gripped her stomach and chuckled some more. "How did you find me, anyway?"

Pebble waved a hand as if her question was irrelevant. "I followed the essence of your power. You are hardly subtle." He began to pace again.

It was making her dizzy. "Must you sweep about like a sea wave?"

He ignored her. "We must think. Only a fool would draw the eye of the gods to her misdeeds. You've been reckless, stubborn, rash and far too impulsive ..." On and on he went.

She was too worn out to argue the truth of the matter.

Abruptly, he stopped pacing. "He will kill me. He now knows that I've been keeping you a secret, and helping you do whatever it is you did that enraged Syn'Moreg. He'll pull me apart limb by limb."

Elika buried her head in her hands and recalled the hunter's hesitation.

He could have slain her, could have shredded her black web, yet he just stood there. She was certain it was not mercy that saved her, but his curiosity.

"He'd have killed you already if that was his wish," she said, trying to offer him comfort, though she found none in those words herself.

Shoran's mercy was a taunt, she was certain, and she heard the whisper of his unvoiced threat. *I'll find you again*. And aye, it frightened her. And fear fed her anger.

"Don't mistake his mercy for anything other than a brief reprieve. He's not rash. He doesn't need to be. If Shoran spared you, it's likely only so that Syn'Moreg could have the pleasure of killing you himself. You must stop your attacks against the mages. Whatever you are doing is upsetting the demigod of the Abyss."

She thought of the dark spider that invaded her dreams. "Might be I want to upset him," she said with a pang of anger as she recalled countless folk who had fallen into his chasm or perished on the cursed bridge across it. He had broken their world. Though the encounter with his servant had left her shaken, she could not abandon her cause. "Look, the way I see it, men will forever be enslaved by the Laifae, unless we fight the terrors that force such existence upon us."

"Not *us*. *Them!* You are not one of *them* of mankind! *You* are one of the terrors."

Her blood chilled at his cutting words. Holding on to the tree, she rose to her feet. "I am one of *them*, Pebble. The humans I mean. I'm not a magic-lover and never will be. Great injustice has been done to Seramight, and I will use what power I have to right it. Might be you should keep away from me and save yourself from being torn apart limb by limb. Go and hide in whatever cave your father has carved until all this passes."

She limped away before she saw the replying hurt in his face. But damn it, his words were just as brutal. Whatever else she was, she was one of *them*—humans. She was born and raised in Seramight amongst men, by *them*. No one else had claimed her. No one else taught her, fed her or loved her. The tane who had found her gave her to a human family to raise. The tane who ripped her from their embrace died soon after and left her alone and unprotected on the street. Penny had found her and cared for her.

Elika swallowed the ache of aloneness. She wanted to go home, to Penny and her pack, to her old city. But that life had been taken from her, by magic, by Syn'Moreg, by the Laifae and the tsaren. Now she would take from them. As long as there was life left in her bones, she'd fight them and take back everything they had taken from men and from her.

~

Elika was roughly shaken awake. With great effort, she opened her blurry eyes. Two shadows stood over her.

"What is wrong with you, girl?" her mistress demanded. "You look half-starved. Have you not been eating?"

Elika tried to sit up, but her body would not obey.

"She's with ague," Meena screeched and jumped back. "Magic is punishing her."

The events of the night before rushed to fill her sluggish mind. She had expended her magic, had watched it bleed. The pain was gone, but her body was numb and weak. She tried to rise again, only to fall back onto her pillow.

Mistress Oblana's lips firmed. "It is clear that you have not been looking after yourself. And now you are lying in bed instead of working. Each day you laze around with some sickness, I shall deduct the full price of the web you are not weaving from your coin."

Elika groaned inwardly. Her mistress sold them for ten silver pieces each. She'd never earn enough to pay off one of those webs. The thought was slippery, fading away like water pouring through her fingers. She closed her eyes, just to rest them a little.

"Meena, fetch a healer. And bring up food, anything the cook can spare. And this, too, you'll pay for, Lika."

It was the last thing Elika heard before she was woken again by a man leaning over her quizzically whilst peering through an eyeglass. A bony finger prodded her arm and shoulder. "You need to feed your girls more, Oblana. It's all very well to starve them, but then what are they worth to you like this?"

Mistress Oblana's spine stiffened. "I feed them thrice a day, which is more than most get."

"Yet she is clearly wasting away." The healer lifted Elika's emaciated arm, then let it drop again. "The simple cure is more food. Feed her up, and she'll be fine in a few days. There's nothing more I can do for her."

After he left, the mistress loomed over her. "Get up and eat every last drop in those bowls." She pointed at the table, where two bowls of stew were steaming invitingly.

Elika took note of her body, and aye, her hunger was fierce. The scent of potatoes, meat and sweet beet propelled her to rise and stagger towards the food.

The mistress stood guard, watching her eat until every drop of hot stew and warm, buttered bread was gone. She need not have bothered. Elika ate until her stomach was full to bursting and aching, and the bowls were scraped clean with the last of her bread. Even so, hunger clawed at her still.

"From now on, you will eat four meals a day," said the mistress. "And you will pay extra for them."

Elika saw no reason to argue. She needed her flesh and strength back before she faced the dark hunter again.

With a huff, and a swish of skirts, the mistress left her alone to wash and dress. When Elika dared to look at herself in the mirror, a gaunt, hungry face she barely recognized stared back. She lifted her shirt and examined her body. It had shrunk overnight, looking sunken and deathly bony.

For a few sluggish moments, she sat on her bed, thinking that she might yet kill herself if she continued to cast magic about. She just could not eat fast enough to replenish it. Yet there were many more mages to unravel, many battles still to fight. And now, there was Syn'Moreg's servant intent on stopping her. She'd need all her strength to fight him. It seemed an impossible task.

The thought faded … and she was falling, falling …

She jerked awake and shook her head to clear it. It was already mid-morning, and ten silver pieces were looming over her ledger of debt. With that daunting thought, she forced herself to rise and limp downstairs to the workshop. As it was, she'd be working late to make up for the time she had missed. Mage Aeon-Rah had procured more of the magical dye from another mage, and an errand boy was sent to fetch it before they ran out.

As Elika sat at her loom, Liffy took in her sickly appearance without surprise. "'Tis what happened to Tikka when she lost magic's favor. It made her waste away until she was just skin and bones. I told her to pray more, but she wouldn't listen."

Elika ignored the barb, focusing instead on weaving the silken web.

At their midday meal, she was given more food than could fit into her stomach, and Meena stood there, watching until every crumb was gone.

When Elika finished eating, the effort to keep her eyes open exhausted her. The next thing she knew, a quiet, surreptitious closing of the door startled her awake. Had someone slammed it, she'd have likely slept through it. But it was the quieter sounds you had to be heedful of.

She was still at the kitchen table. Her head made a pillow of her folded arms. The kitchen was empty. A sensation of something being wrong nipped at her. She unfolded and silently crept to the door. She pried it open a crack and peered out, just in time to see Liffy disappear under one of the courtyard archways into the street beyond. Quickly, Elika followed. The others were having their luncheon on the benches under a greening vine, and they waved at her as she strode past.

Just past the milliner's shop, she caught sight of Liffy. Neither of them was allowed to leave the courtyard without permission from Meena or the mistress. Liffy must know she risked a beating. Despite that, not once did she glance behind to see whether she was being followed.

She did not go far before she knocked on the door of a house which made Elika's stomach plunge sickeningly. The house was fashioned of black strands of Laifae magic and vile adornments of feathers and dead birds with their wings spread wide. Liffy slipped inside through an opening, looking like a bride with a purpose.

Elika darted forward to stop her, but the branches slid over each other and tangled before she could reach her. After snatching a quick look about, she pulled out her knife, ran down the side alley and circled to the back of the house. There, she pressed herself against the sordid wall of the mage's home and listened to the voices coming from the inside. One of them was Liffy's. She sounded … cheerful? There was no fear, no weeping or pleading …

Elika peered through a gap in the strands, which might have passed for a small window. The stench of dead birds and feathers filled her nose. But it was what she saw inside that chilled her.

Liffy was sitting at a table fashioned from stone and black tendrils, smiling at a young man … a young *mage* clumsily pouring her a cup of red-leaf tea, and spilling a little onto the table. He had the same straw-colored hair, and there was so much similarity in their features, Elika had no doubt she was looking at Liffy's brother, Sam. He smiled crookedly, as if he had not yet mastered the use of his face, and one side of his mouth lifted higher than the other. It was not one of those endearing smiles youths bestowed on girls, but grotesque and yet … affectionate.

Elika's jaw hardened. No. It was a lie. It had to be.

Blissfully oblivious to there being anything amiss about her brother, Liffy chatted away. "Magic is punishing her," she was saying as she sipped the tea. "I keep telling her to pray, but she is stubborn …"

The mage opened the cupboard and brought out a plate of hard cakes and jam. He placed it in front of her, then sat down and awkwardly poured himself a cup of the same tea, spilling it as he did so. He wiped the table with a cloth and put a lump of sugar into his cup, smiling with delight as he listened to her chatter.

Elika had never before seen delight on a mage's face and it twisted something sharp and awful inside her.

"And your master, Sam, does he still treat you well?" Liffy was asking, and Elika's stomach tightened sickeningly.

"Aeon-Pinkshoe is kind," said the mage in a voice that sent a shudder of disgust through her. Liffy, however, seemed content to ignore the rasping, inhuman sound. "He brought me more birds for my crowns."

Liffy nodded as she bit into her tea-drenched cake. "My mistress has not taken a cane to me since Lika started weaving her webs. But I do sometimes wish Meena would disappear. Lika is nice enough, but she is … strange, you know. She reminds me of that Sachi girl who begged our father to let her rest in his barn for the night. Do you remember? She was on her way to Terren after the Blight destroyed their temple. She had bare, bleeding feet and was young, but her eyes were old. Do you remember telling me so?"

The mage lied with a nod.

"Oh, Sam. Now that Aeon-Pinkshoe has found a buyer for your beautiful crowns, you'll save enough coin for us both soon, won't you?"

"Soon," he agreed.

Liffy smiled brightly. "I have nearly two sherrings myself already. We'll get to Wavestar, I swear it."

Again, he nodded a lie and poured more tea into her empty cup. Mages were forbidden from going to Wavestar, and Sam was dead.

"You'll love it there, Sam," she went on. "Everyone says it's the most beautiful city in the whole realm."

The mage's smile widened, and it did not seem like a lie. "We will travel to many cities and see many places," he said with a wistful, longing note in his ugly voice. "We will see real rivers made of water and forests that are filled with scent. And we will walk up solid mountains of stone that crumble, and we will touch the cold snow at the top."

Liffy beamed and stood up. "Aye, we'll do that one day. Well, I must go before Meena notices me gone. But I'll come to visit you again soon."

"Soon," the mage echoed and rose to his feet like a clumsy child. "Come back soon, our sister."

She gave him a kiss on the cheek and they walked together to the front of the house.

Elika exhaled slowly, her hand still tight around the hilt of her knife. She ran back to the workshop and was at her loom by the time Liffy returned.

She took her seat at the spinning wheel, spread her dress prettily, bowed her head in a prayer to magic, then smiled brightly. "My brother came to see me whilst you were sleeping. He's saved almost enough to buy us both a passage to Wavestar."

Elika nodded mutely, her hands moving absently as the web in her lap took shape.

~

"Syn'Moreg," she whispered, naming the stone spider in her hand as she closed her fingers around it, battle brewing in her heart.

Outside her window, the screeching winds of the Abyss raced through the streets, carrying upon them the rage of the power that sought her. *I'll find you*, they promised as they went past and vanished.

The night deepened. Everything grew silent, and in that silence her fear for Liffy found its voice. Whatever madness festered in her grief-stricken mind, the foolish girl believed her brother lived on as a mage. Elika could not fathom why the majren indulged her with his shameless lies, but he was a threat to Liffy. One way or another, he would hurt the hapless girl who had claimed him as her brother.

Elika stuffed the spider into her pocket and slipped out through the window. Within moments, she was down on the street, heading towards Maj-Blackfly's house. That was his name. The folk around here said he had appeared at the start of winter and spun his house into the shell of the one burned down by the mages to make room for him. What happened to the previous occupant no one could say, save that he had vanished and had not been seen since. Elika had her own suspicions on the matter.

She snuck to the back of his house, willed the strands to part, and entered through an opening. The house was warm and brightly lit. A humming came from the front room.

She peered around the corner. Maj-Blackfly was sitting in a cozy chair in front of a burning coal fire, crafting circlets made of feathers for the ladies of the court. The circlets were not like any common crowns. There was an ethereal essence to them. The feathers were seamlessly merged with gold strands and small jewels. A few of them lay on the stone table beside him. Try as she might, she could not deny the strange, yet striking beauty of the Laifae craftmanship. It contrasted starkly with the ugly creature and clumsy movement of his hands. The feathers he picked up from the small basket were plain white and grey. By the time he melded them with the gold wire, they morphed and glowed with a sheen of stars and metal. Their beauty stirred the unexplored feminine vanity in her, and her fingers itched to touch those feathers. Then she thought of Liffy being fed lies by this creature, and her awe faded.

She pressed herself back against the wall of dead birds and black strands, gathering the strength to do what she must, thinking of the broken girl whose frail hopes were perched on brittle lies about her brother.

The chair creaked as Maj-Blackfly bent to get another feather. His robe rustled. The wire clicked against the wood of his chair as he patiently turned plain feathers and gold nuggets into crowns worthy of the gods. And as he worked, deep in his throat, he hummed a wordless tune she recognized as one of Pebble's famed creations.

You are one of the terrors, he had said, and those words twisted like a dagger inside her.

Her breathing grew strained. *For Liffy, you must do this.*

You will break her, whispered another voice of reason, and it sounded like Penny's.

She is already broken.

She still has hope. Will you steal it from her?

False hope, for Sam is dead.

"Who's there?" asked the mage, alert and tense.

Elika caught her breath. His robe rustled as he rose from his creaking chair. Then silence.

"Liffy?" He tentatively probed that silence. "Have you come to see us again? We have your favorite plum cakes with jam." His feet shuffled closer, then stopped. "Liffy, our sister?" His voice trembled.

With a silent curse, Elika slipped away the way she had come. Once outside, she ran back home as fast as her feet could carry her, hating her weakness, and knowing that Liffy would pay the price for it.

~

As mid-spring approached, the city grew abuzz with excitement. The Festival of Flowers was upon them, a custom which survived the divide of land and time. Elika thought it might be the only tradition that still united the Daes and Alterrians, who had otherwise grown so far apart.

As in Dae-Terren, strings of flowers were hung on doors and trees, and chains of them stretched from house to house above the streets. Women adorned their hair with fresh blooms, and Liffy looked like she had rolled in a meadow and got covered in blossoms from head to foot. Even Meena was more cheerful and forgot to berate them. She strung flowers sewn from the offcuts of their bright fabrics out the window and instructed them to decorate the workshop and the shrines. It was a welcome distraction and brought with it a sense of respite, for Elika did not want to taint the celebration of life with thoughts of death. Each day, a little more of her strength and flesh returned, and for a time, she thought no more of hunting the mages.

The peace was not to last. She soon learned that here, the festival was tainted with another, darker tradition—the archmage's Spring Parade. This year, it was promised to be grander than ever, and the whole city was caught in the fervor of anticipation. It was all Liffy could speak of, for having only arrived last summer, she had not seen it before. It involved a display of magic by the archmage himself, and everyone knew he was gifted with vestiges of Arala's powers.

"Everyone in the city will attend. Even us," Liffy had said with that grating excitement, whilst Elika's thoughts grew dark with her own anticipation. Soon, she would glimpse the master of their masters, the one responsible for the creation of every *majren* and *aeon*.

For centuries, Tridamor had been flooding the lands with his creatures. They spread like a pestilence through Seramight, settling in every city, town and village. And still it was not enough. It would never be enough, thought Elika, until he exterminated mankind, for that must surely be his plan.

When the day of the Spring Parade arrived, they all set out together, dressed in their finest frocks, though hers still hung loosely on her. The sun was high, and the air was thick with scents of green sap, honey blossom and crushed apples for cider. The mistress walked ahead, with Meena as her companion. Elika trailed close behind with Liffy and the cook. They joined the growing throng of folk all heading the same way towards the temple. There was laughter and excitement aplenty. Yet beneath the festive air, Elika saw what the others did not. The city had changed. The people had changed.

Never had the enmity between the Daes and Alterrians been so stark. Somewhere along the way, the Daes had forgotten to be afraid. They made a point of wearing muted colors, in contrast to the bright, festive cloths the Alterrians wore. Despite the slave bands around their necks, the Daes held their heads high and stared boldly at the silk-clad enemy. Save that the enemy was other men.

Magic-lovers, they cursed under their breaths.

Magic-haters, Alterrians sneered and spat at the feet of the Daes.

Ever do men turn against each other when faced with another threat, she thought bleakly. Like starved dogs, they would tear each other apart and gift this world to their shared enemy.

She eyed the mages in their midst. Not one of them wore a collar. Human laws could not touch them, and the tsaren cared not what their subjects did in the earthly realm. Yet who was there to unite men against the Laifae, the true invaders of their realm of Seramight? Aye, she saw it now. The Rogue Mage had only widened this divide into a chasm no bridge could span. The realization was a poisonous serpent in the pit of her stomach.

An Alterrian shoved past her with a curse. The crowds had grown thick, and their group now huddled like chickens, pushing and shoving at the edges of the sprawling temple square, until they encountered an impenetrable weave of bodies.

Children climbed atop statues and sat on men's shoulders to look over the sea of heads at the enormous domed temple in the distance. Elika wished she, too, could sit on one of those wide shoulders that blocked her view of the temple doors. She was here to see the archmage, but as it was, she'd see only the cracked leather vest of the man in front.

The mistress was clearly unsatisfied with their view as well, for she started to battle through the wall of bodies, shoving her way forward, drawing the others of their party with her. Elika saw her chance to break away. Before any of them noticed, she fell back and allowed the crowd to swallow her. A quick glance about, and she picked a place for herself. She weaved her way through the hoard to the nearest lantern post and joined a group of Dae boys clinging to it.

"Move over," she said, nudging the boy with a shorn head. "There's enough room for me, too."

When they heard her Dae accent, their scowls dissolved, and they shuffled aside, allowing her to squeeze beside them.

With her feet balanced on the stone carvings, she could see well above the heads. The temple spread through much of the western city, and merged with the palace beyond it, absorbing the ancient human Seat of Power into its sphere of dominion. Above the sweeping marble steps, the giant doors were open. Mageguards in red regalia stood in a long line at the base of the steps. With their sharp pikes, they prodded the eager crowd away from the barrier of slithering black strands of Laifae's magic.

Reval's fiery guards were also there, motionless statues at the back who were ... still singing, absurdly, willing Arala to rise from the dead and answer.

Elika's gaze moved to the tall platform spun of black magic, with nearly a hundred aeons and majren gathered there. You could always tell them apart. The difference was as stark as one between a farmer and a nobleman, and not just in cloth and bearing. The majren were the farmers. They held no political ambition and made poor scholars, poor warriors and poor masters. The aeons, in turn, cared naught for craft or trade, only for wealth and rule. Be that as it may, both were as easy to unravel as each other.

At the thought, her heart raced with unbidden temptation and that compelling sweetness of unbridled power. So many mages in one place, so many to unravel. No one would know. No one would find her in this throng. She would show Shoran that she was not afraid of him …

The trumpets sounded. She quickly strangled the impulse and turned back to the temple where the red-robed mageguards were emerging from the doors. They carried the banner with Arala's symbol of the butterfly, which Tridamor now brandished as his own. Then the creature himself appeared —Arala's own favorite creation. The sight of him took Elika aback.

Tridamor was stretched long and thin, two heads taller than the mageguards beside him. A veil of silvery hair fell down his back to the ground. His eyes stretched wide across his face and were too far apart, like a lizard's. He was robed in the silvery green cloth with sunlight shimmering over it. For long moments, she filled her vision with his strangeness, this being who had claimed the throne of Terren, the creator of the abominations she was destroying one by one. And deep in her chest, she nursed the whisper of a newly emerging purpose.

The archmage spread his arms and his deep voice rolled like an avalanche over their heads. "People of Al-Terren. This day we gather to celebrate life in all its glory. Today, we welcome the birth of new life—the majren who will walk amongst us and bring the wonders of magic into your pitiful lives. Today, we will curse those vile fiends who seek to destroy all that is pure and sacred. Glory to the tsaren! Glory to Arala!" Ribbons of light burst from his hands and snaked their way into the sky before vanishing.

His shout was joined by the roar of the crowd. "Glory to Reval! Glory to Ilikan! Glory to Draygan!"

The Dae youths beside her were notably silent. They exchanged dark looks as the Alterrians around them raised their voices in rapturous praise.

"Magic-loving bastards," one uttered, but his curse was swallowed by jubilant shouts.

Another group of tense, sullen youths hung around on the corner of an alley, their arms crossed. The older of the youths, with the look of a leader, slowly turned his acidic gaze on the men who echoed the archmage's revered cry. Something about him and the other Dae youths caught her attention.

She looked closer and saw that all of them were armed, even the younger ones who clung to the post above her, and not just with plain knives. The older youth's hand absently slipped lower and gripped the hilt of a knife. Distractedly, he readjusted it in its holder, betraying a flash of the red blade. Around each of their necks hung an identical, plain string, but the pendant was hidden. She did not need to see it. With a jolt of dread, she knew what they were wearing. Blood-salt, the same crystals that coated their weapons.

Elika's heart raced with a deeper understanding of the undercurrent she had sensed on the streets. The seeds of strife had been in the fallow ground for far longer than her time in Al-Terren. She had watched them sprout the day she killed Maj-Dun'Flower. They had grown with each mage she destroyed, fed by her hatred and their own. Yet this was not what she wanted, what she had hoped to bring about. She had seen this divide before and knew where it led. She only meant to set mankind free, to give them strength to fight against enslavement and take back their city. But what she saw in their faces spoke not of the coming battle for freedom, but annihilation of every shred of magic ... and everyone else who stood in their way.

Another cheer went up and her head snapped back to the archmage. He was floating upon the cloud under his feet.

The Daes nearby grumbled in anger at the brazen show of power. "Look at the bloody fool, thinking to impress them other fools."

The archmage spread wide his long arms. "Release my children, for spring is upon us!"

A roar erupted.

But the sounds retreated abruptly as Elika's world shifted and spun, and her vision filled with the sight of horror, until she saw nothing else and heard no more. For there, emerging from the temple doors was a colony of newly forged majren.

They walked as if they were still learning how to place one foot in front of the other. Their backs were hunched, their arms dangled loosely by their sides, swaying like ropes blown about by a fickle wind. They grinned benignly, placatingly like babes gazing upon the wondrous vista for the first time. On and on they came, row after row, until tens turned to hundreds, and still they kept coming.

A cheer drowned out a woman's wail and a scream for a loved one lost to those abominations. The Daes remained grim and silent as they watched the army of aberrations emerge into their world.

The archmage raised his arms towards the sky, where Reval's island hung witness to the proceedings. "Hear me now. For this, I swear," Tridamor shouted and fire erupted from his fingers. "For every mage the Rogue takes from us, we will birth a hundred more!"

Elika grew sick at his threat, for here before her, the truth of it marched out of the temple gates.

The crowd parted before the procession. Hundreds marched on to enslave thousands. Here and there, women and children wept, for every one of those abominations was once a son, a husband, a father. Oblivious to the weeping of mothers and wives, the lumbering majren grinned with youthful joy, taking in the world that did not belong to them. Then a familiar face among them caught Elika's eye and everything in her recoiled.

"Tom," she whispered his name under her breath.

Tom from *Eagle's Feather* was there, grinning like a dullard, his feet tangling, his arms swaying loosely, else his hands mindlessly pulled on his hair.

Tom was dead.

Her throat constricted, but she could not tear her gaze from the abhorrent sight. She searched for Bobquick, but there were no children among the majren, and she grew frightened for his fate. Then she saw more of the men who had been taken from the tavern that same night. Men who had raised their cups to the Rogue Mage—Skinner the Tanner, Silent Peters, Rollers the Baker, Happy Hans and so many more she knew by name—their dead bodies now possessed, walking, grinning, waving back at the rapturous crowds.

Something dark and cold stirred in her chest, something feral that would not be contained. The world fell away until only she and the vile corruptions remained. And the feral thing inside her uncoiled and roared at the wrong that had to be righted.

Tom's head lolled to the side and righted itself.

She could not return his life, but she could return his body to the soil of his forefathers, to be laid to rest and not torment those who had once loved him.

This had to end, this butchery, this violation.

Rage surged through her, and its claws pulled the fabric of this world towards her and into her.

You can destroy them. You can free men.

Everything around her grew brighter and brighter, and she saw the webbing of the shimmering essence she could grasp and twist. Those same threads that ran through the abominations. She was justice, she was vengeance, and she would show the archmage that the reign of magic in Seramight was coming to an end.

With an internal scream of hatred, she grasped those threads and tore them from the stolen bodies, shredding the light as she did. Then she turned her gaze upon the one who made them. And the whisper of that newly forged purpose grew loud, for she saw his threads too, and knew she could destroy him. She reached for the archmage …

A wall of power pushed her away violently, painfully akin to a rock being thrown at her head. The jolting force snapped her back into awareness. The shimmering essence vanished. The creature in her curled up and grew still.

There was silence.

Everyone was frozen as they stared upon hundreds of majren lying dead on the ground. More mages lay dead beside the temple, beneath the archmage floating on his cloud.

Silence—deep and poisonous.

The archmage stared in horror at his dead creations, then lifted his face and frantically searched the crowd.

"ARALA!" cried Reval's thunderous voice from the sky. "I AM HERE, MY LOVE."

As one, his army stepped forward, their song loud in the silence as they called insistently for the demigoddess to show herself to her one true love.

Then screams erupted and the temple square became a churning sea of bodies, running and tripping over each other.

"Stop them!" cried the archmage. "Find him!"

He spread his hands and fire tore from him. Flames flew over the crowd and blocked their retreat.

"The Rogue is amongst them!" he shouted and pointed at the mass of fleeing folk.

The mageguards charged forward.

The youths next to her jumped down from the lantern post and ran. Elika followed. They came to a jarring halt as flames blocked their exit from the square, and the heat drove them back. Then the flame advanced on them and grew hotter.

Elika got ready to use her own magic, knowing it would betray her to everyone nearby. A shrill whistle spared her. It drew their attention to the older Dae youth waving at them from inside a broken window. They darted for the house and one by one climbed inside. There were eight of them, and more were climbing in behind. They ran through the house to the back, but more flames blocked their escape through the garden.

"To the roofs," the boy with shorn hair shouted.

They raced up the stairs and broke through the roof tiles to climb out. Screams and shouts rent the air and the smoke grew thick. Elika dared a glance below. The guards had surrounded the crowd, grabbing anyone they could, old and young and women with babes … A knife flashed and the guard fell to his knees. Another glint of silver and his body was swallowed by the flood of outrage. More weapons gleamed and more guards fell. The roar of battle erupted as more and more men turned on each other.

"Traitors!" they screamed as one.

Before her strength and courage wavered, she quickly wished for the water to douse the flames …

A waterfall cascaded from the cloudless sky, as if a giant bucket of water was tipped over everyone below. It knocked men and mages to the ground and carried them in a wash as it flowed along the streets away from the temple.

Elika turned and fled, following the boys along the roofs.

In the distance, Reval's army rose on their clouds above the city, circling and singing, heedless of the raging riot below.

"ARALA!" cried the voice of madness.

CHAPTER NINE

One Eye

"We must write about the beginning, our tsarin said, and his fire burned bright around him as he told us the story of his birth. Long ago, when the realm of Alafraysia brushed against God's domain, they crossed into our world and found chaos. They found the branching Black River of our kind and many dreams that shaped our realm. And they found pollution of humankind's invasion, those dreams that did not belong to us but to them. The gods took pity and gave us a gift. They gave us five tsaren—meaning 'world-shapers' in the old tongue of the gods—fashioned by merging streams from the Black River with the Ethereal Essence and Elemental of the Earthly. Five seats of power they created: Fire, Water, Air, Rock and Life. The tsaren gave our realm order, and we rejoiced in the new vision of our world. We had sky, and mountains, and seas and grass. We had fire and winds and sands, as in the realm of Seramight. Save that the fires did not burn, the winds did not stir the grass, and we felt not the silk of flower petals on our essence. The world they had built was but another dream."

The History of Alafraysia and Seramight,
By Mageguard Bluelight

Soon after dusk, the mistress, Liffy and the cook returned sodden, ashen and covered in blood, soot and smoke. Liffy was weeping. Her hair was loose and matted. Mud stained her pretty dress and one sleeve was ripped at the shoulder.

"Where were you?" the mistress demanded, her voice hoarse and shaken.

Elika lowered her head. "Forgive me, mistress. I ran away as soon as I saw them fall dead. Then the flames erupted behind me and I thought we'd all be burned alive ... I was afraid." She looked up and frowned. "Where is Meena?"

"Dead," said the mistress blandly. "Daes dragged her off and butchered her like an animal." Her voice was bland, but Elika saw the accusation burn in her eyes. *You are one of them. You are one of the ones who are making my city fall apart.*

Elika lowered her gaze. "How may I assist you, mistress?"

"Get out of my sight. Resume your work tomorrow."

The mistress limped upstairs whilst the cook shuffled silently to the kitchen.

"I hate him," Liffy said fiercely as tears spilt down her cheeks. "He's a beast."

"Who?"

"The Rogue Mage," she wailed and ran upstairs, sobbing as she went.

Elika refused to allow the guilt to choke her. She was doing it for them, for Liffy, for men enslaved by the Laifae. She repeated this as she climbed the stairs to her room. Repeated it still as she locked the door behind her and climbed onto the roof. The winds of the Abyss were wild, drowning the city with their screech and Syn'Moreg's rage.

Elika ran, fleeing regret and self-loathing that crushed her chest.

~

"O fair maiden, dark of thought
With breath of icy winds.
Upon the clouds, she floats above
And tears of loss she sheds."

The minstrel's soft voice floated through *Eagle's Feather*. It came from a young woman with red strands in her hair and a blindfold over her eyes. Beside her rested a walking stick. Sightlessly, her fingers brushed the strings of a small harp. Elika had never seen her before, nor most of the folk here. All were Daes, all nursing some grief in their ale. Most of the patrons here now belonged to One Eye's gang.

She looked past them, expecting to see Tom at their usual table. But Tom was not there, would never again be there. This was the price of true resistance. Except, she was not the one paying it. Might be Liffy was right to hate her.

Then she spied Bobquick, and her heart gave a little leap. He was sitting at another table, largely hidden by a protective mass of brawny bodies, and wiping angry tears from his eyes. A rough with the black tattoo of a cross over one eye sympathetically pushed a mug of ale in front of him. She might have wept with relief at seeing him alive, save that her heart sank at his newfound company.

Blood Dog sat amongst them, dully playing with his dagger, turning it back and forth with its tip in the rough wooden table. As if he sensed being watched, he glanced her way and abruptly shook his head in a warning. Elika was in no mood to heed it. Especially seeing as Bobquick was gazing at him like a pup waiting for instructions.

She traded three pennies for her ale, walked over and sat next to the boy. He swiped at his eyes and gave her a heart-wrenching smile, strained with grief. "Hey, Lika …"

"What are you doing with them?" She nodded towards the toughs.

His lips trembled. "Tom's dead." His voice was choked.

"Aye, I know."

"One Eye told me he'd look after me," he said with a sniffle. "And promised that no one was ever going to make me their slave. And they have this code … I always wanted to be one of Pocket's men in the old city. One Eye said he knew Peter Pockets."

It would have been better for him to find another good master. Still, with the tensions rising in the city, he might be safer with Rory watching over him. "You're one of them, too?" she asked Blood Dog.

He shrugged. "For now. It's getting dangerous out there for those not clear about where their loyalties lie. Don't you think so mousy?" he asked with a sly smile.

"Besides, we discovered who the Rogue Mage is," Bobquick said with fierce pride.

"You have?" she asked, keeping her voice level and taking a measured draught of ale.

"Everyone's talking about it. It's Northwind."

Elika choked on her ale. "Northwind," she echoed dumbly. Her mind seized. Mite was Northwind, if Bill Fisher was to be believed.

Blood Dog stretched his feet onto the seat in front of him. "Makes sense, that does," he said, unconvincingly, raising his eyes to her. And again, there was that flash of shrewd scrutiny.

"Why him?" Elika asked, keeping both her bewilderment and a pang of affront guarded. Especially with Blood Dog watching her closely, as if he suspected something no one in their right mind should suspect.

"'Cause everyone saw him," said the bald tough with fat lips, as he scraped his fingernails clean with his knife. "He killed a mage on the street in broad daylight, right here in Daetown. Killed him with an ice sword for choking a kid. There's many who saw it with their own eyes."

"Where did he get an ice sword?" Elika asked incredulously.

"He made it with magic," Bobquick said as if it was obvious. "Turned his regular sword into ice. 'Cause he's the prince of the Sacred Crown, like Prince Southfire. And they have gods' blood in them which gives them gods' magic."

"Killed the mage with one strike," added the red-bearded thug next to Bobquick. "Gerrid, over there in the corner, is a guard of the Northern Bastion. Claims it's his captain who's Northwind. Says he calls himself Aeronmite. They say he's the missing son of rebel Lord Silvering, the one who tried to kill the false king in Dae-Terren all those years ago, but got himself killed instead."

Blood Dog spun his dagger on its tip, keeping thoughtfully silent. His silence, and thoughtfulness for that matter, unsettled Elika much more than his crude outspokenness.

"And now Northwind's missing," said Bobquick. "Run off and no one's seen him since."

Elika froze in her seat with fear for Mite. They thought he was killing the mages, and now he was missing. No, Mite could look after himself better than anyone. He was missing, which meant he was hiding. They'd not find him unless he wanted to be found.

The blind minstrel's forlorn voice rose higher.

Elika glanced around the tavern. "Where's Pebble?"

"Not seen him since the attack," said Bobquick. Then his face fell. "Do you think they made him a mage, too?"

Blood Dog barked a laugh.

She saw nothing funny in this and might have suspected as much herself, save that she had seen Pebble since then. But they had parted badly, and she regretted that. A deeper fear for him now scratched away at her, and the screeching winds outside seemed to grow shriller.

He will kill me. He'll pull me apart limb by limb.

"Why don't ye join us?" Bobquick was saying, and she turned her attention to him. "One Eye will buy your freedom, especially since you're one of us." He turned to the toughs. "Lika was one of Bad Penny's gang in the old city. So she knows what's what on the street. Carries a knife, too, and can use it," he said with childish wonder.

Elika froze as the toughs grew equally still and their faces slowly turned towards her.

The red-bearded one smiled. "Was she now?"

Blood Dog cuffed Bobquick on the back of the head. "What did I tell ye about talking too much and telling tales?"

Elika did not know who moved first, them or her, only that they were all on their feet, chairs knocked to the floor. The bald tough reached for her, but she was faster.

"Grab her!" he shouted as she darted for the door.

Three of them gave chase, shoving patrons and tables aside like clumsy bears. She reached the door, pulled and was grabbed from behind. Then she was being crushed against the wall. Foul breath brushed her cheek.

"Be still or I'll cut ye. One Eye wants a talk."

"Got the wrong person," she said breathlessly.

"Why did ye run then?"

"Why did you chase?" she countered. "It's not me he wants."

"Maybe so, but then might be you'll help us find the right lass who rubbed One Eye the wrong way." He chuckled at his own joke, then yanked her back by the hair.

She reached for her knife, but two more toughs grabbed her arms in a vice-like grip.

"Be still, before we decide to tie you up and deliver you as a blood-soaked sack to One Eye. Don't think he'd be too happy to think you hate him so much you had to fight us all the way to see him."

They pushed her out the door.

"Let her go," Bobquick jumped at the bald tough holding her.

He shoved the boy back. "Watch your manners, kid, or I'll teach them to ye. And I'll start by reshaping your curly ears."

Blood Dog grabbed the boy's arm and spat on the ground. "Not your fight, lad, and not your problem either." And to Elika's relief, he dragged the boy into the tavern by his scruff.

She made another effort to wrench herself free.

"Now, now. No one's going to hurt ye …"

"My mistress will if you don't let me go," she hissed and her teeth gritted in outrage as the tough shrugged and shoved her roughly into a waiting carriage.

Four of them climbed after her and caged her between them. Now that no one was looking, she reached for her magic, but it was buried deeper than she could reach and it took her a moment to realize why. Pain shot through her, the type that was all too familiar. It seized and shook her body until she cried out. Just as quickly, the pain vanished.

"Looks like the mouse is possessed with magic, just like One Eye said."

Through a haze, she saw the bald, fat-lipped tough lean away from her with a metal chain in his hands. It was coated in a thin layer of blood-salt.

"He warned us you're dangerous, so he gave us plenty of rope and blood to hold ye. You do anything and we cut ye with these."

He showed her a sharp red blade. "I'll put this chain on you, too. And gag you to stop the screaming. So what will it be?"

"I'll come," she said. "But only 'cause I want to talk to One Eye myself," she lied. The whole of the carriage was covered in blood-salt crystals. Her skin tingled painfully, her magic withdrawn and tight.

"That's a good girl." He grinned.

The carriage stopped outside a grand house at the southern edge of Daeside, where rich pouches lived opposite leafy parks. She was roughly dragged out, marched up the stairs, and shoved through the door into a large hallway with polished stone floors.

A guard came towards them, looked her up and down, and scratched his chin. "Seems a bit young and scrawny for his tastes."

"Tell him that, Toad, not us," said the fat-lipped tough.

Toad was rotund around the waist, and had a squat head on his thick, short neck. "He's in the cellar," he said.

"Well, be a good servant and fetch him then."

"He won't like being disturbed down there." Toad jerked his head towards the back of the house. "You know that, Punch."

"He'll like it even less if ye don't tell him we've found the mouse he's been searching for."

Toad regarded her again, closer this time. "Her?"

"Her."

He looked doubtful, but shrugged and walked off, mumbling. "Too young for what's coming, if you ask me."

Elika tensed and Punch barred his teeth. "Frightened, are ye, mousy?" He leant into her menacingly. "A big cat lives here, who eats little mice like you." He laughed.

"You don't know how many cats I've skinned who tried to scare me."

He laughed harder. "Always liked you kids, the bad pennies as we used to call ye. Got meat on ye for your size. Might be if One Eye doesn't kill ye, you might join us, like Quick told ye to."

"Got a master already," she bit back.

Shortly, Toad returned. Behind him strode a long, lean man with a face reminiscent of a fox's, for he had an overly protruding jaw and mouth. The socket with the missing eye was hidden behind a silver eyepatch. One-Eyed Rory. He was looking down at his hands as he wiped the sticky blood off them with a handkerchief. Not that it mattered. He was covered in far more blood than the cloth could wipe. It was between his fingers, up to his wrists, and soaked into his white shirt. Even his black trousers were slick with it. Her unease grew.

Rory lifted his face, and his eye turned cold and stony. He barely made a motion with his hand, and a knife appeared at her throat and dug into the skin below her collar.

"Got you on a leash, hey, punch sac," she said to Punch.

"Stop your squeaking, mouse," he replied behind her. His breath stank of ale and rotting teeth.

Rory approached them slowly. "There you are, Spit," he said ever so mildly, in that way of his before he'd cut your throat. Though if his expression was anything to go by, he'd not be killing her quickly.

She swallowed past the sharp blade cutting into her skin. Aye, Rory looked ready to murder her. Whatever it was he got into his head to accuse her of, the last thing she needed was to appear guilty. And fear was a sure sign of guilt.

"Rory," she replied calmly. "Not a nice way to greet an old friend."

"Where's my son?" he asked quietly, taking out his own red-bladed knife, as sharp as the murderous glint in his eye.

With that question, her mind froze, and she forgot to be unafraid. The only answer that came to her lips was the one answer she could not give him. *I do not know.*

Her gaze fixated on the knife in his bloodied hand and the soaking red-stained handkerchief poking out of a pocket. His fist tightened around the hilt, for in her hesitation, he had seen her guilt.

"He crossed the bridge …" she blurted out and tore her gaze from the blood on his hand and returned it back to his murderous eye. "Made it to the other side—this side—alive. I watched him do it."

His jaw tightened.

Aye, he'd gut her, faster than she could scream.

"Penny was with him," she added quickly. "And Tiny Timmy, too. They were like brothers by the time they crossed."

"Penny ..." he echoed and surprise flickered in his face. The white fist around his knife loosened. "Penny's alive?"

"Chelik's safe. That's all you asked of me, Rory," she said as calmly as she could. "That was our deal. I kept him safe and made sure he crossed the bridge. I kept my word. He's alive ..."

"*Was* alive last you saw him."

She swallowed. "He is safe, I know it."

"Explain quickly, Spit. I itch to cut ye."

"Look, it's this way. He was with Penny and a fat pouch called Anten, along with Rosy Rose, and Tiny Timmy. It was the safest he could ever be. Safer than he'd be with me. They left before me. I ... I thought to stay behind a little longer. I haven't seen them since."

"Fat pouch, you say," he said thoughtfully, chewing that piece of information.

"Anten and Penny got close. Very close. He won't let anything happen to them. Not if he's breathing. If Chelik was with me, he'd not have done so well."

His gaze dropped to her collar, and he ran his blood-salt knife along it. "Not like you to get caught, Spit."

She fought the pain of blood-salt's proximity to her skin. "And yet I'm here," she pointed out dryly.

His knife paused at the engraving. "Mage Aeon-Rah owns you. How interesting. You know, I can buy you your freedom," he said mildly and lifted her chin with the tip of his knife.

The blood-salt tip burned her skin, and she couldn't hide a flinch from the searing pain. "I'd rather you didn't," she replied coolly. "Don't need you to. My mistress treats me well enough." Sweat beaded on her forehead.

"Magic still got you, hey Spit?" he said and took away his knife, but the tough still held his to her throat.

She recalled Peter Pocket's obsession with her magic. Rory now regarded her in the same calculating way, as if he was imagining all the ways he could use it through her.

His lips twisted in a sardonic smile. "Like being a slave, do ye?"

That irked her, but she shrugged nonchalantly. "Got to earn my keep."

"Fifty sherrings too much to steal for you? Thought you a better thief than that."

"I'm done with the streets and stealing what doesn't belong to me."

"Never thought you so naïve, Spit. Once that collar is around your neck, only by crookery or mercy will it come off."

He must have made another gesture, for the knife fell away from her throat.

She rubbed it, and her fingers came away sticky and bloodied. "Look, Rory, I told you about your son. If you have half the wits of Peter Pockets and a tenth of his men, you likely have enough spies around the city to find Penny and Chelik."

"Seeing as I entrusted him to *you*, how about you find him for me? My men have better things to do than run around fixing your mistakes."

Without Rory, she'd never find Penny. He must know that, which meant he was setting a trap for her, and Elika suspected she knew why.

"I don't think you'd be wanting to snatch me into your gang," she said. "The way I see it, there're some secrets that are best left behind on the other side of the chasm. Peter had this code, which I hear you are enforcing, about traitors and such."

Rory had betrayed Pockets in the end by helping her escape his dungeon. Were these men to learn of it, they'd not look at him the same way, would not trust him to do right by them. And men who lost trust were far more difficult to trust back.

"You threatening me, Spit?" Rory asked, deceptively mildly.

"Only saying how we should try to remain friendly. If we were to go by Pockets' Code—which is now your Code and your rules, the way I hear it—I still belong to Bad Penny's pack."

"That's not how that works, Spit. Not here. You belong to Aeon-Rah now, and he'll sell you to me. Then you'll belong to me."

"Look, Rory …" she began wearily.

He brought his face close to hers. "Do recall that I entrusted Chelik to you and not Penny. You lost my son. For that, I should be cutting your throat, or at least carving out one eye. You have till summer to find him." And just so she did not doubt his sincerity, he dragged his knife down her body and stopped between her legs. "Do you know what we do to bad girls who betray our trust, Spit? Bring him to me, alive and in as good a condition as when I left him with you, or you'll be birthing me more sons."

The knife dug in deeper, but she refused to flinch, refused to be cowed. "I'll find him," she said through clenched teeth.

"Then we understand each other." He moved away, sheathed his knife. "Take her back where you found her," he said to his men. "Tomorrow, I think I'll visit Aeon-Rah and see how willing he is to part with one of his little slaves."

He smiled at her, meanly, and she remembered why she hated One-Eyed Rory.

CHAPTER TEN

hunting the Shadow

"In the beginning, there were five tsaren. Orian, Reval, Ilikan, Draygan and Tirran. The greatest of them, Orian, held the seat of power over life. He was Goddess Neka's creation, and in her godly vanity, she fell in love with it. Orian returned her love, deep and abiding it was. Their child was Arala. She was Neka's gift to him, but he cherished not the child, only the goddess herself. When Orian's obsession with Neka took him to the forbidden realm of the gods, it led to his inevitable death. And for centuries, his seat of power in Alafraysia remained empty. Until Arala claimed it. Her arrival heralded a new era for our realm, for all loved and wanted her, and the four remaining tsaren fought to possess her. Arala reveled in their rivalry, fed it, and declared that she would only give herself to the most powerful of them. Secretly, she became Tirran's lover. When Reval learned of it, he slew his rival and absorbed his Ethereal Essence of Air, and thus took Tirran's throne in our realm. Soon after, he wooed Arala and claimed the demigoddess as his own."

The History of Alafraysia and Seramight,
By Mageguard Bluelight

There were five of them by the well, scrubbing their clothes and linens in the troughs. Liffy brought up a bucket of fresh water and filled the rinsing trough with it.

Elika wiped her brow. Her hands were raw from the rough, acrid soap the mistress insisted on buying from a mage rather than Lonely Linna, a Dae washerwoman who lived at the end of the street. After the Spring Parade, the mistress had sworn she'd never spend another penny with a Dae, no matter that the vile-smelling soap left the skin chapped, red, and itchy.

"I hate the way they are looking at us," Liffy said, casting a glance at the Alterrian women hanging sheets on the other side of the well. "It's not our fault the Rogue killed them mages."

"Don't pay them any mind," Elika replied as she squeezed the water from her spare skirt. "They were friendly with Meena, that's all."

"We didn't kill her either, so I don't know why they're glaring at us and whispering."

Daila stopped scrubbing her sheets to soothe her babe in the basket by her feet. "Can you blame them? All you Daes ever talk about is how much you hate magic. It's not as nice living without it as you imagine." Daila had always been kind to them, but even she had been bad-tempered lately.

"We don't need to imagine," Elika said as she hung her skirt on the line to dry in the sunshine. "Survived well enough without it in Dae-Terren."

"Aye, you did, and look where it got you?" Daila said as she rocked her babe to sleep.

"In Dae-Terren, everyone was born free," Elika said with a pointed nod at the babe. Though the child wore no collar, Daila and her husband gave every penny they had to buy their daughter's freedom.

"What use is freedom when you end up penniless on the street? And it doesn't keep your belly full, now does it?" Old Sticks asked from the bench in the shade and coughed violently. His winter cough had not retreated as the weather warmed, and they suspected he wouldn't see the coming summer. "It's where I was till they put me to work. You can take your freedom and rot in it." Another cough racked his body.

Liffy hung her nightdress on the line and froze, looking towards one of the archways into the courtyard.

Daila straightened. "Who's that now, staring at us?"

Elika followed their gazes and cursed.

Blood Dog was leaning on the stone wall, shamelessly perusing the women with a wicked smile on his lips. They stared back at the ruffian, like startled birds on the verge of flight.

"I'll get rid of him," Elika mumbled and marched up to him, keenly aware of everyone watching her. "I'd not be coming around here, Dog. My mistress is very testy when it comes to Daes. And the guards are never far."

He leant in. "Your guards are puppies, mousy. I've cut more of their throats the last few days than I care to count."

There was a hard glint in his eyes, which made her wonder whether this was not an empty boast.

"What do you want?"

"Me? Nothing. But One Eye wants something from you."

"What would that be?"

"Didn't ask him. Don't care either. Only came to warn ye."

"Why?" she asked suspiciously. "'Tis no concern of yours."

"You want me to tell all them watching us?" He nodded at the others in the courtyard.

Everyone was still eyeing them with grim distrust. Sticks went into another one of his coughing fits.

"Well, you coming or do I have to drag ye?" Blood Dog asked.

"Look, I can't leave now. I'll be flogged if I do. I'll try to slip out later. The mistress …"

"As I said, don't care about the skin on ye back. I've got better things to do than wait on your mistress' pleasure. Let us talk, and then ye can return to playing washerwoman."

Elika cursed again under her breath and followed him. "Say what you came to say and go away."

Blood Dog spat on the ground. "There's been talk among One Eye's men. Seems he's gone all hard for you. Tried to buy you from Aeon-Rah, but the mage refused to sell. Offered five other girls instead, for a fraction of the price."

"There's no mystery here, Dog. Got magic's favor, that's all. Aeon-Rah is earning more from my weaving than he'd get from selling me."

"So I hear. 'Tis why One Eye offered a hundred gold for you, and the mage turned him away."

Her jaw dropped as she tried to imagine that much gold. Then she wondered how Rory could have so much. "Then I'm worth more to him than that," she repeated and wondered whether that could be true.

"Curse the bloody fools. No one, save the king himself, is worth that much. Had Aeon-Rah sold ye, you'd be owing that to One Eye. And the bastard is not fool enough to believe you'd ever be able to repay it. Now he wants something from ye, something worth more than a hundred gold."

"Why do you care what he wants from me? Why are you really here, Dog?"

"'Cause I know you're the Rogue," he said, sounding exasperated.

Her insides jolted. She'd been careful. He could not suspect it. But there was no doubt in Blood Dog's face. He knew. Which meant others might soon follow the crumbs that led to her.

She gave a forced laugh. "Might be you know wrong. Thought you said it was Northwind when last we spoke."

"Ever you blabber and squeak lies. I never said it was 'im. And don't go giving me that murderous glint in your icy eyes, mousy. I know how to gut both mages and men, and little half-breed mice like ye. Your secret is safe with me, anyhow. If it weren't, you'd be in Tridamor's dungeon already. There's a fair price on your head which would tempt the gods themselves to deliver you to him."

She looked closer at him. He was not just a mindless thug, as she often thought him to be. Wisdom lurked deep in his dark eyes, masked by belligerence, by his contempt for the rest of the world, and vulgar indifference to death.

"Who are you, Dog?"

He smiled, showing missing teeth behind his cheek. "I'm who you see, mousy. And don't go twisting what I say. I'd care less than a small fart if they found you washed up in the river tomorrow. I'm only here to warn you that One Eye suspects what I already know."

That Rory might suspect she was the Rogue was not a surprise. He had seen her magic in the old city; had been there when Pockets wanted it for his own.

"Things haven't been going too well for him since the parade attack," Blood Dog continued. "The archmage's guards are hunting his men, torturing some to find out where One Eye's hiding out. Two dogs are fighting over one bone, and that bone is Daetown. And now a third dog's about to join the fray."

She frowned. "Who's the third dog?"

"Lord Snowstorm of Daetown, that's who. But he's my problem to deal with. He wants One Eye dead so that he can reclaim the streets and restore order."

"If you're now one of Rory's men, you shouldn't even be talking to me without him knowing. What game are you playing?"

He leant in, and she smelt decay on his breath. "Listen, mousy. I am nobody's man. Just 'cause it serves me right now to snuggle with the One-Eyed fox, doesn't mean I'll be with him tomorrow. I know what you're trying to do; playing a little assassin in the night, thinking it matters that you kill a few rats. Been there myself, and was better at it than you, 'cause I know the right dog to kill to make it matter."

His confession about being an assassin did not wholly surprise her. Blood Dog was ruthless enough for that. But then, so was One-Eyed Rory. With a drop of warning in the right ear or a gory death, he would make way for Pockets to take control of a rival gang, a street, or a magistrate. But where Rory was poised and dignified when he needed to be, Blood Dog was a greasy, vulgar ruffian with the finesse of a bull on heat. She could not see how he'd be doing anything that mattered to anyone.

"And who do you think I should be killing?"

"To start with, One Eye," he replied. "I'll only give ye this advice once. Take it or not as you wish."

"Why don't you kill him yourself, Dog?"

"'Cause he's not the weed I'm looking to pluck. Nor is he a threat to me."

Her fascination grew. "Who are you hunting? And who's paying you?"

"Who's paying *you*?" he countered slyly. "Look, my hunt is my own. I don't interfere in your business, so you keep out of mine. I'm only here trying to help ye, and blast it if I know why. Got an itch around ye, and not the one I usually get for pretty lasses either. Something's bothering me about ye. That aside, we are a rare breed, mousy, getting rarer too. Any fool can be a mindless killer, but our kind hunts for different reasons. You just need to understand your reason. Anger, vengeance, or pity are not the right reasons. For every move you make, some bastard will counter it. Which is why you need to pick the right dog to gut. And you've been picking off the pups when you should be cutting the head of the alpha."

"You mean the archmage," she said carefully. "I tried … he is protected somehow."

"There you go, blabbering again. Keep your hunts to yourself, mousy, else me or another might find them inconvenient to ours and make *you* our next hunt. Now heed my warning or not, I've done my part by the Fates." He stuck his hands in his pockets and strode off.

Elika watched him, before returning to the courtyard to finish hanging her laundry.

Everyone was eying her suspiciously.

"Who was that?" asked Liffy.

"Just a rough who got lost. I merely showed him where to go."

Nothing more was said on the matter.

Three days later, the crier walked past, shouting about Lord Snowstorm's assassination in the night. His lady and young son had fled Terren for their country estate. Daetown was once again without a lord overseer. A chill ran over Elika's skin as she thought of Blood Dog and his words.

~

Another seventh day when Elika could venture outside, had come and gone, and she was no closer to finding Penny. Rory had given her until summer to find his son, yet a lifetime would not be enough in this city. So she strolled aimlessly through yet another market, asking questions of anyone willing to answer them, seeking familiar faces from the old life who might recognize the notorious Bad Penny.

With every flash of red hair, her heart skipped and turned in her chest. Whenever she spied boys milling on the streets, she imagined that saw Tiny Timmy and Chelik. At every stall of the Winged Folk, she asked about Rosy Rose. Surely, they must have seen a girl with a penchant for blue feathers, perhaps accompanied by a woman with copper hair.

Always, they shook their heads in reply.

Penny and the kids may not even be in the city, thought Elika as she stopped in a mapmaker's shop. Around Terren, there were many outlying farming and coastal villages, and many towns through the land, besides. The mountains to the north were pitted with mines, and when the day was clear, you could see a city of tents at its base, with campfire smoke rising from it. There was a trading town up there, also, where Penny might have found herself living. Else, perhaps, they travelled to Wavestar, the farthest place in Seramight, where men still lived without magic.

Blood Dog's warning came back to her. Aye, Rory expected her to fail, and when she did, she'd owe him a debt only he could name and likely one she'd never be able to repay, like those hundred gold pieces. Nor could she abandon the search. His threats aside, she had to warn Penny that he was looking for them. Sooner or later he'd find them himself.

Elika raked her brain. Pebble might be the only one who could help her. The two-hundred-year-old tane knew every man and woman in the city, if Bobquick was to be believed. And there was no one in Terren who'd not heard of the famed Minstrel Pebble. Even if Pebble didn't know where Penny was, he'd know the right people to ask. But he, too, had gone and vanished.

She had tried to find him in his usual haunts, stopping in every tavern he sang. There was no sign of him in any of them. No one had seen him in *Eagle's Feather* either, since the night of the attack.

"Damned if I know where he is," said Tipps as he wiped dry the clean mugs. "Hasn't even come back for his lute." He pulled it from under the bar to show her.

He will kill me.

"Where does he sleep?" she asked.

"Not a question we ask our patrons." He threw the towel over his shoulder. "Now and then, he pays for a room upstairs. Might be he's back in the royal courts. The bored noble ladies are particularly fond of his giant … ahem … songs. A time or two he'd boasted of a mistress who offered him her bed."

Elika regarded the lute in the innkeeper's hand. "Wouldn't he have his lute with him if he was singing for them?"

The innkeeper thrust it under the counter with a shrug.

Elika left the *Eagle's Feather* with a deepening certainty that some evil had befallen the tane minstrel, and Shoran was to blame.

Dusk had fallen, and she found herself ambling along the street that ran alongside the looming outer city wall. She strode past bastions and grimy prisons beneath them, with bars across windows low at her feet. Outside one such gaol, men in chains were being herded into a prison wagon. The memory of Tom walking alongside other murdered men with those awful, inane grins still haunted her nights. The same fate awaited these prisoners. From the numb acceptance in the faces, she suspected they knew it, too.

With an inward sigh, she approached one of the guards. "Where are you taking them?" She feigned a curious expression.

"Why are ye asking?" he countered. "I'd say 'tis none of your concern, slave. Go back to your master."

"I'm only asking, seeing as my mistress is always complaining we've not enough workers for our workshop. So I thought might be you could spare a few, seeing as you have so many."

"These men are prisoners," he explained slowly, as if she was simple. "And prisoners go to the temple. If you want one of them, then you need to ask the archmage. Now be on your way."

There were no women among them. Elika did not know why all the mages were men. Nor did anyone else she'd asked. Save that women were taken to the mills and mines. Else the pretty ones might end up in a whorehouse.

With a shrug, Elika left him, strolling along without looking back, before turning into an alley and peering around the corner. The guards' attention was once again taken with filling the cages with wretched souls doomed to die. She pushed out her magic. Slick, black tendrils grew out of the ground like weeds. They wrapped and snaked around the wheels and bars of the wagons, as prisoners cried out in fright. The guards shouted and drew their weapons, and slashed at her magic, but she barely felt their strikes. Unlike when Shoran's sword had cut her.

The tendrils pulled the cage apart, and it crashed into a heap where it stood. The prisoners scampered in all directions. More guards poured out from the bastion to join the battle. Elika quickly withdrew her magic, leaving the guards spinning about, their swords drawn, but with no enemy to slay.

A warm spring breeze stirred her hair. She thought of Pebble and his uncertain fate. Might be it was time she hunted the shadow that stalked her. If he was a mage, she need only catch him unawares. Once in her power, she would ask him about Pebble, for she was growing more and more certain Shoran was the one who had him.

~

It was a moonless night and perfect for a hunt. And tonight, she too was being hunted.

She had unraveled a mage to draw Syn'Moreg's servant out. A force of merciless rage was searching for her now. She had found a perfect place to lure him, where the shadows were deep and easy to hide in. She need only unravel another majren, and he would be there.

And she would be waiting.

From the roof, she watched the window across the street, where the majren were readying for bed. There were three of them behind drawn curtains, fearful of the night ahead and the monster hunting them from the shadows. They were newly released into this world, and like frightened pups, they kept close together.

In the distance, a bell chimed the last hour of the day.

Without moving from where she crouched, she reached out and grasped the invading strands of life and ripped them from the stolen bodies. The deed drew her own hunter to her.

The screeching wind came out of nowhere, cold and cutting, whipping her with its judgement. An instant later, his vast power marched towards her, preceded by his wish to destroy. His rage sent ripples through the essence of the world, and a shudder went through her so potent her legs froze in awed terror. Surely this creature was just another Laifae mageguard, bound to his master's power. If so, she would unravel him ... once she learned what had befallen Pebble.

Across the street, the mages' house was now nothing more than stone and charred beams of wood. Suddenly, the stones rose on the wind and flew at her.

Quickly, she gathered her wits and fled along the roof ridge, glancing behind to see that he followed. He prowled after her, calm and certain, whilst a shield of stones circled around him. He hurled one of the stones towards her.

Before it reached her, she slid down a pipe into a secluded garden, pulled out two knives and blended into the shadow of an alcove of the house. A cloaked figure glided gracefully from the roof, riding the wind he had summoned, and landed softly on his feet. Stones landed behind him and formed a wall to block her escape through the garden gate.

Unimpressed, she watched from the dark. Ever do these beings of power brazenly flaunt and brandish their might. Still, there was no denying his was more potent than any she had encountered in this world so far. It burned hot against her senses and charged the air between them.

Slowly, he panned around, his face hidden beneath a hood. She needed only a moment to unravel him, but a chilling sense of danger held her from moving, from sending out even a whisper of magic.

He turned … halted … and slowly turned back to face where she was hiding.

She pressed herself deeper into the shadow. *You have the power to unravel him*, she told herself as she took a steadying breath.

Crunch. A step upon the gravel.

She gripped her knives harder, trying to judge the distance between herself and him.

Crunch. Closer still. Slow, deliberate, as if he was taking pleasure in his dark hunt of a prey to conquer, then to vanquish.

Crunch. He was almost upon her.

Pebble. She had to find him. She took a breath and struck.

Black tentacles sprang out of the ground behind him, wrapped around his legs and violently yanked him back. She stepped out to see him face down on the ground. He raised his hooded head and met her gaze. She kicked him in the face, jumped on his back, struck one knife into his side, and quickly noted that he stiffened with pain. Before he could react, she pressed the other blade to his throat.

"'Tis but a quick swipe to cut your throat," she said quietly over him. "Where is Pebble, beast? What have you done with him?"

His body began to shake underneath her, and she realized he was laughing.

She twisted the knife in his side. He stiffened, laughed even harder, a dark rumble of mirth, but there was a pained note to it. "I hate cocky bastards," she mumbled and cut his throat. He grew still. She moved off him, pulling the knife out of his side. "'Tis your stupid bones I'll be sending to Syn'Moreg. See how he likes that …"

He struck fast, kicking out and knocking her back to the ground, then spun and in one motion cut off the tentacle holding him in place.

She groaned. The pain was akin to a severed limb. With effort, she rolled to her knees and looked up. He was looming above her, as menacing as ever, as if she'd never slit his throat. Worse still, under his hood, his eyes glowed hotter with his fury and outrage.

Might be she did not cut his throat deep enough. She had never done it before, though Mite had taught her how to do it right.

The shadow took a step towards her and she imagined water falling on his head. And it did … save that it did not wet him, nor did he seem to notice as he advanced on her. She scrambled to her feet, backed away, and sent out more of her tendrils to wind around him, whilst she focused on catching his essence …

The ground shook and imprisoning stone bars rose around her. Before they sealed her in, she called upon her magic to tear them apart, and those slick, black strands broke through the stone as through glass. The effort drained her strength, and her legs shook weakly beneath her.

A thread of light wound around her neck. But the shadow's attention was not on her. Black tendrils were darting at him from all sides, trying to grab him. He sent a flash of light after light, imprisoning those strands. It grew harder for her to move, to breathe. The light was binding her, imprisoning her and her magic. With a pang of dread, she realized he was not seeking to kill her, but to subdue her, catch her … and deliver her to Syn'Moreg.

Ignoring her pain, she reached again for his essence and grasped the threads of his lifeforce. To call them threads was to call stone "silk". They were hot, violent and strong, so very strong.

He must have sensed her hold on him, for his head whipped about to face her.

With all her remaining strength, she pulled the threads, threatening to rip his life out of the body.

He grunted, tensed and fury flashed in his glowing yellow eyes, fury and incredulity that she would try to do this to him. The thread around her throat tightened and something hot and hard crushed her chest. Her mistake rushed in on her. For in binding him, she exposed her own essence to his attack.

He had a hold of her soul, and his eyes blazed as he watched her come to realize it. And he watched still as her hold on him grew slippery. He would end her just like she had ended the mages. Slowly, ever so slowly, he pulled, and she gasped as her soul began to drain from her body. A growing sense of detachment muted her terror and pain …

Abruptly, he released her, and she fell to her knees, panting for air.

Wordlessly, he watched her, and she understood his warning; he, too, could unravel her.

He took a step forward and reached down towards her with a gloved hand.

With the last of her strength, she wound her magic around his neck and pulled him away from her. He spun to cut through the thread with his sword, sending another blinding flash of pain through her, and this time she did cry out. But in the moment of his distraction, she willed a swirling fog into existence. It blinded him long enough for her to dash for the garden wall, and using a rope she had set up earlier, she leaped over it and fled.

CHAPTER ELEVEN

Shadow's Whisper

"Alafraysia has no laws such as those men live by. It is the realm of order and chaos combined in perfect harmony. The tsaren rule through might alone. We bow to them, and they leave us in peace. We plead with them, and they grant us our wishes. We offend them, and they punish us. Only three laws are ever imposed upon us. Drink not too deeply of the well, damage not the Silvery Web and disturb not the spider who guards it."

The History of Alafraysia and Seramight,
By Mageguard Bluelight

Dark chanting came from around the corner. Elika pressed herself against the wall as the cloaked figures passed. Tonight, Syn'Moreg's dark worshipers were chanting in the common tongue, a warning for men to absorb into their dreams.

Lord of Darkness and Abyss
Mercy fair and light we seek
Winds eternal rage in anger
Keeping watch over your slumber
Wake not the god of endless night
Where shadow flies unhindered might

The smoke from their lamps left a lingering haze in the streets. After their voices were distant, Elika darted onto the street and strode briskly away, glancing into every shadow as she went.

No one was close, yet her sense of a threat grew stronger. Shoran was stalking her still, tracking her at a distance, as if his nose was honed on her sent. The unnatural wind intensified, and she broke into a run.

She turned onto Yarn Row, stopped in the shelter of a doorway and listened. Silence. Stillness. Yet the hunter drew closer, as if the end for his prey was nigh.

Elika shook herself. She was being foolish. He had frightened her, and the night had engorged those fears. With a last look around, she climbed to the roof.

The window to her room gave way under a gentle probing. Once she jumped inside, it slammed shut behind her as the winds screeched outside.

She locked the window, changed into a nightgown and crawled into bed. The pain throbbing in her body from her latest battle was overshadowed only by her fierce hunger. She ignored both and lay very still, watching the darkness beyond her window, expecting to see those haunting yellow eyes pierce it at any moment.

He did not chase but stalk, as if savoring the hunt. An instinctive wave of terror rode on that thought. Only her certainty that he could not know where she was, calmed her frayed nerves. Death of the majren drew him, not she, else he'd be here by now.

Rap-tap-tap.

Elika bolted upright in her bed.

Another sharp rap came on the window. Peering at her through it was the white-tipped crow. It made a rattling sound, tipped its head, and with a loud screech, flew off.

'Tis nothing but a foolish bird, she told herself without conviction.

The winds outside grew shriller.

She lay there for a long time, afraid to close her eyes, listening, waiting for the night to pass and the light to chase away her terrors. She thought of Pebble and his fate, certain now that he must be dead.

Eventually, the darkness seeped into her mind, and she sought refuge in the dreamless slumber. But even there, she found no rest. In the dark, the shadow hunted, drawing closer, his whisper on the screeching wind. Then the hunter was upon her, crushing her chest until she could not breathe.

She started awake and stared into the glowing yellow eyes. She almost screamed, but the weight of his hand upon her chest and her terror left her breathless. A warm blade was pressed to her throat. It was not metal or stone, but akin to a talon or claw.

"*Amena, fia neda Arala Dia'Neka,*" he whispered.

The whisper was the vortex of a silent storm. There was power in it that rolled over her and through her, and terrorized her with its command. She was but a leaf upon the storm of his strength. Even the hand pinning her to the bed felt as immovable as a mountain.

"I do not speak your tongue," she whispered back, refusing to be cowed, though her voice came out faint as a child's breath.

"You are not Arala," he repeated slowly in the tongue of common men, tinged with a soft, exotic accent.

"I know that," she said and took note of her limbs. Her arms were not imprisoned. He held her down with the heavy press of his hand and the weight of his leg over hers.

"What wind fashioned you? Speak," he commanded, speaking deliberately, as if every word was to be noted and heeded. And the demand was a force that drew the truth from her.

"I … I do not understand," she said on a breath.

"What god birthed you?"

"I'm … human."

"Human?" There was dark amusement in his voice. "You lie to *me*?" The blade pressed harder against her throat. "Why do you attack the web?"

Elika's breathing grew more strained. The faint glow of his yellow eyes filled her vision. There was something potent about the warmth of his nearness, something intoxicating about his scent. Her mind grew muddled.

"I weave webs … for Mistress Oblana. From a yarn dipped in magic," she replied nonsensically.

He lowered his head and whispered in her ear. "Toy not with my patience. What are you? Where did you come from, cub?" This close, she heard his erratic breathing, as if she, too, unsettled him.

There was power in his question that made a lie impossible to speak. Even the thought of lying made her throat close up painfully, and her tongue would not twist against his demand for truth.

She turned her head towards his cheek, brushing his warmth. "Dae-Terren," she whispered.

She could sense his rising frustration in the tension of his body, in the twitch of his arm that held her down. He turned his head to look at her, his face so close his breath caressed her lips and sent an odd tingling sensation from her lips to the pit of her stomach.

For a long, suffocating moment, he grew very still, as if considering her, before speaking again. *"Morta neda veria la fia."*

The rumble of his voice rolled through her like a gentle quake, shaking and reordering everything inside her. Then his lips were on her neck. She arched her back in surprise, reached for the knife she kept under her pillow and lunged at him.

He caught her hand and lifted his face to hover above hers. She wanted to see his features deep in the hood, for she could not guess his thoughts.

"I do not know your magic," he said in a quiet rumble that reverberated through her soul.

She strained the knife towards him, but her legs shifted ever so slightly, parting as if welcoming him closer. He turned his head, noticing her inadvertent gesture. She heated with shame and something else far more primal. Then she reached for the magic inside her and realized that the force of his hand was not only holding her down. The ball of power inside her was wrapped in a cage of its own.

"One day you will, I swear it," she snapped.

In reply, his knife pressed harder into her skin. "Will I, kitten?"

"Kitten? Your master must be a coward to send you to kill a *kitten*. Is this who you are, mighty Shoran, a man who slaughters defenseless girls in their beds?" She made herself smile at him. "Or might be instead of killing me, you'll deliver Syn'Moreg a message from me."

His eyes brightened and dimmed again. "Tell me the message, and it shall reach his ears." Dark amusement dripped from his voice.

She matched it with the most wicked grin she could muster.

> *"To Gods I sing*
> *To Gods I crow*
> *A child's prayer on my brow*
> *I seek to wound*
> *I seek to strike*
> *A child's wrath upon your might*
> *Destruction, death*
> *And vengeance right*
> *Beware the anger of my spite."*

His face shifted and there was fire and challenge in his eyes as he replied:

> *"The gods of night*
> *They rest a while,*
> *But in the web*
> *The spider sits.*
> *Beware, small child*
> *For in the dark you'll find*
> *His poisonous venom*
> *Upon eternal winds."*

Suddenly he was no longer on top of her and she could breathe again. But his body left a lingering warm imprint on hers. She sat up and felt oddly ... cold. The room was empty. The window was locked from the inside. The door was closed.

She jumped out of bed, still clutching the knife in her hand.

Slowly, she turned, seeking the secret way he had entered and left her tiny room. Drawn by some alien sense of things that could not be seen, she touched the wall, where she last caught a flash of his form. For a moment, she thought the wall gave way beneath her hand. A tingle ran up her arm. She snatched back her hand, lit the candle, and returned to the wall to touch it. Solid.

She spun about, thinking she'd never be able to sleep again, seeing as there was no place Shoran couldn't reach her. And now, she'd gone and threatened Syn'Moreg.

She sat on the bed. "What have we gotten ourselves into now?" she said to the magic inside her. "'Tis your fault, you know."

She rubbed the place on her neck where the sensation of his lips still lingered, a hot brand he had left behind, both intoxicating and infuriating. His scent still lingered in the air, and it was only now that she realized it did not have overtones of death. It was clean musk, with an inexplicable scent that did not belong to a human. It put her in mind of summer storms and lightning.

The wind screeched outside, its sound etched upon her soul.

She blew out the candle and pushed to open the window … the wind slammed it closed. She pushed harder, but the wind howled its denial and the window remained firmly shut. Across the dark street, Shoran's hooded shape watched her from the rooftops.

CHAPTER TWELVE

Daetown

"Only humans ever came close to destroying the Great Web. Is it any wonder our kind hates the destructive stupidity of mankind? Never again must we allow their nature to roam free, for our sake, for theirs and that of the gods."

The History of Alafraysia and Seramight,
By Mageguard Bluelight

It was close to dawn. Outside, the wind screeched and screeched. The stifling attic room had become her cage. For days, she had not ventured out at night. For days, the howling winds intensified and pinned her window shut whenever she tried to leave. She had snuck through the sleeping house late one night, only to find the doors downstairs just as firmly guarded by the sentinel winds.

And each night, she waited for Shoran to come through that wall and pass Syn'Moreg's judgement; to smother her in her sleep; to make demands and free her … anything but his abhorrent, mocking silence.

Worse still, she had taken it into her head to lie awake in the dark, reliving every moment of their encounters, every battle they had fought, which inevitably led her to relive his lips on her throat. It was a brand that never fully healed. She raked her hair with her fingers, biting back impotent outrage, whilst the wind howled and howled …

And stopped.

At dawn, it always vanished, like all terrors of the night. She pushed lightly on the window and it popped open with a small squeak. She was outside in an instant. The air was fresh. Beyond the city, the dark sea was enticing, and the distant mountains held secrets she wished to explore. She could flee her prison, hide from him, save that Syn'Moreg's gaze was upon her. He haunted her dreams, and there was no running from them. She had to find a way to defeat Shoran and send Syn'Moreg his bones.

Tomorrow was the seventh day when she was free to forgo her work and chores and venture out in daylight. For now, simply proving to herself that her freedom had not been wholly stolen was enough. She climbed back inside and raced to the kitchen, where she snatched a plate of boiled ham and warm bread from the cook before hurrying to the workshop.

Since Meena's death, nothing short of early starts and late finishes kept the mistress from using her cane on them. Shortly, Liffy also appeared, looking sleepy. She had been given Meena's chores alongside her own, which included being at the mistress' beck and call when she could not sleep with one of her headaches. Liffy often spent half the night fetching tea and wet towels for the mistress' head. Elika was spared most of those tasks. She was to do nothing save weave more of those precious webs for the rich.

Liffy threw open the window before sitting at her loom. Outside, the day was balmy. Spring was morphing into summer, and Elika was running out of time. Soon, One-Eyed Rory would demand his son.

The door below opened, and a voice reached them that always filled her with disgust. That horrid sound of two men speaking from one mouth.

"Why have you been pestering us with these bothersome requests for girls?" asked Aeon-Rah.

"Meena's gone," the mistress replied. "I need another girl."

"Another runaway? You must take better care of them."

"She did not run away but was murdered by the magic-haters at the spring parade."

"Be that as it may, we have no more girls for you. There are too many runaways around the city. The one-eyed thug, who calls himself a lord, is buying or stealing their freedom. The bridge is gone and the Daes are no longer arriving. Everyone on Yarn Row wants more workers, but where are we to find them?"

"Then catch the ones who are already here. You must have many prisoners —"

"The archmage demands all prisoners are taken to the temple. Whilst the mines, the workshops, the merchants, and every trader cry out for more slaves, more servants, more apprentices. And no one wants to pay freemen the coin they demand for their work. Make do with what you have, Oblana. Or pay a freewoman to work for you. And try not to lose any more girls."

A moment later, the door below opened and closed, and silence fell over the house.

Steps sounded on the stairs. Liffy nervously adjusted her crown of flowers as she glanced towards the door, where the mistress stood with the cane in her hand. "Until we find another girl to replace Meena, you will work on your seventh day, too, Lika."

Elika's hands stilled. It was the last thing she could afford to lose. She might as well go straight to Rory and hand him the knife to cut her throat with. "'Tis not our agreement," she said coolly. "Magic hates liars, everyone knows this, and I promised to pray to it at the temple every seventh day," she lied smoothly. "If I don't go to the temple to pray, magic will abandon me."

The hand with the cane twitched. The mistress feared nothing more, and doubt rode on the wings of that fear.

Elika saw it in her face and pressed on. "Mage Aeon-Rah granted my magic the wishes to keep it happy. So it might be best to ask him first. Else he'll only blame me for losing its favor. See?"

The mistress' face darkened. Elika knew the mistress was not so foolish as to do that. She reached the same decision, it seemed. "Then you will also work all night before your seventh day." With that, the mistress spun on her heel and marched out.

There was no avoiding it. Elika worked late into the night, snatching only a few morsels of sleep where she sat at the loom. She startled awake at dawn when a cart rolled past outside the window. The early hues of light had already dispelled the imprisoning winds.

She raced upstairs on quiet feet, fearing to wake the mistress. There, she took out her box from behind the shrine and counted forty-three coppers and twenty pennies. Almost half a sherring, she thought, and was unable to suppress that ridiculous pang of pride. She had earnt every one of those coppers. It was the only thing she had ever possessed that was truly hers. There might not be enough to buy her freedom, but there was plenty to get by for a time, if the need ever arose.

Elika pocketed twenty pennies and returned the box to its hiding place. Today, she decided to leave the house through the window, lest the mistress accosted her on the way out.

It was a grey day, and the drizzle soaked into her clothes before she found her way down to the streets. This early, the city had barely begun to wake. A few servants scurried about their masters' early morning business, and a few farmers carted their vegetables to the market. She gave one of them a penny to allow her to ride on the back of his wagon, with his sacks of parsnips and turnips. When she saw a woman with a basket of rhubarb pies, she became aware of her gnawing hunger. So she gave the farmer another penny for one of his turnips, which she ate raw as they rode. That only angered her feral hunger, and her stomach growled for more.

Warm, fresh-baked smells came from the bakers, and she hopped off outside Sweet Shay's Bakery. His famed jam rolls were the best between Yarn Row and Daetown, and Shay boasted he needed no magic to help bake them either.

"The mistress let you out again, Lika Lass," he greeted her cheerfully when she entered his shop. "Been a while since I've seen you."

"Been busy, that's all," she replied as she eyed his baskets of rolls and pies.

"Want your favorite, then?" Shay was a Dae who had crossed some years ago and bought his freedom and his bakery with his lucky silver piece. His father gave it to him as a lucky charm to protect him against the bridge's magic.

"Aye, make it three strawberry rolls."

"The mistress not feeding ye?" he asked. "You look skinnier than you did the last time I saw ye."

The mistress was feeding her plenty enough for two men. It just never seemed enough for her greedy magic. And her last fight with Shoran had drained her even more.

"You know how it is. And don't bother offering to buy my freedom again. Aeon-Rah won't sell."

He handed her three rolls and took six pennies for them. "Couldn't buy your freedom now, even if I wanted. Didn't you hear? The archmage raised the price to one hundred sherrings."

Elika lowered her roll before she could take a bite. "A hundred sherrings …" she echoed dumbly, knowing she'd not earn that in a lifetime. "That's a whole silver piece."

"And what else is to be done? With the Rogue Mage killing the mages, One Eye freeing the indentured and the archmage carting away every petty crook, there's a shortage of collared workers. Daetown is swelling with runaways, and One Eye is trying to protect them from the mages. Soon, we'll be needing to bring slaves from the southlands. The city needs the collar-bound or the slaves."

"We didn't need them in Dae-Terren," she said, and bit into her roll.

He scratched the back of his neck. "That was there. But here, as soon as you give men freedom, they demand more for their labors. Everyone wants to be a master. And now there's more masters than servants. What we need is more desperation on the streets, and more hungry mouths to feed."

Elika finished her roll and pocketed the other. "Where's Jina?" she asked. "Don't tell me she ran off too?"

Shay's face fell. "Aye, she did. Said there's work in Daetown for any Dae who wants it. I told her she owed me money for her freedom. But she said only slaves and whores are bought, and she was neither. Called me a cursed magic-lover and stormed off. Haven't seen her since. I'm not a magic-lover, just have nothing against it, you know. It can be useful, at times. But now, half my customers think I'm a magic-lover. The other half call me a Dae magic-hater. But the Rogue is getting Alterrians all riled and angry, and One Eye is putting fighting talk into Dae mouths. And now Northwind's long-lost heir is crawling out of whatever dusty larder he's been hiding in to claim his right to Terren."

"They found Northwind?" she asked with a jolt of worry for Mite.

"Aye, and it's not good for the rest of us. Too many cats circling Terren's seat of power, and soon they'll be fighting over that juicy rat."

"Where's Northwind now then?" Elika asked, trying to sound conversational, worried again for Mite. She did not think Reval would be too pleased to learn he'd failed to end Northwind House six hundred years ago.

"They say he's under Duke Warwind's protection. That's all I know. Half the court thinks he's an imposter. The other half are too afraid to speak in his favor. Though no one can deny he has the magic of the Sacred Crown in him."

"He's got magic?" she asked with a frown. Surely, they'd have seen it living with him in the Hide.

Shay shrugged. "They say he has Northwind's power over ice and can't be burned by fire. But then a sword is as good a way to kill a man. I dare say the youth will be dead soon enough. Prince Southfire won't be too pleased to have a challenger. And the archmage will never surrender Terren to the rightful king."

"King?" she echoed dumbly. "Heard it was a crime to even whisper of it." For six hundred years no one was permitted to utter "king" in this half of the world, for it excited the tsaren into any manner of daft destruction.

Shay leant in secretively. "Keep your ears open, lass. 'Tis not *Prince* Northwind they whisper of. Got their imagination going, this youth."

A Dae servant came in with an order from her master's cook and abruptly took Shay's attention. Elika waved to him and left the shop.

More and more folk emerged from their homes until the city was a buzzing hive of trade. As Elika strode towards her first errand of the day, she listened to what was being said on the street and spoke with the folk she knew. And aye, she heard those forbidden whispers of a king in their midst, and her mind churned.

The courtyard of Syn'Moreg's temple was, as ever, quiet in the light of day. The priests were likely abed after their night of roaming the streets and disturbing people's sleep. Overhead, a crow cawed.

Elika met its beady eye. "Thought you could talk," she said to it.

The crow cackled as if laughing.

Elika descended the stairs into a firelit hall and approached the giant stone spider, her boots loud on the stone floor.

Shortly, the priest emerged to greet her. "Aleyala, you honor our humble temple with a visit."

"This temple of yours is far from humble," she replied wryly without taking her eyes off the spider.

"It is humble compared to your glory," he said sagely.

She tore her gaze from the statue to see whether he mocked her, but there was an absurd sincerity in his face.

She chuckled. "If you say so, priest. Did your crow tell you I was here?" She looked up to see it flying overhead.

"The crow is not mine, Aleyala, but yours," the priest replied. "It is you it follows."

"Then 'tis indeed a foolish bird."

The crow cawed in protest.

Elika ignored it. "Do you know the language to which these words belong: *Morta neda veria la fia?*"

"It is the lesser language of the gods. Otherwise known as the common tongue of their realm El'Sandria."

"What do the words mean?" she asked with growing apprehension.

"*Blood does not lie for you,*" he replied gravely.

"Is it a curse?" The Sachi lore spoke of gods cursing men in all manner of creative cruelties.

"It is not a curse, but the test of truth. There is power in sacred words, for each word is bound to the magic of the spirit."

She recalled Shoran's lips on her neck and it tingled afresh with the memory. He was tasting … her magic?

"There is a way to travel between the realms," she said. "The Laifae came to our realm from their own. The gods, too, are said to cross into ours when it suits them."

"When the realms brush past each other the veil parts, and those who know how to find the path can traverse between worlds."

"*How* do I cross from one to the other?" she asked.

"I am not a traveler, nor have I the power to touch the web that binds the three realms. I only know that you must sense the path to follow it. Where is it you seek to journey?"

"I need to find Shoran," she replied.

The priest's eyes widened. "*Lord* Shoran? You have … spoken with him?" He took a step forward, and she took one back. "If you have spoken with him, then you have Syn'Moreg's ear. You must speak to him on our behalf …"

"I have to find him first, priest. Shoran vanished into a wall. How do I follow him?"

The priest studied her far too shrewdly before walking over to a circle of stones beneath the spider. "Come, look into this well."

Uncertainly, she approached and looked into the pit, as endless as the night. Her heart juddered and her feet took an abrupt step back.

The priest stood right at its edge, so close, she felt sick just from imagining him falling into it.

He gazed into that bottomless abyss as he spoke. "Long ago, as Terren burned with Reval's fire, Syn'Moreg emerged from this well, fury burning in his eyes. The priests fell to their knees and offered to give their lives to cool the demigod's rage, for they foresaw a great calamity to come. He paid them no heed, asked for no lives, and offered no mercy. Not long after, he sundered the world and returned to the dark Abyss. We have guarded this path ever since, but he never emerged again. Step closer and put your hand over it."

She eyed him wearily and stepped forward, keeping the well between herself and the priest. She put her hand over the well and felt the wind pull her inwards. The sensation was akin to what she felt on the wall of her room after Shoran had vanished.

"Only a few ever feel the path. Those who have a taint of gods' blood in their veins," said the priest.

"Like the heirs of the Sacred Crowns."

"And their long-abandoned bastards, or the children of those bastards. Those with enough blood of the gods may traverse the veil to other realms. The Great Web links them and it will take you where you need to go. Imagine the path and it will appear. But beware, when you travel, others too can follow. Once disturbed, the Web is slow to still, and the spider will always find you through those quivering threads."

Elika left the Sachi temple, toying with the spider in her pocket, thinking upon what the priest had told her. If she could sense the path, might be she too could traverse to the place where Syn'Moreg's servant was hiding.

She pushed that thought aside. It was time she went looking for Penny ...

An acrid stench of smoke reached her, and she knew instantly what she smelt in it. Overhead, there was a pink hue in the grey clouds. Her feet moved of their own accord, following the wind which carried the warning of death.

As she drew closer to Daetown, she saw blood on the cobbles, broken windows and buildings turned to smoldering ruins. There were wounded, too, and folk hiding in their homes. When she reached the city wall that marked the border of Daetown, she found the roads barricaded with overturned carts and piles of stone rubble.

New gates had been erected and were guarded by toughs with tattoos of a cross over one eye. City guards, bearing the emblem of the Northern Bastion, stood side by side with them, questioning each person seeking entry into Daetown. A banner was flying from the gate, with an emblem she recognized from the gilded gates of the palace in Dae Terren. Northwind's emblem of a crown made of ice.

Archers guarded the district wall. It was more of a lookout and an overpass than a defensive structure, for many archways and roads wove in and out beneath it. Though barricades were now erected across the ones she could see. Farther along, stonemasons were sealing most of those archways and blocking roads into Daetown.

A thug with an axe on his belt blocked her way at a checkpoint. "No one's allowed entry into Daetown without reason."

The metal head of his axe was studded with thick blood-salt crystals, and the tip was coated with it. The weapons of other guards were similarly fashioned.

"Last I heard, this city didn't belong to One Eye. I go where I wish."

"Daetown belongs to us now," he growled. "Lord Snowstorm is dead, and no damned mage will take it from us again. And you'll state your business, *slave*-girl."

"Not a slave," she said. "My mistress pays me a fair coin."

"Calm yourself, Petric. Can't you see she's one of us?" said his companion and turned to her. "What's your need in Daetown?"

"Here for ale in *Eagle's Feather*, as always. Got no business save hearty food and honest talk."

"Well, there'll be plenty of talk to be had today, I can tell ye."

"What passed here?" she asked with a nod at the blood on his armor.

"Blasted mageguards, that's what. Attacked at dawn, when everyone was still abed. The bastards rode on their horses with prison wagons in tow, throwing fire and wind this way and that, dragging honest men out of homes. So, Captain Trian ordered the mages to stop doing what they were doing, for there was no proof of crimes. But the chief mageguard started shouting about a new overlord of Daetown, Mage Birdwing, and telling us to put away our weapons. Well, we did none of that —"

"Took them by surprise, we did," the axe-wielding tough cut in with a chuckle. "Had something they didn't expect. Seems these bloody magic-lovers forgot about the blood-salt."

"They didn't forget," the Dae guard replied. "They're forbidden from using it by Syn'Moreg. Anyhow, we caught Birdwing and his mages. Then we burned the bastards and hung the charred bodies on the city wall over there for others to see." He pointed to where eight charred, mutilated bodies hung by their necks or legs if there was no head left. "One Eye is our overlord now, and no magic-wielding bastard will tell us otherwise."

There was no faulting Rory's ingenuity. He could be smart when he wanted to be. And Peter Pockets had taught him much about conquering men and streets. Daetown was not a small district. She gathered he now owned a quarter of Terren, and all the workhouses and mills within it.

"Archers! Ready!" shouted a voice from the wall.

The guards around her tensed, their hands dropped to the hilt of their swords. The archers pointed red-tipped arrows at Reval's mageguards floating overhead on small clouds. They paid the archers no mind and were content to ignore the dead mages hanging off the wall. Then they were gone.

The bows slowly lowered.

The guard shook his head. "Don't know what to make of them. They flew right by when we were burning their kind, singing like bloody minstrels. Didn't once look our way," he said and returned his attention to her. "Alright, off with you then. Don't go causing trouble."

"No trouble," Elika agreed and left the guards at the gate as she proceeded into Daetown. Everywhere she looked, there were signs of fierce battles. Blood pooled on roads and stained the walls and doors of honest folk's homes. Mages' houses had been burned down, and the fire had spread to neighboring buildings, which were smoldering still, and debris was scattered around as if thrown about by a storm. Many of the folk bore wounds and bruises, and everyone was armed with red-tipped weapons, even the children.

Ahead, she saw kneeling men and women tied to poles. Their bright Alterrian clothes were a stark contrast to the grimmer shades worn by the Daes guarding them. The women wept. Men stayed silent, looking as frightened as the children among them.

"What are you going to do with them?" she asked the closest guard.

He shrugged. "Hang them like the others." He flicked his head towards the crudely erected gallows from which hung four men and a woman.

"They are humans … like us," she said, a little too fiercely.

"They are magic-lovers and traitors." He spat at the nearest man. "And if you don't want to join them, I'd be careful about what you say next."

"I don't love them any more than you, but our fight is with the mages," she pressed on stubbornly. "Not women and children. At least let *them* go."

He grabbed the scruff of her tunic and lifted her to her tiptoes so he could glare into her face. "Listen 'ere, little goose. If you want to trumpet their cause, then do it to One Eye. Our fight is with every blasted magic-lover, human or Laifae. And if you speak for them, you are one of them." He started to drag her to the pole where the others were tied, whilst the other guards snickered nearby.

She dug in her feet. "Don't think you'd want to be hurting me. Got an important job to do for One Eye, one that my life depends on, see?"

He stopped dragging her. "I don't see. What's your life to me?"

"Well, if I can't complete the job my life depends on, 'cause you stopped me, then it's fair to say, your life will depend on that job, too."

He frowned and shook her. "Speak clearly, before I —"

"If you hurt me, One Eye will hurt you," she said blandly. "Name's Eli … Eli Spider."

He released her instantly, eyeing her suspiciously. "Aye, we know of ye. But how do I know you're her?"

She reached into her pocket and pulled out a stone spider. "See?"

He frowned again, as if thinking was difficult for him. "Fine, go, and don't let me catch you talking that treasonous talk of yours again."

"As you say." She shrugged. "Means nothing to me, what such a strong man like you does with frightened women and children. Minstrel Pebble himself will likely write songs of your deeds in defense of Daetown."

He scowled, his fist flexed as he tried to work out if she was mocking him. Before he did, Elika smiled, friendly like, and walked away without a backward glance. And as she did, she pushed out her magic.

"Mages!" the guard shouted, just as she expected.

She glanced behind her to see the guards draw their red-tipped swords and race towards the rising black tendrils at the far end of the street. As soon as they left, she pulled out her knife and ran back to the prisoners and sliced through the ropes binding their hands.

"Go! Get out of Daetown and don't get caught," she urged them as they helped each other to their feet. Then she watched them flee in the opposite direction to where the guards were fighting her magic.

Elika followed suit, and when the guards were no longer in sight, she recalled her magic. Her fatigue was instant and crippling. She sank to the ground. Their blood-salt coated swords cut through her black strands, and every one of those cuts throbbed somewhere on her body. For a time, she sat there gathering her strength, then honed in on the mouth-watering scent of roast meat. She rose with effort and followed it.

Around her, Daetown was brimming with workers. One Eye had drawn every trade into Daetown: cobblers, locksmiths, blacksmiths, backers, anyone who knew how to do anything useful. Paid them fair, too, they said. Those who had no trade to boast of joined his guard. They were everywhere now, young and old, patrolling the streets or leading groups of bound Alterrian prisoners.

The first time she caught sight of men rolling barrels into a dark cellar, she thought nothing of it. The sight grew more frequent until she saw a barrel leave a trail of blood as it was hurried away underground. With a pang of dread, she thought of the mysterious wilting of the fields and the dead animals to the south. And she wanted to yell the truth at the fools heedlessly pushing those barrels along. Were she to do that, they'd likely hang her with the rest of the magic-lovers for spreading lies. So she said nothing, and looked aside, hating her weakness and their desperation.

The smell of roasting meat came from a communal fire in a courtyard off the main street. A fat pig was on a spit roast, tended to by a brawny Drasdane woman. Soldiers still covered in fresh blood from the battle that morning lined up to cut slices from it. Elika gave the woman a few coins and was allowed to join the feast.

Afterwards, she strolled to a more gentrified part of Daetown, known as Wood Lane. It was a small collection of streets, where impoverished Dae gentry lived beside leafy parks. Just the place Anten would settle with Penny and the children.

It turned out to be another long day of asking questions and getting no closer to answers she needed. Aye, there were red-haired women around here. None went by the name of Penny. Nevertheless, Elika stalked each one she was pointed to. And as dusk neared, she was no closer to finding Rory's son.

For a while, she sat under a tree in a park, watching well-to-do folk walk by. Lovers strolled arm in arm, and suited gentry rushed home, carrying scribe cases or rolled up scrolls. Soon, she, too, would be returning home, only to be once again imprisoned by Shoran's blasted winds.

Fighting him seemed useless, seeing as cutting his throat was not enough to end him. His powers and strength swallowed her own. Besides, despite spending all her pennies on food, she was not yet strong enough for another battle. Might be she'd do better to talk with him instead and simply ask him about Pebble's fate in a friendly way. Perhaps he'd agree to a truce and remove his imprisoning winds. Trouble was, she knew not how to reach him … save one way. And it always made him angry. Then again, he was already furious with her, she thought, as her gaze fell on a mage walking past, tugging on the chain of a young servant girl, whilst she stumbled and tripped behind him.

Elika followed him to Apothecary Corner where acrid smells laced the air, and shops sold all manner of foul-smelling cures and colorful tonics. The mage doddered into his shop, yanking the chain attached to his pitiful servant after him.

The hour was still early, so Elika waited and learned from the folk around here that his name was Maj-Healingbalm, and he has been around for near a hundred years. You had to be careful with his cures. More often than not, they indeed cured the said ailment as promised, but then they left you sick with some other malady instead. Else they made your hair fall out or one of your fingers turn black and drop off. Elika would sooner trust a herb witch to cure her of any ailment.

The city grew quiet.

She watched his shop until the last customer left and the majren locked the door. He then retreated to his room upstairs. From across the street, Elika saw the servant girl through a window, sleeping on the floor beside a fire. Maj-Healingbalm remained restless. He moved about in his home, making more tonics, then rearranging his decorations. Mages were collectors of strange items, whose purpose she could not guess. This majren was no different. For long moments, he admired his collection—a glass egg with a dead snake inside, bones of a rodent decorated with paint and ribbons, a polished stick with metal bands on each end. He picked up each piece and turned it in his hands, examining each as if it were a precious treasure.

Night deepened. Elika closed her eyes. There were dozens of mages on this street, and if she allowed her mind to drift, she could find the silky essence of them all. But tonight, she would only unravel one.

She reached out, gathered Maj-Healingbalm's silken strings of life, and pulled. The thud of a heavy body hitting the floor came from inside the house. The wind came instantly—wild and angry. She leant on the wall and waited, trying to be unafraid.

A shadow moved above her. On the roof across the street stood a dark shape with yellow eyes pinned on her. Elika stood where she was, waiting for him to glide down towards her. But he just stood there, looking down at her, no doubt pondering the best way to slowly choke the life out of her.

For a moment, she thought he might turn away and leave, so she reached for his threads, grasped them …

There was a hard burst of air, and she staggered back, feeling as if a rock had struck her chest. She crumbled to the ground and shook her head. Boots and a cloak appeared in her sight, and she was yanked up roughly by her arms.

She stared into a dark hood at a featureless face with glowing yellow eyes. Fury seeped from his tightly held body as he stood there so still, so silent, with his face hidden in the shadow of the hood. In his hand, he held his sword made of darkness itself.

She'd be a fool not to be afraid. She'd be a bigger fool to show it.

"Listen to me, kitten, and heed what I say, for I will only say it once. Cease your destruction." He said it slowly, in that deep voice of his that sounded as if darkness itself spoke through him, each word a firm command.

She feigned a faint, as her hand slipped to the hilt of her knife. As she had hoped, he moved on instinct to catch her. She put the blade to his throat and grinned.

"Wanted to speak with you, beast. Might be you'd do better to heed what I have to say."

He froze, looked down at the knife, and blinked. "You destroyed him and shredded the web to summon me?" His dark voice dripped with outrage.

"Got no other way to find you, now do I?"

He grew very still. She tensed. Then he threw his head back and laughed. It was a deep rumble that reverberated through her oddly, like a violent ocean of mirth. "Ah, kitten, put away your claws before I decide to cut them off."

"Not until you —" Before she could finish, he moved and within a heartbeat he was at her back, pressing her own knife to her throat. She swallowed against it. "Might be if you just listen to me, we might reach an understanding," she said feebly.

His humor had fled. His grip on her tightened. "There will be no understanding between us," he growled low and hard behind her, and the sound reverberated from his chest into her body.

"Shall we battle then until one of us is dead?"

"It shall not be me."

A black tendril of her magic wound tightly around his throat. "Might be it will," she said and swallowed against the knife at her throat. "A trade, Shoran, that will benefit us both. I'll leave your precious majren alone, and you'll remove your winds and never bother me again."

She had no intention of leaving the majren alone, but she needed to know how amenable he was to any agreement between them.

He stiffened at her back, his breath growing more ragged, more angry. "No trade can be brokered. Our paths are joined in life and will be severed in death." He spoke into her hair and lowered his head to her cheek, as if trying to make sense of her, as if breathing her in.

"'Tis clear you do not wish to kill me—"

"As yet."

"As yet," she ceded.

"Though my patience is a waning breeze." The knife pushed harder into the skin of her throat. "What do you seek from the Fates?"

"Our world back. Mages gone. *You* gone. My freedom. Take your windy prison bars from my home."

"The winds trouble you, kitten?" he mocked gently.

"No more than I'm troubling you, it seems."

He stilled. And in that stillness, his scent filled her head. His warm breath on her skin made her dizzy, confused. Her heart sped up, her breath grew oddly erratic. She felt his hand tighten on the dagger, felt the readying tension in his body. She swallowed again, her breath coming faster and faster. But he did not move. She waited, the anticipation of death becoming worse than the end itself.

"Get it done already," she snapped, and the plea came out ragged.

His hand twitched, and she felt his brittle indecision. He wanted to end her now, here. It would be easy.

"I'm not afraid," she lied.

"Why?" he asked in a whisper that pulled the truth out of her.

"Because I would end you, too. I tried. For men, I tried. For Pebble." She closed her eyes for she could not look death in the face any longer. "I'll try again if death is the only way to be rid of you." The truth poured from her lips of its own accord, and it was a relief to her soul to voice it. She braced herself for his retribution.

He released her, abruptly, and she fell to her knees. He knelt beside her, his eyes flashing bright. "Do not mistake my mercy for weakness. The next time you attack the web, I will destroy you." He rose to his feet and took two steps forward.

"Where is Pebble?" she called out.

He stopped.

"Did you kill him?"

Silence.

"Where is he?" she demanded more fiercely.

"Sailing on the winds of fate which take him far from you."

"You killed him," she uttered with a stab of regret.

"Not even gods can kill a dream," he said with rising frustration.

"Aye, they can, Shoran. Many dreams have perished, and many lives were lost with them."

Without giving a reply, he vanished through the solid wall of the building.

"Arse," she mumbled and scrambled to her feet.

She thought she heard him growl, before his essence faded. And the winds screeched louder and harder and yanked on her hair and clothes.

CHAPTER THIRTEEN

Shadow's Lair

"When our glorious tsaren came to rule Alafraysia. They heeded our wishes and drove the phantasms of men from our realm. And we rejoiced. But the kings of the Sacred Crowns grew angry, for men could no longer dream. So they attacked us, and the first war between our kind broke out. It ended when our most beautiful Tsarina Arala brokered peace between Reval and Northwind. And once again, men could visit our realm through the veil of dreams. And we of the Black River despaired."

The History of Alafraysia and Seramight,
By Mageguard Bluelight

Elika pushed against the wall, where days ago Shoran had vanished. She ran her palms over it, probing it. Solid. Cool. She pushed. Firm.

"Where did you go?" she mumbled and reached for that intangible essence. Nothing.

Outside, the winds were shrill. The window was firmly barred and the imprisoning walls loomed. As long as Shoran held power over her, there was no reason for him to release her. The only way out of her prison was to escape and be a threat to him.

On the streets, when a gang invaded your abode, you had to invade right back to remind them they were no safer. She had to go after him, had to show him that he was no safer in his bed. Then might be he'd listen and agree to a truce. The plan was sound. Except, she had to find his lair first.

She pushed and prodded the wall. Nothing.

She leant her head against it, closed her eyes and called on her magic to lead her towards Shoran along the web that bound their worlds. Again and again, she had seen him disappear in an instant as he took a path to another place beyond her world. And she had always sensed his approach, could feel his power draw near, as if they were bound by an invisible thread. With her hand on the wall, she recalled his essence …

And there it was, too faint to grasp, yet there to follow.

Imagine the path and it will appear.

So, she imagined a door, behind which lay his essence.

She stepped towards it. As she did, the sensation of being pulled and falling grew strong. The solid wall flexed under her hands. Her mind reached farther, past the wall, where the door appeared. More than a dream, less than reality. A strange place her feet dared not step towards.

The door might open to the depths of the ocean, or the dark of the Abyss. Maybe death awaited her beyond it. Dire warnings filled her heart, and long ago, she might have heeded them. But she had feared the unknown all her life, and it had almost destroyed her. If she turned away now, she would forever be afraid—of Shoran, of Syn'Moreg, of every thug and rough on the street.

She emptied her mind of all thought, save the path ahead and allowed it to pull her onward, towards the featureless door in her mind. Her hand slipped through the wall as through water. Her arm followed. Another step and she walked through a barrier of biting, icy wind, where a turbulent force pulled her in all directions at once. For what seemed like an instant and an eternity, she was suspended in a place where her body existed with no form or shape. She pushed onward and just as abruptly became whole again, with her feet planted firmly on the ground.

She opened her eyes. Torches in scones dimly illuminated a dark, stone hall that had no beginning and no end. The windows were pitch black; the darkness beyond far deeper than the night. Her skin chilled with ungraspable dread and foreboding. Twisting black pillars rose along the hall to an arcane, arched ceiling. Pale white strands of light webbing danced along the dark stone. In front of her was the only door in the hall. It was tall, bronze and wide. A web was etched into the metal plates.

She put her ear to it. No sound.

Gently, she pushed on the door and peered through the crack into the room. There was a large four-poster bed. A man slept in it. It was too dark to see him clearly. The only light came from a few strange embers in the fireplace that cast out a green, malevolent glow.

She had not seen Shoran's face, hidden as it always was in shadow. But something told her this stranger was him, asleep contentedly in his bed, whilst she, his prisoner, fought against the cage of his making. Soundlessly, she slipped inside and drew closer to the bed.

He was lying on his back in easy abandon, brazenly naked, as if nothing in the three realms could hurt him. Surely, this could not be Shoran. He looked too human, too peaceful, too ... Sachi.

She was taken aback by his features. For a moment, she lost all ability to think, for the face she saw was nothing like she had expected. A Sachi. He was a Sachi—with the same black hair that fell over his muscled shoulders, the striking square jaw, the wide slanted eyes. Somehow, she thought that the servant of darkness would be ugly, twisted, deformed, with the love of cruelty etched in the lines of his face. Instead, there was an arresting quality about him that made her halt and stare. But it was more than his fair face that caught her. When she gazed upon him, she heard a whisper of distant kinship, a home she long forgot. With the Sachi, she had always felt thus, but never as potently as she did now. It was as if deep in her soul she knew him.

Her fear of him began to ebb. He was just a man, gifted with the power of the demigod he served. Yet there was something more than human about him, something altogether ethereal. She could not guess his age, for he was neither young nor old. If Pebble spoke truth, this being was ancient, like the mages and the tsaren.

Unbidden memories seeped into her mind of the night he had come to her room. He was close then, crushing her to the bed, his breath on her neck. She recalled the salty, faintly earthy aroma of his skin, his lips on her neck.

Her gaze dropped to his manhood …

Damn it, Eli, she chided herself and forced her eyes to refocus on his face.

She shook away those errant thoughts, remembering that he was Syn'Moreg's servant. He had imprisoned her in her room, had threatened her, and sought to save the majren from her, and thus, siding with the Laifae. She sought the strings of his essence, but found a wall instead. She groped deeper, harder. If she could grasp his essence, he'd be at her mercy. But yet again, instead of loose threads, his essence was akin to webbing with a strong, tight weave. Whereas, the mages were loose, silken threads, and easy to unpick. Frustrated, she imagined cutting through that dense weave to release the thread she could pull upon.

His eyes flew open and met hers. They were black as night, save for that faint yellow glow. Any doubts she might have entertained about him being Shoran fled. Before he found his wits and leapt at her, she threw out black strands of her magic, wound them around his wrists and pinned him to the bed. Her heart raced so hard, she would surely be sick.

Slowly, he turned his head to look at his restrained wrists, then returned his black gaze to her, filled with dark and terrible amusement.

Calm yourself, Eli. Calm. She had found his lair, and now he was at *her* mercy. She only needed to make him listen.

"Not so nice having your home invaded whilst you sleep," she said menacingly, but her voice trembled in her throat. She cleared it. "Nor being imprisoned in your own chamber."

"It is indeed intriguing," he mumbled, and the rumble of his voice pulsed through the black strands holding him and into her limbs.

A light exploded above her head. She cried out and ducked as a white fireball flew at the wall and turned into snaking lights that crawled over the stone. She straightened, composed herself and regarded her captive coolly. It did not escape her that the fireball could as easily have struck her. She opened her mouth to speak, but then she noticed that there was not a mark on his throat where she had cut it. Not even a scar was left behind. Her treacherous, curious eyes moved over his unblemished skin, down over his chest, to his stomach, and lower still …

Her cheeks burned and she snapped her gaze up to his face.

A wicked smile stretched over his lips. "Oh, kitten, how did you get so terribly lost?" His deep voice rumbled like a distant storm.

With a loose strand of magic, she grabbed the discarded silken sheet lying loose beside him and threw it over his manhood.

His lips quirked, but he made not a move, as if curious to see what she might do next.

"Seeing as I have you at my mercy —"

"Do you?" he asked mildly.

The question chilled her, and she whipped out more of those black, slick strands and bound his ankles.

His lips twitched as if he was trying not to laugh.

Still far too cocky, she thought and imagined a fireball which appeared above his head and hovered there hot and threatening. Yet he gave no sign he even saw it, his gaze firmly fixed on her.

Feeling somewhat safer, she continued. "Didn't come here to kill you, but to talk."

"My attention is entirely yours," he drawled.

She nodded. "Aye, it is. 'Tis how it is on the streets, you see. You find where a man sleeps and they always listen, where they were not so willing to do so before. So let us say we do not want to kill each other, else you know …" She pointed to the fireball above his head. "I could. And aye, you could kill me, too. So, it seems we are at an impasse. Might be your winds can keep me locked in, but they can't keep me from finding you right here, in your bed, naked as a babe. Nor can they stop me from killing you before you remember to wake. 'Cause you know, I've been standing here a while."

"Watching me sleep," he added.

She hated her face for blushing. "Plotting the many different ways I could kill you," she said dryly, adding an indifferent shrug for good measure. "And don't bother reminding me you can do the same. But seeing as you don't want to kill me—as yet—and ... well, I *do* want to kill you, but I'm finding it a little harder than it should be ..." She took a deep breath. She was muddling this. Something about the steady, intent way he was looking at her made her heart race and her mouth babble nonsense. "What do you want, Shoran? Why do you stop me from unravelling the mages?"

"Why do you unravel them?" he countered, speaking slowly. There was genuine curiosity in his question that irked her.

"They steal men's bodies, murder the innocent to take what's not theirs. This world belongs to men."

"This world belongs to both, humans and Laifae. One world there is now, where once were two."

"We live in Seramight, the realm of men," she objected. "The Laifae's realm is Alafraysia. Never seen it and never want to. 'Tis there they come from and into ours. Else they'd not need our bodies."

"The two are merged into one," he said with the worldly patience of someone explaining a simple matter to a child. "The veil is thin. Dreams intrude upon the Earthly, as the Earthy intrudes upon the Ethereal."

Elika did not understand him, but for the shame of admitting it, decided that it did not matter. He only needed to understand her. "They kill men to steal their bodies for their own."

"And men kill the Laifae. 'Tis the endless cycle of the ages I care little for anymore."

"Then why do you try to stop me?" she asked, bewildered.

His eyes flashed, and he leant forward, tugging on her restraints. "You strike that which is sacred. You attack the web."

Elika shook her head. "I attack only the Laifae."

"Your power is unbridled," he said in that tone of restrained impatience, something that should have been obvious.

"Unbridled?" She frowned and saw an answering frustration in his face.

"You delve deep and break the light. You destroy that which must be preserved. Worse still, you do so in ignorance."

He spoke in the common tongue of men, and yet when he spoke, he gave the impression that he rarely used their language, rarely spoke at all. It seemed to cause him effort to be understood. It reminded her of the younger children in their pack and pulled on those foolish strings of pity. Aye, she was a fool, for he was not a man to pity.

"So, if I … um … stop breaking the light, you'll leave me in peace? I already told you, I won't kill any more majren."

"The power unleashed will not be denied. I must contain you."

Everything stilled inside her at his threat and everything it implied. "Do you mean to keep me prisoner until I grow old and die?"

The black strands around his wrists and ankles tightened, mirroring her anger.

"I am yet to ponder what to do with you," he murmured. "'Tis not an easy quandary."

"What will it take for you to leave me alone?" she asked quietly, giving him one more chance at peace. "Name your terms."

"No terms, kitten," he said equally quietly. "You cannot be allowed to run wild. I must tame or slay you. Judgement will come in time."

His words struck her hard. He meant to keep her prisoner. He would never leave her alone. There was to be no peace between them, and only one path remained. Before he could read her intent, she cut the thread of his essence, grabbed it and pulled.

For an instant he arched his back and gasped. Then she felt him slip away from her grasp, like water running through her fingers.

"Yet again, you would try to unravel me into the wind?" Booming laughter burst out of him, terrible in its power.

Then it died, and he sat up, pulling easily against the hold of her magic, and she staggered away from his menace. Out of nowhere, a ball of smoke appeared overhead and doused her fireball. And it dawned on her that she was not holding him down, that her magic was no match for those arms. He was never at her mercy.

She flung out more black strands and waved them menacingly at him. "Keep back and I won't hurt you."

Her threat sounded weak in his dark lair. So she imagined fire into existence to burn his bed, and commanded the side table to jump forward and rear on its legs, and that, too, burst into flames. But he gave none of her conjured magic a single glance, as if she alone could see it.

"Hurt me?" He laughed again and his gaze grew intent. "Do you even know where you are?" he asked and the floor beneath her feet shook and was gone.

The light was gone—everything was gone.

She plunged into darkness, falling sickeningly fast through nothingness, her screams swallowed by the winds. Her mind emptied of everything but terror. She screamed and screamed until she was hoarse, and still she could not stop screaming. Her heart felt as if it would burst, and she pleaded that it would, for she could not bear this torment. She flailed her arms and legs, her fingers reached out to grab anything inside the dark. But there was nothing, save her screams and the eternity beyond …

Suddenly a web of light came from nowhere, wound around her and trapped her. She fought against it, kicking and scratching, fighting and fighting its restraint like a mindless animal …

"Shhh, kitten, I have you."

Arms were suddenly around her, holding her. The web was gone. She clawed and scrambled at whatever it was that was solid and warm, yelping and screaming hoarsely, afraid she would slip and be there again …

The darkness was gone, replaced with shadows and light, and she had barely enough sense left to realize that she was not falling anymore. She wrapped her arms around a warm neck and clung tightly, whilst breathing hard against the crushing terror in her chest.

The arms around her tightened. "*Amaya si niarna*," came a soothing whisper in her ear. "In darkness lives light. To the light, you are bound."

She wanted to speak, but another whimper came from her mouth. She buried her face in the neck and just breathed. She was not lost in the eternity of darkness. It was but another nightmare.

"*Amaya si niarna*," he repeated, and the gentle words seeped into her heart and compelled it to calm.

A fragment of reality intruded. Her mind latched onto the solidity of it. She remembered where she was. She recognized that voice. The scent of man hit her. She lifted her head and stared into black eyes.

She flailed her legs and pushed herself away. He released her, but her legs wobbled beneath her as if they were made of water, and she fell to the floor. She scrambled backward until her back hit the wall, whilst staring at the solid floor through which she had fallen. She could not go back to that Abyss, could not face the darkness. She pulled her knees to her chest and buried her face. But when she closed her eyes, the Abyss raced at her. Her eyes flew open, and she retched whatever meagre contents were left of her last meal that day.

She felt him watching her. A small part of her was horrified at herself for showing him this frightened, wretched creature. She forced the echoes of her screams out of her ears and raised her face.

She shook her head in fear and denial. "Kill me. But don't send me there again." Her voice trembled. It was hoarse, cracked, her throat sore.

He was looking down at her with an inscrutable expression, devoid of anger, almost kindly in truth, and it made her terribly ashamed.

"Do not show me your claws, kitten, for I fear mine are sharper and cut much deeper," he said with a faint note of regret.

He was clad in a black silk shirt and loose trousers. He had sent her there … to the Abyss. And whilst she was falling, he was calmly dressing …

She wanted to kill the bastard.

If he saw her hatred, he gave no sign of it. "How did you find the path here, tell me?"

"I walked through the same door you did." She scrambled to her feet whilst holding on to the wall. Her body trembled, but it was not with fear this time, but weakness.

He turned away and went to stand by the dark fireplace. As he approached, fire burst into life. It was green, like the glowing embers. He braced himself against the mantle and looked at the flames, thoughtful and calm.

"I offered you peace, but you would have war between us," she said, if only to break his silence.

"You know nothing of war and bring me no peace," he said dismissively. "'Tis what to do with you that I must ponder."

"Free me from your cage or you will never know peace."

"I cannot do that." His voice rumbled. "You are far too dangerous to roam the world unfettered. Already you shred the web with your claws. It falls to me to chain you."

He said it so dismissively, she suddenly felt as if she was indeed a wild cub he knew not what to do with, fighting against the bars of her cage, unable to break them without destroying herself in turn. So calmly he stood there, with that breathtaking arrogance, believing it was his duty to own and imprison her until he passed some judgment as to what her existence should be.

The terrible thought broke something inside her and unleashed every fighting instinct she possessed. She would break those bars or break herself against them. She threw out her magic and allowed all her terror and rage to flow into it. The black strands flew out, raced through the walls and tore everything apart piece by piece. The tendrils shredded his bed, latched onto anything and everything, tearing it all to pieces, breaking it, and throwing it at the wall above him. Wild and free, like her rage, the strands destroyed what they could grasp until the walls cracked, and the stone crumbled. The windows smashed outwards, and the winds of the Abyss tore through the room.

Yet he stood there composed, ignoring the destruction she was wreaking, as if it was of no consequence. Debris flew at him, but never reached him, as if he was cocooned inside an invisible shield.

And her magic grew wilder and wilder, whilst she grew fainter and fainter until she realized that she was unravelling.

With all her might, she clung to the essence of herself and forced the magic to return before she became nothing. It crawled back inside her body, spent and brooding. Elika slumped against the wall and realized her terrible mistake. She was fading, her body was fading into nothingness. The room was in shreds, the winds from outside screamed in her stead. She gazed down at her hands and found that they were trembling. There was barely any flesh left on the bones of her arms.

Mistress Oblana won't be happy, she thought distantly and wondered how many coppers she'd take from her for the food she'd need to restore her flesh.

Shoran titled his head, glancing at her over his shoulder with not a flicker of emotion. She had to get away from him before he realized how weak she had made herself, how foolish she had been.

"Stay away from me, beast. Your prison will not hold me." With those words, she staggered out the door, desperately trying to hold herself from flying apart and vanishing.

She was back in the endless hall, limping towards the nearest wall. There, she felt the wavering pull of the veil. She imagined the door to the city, went through and out into a dark street. Her legs were shaking and she could no longer feel her body. The world spun and spun until she was sick from it. She took another step and fell to the ground. Overhead, the stars and the sky were swirling just as wildly. She was dying. She had killed herself. Dimly, she wondered whether the mages felt thus when she unraveled them; afraid, lonely, on the edge of nothingness in their last moments.

A shadow with glowing eyes blocked the view of the Abyss and filled her fading vision. She could not move. It did not matter. Shoran had won. For she'd gone and unraveled herself instead of him. Might be it was always inevitable, it would end thus for her.

"Not the chasm," she whispered her last plea. "Not the Abyss ..." The words faded on her tongue.

He crouched beside her. "Do you wish me to send you to the gods?"

A softly spoken threat?

She shook her head. "I want to … live," she whispered, and the painful truth of that struck her. A tear rolled down her cheek. She was not ready to die, was not facing it fearlessly.

He sighed. "Do you wish to live amongst the gods?" he said it slower, with a note of exasperation.

Her mind swam. Three paths faced everyone after death: to gods, to magic and to men. "Men … my path … to men."

And the last thing she knew of the world was the sensation of floating up and up upon the wind of the Abyss.

CHAPTER FOURTEEN

Choices

"There is no creature fouler than a Tane, a corruption of our ethereal essence, a being that should never be. Yet in Seramight, they are allowed to exist. They are the proof that the two realms are truly one. The first Tane appeared near a thousand years ago, soon after our realms collided. Unlike our kind, Tanes live solely in the realm of Seramight. They cannot cross to Alafraysia, thus betraying their true nature. The tsaren despise them. Yet they cannot bring themselves to destroy the abominations they created inside she-human bellies. We asked Mage Fragrance why that was, and his whispered reply made us shudder and grow cold. They fear the face of their own barren hopes, for in Seramight they see that which can never exist. Unlike the gods and humans, they can never leave behind more than a dream of a child.'"

The History of Alafraysia and Seramight,
By Mageguard Bluelight

Everything spun and spun. Out of the vortex of churning darkness, voices drifted, faint and broken.

"… unguarded … starving … lift her head …" a deep voice spoke.

"She refuses it still … fights … Maxim will hold her …" said a prim feminine one.

"No. Do not fight her … will kill her …"

Elika opened her eyes. Two people stood above her, spinning and blurring with the rest of the room.

A silver cup was coming towards her lips. And she was back in the temple, sick and burning hot in the fires consuming the city. She turned her face away, pushing aside the cup. "No more …

no more blood-salt." She closed her lips tightly, for she was certain she would retch.

The large hand with the cup froze.

A woman's gasp came from somewhere near. "She's been drinking blood-salt … Why?"

Elika turned to the voice. "To destroy the magic in me, lady, for 'tis wicked and draws the Blight towards us." The words came out easily and truthfully, but she sensed a lie in them. "Take me to the bridge instead … the fires burn …"

The woman stepped forward out of the darkness and reordered into a middle-aged matron in a fine dress with a horrified expression on her face. Her lips firmed and her eyes narrowed. She spoke to the shadow holding the cup. "The gods would show her no mercy, Shoran. You know that."

"Aye, I know," he replied slow and thoughtful, as if all the ages were at his beck and call.

Elika laughed deliriously and coughed. "The gods are dead! Else they know not what mercy is. Damn the gods."

Slowly, the cup moved away.

"Do you hate the gods then, girl?" the woman asked sternly.

Elika did not, but she hated being here, wherever here was, hated being sick, hated that she was dying and above all, hated the woman's judgment. "They have abandoned us, lady. Their son destroyed our world. Hate is what they well deserve."

"Us? Who is *us* you speak of?" The woman raised an eyebrow.

"Men," Elika replied weakly.

The woman turned her head to the dark shadow next to her. "She speaks like an Othersider and a commoner of the lowest sort … but neither is possible. Yet she wears the slave collar with Aeon-Rah's mark on it. Whose is she, Shoran?"

"'Tis a mystery I am yet to unravel," he murmured. "Though grave are my suspicions."

"She is … broken." The woman threw Elika a pitiless glance. "See how she speaks of the gods? And hate has festered in her body. 'Tis poison that never leaves."

Broken. She was broken. She felt broken. Elika turned her face away.

"You'd do better to let her die," the woman continued. "She'll be gone by morning. Do not unleash another Elriad upon the world."

Silence.

Aye, Shoran was hesitating, he wanted her dead.

Elika smiled faintly at the woman. "Don't know who you are, lady, but might be you are right. I'm tired and aye, I'm broken. As broken as the world." As she spoke, the last of the strength with which she held herself together began to peel away. She was unravelling. Nothing could stop that now. She moved her hand, reached into her pocket and she pulled out the stone spider. She gazed upon it the last time and sought the strength to face whatever was to come beyond the realm of the living. Her breath grew shallow, strained and pained. She held the spider tight to her chest and whispered, "Name's Eli. Eli Spider … if … if anyone asks … about me."

"Spider …" The woman gasped in surprise and paled. "She's a …"

Shoran stiffened beside her. The knuckles around the cup tightened.

"Who are your guardians, girl?" the woman asked urgently. "Who cares for you?"

The question was crushing. Elika thought of her pack, of Bill and Igla—they were all dead. Mite left. Penny was missing. Who cared for her? A tear escaped her eye and flowed down her cheek. She was alone. She had been alone for so long, she no longer felt the deep, dark hole of loneliness that swallowed her each waking day.

"There's no one, lady," Elika whispered, and her eyes drifted closed. Her arm fell away and she could not hold on to the spider. It hit the floor with a light clunk. She grew lighter and lighter as the last of the magic flowed out of her, leaving nothing behind but the eternal Abyss.

Suddenly, a firm hand was there, holding her head, lifting it up.

"Drink," a deep voice ordered.

Elika moaned and tried to turn away, but the hand was persistent and would not allow it.

"Drink, little spider. Drink the light and live," he urged firmly and tipped the cup at her lips.

Elika had no strength to fight, and the liquid poured into her mouth. She braced herself for salty blood, but the sensation that hit her mouth was nothing like it. The liquid was syrupy sweet. Warmth spread from her tongue, down her throat and chest, and raced through her body like the flood of life and joy. The liquid was life itself, feeding her, solidifying her. It sated the deep craving she had lived with for so long. Her eyes flew open, and she stared into the cup filled with a pale silver light. She grabbed the cup and the hand that held it with both of hers, wanting every drop of that light. Greedily, she drank until there was nothing left. Whatever it was her body had craved, it had found. The magic inside her demanded the elixir at her lips, that which had so long been denied.

Shoran gently wrestled the empty cup from her grip, but Elika wanted more. It was not enough. She fixated on that cup, followed it with her eyes to the other side of the room where it was filled from a jug, and watched it still as it was brought back to her. And nothing else mattered but the cup. She reached for it and gulped its contents, spilling some down her chin …

Stabbing pain struck her stomach. She moaned and put her hand to it.

"Enough for now." Shoran took the empty cup from her other hand. "Your body must adjust to the food long denied you."

"'Tis poison," she moaned and curled on her side over her stomach.

"There's no poison that can kill you, save the blood-salt," he said and rose from the bed.

"How did she survive so long without silversap?" asked the woman.

"'Tis indeed a wonder," Shoran replied as he replaced the cup on the table.

"Seeing as you have claimed her, will you not remove that ghastly collar?" the woman asked with a note of disapproval.

"The choice to be enslaved by Rah was hers, and so it shall be hers to free herself."

Their voices grew distant. And for a blissful time, everything grew dark and stopped spinning.

~

When she came to, her mind was blank. *Eli Spider*, emerged a whisper of a thought. That was her name. She clung to it. Around her, the room was richly decorated. A lazy fire burned in the fireplace. She wondered what day it was. How long had she been here? A sliver of sunlight peered through the velvet curtain. The sun was low, and after studying it, Elika decided it must be evening.

In her hand, she held something. She lifted it. The stone spider.

She rolled from the bed onto her feet. She felt wrong … something was different. The realization that she was not hungry dawned on her. She had known hunger for so long, its absence left her unsettled. She wore a nightdress that was not hers. Someone must have undressed her. With a pang of embarrassment and self-consciousness, she desperately hoped it was not Shoran.

In front of her was a mirror. When she glanced into it, she did not recognize her own reflection. Her body was little more than skin and bone, her jaw pronounced, her cheeks sunken. There were dark shadows in the hollows of her sunken eyes. A memory emerged of her magic destroying Shoran's lair with abandon. Her hand rose to touch the papery skin of her cheek. Never before had she come so close to destroying herself. She and magic were bound. She had come to accept that. But it seemed their joining went far deeper than she had realized. Were she to unravel, there'd be no body left behind.

"You are awake. Good," said a stern voice from the door.

Elika faced a tall, prim woman with an ageing complexion, looking neat and crisp in a dark velvet dress. She had dark blue eyes like Bill's had been, reminiscent of the depths of the sea.

"Who are you? Where am I?" Elika asked and found her voice was still hoarse.

"I am Tane Rosalina, daughter of Ilikan. You are in my house. Get dressed. Dinner awaits downstairs."

"Another Tane," Elika muttered to herself with dull resignation as she looked around for her clothes. Tanes seemed as drawn to her as caterpillars to a spring leaf. Except this Tane clearly thought the leaf was not to her taste.

The woman's stiff lips stiffened even more. "You can wear the dress the maid left on your bed." With that, she walked out and closed the door.

Elika regarded the silken dress laid out on the bed. It was frilly and foolish looking, something a young lady might wear. So she ignored it and found her own pile of clothing, washed and neatly folded on a chair. She pulled on her hessian trousers and shirt, then tentatively opened the door to peer into the hall. No one was about, so she headed for the sweeping stair.

When she passed the window, she stopped to look outside. She was in a part of the city she did not recognize. There was a park with a lake across the wide tree-lined street, and large mansions at the other end of it. She noted the direction of palace towers and the mountains and judged that she was in the southern part of Terren, likely in Gemstone District.

An aged servant came towards her, walking with a haughty air of one who detested anything less than perfection. And she was far from perfection if his brief perusal of her was anything to go by. He lifted his chin even higher. "You are not dressed for dinner."

He was shorter than her, yet he managed to look down at her rather admirably, she thought. "I am wearing the clothes I own."

"The mistress gave you a dress," he said in a clipped tone.

"I am not a doll to be dressed by your mistress," she said, matching his curtness, and took a step to walk around him.

He stepped in front of her. "In this house, the mistress is obeyed. She is a great lady of impeccable breeding ..."

"Whilst I am clearly not." Elika tried to sidestep him again.

His lips turned down. "I suppose it was too much to expect a crumb of gratitude from a ..." He looked her up and down again.

Elika crossed her arms. "From a street rat?" she finished for him. "A slave? A *servant?*" she said the last pointedly, whilst giving him the same perusal along his length.

He spun on his heel. "This way. The mistress is waiting. And she hates tardiness nearly as much as poor graces."

In the dining room, a long table was set for twenty people, though there was only the mistress standing expectantly at the head of it. "Was the dress not to your liking?" asked the tane imperiously.

"She said she is not a doll," the man rushed to reply. "Rather ungratefully, may I add."

"Thank you, Maxim, you may leave us."

The short man bowed, and with a haughty glance at Elika, left them.

"Sit and eat." Tane Rosalina pointed at a chair and lowered herself gracefully onto her own.

Elika's stomach rumbled at the sight of so much food, so she sat down as the lady instructed.

"Are you a fish flopping on the beach?" the tane demanded.

Elika blinked at her. Surely, she was as daft as Bill. "No, lady …"

"Then you do not flop or bounce when rising or taking a seat. That is not how a lady sits down. You do it with grace and elegance."

"As you say." Elika grabbed the bread and chewed whilst tearing off the roast leg of a bird in the center of the table.

"If you manage to gather a grain of patience, the servants will serve you," Tane Rosalina said primly. She sat with her back stiff and upright, whilst the servant placed small portions onto her plate.

"I can serve myself well enough." Elika wiggled her fingers at her. "See? That's what these are for."

The tane's eyes narrowed. "Let us understand each other, young lady. I care not what or who you are. I will not have such insolence at my table, or in my own house."

Elika sighed and stood up. "I don't know why I'm here, lady. Might be best if I —"

"Sit down!" the woman snapped. "And do it gracefully."

Elika regarded the food and lowered herself slowly to the chair.

"You are here not at my invitation, I assure you," the woman continued. "His lordship Shoran brought you here, half dead and looking like a half-starved street cat."

"Didn't ask him to. Why did he bring me here, anyway?"

"Do not speak with your mouth full. He named me as your keeper and instructed me to care for you. And sit up straight. You are not an old fishwife."

Elika froze in mid-bite. She lowered the bird's leg and her other hand rose instinctively to her collar. "I already have a mistress. I don't think you can take me from her."

"Shoran can take you from whomever he wishes and place you wherever he wishes to place you. And why don't you remove that ghastly collar?"

Elika pulled on it. "See, it won't come off. And Shoran has no authority over me. I decide where I go." She tore off another chunk of bread.

"Look at you. A filthy street urchin with the manners of a barbarian. This is what one becomes without someone's authority over them. You call yourself a tsarina?"

"I call myself Eli Spider once of Bad Penny's pack," she retorted.

The woman was ready to snap back when a flustered servant girl rushed in. "A visitor is waiting for you in the guest lounge, mistress. He ... he did not arrive via a door."

Whatever hung on Rosalina's lips died there. She stood up. "We will speak later."

After she was gone, Elika stuffed her mouth, and gingerly left the dining room past the servants standing by the wall and staring ahead like creepy statues. No one looked her way or followed.

In the hall, she could hear Rosalina's raised voice. "Insolent, impertinent girl! I cannot do this, Shoran!"

A deep male voice replied. Elika could not make out what he said and tiptoed to the lounge door.

"It is more than clear that she has lived on the streets her whole life, amongst magic-haters. She has no table manners ...

no manners of any kind. She speaks and acts like a street thug. I would not trust her not to rob me in the night and run off. She is damaged, Shoran. You have seen the scars on her back. You have seen the fresh wounds, too. She respects no authority and wants nothing but to satisfy the basal instincts of the moment. She cannot read and does not seem to even recognize the lettering before her. If she were younger, I might have been able to do something with her. But she is nearly a woman grown. She is wild, untamed and impulsive. She will not be caged by civilization or by you. I cannot help her. Give her to Reval, he's seeking …"

"No," came a brisk, harsh reply. "You will not speak of her to anyone."

Elika's throat tightened around a shame-filled lump. Everything the old woman said was true. But she was not a thief … at least not any more. She thought herself the savior of mankind. The truth was, she was just another pitiful street rat fighting its corner.

She'd heard enough. The tane did not want her here, and she wanted even less to be here. Elika headed straight for the door and stormed out of the house. Half blind, she fled along the street, then climbed up to the nearest roof and ran as fast as her feet could carry her back to Yarn Row. Back to spinning the webs for Mistress Oblana. Aye, she was everything Tane Rosalina thought her to be. Worse still, the tane thought she was hopeless, that she could never change.

Elika swiped her eyes. When had she ever wanted more than that? Her only ambition was to save enough coin to buy her own freedom, whilst setting men free from their own bonds. Somehow it had seemed important that she do something honest and true. Even at that, she had failed. No one in Terren knew who she was, what she had done for men, that it was she who had destroyed those majren. It was Northwind's name they now chanted.

On the edge of Yarn Row, Elika found a way down to the street. Unthinking, she strode into the kitchen of the workshop, meaning to go straight to her room, certain everyone was abed.

But the kitchen was not empty. Mistress Oblana was pouring herself a chamomile tea for her headache.

As soon as Elika entered, the mistress spun on her. "You wretch! How dare you show your face here after running away."

Before Elika could understand the reason for her anger, a stick flew out and struck her in the face. Elika cried out and covered her head, whilst Mistress Oblana hit her and hit her.

"You wretched girl. You run away and now come crawling back. Ungrateful wretch!" she shouted as she beat her.

Elika snatched the stick from the mistress' tired hand and dashed aside to put the table between them. "I didn't run away. I was sick and didn't know where I was."

But her pleas fell on deaf ears.

Mistress Oblana was breathing heavily. "Three days! Have you been whoring yourself? Admit it."

Three days, Elika thought in alarm. "I was sick mistress, unable to return."

"I had to turn customers away. The others are demanding their payments back, for I could not give them a web I had promised."

"I'll work extra hard," she rushed to say.

"And where is the other wretch who went with you? Where is Liffy?" the mistress yelled.

Elika was stunned. "Liffy's gone?"

The mistress narrowed her eyes. "Do not play the innocent with me. I know you ran away together. You will not have your seventh day anymore, nor will you be paid until you catch up on the missed work … yours and Liffy's. Starting tonight. You will work through the night and all day tomorrow. In the morning, I will send for Mage Aeon-Rah. He has been frantically searching for you."

Whatever reply was on the tip of her tongue wilted away. The mistress was wearing a collar. Elika's jaw dropped. "You're …"

"Aeon-Rah refused a hundred gold for you. Until I repay it to him for losing you, I'm to wear the collar." She broke down then, fell into a seat and began to weep bitter, bitter tears. Or might be they were tears of relief. Now that Elika had returned, Aeon-Rah would surely forgive the mistress.

Without another word, Elika rushed upstairs to the workshop. It was dark and empty. She lit a candle. It was barely enough to see by, but the mistress never got over her fear of wasting them. There were rolls and rolls of yarn waiting to be given shape. She sat on the hard chair and winced. Her arms and back were sore where the mistress had struck her, and her face was swelling on one side. Under the flickering light of a single candle she began to weave, whilst the rest of the city slept.

No more adventures. No more magic. She would work day and night and earn her freedom, and then … what was there for someone like her?

She never thought about learning to read. Mite could read. Could Penny? Reading, however, did not earn coin. She had never thought of the future, living only in the wretched present. The future had always been a barren landscape, for there had only ever been two choices for her; to be consumed by the Blight or to face the Bridge. The future had always been death. Yet here she was, and the future was suddenly a wide vista with countless possibilities beyond her ken to clearly see, and just as frightening for it. Might be she'd work hard and earn mistress Oblana's respect. Perhaps she could have her own shop like this one … Or maybe she'd be working here all her life. A spike of panic stabbed her. Everything in her rebelled at the thought. Then what did she want?

Home, came an echo of longing. *My pack. To belong.*

The thought died before taking root. From the corner of her eye she saw a shadow move and take man's shape. She ignored him, hoping he would simply go away.

But he did not. He leant on the wall and watched her in silence.

"What a pretty web you weave, little spider," he said after a while.

Elika ignored his soft mockery.

"Two spiders in a web. Two masters where there should be one," he mused aloud after a long silence. "'Tis a curious mystery Fates give us."

"Leave me be," she said without raising her gaze from her web. "You've caused me enough trouble. Go tell your master he has won. Just leave me in peace, so I can earn honest coin."

He pushed away from the wall and strode towards her, his gait elegant and prowling. Gently, he placed his hand on her shoulder where the mistress had struck her with the cane, and she winced in pain.

His fingers brushed her jaw and turned her face towards him. His eyes flashed in anger, but he spoke softly. "Shall I kill the one who has done this to you?"

"If I wanted them dead, I'd kill them myself. 'Tis what I deserved." She wrenched her face from his hand and resumed her weaving.

"What you deserve? Strange how you have come to believe such a lowly lie. Pain of the flesh does not take away the pain of a tortured soul. It merely masks it."

"I've been hurt worse before. I care nothing for it."

"Tell me, kitten, who was your first keeper? Who found you as a babe?"

As ever, he extruded a powerful compulsion that made her want to tell him the truth, though she knew not what that was.

"Tane Igla said she found me and gave me to a seamstress and her husband," she replied, hoping that would be enough for him.

"Iglasina? She lives then?"

"She and Bill are dead. Got by the Blight."

"But of course, the Blight," he said with a note of scorn. "And where are the folk who were meant to be your parents, who were entrusted with your keeping?"

"They are dead. Died trying to cross the bridge across the chasm your master created."

"And you hate him for it?" he asked softly.

"Aye, I hate him, and you for serving him. So leave me be."

"Why did you not cross with them? Magic would have protected you."

"Another Tane stopped me. Besides, I was too afraid."

"You fear the Abyss? What a confused little spider you are." Elika did not reply.

"Where did Iglasina find you?" he asked after a silence.

Elika's hands stilled. "Why do you ask me these questions?"

"Merely to unravel how you came to be, and thus where you belong."

"I belong here."

"Do you?" he asked mildly, as if he had read her thoughts not a few moments ago, when she had been asking that same question.

She stared sightlessly at the web in her hands. "I owe you no answers."

"Yet I would have them, nonetheless." There was steel in his rumbling voice that brokered no refusal. "Where did Iglasina find you?" he repeated more forcefully, as if determined to wrench the truth from her with the power of his will alone.

"At the back of an alley …"

He moved suddenly and was behind her, his face close to her ear. "*Seeya neda veria.* Do not speak lies to me. I can smell them on your sweet breath. Where did she find you? Speak the truth or let the lie become your prison."

Elika shook her head as the truth was wrenched from her lips. "What she said made no sense …"

He stroked her cheek with a finger. "Tell me her words as she sang them."

"In the bridge," Elika replied, unable to refuse the seductive command.

He stilled, then straightened, took a step away, and she dared not look up, for fear of what she'd see in his face. He lifted her face to his, and his eyes roamed over it for long searching moments. Then he walked aside to examine the yarns of silken threads hanging off the racks. He ran his fingers over them, caressing the yarn, and a strange, replying shiver ran up her spine.

"What a wondrous thing impossibility is," he said absently, then recited,

> *"A silken thread will weave your dreams*
> *And shape your wishes into worlds,*
> *It will give flesh to secret wants,*
> *And then unravel all your hopes."*

"For so long I had pondered the inexplicable, and she chased the impossible. Yet here you are. The dream that began the end and wove tragedy through ages past has born its fruit at last."

His musings were incomprehensible, and she felt there was something important he was trying not to tell her. "Why are you here, Shoran?"

"I might ask you the same, little spider," he replied as he continued to stroke the silken threads meant for her web and study their flyaway texture. "Those hands of yours know their true purpose, yet you do not heed the call."

She looked down into her lap, where the web she had been weaving was taking shape. He was right. She did not belong here. Everything was wrong. The very power of his presence distorted her reality, her wishes, and her dreams. It made her want to lay aside the web and follow him like a pup with a new master.

"I do not want it. I never wanted the magic inside me. If I could get rid of it, I would. I only wish to be human."

"Yet you are not. To wish for it festers only malcontent." He faced her, his hands clasped behind his back. "'Tis a quandary that you pose me. The power in you will always seek its own voice. The purpose seeded in your blood will never ebb. It will grow until it consumes you. I must end you or else I must contain you. One does not appeal to me, the other not to you. Yet those are the two choices before us. One of them, we must choose."

In his eyes, she saw the truth of it, and it was hard not to feel shrunken before him.

"Then to the death we must fight," she said without conviction, knowing that their fight to the death would be short.

He was silent for long moments as he considered her defiant reply. It was a calm consideration, unmarred by any emotion or even some measure of need. Nor was it calculating, for he wanted nothing from her. He simply balanced her decision against his own. She imagined he would end her with just the same meticulous precision and no feelings on the matter. Despite that, she knew better than to appear cowed before him. So, she returned his stare without flinching and waited for his judgement, whilst readying to muster what brief defense she could. She would hurt him, and she allowed that silent promise to pour from her gaze.

And aye, he saw it clearly enough, for his lips curled wryly. "Fearless you are not. Merely foolish. How easy it would be to defy the great power that made you and extinguish you from the web. Yet, I find I cannot bring myself to do so. At least not as yet. Three parents forged you. Yet it comes to me to care for you."

"I'm not a child. I can care for myself well enough."

"Tane Rosalina is expecting you tomorrow morn. As your guardian, I have appointed her as your keeper."

"I don't need a guardian or a keeper. Nor do I wish her charity."

His lips quirked. "Kitten, 'tis not for you to question me, the one who holds the fluttering beat of your heart in my hand. I can crush you."

"Then do so. I will not live in fear of you or any man, mage or god."

"Spoken like a goddess. I applaud you. Perhaps Rosalina was wrong about you after all."

"No. She was right. Everything she said was true. I am nothing but a street rat, a thief … though not anymore …"

He moved his hands, and the air spun and formed itself into a swirling mirror. "Gaze into the silvery pool and tell me what you see."

Elika set aside her web and stood in front of a magical mirror that showed her what she was not. The reflection showed a beauty she had never seen before, yet one who wore her face. It was not a scrawny girl, but a curvesome woman, tall and majestic, in a pale green dress wrapped in a silvery web akin to the one she was weaving. A crown circlet adorned her head, and long strings of gems fell down her long black hair.

"What do you see?" he asked again.

"A lie. Magic lies."

"'Tis not magic that shows you your reflection, but your own heart. The silver water is merely a reflection of your deepest dreams and secret desires, and the truth you hide deep in your soul."

"It shows a queen."

"And so you are."

"It would be a nice story," she said wryly. "A queen of men? Of Magic? Shall I stroll to the palace gates and tell them a magic mirror told me I was to rule?" She smiled sadly at the absurdity of it.

He passed his hand over the mirror and she saw herself as she was now. Thin, drawn and pale, with matted hair down to her shoulders, and a dark angry bruise marking her cheek. She turned away from the ugly reflection.

"You cannot escape what you are, any more than I can ignore your existence. I have shown you a path, but you must walk it."

"You would send me to the old tane, to be dressed and fed and mocked? You'd call it a gift, but I say it's a debt I do not wish to incur, nor do I want to suffer the insults. I haven't earnt my riches. Nor will I be given them."

"To claim what is rightfully yours is never a gift. To accept your nature is not defeat. A butterfly does not emerge from its cocoon to swim in the ocean. For it to do so is not rebellion against the Fates, but needless suffering and death."

"I do not fear suffering —"

"It is not only *your* suffering I speak of. No one can make you a queen. 'Tis for you to grasp your birthright and become one. Much is yet hidden from you. Of the past, of the present, of what you are and the cruel winds that bore you, and the power you are destined to wield. Even your true name is hidden from you."

"I'm Eli ..."

"Eli Spider of Bad Penny's pack. Elika, Lika. Aye. Those names you have lived by, and much have I learned of you these last days. Yet you have another name, the one your mother gave you. And when you are ready, to become what you were born to be, I will restore that name to you. And you will know your true nature." His voice deepened and darkened as he said that, as if it was a threat. "I will give you time to make your choice. Take the path I offer you here in this world or return with me to the Abyss and face the merciless truth of what you are. For only truth or sword can stop the path you have set yourself and the world upon."

"You give me no choice."

"Few choices and paths there are for one such as you … and one such as me."

He turned and marched straight at the wall and vanished. The wall shimmered and stilled.

~

Last night the winds had not returned. Shoran had released her from her prison, but she was not free. Would never be free. In her lap, her secret box was empty. Her coins had been stolen, and with them her hopes. Even the pouch behind the chamber pot under her bed was gone.

Mistress Oblana had no reason to steal from her. And whatever else she was, the mistress was compelled to account for every penny, every debt and expense. She'd likely be at a loss as to how to record the stolen loot in her ledgers.

It could only have been Liffy. The girl had wisely run away. Might be she'd find her way to Wavestar after all.

Elika closed the lid. The empty box mocked her naivety. She returned it to its place beneath the shrine to magic as steps approached outside.

The door opened, and the mistress came in. "Aeon-Rah waits for you downstairs." She still wore the collar Aeon-Rah put on her.

Elika followed the mistress to the workshop, where four girls Elika did not recognize were working on looms and spinners. The youngest could not be more than six. Aeon-Rah was watching them without expression.

He turned to Elika when she came in. "Where is the other she-human?" he asked her.

"I don't know," she replied, though she had her suspicions.

"I dare say the city guards will find the wretch soon enough," said the mistress placatingly. "And when we find her, she'll wish she never betrayed me."

Despite her own bitter sense of betrayal, Elika hoped Liffy wouldn't be found.

Out of nowhere, a tendril of magic wound around Elika's throat and before she could react, threw her against the wall. Everything went dark. She lay there for a moment stunned and in pain.

"We will teach you a lesson about running away," hissed the mage. "You and these other girls will learn it."

The other girls watched silently as another strand struck her across the face. Then her neck began to burn, as the collar around her throat grew tighter and tighter. Elika grabbed it and tried to pull it off. But it grew tighter still until she could not breathe and her head felt like it was afire. Desperately, she clawed at her skin, unable to cry out, to scream, to gasp for breath.

Aeon-Rah watched on without mercy. "The one-eyed thug has been demanding we sell you to him. And when we refused again, do you know what he threatened us with?"

In her panic, Elika could only claw at the collar tightening around her throat.

"Please, your eminence, do not kill the one who has magic's favor?" the mistress pleaded urgently. "She'll be a good girl from now on."

The mage ignored her and took a step closer to Elika. "He told us he would end us. Then his men threw vile blood-salt on us, and as we writhed on the floor in pain, he pierced us with the blood-salt dagger. He promised to return and do much worse to us unless we sell you." Another strand of magic struck her. "Every pain he inflicts on us, we will inflict on you. And since he made you his whore, we shall make you ours also, and we will send him flesh from your bones, staring with your hands."

"No," screeched the mistress. "Please, I need her webs. You need her to weave them. Think of the gold she brings us. Surely magic would not approve —"

"Silence, she-human." He struck the mistress, and she stumbled back. "If not her hands then we will take her feet, so she never runs away again."

Everything was growing dark, and Elika's fingers could no longer claw at the choking collar. Another magic tendril wound around her ankle. Then an axe appeared in the air above her. It rose above her foot …

"No!" With the last of her strength, she pushed out her own strands of magic. They wound around the axe. The shock in Mage Aeon-Rah's face unbalanced him enough for her to roll from under the axe and grab the threads of his essence. She pulled and suddenly she could gasp for air. She took a deep breath.

The mage's eyes grew wide. "No … it cannot be … Arala?"

"Name's Eli," she said hoarsely as she rose to her feet. "Eli Spider," she added and yanked the life from the body he had stolen.

The body hit the floor with a heavy thud. The collar from her neck fell away. Five more followed, from the necks of the mistress and the girls in the workshop.

Mistress Oblana's eyes were wild with horror as she stared at the shriveled corpse of a man possessed by Aeon-Rah. Nor did the mistress raise her face to see the girls freed by his death flee her workshop.

"You …" the mistress gasped and staggered away from her. "It was you …"

By tomorrow, everyone would know she was the Rogue Mage. With that realization came deep relief. Her fate had been decided. She could not hide anymore, could not run from what she was.

The mistress recoiled as Elika walked past her, down the stairs, and out the door of the shop. Outside, she kept walking. The wind swirled around her. *I know what you've done*, it whispered. A hooded shadow appeared in the mouth of an alley. She ignored it, feeling numb save where the mage had beaten her and the burning bruises around her bare throat. Then the shadow vanished, and the wind stilled.

Shoran was right. She had allowed herself to be punished. For the pain in her flesh masked the greater pain in her soul for all she had lost, all she had done, and all she had hoped to be.

Without thinking, she picked the pocket of a merchant carrying rolls of cloth to his wagon. Then she picked another pocket, and another. She was a thief. She would always be a thief. She had hoped for more, to do better, yet why fight who she was. Liffy was right to steal from her. She was right to set herself free no matter the price. A part of her was proud of Liffy. If the girl had not robbed her, Mistress Oblana would have found a way to take more and more until Elika's freedom was as vague a dream as her being a queen. Were she to see Liffy, she would not demand her worthless coppers back. More than those wretched tokens of her labors now filled her pockets. Yet a deeper sense of grief told her that she had lost something worth far more than those coins.

She picked another pocket. There were plenty of rich pouches around this city. Aye, Rory was right. Streets were her life, her freedom. Not futile servitude with no hope of escape. She stuck her hand into another pocket, deftly taking out a silver coin and pocketing it just as swiftly.

Her feet took her past Maj-Blackfly's house. She stopped when she saw it, for it was nothing but a burned-out shell. No one knew what had happened to him, save that one night he was gone, and the magic with him. Might be he had run away with Liffy, as they had dreamed. Elika hoped that was their fate, and she walked away without looking back.

She took a few turns until she found a perfect place to leap, climb and jump onto the roofs, using a gutter pipe, balconies and window ledges. When she was there, her heart finally slowed. She sat on the roof and gazed over the world before her. She had a new life to forge, and that in itself was more freeing than the loss of her enslaving collar.

Above the city, Reval's island continued to spin. It was upside down again, yet shapes moved through the gardens of the palace as if they did not know it.

A flash of gold drew her gaze towards the harbor. There, a giant ship with four masts and golden sails rose above the roofs of the warehouses. And those sails were flames of hope, beckoning her closer. Her feet replied and moved towards them, until she saw the grand ship being readied for departure.

It did not look like a common trading ship. The crew were neatly dressed in uniform and the captain watched the harbor restlessly, as one might when waiting for an important guest. A fancy emblem of an unfamiliar noble house was painted in gold onto the hull. Above it, were the symbols of their language that she could not read. She knew not why, but suddenly she wanted to read those letters, wanted to know where that ship sailed and why. Might be she could sneak aboard and see where it took her.

There was a vast world out there. The world she knew nothing about. Her whole life she had dreamt of seeing the lands beyond Terren and imagined visiting the cities of tales that had once crowned the kingdom of Seramight. Those cities they once thought lost were here and prospering, and within her reach. She wanted to sail to the edge of their world and gaze upon the Sea of Fire and the cursed lands of ragged mountains where even the tsaren dared not venture.

Excited crowds began to gather around the ship, as more and more folk converged on the streets. Elika grew curious and waited with them until she saw the cause of the commotion.

A procession came into view, bearing the same colors flown by the ship. Magnificent horses carried fine lords in shining armor. They rode slowly, allowing the folk around them to feast upon their majesty and dazzling glory. At the front, the captain of the procession held a white banner with an ice-laced crown on it. Behind him, atop a great black stallion rode a majestic lord with a velvet mantle over his shoulders. For a moment, Elika forgot to breathe. Mite. The man in a royal cloak, riding like a king of old among his people was Mite.

He looked more handsome than she remembered, and she desperately searched his features for the boy who had left her by the bridge. The boy who had slept on the floor with the rest of them and fought and stole and killed to keep them safe. But there was no trace of that boy. Instead, the lord riding past was colder, harder, his eyes staring straight ahead as if nothing around him mattered.

"Northwind! Northwind!" the crowd chanted feverishly.

"Northwind!" the women shouted and threw flowers at him.

"Northwind!" Daes and Alterrians alike, united at last in their cries of adulation.

Yet he saw them not, acknowledged not the rapturous crowd. He had aged beyond his years, and lines of bitterness were etched upon his youthful features.

Oh, Mite, what happened to you?

I will wait for you on the other side. His words so fervently spoken. Empty words, unwitting lies and childish dreams. The son of the nobleman had always been an imposter in the world of orphans and street gangs, whether or not he thought himself to be so.

The purpose seeded in your blood will never ebb. It will grow until it consumes you.

Mite could no more escape his fate than she could hers. This magnificent stranger, proud, tall and strong, was not Mite, but Prince Aeronmite Northwind, the heir of the Sacred Crowns. Sadness engulfed her for him, for them all, for the Fates that could not be fought.

On his hand that held the reins a blue stone flashed in the sunlight, and even from up here, she recognized the ring he had given her in that other life. The ring she had given to Penny in turn to return to him. Her gaze fixed on it. He had seen Penny, which meant she was alive, and he knew where she was.

The thought died abruptly, as Elika's gaze shifted to the rider beside Mite. A beautiful lady, with dark hair, jewels and a glorious blue dress. The outer skirt of her silken gown was fashioned from the web that Elika had spun with her own hands. The woman's eyes kept darting to Mite, her smile mysterious, the type of smile a woman bestowed on her lover.

Elika looked down at her rough, blistered hands. Nothing like the lady's hands. He was a prince and she a bastard of unknown parentage, an orphan, a thief, a wild, untamed street urchin with no manners to speak of. She imagined herself riding beside him.

The court and the gathered crowds would have laughed at him and at her.

The slow clip clopping of hooves as they rode past filled her ears.

Her fingers rolled into fists.

The image in the mirror Shoran had shown her flashed in her mind, a cruel taunt of everything she was not and could never be. She imagined being that woman, coming to stand before Mite, showing him that she, too, was more than she appeared, showing him that she could have been that woman riding beside him, and that he had made a mistake in leaving her behind. She imagined the regret in his eyes ...

And it gave her no joy, only sadness and grief.

She moved to follow the procession and the weight of her pockets, filled with stolen loot, dispersed the image of that queen. The image she had seen in the mirror vanished. It was replaced by an image of her future—aged before her years, living on the streets, a thief, a bitter maid, a murderer, fighting off letches and nursing an unwanted babe.

No! Elika pushed that image aside. She would not be that woman. She would be more. Seeing Mite now, she realized that she could never accept that fate for herself.

The procession reached the ship, and Mite dismounted from his horse. He reached up and assisted the young lady from her own. Behind her, an older man bearing the same emblem as the ship, watched the two of them closely, like a father intent on a match.

Then a red-haired man in the guard's uniform she recognized, pushed through the crowd towards Mite. They clasped hands like old friends and spoke in lowered voices. She had seen them together before at the docks, and knew they were close. Mite patted him on the shoulder and the red-haired man nodded and left.

Another figure tore her gaze from them, and her heart shook with the sense of betrayal. Pebble. Alive and clearly excited about the journey ahead as he watched the procession from the deck of the giant ship. For so many days she had lost herself in worry for the minstrel, convinced that he was dead, or imprisoned in a grimy dungeon. Yet there he was, with a shiny new lute over his shoulder, striding towards Mite, whilst gazing at the horizon as if it was a pot of honey.

He whispered something in Mite's ear and received a nod in reply. Then Mite offered his arm to the young woman. She took it graciously, the perfect image of a shy, blushing bride, as he led her aboard the ship.

Pebble turned suddenly, as if Elika had summoned him, and his gaze rose to the roofs and lingered on her. She had been unkind to him the last time they had parted, and she had come to regret it.

He pushed his way through the crowd towards her, and she left the roofs to meet him on the ground. In the sea of heads, it was easy to find the giant who loomed above them.

"I thought Shoran had killed you," she said resentfully. "Might be he should have," she added with a pang of hurt.

Pebble was clearly taken aback. "Why would he kill me?"

"You told me he'd tear you apart limb by limb."

"I'm a minstrel. I'm prone to spinning dramatic tales," he said apologetically then rubbed his shoulder. "Though he almost did when he caught up with me."

"Why didn't you come to find me? I thought you dead."

He scratched his head, looking abashed. "Shoran was very angry with me. He said I was indulging your foolishness, and that I should have sent word to him as soon as I knew of your existence. He was right, of course." Pebble could not meet her eye and she saw more in his avoidance than he dared speak.

"You betrayed me. You told him where to find me."

His face grew haunted. "We spoke. He asked me questions, many of which I didn't know the answers. And aye, I told him what I could. Shoran has a way of asking that twists your tongue into telling the truth."

She knew it well enough herself. "So you've been hiding from me."

He rubbed the back of his neck. "Not exactly ... I was ... busy," he said evasively. His gaze to the ship betrayed him. "I cannot help you anymore, princess. He forbade me anywhere near you. Forbade me to even sing of the Rogue Mage."

"And you do everything he tells you to do?"

"Aye," he said with a frown as if she asked a foolish question. "We are his people."

"His people?" she echoed and recalled the way Tane Rosalina spoke of Shoran. "What do you owe him?"

Pebble's face grew serious. "A thousand years ago, the mages decided to massacre the tanes. All of them. The mageguard, led by Archmage Wisestar, would have succeeded, save that Shoran intervened. He saved my kind from extinction and laid claim to every tane. We are now under his protection. He is ... our king, you might say. Though he rarely asks anything of us."

She recalled one of Bill's stories from long ago, of the dark age in which the tsaren turned their backs on the slaughter of their bastard half-breed children. Though the humans tried to stop it, the mages were too powerful and too determined to destroy every tane in the land.

"Why would the mages kill the children of the tsaren?" she asked, bewildered. "And why would the tsaren allow it?"

He flinched at her question and seemed afraid to look at her. "You truly do not know what we are?" Pebble shifted on the spot, looking embarrassed. "He said as much. But I thought perhaps ..." He shook his head and looked aside. "'Tis why you do not hate us. But one day you will, tsarina, when you realize what is denied you, what is denied all the tsaren and the Laifae." There was anguish in his voice.

"Pebble ..." she began gently.

"Please, ask me no more of it, for I would not have our parting mired with your disgust and contempt. We are their children, but not as they would wish us. 'Tis all I'll say on the matter. Today, when the sea rises again I must leave on that ship. Shoran gave me another task, one which promises me songs to last the ages."

"You're going with Northwind." She gazed towards the grand, gold sails. "What are you up to, Pebble? What is Shoran up to?"

"I am accompanying the prince and Duke Warwind to Ilikan's court. Prince Southfire and Reval banished Northwind from the city. They would have had him killed, but half the dukes threatened rebellion and war if the heir to the Sacred Crowns was murdered."

"You know … Aeronmite," she said as a river of questions rose in her mind about him but could not find voice.

Pebble smiled sadly. "I know him, and I know he'd do better without echoes from his past crossing his path."

So he knew of hers and Mite's past. She wondered how much Mite had told him.

"What's the name of the ship?" she asked. For some reason, it seemed to matter.

"*War Wind*. Named after the duke who owns it."

"Pebble, why are you truly going with him?"

"Because he is another fool who needs my help, and Shoran needs me to watch him. Besides, what minstrel would miss the beginnings of the greatest song of our age."

"I need your help, too," she said a little resentfully.

"I can no longer help you, tsarina. Nor do you need me. You have another guarding you now."

She had no one, but there was no use trying to convince him. "What's Mite going to do?" she asked instead.

"Northwind plans to return a king. That's the purpose of his journey. He will take Terren by force if need be."

A pang of pride hit her for Mite. Men needed a king to protect them, and there was no one better than him. Aye, she saw them today, Daes and Alterrians united in their cry for the return of the human king. He was their true flame of hope. Mite would be the city's savior. The Rogue Mage was dividing them, whilst Northwind was uniting them. If anyone could get the city to rise against the mages, it was he. Aye, men would follow Mite. The realization sent shards of understanding through her, and she saw with unshakable clarity, her purpose.

"My task is not yet done," she echoed her thought.

Pebble breathed out. "There's only one thing you need to do."

"What's that?" she asked with a frown, wondering if she betrayed her thoughts.

"Nothing. Do nothing, princess. Do not use your magic. Forget your foolish quest to kill every mage in the city. Everything's different now. There's Northwind. This city is rightfully his, and he will claim it one day."

But doing nothing was not a choice she could make. She would help Mite any way she could. He shall be king. She'd make certain of it. Until he returned as king, she could not abandon men to the mercies of mages, not when she had the power to help them.

But first, she had to find Penny. "If you know Mite, then you must know Penny. I know they've met."

"Ah, the beauty with the hair spun of fire. She has crossed my path a time or two. Had a few unladylike things to say to Aeronmite." His chest rumbled with laughter. "Never seen the prince so abashed in the presence of a woman."

"I need to find her."

Pebble bowed dramatically. "Then let it be my last gift to you, princess. She lives on Silver Tree Side, the house with green curtains. But for now, great songs await to be discovered, and I must find them. Look for my return and I shall share them with you."

And she watched him stride to the ship, towards Mite, never once looking back.

A short time later, sailors finished loading the ship with crates and barrels for the long journey. A white-tipped crow landed atop the mast and cawed loudly, as if it was also excited by the adventure ahead. No one paid it any mind.

As the sea rose, she still stood there, watching the ship carrying Mite and Pebble, and the damned bird, too, set sail for distant lands. It sailed under Reval's island in the sky, and further still towards the southern horizon.

When she could no longer see its golden sails in the dusky sky, she left the harbor and made her way to Silver Tree Side.

CHAPTER FIFTEEN

The Debt

"When the realms of Alafraysia and Seramight merged, the tsaren reformed themselves into the earthly form to be found as babes by the humans. The foolish men mistook the babes for the sacred children of the gods. So is it any wonder that once our glorious tsaren learned of this misunderstanding, they continued to allow humans to believe it? For centuries, the tsaren travelled the lands and gathered worshipers amongst mankind. The most loyal of those offered themselves to be merged with the Laifae, to give rise to us, the mageguards. The illusion was destroyed when Reval attacked the Sacred Crowns. Never again, since the Sundering wars, have men offered themselves freely to allow our kind a body with which to explore their world."

The History of Alafraysia and Seramight,
By Mageguard Bluelight

Behind the heavy green curtains of a stately house, moved the shadow of a woman's shape, outlined by the light of a bright lantern. Elika would know that shape anywhere. As a child, she had spent countless hours watching Penny move about their hideout amongst the pack of hungry orphans.

Seeing her now, Elika could not bring her feet to take those last few steps across the streets towards the door with cheerful flower pots beside it. Were she to take those steps, her lonely, aching heart would surely never let her leave again. So, she savored the warm sight of that which she could not have and allowed herself to be soothed by the relief that Penny and the children were safe.

Anten had done well for them. It was not a large house, sheltered in a quiet street of many such. Silver Tree Side in the Temple District bordered the palace grounds. In this part of the city, lived honest folk, who served and traded with the palace and the many temples nearby. The Sachi built humble temples for every god they worshipped. There were old temples for the tsaren, grand and audacious in design, where priests and priestesses spent their lives praying for mercy from the great powers that caused untold destruction on some whim or spite. There were other, lesser temples which worshipped not gods, but knowledge and wisdom and Fates. Those were for scholars who spent their days rereading old scrolls and thinking upon things that did not matter to the hungry, sick or desperate. Elika always thought scholars to be children of indulgence, an idle body, and an easy life.

Across the street, she watched Anten return home, dressed in the suit of a clerk, carrying a stack of leather-bound parchment in one hand and a scriber's case in the other. His fingers were ink-stained. He did not wear a mage's collar, and that eased every fear she had been nursing in her heart for Penny and the children. When he opened the door, delighted screams greeted him, Rosy Rose's voice amongst them. There was a flash of a pretty blue dress and the door closed again.

Elika would have left them in peace. They were not the pack she had left long ago. Their story had ended at the Bridge and began anew in this world. She would have walked away, content in the knowledge that they were safe and well. But if she had found them, then Rory would too. He had given her until summer, which was here already if the ripeness of plums and the flowering of the blacknut tree were anything to go by. Penny had to be warned. Yet shame held Elika back.

Aye, she was ashamed to bring the past to their door, ashamed of what she had become. Ashamed that she had not tried to find them without Rory's threats. But there was no avoiding this.

Taking a deep breath, she strode towards the door, raised her hand to knock, and froze as Penny's laughter rang out.

Elika tightened her fist and knocked loudly.

The laughter stopped. The door opened.

In the light of the oil lamps, Penny's hair shimmered like fire.

For a moment Penny just stared as if she did not recognize her, then her eyes widened. "Eli?"

Elika tried to smile. "Hey, Penny."

Suddenly, she was being crushed to Penny's chest. A hand stroked her hair. "You made it across. You came." Penny pulled away and frowned as her gaze roamed over the bruise on Elika's cheek, and on her neck where Aeon-Rah had tried to strangle her.

"Said I'd follow, didn't I?"

Anten appeared behind Penny. "Oh, you're here. Good. We're just about to sit down for dinner." He said it blandly, as if Elika had never left, then turned and walked away. "Got wine if you want some," he threw over his shoulder.

"Prefer port myself," she flung back and couldn't help but smile.

"Come inside," Penny said. "You look … hungry. Are you living on the streets? 'Cause there's no need. Now that you are here, there's a bed for you."

Elika stepped inside just as three small, well-fed faces appeared in the lounge door, eyeing her warily. Chelik was amongst them—healthy, happy, clean and well-dressed. *Damn Rory*, she thought. The boy did not belong in his father's world. Like the others, he had grown since she last saw them.

"I thought you were dead," said Chelik.

Rosy Rose has grown more than the others. Her form was now long and slim. She wore blue and silver feathers in her hair, and on her shoulder, perched a glorious and haughty bird, the owner of those feathers.

"You must have dinner with us," Penny said.

Elika shook her head abruptly, refusing to follow. She stared at the tiled floor, for it was too hard to look at Penny. "I … I need to talk to you," she said and her eyes inadvertently darted back to Chelik.

Penny saw, stilled, and her pale eyes turned to ice. Then she smiled and said with forced cheer. "Very well, let us speak alone by the fire."

She led the way to a small guestroom along the hall and closed the door behind them, then sat on the settee. "Sit, Eli," she said in that way of hers, which made every kid in their pack jump to do her bidding.

So Elika did as she was told. For a moment, she tried to find the words to speak. "You've done well for yourselves," she said, if only to ease the tension between them.

"Anten got himself work with the priests in Reval's temple. He's transcribing old records onto fresh parchment before they crumble away completely. They give us enough to live comfortably. There is a spare room upstairs …" She stopped, seeing the refusal in Elika's face.

"How are the children?" Elika asked before the silence deepened.

Penny told her that Rosy Rose took her studies with the Winged Folk, who gave her a young bird of her own. The old woman, Edna, had been teaching her how to collect its feathers, when to do so and how to fashion beautiful charms.

"Rosy Rose sells her feathers and charms at the market with Edna," Penny added proudly. "Chelik is Anten's apprentice. He's helping him to scribe and reorder old documents so they can be found easily by priests. Timmy has apprenticed himself with a blacksmith. Says he wants to make weapons for Northwind's army." As Penny said that, something caught in her voice and her gaze sharpened on Elika.

A look passed between them, in which Elika answered Penny's unasked question. Aye, they both knew who Northwind was.

"Penny, I'm sorry. I'd not intrude upon your happiness …"

"You are family, Eli, and always will be."

Elika gave her a small smile. "I'm here about Chelik."

Penny stiffened again. "One-Eyed Rory. Is that where your bruises came from?" she asked with the steely calm that would have terrified anyone who knew Eight Dagger Duggie's daughter.

"Don't go looking for your knives, Penny." Elika smiled faintly. "Had a run-in with a mage who tried to make an example of me to the others. He's dead now and I'm free."

Penny nodded. "Good."

"Rory wants his son," Elika said flatly.

"He can't have him. Chelik is ours now."

"'Tis what I told him. But Rory wants to see him, to make sure he's safe. I owe him, Penny. He entrusted Chelik to me."

Penny considered that. Then fear flicked in her eyes, before vanishing again behind an impassive expression. "How did you find us?"

"Not through Rory. He doesn't know where you are. He's been tearing the city apart looking for me and Chelik. I told him Chelik crossed with you. I won't tell him where you are, but it's only a matter of time before he tracks you himself."

"How did you find us, Eli?" Penny repeated in a cold voice.

"Pebble. He told me."

That set Penny aback. "Oh … and Mite?"

Elika shook her head. "Have not spoken with him."

"He doesn't know you crossed."

"No. Don't want him to either."

Penny looked troubled. "Mite came to see us."

"You mean Prince Northwind," Elika said and cringed at the harshness of her voice.

"He wasn't a prince when he found me, but captain of the Northern Bastion. One that overlooks the bridge," she added, as if it held some meaning. "I gave him the ring."

Elika nodded. "It was his. Did you know … about his past? Has he ever spoken to you about it?"

"Mite never spoke of where he came from. But when I first met him, I had my suspicions that he was fed with a golden spoon as a babe." Penny went quiet, as if waiting for her to say something more. When Elika didn't, she said abruptly, "He asked after you."

Oddly, Elika's heart hardened at that. "I dare say he asked after all of us, all the ones who didn't make it."

"I told him you were … dead," Penny said blandly, yet Elika saw a slight wince. "When the bridge vanished … we thought you stayed behind. No one saw you cross."

No one looked. No one waited.

"I understand. Don't berate yourself, Penny. It matters not whether Mite thinks me alive or dead. He set sail tonight for other lands. He's gone." Again, Elika's heart morphed to stone. "Don't tell him I'm alive. I don't want him to know."

"Do not judge where judgment is not due. Mite is not to blame for anything that happened."

Elika could not find it in her to agree.

"Eli … I think you need to speak with him. Find him. He'll want to see you. When he learned you were dead —"

"No," Elika interrupted sharply. Then said more gently, "I have another life now. As does he. He has his own battles to fight. And I have mine."

Penny looked aside, saddened. "I fear you may come to regret your anger."

"We need to decide what to do about Chelik. If Rory sees he's well and prospering, he might let you keep him. I'll try to convince him."

Penny pondered this, but remained unconvinced. Elika could see it in the grim set to her lips. "Speak with Rory and arrange to meet in Daetown, just the three of us and Chelik. No one else."

"I'll tell him," Elika said and noticed that Penny did not wear a bloodstone ring on her finger. "I thought you'd be wed to Anten by now."

A shadow fell over Penny's face, and hurt, so much hurt. "Anten's wife is alive," she said dully and looked into her lap at her hands.

Elika suddenly recalled that Anten's wife had taken his babe across the bridge. The babe died, but his wife reached the other side. But at the time, many believed there was only death to be found there … or rather here, on this side.

"Oh, Penny … I'm sorry."

Only death could break the bond forged before the witness of the gods and sealed with blood.

Penny smiled, a little bitterly. "It took us a while to realize it, too. I'd not care, only that it's sometimes hard to look at him and know there's a woman out there with a greater claim to him than me. Anten pretends it does not matter, but I see the shadow in his eyes."

"Can you be sure she's still living?"

"I tracked her down. She's alive and newly wedded to a rich merchant, for she believes herself to be a widow. Her crime before the gods is through ignorance and innocence. They will not punish her. But us ... we know."

"It doesn't matter ..." Elika began but was stopped by the crying of a babe.

Penny closed her eyes as the sound drew closer. And Elika realized the true tragedy of it all.

Anten walked in cradling a babe with round eyes and short red hair, just like Penny's. "She's hungry," he said

Penny was instantly on her feet, taking the infant from his arms. "This is little Eli," she said. "We named her after you."

Elika was speechless. Then she saw something that chilled her blood. The babe wore a collar. Elika clenched her jaw. "Who's the mage who claimed her?"

Penny's smile vanished. "Chelik had enough coins, given to him by his father, to buy his own freedom, and Timmy's too. Anten bought mine first, then worked to buy his own and Rosy's. We'll buy Eli's freedom, too, before she's old enough to be placed with a master."

"Babes are born free," Elika said. "You shouldn't have to pay for it."

"Mage Aeon-Stonefish is not a cruel man," Penny said. "And don't look at me like that, Eli. We'll earn her freedom before she is of age to work."

Elika gritted her teeth. "I'll kill him."

Penny's expression shuttered. "If I wanted him dead, I'd kill him myself. Stonefish gives us no trouble. Nor does he demand that I work for him on Eli's behalf. Were he to die, another mage would take his place, one who won't be so accommodating."

Elika said nothing, noting how the bruising on her neck still burned. And it became hard to look at the babe with the collar around her neck which the mage could use to strangle her when the mood took him.

Penny must have seen those thoughts, for she hugged the babe tighter.

The babe with red hair was one of their pack now, and Elika knew that as long as she breathed, she'd continue the fight for them. Damn Shoran and his threats. She'd unravel every mage if it meant never seeing another human babe with a slave collar.

But then, Blood Dog was right. She needed only to unravel one to save thousands. Tomorrow, she would go after the one who made them all. She'd go after the archmage, and she would help Mite restore the world to rights.

~

Elika waited as Rory paced beside his desk, whilst a young, nervous-looking priest scribbled on a parchment.

"Lord Merilan ..." Rory chewed it on his tongue, as if tasting the flavor. "It sounds too ... soft."

The late Lord Snowstorm's residence was a large mansion with stables at the back. When his lady and son fled the city for their country manor, they left everything behind, including horses, terrified servants, and their household priest. He was as slim as a sausage, with narrow shoulders and a boyishly smooth jaw.

"My lord," the priest began anxiously. "House Merilan is the only noble house which has no known living contestants. No one will dispute your claim."

Rory stopped pacing and turned to the scribe. "No one will take a lord with a name like *Merilan* seriously when he stands next to Northwind or Warwind. Now that's a name I could wear. Warwind. What do you think, Spit?" He turned to her. "Does Merilan sound majestic or frightening or awe-inspiring?"

She shook her head.

"See, a street urchin knows more than you do, priest. Now stop quivering like a maid in a brothel and go back to your books. You told me the library upstairs had the complete lineage of noble houses. So go through it again until you find me a name that will send fear into the hearts of warriors."

"Of course, my lord." The priest hurriedly gathered the parchment on the table. "It may take time ... so many houses have come and gone … and the recent records from the Otherside are missing altogether. If you would but permit me to return to the temple … I might be able to …"

"Escape?" Rory said mildly.

"No, my lord. I would never —"

"I pay you well, do I not?"

"You are very generous, my lord." He bowed as he spoke.

"And I need a scribe I can trust."

"I am honored to serve you."

Rory waved him away. "Your sniveling is making me itch to throw you out the window. You have three days to bring me a name and title deeds."

The priest bowed and fled the room.

Rory turned to her. "Now, Spit. It's been so long since you've come to see me, I was beginning to suspect you don't like me." He did not look as if he wanted to murder her, which was a small relief.

"Been busy, that's all, looking for Penny and your son," she replied dryly. "In this vast ocean of a city."

"Seeing as you are here and cocky, I suspect you found them. I was not relishing cutting you to pieces." Then his gaze dropped to her neck. "Am I to assume Aeon-Rah's dead, then?"

She shrugged. "Something must have got him. Nothing to do with me. Matters not to us anyhow. We had a deal, and I kept my side of it. Found your son. He's alive and well, and free."

Rory walked to the bar and poured himself half a tumbler of rum, sat behind his desk, and threw his feet on top of it. "Then why is he not standing here with you?"

"He's happy, Rory. Anten is doing well for them."

"As well as me?" He spread his hands over the lavish study that had once belonged to Lord Snowstorm.

"Can you give him mother's love?" she bit back. "Your son lacks for nothing. Penny loves him as her own."

"So, Penny refuses to return him. Claimed him as her own and sent you back to me to negotiate a meeting, to let me see for myself."

"When you gave him to me, you told me you didn't want him to be like us. He's not seen such things as we have. Things that we do. He need never see such things."

Rory studied the color of his drink, turning it in the light, this way and that. He took a sip and savored it before swallowing. "Kelpian Rum, from the Maysea Islands in Meramer. The best this world has to offer. Trouble is, this rum belongs to Ilikan. The tsarin controls the islands, and no one can sell a drop of it without his permission."

"Then where did you get it?"

"Fished twelve barrels of it from the sunken ship Reval destroyed. Lost three men doing it too. Drowned, poor sots. Do ye know how much twelve barrels are worth? A hundred gold pieces." He went silent, waiting for her to absorb his words and everything they signified. That much gold could buy the freedom of half the city. "Aye, I see you understand. That's enough gold to buy the freedom of ten thousand men. Enough gold to buy an army."

"What do you need with an army, Rory? All those men to feed and clothe and their families too."

"Every nobleman needs his own army. And an heir to follow 'im."

"You're not noble born."

He toyed with the feather of the quill the priest had left behind. "Oh, but I am, at least as far as the deeds to the titles will show. 'Tis what matters. And when Northwind returns, he'll back my claim."

"Why would Northwind back you?" Elika asked with a frown. Mite and Rory only ever showed mutual tolerance and grudging respect for each other in the old city. Neither liked the other.

Rory smiled knowingly. "Mite and I have become reacquainted recently. He's changed, ye know. Rather grim and miserable. Heartbroken, I'd say. Maybe one of his ladyloves tired of him roaming around the city."

Elika refused to show any reaction, despite her heart flipping over in her chest. Aye, that was Mite, though she'd never known him to be heartbroken over his ladyloves.

"See, if we're to do business together, we need to be frank with each other, Spit."

"Name's Eli," she said. "Might be we'll start with that."

"Gone up in the world, out Little Mitey has. Struck me hard in the gut it did, to learn that he was Lord Silvering's heir and we never knew. It's a good thing Pockets is dead. I'd hate to think what he'd make of that. Did ye know, Mite was Northwind?"

"Found out only after he left. None of us knew. What does it matter, anyhow?"

Rory sipped the rum. "At the moment, it doesn't. Only that me and him had a nice long talk, spoke of many things such as how we might take back the city. Oh, and I know it wasn't Mite who's been killing them mages, but *you*."

Elika forced herself to chuckle. "You think too highly of me, then."

"I thought we agreed to be honest with each other, El," he said coolly. "Had my suspicions as soon as I saw ye. I mightn't be able to read, but I'm not a fool. I've seen your power in the old city. Saw your magic tear them golden gates apart for Pockets' rebellion. And I've heard of what Mite can do, being of the Sacred Crown blood. The magic they wield is different to the one *you* wield. So I thought to buy you from Aeon-Rah, and thus test you. If you're the Rogue, then you'd likely kill him before he sold ye to me. And if not, then I'd still have your magic in my ranks."

"And if it was me?"

"If it was you, then we can do very well for each other. Pockets was right about the benefits of having a mage on our side. This world as it is doesn't suit us. None of us wanted to be here, on this side of the bridge, but the Blight drove us this way, anyway. It's time we took Terren back."

Elika ran her hands through her hair. "Rory, there's something you don't understand about the Blight —"

"I don't need to understand anything about it. I only need to wrestle the control of the streets from them bastards, whilst Mite goes and plays king. And might be he'll return with an army, as he promised. And when he does, I'll add my own to his. For this, he'll anoint my lordship, give me lands, and make me the overlord of any part of Terren I choose. And I get to have a place in his court."

Elika regarded him wearily. Mite made a deal with Rory? She just could not see it. "Why would he come to you?"

"Because he has too few friends, especially those who know the streets and can gather Daes to his cause. Terren is a fortified fortress that can withstand any attack from the outside. So he needs an army on the inside as well, one he can trust to stand with him. And he can't trust the Alterrians."

"Nothing wrong with being ambitious, but I'm not one of your men, Rory, and I'll never join your gang. I'm only here about Chelik."

He considered her. "What do you want, Spit? You'll be well looked after, and you'll get the creamy share of all plunder. Might be King Mitey will make you a grand lady, too."

"I'm done with the streets. Want to do better for myself. But might be I could help you in exchange for one thing."

"I'm listening."

"I'll kill the archmage. He's the only one who truly stands between Northwind and Terren. He's the only one besides the tsaren who can make the mages. I destroy him, and the city is without the one man who can crush Northwind's ambition. No more majren coming out those temple doors."

Rory was no fool. He knew she offered him the one thing both he and Mite needed to take this city.

"And in return, ye want what?" he asked, though she could tell he already knew.

"I want you to leave Chelik and Penny alone. Let Penny raise Chelik. Might be when you're a true lord with your own keep, someone important in Northwind's court, you can show him what you are and give him a choice. Or might be you'll find yourself a fine lady and have more sons. True heirs to your name. The nobles have this thing about bastards, see?"

He swirled the last of his rum. "Always liked you, Spit. If only my scribe had your gut. These blasted priests are worse than wailing babes. Tell Penny to bring Chelik to Dune Ash Street tomorrow at midday. I'll keep my distance, for now. But I want to see for myself that he's well. You kill the archmage, and I'll let Penny keep Chelik … until he's of age." He flung his feet off the table and leant towards her. "Now, I want to show you something. As a gesture of our friendship and newfound honesty between us."

He rose and bade her follow him through the mansion, past colorful guestrooms and richly decorated hallways, down the wide, spiraling stairway and into the windowless underground level of bare stone rooms. Lanterns burned intermittently along the walls, keeping the cellar gloomy and eerie. Most of it was used as food storage with rows of wine barrels.

Two guards were rolling dice beside a narrow stair. The older one was fleecing the younger lad of all the miserly possessions in his pockets.

Rory opened another door into a corridor lined with windowless prison cells, and the stench of blood hit her. Her body recoiled. The tingling on her skin warned her there was more here than blood. She hesitated on the threshold of what was more like a dank dungeon than a cellar.

"What's down there?"

"Come and see. I think you'll be pleased." His lips stretched into a parody of a smile. "But of course, it must affect you just like *them*."

Elika did not miss his sly insinuation. Always on the streets, there were "*us*" and "*them*" who were not to be trusted.

"Not a friendly thing to say now, is it, Rory? Thought we agreed to be friends."

"But we are," he replied smoothly.

She did not believe him. Still, she followed him, keeping her hand close to her knife and her magic at the ready. Wine barrels gave way to barrels of blood-salt stacked three high along the wall. Her skin tingled painfully, like needles stabbing her everywhere at once.

Rory stopped outside a prison cell and looked through the bars, his face hard and merciless. Tied to a wooden rack was a naked man, moaning and groaning, unaware of their presence. His tortured body was painted in blood ... no, not blood, but blood-salt.

"Why?" she asked with breathless horror. "Just kill him."

Rory might be cruel, but she'd never known him to take pleasure in another's torment.

He gazed dispassionately at the mage. "I know what they are, El. I suspect you do, too. This one was once one of my men. Flint Finger, we called him. Cunning bastard and loyal. He'd do anything for you if you asked. He's dead now, yet his body remains. The creature in him doesn't know who we are. He doesn't recognize any of us. Calls himself Silverstar. We pored blood-salt down his throat, yet it didn't kill him. He throws it up and screams. So we tried to drown him in it, and still, he lives. The last mage, we disemboweled, cut off his head and limbs, and still magic poured out of him, and his limbs moved, whilst his head stared at us and silent pleas came from his broken mouth. We thought the only way to kill them without using magic was to burn these abominations alive. But then we discovered another way." He opened the door of the cell, strode forward, and picked up a red crystal dagger on the table beside the rack.

The mage's eyes grew wide with terror.

"Rory ... I can end him ... don't ..."

He stuck the dagger in the mage's chest.

Elika flinched and looked aside, feeling sick.

The mage screamed, writhed and shook. His body arched, but the ties held him down. On and on it went.

"He's not dying. Stop it," she said, keeping her voice as calm as she could, though inside she, too, was screaming.

"Wait. It takes a little time to work ..."

The mage moaned and wept and pleaded in the silence Rory's words left behind. She reached for the mage's essence and pulled on the strings of his life. His moans stopped.

"There, see? He's dead," said Rory.

The body was finally still, the corpse it left behind was grey and bruised, and stank of rotting flesh.

"We learned a lot from this bastard about his kind and their realm, Alafraysia," Rory said, whilst still staring at the body. "He claimed it was not their fault our two realms merged. He didn't know why they did. Said only the gods had the power to make it happen." Rory turned away from the mage and faced her. "When

I heard the mages were being found dead with not a mark on their bodies, I wanted the Rogue to be one of my men. Didn't realize that was you at the time. Only after I saw you did I piece everything together. Aye, you used their magic to help the rebellion. I saw ye. Others saw the same dark magic tearing through the roofs of the houses on Rift Street. Funny, this thing, you being the Rogue. Magic killing magic."

"Like men killing men," she replied dryly.

"The Rogue Mage inspired us, see?"

"I don't think you needed inspiration."

"Like you, we've been hunting them in their beds. The city is ours, El. The Daes are lining up for their red daggers. The mages try to attack us, but we push them back." He strode to a barrel beside a wall and opened it. "Did you know that blood-salt is illegal in Seramight, by Syn'Moreg's decree?"

The barrel was filled to the top with red crystals.

Elika flinched. "Rory, you can't use it. The Blight ... it was caused by blood-salt."

"Why would it cause the Blight?" he asked dismissively.

"I don't know. Ask the priests or the mages. Only know what I saw. If you destroy magic, you destroy everything else that's living."

"I think you got it all wrong, El. Besides, what choice do we have? Allow them to enslave us, kill us, possess our dead bodies until no more men remain? I'd sooner see our world destroyed than give them another piece of it. We'll be taking it back. Northwind will be king, and then he'll deal with the tsaren."

"And Syn'Moreg?" she asked.

"And him, too. Even the gods can be killed."

And her too, he left unsaid, but she heard it anyway, saw the way he regarded her with equal coolness as he did the dead mage.

"Had enough death for today, Rory. Got things I need to get on with." She turned on her heel to leave the horror beneath his mansion.

"Don't forget to kill the archmage, now will you, Spit?" he said as she walked away, and she felt him watching her leave.

~

The night was draped in the salty balm of the sea. It was peaceful up here on the roofs, under the gaze of the moon and the silent stars. For a long time, Elika watched Reval's island turn and turn as it circled the city. And she drifted to sleep to the forlorn songs of his guards as they searched for Arala, and the dark chanting of Syn'Moreg's priests.

She knew not how long she had slept, but the moon was still high when something disturbed her. Even before she opened her eyes, she sensed a presence near and knew who it was. Shoran sat on the edge of the roof, facing away from her, watching the stars. She did not move, and he did not turn to see whether she was awake but spoke to the sky.

"El'Sandria. 'Tis the name of the celestial realm," he spoke in a quiet rumble. "Days there are long and slumbering, and time drifts upon the sea of eternity. There is no night there, only light. Rare are babes in the realm of the gods, and each is precious to them. But time is not kind to their children, for like the gods they do not age, and cannot grow in the realm of light. The gods carry their babes to the Sachi of Elder Valley to be raised. The sacred children are nurtured and worshipped. They want for nothing, suffer no harm. When the babes grow to adulthood, the gods return for them. Always. No babe is ever abandoned. Each one is loved. They take them back to El'Sandria and teach them about their powers and the inviolate laws of Nerasky. 'Tis the name of the Abyss you fear." He tilted his head towards her. "Injustice has been done to you, one the gods will atone for. But only if you do not provoke their wrath."

"I'm not Arala," she said and sat up, wondering why he was telling her the story.

"I know that," he said dryly without turning to look at her.

Elika moved to sit next to him, keeping her distance, yet his warmth still reached her. "Igla tried to convince me I was her. Bill thought she was daft for thinking so. I thought Bill was daft for thinking me to be a tsarina."

Shoran said nothing, but his lips twitched into a beginning of a smile.

"Arala died when she forged the bridge," Elika said.

"'Tis not so. Arala did not perish when she spun the bridge across the Abyss."

"Then she's still alive?" Elika asked as she watched Reval's island draw closer again.

Shoran turned his head, his eyes dark as the night sky, faintly aglow with the light of stars. "Arala is dead," he said and seemed to probe her face for some understanding of that.

She nodded to the island. "Then someone should tell Reval that."

"When he learns the truth of Arala's fate, it will destroy him. And he will destroy in turn." Shoran turned away again and for a while, they sat in silence. Then abruptly, as if embarrassed by it, he placed a cloak in her lap. "'Tis dangerous to look like a runaway servant with no collar. The cloak will make them see you as a wealthy lady."

Elika dug her hands into the feather-soft fabric. The cloak was black, and though thin, it was very warm. She knew not what to make of his gesture. To thank him seemed trifling, and she doubted he wanted that.

"Is it magic?" she asked instead. "Feels warmer than it looks."

His lips quirked. "It was made by human hands, from the down of the Blacksnow Mountain goat." He pointed at the mountains to the west, sundered by the chasm. "See the distant white peak merging with the cloud." She could barely make it out. "There is a tribe of mountain folk living there, the Neareed. You will recognize them by the white furs they wear and the silver sheen to their hair. Every ten years or so, when the winter is mild and spring arrives early, the pass to their lands melts and they bring their trade of wools and furs to Terren."

Elika ran her fingers over the wool. "Don't think I'll ever get used to seeing how many different folk there are living on this side of the chasm," she said wistfully. "All my life I stared at the deadlands. For so long we believed there was no one left alive on this side. It was just us left in the world, in Terren ... our Terren.

To see the lands and men flourishing here …" She shook her head. "It makes me glad … and angry. So many died, fearing to cross. Such a wicked lie …" Again, she shook her head. "Whose magic was it that showed us the lie?"

He said nothing for a long time, and she thought he would not answer. Then he did. "Arala's."

It was the last name she expected. "Why? Why would she do that?"

"Because she was trying to protect a secret," he replied distantly. "Her secret. She needed time, and she needed humans to stay behind a little longer."

His words were an echo from the past. "A tane said that to me once. When my parents took the bridge, she held me back and said I needed to stay back and hold the world together a little longer. I never understood what she spoke of."

He was silent again. Then, "Tell me about your magic."

Elika tensed and met his dark gaze. "It just came to me … after I stabbed the bridge."

He flinched and pain flashed in his gaze before he abruptly looked aside. He ran his hands through his hair. "'Tis a tragedy that will come to haunt you, Aleyala."

"I regretted it," Elika said with a shrug. "After I crossed, that is. The bridge saved my life."

There was another long silence before he spoke again. "What mastery of magic do you favor?"

"You mean what can I do with my magic?"

He nodded slowly.

He seemed genuinely curious, but she knew better than to reveal her weapons. "Might be if you tell me what you can do, I'll tell you what I can do," she said wryly.

He smiled mildly. "I have seen your magic, kitten. 'Tis not what I am asking. What well of power do you draw from?"

"The only sacred well I know is the one we use to cleanse our souls of earthly grime and refresh cloths upon our bodies."

He frowned and looked at her quizzically.

She chuckled. "See? Not so easy to understand cryptic talk. I speak of the water well you find in every courtyard."

A surprised laugh escaped him, a deep rumble which he quickly stifled.

She sighed. "I know nothing of my magic, why I have it, and why it leaves me hungry. Why every time I wish for something it replies, even if I don't truly want it."

"'Tis the well of the Ethereal Essence you draw upon. It is the Laifae's magic, and it is fleeting," he said. But in his face, she saw that he left much unsaid.

"Fleeting but destructive," she said gruffly. "The fire brought to life by magic still burns."

Again, his eyes roamed over her face as if he was trying to understand her. "'Tis fear that gives Laifae magic its power. Their fire holds no heat and does no damage. If you do not fear it, then it will not burn you. But in this realm, if you believe it is real, you will add earthly magic to it and it will burn you as surely as a real fire."

His words echoed the priestesses' teachings in the temple of Arala. *To defeat magic, you must not fear it*, High Priestess Herra had taught them.

Elika took out the stone spider, just to show him. "'Tis not fear that makes the stone move." She wished for the spider to walk on her palm, and so it did.

"'Tis the well of the celestial spirit you tap into now, the most dangerous and destructive of all powers to wield. And one who wields the Spirit need never fear the fire, be it real or not."

Elika put away her spider. "The way I see it, all magic is dangerous."

She wrapped herself in the cloak he gave her, and lay down again beside the warm chimney, thinking upon what he'd told her, whilst watching his back. They spoke some more, until she grew drowsy and could speak no more. When she awoke at dawn, he was gone. But he had left behind a strange sense of absence, and the roof seemed lonelier than before.

~

Rory was waiting for her, leaning on the corner of Dune Ash Street, watching folk go about their business.

"They are late," he said when Elika joined him there.

She shrugged. "If Penny says they'll be here, they'll come."

She watched a group of children chase a kitten and try to trap it between them. The kitten hissed and spat and clawed the girl who picked it up and wrapped it in a shawl, cooing over it.

A flash of red hair caught Elika's eye. Beside her, Rory straightened. In the distance, Penny was strolling in a fine dress, looking like a proper lady, her hair styled in Alterrian fashion. Beside her, Chelik wore a fine suit and a smile on his face as he peered into the windows of the shops they passed.

Penny gave no sign that she saw them, but Elika saw the subtle firming of her lips. She stopped to allow Chelik to look through the window of the sweetmaker.

"He's grown, hasn't he?" said Rory with pride.

"You won't find a better mother for him than Penny."

"He looks happy, too," he said with a note of longing.

"'Cause he's safe, and far from the troubles of Daetown."

"He looks like me, doesn't he?"

Elika did not see it herself. "Aye, he does. Though I expect he'll grow to be much more handsome than you."

"I think ye may be right, Spit. He's a handsome lad, as I never was."

Penny turned then and resumed walking. Elika barely saw her hand move, but an instant later, a small dagger flew past Rory's good eye. It grazed his ear and embedded between the joint in the stone. Rory didn't move, but his lips curled into a wry smile. "Warning taken, Red. Keep my son for now." And with that, he walked away.

CHAPTER SIXTEEN

The Making of a Tsarina

"Though he tells us we … rather I … am one now, one spirit beside his own, inhabiting his body, we know it is not true. We are many inside this man. He cannot understand it, though our minds are often joined. Yet he argues and argues until we can stand not the sound of his voice, or the assertions of his small, human mind. Reval tells me the man will die a natural death if I but wait. Then the body will be ours. We grow impatient, and poison tempts us to be rid of this body's inhabitant once and for all."

The History of Alafraysia and Seramight,
By Mageguard Bluelight

At dawn, the doors of the archmage's temple were dragged open by black strands of magic. Soon after, a wagon carrying prisoners arrived at the side gate. The mageguard at the gate walked around the wagon, peered into it, and waved it through. It disappeared behind the stone wall.

Elika pushed off the wall, and with her hands in her pockets, strode to the temple doors, where two mageguards stood sentry. As she tried to walk past them, they wordlessly blocked her with the crossing of their long pikes.

"That's a very grand temple," she said with feigned wonder. "I'd give anything to peek inside it."

The mageguard scowled. "Entry is forbidden to anyone but the courtiers."

"But how am I to pay homage to the archmage?" she asked in feigned dismay, whilst probing the essence of these mageguards. Theirs was harder to grasp than the majren's. Some faint power protected them. Still, she could end them regardless and slip inside. But behind them, inside the temple, there were more mageguards alongside human ones. Too many for her to fight alone.

"Pray at another temple," the mageguard snapped. Then his eyes narrowed on her. "Where is your freeman's mark?" he demanded and tried to grab her.

But she was quicker, as she jumped back and ran.

A wall of fire appeared in front of her. She skidded to a halt, then covering her head with her hood, she willed herself to be coated with water, and dripping wet, ran through the hot wall of flame. Mageguards never chased, save on their horses. The mages were slow and awkward, and sent human guards running in their stead. Not long after, she found herself alone and dry as if the water had never touched her. The magic was fleeting, just as Shoran had said.

Later that day, she returned to the temple, and watched highborn ladies and lords go in and out of the prayer hall. The temple itself was enormous. Were she to sneak inside, she'd be no closer to finding the archmage than she was now. The way she saw it, she'd have to be a tsarina, in truth, to demand an audience with him.

A cold shadow fell over her, as Reval's island passed overhead. *Arala … she could pretend to be Arala.*

She laughed the thought away, but it returned like a hungry puppy. And she could not help but think of the queen in the mirror Shoran had shown her.

Reval was seeking Arala, and he had demanded the archmage find her and deliver her to him. Might be she could confess to being a tsarina, demand to be brought to stand before the archmage …

Tane Igla's mocking voice from long ago cut through her plans. *Ha! Look at you, drab and scrawny, like a drowned rat, half-eaten by fleas. Where's your might and majesty, where's your wisdom and grace? You, my dear, are no goddess. At least not yet.*

Were she to show those mageguards her magic, they'd likely attack her, bind her in magical chains, or blood-salt, and take her straight to Reval. If she wanted to be treated like a tsarina, she had to look like a queen and act like a goddess returned.

When her eyes settled on a young lord leading his lady by the arm, she saw instead Mite with a fine lady on his arm heading towards the grand ship.

She could be more, would be more. Damn Shoran, she thought and grinned despite herself. He gave her a path and might be she'd use it to destroy the man whose death would free this city.

~

She pounded on the door with the heavy brass ring. The demanding echo went through the house twice.

A moment later, an annoyed servant flung open the door, his nose tipped up above a pointed chin. "The hour is late for … Oh. You are back," Maxim said flatly, with a note of disappointment. "Seems I'll have to inform the mistress of the bad news." He stepped aside and looked straight ahead at the wall as Elika walked inside.

"I was told she was expecting me."

"She was, indeed. Five days ago." He scrunched up his nose. "Has my lady found herself inside a fish barrel?" he drawled. He himself was as neat and crisp as sugar-glass. There was not a speck of disorder about him. His hair was oiled back, and not a strand poked out of place. Not a fleck of dust marred his starched jacket, not the slightest stain mired his white shirt.

She shrugged. "Bought a fish pie earlier. But don't worry, I clean up pretty well." She winked at him.

He closed the door behind her. "Perhaps you might consider cleaning up before offending my mistress with that uncivilized stench."

He was interrupted by a prim voice. "You are late." Tane Rosalina stood at the top of the stairs, regarding her as if she was a diseased dog begging at her door. "I was expecting you days ago. In the morning," she added, as if Elika had committed a double offence with arrival at night.

"It's a long walk from Daeside," she replied with a hint of humor.

The tane remained unamused. "You shall learn that I value punctuality and honesty above all else. Maxim, take her to her room and give her a thorough bath. I can smell this creature from here."

"At once, mistress." Maxim bowed and led the way upstairs to a set of double doors. He pushed them open. "These are to be your chambers. Your maid will attend you shortly."

"Don't need a maid," she said as she stepped into the room, the same one she had woken in before. There was a four-poster bed with plush curtains, a tall window overlooking the gardens, and a warming coal fire.

"Every lady needs a maid," he said with a lift of his chin.

She raised an eyebrow at him. "Do I look like a lady?"

"Indeed, you do not. Hence, I suggest you ask the maid to repair this tragic oversight."

Elika ran her hand through her hair. "This may yet be the most foolish thing I've done," she mumbled to herself.

"I will bring you some tea and leftovers from dinner. It is late and the servants are abed." Maxim sniffed the air. "I'll have to wake the poor footmen to bring your bath." He marched out.

Elika strode to the windows. They rose high into the ceiling and were too far from the ground for an easy jump. Nor could she climb to the roof from here. This would not do. She had never slept anywhere where she could be trapped or cornered with no escape onto the roof or ground. She opened the window and looked out. Further along the wall, a vine was rambling over the stone, which she could easily climb down into the garden. She took a quick note of the ledge leading to it and planned a way down using the thick stalk. Satisfied, she closed the window and turned back to the door.

A sleepy young woman stood there with a puzzled expression on her face.

Elika grinned. "I suppose I'm the worst-looking lady you've ever seen."

The maid seemed to catch herself and curtsied. "I'm to assist you, my lady."

"Name's Eli."

"As you say, my lady," she replied with another curtsy, and turned around to instruct two boys where to set the round wooden tub they were dragging between them. She then sent them to fetch warm water. Before long, the tub was full, and the maid arranged soap and a scrubbing brush on the stool beside it.

Then she laid out a nightgown on the bed and stood there waiting expectantly.

Elika sighed. "I can wash and dress myself well enough. Might be it's best you just return to your bed."

Without a word, the maid curtsied and scurried away on light feet.

Elika undressed and climbed into the bath. She scrubbed herself thoroughly, washed her hair, and emerged to dry herself with a cloth the maid had left behind. A knock came on the door. She quickly threw on the nightgown, just as Maxim came in with a tray of food. He placed it on the table and turned to the maid behind him who was carrying a pile of clothes.

"These are for tomorrow," Maxim said in a tone that told her there would not be another discussion about what she was to wear. "Hinna, take away those rags and … burn them."

Elika opened her mouth to object, but upon seeing mild disgust in the maid's face as she lifted them with the tips of her fingers, decided against it. "Want my cloak back though," she said, and the maid curtsied in reply.

Then she was left alone. She ate, without savoring the food, and sat on the bed with bone-deep weariness. There was no going back. She knew not what future awaited her, but she lamented the past and grieved for the girl she had been. Aye, she had become a stranger to herself. She curled up on top of the bed. Her mind drifted to Mite. Then his image dissolved to be replaced by a Sachi man with glowing yellow eyes.

~

The table was laid with enough food to feed half of Daetown, thought Elika, whilst the tane took her time explaining where every morsel came from, as though the dishes themselves were guests. Three birds came from Hunter's Forest. Exotic fruits were from the orchards of Springlands in the southern lands. And vegetables roasted in honey were from Shirefarm village just south of Terren.

Elika was dizzyingly hungry. Yet she was not allowed to lift her hands from her lap. She was instructed to sit there demurely whilst the tane ate her food. And watch as the tane tore a small piece from the steaming bread whilst the servant placed more carrots on her plate.

"You can glare at me all you want, girl. This is a lesson in patience you will learn quickly, for I have no patience to teach it to you slowly."

"Hunger is a lesson I'm well familiar with."

"This is not a lesson in hunger. Merely one in not surrendering to your basal instincts and eating like an animal." She nodded to the servant standing guard behind Elika.

Instantly, he stepped forward to lay small portions of food on her plate. She half expected him to chew it for her, lest her jaw was strained.

Then another servant stepped forward with a jug, filled her cup with the silver liquid and stepped back. At the sight of it, a craving so deep and cutting hit her, it was all she could do not to grab the cup and drink the silvery honey.

"I can see you know what it is," said the tane. "At least your magic does."

"What is it?" she asked as she defied the urge to reach for it.

"Silversap. It feeds the magic inside you. Whilst the food before you nourishes your earthly body, the magic in you has been starving. Shoran left you a jug of the sap to allow you to gain your strength. You may drink it."

Elika's hands were instantly on her goblet. As soon as the silvery sweet syrup touched her throat, she tipped back her head and downed it in a few gulps before she could stop herself. It rushed through her, surged through her blood, a lifeforce that awakened every part of her body, enriched her soul, and filled her essence. The world grew brighter. The colors changed and became astounding. The air tasted fresher, and her thoughts grew clear and vivid. She smiled in a blissful daze, marveling at the wonder of the world and light and the essence of life vibrating around her …

"Damn it, girl, do not drink it all at once. You have starved your magic, and now you drown it."

The cup was empty, but the craving only intensified. "I would like more." Her voice sounded odd to her ears, deeper, more powerful, and yet more distant.

"This is enough for today. Shoran left clear instructions. You are not to overindulge. Eventually, you will learn to harvest Silversap yourself."

"Where do I harvest it from?" she asked eagerly.

"'Tis for Shoran to teach you that. I am here to teach you manners. Eat. But you are not to use your fingers. You no longer live on the streets, so there is no need to eat like a stray animal."

Elika strangled a retort for the prickly tane and picked up her knife and fork. Penny taught them manners, and she knew how to eat without being told.

"Do not stuff your mouth so your cheeks puff out. Small portions are enough."

Elika cut less for her next bite.

"And do not chew so fast. Mealtimes are meant to last."

She began to chew slowly.

"Back straight."

She straightened her back.

"Don't slouch either … your nails need cutting and cleaning. Have you been digging in the mud? I will speak with your maid. Sit up straight, I said."

Again, Elika straightened.

"Try not to drop your food into your lap."

"Tane Rosalina —"

"Do not talk with your mouth full."

She had but a morsel of food in her mouth. She swallowed it, before proceeding. "I have one request."

"It is not polite to ask for things at mealtimes. But rest assured, Shoran has instructed coin is not to be spared on what you want. So simply let your maid or Maxim know what it is you need or desire."

"It's not coin I wish for … but … some freedom … to go to markets."

The Tane lowered her hands into her lap and looked steadily at her. "You are not a prisoner here."

"What are my chores?"

"Chores?" the tane echoed. "I have servants, better trained ones than you could ever be. You are here because Shoran wills it. I am to look after you until you can look after yourself."

Elika chose not to point out that she could look after herself well enough. "Do you always do what he demands?"

The tane shifted in her seat in discomfort. "One does not deny him."

There was more to it. Elika saw it in her face. "Pebble told me he's your master."

Lady Rosalina's fingers twisted the silver ring on her hand. It caught Elika's eye, for the ring had an amber stone with a black spider inside it. "He is more than a master to us. I owe him my life. I owe him all I am today. Ilikan ripped me from my weeping mother's arms and threw me into the ocean where he summoned a great wave to whisk me away, far from any land so that I might drown. Save that I did not want to drown. I wanted to live. So I floated for many days, with only tears for comfort and fish for company. Eventually, someone whispered to Shoran what Ilikan had done. So he found me adrift in the ocean and gave me to a noble lady cursed with a barren womb, but who craved a child of her own. Of course, Lord Shoran punished Ilikan, and forbade him to harm any more tane babes."

"I can't understand such cruelty towards their own children. Why would the tsaren do this?"

The tane stiffened. "Enough of your foolish questions. I will not tolerate insolence. Now, finish your breakfast. And straighten your back. Today, Master Goldgrace will teach you letters and numbers."

~

"No," Elika said abruptly. "I would rather be ignorant than be taught by a mage."

"Why does she-human speak so ungraciously to us?" Mage Goldgrace asked, sounding wounded. Though he stooped in his natural posture, he straightened tall in his indignation.

There was something ancient about him, though in appearance he was not much older than Tane Rosalina. A fog of perpetual tiredness hung about him, as if he had not slept in centuries. His eyes were of no discernible color, as if the mage could not decide what they should be. So they shifted like pearls in the light— white, then pink, then faintly blue. His hands were equally restless, tugging and pulling at his robes and belt and strands of lace around his sleeves.

Fighting back her deep-seated revulsion, she turned to Lady Rosalina's unyielding face. "Surely there is a human master, perhaps a priest, who can teach me letters."

"Lord Shoran sent Master Goldgrace to teach you. I do not question his reasons. If you wish to do so, then ask him when you see him next. Until then, you are to learn your letters. And do not slouch. Straighten your shoulders and stand tall, girl."

Without another word, the tane departed from the library, her back straight, her shoulders pulled back.

The door closed.

Elika eyed the mage. "How long have you had that body?"

He straightened, eyeing her back uncertainly. "Milikan died eight hundred years ago. He was a … friend. I miss him greatly." Grief briefly touched his eyes.

"Did you kill him?"

"Kill him?" He raised his voice in outrage. "I'm a mageguard ... brought to the earthly realm by Tsarin Ilikan himself. Milikan and I were one until old age crippled and killed him."

"You refer to yourself as '*I*'," she noted.

"Milikan taught me to do that. He was a scholar and taught me that there was freedom in loneliness. I was afraid to be alone. He taught me how to be a rock in the stream of the river I came from. It helped me when he ... died." There was such a forlorn expression in his face, she had to look aside before she got it into her head to pity him.

"If Ilikan made you, why aren't you serving your tsarin in his court?"

He sat in the tall chair beside the fire and his shoulders slumped. "I ... we ... were banished. In the Sundering War, I helped King Southfire save his heir before he was slain by Reval. I smuggled him out of the besieged castle and gave the boy to humans to hide. For that, Ilikan cursed me as a traitor and banished me from his court. To be cursed by a tsarin is to be cursed by all. I have no place amongst my kind here."

Elika fought off another unwelcome pang of pity. "Then why don't you return to your own realm?"

He looked haunted as he replied. "Only the tsaren can release us from this world. I am trapped here and cannot return to Alafraysia." He rose to his feet. "But we are not here to reminisce about days long past. I am to teach you letters. Master Shoran informs me you are to start with the common tongue of men. When you have mastered it, we will learn the runes of the Laifae and the tsaren. And after that, you will learn the language of the gods."

She looked at the books on the study table. The thought of being able to read was far more compelling than her dislike of the mage. So she sat and Mage Goldgrace placed the parchment, ink well and another book in front of her. He was so close, she could smell him.

"Why do you not smell of death like the other mages?"

He stepped away, looking oddly embarrassed. "The flesh eventually stops decaying, and we learn to ... mask ourselves.

When Arala was alive, she could restore our flesh, for she was the daughter of the gods."

Elika looked down at the parchment, trying not to imagine what a dead body would look like after six hundred years beneath the Laifae illusion. "What letters are you teaching me today?" she asked and did not look at him again until the lesson had ended.

~

Before long, Elika lost count of the days. If she thought they would be filled with ladylike idleness, she could not have been more wrong. The tane kept her busier than even Mistress Oblana had done, with the strict routine of lessons on everything that Elika was not. And these, she could not escape even during her mealtimes.

With merciless rigor, she was taught how to eat, how to drink, how to dress, walk and speak, and even how to breathe. If she moved her hand too quickly, she was reprimanded for moving like a brute. If she sighed, she was told a lady never sighed in frustration, only in admiration. When she yawned, she was berated for her rudeness and uncivilized manners.

"One does not yawn in the company of others," Lady Rosalina had told her.

Each morning she had lessons with forlorn, tired Mage Goldgrace. She hated those the most, for the more time she spent in his presence, the harder it grew to despise him. There was humanity about him she had refused to see in other mages. He never raised his voice to her, never brandished his magic. And it distressed her that she was coming to prefer his mournful company to Lady Rosalina's.

When she worked, he occupied his hands with items he carried in his pockets—those strange artefacts the mages were prone to collect. He loved the feel of feathers and silk and soft pieces of fur. Once, whilst she scribed words from a book, he absently sowed the ripped lace on his robe.

"Surely you can just use your magic to fix that?" she had asked.

"'Tis folly to waste it so needlessly, when the hunger is so hard to sate," he replied without looking up from his work.

To hear him speak of the hunger she knew so well was almost the undoing of her disdain. It was a similarity she did not want to acknowledge yet could not escape. Understanding and compassion meant acceptance, and she could not accept what the mages did—enslavement, murder, invasion of another's world. She forced herself to recall the collar around the neck of Penny's red-haired babe, and those echoes of sympathy vanished. *Seek not a kindred spirit in a foe.* It was a lesson you learned quickly on the street.

After the morning lessons, she had lunch with the tane, where she was endlessly reprimanded. If Elika sat in silence, she was accused of sulking, which was unbefitting a lady. When she spoke, she was berated for speaking like a common tavern wench. There were so many different types of spoons and knives and silly-looking forks, that she often forgot which to use with what dish. And was again berated.

After the midday meal, more lessons followed, each with a different master. There was the master of dancing and singing, with his effeminate charm and amiable smiles. Then there was a pretty minstrel who was in love with Pebble. From her, Elika learned to play a harp, a flute and a lyre. Each day she was instructed on how to walk, or rather glide like a lady, to carry herself with decorum and grace. She was taught how to address a tsarin, a duke, an archmage, and every official with a title beneath them.

Sometime in the summer, she had turned seventeen. She did not know the day of her birth, only that she was born in the summer. That knowledge seemed ingrained into her soul.

As autumn arrived, and the trees grew golden, she was taught how to ride a horse. It turned out this was Lady Rosalina's favorite activity, and she took charge of the lessons—to Elika's dismay. Once again, she could do nothing right. Her posture was wrong, the way she clumsily handled the animal, and even the cut of the attire she wore was unbecoming. They would ride to the park, escorted by two footmen. These excursions were always early in the morning before the other riders of noble birth came out for their morning jaunts and strolls. As soon as they appeared, Lady Rosalina would return home. Elika suspected it was because of the questioning glances the nobles cast their way.

"Why do they stare at us?" she asked one day of the tane.

"They know me, but they do not know you. 'Tis better if they see less of you, at least with me. There is a hunt for a Dae girl said to be the Rogue. They might mistake you for her."

Elika said nothing in reply. The tane no doubt knew everything.

Much later, Elika learned that in the days of the human kings, tanes born to noblewomen were welcomed at court. But since then, the archmage had banned tanes from his court. This did not sit well with many noble houses who revered them for their long lives and peaceful ways.

"My kind hold no ambitions for power and are often useful to the nobles. At least in aspects of history and accurate records of the days long past," Lady Rosalina had explained. "But they are forced to shun us. And Prince Southfire dances to the tune played by the archmage."

Not all nobles shunned the tanes, for Lady Rosalina received many invitations to private dinners and gatherings. A rare few of which she accepted. On more than one occasion, Elika watched her leave the house in a glorious dress and sapphire gems, to be taken away in a fine carriage.

"And once you forge me into a proper lady, what then?" she asked the tane one day as they rode back from the park. "Will I be presented to other noble families or perhaps to court?"

Tane Rosalina gave her a long sideways glance. "Do you wish to be presented to the court?"

Elika thought of the archmage. "Aye. Can you arrange it?" she asked as they drew closer to the stables at the back of the house.

"When the time is right, you shall be presented by Shoran. Not before then, and not before you are ready. Else you will merely embarrass yourself and me."

But as winter approached, there was no sign of Shoran, or when Elika might be deemed ready.

Often, by the time dinner came about, she could barely contain her simmering anger at being berated for her every minor offence to etiquette. No matter that she did everything the tane demanded and tried hard to please her. Silences at dinner were often long and tense. The long hours after that surely made up for those silences, for after dinner, she would read to the tane in the library, whilst the old woman dosed in her chair by the fire. If Elika stopped reading, Lady Rosalina would start awake and demand she read some more.

The days merged into each other. Rarely now, Elika continued her nocturnal forays into the city. And when she did, it was to seek news of Northwind and the happenings in Daetown.

The tane hated gossip and spoke in a vague, disinterested way about what was happening in the streets. "Focus on your lessons and not on what the rabble is doing," she would say when Elika asked for news.

So she went out and learned on her own that there was an uneasy truce between Terren's seat of power and Daetown. This had been orchestrated by their new Dae overlord of noble origin, Lord Nightkill. He had taken charge of Daetown and petitioned the archmage and Prince Southfire for a peaceful resolution to the conflict on the streets. So far, it was said that messages were being sent back and forth between them. Though what was said or negotiated no one knew save the one-eyed lord himself.

But the end of autumn brought with it dire news. It was from the maid Hinna that she learned of Northwind's imprisonment by Tsarin Ilikan. After that Elika spend night after night seeking news of Mite.

She found it in *Ilikan's Water*, the tavern at the far end of Wharf Street that was frequented by the guards of the Northern Bastion. She had been there before. The ale was cheaper than anywhere else, and Milly, the tavern keeper's wife, made the best fish pie in the whole of the city. Many sailors drank there, and there was gossip aplenty from across the realm. And it was in this tavern that she had come upon the red-haired guard who was friends with Mite.

He was drinking with his companions, but there was no cheer in his face. Elika sat at a table close enough to listen and shortly learned his name was Trian, and he was the new captain of the Northern Bastion.

"We must do something to help the captain," one of the guards at the table blurted out. His companion nudged him with a nod at Trian. The guard flushed red. "Um, sorry captain. Just catches your tongue, you know."

The red-haired captain waived that away. "No matter. Aeron was the best damned captain we've had in a decade."

"Surely you can do something, captain. Who's to know what Ilikan is doing to Northwind in that watery dungeon of his? What if he kills him?"

Captain Trian stared at his ale. "There's nothing we can do. We can't abandon our post. If I know Aeron, he'll get himself out of the mess he got himself into. I warned him against going to Ilikan. But Warwind convinced him to go anyway, thinking Ilikan would ally with him if only to dismantle Reval's power over Seramight."

"I heard he means to use Northwind as a peace offering to Reval," said another guard.

"'Tis not peace he wants, but control over Terren's harbor. Thinks it's his since it touches the sea. None of the tsaren want Northwind restored to power. It would mean the end of their reign."

The men grew silent then, knowing that ears were trained on their conversation, and not just her own. As if he sensed her watching him, Trian turned her way. She quickly looked aside, but something about her caught his attention, something akin to a vague sense of recognition. His gaze lingered a little too long, before he turned away. When he did, she left the tavern, and was careful not to be seen by him again.

When autumn turned to winter, the changing winds brought daily flurries of snow and news of Northwind's escape from Ilikan's prison. Mite was safe in Wavestar, in Duke Firewind's court. Daetown was abuzz with excitement. The news was a fresh wind in her increasingly stale life. It propelled Elika to try even harder to learn how to be a perfect lady. Though were she to believe the tane, she was no closer to convincing anyone of her noble birth.

Soon, she told herself. Soon.

~

Outside, the snowstorm howled and whistled through the cracks in the house. Elika stared sightlessly at the mirror, whilst Hinna ran a brush through her hair with gentle patience. It was their nightly ritual, insisted on by Lady Rosalina. Hinna was shy and rarely spoke unless Elika asked her questions. Though her parents were both Dae, she had been born in Al-Terren. Elika gleamed little else from her, save that she was recently wedded to a locksmith. And though he was much older than she, he was still fair to look upon and treated her well.

"Did he buy your freedom?" Elika asked.

"Lady Rosalina buys the freedom of all who serve her. She's a kind lady."

On her hand, Hinna had the freeman's mark. Elika refused to be branded. Although with the increasing number of runaway slaves and servants, more and more folk were being stopped on the street and their marks checked.

Lady Rosalina had given her a pair of gloves to wear, stamped with the royal house of the tane's adoptive mother. The tane herself wore nothing but the spider ring upon her hand. It was protection enough against being accosted. More than once Elika had caught mages eyeing it with equal disdain and weariness.

There was a knock on the door and Hinna went to open it.

"The mistress requests your presence in the library, my lady," said Maxim.

Elika flung her hair behind her shoulder and threw on the robe over her night dress.

"My lady," Hinna protested. "You must put on a suitable dress, or the mistress will be angry. I must also dress your hair."

Elika sighed in frustration. She was wearied and ready for bed. The last few nights, she had little sleep. She had spent them in Daetown, seeking news of Mite.

"It is late and the mistress knows this," she said. "Besides, I dare say she'll not sleep unless she finds another reason to reprimand me."

"My lady, please ..." Hinna pleaded. "The mistress is already angry with you for spending too much time in the kitchens."

Though most of the servants kept a polite distance from her, the cook was chatty and always slipped her sweet pastries when there were any to be had. Besides, the kitchen was the warmest place in the house. The tane did not feel the cold, at least not like humans, and she hated the smell of smoke from coal fires. So only a few were burned around the house, despite the snow blanketing the city. Often, Elika shivered next to her, whilst the old woman was content in her summer dresses. Lady Rosalina also seemed immune to any manner of winter ailments that constantly afflicted the servants of her house these days.

Elika ignored the maid's pleas and marched downstairs. Aye, she was supposed to be dressed appropriately whenever she left her room, but damn it, it was late and she was ready for bed. All day, the tane had berated her. Elika could do nothing to please her, though she tried hard not to give her any cause for complaint. Her gliding was compared to a duck wading through mud, and her eating habits to pigs. Even Maxim took pity and whispered to her not to take too much notice of the mistress' unkind words. Elika suspected the cruel words were meant to flay her pride, to humble her into mindless obedience. Most certainly, the mistress did not treat any of her servants this way.

Elika flung open the door to the library and froze. Beside the mistress stood Shoran. Her heart gave an odd bounce and her cheeks grew hot, though she knew not why, save that his gaze was intent on her. She had not seen him since the night he had sat beside her on the roof and given her the cloak, which she always wore on her forays into the city.

"What are you wearing, girl?" the mistress demanded aghast and turned red.

Elika wrapped the robe more tightly around herself. "You did not tell me we had a visitor," she said calmly, though she was anything but calm.

"Are you a street urchin or a lady? We have been working hard to remove that barbarian accent of yours. Speak as you are taught to speak."

Elika flinched at the reprimand. For some reason it shamed her far deeper in front of him. "I'm still a Dae," she replied quietly.

"Outside your room, you must always dress as if you are about to receive a visitor. We have spoken of this," that tane continued mercilessly. "She is a mutinous student, Shoran, as you can see. But we are making progress, nevertheless, despite her current attire."

He remained silent, but his eyes took her in, flicked in brief perusal and detached approval, as one might when examining a newly healed wound.

Hot now with the humiliation of being chastised in front of him, she lowered her face before her anger got the better of her.

"Do not stoop, and do not play coy, girl," the tane berated her. "This false acquiescence is contemptible. Lying does not become you."

There were rare times in Elika's life, when such potent anger built in her, it caused her head to pound and light to explode behind her eyes. She closed them momentarily against the assault, then raised her gaze to the tane. In her temples, blood was pounding. There was no holding back the surge of fury.

A cynical smile touched her lips. "Does it not? And yet it is what you are wanting from me every day."

"I want you to become a lady worthy of who you are."

Elika lifted her head higher. "Lady Rosalina, you are gravely mistaken. You seek to turn me into a liar and nothing more. I am not who you think me to be, nor who you want me to be. I have been raised on the streets and have seen death and cruelty enough to last a lifetime. I have stolen, lied, walked past abandoned babes, killed men without remorse and watched them burn without pity. Do you think a few silly dresses and foolish dance lessons will erase my past and make me forget who I am? Do you think I can forget what the tsaren and Syn'Moreg have done to our world, and what it turned men into? Do you know what men did to each other in the end? What they did to pretty ladies like you? They beat them, raped them, then tied them to the stake and burned them alive in the blood-salt fires. This farce I am forced to endure is nothing but a lie."

She wanted to shock the tane, and it was clear she had done that. Though she spoke calmly, rage poured out of her and formed itself into a force she could not contain, and the air itself charged around them.

She saw Shoran tense with readiness, but Lady Rosalina gave no sign that she had noticed. Instead, she reddened with outrage, straightened tall and clasped her hands together. "If this is so, then why are you still here, living this *lie* as you call it? You are not a prisoner."

Because I want to kill the archmage and I need to trick him into believing me to be what I am not. Because I want to show Mite I can be more. Because I want to be more.

"'Tis Lord Shoran's will, is it not?" she said with a wry twist of her lips.

"It is as I suspected. You care not for civilized ways. There is no hope for you. Not until you learn to humble yourself before your betters and rise above the mud you came from, girl. Not until you want to be more ..."

Elika closed her eyes against the fury roiling in her. The last time she released it, she had nearly destroyed herself.

"At every turn, she fights me, Shoran ..." Lady Rosalina went on until her voice was poison feeding the coiling snake of rage and hate.

Elika had tried so hard to please; had done everything the tane demanded. It was never enough. The tane's words were cutting and unjust, and she wanted nothing more than to shake the house apart just to stop the onslaught of this derision.

The ground trembled, there was a crashing sound, and the tane cried out.

Suddenly a warm, gentle hand pressed against her cheek. "*Morna frya deari.* Still the fire in your heart."

Elika's eyes snapped open and met Shoran's fathomless, dark gaze. The ground stilled. The gentle command flowed through her, warm and compelling.

"I cannot do this, Shoran," the tane whispered. "Take her away. She is Elriad returned, can you not see?"

"Leave us, Rosalina," he said.

From the corner of her eye, she saw the tane rise from where she had fallen to the floor. Without raising her gaze, she walked out stiffly. The door closed with a prim click.

"Such a deep sea of anger and hate for one so young," he said softly. "Be careful of wading into it, lest it drowns you. The world is not as dark as grief would have you see it."

For a moment she could not move. No one had touched her so gently in so long—not since Penny when Elika was still a child. No one since had looked at her with such deep compassion. With so many young in their pack, they vied endlessly for Penny's love, a love she had little time to bestow on them all. The hand so warm and soft upon her cheek brought out all those childish longings. For a brief moment, it swept away the unending loneliness, the deep fears she nurtured, the wretchedness in her soul.

"It is far darker than I wish it to be," she whispered back, afraid to lose the steadying hand and the odd, brief peace it gave her.

His thumb ran along her cheek. "I can take you from here, to a place where the troubles of man will not reach you. Where you will be loved and cared for. Where flowers will be laid at your feet and your days will be carefree and warm. Where you need never know pain again."

The seductive words were honey, and she turned into his hand wanting to believe such a sweet promise could be true.

"Just say the word, and I will take you there," he said as if he read her doubts.

There was a frightening power about him that seeped from his pores. Today, it was quiet, unimposing, and yet this close it was still like a hot brand. And it was hard not to believe him.

She met his gaze and sadness filled her. Even if he could take her from everything in this world, she could not go, could not abandon men to their fate. She had to kill the archmage. And maybe … after that …

"Might be if there is such place you should take all men there. I cannot go until the world is set to right."

Abruptly the hand fell away, leaving her cold and bereft of his warmth.

He walked aside to the table, and her heart resumed its beat, pounding as if she'd been chased along the streets. He did not move like other men. There was a fluidity about his movements, a grace beyond that of any human.

"Fates have shown little kindness to Lady Rosalina," he said and turned around. "Much cruelty was done to her before I offered her protection. That cruelty taught her to fear those who despise her kind. And thus, she fears you."

"I do not despise the tanes. It is not fear, but contempt she feels for me."

"She cannot tell one from the other. Shield your heart against her words." He looked down at a leather-bound book on the table and his fingers ran over the cover. "I am told you can read and write now."

"I'm well versed in the common tongue of men. The Laifae symbols are too many and confusing. Master Goldgrace feels quite offended by my lack of appreciation for his beautiful language. But to my ears, it sounds like a pack of mewling cats. The language of the gods is far more beautiful. Though I only know of it from you …" She trailed off, wondering why she was telling him this nonsense, speaking rapidly as if afraid he'd leave before she finished.

He tilted his head at her and lifted the gold-trimmed leather book he was caressing. "I came to bring you this tome. It will teach you about the gods and their realm."

She blinked. "The gods are dead. I care not for them."

"Do not confuse ignorance with rebellion. Put your anger aside. The gods are not dead."

Elika crossed her arms. "The priests say they are."

He lifted an eyebrow. "The Sachi priests said thus?"

She shook her head. "Reval's priests, in the old city. The Priests of the Nerabyss too, and those in temples built for the tsaren. They said Syn'Moreg is the last god alive, and even he, they suspect, might be dead. The Sachi priests are stubborn," she said pointedly with a perusal of his Sachi features, and his lips quirked in amusement. "They refuse to believe the gods have abandoned men. Be they dead or not." She shrugged, for in truth she cared not whether or not they were dead.

"Ever men think that gods have nothing better to do than answer their prayers. Even were it their will to do so, they cannot traverse the veil to this world until the realms brush against each other. This book will help you understand what they are and why they do what they do."

Elika studied his features. "You are a Sachi," she said.

He took a while to reply. There was a way about him where every word he spoke was weighed and measured before he spoke it. "My mother is a Sachi. Long ago, I was one of them."

She studied him more closely and reminded herself that despite his features, he was ancient. Might be he had been human once. Now there was something otherworldly about him. He must be a mage, for what else could he be?

"The man whose body you wear, is he … dead?"

He struggled to hold back a smile, and his harsh lines eased. "The man to whom this body belongs is very much alive and speaking with you now. I am not a Laifae."

"You are not a mage?" She was confused. "But your magic—"

"Comes from another source, as does yours," he finished for her.

"Can you teach me … about magic? Might you have books about it?"

He replaced the book he was holding on the table. "I cannot teach you what you are until you are ready to accept the truth about who you are. The lessons you should have learned as a babe, have not been taught you. You are blind and unaware. It falls to me to guide you to your awareness."

"I am aware," Elika said stubbornly.

"Then tell me who and what you are."

She pursed her lips and stared at the floor to get away from his probing gaze. In truth, she did not know ... did not want to know.

He spoke into her silence. "You have lived as a human all your life, brief as it was. It is all you have ever known. Take it away and what have you left?"

Speechless, Elika gaped at him. He had read her deepest fear; knew her heart like no one else.

Then she saw it. His understanding was deeper than the rippling surface of his words. He knew her fears because he had known them himself. And as she looked at him, his Sachi features called to her, his black eyes were a fathomless Abyss she feared to get lost in. Always, when he was near, she felt close to home, that unsettling sense of kinship, of safety ... and more.

"I cannot take you from this world without showing you the door to another," he continued. "When you are ready to cross, you will know all." He lifted his hand from the book and strode to the bookshelf.

"Are we kin?" she rushed to ask before he disappeared. "Are we ... the same?"

He stopped; looked at her over his shoulder. "Blood does not tie us. The gods do and the path you have set us upon." And with that, he vanished into the bookshelf.

Elika walked towards it and put her hand on the shelf, savoring the sinking sensation, a well she could fall into and find him in another realm. She stood there for a long time, wanting to follow him, resisting the urge.

CHAPTER SEVENTEEN

Mage Goldgrace

"Man is the only being who dies from the decay of the flesh. It is a sickness, a curse, a punishment bestowed upon them by the God of Death, Moreg. Though we sought records to discover why the god cursed them, no written memory of that exists. It was Reval who told us the tale, which was passed to him by Arala. Long ago, Demigod Elriad led the rebellion against the old gods' rule and sought to claim the much-coveted world of Seramight. The humans—who too were eternal by Neka's design—joined his army and thus betrayed the gods. For that, Moreg cursed them with the rapid decay of the flesh and untimely death. Absurdly, instead of groveling on their bleeding knees for forgiveness, humans have somehow learned to live with the curse and forgotten that once, long ago, they too were blessed with eternal lives."

The History of Alafraysia and Seramight,
By Mageguard Bluelight

Breakfast was a miserable affair. For once, Lady Rosalina's cool silence was unwelcome. The tane did not comment once on how Elika ate, or that her back was not as straight as it should be. So there was no distraction to be had from her restless thoughts of Shoran. His visit had left Elika deeply unsettled. She had barely slept last night, thinking upon every word he had said, his every gesture and every glance, whilst nursing the imprint of his palm upon her cheek. For want of sleep, she had read by the light of the candle the book he had given her, until her eyes could not stay open. And then she dreamt of the gods and the realm without darkness, rich with sacred orchard trees, their fruit heavy with the nectar they fed upon.

The tane spoke suddenly. "Lord Shoran brought you more silversap. Though he instructed you are to drink it sparingly and not to use your magic needlessly."

Elika had already eyed the jug and stifled the itching craving to reach for it. The servant stepped forward and poured a miserly measure of it into a silver goblet. Fighting the urge to drink it in one mouthful, Elika took a sip.

She then cleared her throat and said, "Tane Rosalina, I am grateful for your forbearance with me. You have shown me great kindness in allowing me to stay here. Please do not think me ungrateful." She placed a small piece of bacon into her mouth.

"It is not your gratitude that worries me, girl—I seek it not— but your hate-filled heart. When combined with great power, hate is a dangerous force."

My heart is not hate-filled. Elika opened her mouth to object, but words never left it. She hated. She could not deny it, but she hated because of her love for mankind, for the innocent dying on the streets.

"Love breeds hate," she replied and cut another small piece of her bacon. "Would you not hate those who harm the ones you love?"

"No. I would fight for those I love, but never hate for them. Gods do not hate, girl. If they did, we would not be here. One god alone has the power to destroy the three realms, and both men and the Laifae have given them much cause to hate. But power must not be guided by hate, only by wisdom and justice."

Long after breakfast, Elika pondered those words. She had retreated into the library and was reading Shoran's book about the gods when Master Goldgrace arrived. He had a fat tome under his arm, which she knew was another of his history books that made her eyes heavy with sleep when she read them.

He stopped when he saw her, seeing something of her thoughts in her expression. "Lady Elika, you seem ... determined."

"You once told me that you wish to return to your realm."

He looked wistful. "I … we dream of home. It is lonely to be one."

His words stumbled her, for they mirrored her own heart. And she hated sharing that pang of understanding with the mages, for to do so would be to acknowledge something she could not afford to see.

"Would you grant me something in return if I could send you there?" she asked carefully.

"Only a tsarin can free me from this body, from this realm. And they will not do so, for I have been banished and punished."

"And if I could?" she persisted.

He started, frowned, then gaped at her. "Reval … he seeks Arala. His mageguards roam the city each day, calling to her. You are she … you are the Rogue Mage." Suddenly he was on his knees at her feet. "Free us, my tsarina, return us to our realm. We live in your light."

"I will do that if you answer my questions."

"Anything. Ask me anything, my queen."

"Why can only Tridamor make the majren, and not you?"

"Arala gave him that gift … *you* gave him that gift. A demigoddess can reshape life to her own design. 'Tis the magic of celestial spirit. Gods have the power to touch and draw upon the light of the Great Web."

"There is no one else with that gift?"

"No one, only the tsaren and the gods themselves."

"Then Tridamor would welcome me into his presence?"

He shook his head. "No, he would be too afraid to allow you near."

That took her aback. Her plan was to be admitted to him as a tsarina. "Why?" she asked.

"If you are Arala, then he is your creation. A mage is always bound to their master, a mage cannot abandon their master in a time of need. To do so is treachery of the worst kind. After the world was sundered, Arala asked Tridamor to help her forge the bridge. She needed his strength and his sacrifice to save herself. But Tridamor was afraid to die, and at the last moment he abandoned her, so Arala unraveled instead of him."

"How is it that Reval has not killed him?"

"Tridamor claims that Arala drained him of strength, and he was ready to die for her. But when he came to, he was still alive, and she was gone and the bridge was forged."

"How do you know this?"

"I was there. I was one of the few who witnessed it. Tridamor broke from the contact at the last moment, leaving Arala without his strength. He is terrified of your return, and he seeks to find you before Reval does. He will try to kill you."

"I must get close to the archmage to unravel him."

Goldgrace rose to his feet. "I could not allow it, tsarina. It would be too dangerous. You must go to Reval. He will help you. I must tell him …"

"No," she said harshly. "He must not know."

The mage began to pace. "My queen, it will not be easy to unravel him whilst he surrounds himself with powerful mageguards loyal to him."

She recalled a wall of power protecting Tridamor. "An archmage is not the same as a majren," she said thoughtfully. "How are they different?"

"A majren is a small drop of the river. A mageguard is a pool, whilst an archmage is a lake."

"So, they are … larger, more powerful," Elika said.

"They are … deeper," he replied. "But no one is deeper than you, tsarina. You are the sea. You can tear us apart altogether and kill us instead of returning us to our realm."

A horrible understanding crashed into her, one she had suspected but feared to admit. She was killing them and not returning them to their realm.

"Do you know how I must do it? So as not to kill you."

He stopped pacing. "I know little of tsarin's magic. It is deep and boundless within our realm, but … bound and shallow in this one. Yet a tsarin's power is vast and linked to your emotions. Your thoughts and feelings can raise a storm. You can sense the Great Web around you, and if you tap into the elemental well of power, you can turn dreams into reality. It is how Reval can change the winds, and Draygan can make the ground tremble."

"If I am angry, my magic is more powerful."

"And it will drain you faster."

"Tell me how to send you back to your realm."

"Our realm," he corrected and chuckled. It was an odd sound between a child's giggle and a wheeze.

"If Alafraysia is my realm, then how do I get there?"

"Tsarina, you can go anywhere your heart desires in Alafraysia or Seramight. The realms are one. You need but to wish it and follow the path home. You need but to see it to step through the veil. Look closely, for your eyes are not as blind as mine. Your flesh is true, whilst mine is but a dream woven into a dead man's body. Look and you will see."

She did, but saw only the world as it was. Then she focused, drawing on the essence flowing through the world. Everything shifted ever so slightly, as if she was in two places at once, seeing both at the same time. She looked at the bookshelf, and suddenly there was a white fog drifting through the shelf into the room. She looked at the sky and saw a purple mountain, faint as a spider's silk, then it vanished. And when she turned to the mage, the skin of his face was translucent. Beneath it, she saw a black, churning, fluid-like creature, its strands wound around a human skeleton. It was an awful, startling sight, and she looked aside, losing her focus. The mage returned to the form he wanted to be seen in.

"What made it happen?" Elika asked, horrified by all it implied. "What made the worlds merge?"

Goldgrace's shoulders drooped. "No one knows for certain, but only a god has the power to make it happen. Some say it was Syn'Moreg, others that it was Arala. Others yet, claim it was both of them, working together to unite the realms into one."

"Then why do the gods not sunder the realms apart?"

"It is said that they cannot. Else they do not care enough to try."

She pondered it briefly, then decided such things were for the gods to solve. Her fight was only with the archmage.

"Shall we resume our lesson?" she said to Mage Goldgrace.

He wrung his hands. "Mistress ... if I ... if we may ... we are ready, tsarina. You need us not to teach you anymore. We wary of being one and wish to rejoin the Black River."

She knew better than anyone the longing for home. "If you are certain, then I will do as I promised."

She felt for his essence, grabbed it ...

"No!" he cried and fell at her feet, grabbing her dress. "Please do not kill us."

"Kill you?"

"You are ripping me apart, tsarina. I wish to live."

She fought off a rising sense of horror. "What should I do?"

He placed her hand on his chest. "I need but a whisper of your will. A small push, nothing more. Alafraysia is all around us. You see it, do you not? I am but a step from home. Push me there, do not rip me from the web. The river of our people awaits my return."

Elika gently pushed at his essence. "Go home, Goldgrace."

"Thank you, tsarina," he said and with a smile crumbled to the floor.

Nothing more was left of him but a yellowing skeleton of a man who died long ago, still clad in Goldgrace's robe.

The door opened. Tane Rosalina came in. She stood there, staring at the skeleton on the floor, then briefly closed her eyes, took a deep breath and said, "I cannot keep you. I cannot help you. Please, you must leave, tsarina." She turned away and closed the door behind her.

CHAPTER EIGHTEEN

The Tower of The Abyss

"Since our gracious and beautiful Arala arrived in our realm to take her father's seat, she had always been restless. Ever the draw of the Earthly turned her gaze towards Seramight. Ever, when our realms brushed past, she crossed the veil into their world, and roamed the lands until the spheres drifted apart. And when she returned, she was withdrawn and unhappy. Though Reval tried, he could never ease her longing for the world of man. Then another, darker and more compelling longing gripped her heart, one which Reval was powerless to fulfil. Arala grew more and more unhappy, and she no longer cared to shape our world, or for the happiness of our river. Then one day she vanished. With the cycle of the spheres at the maxima, there was only one place she could have gone. To the Tower of the Abyss. The one place no being, save the children of the gods, could follow."

The History of Alafraysia and Seramight,
By Mageguard Bluelight

Maxim shifted apologetically and placed a leather bag on her bed. "The mistress says you are to take anything you wish. In the morning, I will drive you anywhere you wish to go." He placed a fat purse of gold pieces beside the bag. "This should be enough to settle you in a comfortable place with your own servants. May I recommend a nice tavern for now? The Golden Ladle is particularly fine, where wealthy merchants and travelling noblemen often stay. It will be safe for you there. The mistress will, of course, speak with Lord Shoran about providing you with your own mansion … perhaps nearby."

Elika mustered a smile. "Do not worry about me, Maxim. I am not a helpless child, I know my way around the city. And I'm sorry for all the trouble I brought you and your mistress. Tell her I'm grateful for everything she's done for me, and for the home she gave me."

A sob came from the corner, where Hinna was folding Elika's clothes into a neat pile. "The mistress is being unkind," she said and blew her nose into a handkerchief.

Maxim shifted uncomfortably. Of the servants, only he knew why the mistress was casting her out. It was Maxim who had helped her wrap the skeleton of Mage Goldgrace in a hessian sheet and sew it shut. It was he who had dragged it with her under the cover of darkness to throw into the river in the eastern district of the city. It was this poor beleaguered butler who had to lie to the other servants when Elika made the whole house shake with her ill-suppressed magic. And it was Maxim, who always interjected when Elika and the tane clashed in temper and reason.

There was a loud, demanding knock on the door downstairs. "Open in the name of the archmage."

"Pardon me. I will be back," Maxim said and rushed downstairs.

Hinna followed silently behind, leaving Elika alone.

Elika took off her silken dress and threw it aside, before changing into the split leather skirt she wore when horse riding. She pulled out a small bag she had bought for just such an eventuality, and stuffed into it a spare shirt, a pair of trousers and underclothes. The purse of gold was tempting, and the old thief in her rebelled at leaving it behind. But she could not take Lady Rosalina's coin. She owed her too much, as it was. Besides, the couple of sherrings in Elika's pocket would see her through comfortably, until she came up with a plan.

"Bring us the tane. She is to be questioned," demanded a loud voice belonging to a mage.

"The mistress is abed." Maxim's droll voice was loud enough to carry upstairs.

Elika pried open the door and listened.

"Then you better wake her. Here, read this. It comes from the archmage. Every tane is to be questioned about the whereabouts of a young woman who once belonged to Aeon-Rah."

"There is no such woman here," Maxim said with bored patience.

"We have had reports of a young woman staying with Tane Rosalina."

The tane suddenly appeared. Elika flung open the door and grabbed her arm. "No, they will kill you," she whispered and tried to pull the mistress into the room.

Lady Rosalina shook her off. "Nonsense, girl. He will hot harm me."

"I … I can unravel them," she offered.

"No. I do not ask that. I will speak with them and answer their questions. Be sure to be missing by the time they search the house." Tane Rosalina continued on her way. "Maxim, what is this disgusting noise about?"

"They wish to ask you questions, but it is late."

"'Tis impertinence of the worst kind. Has the archmage forgotten his manners?"

"You must come with us, tane," the mage said, disgust dripping from his voice.

"My name is Lady Rosalina, daughter of Ilikan, and you would do well to remember that. What are these questions about?"

"The Rogue Mage. The one who has been killing the mages."

"And what is that to do with me? The city is a violent place. If one mage turns on another, 'tis not my concern."

"'Tis not one of ours. Only a tsarin can unravel a mage, as you well know."

"I still cannot see why you are here, unless you think I am a tsarin."

"Because the tanes know of the girl, the one with the power of a tsarina, and keep her secret. Though you are a terrible abomination, an outrage of natural order …"

"You stink of a dead man's body and yet speak to me of natural order and abominations?"

"… you possess sight which we do not. We know one of you is harboring her."

"Blind as an eyeless worm," said Rosalina with contempt.

"The human eyes are blind," he said in indignation. "You do not have human eyes and thus see what we cannot. So enough of this prattle. You have been seen with a young woman. You will come with us to answer questions."

"Do you recognize this ring? I am Syn'Moreg's subject, and you may not take me anywhere without his permission. As well you know, mage."

A hiss. "Then we will search your house. Step aside."

"Maxim, please assist this rude, insolent creature. You can begin with the basement, for surely that is where I would hide this so-called Rogue Mage if I had him."

"Aye, mistress, at once. This way, my lord."

Whilst Maxim took the mage below, Elika rushed to tie her bag. She slipped her knife into her boot, pocketed the spider token, shoved Shoran's book into the inside pocket of her cloak, and pulled on her gloves.

Silently, she climbed out the window. Much of the wall was covered with a thick rambling vine which had flowered all summer and sent a nightly fragrance into her room. It was bare now, and the twining branches were covered with frost. Within brief moments she was on the ground, running for the back of the garden, where she climbed another rambling vine over the outer stone wall.

The street beyond was silent with only stray, mangy dogs sniffing around for food and bored-looking cats watching them from high on the walls. For want of a direction, Elika headed towards the archmage's temple. There lay her purpose. She was careful to keep out of sight of the guards, the drunks and the roaming mageguards on horseback.

The city bells had struck the second hour of the new day by the time she reached Temple Square. Floating magical lanterns lit the temple from the base to its domed roof. She found a place to sit where shadows hid her. If Goldgrace was right, marching to the gates and announcing herself as Arala would likely get her killed or captured. Tridamor, it seemed, had his life to protect against accusations of treachery. So how was she to get close?

The cold seeped through her clothing and nipped at her mind, and no ideas came to the fore. She sighed and her breath steamed. It was too late to find a bed for the night. Tomorrow, she would pay for a room at a respectable inn in Daetown. Then she would find a way to get inside that temple.

The cold finally reached her bones, and her limbs grew numb, making her drowsy, then sleepy. A part of her wished for a quieter life, where she would never spend another night sleeping in the street. Where men lived in peace, and magic was back in its own realm. And flowers would be placed at her feet. There was light and warmth, and she was riding through a meadow on a horse …

Her head lolled and bounced back, startling her awake. Arms were gripping her shoulders. She snatched the knife from her boot and lashed out, cutting the shadow looming over her, then jumped to her feet and staggered back.

She shook her head to clear it. *Fool you are to fall asleep in the street in the cold.*

A shadow stepped towards her. She warded it off with the knife. "Keep back. I've no coin to give you." Her limbs were frozen numb and unbalanced.

"Keep your coin, kitten."

With an inward sigh, she lowered her knife, then slid down the wall to the ground and hugged herself. "How do you always know where to find me? I haven't unraveled any mages tonight. As yet," she added just to prod him.

He sat down across from her and put his head back against the wall, as if wearied by her. "You killed Goldgrace. Why?"

"You cannot kill a man twice," she replied mulishly. When he said nothing, she hugged herself tighter and sighed. "I did not kill him but returned him to his own realm. He wanted to go home and asked me to free him."

"Tane Rosalina refuses to have you back. She is … disturbed."

"I do not wish to go back. She despises me."

"She fears you."

A small, ironic smile escaped her lips. "'Tis truly madness that she fears me more than she fears you and your world-destroying master."

He considered her in silence, then he ran his hand through his hair. It was such a human gesture that for a moment, she forgot he was not. He took out a purse and threw it to her.

She caught it. It was heavy for its size and she suspected it was filled with gold pieces. She threw it back at him. "Don't want your coin."

"You would rather steal than accept what is freely given?"

She heated in shame. "Nothing is ever freely given, Shoran. I'd rather steal than owe more than I can repay."

"How cynical you are. And how tragically misguided." He held up the fat pouch. "There is no need for you to steal."

Elika flushed with self-awareness. "Only whores take money from men they are not wed to."

He tilted his head as if considering her words. "You were once part of a gang of thieves, were you not?"

"We were a pack ..."

"You shared your plunder?"

"Aye, though we called it our finds. We did not plunder ..."

"Then think of this as me sharing my *finds*." Again, he held out the fat purse.

"We are not a pack." As soon as she said that, she sensed the lie in her words. There was something about his very essence that spoke kinship. The sensation was unsettling.

"How does one become a pack?" he asked with a slight tilt of his head.

"It's ... agreed upon. We bring orphans into our Hide where we live together and look after each other."

Silence, a pointed one as his brow lifted. Damn him.

"We are not a pack," she said more firmly.

He turned the purse in his hand thoughtfully. "You cannot sleep on the streets. The cold will get you if not the predators."

"Look, I've been looking after myself for a long time. In the morning I'll return to Daetown and find an inn to stay in, whilst I ..." She stopped herself before she betrayed her plans. Then blurted out, "… find a way to earn a living. Might be I'll sew dresses."

He stared flatly at her, and she had a distinct feeling he was not impressed by her explanation. Or believed it. His gaze then drifted to the archmage's temple.

"So, you see," she continued before he divined her plans. "You've no need to worry about me. Flattering though it is to have the servant of the dark lord, destroyer of the world, showing such interest in me and my affairs." She said it in a way that made it clear she was not even slightly flattered. Then she rose to her feet and curtsied mockingly. Though with perfect grace, just as Tane Rosalina had taught her. "My lord." She turned to leave him.

A firm hand wrapped around her arm. "You will stay in the tower until the great wind whispers wisdom to me as to what to do with you."

"Do with me," she repeated slowly. "I'm not yours to do anything with."

"The night is cold and will grow colder," he said with more force.

As if he called it forth, snow began to fall, thick and heavy. The type that buried sleeping men in the street by morning. Were she to fall asleep, she'd likely be dead by dawn. Still, the thought of going with him to his tower filled her with dread and made her insides skip and flip in an unsettlingly giddy dance.

"I'd rather not be your prisoner." She tried to yank her arm back.

His hand tightened around it. "Show sense and do not fight me. I mean you no ill will," he said in a quiet rumble that sent waves of apprehension through her.

He strode towards the wall, pulling her with him. A single blink later they were in the dark hall with one door in it. He released her instantly, and only the sudden warmth of his tower stopped her from running back out the way she had come.

Shoran opened the door—the only door in the long, long hall. "This is to be your chamber."

Elika approached it suspiciously. The last time she was here, the only door she saw led to his room. She peered inside, keeping her distance from Shoran, and was relieved to find a different bedchamber. It was very feminine with remnants of another female's possessions: a brush beside the mirror, a golden dress discarded on the chair, gemmed shoes beside the bed.

Something cutting and unpleasant ran through her chest. "This is another woman's room. Your ... mate," she added lamely.

"This was once Arala's room," he said.

It was the last thing she expected to hear. "Arala ... she lived here?"

"For a time," he said and again looked at her in that odd, searching way, as if he was trying to see inside her mind. As if something about her puzzled him.

"I'm not Arala," she said.

"I know that," he said with a hint of dry humor. "You can stay here, nonetheless. You will be safe and undisturbed. She left behind things she will no longer need. Make use of them as you wish."

He turned to leave.

"Where are we?" she asked. "What is this place?"

He stopped. "The Tower of the Abyss," he replied without turning and strode down the long corridor until shadows swallowed him.

~

Echoes of Arala haunted the room. The elaborate, silver brush still held silken strands of black hair. The priceless jewelry had been carelessly discarded. There was no dust anywhere. Elika imagined that at any moment, the demigoddess would stride through the door and smite her for daring to invade her chamber.

Elika started a fire in the fireplace; it had been laid and was ready to light with a candle. As she warmed through, her eyes grew heavy. She lay on the bed expecting a scent of perfume, but there was no scent left behind, just clean silk sheets. For a long time, she lay awake, waiting, listening to the silence whilst Arala's echoes warned her away. If this was the Tower of the Abyss,

Syn'Moreg must be somewhere near. The curtains were drawn, but Elika dared not approach the windows. Through the parting, she had glimpsed the oppressive darkness beyond. The type of darkness that made it hard to breathe.

The warmth of the fire finally lulled her to sleep. She was woken by the smell of food. A tray with eggs and bacon had been placed on the side table by the door. The door was closed. No one was around. Outside the window, it was still dark, so she knew not how long she had slept.

Elika pulled on her boots, sat on the edge of the bed and gathered her thoughts. The food beckoned. She was hungry ...

A frightening thought came to her. She rushed to the door, yanked on the handle ... and staggered back as it opened. With a sigh of relief, she closed it again, then sat on the chair with her back straight and shoulders pushed back. She ate the food the way Lady Rosalina had instructed, taking small bites, chewing unhurriedly, cutting each piece with a knife and fork without clinking loudly on the plate.

When she had finished, she approached the mirror into which Arala had gazed. Elika's eyes dropped to the brush with black hair, the same color as hers, as Shoran's, too. Her hair was mussed from sleep, but her hand hovered above Arala's brush. To touch it was to acknowledge some deep secret—knowledge that must never emerge. Her hand moved away, and she used her fingers instead to untangle her hair.

There was a discarded dress on the chair, gold, shimmering, very slender, and too long for Elika's height. On the table lay a decorative collar made of gems. And beside the chair were slippers for a foot larger than hers.

Needing to get away from another woman's presence, Elika grabbed the book Shoran had given her and strode to the door. She flung it open and all but ran out of the haunted room.

It was no better on the other side. The dimly lit hall of black stone stretched into eternity. There were no doors she could see. Her feet moved forward, but the hall just stretched on and on, weakly lit with pools of light from torches. Behind her, the door to Arala's room was gone. So Elika walked on and on, and still no doors or stairs appeared. The bottomless Abyss taunted her behind the windows.

Panic bloomed in her chest. There was no lock on her door because there was nowhere to flee. She was a prisoner, else this was a terrible dream. Her pace quickened, then she started to run. Walls rushed past with no way out. Elika stopped and spun around. Everywhere she looked, there was just endless hall and the Abyss beyond.

"Shoran!" she cried out as she searched for his thread, for some essence of him nearby.

A faint light appeared in the distance. She ran towards it and his thread grew stronger, pulling her towards the man she wanted to see. The light grew into a doorway. The door was ajar. She burst in and came to a staggering halt inside a vast library. Shelves of books and scrolls rose into the ceiling with balconies and ladders everywhere. Shoran stood at one of the windows, watching the darkness beyond with his hands behind his back.

"Why have you bound me with your thread?" the dark voice asked.

"The hall … I was lost." Her voice sounded small in the space between them. She composed herself and stood taller. "I've come to speak with you."

He remained silent.

She stepped further into the room. "I've brought your book back."

Silence.

She suspected that he rarely spoke, that he lived here alone, in this forlorn, forgotten place. And his silence became stark and bare, as if his very soul was flayed by loneliness.

She placed the book on the table and walked to the shelves. All the tombs she could see were written in flourished symbols of a language she did not recognize.

"May I borrow another?" she asked, as she sought one writ in the common tongue of men. But there were so many shelves, it would take her years to search through them all.

It took a moment before he replied. "My library is at your disposal."

She ran her finger over the spines of books, wondering what secrets they contained. "Do you have a book about … Syn'Moreg?"

His shoulders stiffened, and he spun around. "Syn'Moreg."

"You gave me a book about the gods, with names and histories of the most famed of demigods. But Syn'Moreg was not one of them. He is the son of god Moreg. There must be books about him."

He stilled. "All such books in my collection are written in a language you do not speak. Mage Goldgrace was to teach it to you, but you decided to … send him away."

"The book you gave me is written in the language of common men."

"I translated it for you," he said dryly.

She blinked. "You did?"

He did that for her? Her gaze was drawn to a long table with an inkwell and parchment, and many open tombs. She imagined him sitting there and patiently transcribing the whole book to give to her, so she could read it.

"There must be many books about him written by priests in the common tongue," she said at length.

He moved towards her, stopping close enough that she could feel his heat and the power he emanated. Her breath caught, her heart did a skip and shied away in fear of being seen doing such a foolish thing.

Thankfully, he faced the shelf and did not see it. He reached up and pulled out a book. "A human priest wrote of him long ago. It is conjecture mostly. Yet seeds of truth you'll find beneath the lies and baseless fears."

He held it out to her. For a moment, she could not tear her eyes from his, and she was drifting, falling into those bottomless, black pools. Her gaze flicked to his lips, the softer texture of the bottom one. Those lips firmed, and she quickly dropped the focus of her errant eyes to the book in his hand.

Gingerly, she took it from his long fingers, whilst absorbing their strength and elegance, the fingers that had brushed her cheek so gently …

He stepped away, and it was as if cold water hit her and snapped her out of a foolish daze.

Her gaze refocused on the book. *The Dark Powers of The Three Realms.*

"He's here," she whispered without looking up, embarrassed by those foolish, errant thoughts. "Syn'Moreg is close. This is the tower which is said to be the way to reach him."

Slowly, Shoran nodded.

"Does he know I'm here?"

"There is little he does not know," Shoran replied.

Elika hugged the book to her chest. "He haunts my nights, invades my dreams." She spoke quietly, fearful the spider might hear her.

"He does not haunt your dreams, but you haunt his," he said with a note of bitterness as he retreated to the window.

"Your master is cruel, but I think you are not."

"Cruel?" he echoed softly.

"He broke the world. Mages enslave men, else they murder them to possess their bodies. You said your mother was human. Surely you must feel compassion for them. There must be something you can do to stop this. I ask only that you try." The request sounded naïve even to her ears. Still, she had to ask if only to find out if he could ever be her ally.

Silence. And in that silence, she read his answer, and the walls closed in around them. He would do nothing without Syn'Moreg's command. Disappointment washed through her.

"I want to speak with Syn'Moreg," she said abruptly. Why deal with his servant when Syn'Moreg would be the one to decide their fate? Might be he would listen.

"And what would you say to him?" his tone turned mocking again. "What do you desire of him?"

"It is not for me I would speak, but for men."

"How brave and brash you are."

"Don't mock me. He sundered the world and gave half to men and half to magic. He knew the half he gave to men would die."

Shoran's eyes grew hard and angry. "Aye, he knew. Save that he did not sunder it to give half to men and half to the Laifae. He sundered it to undo another's wrong. He sundered it to save the other half of the web before it burned in the fires started by men and the tsaren. The fools threw blood-salt into Reval's flames and nearly brought about the end of the three realms."

Elika started at that revelation. "'Tis not what men say. Everyone knows Syn'Moreg gave this world to magic."

"They know little at best, and nothing for the most part. Two worlds have merged into one. It belongs to both."

"Then … this half of the world does not belong to the Laifae … or the tsaren," she said slowly as her mind choked on the lie they all believed.

His lips curled cynically at her dawning horror.

Mages enslaved men, believing this world was theirs. Men had been deceived, else they had deceived themselves. The priests spoke as if they knew such things, yet who proclaimed it so?

"Why did you not tell them … the men … the mages?"

"And they would listen?" he mocked. "They listen not to that which does not serve their purpose. It is for them to mend the rift between their races. My task is only to protect the web." His gaze returned to the Abyss beyond. "Why don't you come to this window and see what lies beyond your fears?"

Elika watched his back, unable to leave, to move away, wanting to move closer to him. But then she looked past him at the starless void beyond—at nothingness and death. And she saw that he was as much a part of that darkness as the darkness was a part of him. She dared not step closer towards either of them. "There is nothing there I wish to see."

He did not reply and she left.

CHAPTER NINETEEN

The Orchard of Elder Valley

"The location of Elder Valley is a well-guarded secret. Though it is well known that there are two ways to reach it. The first is as a demigod who can traverse the world in the blink of an eye. The other way is to cross the Sea of Fire, the Mountain of Bones and the Pass of the Blind. Many fools had perished trying to reach the mythical land where the children of the gods run wild and free, to the land which is never touched by cold, and where the trees are always fruiting. Many a prince of the Sacred Crown sought to find his way there and return with a demigoddess bride. Only one ever succeeded. As the blood of gods thinned in the heirs of Sacred Crowns, and magic faded from the world, the sixth King Northwind made the perilous journey across the Sear of Fire and found the sacred lands. He returned with Arala, daughter of Goddess Neka, as his young queen. And the world was never the same again."

The History of Alafraysia and Seramight,
By Mageguard Bluelight

Men with any sense were abed. Even the mageguard had retreated from patrolling the wintry streets. The cold was piercing and the snow so thick, even villains shied away from this night, preferring spiced ale by the fireside or the warm flesh of a whore. It was the perfect night for her foray, though Elika would sooner be abed herself instead of watching the snow-capped domes of the archmage's temple.

The temple and its grounds were a fortress upon a rise in the land. It encompassed the palace within its walls and the great halls of the court. Torches burned along the wall, and guards patrolled the lookouts. There were two main entrances into the keep; one to the west leading into the temple, the other to the south leading into the palace itself. She had walked around the grounds, noting servants' entrances and smaller gates for deliveries. There was a separate entrance for the prisoners, which led to another enclosure within the grounds bordering the prayer hall.

From the roofs of the tallest building nearby, she looked over the wall and spied the stables, the mageguards' training yard and vast gardens. Mageguards were stationed at every entrance both inside and outside the grounds. For days, she has been searching for weaknesses in the temple's defenses, looking for boltholes, blind corners, and pockets rarely touched by the gazes of guards. And she had found one such weakness.

It was a foolish construction, in truth. A low roof ran from the eastern servants' entrance towards the stables outside the walls. A stream of messengers arrived there each day, leaving their horses to be tended, before riding away again. She had followed some of them, to discover that most were servants running errands for the denizens within the walls of the keep. They carried missives, orders and payments to shops, and an occasional request to a whorehouse. Upon which, a young woman would be seen leaving with the messenger to return to the keep.

The low roof between the wall of the keep and the stables was built under a small window, wide enough for Elika to squeeze through. She had watched it for three days and nights, and never saw a light, nor movement of any shadow.

This night deepened. The moon had set. The guards grew sleepy and inattentive, huddled around the torches and pot fires to warm themselves. When none were facing her way, she crept to the stables. From there, it was little work to climb to the low roof. The guards on the wall had turned their backs on the city, and her dark cloak would hide her from any straying, sleepy gazes.

She scurried along the roof and pressed herself against the wall beneath the window.

Silence. No calls of alarm.

She pulled off her gloves and grasped the icy stone of the wall to climb up, but there was little grip to be had, for the stone was covered in ice. Her foot slipped. She tried again, pulled herself up, but found no purchase. She looked up at the window. It was an impossible climb …

Magic. She could use magic.

Tentatively, she sent out her black tendrils. They emerged from the skin of her hands, burrowing out of her flesh like maggots, and she bit back a cry of disgust at the horrid sight.

Don't look, Eli, just climb.

Feeling queasy, she looked away, but still felt them crawling along the cold stone and gripping the rough surface. The tendrils then emerged from her feet and boots, like wriggling snakes. She shuddered, and keeping her eyes on the window, began to climb. When she reached it, she wedged her knife into the slit in the window, and after a little digging and probing, found the lock. A moment later, she crawled inside.

The magic wormed its way back into her skin, and she ignored the vile sensation. Around her, the room was reminiscent of an unused storeroom, for it was too small for anything else. She left the window slightly ajar for a quick escape and pressed her ear against the door.

Silence.

She pried it open.

Creak. The sound seemed loud enough to wake the keep.

She froze, listening.

Silence.

She opened the door a little more and peered into the corridor.

No one was about.

She slipped through the crack and left the door ajar just enough so that it drew no attention or hindered her escape.

Torches burned at the end of the hall. Quietly, she crept towards them, counting doors and windows from the one she had come through, until she came to a stairway. Voices rose from downstairs—guards arguing about luck and women as they rolled dice. Elika went up, and the voices grew distant.

At the top of the stairs, she found another corridor with storage rooms along it filled with crates and boxes. On and on she crept along the upper levels of the keep towards the main temple, being careful to memorize each turn. Today, her foray was only to explore the vast temple, and probe it for secret ways. So, she avoided the main walkways, where guards were always posted, or servants rushed back and forth as they tended to the demands of their masters.

A sound …

She pressed herself against a wall inside an alcove.

Humming came from somewhere deep inside the temple, then a scream of agony. Her blood chilled.

She peered out, and seeing no one, raced towards the sound. The passage led her to a swirling balcony above a vast hall. Keeping behind the column, she peered around it and gazed down. Chained prisoners were on their knees beside a pool with swirling and bubbling black liquid. In front of them stood the archmage, dressed in gold robes, chanting in the language of the Laifae as he pulled on the churning liquid. The black strands rose and fell to his command and grew restless with impatience.

Mage Goldgrace had taught her their language, and she understood the archmage's words.

"Sacred light I call upon, in the name of Arala's grace. Sacred light I call upon, to part the veil and bring them forth."

As he chanted, two mageguards grabbed one of the men and pushed him towards the black pool. His head was thrust into it. The man struggled, then his body jerked and shook. A muffled scream wrenched from him, terrified and pained. Then he stilled, his shoulders slumped, his body now limp. The mageguards removed his chains and lowered him to the floor.

His body jerked again, and he opened his eyes.

"Hail, my kin. Gladly we embrace you in Seramight," said the archmage magnanimously. "I name you Feathersoft."

The body moved and rolled, the limbs flailed in different directions. Mages helped him rise, but his feet tangled and he fell. His arms flopped without control. He made a noise, guttural, incomprehensible, then hoarse words emerged from his throat. "We are broken." His lips did not move.

"You are whole. The human body is confining," replied the archmage. "You must move as one now, think as one, else the body will not obey your wishes." He then turned to the guards. "Take him away. Put him in the nursery with the others."

The mageguards dragged the majren away. They repeated this again and again until all the prisoners were gone, and only the archmage and one mageguard were left behind.

Elika lowered herself to the floor where she was hidden by the bannister. Anger pounded in her temples. This was her chance. Might be it was her only chance. She steadied her breathing and forced herself to put aside the vile images of those poor men being drowned and invaded by another creature.

"Your eminence," said the mageguard, his quiet, hissing voice carrying strongly in the echoing hall. "A reply has arrived from Captain Firesong."

"Firesong," the archmage spat. "So Reval deigns not to reply to me himself but sends his arch to do so in his stead."

"His grief is tainted with hope. His mind is twisted by Arala's refusal to return to him. He believes you are hiding her, or else you want her for yourself."

"Ramblings of a madman. I cannot sense Arala. If she has returned, we are no longer bound. I have not sensed her since the fog lifted."

Elika held her breath and reached her senses towards the archmage.

"We have relayed this to our illustrious tsarin time and again, but he is blind with despair and anger," the mageguard replied placatingly.

"And what does the captain say to our request?"

"It was the same reply. None of Reval's mageguards will be sent to our aid against the Dae rebellion until Arala is returned. He says the city was entrusted to you for guardianship and … ahem … it is your task to guard it."

"So Reval seeks to make me look a fool and take the city from me?" the archmage said thoughtfully. "He wants the imposter prince to attack us."

"Your eminence, perhaps we should accept Lord Nightkill's demands. If we give him what he desires, he will turn Daetown against Northwind."

Elika stilled and strained her ears to hear more. What was Rory up to? She'd kill him herself if she thought he meant to betray Mite.

"Only fools trust the word of a liar," replied the archmage. "And we know the one-eyed *lord* is nothing more than a street thug."

"Still, what have we to lose if we cede to his wishes? He is greedy and ambitious, and such men are easy to bend. We will twist and stretch him to our design. And if he betrays us we will strike and destroy the rebel hold."

There was a thoughtful pause. "Perhaps you are right, Grimday. I will consider my reply to him carefully."

Elika had heard enough. She closed her eyes and sought the threads of the archmage's essence. *He is a lake. She is the sea.*

She reached for the pool of his magic, and once she found it, she felt its depth. And for the first time, she felt not one or two presences, but many. Layer upon layer of consciousness. And she knew what she had to do; she had to unravel them all. So she sought their individual strands, but there were too many. As she grasped one, another slipped away.

A wail echoed through the hall. "I'm under attack! I'm under attack! Find her! The Rogue Mage is here." The voice that screamed was a chorus of voices, awful and terrible to hear.

Something hit her mind so hard she staggered from the force. Her head pounded as if she had been struck by a stone.

"Arala!" he screamed. "Show yourself."

A power surrounded her. It came not from the archmage but from all the mageguards nearby. Flames rose everywhere at once.

"Arala! Why do you hide?" he called out. "Am I not your ever-faithful servant?"

An impenetrable wall made of hundreds of layers of webbed consciousnesses had formed between her and him. She was too far, and too many stood between her and Tridamor. Then black strands emerged from the stone and began seeking her as they crawled over the floor and walls.

Elika rolled to her feet and fled the way she had come, jumping over the black strands as she went. As she raced through the fire, she forgot not to be afraid, and the flame grew hotter as she grew more frightened, for fear gave their magic power to hurt.

It is not real, it is not real, she chanted as she ran, forcing herself to believe it, and as she did, the heat retreated.

Shouts came from behind her. She threw out a wall of black webbing and raced ahead. Something sharp cut through it. Ignoring the pain, she imagined a stone wall behind her. And so it appeared, blocking the way across the hall. Elika grinned with relief …

A mageguard walked through the wall as if it was not there. And she cursed the fickleness of magic, grasped the mage's essence and …

"Mistress," he cried in pain.

She took a calming breath, for the creature was now in her grasp. She shifted her vision and another world with a purple sky and mountains suspended from it like jagged teeth. Then she saw the black, shifting creature wound around the skeleton of a man. Gently, as Goldgrace had instructed, she pushed it back into its realm.

The skeleton of a man fell to the floor. More mageguards walked through her illusion of a wall. Elika turned and ran, outpacing the much slower mages. She burst through the door she had left ajar, took three steps to the window, crawled onto the ledge and dangled off it.

An arrow hit the wall beside her. Then another. She flung out her magic strands and slid down the wall. An arrow pierced her hand, and she stifled a yelp of pain … save it did not hit her hand but the black strand holding on to the ledge whilst she dropped to the roof. More arrows whizzed past as she darted over the stables and jumped to the ground.

Guards were waiting for her with swords drawn. As soon as they saw her, they charged. Elika pulled out a dagger, ducked under an arm, and sliced through a thigh. The guard cried out and fell to one knee. She avoided the downward strike of a sword, took out her other small knife and threw it at the guard blocking her way. It found his throat. He gripped the knife. Blood poured through his fingers. Two others tried to grab her, but in their armor, they were as clumsy as fat cows. She ducked past them. One grabbed her hair. She spun in his grip and cut his arm. He released her with a hiss, and she bolted along the street.

Arrows flew past. Footfalls sounded behind her. She leapt up at the nearest balcony and pulled herself up. Without looking down, she grabbed the rainwater pipe and scrambled up it to the roof like a spider. Another arrow struck the wall by her head. She lay flat as another arrow flew past. Quickly, she crawled behind the nearest chimney and placed a hand on the warm stone. She searched for the dark path towards the tower, groping blindly for Shoran's thread, his essence …

"'Tis her, our glorious queen, I see!" called a lyrical voice, and Reval's mageguard rose on a cloud above the roofs. Then another and another joined him.

"Arala, oh sacred flower, return to your king," they sang as they flew towards her, chains in their hands.

Overhead, the sky exploded with fire, and a ribbon of flame streaked across the clouds, forming shapes of flowers and exotic birds.

Sweet Neka, he's madder than a grasshopper in a jar.

Elika closed her eyes and reached with all her might towards Shoran. The stone moved beneath her hand and she was sinking, sinking into darkness. She fell through, pulling on the thread in her grasp … and fell forward and down, onto her hands and knees.

Stone floor … green, flickering light of that strange fire …

Bare feet appeared in front of her.

She looked up, past the black silk trousers and shirt, and into dark eyes dimly lit with golden light.

"Why is there blood on you?" asked the darkness.

"It's not mine," she replied and jumped to her feet, spun and faced the door, waiting for the mageguard to charge in after her.

"They cannot follow you here." His dark voice came from close behind.

"I followed you here," she said.

He moved closer still. "Who is following you?"

His voice was so soft and seductive; it washed through her like a kiss and shattered her concentration. She turned and realized she was still holding a bloodied knife.

She lowered it. "Reval's mageguard," she admitted reluctantly.

His gaze darted to the knife. "'Tis men's blood you wear."

"They are following me, too," she ceded wryly.

"Why?"

She clamped her mouth shut before truth fled from it. Then shrugged nonchalantly. "Might be they don't like me."

He was silent, considering her, clearly not believing her. "Trust me," he said, his gaze intent.

And those words, so gently spoken, nearly undid her. She saw then that she was in his bedroom, the one she had destroyed the last time she was here. It was restored to what it was, as if she had never torn it apart. Truth tickled the tip of her tongue, wanting to escape, but she recalled whose servant he was, to whom he was beholden.

"You are his," she said quietly.

"I can be yours."

And those cruel, devastating words whose meaning she could not wholly fathom muddled her head.

Trust not those who trust you not back. Penny's voice came to her through the mud of confusion. And it was the voice of reason she latched onto before she said something to betray herself.

"Do you trust me?" she asked him in reply.

Silence. Aye, he considered it. The question stumbled him as much as his words stumbled her.

She smiled sadly. "Easier to ask than to give, hey Shoran? Easier to take than to make," she added cheekily, an old saying on the streets.

From the corner of her eye, she saw a silver jug and a goblet beside it. It brought to the fore her fierce hunger. She had used her magic, spent herself, and her head buzzed with the want of the silvery liquid. Her hands began to shake.

She returned her knife to her boot, wiped the blood from her hands onto her trousers, strode to the jug, poured herself a goblet, and downed it at once. It hit her with the sweetest force as life and light rushed through her blood. She moaned in ecstasy, then poured another measure and drank it too. Light exploded around her. Everything grew brighter and more beautiful. She poured another goblet … a large hand wrapped over hers, stopping her from raising it to her lips.

"No more." His voice was distant. "Drink not too deeply of the well, for it will drown you."

He took the goblet from her hand. She spun to face him, hostile at first, then breathless. She was swimming in life and joy as if she had been born anew, and he … he was breathtakingly handsome …

"It will pass," he said, taking a step away from her and sipping from the goblet himself.

Warm embarrassment cleared her thoughts somewhat, enough for her to see something she had not noticed before. The weariness in his face was not because of her, but because of his own spent magic. He looked worn and drained of his usual vigor. Always, he had a jug of silversap to hand. He was using his magic … but not on her. What was he doing? Where was he expending his magic?

Slowly, the delirium faded, the light grew dimmer, and the euphoria vanished.

He picked up the jug and looked inside it. "Come, we will refill it. It is time you learned where to harvest your strength."

He took her hand, and strode to the door and through it, emerging outside …

Elika suddenly gazed at the magnificent vista of rolling hills and meadows covered in early morning mist. Surely, they had left the realm of men. The air was warm and balmy, though it was mid-winter. It was dawn, and the sky was a battle of purples and gold of the like she had never seen before. They stood on the edge of a grove of old trees with silvery leaves and bark, and strange fruit she did not recognize. Jagged, tall mountains encircled them far in the distance.

"Where are we?" she asked, for surely, there was no place more peaceful and serene, save the realm of the gods.

"Elder Valley," he said and released her hand to walk ahead into the trees.

"Where the gods bring their children to be raised?" she asked in astonishment. "I thought it a myth … it's not on any maps."

"Few know of its existence, for only a few can ever come here. This is the Sacred Orchard of Gods' Wood. These trees tap into the wells of power. Their roots feed upon the Great Web's light." He stopped beside one tree, extended his finger, and it elongated before her eyes into a black, hooked claw. It cut into the bark and silver liquid poured out of the tree. He placed the jug and kept it there until it was full. The claw turned back into a finger, and he ran it over the wound, sealing it again. He reached up to pluck a fruit and offered it to her.

It reminded her of an apple, only it was red with silvery veins. Gingerly, she took it.

"The fruit is for the children of the gods. It feeds and nourishes them as they grow. The sap of the tree is far more potent and is used to restore strength and vitality when it is drained. Those who overindulge, drown."

She bit into the fruit. It tasted like a blend of strawberry and apple. Silver juice flowed down her chin. The fruit was less potent, yet still sent a pulse of life and vitality through her veins with each bite, as if awakening her from a wintry slumber.

"The first kings of the Sacred Crowns were demigods who could cross the veil to this land when their power was drained. Here they fed and feasted and rested. Too often they overindulged, and mankind paid the price. As generations went by, the blood of the gods in their veins thinned, until their descendants could no longer reach these sacred trees. Only by traversing the perilous Sea of Fire could they find the pass into this valley and harness the power they coveted. Many tried. All failed but one."

"Arrain Northwind who married Arala," she said, recalling the tale in the book about the gods that he had given her. It was written by a demigod Orolan, who was said to have witnessed everything he wrote. "How did he cross the sea without burning?"

"By some design of Fates, Arrain was more powerful than his predecessors, and his magic shielded him against the fire. Orolan, who foresaw their entwined fates, then showed him the way. Worthless old bird that he is," he added with a note of annoyance, as if he knew the demigod himself. "Arala used to run through these woods, feasting on the fruit with abandon," he said at length, and there was a hue of regret in his voice. "She would sing and dance and cast light upon the trees. It was how King Arrain found her. And he too partook of the sacred fruit and filled his body with the power long denied him."

"They say Arala was beautiful," she said, probing a little deeper where she knew she should not.

"Beyond compare," he replied, and again a note of sadness crept into his voice.

"You and she were close," she said awkwardly and swallowed a pang of bewildering jealousy.

"We were raised together as children, in my mother's Sachi tribe."

The pang of jealousy intensified.

"When she left with Northwind as his queen," Shoran continued, "she took cuttings of these sacred trees with them, as a gift to her beloved and to mankind. From these silvery cuttings, she planted silver orchards of the sacred fruit. And from them, she fashioned other fruiting trees of El'Sandria: apples, oranges, peaches and countless others. None of the fruit trees are native to this world. Though the gods were angry, Neka forgave her daughter's unwise gift to the young king."

Elika could not imagine the world without fruit and jam and apple pastries. "'Tis one transgression I could forgive the gods," she said with a grin, and recalled the story of the silver-leaved orchards, which were all burned down by Syn'Moreg, save those in Arala's personal gardens.

"Indulgence always claims a price," he went on to say. "In her folly, she planted these orchards where any man could partake of the silver-veined fruit. It strengthened the blood of the gods, and men with the slightest drop of it could once again drink from the wells of power. And the world grew more perilous. The Laifae were not responsible for all the ills born of magic."

As he spoke, she searched his face, trying to grasp what it was about him that did not belong in their world. There was an agelessness about him, melded together with an age-worth of learning and knowing. And in his eyes, she saw the depth of wisdom and world-weariness of a wrinkled old man.

"How old are you?" she asked tentatively.

His lips tilted up sardonically. "I was born two thousand eight hundred years ago, as measured by the turn of days in Seramight."

Elika gaped. The import of his words sank in slowly. The number of years he had lived was incomprehensible. Then her heart began to race, as ever so slowly, a suspicion dawned on her, one she dared not entertain. The silver leaves whispered in the breeze. Her gaze locked on the jug of silver liquid in his hand. He was not a Laifae, his mother was a Sachi, but he was not a human …

She raised her face to his. Dark amusement shone in his eyes at the slow awakening of understanding in her mind. And in his fathomless black eyes, she saw the ages of man pass, saw eternity and loss and loneliness of time unending.

He was not human, he was not Laifae or a mage or a tane …

And here, surrounded by the sacred forest of the gods, understanding crashed into her.

His smile widened and darkened, as he read her realization, and waited for her to accept the truth she had so long denied.

"You're a demigod," she said on a breath, and that truth fell between them. It took her breath away, terrified her. It was one thing to hear old stories of gods or read of them in crumbling pages, and quite another to face one in the flesh. A demigod stood before her. A being with the power to destroy the world. Even the lesser of them could fell an army of mere men.

A wicked glint in his eyes mocked her for not seeing it sooner, laughed at her for being such a fool.

Her jaw went slack, and she could not look away, could not stop taking in his features so different to men, and yet so alike …

Aye, she was a fool for thinking she could kill him. Irritation followed that thought. She crossed her arms and kicked the stone beneath her foot. "You might have mentioned it before."

A low rumble of laughter came from him. "To what purpose?"

Then another thought pushed its way to the fore. "Why did you bring me here, to the sacred forest meant for the children of gods?"

He cupped her face and brought his close to hers. "Ever you deny that which you fear most. 'Tis here you should have been raised, Aleyala, daughter of the gods. This orchard is yours to plunder."

Elika stepped back. His hand fell away. "No. You are mistaken."

"We are kin, kitten. 'Tis a cruel fate that led to you being uncared for." He opened his palm. In it lay a ring with a spider on it, like the one Lady Rosalina wore. "Take this, and no one shall ever harm you again."

Anger and shame bloomed in her chest, and that deep resentment that follows abandonment. "I do not need your or your master's protection. Nor am I a child anymore, be it a godly one or not. Take me back to the tower."

His fingers closed around the ring. "'Tis the path you have travelled, and the same path you can tread. Turn and seek it with your mind." With that, he strode forward and vanished.

She ran after him and straight into a tree.

She cursed, rubbed her head, then felt for the path and returned to his dark hall. There was no sign of Shoran.

CHAPTER TWENTY

The Dark Path

"Through our long searches, we never found the answer to the greatest question of our time. Why did our realms collide and merge? Was it the act of an angry god, or another celestial disaster? When we asked our liege Tsarin Reval where we might find the answer, he grew angry and the fire of his flesh grew hot. We feared he might sunder us from this body and send us back to the land of dreams. 'Seek not what is dangerous to touch,' he said. 'Ask not what your mind cannot grasp. 'Tis merely a tragedy that came to pass, borne of impossible dreams that could not be spun.' He turned away, but not before we saw a flash of grief."

The History of Alafraysia and Seramight,
By Mageguard Bluelight

*R*uby's *Red Lips* was a rundown whorehouse, from which the lowliest wretch would not be turned away if he had half a broken penny to spend. And those lowliest wretches now cast crude and leering glances her way. Others were more threatening and violent in their intent. Elika knew it was not just the neat clothes she wore, which were worth more coin than they had on them. Tane Rosalina's instructions had etched themselves deep into her skin and bearing, and that rankled them more than what she wore. So they eyed her to see whom she went to meet, whilst she paid them no notice as she strode past.

The whorehouse was grimy, with stained floors and the stench of old ale mixed with ripe sweat and pungent, sickly-sweet perfumes. The thick, scarlet curtains hiding the windows were frayed at the edges.

Elika's gaze flitted past the bawdy whores and sordid gropes of their patrons, past base desires of men and lewd kisses. Her gaze skipped past a girl too young to be a whore pulling an old letch up the stairs, and finally found Blood Dog. He was drinking deeply of his ale whilst fondling a half-dressed wench in his lap. He slammed down his mug, buried his face in her voluptuous, sweaty bosom, and growled like a playful puppy.

Elika sat across from him, ignoring the whore's annoyance at the intrusion. "Hey, Dog."

He froze, raised his head, and cursed. "Don't ye see I'm busy? Unless you are here to sit on my other knee." He patted his spare knee in case she didn't know where it was. "Then come along and join us. Else scurry off and leave a man to his needs." His reached into the woman's dress, pulled out her tit, and licked the nipple.

"Want to talk to you," she said, ignoring his sly gaze and the woman's naked tit. She'd seen worse. If he thought to scare her off, he'd be disappointed.

"Bloody hell, find another to blabber with. My balls are full to bursting, and my cock's hard enough to impale a tree." He put his hand under the whore's skirt. She threw back her hair and nipped his ear, whilst her hand travelled to his lap.

"It's about them dogs you talk about cutting the heads off," Elika said flatly.

He cursed again, yanked out his hand from under the woman's skirt and put her aside. "Listen, love," he said to her. "How's about I give ye a copper to wait over there till this mouse scurries away and leaves me alone?"

The woman took the coin. "Might be we'll go upstairs when you're finished here, puppy, where there are less mice around."

Blood Dog's gaze followed the buxom wench longingly, then turned back to Elika with a face that promised murder. "I thought we agreed not to talk about things that didn't concern you."

"It concerns me, Dog. Anything you do to harm men concerns me."

He laughed. "My, aren't you a fierce one? I dare say some lucky bastard will thaw that icy gaze of yours one day."

A lush serving wench brought them their ale and leant over Blood Dog to get him to notice her bursting bosom. "Hey, Dog. Keeping fancy company these days, are ye?"

Dog slapped the tavern maid on her arse. "No one's finer than you, Silks."

She roughed his hair and took away his empty mug.

When the maid was gone, he sat back and took his time perusing Elika in that debauched way of his that made her want to pull a knife on him.

"Cleaned up, did ye? Got yourself a rich man?"

"It's not like that. Just found a mistress who wants to turn me into a proper lady's maid. Likes to dress me nice and nags me about keeping my back straight."

"Is that so?" he drawled. "Now how about you tell me the truth instead, Prunny. I'm not as stupid as I must look to ye. Besides, you came to find me. So, what do you want?"

"As I said, got a big dog to hunt down." She glanced around to make certain no one was close enough to hear. "And you said you used to kill when killing needed to be done. And I suspect you are doing it still. It was you who killed Lord Snowstorm of Daetown. Though you also said you killed the right people to make it matter to the bigger game. Lord Snowstorm only mattered to Rory, not to anyone else. Now men are turning against men, instead of turning against mages. Why him? Whose side are you on, Dog?"

He took a swig of his ale. "Damn it, but there's something about ye that's been plaguing me. Ye look familiar ... more so now that there's flesh on your face. Yet I can't place it." He put down the mug. "We're on the same side, mousy. If we weren't, they'd be fishing ye out of the river. 'Cause you're a barb in my cock. Not sure what to make of ye. Be that as it may, listen closely and learn. To hunt a big fish, you need first to isolate it. Then you need to bait it. Lord Snowstorm was a weed in my scheme that needed plucking."

It was a strange thing to say, and some memory tickled at the back of her mind, just beyond her reach. "Who are you hunting, Dog?"

He leant in, and his face morphed into one of a shrewd, hard man, with intelligence and belligerence in equal measure. "I told ye to keep out of my business. But tell you what, seeing as you are halfway to getting yourself killed, I don't see that it matters. Southfire. He's the poor bastard I'm after."

That took Elika aback. Then she chuckled and sat back with a wide grin, which clearly annoyed him. "Surely you've looked in the mirror recently. You'd not get within a league of the prince of the Sacred Crown. They'd smell you coming before they saw you. Besides, what does a whoring street drunk like you want with the prince?"

He scowled. "Southfire is Reval's ally, and he bows and prances around Archmage Tridamor like a jester. Three masters united against men. We need to break that union, mousy, before Northwind makes his own claim on the realm. Like I said, we're not on opposite sides. At least not as yet."

Elika's grin fell away. "You are working for Northwind?"

"I kill for no man. My purpose comes from the gods themselves. Their blood runs in my veins. I'm one of King Eshan Westwater's miserable descendants."

Elika shrugged at the greasy man. "Every man on the street claims a drop of god's blood in their veins. Might be all of us are a descendant of some king or other. Plenty of their bastards are said to have run around the kingdoms, seeding even more bastards in unsuspecting women."

He laughed roaringly, then drank to drown his mirth. "As you say, mousy. Ye right, of course. There's no crown in my future. Only ale and whores. But blood is more than what keeps your heart beating and my cock erect. It's your life source and your purpose. No blood is more demanding than that of the gods. Even a drop of it fills ye head with all manner of wild ideas about the future and what one must do. Ye can't fight it."

"And your blood tells you to help put Northwind on the throne?" she said slowly, unconvinced.

"Never said that, now did I? Not my problem which bastard takes the crown, nor does it matter in the end. They're all alike. My task is to break the nest of serpents, which threatens the three realms. 'Tis about balancing the Fates against the inevitable end of light. If we don't, then the Abyss will swallow us all sooner rather than later."

Again, something about his words nipped at her mind, for they reminded her of something she had read.

She shook her head slowly. "You are but one man. Your ambition is too great. Might be we are both fools to think anything we do matters."

He leant in. "Listen, mousy. Don't ye listen to those who'd tell you one man can't change the world. A knife in the dark is the only sure way to carve the shape of the future. There's those who, like One Eye, brazenly crave power and will do anything to get it. But his power is trifling and fleeting, and another like him will take his place when he's gone. Now there's others like you and me who hold great power without wishing for it. And that power wants its say on matters, and it wants freedom from any cage you put it into. The sooner you accept that, the sooner you'll see your place in this world."

If she didn't know any better, she'd think she was sitting in front of a Sachi priest. And his words sent her mind into the sky towards greatness on the soaring wings of possibilities. The harsh, ringing laugh of a whore brought her back to where she was.

"No groping till you pay for it, you cheeky bastard," said a shrill, indignant voice.

Elika glanced around and the illusion he was spinning was broken. "So, is this your place in the world?" she said. "If this is where the gods sent you, then I hold no kinship with your cause or theirs."

He sat back, grinned and stretched his legs. "Even the mightiest gods need a respite from setting the world to right, mousy. And seeing as you are in the same place as me right now, I'd be heedful of casting your mighty judgement about."

Elika sighed. He was right, of course. Here she was, seeking help from the drunk letch in a whorehouse. Who was she to judge him? "Thought you might help me, that's all. I'm hunting the archmage and need to get close to him to do it. Just don't know how … anymore."

"Ah, so that was you who got Tridamor hot and flustered and pissing his pants when an intruder attacked him in his own temple. Don't know how you got in, but I dare say you've locked yourself out again, ye clumsy mouse. Not sure even I can get into that temple now."

He was right to berate her. She had chastised herself, too. Since her failed attack on the archmage, he had trebled his guard and made certain no window or door was unguarded.

"Look, it's not hopeless as yet. I got myself trained as a lady, so I might just walk in as … Arala." She forced the name out of her mouth, though it did not sit well on her tongue.

Blood Dog roared with laughter. "Aye, I can see it. Except, as soon as Reval gets a whiff of Arala's whereabouts, he'll be there faster than a bull on heat in a barn filled with cows."

"Aye, I thought so, too. So, how do I sneak into the court with them lords and ladies as one of them without being stopped and questioned?"

"You need to go with a lord, that's how. A young niece from the countryside gentry, who's come to Terren to find a rich lord to wed."

"That's the problem. I don't know any lord."

"Aye, you do. Lord Nightkill." He grinned slyly.

"You mean One Eye," she said uncertainly. "Not sure I can trust him. He's up to something. Overheard Tridamor and a mageguard talking about it. Sounds like he's been looking to make peace with them."

"Listen, mousy. I'm not a boiled-sweets jar of possibilities for you to peruse. If you've been trusting One Eye before, then you're a fool. I warned ye about that, didn't I? You don't need to trust him or like him to use him for your own ends. So, it's either him, and I can help, or find your own way to do it."

"What if he betrays me to the archmage?"

"He won't. 'Cause if he does, I'll slit his throat."

There was such crude honesty about the ruffian, she thought he might yet be the only man she could trust. It was a sobering thought, and it made her reach for her ale. He was right, besides.

She had no other options, and she didn't need to trust Rory, she only had to watch him closely.

"Very well. What shall I do?"

"Tell ye what. Come and meet me this evening on the corner of Westway Parade, dressed like the fine lady you're meant to be. If you impress me, I'll take ye to Nightkill myself and help you get close to the dog you're after. Be sure to arrive in a nice coach. Right now, I got my own needs to take care of."

He waved over his whore, who was waiting patiently at the bar. She grabbed two foaming tankards and approached with an exaggerated sway of her hips.

Elika finished her ale just as the whore arrived and plopped into Blood Dog's lap with a giggle.

"Tonight then, Dog," Elika said and left them.

In reply, he mumbled something from inside the wench's cleavage and waved her off.

On her way out, a drunk grabbed her wrist. "Hey there, beautiful. How about you sit on my knee and give me those sweet red lips of yours?"

Elika was about to cut him, when Blood Dog's voice called out. "Bizzer, ye touch her again and I'll cut ye arm off at the shoulder and carve ye eyes out of your head."

The drunk snatched away his hand and turned back to his ale.

No one else bothered her on the way out.

~

"Well, look at ye, Spit, you do clean up well." One-eyed Lord Nightkill looked her up and down with an appreciative twist of his lips. "And you have grown since I last saw you. I almost didn't recognize ye."

Blood Dog stood to the side, leaning on the wall with his arms crossed, taking his own fill of her body, no doubt.

Elika straightened, tall and proud, as if she was Lady Rosalina herself. "You will address me as Lady Fair," she said in her best Alterrian accent.

"Magnificent," Rory said as he circled her, shamelessly perusing her figure. He felt the silk of her dress between his fingers, and it was all she could do not to step away from his touch. "This silk must have cost ye a fair silver. I can see why Pockets was so enamored with you, telling me to look deeper beneath the rough."

One-Eyed Rory had a few more scars on his face since she had last seen him. Just like Daetown itself. There were shadows in his face too, and the haggard lines of a leader under siege.

"Now that you have finished perusing, shall we talk?"

"Then talk. What brings you to me, Spit?"

"Our arrangement. You want me to kill the archmage, and I need to get close to him to kill him. The only way is to be presented to him in court … as a lady."

He threw back his head and laughed. "Oh, Spit. You'd do better to be presented to him as a whore. I can pass you along as one … but a lady." He laughed again.

Rory's mirth stung, though she expected it. It reminded her that she was an imposter, as much as Lord Nightkill himself, and it was hard not to think of Mite and how magnificent he looked with a proper lady beside him.

"If you could present me as your cousin …"

"As my mistress, you surely mean."

"A cousin," she repeated more firmly. "A relative of proper breeding will only strengthen your claim to the name you stole. Surely a lord of such worthy stature as yourself would have an extensive family of noble birth to vouch for you."

"Spit. I'm hard done meself trying to convince the court that I'm a lord. The blasted dukes are combing the records and looking for ways to deny me my claim to the title deeds. They already call me an imposter. They'll skin me and hang me at the slightest proof that I am one. But my titles are verified by the priests and there is naught they can do. But if I bring a … a woman of any less breeding than a full-blooded lady claiming relations, they'll laugh at me, before flaying me alive. I'd do better having a goat hang off my arm. At least then they'd see me as a man of strange tastes, rather than a man of weak ones. Do you see what I'm saying? Find another way, El."

"I will not betray us," she insisted. "Let us have dinner and I will prove it." She curtsied perfectly, just to show him.

Blood Dog cleared his throat then. "If I may, *my lord*."

Rory's grin fell away. "Don't mock me, Dog, or I'll cut off your ears."

Blood Dog grunted at that and continued, regardless. "Mousy is right. Nightkill bloodline is distantly related to the old seat of Killray town, somewhere south-east of here." He waved his hand. "Doesn't matter where. But I did some asking, and the old lord is about to die …"

"And how do you know he's about to die?"

"'Cause it suits us that he does …"

Elika flinched. "Might be there is no need to kill him," she said, sounding naïve even to her own ears.

Blood Dog turned his shrewd gaze on her. "Not a palatable feast for you, queeny? You'd best be stripping off that squeamishness of yours, for there's no way of getting where you want to go without death along the way. The man is on his deathbed as it is. His family's cursed, see. Long ago, one of them offended some god or other. The lord's got a daughter. Lady Fair, her name is, which is why I gave it to ye. Except she's been tainted with disfigurement from an illness when she was young and has not been seen in public since. Except, upon the death of her guardian, she will make a miraculous appearance, and she'll be telling everyone of the kindness her distant cousin, Lord Nightkill, has shown her. Her father had, of course, accepted him as his kin, for there was no denying the distant relations and similarity of features."

Rory rubbed his long chin. "Then why didn't her father present me in court already?"

"He has not been to court since his daughter's affliction. Embarrassment, I believe. Else they fear his curse."

"And what happened to her disfigurement?"

"Cured by prayer, and magic of course."

"And they'll believe that?" Rory raised a brow.

"They'll believe you 'cause no one will want to be the first to insult the lady by calling her a liar. Besides, look at her face."

Rory did. "What of it?"

"It's riddled with Sachi features, ye damned fool. All ye have to do is claim she's never had a disfigurement but was instead conceived in secret to another woman with the blood of gods flowing strongly in her. A Sachi woman from the mythical Elder Valley. It'll give them a believable reason for your interest in the girl."

"The Sachi are disdained where we're from," said Rory.

"'Cause where we are from, they forgot much that is still remembered here," Blood Dog replied. "'Tis the taint of gods' blood the nobles here covet in their wives and mistresses."

"And what will you do with the real Lady Fair?" Elika asked.

"She'll be looked after as she was before her father's death, in his keep under lock and key with servants to tend her."

"And the servants?"

"Will be loyal to the one who pays them and will keep their silence if they don't want their throats cut in the middle of the night."

Rory considered it. "Having a cousin of noble blood does lend me standing in court. Though you may be barking too soon, Dog. Both Southfire and the archmage are refusing to allow me entry to court."

"This is why you need the lass. Spin a tale they'll never believe, yet which will nevertheless intrigue them. She's your bait, and you just need to catch a fish to take her and you to Southfire. As you said, she'll have to go as your mistress. One who is madly in love with the ragged new lord," Blood Dog added with a wink at Elika. Before she could object, he carried on. "Unless you want to be fighting the lecherous advances of every lord. You'd do better going as his love-stricken mistress, and under his protection."

"My love." Rory leered at her tauntingly, taking a step closer and circling his arm around her waist.

She was ready. A knife appeared at his throat. "You got your whores, Rory. I'll not be one of them. I just need to get inside the court, 'tis all."

"And how do you propose to convince them that you are in love with me, if you flinch when I touch ye?"

Elika stepped away from his arms. "I'll play my part when it matters."

"Ah, Spit, you need to get your bits stretched. Has Mitey even kissed ye?"

Her cheeks warmed.

Rory laughed. "Get yourself a man, mousy, else you'll never fool them."

Blood Dog sniggered behind her.

"I am a lady. Chastity is expected and desired."

Rory shook his head. "There's not a lady in court who has her chastity intact by the time she's your age. They are worse than dogs on heat. And do you think anyone would believe that a woman on my arm is pure? Damn it, if I had a lady in love with me, I'd have her skirts up behind the nearest door before she could confess it. You can't go to court blushing like ye are now. The lords will be sniffing all over ye and I'll be expected to defend you. The only way to do that without spilling blood is to stake a claim on you. See?"

Elika stepped away again. "I'll play my part. You just play yours."

He bowed mockingly. "Will my Lady Fair ask anything else of me today?"

"Just one more thing," she said grimly. "I learned something … something that matters." Her skin chilled just to think of it. "I need you to let everyone know … start a rumor or shout it from the bell tower."

Rory's face grew serious. "Tell me."

"You know how the priests used to say that Syn'Moreg cut the world in half to give half to men and half to magic?"

"Aye," he said slowly.

"It's a lie. He cut the world in half, but never gave the other half to the mages."

Rory went very still. "And where did you hear this?"

"I'd like to know this myself," Blood Dog added, his gaze sharp and probing.

"Doesn't matter, now does it," she said evasively. She did not want to utter Shoran's name. "Just thought men should know. The lie must end."

"She comes to wound, she comes to strike," Blood Dog muttered, and Elika's skin chilled. There it was, that deep knowing in his eyes, and wisdom she did not like seeing there, for it made him far more dangerous than she already knew him to be.

~

The door opened for her before she knocked.

"You are late, my lady," said Toad. "Lord Nightkill grows impatient." Rory had been trying to polish his ruffians into behaving and speaking like proper servants of noble houses, and Toad took to his new role with greater aplomb than the others. "Did I do better this time?" he asked her with a grin, whilst proudly stroking the front of his starched shirt.

"Aye, Toad, I've not seen a more convincing butler."

"They're in the dining room, waiting for you," he said as he led the way. When they entered, he announced her presence. "Lady Fair, my lord." Then he winked at her on the way out.

Blood Dog was sitting back in the dining chair, grimly eyeing her in that disturbingly solemn way, devoid of his usual leer. He had taken to being more thoughtful around her whenever the three of them sat down to dinner in Rory's lordly dining room and discussed their plans.

Tonight was no different. It was their last practice dinner before Lord Rainshore's house party, which Lord Nightkill and his companion were invited to attend. The invitation was not issued out of generosity. Rory was right about the nobility shunning any lords, especially Dae ones claiming distant blood relations.

It was from Toad that she had learned of the hosts omitting Lord Nightkill from their invitations. At least until rumors of unfortunate accidents, suspicious ailments and untimely deaths circulated through the noble circles. Soon after, a frightened, newly made widow issued the first invitation to Lord Nightkill to attend a private dinner. After that, more invitations arrived each day.

"These lords piss themselves more than my nan does," Toad had told her and chuckled. "Show them a knife and they weep like children."

To Elika's frustration, Rory still went to these alone, seeking to imbed himself firmly into their midst before bringing his distant relative and "mistress" with him. The seeds of lies had to be planted first, so as not to surprise anyone with her arrival. Or so he claimed.

Each night at dinner, he watched her closely, and she saw doubts scratching away at him. It stung, for she carried herself perfectly, and made only a few etiquette mistakes, small enough that no one would notice. Unless they were watching her as closely as Rory.

Blood Dog came along each day, eating his fill and counselling Rory in the ways of nobility. "You've muddled your sway with Lady Willow," he was saying now to Rory, as he stabbed the tip of his knife through a slice of lamb. It dripped blood and juices as he lifted it to his mouth. "I told ye not to make overtures …"

Elika was at a loss as to why Blood Dog, with the table manners of a hungry beggar, was counselling Rory. Nor why One Eye was paying him any heed.

"I was complimenting her," he said coolly.

"Damn the fools. 'Tis not what ye think ye're saying, but what she thinks you're thinking."

"I'll make amends," Rory replied icily.

"That well is dry. Lady Trista is the one you should court favor from. Her lord husband can't stand the sight of her, and she craves affection."

And so they went on speaking of this lady and that lord, and how Rory should act around each of them. Elika ate and listened and pondered how this ruffian knew such intimate details of the nobility's ways. What troubled her more was that Rory did not question Blood Dog's advice. She had watched them and knew that neither trusted the other, or liked the other for that matter. It was clear that Rory had come to rely on Blood Dog's counsel, his odd knowledge of the noble houses and who they were. What Dog was hanging around for, however, she did not know, neither was he willing to share.

So she watched him, and now and then, something about him would make her start and stare, something subtle. A gesture, a glance, perhaps a mask would briefly lift … something fleeting she could not quite grasp, yet it made her weary of him.

He saw her studying him now and cockily bit into another juicy piece of meat hanging limply off the tip of his knife. A hint of sly amusement shone in his dark eyes, mocking her confusion. *Go ahead, see if you can unravel the mystery, mousy*, she could almost hear him saying. Though she, too, caught him staring at her with the same puzzlement, when he thought she wasn't looking.

Rory cut his steak like a proper lord. Evidently, he had his own training in how to pass for a noble-born. "Have you managed to *persuade* the captain of the Southern Bastion to join us?" he asked Blood Dog.

Elika's attention sharpened. Northwind was gathering an army on the border of Wavestar. The streets were abuzz with the news, and the rebels had grown more brazen. Captain Trian had called upon the captains of the eight bastions around the city to defend men against mages. But only three had picked up Northwind's banner. The rest remained loyal to Prince Southfire.

Yet what troubled her the most was that whilst Rory still spoke of the rebellion, he made no mention of his dealings with the archmage. No matter that she carefully tried to probe him for some hint of it.

"The captain of the southern outpost is holding firm against us," Blood Dog replied. "And before you ask, killing him won't matter. It gains us nothing. His whole bastion is loyal to Southfire."

"Three out of eight is not enough to take the city," Rory said and sipped his wine. "When the archmage falls, Southfire will step in to take power. I dare say he is counting on the Rogue to kill the archmage and clear the way for his unobstructed rule."

"Northwind will obstruct him," Elika said.

"Not if more than half the city believe that Mitey is an imposter. Most Alterrians won't accept a Dae trying to usurp the rule and law of their city. They'd sooner have Southfire. Our numbers are great, but theirs are greater. We need at least another three captains on our side."

"I'm working on Captain Godsbane." Blood Dog shrugged, as if Rory's concern meant nothing to him. "If we can get to his wife and son and take them into our care, I dare say he'll bend to our cause."

"Then why are they not in our care already?"

"'Cause you've got to pick your time." Blood Dog gave him his usual answer. "Can't go rushing and blundering about. Godsbane is guarding his mansion with more men than Prince Southfire's personal guard. Especially after what your men did to Lord Farrain and his family." Disdain laced his words. "Might be if your men were less brutal in their dealings with the nobles ..."

"They've been punished. It won't happen again," Rory replied dismissively.

"There's another problem," Blood Dog said with a pointed look in her direction. "The people are turning against the Rogue Mage. They blame *her* for the discontent and violence in the city. Most are now thinking it's Arala herself who's returned in the guise of the Rogue."

Elika stilled. She hated the way Blood Dog turned his intent gaze on her again, as if considering the truth of the absurd rumors. She'd rather he leered at her.

"No doubt that is the archmage's intention," she said, hoping to distract him from whatever wild thoughts bore into his head.

"Are the people turning against *me*?" Rory asked without looking up from his plate as he toyed with the uneaten piece of honeyed parsnip.

"No one as yet suspects your link with the Rogue," Blood Dog said. "Perhaps if they did …" He left the rest unvoiced.

"Then I don't see why their feelings towards the Rogue should concern us," Rory said and placed his hand over hers.

He'd done that before, and it was all she could do not to react, though her whole body recoiled. She did everything not to pull away from the gesture and kept her face pleasant despite the disgust and the sense of violation. Shoran's face flashed in her mind and absurdly she felt as if she was betraying him.

Rory's lips twitched in amusement. "My love, I do believe you may be ready for your introduction to society three days hence. Try not to embarrass me."

She gave him her most adoring smile, though she was certain it did not reach her eyes. "Of course not, my lord." She casually pulled away her hand and rose to her feet. "I have much to do before then, so if you would excuse me." She curtsied with a strained smile and walked away gracefully, knowing both of them were watching her.

When she was out of sight, she raced upstairs, unlocked Rory's study with a lockpick, snuck inside and silently closed the door behind her.

She strode to his desk, where there were piles of letters and brief correspondence. She sieved through them, reading quickly. Most were amorous letters to various ladies, threats to their lord husbands, orders for merchants and receipts. One was a brief note from Captain Trian that read:

Mages are still blockading the southern entrance. The western tunnel has been destroyed by Southfire's spies. We urgently need access to the harbor. Lord Truestar.

Elika frowned. The captain was working with Rory. Did he know Rory was making his own demands of Tridamor, which would work against Mite? She sieved through the other papers, looking for proof of what Rory was doing.

She found another letter, in which she read:

Lord Nightkill,

The archmage graces your request for dukedom with his consideration, which he will pass in due course. Though he has gravely declined to cede your foolish wish for the control of the harbor, for it belongs to our illustrious Tsarin Reval, who has appointed Mageguard Whitemoth to be its overseer. As to your third beggarly demand, the Archmage Tridamor is very busy with matters more pressing to the running of the city, and thus cannot meet with you. Instead, we will send one of his representatives to speak with you when it pleases us to do so. When we do, we expect to forge an agreement for our alliance. In the meantime, during this truce, we expect order to be maintained …

"Hey, Spit."

Elika's head snapped up. She lowered the letter. There was no denying what she was doing here, and by the looks of his face, he looked ready to murder her. So she decided on the attack instead. "Seems you've been less than honest with me, Rory, and seeing as it was you who wanted us to be friends."

He strode into the room and threw his overcoat onto the settee. Knives were strapped to his sides over his tunic. "Not an honest thing, going through a man's private things."

"Both of us are thieves. But I stole nothing, save information. What's your play, Rory?"

He prowled to the desk and circled it. Elika moved as well, keeping the table between them. He flung himself down on the chair, threw his feet up and picked up the letter she was reading.

He snorted at the contents. Evidently, he too could read now. "The bastards are not as stupid as I hoped them to be. You're thinking I'm playing Northwind foul?"

"Crossed my mind, that did," she said carefully. "A whole dukedom for you. That's more than Mite promised."

He grunted. "I wanted the harbor more."

She frowned. "Why?"

"'Cause with the control of the harbor, we'd have control of the trade in the city, and that gives us control over Terren. But the bastards cut off roads from Daetown to the harbor. So now we can't trade with the ships directly, other than going through the archmage's merchants in Trader's Quarter. They've been squeezing us, El. Don't have enough metal, or coal, or food. The harbor is the key."

"Give them what they want, so they give you what you want."

"I brokered for peace, to give us time to rebuild and regroup until King Mitey returns. We can't hold off attacks by the mages whilst the boy sits back and ponders whose army he'd sooner have. The only way I can hold them back is to make them believe I'm greedy enough to switch sides. I don't need their blasted dukedom. I just want the harbor. With the coin and power, it'll bring me, I'll buy ten dukedoms myself."

Elika sighed. "You're not an easy man to trust, Rory."

"And you're wise not to trust me, Spit. Now be off with ye. If I catch you going through my things again, I'll be taking off your ear."

"As you say."

Elika left him in his study and felt his gaze bore into her back. She wondered whether One-Eyed Rory was truly a genius master overlord of the streets or the best liar she'd ever known. Though his explanation was sound, she knew that men like him only ever looked after themselves. The rest were to be trampled on in pursuit of power and ambition. And she could not help wondering if she and Rory were working against each other.

CHAPTER TWENTY-ONE

The Reign of Terror

"Dare we write these words where Reval might see them? Yet 'tis the task he set upon us, and in this, we must stay true. Northwind had captured Arala, but he never abducted her. She went to him. Captain Firesong of Reval's Mageguard led his army against the Sacred Crowns in the war that sundered the two realms, and he witnessed much that Reval speaks not of. So, we asked Firesong how a mere human, with barely enough blood of the gods in his veins, could capture and imprison a demigoddess. Blood-salt, he replied. The gods call it the Stone of Chaos, for it is poison to the Great Web and siphons the light into itself. When bound to your flesh, it severs the link to the wells of power. And with the chains fashioned from red stone, the eighteenth King Northwind subdued Arala, daughter of Goddess Neka."

The History of Alafraysia and Seramight,
By Mageguard Bluelight

The spider no longer haunted her nights—Shoran did. His face, his silences, his cold, calm rage. Even his otherworldly patience, as if neither weapon nor all the ages, could touch him.

The endless dark hall stretched before her, like a terror born of nightmares. Yet she had never felt safer. There was a brooding, slumberous mood about the tower, the silent gloom of a place where shadows came to rest.

Elika had deciphered the tower's secret and since then had never been lost, for the corridor always led her to the one place— where she wished to go. She need only wish for the library, or Arala's room, and the door would appear. Yet she rarely saw

Shoran. When she sought him, a door would materialize, but the room beyond would oft be empty, with only a few signs of his recent presence—glowing embers from a recent fire, an empty goblet, his lingering scent.

She sought him now.

Her meeting with Rory and Blood Dog had left her unsettled, and somehow unclean. Everything in her rebelled at posing as Rory's mistress, yet she saw no other way to get close to the archmage. Lonely was the path of lies and wickedness, for there was no solace from it.

A door appeared in the distance. Beyond it lay a cozy room, with a single plush chair beside the fire. Velvet curtains covered the tall windows that looked out to the eternal night. There were books on shelves and dark crystal globes. The room was empty. She sighed, wearied by his absence, and determined to wait. She took a seat beside the dancing green flame. As the warmth displaced the chill in her bones, she grew drowsy.

She awoke abruptly, uncertain what had disturbed her, save that there was a chair across from her, where there was none before. A shadow sat in it, watching her sleep, and her heart skipped with some secret longing.

She uncurled and straightened in the seat. It was hard to look at him and not be torn by shame at what she was conspiring to do. A part of her wondered how much her sleepy face betrayed. There was an unnatural stillness about him that gave the impression of being all-seeing. His calm presence was so steadying, she wanted to confide in him, to tell him everything and seek his council. But his silence was deeper than the bottomless Abyss beyond the walls. And might be it was that, which made her remember he was Syn'Moreg's servant.

So she looked aside, unable to look at him and just not feel.

"'Tis guilt and shame I see in your eyes," he said. "The dark path once taken will taint you irrevocably."

His perception was chilling.

"Might be I'm already tainted," she replied and found comfort in his gaze devoid of judgement. "You have been kind to me," she said with a stab of regret.

Silence. Thoughtful and wearied. Beside him on a small table sat a goblet filled with silversap.

"You know I won't stop fighting them," she said, and it was a relief to confess to him even this much.

Silence. He sipped from the goblet, his ancient eyes never leaving her.

She sighed. "Shoran, if we are to remain enemies or be …" She blinked, lost for words. They were not friends. Yet here they were, sitting by the fire in companionable silence.

As if he read her confusion, one side of his mouth lifted in gently mocking amusement. It annoyed her.

"If we are to oppose each other," she continued more assertively. "I need to know what our battle is to be. On the streets, when opposing gangs—great powers, if you like—have conflicting purposes, they outline their positions, lay out the stakes of battle, and if no agreement is reached … well, then we battle. So, will you stop me? Will you interfere?"

There was a long silence before he spoke. "I am not one of your thugs or gangs. I live not by the laws of the street but by those of the gods. If you seek to meddle in the world of men, so be it. The consequences will be etched upon your soul for eternity to come. The price will extract itself and will be paid. But if you strike the web, there will be a reckoning between us."

His mild words were a stark contrast to his ominous gaze. Even now, he saw her as a threat to the Great Web.

She shook her head in denial. "I'm not the evil that haunts this world. That's your master's domain."

He watched her. Silent.

And she recalled Rosalina urging him to let her die. *Do not unleash another Elriad upon the world.*

"Who is Elriad?" she asked. There was no mention of him in the book about the gods, which in itself was strange.

Again, Shoran was slow to reply. "He was the son of Moreg and a human woman of no consequence. Moreg was late to learn of his existence, for his mother hid him from everyone until he was a full-grown man and she an old woman. By the time Moreg came to claim him, bitterness and ambition were seeded in

Elriad's heart. Worse yet, hatred had poisoned his soul beyond healing. He dreamt of power, of dominion over the realms, of being the master of Fates. He found support amongst other demigods, who were wearied of living by the laws of the light and the rules of their righteous parents. They started a war in the celestial realm. The war spread to Alafraysia and Seramight, and the three worlds were enshrouded in destruction and death. Countless died, gods, demigods, men and the Laifae, before Elriad was finally killed by his brother."

"Syn'Moreg," she said. "He was destroyed by Syn'Moreg."

His silence was her answer.

"Syn'Moreg sundered the world. Countless died then and since. Why do the gods not destroy *him*?"

"Be careful, kitten, in casting your judgement, for it will come full circle back to you. The truth is far crueler than you know it to be. The wrong done to the world goes far deeper than Syn'Moreg. One day you will learn it, and if your heart is not ready to bear the price that is your burden to bear, it will break you."

The words, though softly spoken, were somehow cruel and frightening. "What are you not telling me, Shoran? You know … who I am."

"Who you are and what you are," he replied, and suddenly she did not like the way he was looking at her, or the bleakness in his gaze that probed the depths of some terrible fate awaiting her.

The Abyss closed in on her. She had to get away from him, from this wretched, lonely place, from the dark musings in his gaze.

She rose to her feet. "I only wish to set the wrongs to right. I do not seek power or dominion."

"Hot burns the fire of the just, young heart untouched by the cruel wisdom of the ages." He turned his gaze to the fire. "A wrong can never set another wrong to right, but only seed the weeds of further vengeance. And a soul poisoned by hate can never heal the world, only break it. Be careful you do not unravel all that you hold dear, Aleyala."

She left him alone in the gloom of his forlorn room, her heart aching for the lonely man behind that giant door, for what she had to do, and for the ones who must suffer to free men from Laifae's hold upon their world.

Dark was the path ahead, and she would walk it.

~

The Reign of Terror began everywhere at once in the city. It came at dawn the day after she had spoken with Shoran. Prison wagons rolled by as mageguards led men from their homes. Both young and old were dragged out and shoved into cages. Most were Daes. Elika watched from the roofs as some fought back. Red daggers flashed. Mages cried out. Black strands lashed out, winding around the throats of those men who resisted. A far too familiar sight.

She sent tendrils of her own magic to break the cages apart and free the men inside them. Mageguards burst through the street on horseback, sending fiery whips at the fleeing men. One caught a woman shielding a child and she screamed as flame engulfed her dress.

Elika wished for water and it came from the air, soaking the woman and quenching the flame.

"She is near!" shouted the mageguard with a fiery whip. "Find her." *Find her, catch her*, hissed more voices inside him.

Elika pushed out her magic, wound her tendrils around the mageguard's neck, and threw him from the horse. Men were upon him, stabbing him and her tendrils with knives and daggers made of blood-salt. She stifled a cry of pain and pulled back her magic.

Reval's fiery mageguards floated above the roofs, singing absurd songs about his love for Arala, ignoring the chaos on the streets, caring neither for the dying mages nor for the slaughter of men. Before they spied her, she found her way down and merged with the folk on the street.

Rory did not keep the cruel truth from the folk. He paid every crier to proclaim that Syn'Moreg never gave this half of the world to the mages, and errand boys told everyone on the street who might not have heard.

Elika knew that the archmage would not allow her failed attack against him to go unanswered, yet his brutality still shocked her. The criers walked past, announcing that anyone harboring the Rogue would be punished. And once again, Tridamor proclaimed that the coming Spring Parade would be grander than the last. He had sworn that for every mage the Rogue Mage unraveled, for every mage burned at the stake, a hundred more would rise. It was a promise he seemed eager to keep.

Every day, the mageguards rode out in force, breaking down doors, invading homes, and dragging men from the streets. Men fought back for their lives, women fought for their men, and more and more children were orphaned. At first, only the Daes were hunted by the "flesh collectors", as they came to be known. By the end of the second day, the Alterrians began to fill the prison wagons destined for the temple. At least those who began to question whether the tsaren and the mages were indeed their rightful overlords.

This world did not belong to magic. Syn'Moreg had not gifted it to the tsaren. For six hundred years, men had believed that lie. Now Elika saw confusion haunt the faces of the Alterrians, who until now believed that they were the intruders in their own world.

Merciless was Tridamor's brutality, but in it, she saw his weakness. It seemed he did not wholly understand humanity. In his haste to punish and to cow, he gravely miscalculated their reply. For as terror rained upon the streets, more and more Alterrians joined the Dae resistance of Daetown. Their prince, Southfire, was not protecting them, so they allied with those who would. They allied with Northwind's supporters.

She passed them now on the streets as they dragged another blood-soaked mage towards the pyre. She looked aside as they tied him to the post, and she closed her ears to his screams. After walking a little way off, she reached for his life's essence and gently released him from his torment, returning the Laifae to his realm.

A few streets along, a convoy of prison wagons passed by and came to an abrupt stop. A group of a dozen youths, holding blood-salt laced torches, blocked its path. "Let them out, pig, or we'll burn you all to ash," one shouted.

Elika watched the scene from a distance. A slick red line of oil and blood-salt was spread across the road. More youths ran behind the convoy and poured more oil on the ground behind the stationary wagons. Then they threw flaming torches at it. Red flames roared into life and blocked the mage's retreat.

The escorting mages shied back. "Insolent humans," one hissed. "Get out of our way."

"Burn the bastards," shouted a prisoner from the wagon. "We're dead anyway."

"Shut up, you fool. I don't want to burn," said another in reply.

The mage took out his flaming whip and lashed at the youths blocking his path. The oil on the ground burst into flame. An instant later, a red-tipped arrow flew from the flame and pierced his chest, then another and another. Elika looked up to see from where they came.

In the windows above, city guards with an emblem of an ice crown on their jerkins were loosing their arrows at the mageguards. More men ran out of the abandoned buildings and broke the wagon locks to release the prisoners.

Elika turned around and walked away from the flames and the red smoke that painfully burned her lungs.

On the border of Daetown, daily battles tested their defenses at the barricaded streets. Day and night, a joint force of mages and city guards loyal to Southfire probed the boundaries of the rebel stronghold. But last night, the guards of the Northern Bastion joined Rory's men to drive back the attackers and lay claim to more streets surrounding Daetown. By dawn, they had shifted their defenses to encircle the newly captured territory.

Then she saw something that always made her stomach plunge with dread. Dozens of animal carcasses hanging upside down, their blood draining into buckets. Once full, the women poured the blood into waiting barrels. These were sealed and loaded onto carts. Rory's words haunted her. If men could not have their world, neither would the Laifae. Men would destroy everything and everyone in it before they surrendered.

She understood only too well that desperate need to fight to the end, no matter the price. Like them, she had been fighting to survive for too long to know any other way to be. There was no stopping the flow of blood, no quenching the blood-salt fires as long as the Laifae invaded their realm. The defenders painted the roads with blood-salt. The fighters covered their clothes and bodies with it, to stop the black strands from grabbing them.

Day turned to night. The city was aglow with torches. Around Daetown, blood-salt bonfires were lit where there was enough room to light them. The red smoke kept the mages away, and as the wind shifted, it shrouded the western city. At least there, people would get a peaceful night's rest.

A familiar, cutting wind blew past and vanished. She tilted her head and listened, then sent out feelers along the essence of the world, and sensed his anger vibrate through it. Inexplicably drawn to it, she walked towards him. Out of nowhere, men and women were fleeing past her. She grabbed the arm of a girl to stop her. "What happened here?"

The girl looked behind her. "The bonfire … it just blew apart. You better run. There must be a mage around."

Elika released her and the girl ran off.

The wind screeched past again and vanished. She followed its direction, tracking the disturbance in the essence.

A white-tipped crow cawed above her.

She came to another red bonfire. As she watched, the ground shuddered and shook and split, and the bonfire sank beneath the earth. Women tending the flames screamed and scattered in all directions, whilst the ground resealed itself.

Elika scanned the streets and saw the hooded shadow watching the chaos he had created. His interference irked her. She'd rather he interfered to save men from mages, then might be men would not be setting fire to blood-salt. She flung out her own flame and it roared to life where the other one had been.

He turned his head and stared straight at her. Then he walked towards the darkness and vanished.

"Coward. Running away?" she muttered.

"Hardly," said the dark voice behind her.

She started and spun to face him.

"Are you challenging me, kitten?"

She crossed her arms, refusing to be cowed by the dark warning in his voice. "Let them be, Shoran. Blood-salt is all they have. Else, why don't you use that godly power of yours and stop the mages and the archmage from killing them?"

"The fire you started is getting away from you," he said mildly, mockingly.

"Syn'Moreg started the fire," she bit back.

His lips curled sardonically, and the faint glow in his eyes brightened.

She ignored his silent menace. "You must do something."

"Must I?" His menace deepened. "And what would you have me do? Crush Northwind, Southfire, Tridamor, the tsaren, or the men who are feeding the fires with blood-salt. Do you truly think any death I can summon upon any of them will end this? 'Tis a deep path you have carved. So now we must walk it." As he spoke, his restrained anger bloomed into a potent force, and his voice grew deeper, darker. His power reverberated through her, and she suddenly saw not a man but a demigod before her. One who could command the very essence of life and make mountains bleed fire.

"Help them," Elika pleaded, her voice rising. "Save them. I know it is within your power to do so."

His anger encompassed her now, threatening to tear her to pieces unless she abandon her self-destructive demands of the powers she should be bowing to.

"You plead with me, beg me to help them, little spider?" He laughed, dark and bitter. "Again and again, I have sought to save them, with fear and threats, with compassion and mercy, with magic and power. Each time, I destroyed more than I saved. Men, Laifae, the tsaren, they will do what they will, heedless of what I demand of them. Were I to become involved, it would bring nothing but further destruction. Were I to command them to stop, they would make their own demands. For ages past, they war. For all ages yet to come, they will never stop fighting until everything around them is dead. Side by side with love lives hate, and I cannot destroy hate. Nor can I quench it." Frustration entered his voice.

"You are a demigod —"

"The demigods are forbidden from intervening in the wars between the Laifae and the humans, between Seramight and Alafraysia. To do so would be to choose a side to favor, else each would accuse them of betrayal, and the war would turn against the gods. The gods do not war, they destroy. So it was before, and so it must never be again."

"Then why are you here?" she asked, her own frustration breaking through. "You are interfering now."

"I quench fires that should not burn. I protect that which must not be destroyed. These fires burn more than the lives of the Laifae. The web must be protected."

"Do you care for naught but Syn'Moreg's damned web?"

His eyes flashed. "'Tis all there is left to care for."

She looked aside, feeling strangely wounded by those careless words. There was no help from the gods. No help from Shoran. The archmage had declared war against mankind, and against her. Turning away from the suffering of men would surely etch a far deeper scar on her soul.

"Then 'tis your burden to bear," she said with a nod. "I'll make no more demands of you. Though tell me one thing, will you come to the aid of the Laifae when I choose to destroy them all?"

Her question was met with silence. And oddly, his rage died, to be replaced instead with the wave of despondency, the despair of a certain inevitability. "I do not wish to destroy you," he said, and his voice cracked under the strain of some emotion.

She nodded without looking at him, understanding his threat and his veiled plea. Her own heart was aching. *Yet it might come to that after all.*

She stuck her hands in her pockets and walked away.

~

Elika cast away the remnants of the sacred fruit, took out her knife, and scored the silver bark until the liquid flowed freely from the wound. She placed a cup beneath it, and when it was full, drank it all. The sensation of pleasure and joy coursed through her body as it replenished her strength.

Beams of sun fought through the silver leaves to warm her face. The forest was alive with the chatter of birds and the fluttering of their wings as they danced from branch to branch. Too greedily, she drank another cupful, before turning her face to the sun. When the rush of euphoria subsided, she strolled through the orchard, savoring the peace before the night ahead.

The tree from which she harvested continued to bleed its sap, for she didn't know how to heal it. But she knew Shoran came here often and healed the wounds on the silver trees she left behind. One day, she determined to ask him if he could teach her that magic. She finished the last of the silversap in her cup and replaced it behind a protruding root beneath one of the trees.

When she returned to the dark tower, a door was before her, one she did not wish for, save in the deepest recesses of her heart. She lingered outside only a moment, thinking about the man beyond it, then she turned away and returned to the streets of Terren.

~

It was late in the day when she arrived at Rory's mansion. He was already dressed for their dinner at Lord Rainshore's mansion, and a gold patch covered his missing eye. He was clean shaven with his hair tied back neatly. Despite his perfect lordly attire and bearing, there was no masking the faint echoes of a dangerous thug around the edges. The streets were too deeply ingrained into him. Into them both.

"You are late, my dear," he said with mild irritation, as he adjusted his sleeves. "Your maid is waiting for you upstairs."

"Want to talk to you ... my lord," she said coolly.

Rory halted mid-preen. "And what ails you, my love?"

"Thought you had a truce with the archmage. What broke it?"

"Nothing broke it. The bastards have their own way of looking at things that's different to ours. They have not been attacking Daetown, merely keeping order on the streets by removing suspected rebels from their homes. So far, they have only fought when attacked."

"That makes no sense. It's not what I saw."

"Indeed," he said dryly. "You cannot trust the bastards, El. Their truces are as fluid as their excuses. Now go upstairs and get ready."

Killing the archmage was the only way to fix this, she thought, and with firming resolve, walked past him.

"Oh, and darling, I must insist that until this is done, you spend your evenings and mornings in this house. It cannot come out that you live away from the protection of your distant *cousin*."

"As you say, Rory." She strode upstairs into her chamber and closed the door behind her. When she turned, the maid gasped in surprise. Elika was no less shocked than the maid.

"Liffy," she whispered.

The girl was staring at her with wide-eyed fear.

Elika took a step closer, and Liffy dashed aside. "Keep away from me."

"Not going to hurt you."

Liffy no longer wore the crown of flowers, nor ribbons in her hair. Her frock was plain and unadorned. She looked older for it. "I thought you were dead," she said sulkily.

"Is that why you stole from me?"

Liffy flinched and took another step away. "I'll pay you back … when I have it. Though it's hard to save enough."

"I don't need it. Keep it."

Those pale eyes roamed over Elika's attire, settling on her neck where once there had been Mage Rah's band of ownership. "You're free now," she said in an oddly dead voice. She also wore no collar. "Heard the Rogue got Mage Rah." Hatred laced her words whenever she mentioned the Rogue. "Some are saying it was one of his girls, and that she was Arala."

Elika nodded carefully. "Heard the same. Frightened me, it did, thinking she was so close. What are you doing here, Liffy?"

Her face grew resentful. "Don't have a fancy lord lover who'll look after me, so I got to work."

Deep, frightening suspicion took hold of Elika. This could not be a coincidence. Rory was smarter than that. "Tell me how you came to be here?"

"Lord Nightkill's men came to see me and said he wanted to help free me, 'cause I was a Dae and they look after each other. They said I'd live in a nice house and never be beaten again. And that I could be a maid to fine ladies, and maybe one day be a fine lady myself. So I ran away and they brought me here. They used a saw tipped with blood-salt to cut through my collar. It took them no time at all."

"Liffy, you must listen to me," she said and reached into her pocket for all the coin she had, then held the pouch out to the foolish girl. "Take this. There's enough here for you to get by on till winter. You are not safe in this house. You must leave."

She did not trust Rory. He never did anything out of generosity. There was only one reason he would bring Liffy here. *Behave*, he was saying, *or your friend will suffer.*

Liffy shook her head. "You always want to take everything from me. First, you stole my magic. Now you want to steal my happiness. Lord Nightkill is kind and pays me more than the mistress ever did. And he never beats me. I told him me and Sam are trying to save enough to go to Wavestar, and he said he'll help us. I just need to work here and pay off the debt to him for setting me free."

"You told him about Sam," Elika said with a chill of premonition, remembering the burned-out shell of the mage's home. "Liffy ... have you seen Sam recently?"

"Lord Nightkill said he saved Sam from a cruel master, and that he is now safe and working for him as well. I haven't seen him since I ran away, but Lord Nightkill promised we'll be reunited soon."

Elika's heart sank. But she had no time to convince the girl of Rory's lies. She wondered whether Mage Blackfly was still alive.

She doubted it. Either way, Rory was waiting impatiently down-stairs.

Elika pulled back her shoulders as she recalled that she had the part of a lady to play. Liffy must not suspect her to be anything less than that. "My lord expects you to serve me," she said with a lift of her chin. "We have a gathering to attend."

Liffy's face grew thunderous and petulant at once. "How may I assist, *my lady*?"

"You will help me dress."

On the bed lay a blue silk dress, with one of Elika's webs over the dark skirt. Aye, Rory was toying with her to unsettle her, or perhaps merely reminding her where she had come from and what he could do for her.

With a sigh, she began to change into her evening gown. Sullenly, Liffy assisted, though her hands were rough and unkind.

Elika ignored her enmity and sat in front of the mirror. "Can you style my hair as the ladies wear theirs in court?"

Liffy nodded and picked up the brush. She ran it roughly through Elika's hair, then pulled and tugged as she braided and twisted it, before pinning the hair in place.

Elika did not pay her any attention, for her gaze was caught by the reflection in the mirror. With her face in the mirror right next to Liffy's, it was impossible to ignore the stark difference between them. Her own face held the same subtle oddness she saw in Shoran's features. It was a subtlety she could not quite grasp, an exotic union of features that was not quite as it should be. It was the shape of the bones, the eyes, the slant, the skin itself was subtly alien in its hue and smoothness. Not quite human …

Human. Liffy was human.

Elika rose abruptly, desperate to get away from her own reflection.

"I'm not finished yet," Liffy protested.

We are kin, he had said.

What was she? Daughter of the gods, Laifae …? Was any part of her human, some small part of her perhaps, that came from the Sachi race? Why else did she look so much like them, like Shoran whose mother was a Sachi?

The door burst open and Rory strode in without knocking. "It's time to go. We have been delayed enough. Put on your jewels."

"Her hair …" Liffy began.

"Is perfect," he snapped. "Bring her the travelling cloak."

Elika took a breath and composed herself. It mattered not what she was, only that she had to destroy the archmage. She took the sapphire earrings from the box Rory had given her and clipped them to her ears. Afterward, Rory impatiently fastened a matching necklace around her neck. She hated the touch of his cold, abrupt fingers against her skin, but she held still and kept her mind blank.

Downstairs, Blood Dog was waiting in the hall. When he saw her, he grinned and unashamedly perused her body, lingering on her chest, before moving lower. "Sweet Neka, the mouse has grown into a princess. Who'd have thought."

"Is the carriage ready, Dog?" Rory asked as he pulled on his gloves.

"Aye, it's outside," Blood Dog replied, sounding bored. "This way, *my lord*," he said mockingly and led the way.

Rory glared at his retreating back but said nothing in reply. He escorted Elika to the carriage and sat across from her, whilst Blood Dog jumped into the coachman's seat.

When the carriage jerked and moved, Rory spoke. "I assume the maid is to your liking." He kept his face impassive, with only a hint of polite curiosity.

"She is very competent," Elika replied coolly. "What do you want with her, Rory? Why did you bring her?"

"Why so suspicious, Spit? I thought you might want a friend close by."

She did not believe a word of it. Aye, he was a sly fox.

"Except, she's not a friend. Doesn't like me, you see."

"But do you like *her*, Lady Fair? That was what I asked, after all."

Icy shiver ran up her back, and she said nothing more on the matter.

It was a short journey, and soon the carriage came to a stop. Blood Dog opened the door. Rory dismounted, a perfect lord in every part of his bearing. He offered his hand to help her down.

Ahead, lords and ladies were making their way up the marble steps of Lord Rainshore's mansion. With her first glimpse of the splendor, the dazzling jewels and bright silks, every doubt Elika had ever nursed surfaced to the fore and mocked her. *Imposter*, said their gazes when they brushed her with their careless regard. In those smiling faces, untouched by the horrors on the streets, she saw pride and innocence, greed and dignity, vulgar wealth and sheltered life beyond the reach of the suffering masses. But it was their casual disregard of anything that did not glitter that struck Elika to the core.

Rory led her towards them.

The intense aroma of clashing perfumes pushed aside the natural reek of the streets and masked the faint stench of blood-salt smoke. Rory pressed ahead, and they were engulfed by bodies and silk, talcum and gems, smiles and polite chatter. And it was hard to remember that even now honest, hardworking folk were fighting and dying just a few streets away.

Rory leered at her. "Smile dear, you look like you want to flee."

And she did. She put on her best smile, demure and yet confident. Lady Rosalina had instructed her how to smile, absurd though it was. There was a smile for every occasion, and upon entry into a host's home, a lady must appear polite and interested, and not smile too much or too vividly.

They entered a bright, marble hall illuminated by countless candles in sconces overhead and along the walls.

"Lord Nightkill, welcome to my home," said a fat lord with strained politeness. A tall, slim matron stood beside him, her smile equally disturbed. "Ahem. I am delighted to see you here." He appeared to be anything but delighted.

"But of course, how could I refuse a man of your stature?" Rory replied smoothly. "May I present Lady Fair, my very fair, distant cousin?" He smiled and kissed her hand in the way that made her skin crawl and would have sent Lady Rosaline into blushing fits and lectures of impropriety. Rory as much as shouted atop his voice that he was bedding her.

Elika schooled her features and fought the instinct to pull her hand away from his lingering lips. "My lord, you are such a flatterer," she cooed.

"Ahem," Lord Rainshore cleared his throat and his jowls grew red. "My lady, you are far fairer than rumors suggested. I was told of a ghastly curse."

"The rumors, as you can see, are false," Rory replied smoothly.

"But of course, I meant no offence."

"I am told you have taken control of Daetown," his lady wife interjected.

"I had little choice in the matter, since Duke Snowstorm's unfortunate demise. Somehow, the magistrate managed to convince me of my duty to this city. Truly, I would see the entire district burned down along with the rabble that roams its streets."

"But of course. They say One Eye is removing eyes from his opponents. Dare I say that was how you lost yours?"

Trust Rory to coat lies with confusion, thought Elika. Half the lords suspected he and One Eye were the same man. The other half knew not what to believe. Both, however, thought it best not to voice their views on the matter.

Rory smiled. "Indeed. We fought, and the vile thug stabbed me right in the eye, laughed whilst he did it too. I hear it is his ambition to blind every lord in the city who's loyal to Prince Southfire."

Lord Rainshore cleared his throat again. "Then let us hope the mageguards get to him first."

"Aye, and take out his other eye," Elika added with a pleasant smile.

Rory's gaze glinted with mild menace at her barb. "But of course, my dear."

"Oh, let us not speak of such dreadful things," Lady Rainshore said beside her husband. "I trust you will restore order to Daetown shortly, Lord Nightkill."

"I will indeed, as soon as Prince Southfire heeds my request for more city guards to be placed at my disposal. So far he has been … ahem, refusing to aid me. It is almost as if he cares not whether there is order on the streets."

"But that is quite terrible," Lady Rainshore said with unfeigned dismay, and Elika could not help but admire Rory's skill in seeding doubts and malcontent into people's minds.

"Indeed, it is, my lady. But what can one man such as I do?"

With a curt bow to the hosts, Rory led her into the guest room where a suffocating crowd of lords and ladies had gathered. The room was too warm. The candles dripped their wax along the sconces on the walls. Music came from a balcony overhead, where a group of minstrels played a cheerful dance. She imagined Mite strolling through here like a lord of his own realm. Aye, he would not need to pretend to be one of them. He was born to this world.

Rory led her onward, introducing Lady Fair, spinning tales of her father's ill health and unfortunate death.

"The old rotter had conspired to keep his beautiful daughter from court, for fear of losing her to a husband," said Rory with shocked outrage.

Elika added her part, thanking her cousin for looking after her and her father in their most difficult time. And she smiled and curtsied and said the right things, whilst sinking deeper and deeper into the lies they were spinning.

"My dear, I thought we should go for a ride together in the park tomorrow," Rory purred as they strode along, whilst eyes from around the room followed. "I would love to see you atop the mare I bought you." He was enjoying this far too much.

She forced a smile to her lips and gazed at him adoringly. "As you wish, my lord."

His hand landed softy on her waist, and the whispers about them grew loud enough to hear.

"… a mistress …"

"Poor girl …"

"… destitute …"

Elika's face grew pained from her false smiles.

"Northwind ..." She heard the name in the hum of voices, and soon, there was talk of little else around them.

Rory joined a small group of lords with glasses of port in their hands and bored wives by their sides. They acknowledged him briefly, and each bowed to her, before resuming their conversation.

"Northwind is trapped between Duke Warwind and Duke Firestorm," one of them was saying. "Each has a daughter they want to plant as queen on Northwind's arm, in exchange for their army."

"You mean plant in his bed." One of the lords chuckled. "Northwind is quite a rake. Indeed, he has already made an enemy of Nerabrow after seducing his oldest daughter."

"They say she's carrying his bastard."

Aye, Elika had no doubt of that. Mite was a letch with more lovers than hairs on his head. He would never change. Unbidden, images came to her mind of Shoran, alone, silent, staring forlornly into the dark Abyss.

"Lady Nerabrow is likely carrying Duke Southfire's bastard. She's hardly the innocent she plays herself to be. The lady is ambitious. I dare say she'll wait to see whether Northwind or Southfire will come out on top before declaring the father of her child."

"That won't suit Warwind's agenda," said another. "He's been known to make his own bastards disappear lest they challenge his true son and heir."

They went on to debate which daughter Northwind should choose, that was to say whose army he wanted the most, Warwind's or Firestorm's. Mite wanted both. He had demanded that they send their joint armies, and once he won the throne of Terren, he would choose his bride. The dukes refused, of course. Both wanted him to name his choice, for neither was willing to commit their support without certainty of linking their blood to his.

"Northwind needs to recall what his bloodline owes Warwind," an old lord droned, and everyone was compelled to fall silent and listen. "If not for Jeoran Warwind coming with a thousand men to the aid of Terren and its twelfth King, Southfire would have taken the city a thousand years ago. Warwind saved Northwind then, too, and won his beloved sister's hand and the Duchy of Windhay. Now it's Northwind's turn to wed Warwind's daughter for his army's aid."

"Can't blame Southfire for coveting the gem of the four kingdoms," another lord said dully. "'Tis the sea breeze they love. Their own lands are far too dusty."

The charade continued late into the night, as they dined, and danced and flirted. Rory remained sober, feigning boredom, whilst his eye remained sharp and trained on the stifling scene of obscene wealth, swirling silks and jovial disregard of all that was wrong with their world. Elika's need to escape this lie grew stronger with each passing hour. She needed fresh air.

"There's nothing more for us to do here," she whispered to Rory. "Let us leave. It's best to leave early, so as to be noticed doing so."

"Oh, what a bore you are." He sighed exaggeratedly, though she suspected he was as eager to leave as she. Then more loudly. "Darling, you look tired, we must of course retire."

Between them and the door, there was more bowing and curtsying, stilted farewells and insincere promises of invitations to come.

Then cool air hit her face and she inhaled deeply of the night. They climbed into their carriage and Blood Dog drove them away.

"You were truly mesmerizing, Lady Fair. You surprised me indeed," said Rory in his affected accent. "Looks like Pockets was right about you after all."

Elika gazed out the window. A prison wagon rolled by, and then another and another, each one filled with men, some clearly dragged from their beds, others looked beaten and broken. One of the men was praying, but there was no help to be had from the gods. She, too, had begged one for help and been refused.

"Indeed, you have enchanted many with your beauty," Rory was saying.

More prison wagons went past and each shredded her soul a little more.

She thought of those shimmering ladies in silk, and the fat lords laughing over their glasses of port.

Another prison wagon rolled past; another scrape against her senses.

She could not be like them, like those men and women who could ignore the crimes committed against their own kind.

The thought wormed its way into her, settled in her and dared her to feed it. "Turn the carriage around, Rory."

He must have seen what she intended in her face. "No. We cannot save them all, nor can we risk being recognized."

Blood Dog slowed to turn the corner, and she used the moment to throw herself out the door, jump to the ground, hike up her skirts and run as fast as she could.

She heard Rory curse, heard the wheels come to a stop and the horses rear in surprise, heard him shout at Blood Dog to follow. Then they both gave chase.

She knew Rory was fast, and in the old days, he might have caught her. That was then. Now she had magic. She threw it out and sealed the way behind her with black tendrils, then ignored the frantic cuts of their weapons trying to break through.

The archmage's temple was near, and she reached it just as the last of the prison wagons rode through the gates. She knelt and touched the ground, acutely aware that Rory and Blood Dog were not far behind.

She pushed out her tendrils through the ground to attack the wagons, sent the black strands to rip the gates apart and allow men to flee. And when she saw men running out, with mageguards chasing them, calm descended on her, for she suddenly knew what she had to do.

This had to stop. No more. If the archmage wanted to war with her, then war he would have.

She closed her eyes and drew upon every shred of her magic, and upon the essence of the world. She gathered it into herself, and the ball of power grew larger and stronger, and still she pulled until it burned hot and was ready to do what she demanded.

"Fire," she said and pushed that command outwards, willing it to descend upon the temple and everyone within. Then she opened her eyes and saw the flame, an ethereal shadow without heat or substance. And she fed it her magic, fed it the ball of power inside her, and the flame grew fierce and hot. So hot, it reached her where she stood.

Mages raced out of the temple and cast their magic to quench hers. They sent wind and water … Without thought, Elika ripped the essences from their bodies and fed them to the flame. The mages became half-rotten corpses of men on the ground, whilst the flames rose higher into the sky. And those decaying corpses became the mirror of her soul.

You are one of the terrors.

Bells began to ring. Men ran out of their homes. City guards raced towards the flames. Shouts for water came from everywhere. Men formed lines to the wells and passed filled buckets from hand to hand. Elika strode into the dark, away from the flames and mayhem.

For mankind, she would be the monsters' monster. For humankind, she would be this monster's fear in the night. She would be the terror come for them.

As she walked blindly along the street she had no name for, she reached for the Laifae essence, and found them all. So many mages around, sleeping peacefully, like those men had been when the monsters came for them …

Stop, whispered a small, frightened voice in her mind … and faded.

It was too late to stop, she thought and grasped those strands of the Laifae, too late to save herself.

And she pulled and ripped the Laifae's essence out of the bodies they had stolen. She gave them no mercy, for they showed men none. But it was not enough, for power was all-consuming and demanded more. She walked and ripped and ripped, and the essence of the world trembled. She felt the vitality fade, felt the fabric of their world unravel. And still, she pulled and tore that which was holding everything together. The archmage had started this and she would end it.

No more.

She reached out further and further and drew the essence of every mage she could find onto herself, drew them and ripped the monsters apart.

The wind intensified.

He was coming.

She turned into another street and found more of them, reached out as far as her waning strength allowed and shredded them, too.

But it was still not enough. It would never be enough until every invader was vanquished, and men did not fear to sleep in their beds at night.

The winds screeched and grew piercing.

She would kill every Laifae in the city, she would …

A sword appeared at her throat. An arm wrapped itself around her waist, pulling her back against him. "I warned you," hissed the darkness.

Elika fought him not. Relief flooded her and silent tears left her eyes. "I cannot stand aside and watch men slaughtered—murdered in their hundreds … in their thousands."

In the tight strength of his body, she felt his barely restrained rage, the need to destroy. "You have murdered. You crave to murder hundreds, thousands," he whispered in her ear. "Yet you do not understand what it is you do. The river cannot replenish. Once it is gone, there is only desert. You are destroying them."

"I destroy monsters," she said as tears rolled down her cheeks, for those words sat hollow in her chest.

"Your soul is growing dark." The sword pressed harder against her neck and she felt his internal battle. "You crave destruction." And it was not her he was speaking to, but himself he was trying to convince. "Hate has poisoned you. I cannot heal you." His breathing grew ragged.

She allowed her head to fall back against his shoulder, opening her throat to his blade. "How many times must we do this dance, Shoran? You have your path, your own reckoning, and I have mine. Am I your monster? If so then you must end me. Else let me destroy the monsters who would destroy me and all that I love." The last words choked her. Her heart jolted and her hand moved to cover his around her waist. "End me, for you will not stop me otherwise."

His hand twitched. Then a violent roar burst from his throat. He pushed her forward and she stumbled. He turned and slashed the wall of the house with his sword, cutting through stone as if it were flesh. Lightning flashed overhead, the ground shook and Elika fell to her knees. The shadow stepped towards her, his eyes aglow with hot yellow flame, his sword steady and resolute in his hand. She had pushed him too far; this was her end. He had warned her. And yet she was not afraid, for she had known this was always to be her end.

But beyond the enraged features of the demigod, wild in his vengeful fury, she saw a flash of desperation and raw despair. He advanced on her. She refused to look aside, she would look nearing death in the eyes.

"For men," she whispered a prayer to herself, seeking courage in the truth of her cause. "For men, I give my life."

But the sword did not rise. Instead he bent down, grabbed her arm in a steely grip and yanked her up to him.

"Time to show you that which you deny," he growled. "Time to face the price of your *justice*. For if not the sword, then truth shall end you."

She stumbled in his wake as he pulled her through the wall into the Tower of the Abyss, and into the hall with no beginning and no end …

A door appeared in the distance, ending the fathomless hall … no not a door, but a maw to the void.

"No!" She clawed at his hand and dug in her heels.

He lifted her off her feet. She kicked and fought as he clasped her to him and walked onward toward the Abyss.

Strands of her magic flew out, seeking to wrap around his legs, his neck, the walls around them. They slowed him not. Effortlessly, he bound and imprisoned them in a web of light.

She cast out flame and water to block his path, but they parted before him as if they were his to command. She clawed at his arm, kicked and screamed and thrashed. "Not there …" she gasped. "Please …" she pleaded. "Just kill me!" She pulled at his hair and scratched at his skin, but he just walked and walked, sure and steady toward the endless void.

"'Tis time you learned. 'Tis time you saw," spoke the darkness through him, as he dragged her closer to the fathomless Abyss.

And into it.

Elika screamed.

The winds gripped her, ripped her breath from inside her chest, and screamed back. Fierce and wild like him, they pulled her out of his arms, and she was falling into that nothingness, toward eternity and all the other lost souls trapped within.

Her chest was rising and falling, but she could not grasp enough air.

"Open your eyes," said the darkness into her ear.

His voice broke through her panic, and she realized she was not falling. He held her firmly against him, and she clung to his imprisoning arms.

His forehead rested on her head. "Look towards your fear and see," he said, and it sounded like a plea.

"Don't let me go. Do not let me go."

"I will never let you go," he whispered—a dark threat, a seductive promise.

Something in her reacted to it; the frantic beat of her heart changed its rhythm and she turned her face towards his lips. "Please …" she pleaded.

"Open your eyes, little spider." His breath brushed her cheek.

"I can't," she panted as terror seized her mind and her limbs. "I'll fall."

His hands tightened around her. "Open them or I will throw us both into the Abyss of Nerasky." The threat held such a note of despair that she knew he meant it.

Her eyes flew open. She looked down. He was standing on a stone edge above sheer darkness. Her feet dangled above his. She raised her face seeking anything but the void to rest her eyes on … and froze.

The sight that filled her gaze was more terrible than the Abyss, and yet more glorious than all the light and life of the world. For there, in the fathomless darkness, she saw the web she had only ever seen in dreams. Its strands of starlight pulsed like stars in the sky on a windy day. It was in truth a spider's web, but the pattern was more breathtaking than anything she had ever woven. Something primal turned over inside her and became a craving, a ravening greed. She wanted to go towards the web, to touch those strands and know their vast, endless power. It filled her soul with want beyond the need for food and air—a want so deep it shook her to the core.

"It's magnificent," she said in breathless wonder. Such paltry words, as small and inconsequential as specs of dust upon the glorious light.

"Look closer and see." His voice was strained, and she heard his ragged breathing, felt his chest rise and fall, felt his barely contained tension, as his face turned a little and he furtively breathed her in.

She looked past the light, took in the whole web and her heart came to a stumbling crash. Strands were flailing loosely in the wind of the Abyss, just like Bill Fisher once told her, just like she had seen in her dreams. Everywhere she looked, the web was faded, sickly, as if rot was spreading through it. So many holes, so much decay and destruction … and fire … red fire …

In her heart, she knew what it was, what it meant.

Then she turned her head to an even more terrible sight. The web was sundered. The other half was dark, lifeless and broken. Its strands were barely visible, for they were grey and wilted, limply flailing in the unforgiving wind.

"Do you see the destruction you weave?" A whisper brushed her ear, and his warm lips briefly touched her skin and retreated. And she wanted them back on her skin. "The essence you feel running through the world, the magic you draw upon and pull onto yourself is the very light you are destroying when you rip it apart. Stop your destruction."

"Enough," she said and her voice broke on a rising sob.

"You know the laws of the gods."

"I know," she replied brokenly. She had read of this in that book he had translated for her.

"Those who damage the web must repair it or be punished." He took a step, pushing her forward. "Will you repair it?"

She dug her fingers and nails into his arms. Beneath their feet, there was nothing but the endless Abyss. The dark eternity of falling through it, screaming and screaming until her voice was gone.

"Please," she whispered though she knew not for what she pleaded. His tenderness, his mercy, his lips upon her skin. For him to end this torment.

Abruptly, she was yanked back, and the stone wall sealed the darkness beyond. The endless hall surrounded them.

For a long moment, he did not move. He was breathing harshly, as if composing himself and her, his arms tight around her. Nor did she want to move. He was her tormentor and her anchor. She dared not lose his nearness whilst her mind battled the vision he had shown her. Whilst the world as she knew it broke apart into pieces around her. And she knew not how to piece it together again. Her nightmares and dreams and everything she knew churned and blurred into a new and alien reality made of Bill's wild stories.

"*Morna frya deari,*" Shoran's whisper brushed her cheek. "Still the fire in your heart."

Arms tightened around her, Shoran's head lowered …

Abruptly, he released her and stepped away.

She stumbled from the sudden absence of his strength but did not fall.

His eyes were glowing with anger and heat, and something more she dared not probe.

Her skin still held the imprint of his arms, still burned where his lips had brushed against her cheek. She hugged herself, else she would surely break apart. "I did not mean to attack it … the web." Her voice sounded small between them.

"Your power is uncontained. You did not merely kill the Laifae but shredded their very souls. You draw upon the web to feed the magic in you, the essence of life which you then destroy. You destroy more than all the blood-salt fires in the city. If you shred the web, if you extinguish its light, men will die as surely as the

Laifae. Cease your destruction or by the laws of gods I will have no choice but to end you."

There was torment in his eyes. It was not a command, not a demand but an anguished plea. He did not want to kill her, but he must. She was the evil come to destroy the world. She was the monster he had to vanquish to save it.

"Teach me," she said. "How to use magic and not destroy the web."

His face shuttered and grew cold, as his eyes focused on her, as if seeing her for the first time. The dark gaze roamed over her, took in her dress, her earrings, the jewelry and styled hair now mussed and falling out of its pins. Slowly, his gaze returned to the jewelry, the low neckline of her dress and his lips pursed ever so slightly. She knew how she must look, understood the ugly suspicions in his mind, though the truth was no less ugly.

Then his gaze finally rose back to hers. "Until you release darkness from your heart and drain poison from your soul, I cannot teach you. 'Tis forbidden by the gods to teach such things to those who seek to use them to destroy. I cannot unleash the power of such evil on the three realms. Already I am remiss in my duty to end you," he added bitterly and strode away angry, unforgivingly so.

As she watched his back, she realized with a stab of hurt, that she was *his* monster.

CHAPTER TWENTY-TWO

The War Council

"Of the four Sacred Crowns, the most enlightened line of kings was Westwater. It began with the demigod Eshan Syn'Anav, son of Anav, the god of sea and water. Instead of breeding bastards or a plenitude of ambitious heirs, the first Westwater king had only one son and one daughter. He loved and treasured them both, and his reign was long, for his son was content to remain a prince of the crown. It was his children's children who conspired to overthrow Eshan after a thousand-year rule. Nor were they driven by ambition, but rather by his growing neglect of his kingdom. The removal of the king was a peaceful affair, though it took decades of arguments and persuasion. Eshan eventually left Seramight to return to El'Sandria. Westwater Crown rarely warred with the land kingdoms, and always in defense at their instigation. And where generations of Sacred Crowns have come and gone—with Northwind reaching eighteen kings before their demise—Westwater had only five. The fifth and last king, Elrik Westwater, changed the long tradition of neutrality when Ailing Northwind abducted Arala. At the time, King Elrik had ruled his kingdom for four hundred years and was the oldest king amongst the Crowns. He was also said to be the only one to have Syn'Moreg's ear."

The History of Alafraysia and Seramight,
By Mageguard Bluelight

Smoke from the ruin of the temple still swathed the city and dark clouds gathered overhead. There was an unnatural silence in the streets and a sense of brooding peace akin to a calming breath before a plunge. How long had it been since she faced dawn with no sign of battle, no ringing of the bells or the singing of Reval's blasted mageguards?

She strolled the streets all night, haunted by what Shoran had shown her. Although she had fled the tower, had fled him, she could not flee the twisted tangle of emotions that followed her still. And in the darkest hours of the night when the Abyss seemed so close, it stirred unbidden feelings, and thoughts that did not seem her own. She forced herself to think of Mite. But his face dissolved and was replaced with Shoran's dark eyes lit with anguished rage, his sword at her throat, his lips on her hair, her cheek, his breath upon her skin as he whispered threats and dark promises. All night she had fought an aching need to go to him, to fight him and have him hold her near.

As daylight returned, the dark musings faded, and wisps of foolishness replaced the thoughts and longings of the night before. When the rays of sun pierced through the smoke haze blanketing the streets, she recalled the glorious strands of the web, the light of life and magic, now broken and decaying.

You have murdered, he had whispered. There was no accusation, no judgement, only truth. And that truth was a stain upon her soul.

Elika knocked on the door. Shortly, Toad opened it and started. "You're back ..." He glanced over his shoulder. "He's fuming. I'd not be coming here if I was ye."

She had nowhere else to go. Besides, there was Liffy to think of, whom Rory had lured for just such an eventuality. And Elika still had to kill the archmage. She knew that her fire last night had not reached him, for the folk had been bemoaning it this morning.

So she strode past Toad. "Where is he?"

"In the library. But he's not alone. I'll take ye to him then ... if that's what you're wanting," he added uncertainly.

Elika knew her way and marched ahead with Toad trailing unhappily behind. Muffled voices came from behind the door to the library. Toad opened it a crack and poked his head through. "Pardon me, m'lord. But ... ahem. She's back."

Elika strode in past Toad, ready to face Rory's wrath. The light of the Great Web was imprinted on her mind, and there was nothing she could face that was more terrifying than what she had seen last night.

A man wearing the uniform of a captain was with Rory, leaning over the map of the city stretched across the desk. She recognized him instantly, even before he turned his face to her, if only by his hair, the color of an overripe carrot. Lord Trian Truestar, captain of the Northern Bastion, whom she had followed a time or two to learn any news of Mite.

Rory looked up and stared at her, as if he, too, could not believe she'd dare return. Toad slunk away, closing the door behind him.

"Didn't expect to see you again, Spit," said Rory, his one eye dripping with fury. It held no less menace than having both eyes glare at her. "Thought you had more sense than to bring me your hide to flay."

Elika strode forward. "Still got a job to do, don't I?"

The captain was eyeing her curiously. A frown of recognition touched his brow, as he no doubt wondered where he had seen her before. They had never spoken, but he had laid eyes on her a time or two in the tavern he frequented.

She halted when she saw Blood Dog lying on the settee, his hands behind his head and his booted feet dangling. His eyes were closed, and she thought he was asleep until he spoke. "I can feel your icy gaze burning holes in me, mousy."

"Just wondering if you're sleeping," she said and turned back to Rory. "No point glaring murder at me, Rory. You know you need me."

"Who is she?" the red-haired captain asked him.

Rory was leaning his fists on the table, and she could tell from the tension in the room that they had been arguing before she arrived.

"No one you need to worry about," he said carefully.

Blood Dog barked a laugh. "Aye, he does, you blind, one-eyed fool. We all do."

Elika had never seen anyone insult Rory and survive long past the end of the insult. So it was a surprise when he merely ignored the ruffian lying on the couch in his sweaty shirt and mud-stained boots.

"You are Mite's friend, aren't you?" she asked the captain.

"Mite?" he echoed in surprise.

"Name's Eli. He might've mentioned me."

His jaw dropped, and his eyes widened as if in recognition. "You …"

Rory smiled with a hint of cruel amusement. "*Her.*"

Then the red-haired man growled in frustration and cursed the vilest of curses she had ever heard. He ran his hands through his hair, looking at her in horror, then spun to face Rory and leant his fists on the table. "Northwind must not be told. Not now … not … yet." Then his back slumped and his head hung between his shoulders. "Not ever," he mumbled to himself.

"Must not be told what?" Elika frowned at his bizarre outburst. "That I'm alive? He won't be. He's got enough of his own troubles to worry about."

"I have no intention of telling him," Rory said. "And seeing as Spit here wants us to be honest, this is your Rogue Mage. The one who burned down the temple last night."

Again, the captain swore. Studied her with a clenched jaw. "I'm Captain Trian of the Northern Bastion," he said with a reluctant bow. "Though I suspect you already know that." His eyes roamed over her face as if he was searching for something in it. "I assume Aeronmite doesn't know … about what you can do," he added accusingly.

"Didn't know myself till recently," she said.

His jaw ticked. "Some say you are Arala."

"I'm not."

"What possessed you to attack the temple?"

"The men they were going to murder," she replied dryly.

Rory crossed his arms, unamused. "As I told you, captain, it was not done at my command, despite your accusations. As you might imagine, I have no control over this little treasure."

Captain Trian straightened, tall and somber. "Then this stops now," he said to her. "If you ever cared for Aeronmite, if you owe him any crumb of loyalty and allegiance, you'll do nothing like that again unless you speak to me first."

His anger was all too reminiscent of Shoran's, though Trian wasn't speaking of the Web. Something else was terribly wrong. She could sense it in the silence of the city. "What passed last night?" she asked wearily.

"The archmage has called off the Spring Parade," Trian replied. "The aeons and majren are taking what they can carry, along with their slaves and bonded servants, and going to the palace district. Those who are staying behind have sealed themselves inside their homes, and attack with magic anyone who comes close."

Elika found it hard not to smile. "The mages are leaving Terren."

"I'm surrounded by bloody fools," Blood Dog groaned as he threw his arm over his eyes.

The captain ignored him. "Don't look so pleased, Rogue. 'Tis, not a victory. Tridamor has recalled all the mageguards off the streets and barricaded them inside the palace grounds. They have raised magic defenses and are now in the midst of their own council."

"The truce I secured with the archmage is now broken," Rory added.

"What he's trying to say," Blood Dog cut in with a yawn. "Is that you have started a war."

"The war was already here," she said. "Daetown has been under attack all winter. And Mite is raising an army ..."

"That was not war," the captain replied, his voice rising. "A few battles and skirmishes. Until now, the archmage was trying to crush unrest and small rebellion pockets. Now he believes ... no, he *knows*, that the Rogue Mage has cornered him, and he needs to fight his way out."

"The war was meant to begin with the death of the archmage," Rory said. "And that was not meant to happen until Northwind was ready to march towards Terren with his army."

"*He* would have started the war," Trian said. "When he was ready to defend the people of Terren. When *we* were ready."

"And we're not ready," Rory added.

Understanding dawned on Elika. Terren had no army to defend the people against the combined might of Prince Southfire and Archmage Tridamor.

"And, my dear," Rory continued. "Tridamor will now be extra watchful of anyone trying to get close to him. He will suspect traitors and assassins everywhere, especially those of the feminine nature."

"I can get close to him. Just give me time," she said, her mind racing. It was not lost. She could fix this. "If we get close to Southfire, we'll get to Tridamor. The fat Lord Shorgray is rather intrigued by you," she said to Rory. "The last three gatherings, he's barely left your side. He is nursing secret sympathies for Northwind, of that I'm certain. He's also the brother of Duke Orland, who is inside Southfire's council."

Rory nodded thoughtfully. "I've already marked him for our side. Might be I'll send him an invitation to a private dinner with us."

Blood Dog grunted from his settee. "The only thing you need to know about him is that he's sweating his balls over the debt of fifty gold he owes Mage Aeon-Butterhoney. Offer him the purse of gold in exchange for an introduction to Orland and he'll lick your balls to seal the deal."

"How do you know this, Dog?" Captain Trian asked with a frown, and Elika wondered the same.

"I know 'cause everyone knows. Don't ye people ever talk to anyone?"

A faint smell of whisky and stale ale reached her as Blood Dog spoke, and the strong perfume of incense you'd find in the more expensive whorehouses. Elika looked closer and noticed that his boots were far too shiny and new-looking compared to the rest of him.

"We don't have long," Trian said, turning back to her and Rory. "This morning, my men spied dozens of messengers riding out from the palace in all directions. All of them mages. I have a few men following them, but we think they are calling on the mageguards from other towns and cities."

"The archmage is building an army," Elika said. "You must tell Mite. He must return without delay."

"I've sent a man to Wavestar on a ship that left at dawn's high tide. Aeron will soon learn of everything that's transpired. But we need to hold out until he arrives." Trian turned to the map of Terren, held open by stones on the corners.

Elika took it in quickly, with a sinking sensation akin to falling off a roof. Blue and red stones were placed along each city wall. The blue stones surrounded Daetown, two nearby districts, and encompassed the Northern Bastion. All in all, Northwind's colors held less than a third of the city. The red stones were a rash taking over the map. They guarded the walls of the rest of the city, all the gates, and the harbor, too. The rebels were hopelessly outnumbered, whether the archmage was dead or not.

Trian leant over the map. "Only two other bastions have joined us." He pointed at the Northern, the Eastern and a smaller one between them. It was more of an overspill from the other two than a true defensive tower.

"The Northern Bastion is the largest in the city," Rory said, whilst studying the map. "Dog," he threw over his shoulder. "If you're finished napping, might be you'd like to join us."

"Seen your bloody map already. Don't need to see more than that," he replied without moving his arm thrown across his eyes.

Trian moved two blue stones over the Northern Bastion. "I have a thousand men at my command, but they are no match in armor, weapons or training for Captain Smokeheart's legion. He commands the defenses of the palace and the southern and western walls. The five bastions are all under his overriding influence. They will not join us." He ran his finger over the wall that encompassed two-thirds of the city, and Elika saw their predicament. The captain's next words confirmed it. "When Northwind brings an army, he'll be attacking from the west and south. Both are strongholds of Captain Smokeheart's battalion."

"We'll be attacking them from behind," said Elika with little conviction, for it would stretch them too thinly.

"Aye, he knows that, and he'll be looking to destroy our defenses long before Aeronmite gets here."

Rory scratched his chin. "We need to take charge of this wall." He tapped his finger on the line that had once marked the boundary of the old city. "If we can take it and hold it, we'll control half the city. And it brings us within an arrow's flight of Captain Smokeheart's flanks." He moved his finger to one of the towers on the outer wall. "The Rise Bastion is under the command of Captain Foxhunt. He's only got five hundred men. I honestly thought he'd join us."

Captain Trian's jaw tightened. "He's a good man, but he won't go against the will of the masses, and the masses are crying for Southfire and the death of the Rogue. Especially after last night. If Foxhunt sees that men are turning to Northwind, he'll change his allegiance. He holds no love for either of the princes."

"Foxhunt might care for neither prince," Blood Dog said from the couch. "But his men sympathize with Northwind. Terren is his by right, no matter which side of it he came from. Remove Foxhunt, and his men will be yours. You can take the whole damn bastion into your flanks and place your own captain to nurse them."

"Then remove him, Dog," Rory said without looking away from the map.

Elika saw the shadow of contempt in the captain's face when he looked at Rory. The captain did not like him. Only Mite and his cause united them in an unnatural alliance. The captain was himself a lord, and she suspected he knew everything he needed to know about One-Eyed Rory from Mite.

"I want to speak with Foxhunt before we try force," Trian said. "I might be able to convince him."

"You've already tried. As have my men," Rory replied. "He is beyond corruption. And the archmage will try to recapture the city before Northwind is wed."

"I'll talk to him again," Trian insisted with more force.

"Might be if I kill the archmage before then," she said. "It'll give us more time."

"No," the captain said harshly, turning to her. "If you kill him before Aeronmite marches, you will hand the city and victory to Southfire. Only the archmage is keeping him from proclaiming himself king. As soon as Southfire does, the dukes will align behind him. The people will do, too, if only to avoid war and bloodshed. Most want an Alterrian king and not a Dae one. At the moment, Terrenians believe that Northwind alone can deliver them from the archmage's tyranny."

Elika nodded. "I see. We hole ourselves like rabbits and wait for the archmage to send his army against us whilst we wait for Mite to take his fill of half the ladies of the court before deciding which one he wants to wed."

The captain winced and suddenly he could no longer hold her gaze. He turned back to the map and ran his hand through his hair. "He thought he had more time to convince both Warwind and Firestorm to align with him without the wedding. They will not. My messenger will reach him in four days. If I know Aeron, he will race back with an army, even if he has to steal one." A wry smile, reminiscent of brotherly affection, touched his lips.

Aye, there was a past between them. She saw it that day when Mite raced to the burning ship. They were close, and their friendship likely began on the other side of the bridge, for Trian was also a Dae.

"When did you leave Dae-Terren?" she asked him.

He looked at her wearily. "Ten years ago."

"You knew Mite before that," she said.

His lips curled. "We were like brothers as children. We grew up together and became orphaned together."

"In Lord Silvering's rebellion," she said, thinking yet again how little she knew of Mite. He was indeed a stranger to her, with another life he had kept hidden from their pack. He had a past, and friends she knew nothing about, and adventures that went beyond keeping their pack fed and safe.

Rory and Captain Trian returned to making their defensive plans. Elika listened, but her mind kept drifting to the light of the Web, to Shoran's whispered threats and secret kisses.

By the time they were finished, Blood Dog was snoring loudly.

The captain cast her another unreadable glance and after a curt bow began to leave. She stepped in front of him. "Don't tell Mite about me."

His lips twisted wryly. "May he forgive me, but he'll not hear of you from me," he said dryly, bitingly. Then more quietly. "In turn, I ask that you stay away from him. He needs no ragamuffin ghosts from his past haunting his present. He's been through enough. Leave him be." With that barbed reply, he stepped around her and strode out.

Ragamuffin. That was how Captain Lord Truestar saw her. Not worthy of a lordship's notice. Those words should not have stung as they did. Did she expect pretty clothes and better manners would strip the grimy streets off her skin?

"Now, my dear," Rory's voice came from behind her. "I think we must set new rules, which you will abide by if you wish to continue our alliance and help our Mitey become king."

"What do you want, Rory?"

"From now on, I need you to do exactly as I say. No more Rogue doing her own thinking."

Elika nodded. "As you say. No more thinking."

Blood Dog snored loudly behind them.

CHAPTER TWENTY-THREE

Duke Orland

"History records many great wars where men sought to cleanse their world of our kind. Each one involved burning everything and everyone infected or possessed by "magic", as they called the wondrous gift of tapping into the wells of power. No war, however, has been as damaging to men and the Laifae as the Sundering Wars. Our liege, Reval, was in large part responsible for the destruction, for it was he who set the world afire. Men, in their stupidity, simply threw blood-salt into the flame and turned the flames he had wrought against him. It was then that Syn'Moreg emerged from the Abyss, put out the fires, and in his rage, sundered our joined realms. Though humans think only Seramight is sundered, the great chasm of the Abyss runs through Alafraysia also, a dark scar we fear and avoid."

The History of Alafraysia and Seramight,
By Mageguard Bluelight

Rory and Blood Dog circled her thoughtfully, assessing her as one might prize horse flesh to be sold to the highest bidder. Rory always gave exact instructions as to what dress she was to wear, how her hair was to look, and what jewels she was to adorn herself with. Tonight, she wore emeralds, for they were said to be Duke Orland's favorite stone.

"I do not see how dressing me like a whore will get me closer to Prince Southfire," she said. "I am certain he has plenty of whores at his disposal."

"You're not dressed like a whore," Rory replied, walking around her appraisingly. "Aye, the dark green's a little more brazen than what you're used to, and the low cut most definitely highlights your womanly attributes. It's what we need to intrigue the letches of the court."

"Now listen here, queeny, and do not scowl." Blood Dog added his voice to Rory's. "There's two ways for a beautiful woman like you to rise to the top in the court. Ye either do it through inheritance and chastity needed to bait a duke, or shameless promiscuity. And Lady Fair has no inheritance, no titles, nor enough lands to interest a duke."

"And tonight, we need to interest Duke Orland," Rory cut in.

"And seeing as Lord Nightkill here doesn't have any standing worth spitting on, he can't gain ye an invitation to Southfire's inner circle. Only notoriety will propel either of ye to get close to him and the archmage. The only interesting thing about this bastard here posing as a lord is you, queeny, and their belief that you're in this bastard's bed. And the only way you'll get into the palace is as a mistress to the duke who's the chief advisor to the prince. So, swallow back that bile and smile like a woman who wants to bed a duke."

Elika nodded lifelessly as she fought the assailing thoughts of Shoran. She looked like a courtesan, down to the dark red paint on her lips. Dread settled in her stomach at the thought he might find out about her growing notoriety in the noble circles. Might be Shoran already knew, for she could not forget his face the last time he had looked upon her, when he took in her dress and the jewels she was wearing. Aye, she looked like she was dressed as another man's mistress.

In his hand, Rory was twisting and turning the invitation he had received from Duke Orland to join him for dinner. Blood Dog had been right, fifty gold was all it took for the fat, indebted Lord Shorgray to beg an invitation for them from his brother the duke.

"It'll be up to you to impress him, El," said Rory. "The over-preening, arrogant bastard despises me. I met him once at Lord and Lady Deringer's tea party. He'd hang me by my balls off the nearest tower if he could. And that hate is its own lure to one of his elk. If we make him think I have something I shouldn't have, his pride will chafe. The man is a letch, and he'll be intrigued by you, Spit. Of that I'm certain."

"Aye, he will, for you have something that always gets them salivating over ye, mousy," said Blood Dog. "Ye have the look of a Sachi. So just be sure to tell them Lady Fair has the blood of the gods in her. They suspect a drop of it already, I dare say."

"If you say so, Dog," said Rory. "Now shall we go?"

They left the mansion and climbed into the waiting carriage. Blood Dog was their coachman again, and shortly they were riding through the streets.

A thick fog blanketed the city. So thick, she couldn't see houses across the street, and she couldn't guess how Blood Dog found his way through it. The city was eerily silent. Shadows of men passed by not a few paces away. From a distance came the slow clip-clopping of hooves, and the slow rolling of carriage wheels, the sounds dull and echoing. The horse and wagon suddenly emerged from the fog and she leant back in her seat, startled by their nearness.

As they rode, Rory continued his instructions. "When the duke asks you to dance with him, be sure to accept. And do not flinch when he makes an improper or suggestive gesture. It's time you started to use your womanly gifts. Now, don't glare at me with those menacing eyes of yours, Spit. If Orland pays you more notice than he does any other lady, rumors will be rife, and they will reach Prince Southfire. The prince will not allow his most loyal and valuable vassal to show interest in any woman he does not know. He'll want to meet you."

Since the night she had burned down the temple, Rory had been aloof around her, cooler and harder. Sometimes, like now, she caught a brief but potent look in his eye that measured her as a threat. Elika had no illusions that their alliance was threadbare and grew more so each time he glimpsed her powers. There could never be trust where there was fear. And she was coming to suspect that deep inside, Rory was beginning to fear her. It was the last thing she wanted, for fear always led men to act in unpredictable ways.

So she gave him a firm, reassuring nod. "I'll do as you say. I'll get us inside that palace."

When they arrived at Duke Orland's mansion, Blood Dog jumped down and opened the door for them. "Listen, mousy, there's no secret to how beautiful women interest men," he said, blocking their way. "You just have to rub 'em a little. When the duke glances your way, look him in the eyes longer than appropriate and give him a very slight, secretive smile. Not too much, just enough to pique his curiosity. Then pay him no attention until he comes to you." He stood aside then as they dismounted.

Faces turned towards them and regarded them with an expression one might bestow on mummers sent to entertain them.

Undaunted, Rory strode into the house with her on his arm, towards their host, Duke Orland. He was younger than she had expected, with narrow eyes that spoke of unshakable mistrust of the world and everyone in it. He also had the features of a man who hated to be denied. There was an impatience about him, stemming from the natural boredom of one who has everything he desires. And he took in the scene with a gaze that was restless in pursuing and quick in dismissing.

As they approached him, the duke's gaze skipped over her and focused on Rory with unhidden contempt. There was such depth to the duke's enmity, Elika grew certain their plan was about to fall apart.

She thought quickly, remembered what Blood Dog had told her, and made her move. It was easy to interest bored children with anything that broke up the monotony of their environment. She didn't think it would be too different with men seeking their next distraction. Reaching up to her hair, as if to adjust it, she flicked a pin to the floor, and a curl fell out of her perfectly styled tresses. She stopped, feigned embarrassment and whispered into Rory's ear, "Make him wait."

He stopped instantly, following her lead, feigning concern at the slight disarray of her hair.

The duke's gaze drifted towards her, and whilst Rory tucked the curl behind her ear, Elika glanced at the duke and gave him a small, embarrassed smile. And that was that. The duke's attention was hers as they strolled towards him. Shamelessly, he perused her from top to bottom, and back again.

"Lord Nightkill, 'tis indeed a … pleasure to have you in my home," he drawled. "And Lady Fair, I am intrigued indeed. I have met your father a time or two, and I must say that you look nothing like Lord Killray. I would swear he was cuckolded by his late lady wife." He said it loudly enough for others to hear. It was a calculating insult to them both, and she knew he was testing Rory. When insulted, men were commonly prone to either defend themselves or offend in turn.

Rory was smarter than that, however. He stiffened, glanced around, and whispered loud enough for everyone nearby to overhear. "Do not be unkind, your grace. This is not the child of the first Lady Killray, who died birthing a stillborn *son*, despite popular misconceptions bred by the lord himself about the child surviving. This is the daughter of her father's second wife— whom he wed in secret inappropriately soon after the death of the first. Indeed, Lady Fair's mother was a Sachi of noble birth … an *Elder* from the Valley, I'm told. And it is why he kept his daughter hidden from society for so long, fearing the same ridicule you now bestow. Or worse, fearing the letches who might trick her into marriage for her blood."

"Her blood?" The duke raised his eyebrows.

"I assure you, her blood is impeccable. The documents of her secret heritage are safe with me. And, tell no one this, but the blood of the gods flows as strongly in Lady Fair as it did in her mother." He then turned a salacious gaze on her. "Isn't that right, my dear?"

She looked aside shyly. "You know it is, my lord. You have seen as much yourself. It's why magic favors me so."

Rory put his arm possessively around her waist. "Indeed, I am lucky I found her before anyone else did."

And there it was, a flicker of greed and annoyance in the duke's gaze, aimed at the man he viewed as unworthy of gods' spit, never mind their blood in his mistress.

As Rory led her away, Elika glanced back to see the duke watching her still. She smiled and looked away, then proceeded to avoid meeting his gaze for the rest of the evening. It was easy to do, as more and more lords kept approaching her, seeking the truth of the rumor of her secret parentage. And one lord's interest quickly becomes another's.

Rory played her jealous protector, keeping them from ambushing her alone. She knew it was not out of any care he had for her, but to frustrate the interest of the others. Ever men crave the fruit just out of their reach. Though even Rory could not stop unwanted hands secretly brushing her back, whispered requests for a private assignation dropped in her ear, or sly offers to whisk her away from the imposter lord. And all the while, Duke Orland continued to watch her from afar.

"The duke's intrigued by you," Rory said quietly to her once they were alone again. "Now flirt a little with the fools paying homage to you, my dear. Orland most craves that which others covert and possess."

Before long, Duke Orland made his way towards them, determined and flushed. "Lady Fair, you have stolen the attention of every lord in this room." He raised her hand to his lips and they lingered there.

Rory cleared his throat and placed himself between her and the duke. "Your grace, you are far too observant. I weary of fighting off the attentions of these rogues from my fair cousin."

The lords around him laughed.

"We were just discussing the fog," he continued. "Lord Greywood was just commenting that it must be Reval's doing."

The duke tore his gaze from Elika and seemed annoyed to be forced to converse with Rory. "It is not Reval. The archmage has received word from Reval's court, denying any involvement." He turned back to her. "Lady Fair …" the duke began.

"Then I dare say it must be Ilikan," Rory interrupted, and once again inserted himself between the duke and Elika. "Or perhaps the Rogue?"

"This is not Ilikan's doing," the duke replied with increasing irritation. "Which leaves the Rogue as the only other culprit."

"No doubt you know such things better than I," Rory said. "I suspect the prince and the archmage will solve this mystery shortly. After all, it's only the fog that's keeping his mageguards and Southfire's soldiers from attacking the rebel stronghold."

More lords voiced their views on the matter.

Elika passed her gaze over the room, allowing the hum of the crowd and the flow of music to drown their argument. Suddenly, her skin prickled with recognition. Lady Rosalina stood at a distance, watching her with an appalled expression. Before she could stop herself, Elika blushed at the lie she was presenting. The lie that Lady Rosalina helped her perfect.

You, my dear, are no goddess. The words from another proud tane rang in her mind, dousing her in doubt and humiliation.

"My love," she said to Rory. "I will leave you to discuss such complex matters in peace, for I wish to speak with a lady who owes me a favor."

"But of course, my dear." He smiled approvingly and turned back to the duke. "Surely the archmage means to put an end to this rebellion before they overrun Terren. What use is magic if it cannot defend us against the rabble attacking the city?"

She detached herself from Rory's arm, lifted her head high and glided through the room towards the tane watching her with unhidden dismay. Despite the barbs of doubts Lady Rosalina always seeded in her skin, Elika smiled as if the world was hers to command.

"Lady Rosalina, I am surprised to see you here," she said, being careful not to allow the Dae accent to slip through the mask.

"Duke Orland is a friend and owes me more than one favor," she said stiffly. "When I heard rumors of this mysterious Lady Fair gracing the circles on the arm of an imposter lord, I could not help but confirm my suspicions." Her gaze darted contemptuously towards Rory.

Elika felt her cheeks flush. She knew what Lady Rosalina had heard and to what she was alluding. But there was no avoiding the stain, which she'd likely never wash out. Yet the judgment of the tane still irked her. "Is this not what you trained me for?"

Tane Rosalina lifted her chin and stood prouder than a queen. "I did not train you to be some commoner's whore." The tane looked aside in disgust and clear dismissal.

Elika knew not why she always allowed the tane's caustic words to cut her so deeply, nor why anger flooded her so readily when faced with this woman's judgement. "You forget yourself …"

"Oh, do not pretend to be an imperious tsarina now. I can see you are not. It is clear to me this is some game you are playing. What are you up to, girl? Shoran will …"

"Shoran is to hear nothing of it."

"Ha! He has already heard of this, my dear. Who do you think I learned these appalling rumors from?"

Elika's insides jolted painfully. "He sent you to discover their truth?"

"You are so much more than this," the tane said, her face crumbling.

"Lady Rosalina. Your manner is somewhat less than ladylike."

That brought a surprised raise of her brows. "My manner … you impertinent …"

"Am I or not your tsarina?" Elika said quietly, whilst putting power into her voice, and somehow hiding the tremble in her heart. She had to believe herself to be a tsarina. If she could not convince Lady Rosalina of her noble heritage, she'd never convince anyone in court. She'd be ousted as an imposter. Gently, she pulled on the surrounding essence, knowing the tane would feel the power of it. "Next time you call me a whore, I will not be so forgiving."

Lady Rosalina hesitated uncertainly. "Sweet Neka. I truly cannot tell whether you believe this or not. Whether you are taunting me or commanding me." Nervously, she twisted the spider ring on her finger.

"We will speak again another time." Elika inclined her head graciously and walked away.

Through dinner, Lady Rosalina continued to eye her from the other end of the table. Elika sat close to Duke Orland, with Rory between her and the irritable duke. More than once, he had attempted to catch her alone, but Rory was careful to never allow them more than a few brief exchanges of pleasantries. And the ploy of feeding the duke's frustration was bearing fruit. As the evening progressed, the duke's fixation with her was unshakable. He all but trembled with the need to speak with her alone.

As always at such gatherings, Elika listened to multiple conversations at once. There was much information to be gleamed of the happenings in the court, concerning intrigues, indiscretions and weddings between the noble houses. But it was news of Northwind her ears sought. Invariably, the talk soon turned to it.

"He has fled Duke Firewind's court," Lord Refrain loudly informed the old, half-deaf matron at the far end of the table, and everyone fell silent.

One-Eyed Rory and Blood Dog had carefully studied every noble house in the city, and Elika knew that most present here were loyal to Southfire. Those who were not, remained wisely silent whenever Northwind's name was mentioned.

"Why has he fled, eh?" the old matron asked just as loudly, turning her best ear towards him.

The hum of conversation resumed and drowned out Lord Refrain's answer.

Northwind was suddenly on every tongue.

"Damned fool, that boy," said an old lord.

"… such an insult to Duke Firewind. What the boy did to his daughter …"

"Poor girl …"

"Firewind will demand justice …"

"… carrying his child …"

"What did you say?" the half-deaf matron asked loudly.

"I said Northwind has seeded his daughter with a bastard and refused to wed her," Lord Refrain shouted.

A gasp of shock. "Lady Kristina is carrying Northwind's child?"

"Aye, and Northwind's fled to Windhay. He's now hiding out in Warwind's stronghold and is instead engaged to *his* daughter."

"Perhaps she, too, is carrying his child."

Laughter rang out around the table.

Elika's appetite fled. She listened to their disdain of Northwind with a strange numbness in her heart. Once it might have stung.

"Firewind has sent his army in pursuit towards Windhay demanding Northwind's head."

Rory muttered a very unlordly curse under his breath.

Across the table, there was muttering, anger and confusion. The food she had eaten sat heavily in her stomach. Mite was meant to be more than that. He was meant to be better—an example of honor and righteousness. At a time when he needed an army, and when Terren needed him more than ever, he was forging enemies from friends.

"Firewind won't get within sight of Windhay," said one lord. "Wind Valley is held by Warwind's two sons."

"Firewind's army wields the weapons of the gods themselves," someone said. "Weapons that can slay mages and gods alike, and sunder stone to pieces. It was why Northwind went to him."

"Then why did he run instead of marrying Lady Kristina?" asked a young lady in a blue dress with an eye for Duke Orland. "What does Warwind have to match such a gift?"

No one had an answer to that.

"If every time a man seeded a bastard where he shouldn't have brought about war, we would forever be fighting," Rory said and was joined in laughter by others at the table.

The lords and ladies went on to laugh at Northwind's brazenness, bemoaning his libertine ways and pondering how many bastards of his were running around different courts.

"The boy is a fool," said their host, silencing them at last. "Firewind's hatred of the tsaren is matched only by his hatred of Prince Southfire. Perhaps his army is not as large as Warwind's, but it is unrivalled in battle. Without Firewind's support, Northwind is as good as defeated. Now, shall we raise our toast to victory and enjoy the rest of our dinner?"

Elika tried to recall Mite as the man who protected their pack, as the one who took care of their messes, the one who was solid, dependable and *noble*. The man they now laughed at was not the boy she knew, nor the man she believed him to be. Slowly, it dawned on her that Mite was about to become a father. He had fathered a child … a bastard child.

Oh, Mite. How could you? She thought sadly and forced a polite smile to her lips as Duke Orland turned his attention back to her.

CHAPTER TWENTY-FOUR

Shadow's Kiss

"Tis not our interest to delve too far into the insipid past of humanity, save to say that for much of its history, Seramight was divided into hundreds of tribal kingdoms. It took but four demigods to conquer the uncivilized lands and divide them into four kingdoms of the Sacred Crowns. Or so the songs tell us. In our study of that time, we came upon ancient texts which speak not of four but five kingdoms of Seramight. There was and still remains, a forgotten fifth kingdom no demigod or king has ever conquered, for the army guarding it, is not wholly human. The kingdom is vast, spreading from the border of the Mountains of Fire past the edges of the known lands to encompass the Elder Valley. It belongs to Syn'Moreg."

The History of Alafraysia and Seramight,
By Mageguard Bluelight

"**M**agical items for sale," a drunk voice called out from the fog. "Charms and wards and wish-granting mice."

Elika walked by without slowing. If the drunk had magic-fashioned items, he wouldn't be shouting about them if he wanted to survive the night. Such items were now in short supply. Else, an aggrieved magic-hater might cut your throat for having them.

In Daetown, every mage's house was now an abandoned shell or a burned-out ruin. Indeed, magical or not, merchants across the city had little enough to sell as it was. Alterrians grumbled and cursed the Rogue. They cursed the magic-hating Daes and Northwind. Truth of the matter was that the archmage had closed six of the seven gates into the city. This, too, he had blamed on the Rogue.

With the war looming, traders had been bypassing Terren, headed instead for other cities to the south. And there had been reports of merchants being robbed along the way by small bands claiming loyalty to Northwind. The king's war tax, they called it. Although Elika doubted they had anything to do with the war or Northwind.

The city wall of the Northern Bastion emerged from the fog. From below, she could not see the top of the bulwark, save for the faint light of the torches breaching the mist. Elika walked around its base until she came to a set of stairs. She knew there were archers up there, twitchy and uncertain, listening for the enemy to sneak up on them.

"I'm coming up," she called out through the fog. "A friend. Don't loose your arrows and put holes in me."

"What do you want, girl?" a voice shouted back.

"Here to see Captain Trian."

"And does he want to see you?"

"Are ye a pretty wench?" another voice called out. This one was an Alterrian.

Muted laughter came from the fog.

"Tell him Lady Fair is here to see him," she called back and the laughter stopped.

Elika climbed the stairs, and the bastion's many defenders came into view, Daes and Alterrians both. Usually, the Northern Bastion overlooked the sea and the place where the bridge had once linked the two halves of the world. Now, they saw naught but the fog swirling around them. The red-haired captain materialized out of it and cursed under his breath. "Did One Eye send you?"

"No. Here on my own. Want to speak to you about Mite."

His jaw tightened and he looked even less pleased about that. He glanced at the soldiers around them, who were pretending that they weren't intently listening to what she had to say. The captain jerked his head for her to follow and led her into the bastion tower.

"Curse this blasted fog," he swore as they walked. "Dare I hope this is your creation and you can make it vanish?"

She grinned. "Don't know who made it. But it's the only thing keeping peace on the streets. Thought you'd be pleased."

"The fog might keep the archmage's army away, but it's also keeping my men from capturing the rest of the old city wall. By the time Aeronmite returns, we'll be in no position to aid him."

He strode into a captain's study. As soon as she beheld it, Elika knew it had once been Mite's. There was a sense about it, his way of arranging things that must have stayed with him from the Hide. Clear access to boltholes, or rather the window and the door. The table was set at a strange angle to allow him room to fight off an ambush. Weapons were within easy reach, no matter where in the room you stood. There was a shirt on a hook, which was too large for Trian, but would have fitted Mite.

Trian sat at the table. There was a bowl of cold stew and a mug of ale. "What is it you want to talk about? Be quick about it. I want to return to my dinner."

She crossed her arms. "Look, I don't know why you don't like me, and I don't care either. Only, I know you and Mite are close."

"We are brothers, in every way but blood. Our fathers were like brothers too."

"Then how is it I've never seen you when Mite lived on the streets?"

He cringed abashedly. "I was apprenticed to the priests and snuck Mite into the Temple of Reval whenever he needed. Then I took the bridge and Mite stayed behind. I didn't learn why until we met again as men. We were parted for eight years before he crossed."

"You were waiting for him," she said, with a twinge of old hurt and that haunting sense of loneliness.

"It's why I took the post with the Northern Bastion," he said. "Though the Southern Bastion would have rewarded me far more generously."

Despite her own dejection, she was glad Mite had someone waiting for him. "Then like me or not, you have a friend in me, too."

It seemed to be the last thing he wanted to hear. He ran his hand through his hair. "Look, I've no argument with you. I just need you to stay away from me … and from him."

"I'm trying to help him. He'll make a great king. Or so I thought until … Lady Kristina," she blurted out awkwardly. "'Tis not the Mite I thought I knew. Have you had word from him? Is what they are saying true?"

Trian drank deeply of his ale whilst struggling to hold her gaze. "Aye, 'tis true," he said with an edge to his voice. She could tell he was unhappy about it, too. "Nor did it surprise me that he got her with child. What surprised me was that he abandoned her and left Wavestar after he received my latest missive."

"What was in the missive?"

"Nothing to make him act thus. Only that we have taken parts of the city, and the Rise Bastion has joined our flanks following the disappearance of its Captain Foxhunt." She caught a flash of anger before his face shuttered.

They both knew well enough that the missing captain would not be returning.

"Has Mite written to you?" she asked, certain that he held back more than he shared.

She saw him wrestle with himself. He did not trust her, that much was clear. "I have received only one missive from him since spring, and that was to tell me that Duke Firewind was playing him false. That Firewind's allegiance is not to the Sacred Crowns. I could make no sense of it. The Duke of Wavestar hates the Laifae and their tsaren, and his house has always been unfalteringly loyal to the Sacred Crowns."

She thought about it. "Wavestar is said to be indebted to Syn'Moreg."

"Aye, there is a past there, though I've never found texts relating to it in the priests' archives. Nor does it explain why Firewind would play Aeron foul."

His answer was not what she had hoped for, for it left her no less baffled by Mite's actions. "At least he is leagues closer to Terren," she said with a sigh. "Windhay is but ten days' ride on horseback."

He eyed her wearily. "The wedding is in twelve days," he said, and she got the impression he did not want to tell her that either. "Aeronmite is to wed Lady Mirana, Duke Warwind's daughter."

A powerful pang went through her and quietened again. In truth, she did not know what to think, to feel. She felt much, and yet oddly too little. Sadness, regret perhaps, a little pain, but above all else a certain sense of finality, of a fading future that had once tickled the edges of her childish hopes.

"And after that, he will march on the city." Her voice sounded distant even to her.

"Aye, then he will march with Warwind's army," Trian said, watching her closely.

With mid-summer approaching, the weather was warm, and fields of crops and orchards were ripening. They had seen good rains this season, and the harvest would be plentiful enough to feed an army on the way to Terren.

"Then I have less time than I thought to get close to the archmage," she said and turned to go.

"Eli?" He stopped her, and his voice was kind, regretful almost.

She turned back, surprised to hear her name on his lips.

"Do not trust One Eye," he said after a moment, and she thought he meant to say something else before he looked aside. It was a wasted warning. Only a fool would trust Rory, and she suspected Trian knew it well enough. Still, she nodded her gratitude and left him there looking morose and toying with his cold stew.

~

Mite was to be wed. That thought permeated her blood, confused her, grieved her and yet lightened her somehow. It was as if a string holding her back from yielding to some secret desires of her heart had snapped.

She returned to Rory's mansion, where she had been spending her nights sleeping. After she had dinner in her room and Liffy took away the tray, Elika locked her door and before she could stop herself, walked through the wall into the long, dark corridor.

When had it begun to feel like home?

Her chest constricted and grew tight. There was an ache there that just would not be soothed. She had not sought Shoran since he had dangled her over the edge of the Abyss. Nor had he sought her. He had been angry then, disdainful of her.

The ache in her chest grew stronger.

She wanted to see him … No, she *needed* to see him.

Home. He made her feel like she was home. It was a dangerous thought, perilous to her heart.

A door appeared in the distance. Her feet moved towards it and faltered outside. She placed her hand on the door. There was movement beyond it, a rustle of parchment.

Was he still angry with her? Worse still, was he indifferent?

When did you grow so foolish? she chided herself, whilst trying to find the courage to push on that door.

Aye, she feared him. Feared the pain he might inflict on her heart, the sensations he was stirring in her, the enticement of an unspoken promise, and the replying yearning in her. Yet he was devoted to no one but his vile master. He served no one but the gods and cared for nothing but the web. And yet her heart craved more from him. She knew not what, only that she wanted more.

The sounds stilled. She pushed on the door and found herself in a dark study, with shelves of scrolls and a stone desk.

He was not there.

A crumpled note recently thrown into the fire shriveled and turned to ash before she could glimpse its contents. Curiosity burned fiercely in her. Without thought, she followed him through the lingering ripples his passage left behind.

She emerged on Harbor Street beside the calm sea shrouded in eerie moonlight peering through light fog. A ship was being loaded under the cover of darkness with a cargo of crates and barrels. The fog thickened again around the warehouses. The whole city beyond the harbor was shrouded in impenetrable mist, yet it parted like a veil before Shoran as he strode into a side alley. At the sight of him, her heart leapt painfully in her chest. Just to look at him muddled her mind. He was wearing his cloak. His boots were muddied and she pondered where he had been.

He strode ahead and turned into *The Thirsty Dagger* tavern. Elika raced after him and peered through the window. *The Thirsty Dagger* was not a tavern one walked into stinking of coin. The folk here would take the clothes you wore and the fine undergarments, too, if they thought they'd get half a penny for them on Salve Row. Inside, Shoran looked strikingly out of place; a lord in a tavern filled with rough-clad local workers, stained from the day's labors, and every manner of ruffian you'd find in the lowliest places in Terren. They cast gazes Shoran's way, measured him, and turned aside again. There was a sense of menace about him even the most desperate wretches would be loath to test. And even the blind would surely sense the power that always shrouded him.

Shoran sat at a table in front of a cloaked woman. Her fingers were long and bore many shining rings. When she turned her head, Elika saw with a pang of jealousy that she was striking, her smile lush and suggestive.

Elika could not see his face as they spoke, yet there was tension in the set of his shoulders. Then the woman handed him a letter, brushing his hand as she did so. He pocketed the note without glancing at it, rose to his feet and made to leave. Elika burned to know what the letter contained.

The woman was suddenly close to him, her hands on his chest.

Elika's heart leapt painfully.

He looked down at the woman and gently pushed her aside. Without another word, he headed for the door. Elika leapt away from the window and hid behind the corner of the tavern.

The door opened.

"Shoran," the woman's voice called out, rich and sweet as honey.

Elika heard his steps falter.

"How long do you think you can avoid war with your silly little fog?" the woman asked slyly.

"As long as I can, Meyara," he replied.

"Still trying to interfere in their petty squabbles? And I thought you might have outgrown that weakness of yours for humans. Or are you doing it for *her*?"

Silence.

"You know that only Arala has the power to do what she did to them. They did not return to Alafraysia. They are … gone. Their magic was useless against hers, against the *tsarina's*. She wields the magic of the gods and yet she, too, is of the Black River. Reval is not a fool. He suspects you know where she is. He wants her back. She is not yours to keep."

His silence was loud in Elika's ears.

"He knows that long ago you seduced her, that you love her still, and he hates you for it."

Another pang of pain. She had suspected as much, of course. Still, to hear it confirmed was a torment in its own right.

"Then he knows nothing," came the dark reply.

"He believes you are keeping her prisoner in that tower of yours. He has sent a crow to the gods demanding they interject on his behalf … and Arala's. He seeks justice from them."

Silence.

"Neka will destroy you if she believes you are coveting her daughter. You know this. Reval is plotting your demise. One more transgression and the gods will end you."

Silence.

You are not, Arala, were his first words to her. Thinking back, Elika now considered that perhaps he, too, had been searching for the demigoddess but had found her instead. And she knew enough about men to know why they sought beautiful women.

The woman's voice dropped to a murmur. "Has she returned? Is she with you? I want to speak with her. She will want to see me …"

"Tell Reval that Arala is dead." His words were abrupt, angry. Then he marched away, his steps long and brisk.

"Mistress," hissed another voice from nearby. A mage. "Our spies tell us the priests of the Spider's temple have seen her, Aleyala, the daughter of the gods. They say she speaks like a Dae."

"And have you questioned them?"

"We have, but they refuse to tell us anything more, though they scream loud enough for mercy."

"They will not speak to anyone but Syn'Moreg," she said dismissively. "But it matters not. We know she is in the city. And if she talks like a Dae, and dresses like a commoner, she is likely hiding among them."

"Our spies are seeking any sign of her in Daetown," he replied. "There are also rumors of a lady come from obscurity into the light in noble circles. She is marked with the features of the gods."

"Indeed, I have heard those rumors," the woman said thoughtfully. "I think it is time we had a closer look at this new marvel. Come, Yellowtoe, tell me all you have learned of Lady Fair."

Elika waited until their voices retreated, then poked her head around the corner to see Shoran's form get swallowed by the fog.

She ran after him.

Only a faint essence lingered where he had vanished and she followed it through the veil to emerge into an unfamiliar hall. It was opulent and lined with paintings of richly dressed men and women and their children. Instead of the Abyss, the large windows faced a city made of tall, white towers and spires beside the moonlit sea.

It took her a moment to realize that she was no longer in Terren. The window belonged to a castle on the high rise in the heart of the city. The streets below were dark, lit only by a few lanterns, but she could see that the white stone houses were human-built, and there were no mages' homes amongst them. The folk she saw below in the castle grounds did not dress like Al-Terrenians either. Their fabrics were plain spun of light cotton and the fashion favored looser styles of clothing.

Muffled voices came from behind her … one raised and frightened, the other deep, dark and quiet.

Elika turned to face an ajar door, then snuck closer to it.

"Your guards will not help you."

"Who are you?" said a man's agitated voice.

"Need you ask?" came Shoran's dark reply.

"Why are you here?" The man sounded even more afraid.

"I am here to remind you of the agreement, for it seems you have forgotten where your allegiance lies, Firewind."

"I have not …"

"You have forgotten who your army belongs to, who they serve and who they fight for." Shoran's voice was menacingly silky.

"The agreement allows Wavestar to defend itself. My daughter's honor has been attacked."

In reply, Shoran recited:

> *"Upon the light, upon the might,*
> *The shields and swords of Wavestar*
> *Shall never pass beyond the city's sight,*
> *Until they rise to heed the cry of El'Sandria."*

"Your daughter's honor forms not any part of this agreement."

"Northwind seduced her," the man screeched. "And left her unwedded with his bastard in her belly. I demand justice."

"And justice you may seek, but you will recall the army you have sent, back to the borders of *my* land. You will not use the army pledged to the cause of the gods for personal vengeance."

Her mind raced. Shoran's land … Syn'Moreg's army. Lord Firewind's army could never have been used by Mite. They could not have left the city.

There was a moment of silence before the duke conceded. "I will recall them. But by the laws of the gods, 'tis my right to avenge my daughter."

"Then avenge her," Shoran said dismissively. "But do not forget your duty to …" He stopped abruptly.

"My lord?" came the duke's quizzical voice. "Did you hear something?"

Elika tensed. She had not moved, so might be he heard her racing heart or strangled breath.

"'Tis nothing," Shoran replied, slowly.

"Northwind is back. Surely you will not allow this pup to claim the cursed throne unchallenged."

"Northwind is not fit to be king. Yet the Fates are not for me to challenge. Do not overstep your authority again, Firewind." His voice drew closer as he spoke.

Elika dashed behind the nearest stone statue, just as Shoran marched out of the room and left again through the opposite wall of the hallway.

She waited a heartbeat and darted after him and into his vast library.

He was not there …

Hair stirred on top of her head under a gentle breath. "Spying?"

She spun around and found herself facing a broad chest. She stepped back and shrugged one shoulder nonchalantly. "How else am I to learn what's what, and what it is you do for your master?"

His lips lifted at the corners. "And what did you learn?"

Elika crossed her arms. "I heard what you said about Northwind."

His face darkened.

"Mite's not the same as the last Northwind who abducted Arala," she said too quickly and realized what she had given away.

"Mite," he drawled, stretching the name between them.

"I meant …"

"I know all about *Mite* and where he hails from." He strode past her, putting a distance between them. "What he is to you."

Her face grew warm. "It's not what you think."

"Is it not?" He turned and aye, she was certain those rumors had reached his ears, though she saw no judgement in his face, no recrimination, only coolness. "Dare I suspect your ploys and games are merely a means to get close to Northwind?"

She flinched. "Look, Shoran, what they say … about me …" she began and stopped. Denial seemed useless. There was no explaining what she was doing without explaining why. It became hard to hold his gaze. "Look, I'm not here to talk about what was or wasn't between him and me. Any more than I care to discuss what was between you and Arala." She waited for his reaction, certain she unsettled him, but none came. He watched her impassively, waiting for her to continue. She sighed inside. "Men need Northwind."

"Do they?" he said dryly.

"You told me you cared not for the affairs of men and the Laifae, yet there you are, bringing about the fog and meeting strange women."

"My purpose is now bound with yours," he replied. "Where you dabble, I must watch and counter. Where there is danger to the web, I must protect it. The blood and salt are being gathered once again in Northwind's name. The past is once again repeating."

His words chillingly echoed those Bill Fisher had once spoken to her, when he had begged her not to return the ring of the Scared Crown to Mite.

"Mite doesn't know, but he'll listen," she rushed to defend him again. "Once he's king and learns what blood-salt does, he won't use it. He is just and fair and steadfast."

"I know what he is, kitten. I have spoken with him." His face grew hard and angry. Clearly, he did not think Mite was any of those things.

"You spoke with Mite?" she said on a breath.

"How else am I to assess the threat he poses to the web?"

"'Tis all that matters to you, the damned web," she said in frustration and cringed at her outburst. For she had seen it herself and understood what it was he was trying to protect. But she wanted him to care about folk on the street ... about her.

"There are no greater cares. Without the web, all your hopes and dreams will turn to ash."

"Give Northwind a chance to set the wrongs to right before you condemn him. Despite his lecherous ways, he will make a good king."

He regarded her with a wry upturn of his lips. "How young you are, how fierce and yet naive. Ages upon ages, across countless lifetimes of men, I watch them. Again and again, I see their very nature set them on the same pattern of destruction. Northwind is not the savior you believe him to be. Bitterness runs strong in their blood, the bitterness of being less than a god."

She hated the doubts he was seeding in her mind. Mite had never let her pack down ... until he had left them. Then she thought of Lady Kristina and knew not what to think.

She rubbed her eyes. How many times had she seen him pummel away at one of his many lady loves? Yet here she was, seventeen or maybe eighteen now and she had not even been kissed, whilst half the court believed her to be Lord Nightkill's mistress. It was laughable, in truth.

"Do not burden yourself with woes that have been around for millennia, and will be around for many millennia more," said Shoran more gently.

She met his gaze. Her heart always skipped and danced when she looked into his eyes. He was watching her intently again, as if trying to read her thoughts. A longing struck her, a curiosity perhaps, one that was long overdue.

As if he recognized those thoughts, he stiffened and walked aside, silently denying her leave to voice them.

"Kiss me," she said regardless before her courage fled.

He stilled, weariness entered his face. "No. Though you flatter me, little spider, I am not the man for you." He turned away, looking ready to flee through the shelf stacked with books.

"Coward," she said.

He froze, and despite not facing her, still managed to look potently menacing. "You yearn for another. I will not indulge your whim."

"I do not yearn for Mite. It's only that …" *She yearned for Shoran.* "Only that I've never been kissed," she said quickly and felt her cheeks heat. Penny and Mite protected her from the letches, and most of the time, she posed as a boy. But girls younger than her in their pack took lovers. She had often heard sisters Els and Mills speak in hushed whispers of their conquests and attractive city guards when they were not fifteen years of age. "I only want to know what it's like … why Mite is such a rake. It must be nice."

He spun around with surprise and disbelief, his gaze roaming her face in search of a lie.

"'Tis true. No one's ever kissed me," she said again, blushing furiously now.

"Then Northwind is truly a fool, who should not be king." He uttered it so seriously, it took her a moment to grasp his words.

A jest … from Shoran.

A chuckle burst from her. "I'm seventeen … maybe eighteen. 'Tis summer now. And I know I was born in summer …"

"You emerged into this world on the eve of summer," he corrected her. "You are two moons past eighteen, as measured by Seramight's cycle of days, and six hundred and five years from the day of your *creation*. Which is also your celestial age."

Her mouth hung open. "How can you know that?"

"The celestial hour of your creation is stamped inside the rune on your lower back. Beneath the scars." His jaw clenched when he said that. "And beside another rune which marks the hour of your birth."

"Six hundred …" she uttered, a little dazed. "Then it's even worse than I thought," she said grimly. "I know I'm not a beauty. I wouldn't ask, but … might be if you close your eyes …"

Again, his jaw clenched. "Your beauty is not brazen like Arala's, yet no man would shy away from gazing upon you."

Arala's name on his lips stung. She did not want to think of them together right now. "Then kiss me … just this once."

He stood there, clearly torn.

Then his feet moved towards her. As he drew closer, she trembled slightly in her nervousness, hoping she hid it well enough that he didn't notice.

His hand was on her cheek, strong and warm and oddly rough, like a worker's palm. His body filled her vision, his shoulders, his chest, and her heart raced with the instinctive fear of how much bigger he was than she. With those hands, he could crush her, hurt her. Yet his touch was gentle and steady. In his face, there was an odd expression, and she recognized it as a secret longing. Did he want this, too?

"Have … have you been kissed before?" she asked breathlessly, stupidly, as nervousness overrode her sense. He was ancient, and he was handsome, and he was a man, and Arala's lover besides.

But he did not smile, did not laugh at her. His face lowered. Her lips parted, and she held her breath. Then his lips were on hers, soft, gentle, pliant. She kissed him back, moving her lips as he was moving his, acutely aware of her own clumsiness amidst his expert touch. His other hand was on her waist, pulling her closer. Heat built between them, and her hands moved up to tentatively wrap around his neck. Her mind filled with his scent and the building heat made her drowsy. Her lips began to move more demandingly …

He stepped away abruptly, dropping his hand from her waist and then, more slowly, from her face. Then he turned away and marched towards the door as if he could not flee fast enough.

It took her a moment to gather her wits, and he was almost at the door when she said rather flatly, "That was not … what I expected." She allowed disappointment to fill her voice.

He stopped mid-stride.

"It was … nice, I suppose …" She trailed off.

He spun around, his face darkening. "Nice," he repeated.

"It just … well, it looked *nicer* when I've seen other men kiss women. Might be it's been a long time since you've kissed a woman. Or perhaps … well, you kept your eyes open and maybe … you know, you were wishing for someone else."

"I was not," he growled.

"Then, do you think you might kiss me like you *want* to kiss me?"

Such outrage filled his face, it was hard not to laugh. And it was all she could do to keep her face politely curious as he crossed the distance towards her in a few long, brisk strides.

"There was nothing amiss with that kiss," said the deepening voice of darkness, and it sounded like the command of a demigod not to be denied.

Elika crossed her arms and shrugged. "Seen Mite kiss plenty of girls, and … well, you know, it leaves them breathless, and weak at the knees. And I'm not breathless." Indeed, she did everything to force her breath to be steady, when his nearness was wrenching the air out of her. She examined her feet. "My knees are also rather solid, not wobbly as they are meant to be." She stamped her foot on the floor to show him. "See?"

The irritation in his face deepened, as did his voice. "I do suspect you mock me."

She shrugged again. "Just wanted to do it right, that's all. I guess I could ask someone else."

"Ask someone else," he repeated slowly in such a menacing way, she almost chuckled. "Such as Duke Orland. Or perhaps Lord Nightkill."

She cursed her face for heating but kept it impassive despite that. Last thing she wanted was to make him think he could rattle her with such accusations. She shrugged. "Them. Someone else. Does it matter? Or … I might let you try again if you prefer. I know men hate it when women think little of their kisses. I guess it shreds their delicate masculine pride …"

Before she finished speaking, he pulled her into his arms, crushed her against him and silenced her with his lips. They were wild and roaming. His hands were everywhere at once, pulling her tightly to him, running along her back, her sides … brushing past her oddly swollen breasts, which sent a jolt of shock through her and wrenched a moan from her throat. His heat melded with hers, setting her body afire. Her head spun and spun, and her fingers tangled in his hair. She pulled him closer and closer, and still it was not enough … he was drowning her, and she was floating and aching and wanting …

Abruptly, his heat was gone. He released her so fast she wavered from side to side like a drunk, confused, breathless, and hungry for everything his wild gaze promised. A dark smile touched his lips, angry and yet absurdly smug. His gaze drifted pointedly to her shaky knees. Before she could gather enough wits to speak, he was gone.

For a long time, she allowed her lips to tingle and savored the taste of him on her tongue as she fought a terrible yarning for more of his touch. The first thought that broke through her daze was that Mite would always be a letch if this was what lust felt like.

CHAPTER TWENTY-FIVE

The Wedding in Windhay

"Reval keeps his silence about the merging of Alafraysia and Seramight. He speaks not of the time a thousand years ago, when the Ethereal and the Earthly realms tangled, and two worlds became one. So we sought the records of the human priests. Yet even there, no one could glean the cause of this disaster. When the realms mingled, so did their magic. The tsaren were forced to take on a new form, merging their ethereal body with the earthly. Since then, the tsaren sought neither the truth behind the calamity nor ways to undo it. Their indifference festered the suspicion in the minds of the human kings, that this was not an accidental collision of the worlds but an invasion of the Earthly realm. Generations of Northwind kings fed this belief until they knew no other purpose save the need to undo this disaster. Gradually, they poisoned men against the tsaren and us the Laifae. In the secret writings of the last king Airling Northwind, which we found in the vaults of the archmage, he claimed that Arala was the one to merge the worlds. She was the only one with the power to do it. King Airling gave no reason for her crime, for she refused to confess it, even when he caused her great pain."

The History of Alafraysia and Seramight,
By Mageguard Bluelight

Men rejoiced when they heard Northwind was but a hundred leagues away and soon to be wedded to Warwind's daughter … and his formidable army. They raised toasts to King Aeronmite and his young bride, to the return of the sacred crowns, to the army that would race to save Terren … as soon as the royal wedding and bedding were over and done with.

"I hear the bedding was done long before the wedding," a guard sneered to another, and Elika hated to hear Mite so mocked.

"Then he'll get here faster," the other replied.

And in their rejoicing, men lit blood-salt bonfires, and the fog which Shoran sent to protect them turned red … and vanished. Or so folk said. But Elika was there, and the fog did not vanish, not like the tsaren's magic. Ever so slowly it faded, until they saw the sun peer through it. By nightfall, only wisps of Shoran's magic remained.

By dawn, it was gone altogether. That same day, the archmage attacked Daetown.

The bells rang before the army of mages arrived. Earlier, the scouts delivered the news that a force of mageguards was marching towards them from Temple District. Both Elika and Rory were among the defenders, waiting for them up on the parapets of the old city wall that overlooked the harbor. He did not wear an eyepatch over his empty socket. With him, that always meant his hands would be stained with blood before the day was out.

He grinned as they waited. "Bastards are taking their time getting here. It's a long walk for their dead, rotting legs."

Elika glanced up at the island in the sky. "I thought Reval would be the first to attack us. Why do you think he's keeping his distance?"

"'Cause he is punishing Tridamor. Likely looking for a reason to kill him that won't upset Arala if she ever returns. Wants to see the bastard fail. He's been too secure in his power, you see, Spit. With no wars to rattle him for six hundred years, it made him complacent and stupid. Been too easy for him for too long. Remember that, El, there's always a bastard with a knife wanting what you have and waiting for you to slacken your guard."

Around them, Captain Trian's soldiers were tense and ready. Barrels with red-tipped arrows stood beside the archers, and torches were lit along the wall. Overhead, Northwind's banner with the ice crown flapped in the wind. The city guards wore the same emblem on the chest of their armor.

Beside the orderly city guards stood another army made up of the disorderly, rag-tag forces of Daes and Rory's men. The red tips of their brazen assortment of weapons gleamed in the morning sun. Barrels with a mixture of blood-salt and oil were stacked along the parapet, and children were filling round sugar-glass bottles with the vile liquid, before corking them and stacking them in baskets. Girls with blood-covered hands ran along the wall, placing full baskets beside the feet of waiting soldiers.

More barrels were being rolled up the stairs to the wall. Elika edged as far away from them as she could, but her skin prickled painfully, nonetheless. And in the dreadful wait, her vision was filled with the web of light, broken and burning with dark red fires.

But what choice was left to them? she thought. Towards them now marched an army of magic, intent on conquest, destruction and enslavement.

The ground rumbled.

"Archers!" Captain Trian roared and the guards drew their arrows. Wide-eyed children grabbed the round sugar bottles and peered over the edge.

From the ground beneath them burst giant black tentacles. They raced up the wall, breaking through stone and earth.

"Arrows!" Trian shouted and a rain of red-tipped arrows fell on the black strands of the Laifae. Many recoiled, but some found their way to the top to grab men and drag them over the side of the parapet to their deaths.

"Burn the bastards!" Rory shouted.

The children threw glass jars over the wall, coating the tendrils in blood and oil. Elika grabbed a torch, lit it from a scone next to her, and threw it. A black tentacle erupted in flame and retreated.

Another fat tentacle came at them. Elika pulled out her dagger and cut through it. Black blood covered the wall and the stump vanished.

Rory stared at her, his hands frozen over his red-bladed sword. His gaze took in her dagger and she knew what he was thinking. Her blade was not coated in blood-salt. It should not have been able to cut through the black magic strands.

"Behind you!" she cried.

Rory spun and cut through the tendril racing at him.

Below them, more and more slithering strands came at the wall. She panned around and saw a line of mageguards, far from the reach of the arrows. Their faces were strained, and one of them collapsed to his knees, his head lowered, his power drained. Another stepped forward to take his place.

She caught movement in the corner of her eye, turned and sliced through another black tendril and another.

Smoke rose on the air as torches were thrown over the side. A red-robed mageguard conjured a ball of fire and it flew at the wall. It hit a group of Drasdanes, their hair and fur caught fire.

Quickly, Elika thought of water and doused them with it. But the water she conjured was merely an illusion and had no effect.

"No!" a scream burst from her throat as she watched men writhe on the ground. She turned her face up to the clouds and called upon them to drop from the sky. The clouds vanished and water fell on top of the burning Drasdanes, dousing the flames.

"ARALA!" boomed the voice of thunder over their heads. And Reval's island raced towards the battle, spinning as it went.

Tridamor's mageguards fell back, as Reval's mages swarmed above them on small clouds, singing and calling for Arala.

Rory stared at them, lowered his sword and turned to her. "Do not let them catch you. Go!"

She shook her head as another ball of fire flew at the wall. "They don't know who they are looking for …"

Words died on her tongue, for it seemed they did. They were heading straight for her, drawn towards her magic.

"Go!" Rory shouted. "We do not need you here. Go!"

She moved, running into the nearest tower and sprinting down the stairs. She burst out the door onto the street and pressed herself against the stone wall. Above her, red-tipped arrows flew at Reval's mageguards. But they cared not for them, as the arrows burned to ash in the air before they reached them. All the while, their faces turned this way and that as they sought her amongst the defenders. Elika dared not release her magic, lest it drew them. Instead, she did the hardest thing she could—she walked away, whilst more men and women raced to the walls, rolling barrels filled with blood, arrows, or oil for the fires.

When she could no longer see the flying mageguards, Elika pressed her hand to the ground and reached out towards the mages on the other side of the wall. Carefully, so as not to destroy them, she sought their essences, and ever so gently, pushed them out of Seramight and back into their world.

The effort drained her, for it drained much more of her strength to show mercy and not kill them. Far easier it was to destroy.

A cheer erupted along the besieged city wall. This battle, at least, was over.

"ARALA, MY LOVE, MY FIRE IS YOURS TO COMMAND!" Boomed the thunder and Elika grew to hate that voice.

~

The tree at her back was her anchor. The soft shudder of leaves in the breeze was a balm to her shattered senses. Behind her closed eyes, she saw death and fire and blood-salt. Though the meadows of Gods' Wood were blooming with sweet flowers, her nose was filled with acrid smoke, whilst in her ears echoed the screams of the dying. She took another deep drink, and the silversap spreading through her blood replaced those images with ecstasy and a mindless swirl of sensations. A brief relief which she knew was not to last.

A hand wrapped around hers.

Her eyes fluttered open as a large hand took away the empty cup. Shoran was crouching in front of her. "Do not take too much. Once drained of its power, your body is a bottomless cup. You must first allow it to heal with rest, then replenish it slowly. Each sip takes time to nourish."

"No time," she said faintly. "The archmage is killing them."

"'Tis not your war."

"It's everyone's war. Mine, yours and above all Syn'Moreg's. Might be it was he who merged the realms, for it was he who sundered them. Besides, it was you who shrouded the city in fog to stop the war, was it not?"

"A small mercy I gave them, and more time to find a way to avert this bloodshed. 'Tis all I could offer."

"Is there a way to unmerge the realms?"

He looked down at the empty cup in his hands. For a long time, he was silent. His body was so still, it seemed he had stepped outside of time and place and had become an image on the tapestry of their world.

Elika waited whilst he found the words, or else a will to share with her what he must surely know.

At long last, he lifted his face, his eyes searching hers for what she knew not. "The answer lies hidden in El'Sandria."

"In the realm of the gods? Then why have they not untangled our worlds? Did they do this?"

"Not the gods but Arala." His lips firmed and once again he looked aside, as if it pained him to speak of her.

"Arala did this?" she echoed. "Why?"

He ran his hand through his hair. "She wanted that which the Fates denied her."

"What did she want? What could be worth this misery, the endless wars and countless lives lost? 'Tis the arrogance of spoilt gods to indulge their whims, whilst the lesser beings pay the price."

Shoran briefly closed his eyes as if pained. "Ask me not that which will undo you. Too little you yet know, and truth deny you still, though you must surely suspect it now, Aleyala."

Her heart tripped on some deep-seated horror. As if his words had cracked open a fissure to a terrible revelation she had been battling to keep buried in the dark recesses of her soul.

"Can the gods undo it?" she asked. "You are a demigod, like she was. Can you undo it?"

He shook his head sharply. "I have tried and failed." A haunted look came into his eyes. "Nor can the gods wield the power that merged the realms. There may be one who can. Though I am not yet certain."

"Who, Shoran? If there is a way to undo this ..." She touched his hand, and at the warm contact their kiss tore through her mind—his lips on hers, his hands pulling her tight against him ...

Abruptly, he rose to his feet, breaking away from the contact. "'Tis dangerous knowledge, which your reckless nature will abuse were I to offer it to you."

Disappointment swelled in her. Always, it felt like a betrayal of what she thought him to be, of her feelings for him.

She looked aside and nodded. "As you say. Your secrets are your own."

She bounded to her feet and began to walk past him, but his hand flew out and gripped her arm. "'Tis not for you to know. For there is nothing you can do with such knowledge other than destroy yourself and I will not allow that." With those dark words, he released her.

Without looking at him, she walked away, her chest constricting. And it seemed that each time she saw him, it grew more and more difficult to leave him again.

~

"Where is Blood Dog?" Elika asked as she paused outside the carriage door. Toad was holding the reins, grinning widely. He winked at her.

Tonight was the most important night of their plan, and not having Blood Dog here sent a bout of apprehension through her.

"The dog is feral," Rory said with annoyance as he climbed into the carriage. "He comes and goes as he wills. Don't know where he goes or why, but most days he just drinks himself into stupidity and whores until his cock is bleeding."

Elika climbed in after him. "Never known you to tolerate that in your men."

The carriage rolled forward.

"Dog is not my man," he replied whilst adjusting the laces on his sleeves.

Blood Dog had told her as much himself. "Then whose is he?" she probed, curious to unravel the strangeness of their reluctant association.

Rory studied her through his good eye. A gold patch hid his hollow socket. "As I said, he's feral. I knew him in the old city only because Pockets knew him. They had many dealings over the years. He was the only man Pockets was weary of. Dog is loyal to no one but the gods. Or so Pockets always said. One does not go to Dog for his services, he comes to you when it suits some whim or cause of his."

She frowned. "So he came to you, and you and Pockets let him do what he wills?"

Rory leant forward. "There are powers that walk in this world, both dangerous and benign. When they appear at your door, offering to help you, no matter that they might look like a beggar, only a fool turns them away. Dog came to me. Told me the Fates have sent him and he'll help me get what I want. Gave no reason for it, asked nothing in return. Not even coin or ale. Nor did I care for his reasons. If the Fates sent him, then I'll listen."

"Didn't know you were superstitious, Rory," she said, even as her hand drifted to the spider token in her dress.

"Pockets knew more than he shared with me. Even so, I don't trust Blood Dog. There is no reason I can see for what he does, for the men he chooses to slay, or for the switching of his loyalties. And aye, his loyalties are fickle. At the moment, he is eager to restore the crown to Northwind's head. Come tomorrow, I suspect he'll betray us."

"What makes you think that?"

Rory leant back in his seat. "Because he was the one who forewarned King Tesman of the rising rebellion by Lord Silvering, Mite's father. 'Tis one thing I have learned from Pockets. Blood Dog was the reason King Tesman kept his crown. And it was he who assassinated Lord Silvering's lady wife and their daughter but failed to kill the lord himself and his son."

"He killed Mite's mother?" she echoed numbly. "He was the assassin the king sent to kill them."

"No one sends Blood Dog to kill. He kills who he pleases. So if he's not here, and not whoring, then he'll be murdering someone. Still, I cannot help but wonder, why help Mitey boy now after betraying his father and trying to murder the last heirs of Northwind's line?"

Elika had no answer to that. Nothing about Blood Dog made sense. Worse still, how was she to look at him again and not see the bastard who slew Mite's mother and sister and orphaned him in the end? Everything Mite lived through was because of him. Rory was right not to trust Dog. A man of fickle allegiances was far more dangerous than any other of his ilk.

The carriage drew to a stop outside Lady Wianna's mansion. She was a young widow, whose husband had perished in an unfortunate dispute with a mage over a magical necklace which had strangled his mistress. Lady Wianna, it seemed, bypassed the required period of grief, and instead opened her house to parties and prospective lovers. She most certainly found Rory intriguing when they were introduced.

Rory's mind, however, was not on the salacious lady. After the pleasantries were exchanged, he led Elika to the dance floor. "Now, Spit. Mitey's wedding is in three days," he said, his voice shrouded from prying ears by music and the thrum of voices. "Warwind's army is ready to march. The mageguards are pressing us on all sides. Today, I need you to show your feminine wiles with Duke Orland and do whatever it takes to convince him to present you to Prince Southfire."

"I know my task. We've spoken of this for days."

He held her far too closely as they spun in a dance. She hated these moments, hated the feel of him. Hated those endless thoughts of Shoran when she should be thinking of their plan.

"He is watching us now," said Rory.

Elika turned her face to catch the duke perusing her in that lewd way of his, his salacious thoughts clear for all to see. A sickness settled in her gut. She knew what Rory was referring to, knew that they had little time left to find their way into Southfire's court.

Rory must have sensed her tension, for his voice grew hard and cruel. "'Tis a small sacrifice compared to the lives of men and women dying on the wall of Daetown. 'Tis a small price to pay compared to what your failure will cost this city, *Lady Fair*. If you fail, Mitey will not find the welcome he expects when he returns."

The sickness in her stomach increased. Rory was right, of course. What was her sacrifice compared to the wounded and dying, to the swelling grief that was breaking the hearts of Daetown folk as they burned their dead? Day after day they were fighting off waves of attacks from the mages.

"Very well," she said, steeling herself for the task ahead, as a piece of her shriveled up inside. "Give me a moment alone with him."

The music stopped and Rory released her. With a bow he left her, allowing Duke Orland to pounce. "My dear, your cousin is far too protective of you."

Elika took a breath and turned with a coy smile. "He is rather dreadful, is he not?"

The duke kissed her hand. "Makes me wonder how it is he was so remiss to leave you alone amongst these letches."

"A brief respite, I assure you, your grace. He will find me soon, do not fear."

"You look deliciously flushed. I dare say you need fresh air after that dance. It is so crowded in here … unless you wish to dance with me?"

"'Tis the escape from Lord Nightkill's attentions for just a few moments I seek. He can be so very demanding."

Duke Orland's gaze heated, and her stomach churned. She placed her hand on his arm and he led her outside onto the terrace and the lantern-lit garden. They were not alone. Couples were disappearing into the shadows of the trees and the maze of flowering hedges.

The duke took a more secluded path into the lower part of the garden, beneath the terrace wall, out of sight of others.

"My lord …" she began but was abruptly rendered speechless as the duke pushed her against the wall and tried to kiss her.

Quickly, she turned away. His lips hit her cheek.

"I tire of your teasing and these games you play," he snarled. "I can see you watching me."

She wrestled with an instinct to fight him off and instead playfully tangled her fingers in his hair. "Your grace, I play no games. Nor do I deny your power over my heart. Only, I fear what Lord Nightkill would do were he to see us. You know how possessive he is."

The duke softened. "Do not fear, my dear," he said, as his hand pulled down the shoulder of her dress. "I am a duke. He can do nothing to me." He kissed her bare shoulder.

Gently, she pushed at his chest. "But he can do terrible things to me."

The duke froze. Pulled away. "He hurts you," he said in disbelief.

She looked aside as if ashamed. "He ... he is very jealous. You have seen it yourself."

He frowned. "Aye, I have seen it."

"He will not let me out of his sight, your grace. He fears another man of greater wealth and power will steal me away, before the archmage grants him the right to wed a lady of noble birth."

"'Tis despicable," said the duke. "A rogue like him has no right to a fine lady like you."

"I see it now, of course. But my father kept me hidden for so long ... then Lord Nightkill came to us and I ... I was foolish. In truth, he covets only one thing more than me," she whispered in confidence and glanced around.

"And what is that?"

"I should not speak of it, for he punishes betrayal."

"I assure you, I will repeat nothing you reveal to me. What is it he desires more than you?"

She stroked his chest. "Not what, but who." Again, she glanced around. "Southfire. He craves to be introduced to the king ... ahem, pardon my foolishness, of course I meant the *prince*. But please do not tell Lord Nightkill I told you. He is so proud ..." She quickly yanked the duke into the shadow of a bush and peered over his shoulder. "Shh. He is out there now, looking for me." The duke tried to peer around her, but she pressed him back against the wall. "No. Please. He must not see us together," she pleaded into his chest. Then raised her eyes to meet his. "I know not how to escape him, your grace. Save being whisked away behind the palace walls where he cannot reach me."

The duke lowered his head. "I could arrange that ..."

Elika made her eyes widen. "You could?"

"Of course. The prince and I are very close. I am one of his most trusted advisors."

Elika smiled coyly. "Oh, your grace, what I would not give just to lay my eyes on the true prince of the Sacred Crowns. Is it true there is a glow about him of the godly light?"

The duke guffawed. "'Tis rumors, nothing more. Perhaps ... I could introduce you to him. But my dear," he leant to whisper into her ear. "After the introduction, I do not wish you to play coy with me any longer. I tire of this game."

She pretended to think about it, then shook her head. "I cannot. My guardian would never allow me to go unescorted, and he would trust no one but himself to keep me safe from the advances of others."

"I will insist ..."

"No, your grace. There would be a scandal. But ... let me think ... Aye, it may work. My lord, if you would just find a way to distract my guardian when we are in the palace ..." she pleaded breathlessly. "If Lord Nightkill is taken to court, he will be obsessed with King ... I mean *Prince* Southfire. He will most certainly neglect me. And then ...perhaps you might conspire to remove him from the palace, and I could be left behind ... with you."

His finger ran along the top of her breasts. "Hmm. And you would want that, my dear."

It's not real. Think of the dead and the wounded. Think of Mite ... But it was Shoran's face she saw.

She pushed it out of her mind and forced herself to smile at the duke, as she pressed herself against him. "I would rather be a duke's mistress than a lord's whore, your grace. Nor do I wish to be a pauper's wife. I am not ashamed. I know my lands and titles are meagre."

"Then I think we can arrange an introduction to the prince. I dare say he will find you a position in court." He kissed her.

Elika fought revulsion and an overwhelming instinct to push him away, and kissed him back, running her hands over his chest, pressing herself against him. Just as he started to growl with lust, she pulled away and glanced over her shoulder. "I must leave, your grace. Please give me a moment to return before you follow. He can see how I gaze upon you, and already suspects me false." And with that, she pushed herself out of his arms and raced back up the path towards the mansion.

As she ran up the terrace steps, she caught a glimpse of a dark figure watching her from the shadows of the garden, yellow eyes glowing hot in his hood.

Hairs on the back of her neck rose. She suddenly wanted the ground to swallow her and send her to the Abyss. It was all she could do to ignore him and rush back inside, her heart twisting and knotting in her chest.

There, she grabbed a glass of wine and drank, if only to rid her mouth of the duke's taste. Rory was beside her in an instant. "Well played, Lady Fair. I must say, you surprised me. I was watching you from above."

"I am ready to leave, my lord," she said, as she saw the duke return, his gaze on her. "Lead me away and look angry with jealousy."

"But of course," he mumbled, then more loudly, "My dear, I must insist we leave now. Where have you been these last moments?"

"I only sought fresh air …"

"Alone, I hope," he barked as he led her away through the curious, snickering crowd.

Elika looked over her shoulder at the duke. He was still watching them, his lips upturned in a victorious smile. Behind him, outside the glass window, stood Shoran.

~

Tomorrow, Mite would be wed.

The sobering thought cut through the haze of her waking mind. It seemed the closer drew that inevitable hour, the heavier grew her heart with bittersweet regrets and longings for things that could have been.

Elika did not want to dwell on the past, but her treacherous mind conjured images of Mite's hand, reaching to her, willing her to take it and cross with him into the unknown. And it was hard not to ponder what might have been had she taken it. Might be it would have been her who was to kneel before the priestess and swear an eternal bond and loyalty to Mite.

Don't be a fool, she scalded her naivety. *You'd be bedded, with child and abandoned. What army could you have given him? What allies would you have brought?*

A craving deepened in her chest. She wanted to see him, just once, before his wedding day, just to convince herself that whatever foolish longings she had harbored once were truly gone, and the choices they both made would not haunt them the rest of their lives. Or might be she just needed to see him, to witness the pivotal moment of his life. Might be she owed him that much.

Liffy entered the room with a bowl of water. "Oh, you're awake. Lord Nightkill is waiting for you in his study. The captain is with him. I'm to help you get ready," she added resentfully.

It was a routine they had done endlessly, yet Liffy was still aggrieved to be her servant. Elika understood it, and it did not sit right with her either.

She rose with an inward sigh and went through the motions of readying herself for the day ahead, before going to Rory's study.

He was in good spirits today and grinned as she entered. In his hand, he was turning over a gilded invitation written in flourishing letters. "Compliments to my lady." He bowed and showed her the note. "It arrived this morning from court. Lord Nightkill and Lady Fair are to be presented to Prince Southfire during the Harvest Ball."

Captain Trian was with him, watching her closely and as grimly as ever, as if he half expected her to throw her magic at him at any moment.

Elika nodded lifelessly and walked over to examine the map they were studying before she arrived. To claim half the city, they needed two more garrisons.

Trian and Rory went back to discussing just that.

"I've spoken to Hawkheart," Trian was saying. "He'll do nothing until the archmage is dead, though he's greedy for Northwind's approval and seeks only to have his ancestral lands restored to him."

It was not the first time they had discussed Captain Hawkheart. He came from an ancient house and a long line of vassals loyal only to Northwind's Crown. For that unfaltering fealty, they had lost their titles and lands after the Sundering War.

"Bloody coward," Rory spat. "No doubt waiting to see whether it's worth risking a sword through his neck."

"He said he can fight the men, just not the mages," Trian said. "He asks for barrels of blood-salt to be smuggled into the cellar of his garrison for when the fight comes."

"I'll send my men to equip him," Rory replied. "Which brings us to the matter of the tunnels. Your men lost control of the southern passage and now we've got no way to smuggle supplies to and from the south. You swore they'd defend it with their lives."

Trian stiffened. "And they did. The mages buried the tunnels and my men with them."

For many days now, Southfire and Tridamor had sealed the gates in the north of the city, and sent ships to block the harbor, thus strangling most smuggling routes into the city. So far, that did little to stop the flow of supplies, for Rory had set up underground links with other districts of Terren for anything they lacked. And he was fiercely protective of them.

"The buried passage doesn't matter, anyway," she said. "The supplies are drying up across Terren. If Mite doesn't get here before the end of summer, we'll be running out of food, arrows and everything else we need."

As soon as she thought of Mite, her heart tripped. Just one more time, she wanted to see him.

"She's right," said Trian. "Southfire and the archmage will starve the entire city into submission. They are not allowing even the women and children to flee."

"Then they can fight," Rory said dismissively.

And so they went on, planning attacks on this or that garrison. Sending spies through the tunnels and stealing supplies where they could, to feed their growing army. Through it all, Elika's thoughts kept drifting to Mite and his impending wedding in Windhay.

It was a hundred leagues away, but Shoran could take her there faster than she could blink. He traversed the realm in an instant and she had followed him with laughable ease. He could show her the way to Wavestar. Save that she could not bring herself to ask him. Then how did she reach a place she had never been to?

"Blacksmiths have been asking for more coal for their fires," Trian's voice cut through her thoughts. "They are running low and we cannot equip fast enough everyone who's coming to us wanting to fight. We are short on armor and weapons and even the damned boots."

Rory scratched his chin. "I'll set my men to the task of getting you more coal, and armor, too."

Elika suspected the procurement would involve looting the homes and shops of magic-lovers for the supplies they needed.

Trian knew it, too, if his stiffening expression was anything to go by. He kept his silence, though, and with a curt nod, left them.

Elika started to follow him out.

"And where are you going, Lady Fair?" Rory stopped her.

"Got things I need to do," she said. "I won't be going to Lady Wicker's dinner today. The way I see it, there's no need for me to be there."

Rory did not look pleased. "Duke Orland will be there."

"Tell him I'm indisposed."

"I thought we agreed you would do nothing without my permission."

"This is a personal matter, Rory. And I'm not one of your men to command. I got us an invitation to the palace. Now I have my own things to take care of." With that, she strode off and felt Rory's gaze bore into her back.

When she was alone, she put her hand on the wall, stepped forward and into the dark tower. She reached out to Shoran and sought that inexplicable thread connecting them. A door appeared. But there was no sign of him inside his study. Still, he had been there recently. There was a jug of silversap, and a half-full cup on the table. She took a sip from it and recalled Shoran's lips on hers.

She then examined the bookshelf, passing her hand over it to find the wake of his recent passage.

A tug on her hand. There it was, a disturbance in the veil. She allowed it to pull her to where Shoran had gone.

She emerged in a small room, with a bed, wash basin, and clothes scattered on the floor. From below came many voices and the sound of clicking mugs. The smell of charring meat and cooking smoke drifted up through the floorboards. Everything told her she was in an inn.

There was nothing about this room to suggest it was Shoran's. The clothes were not his. Amongst the male clothes, there were lacy feminine undergarments …

The door opened.

Elika darted behind it as a mountain of a man walked in with a lute hanging over his shoulder.

"Pebble?" she whispered and he spun around.

His jaw dropped. "What are you doing here?" He was clearly not pleased to see her.

She pushed the door to close it and stood in front of it. "Shoran was here to see you."

"How did you —?"

"Where is this place?"

Outside, houses were built of common grey stone and wood. More wood than stone, in truth, and instead of coal, wood logs were piled beside the cold fireplace.

He frowned. "You do not know?" He strode forward and picked up clothes off the floor. "We are in Windhay." He swept up the dress and undergarments and threw them on the chair.

"Where's the woman to whom those belong?" Elika bent to look under the bed, for surely she would not have left naked.

He waved his arm at the window. "The lady had to leave in a hurry, so she borrowed my clothes so as not to be recognized."

Elika recalled that Pebble was famed not just for his ballads, but also for his inappropriate mistresses—mainly wives of lords and wealthy merchants. "What are you doing here? I thought you were meant to help Northwind."

He bowed dramatically. "And I am doing just that. What is a minstrel good for, save turning fools into legends and beggars into kings? I am spreading gallant songs and tales of Northwind, trying to heal the bleeding cut he has inflicted upon his honor."

"Lady Kristina," she said, understanding, and looked at the floor.

Pebble sighed. "When I sailed out with him, I thought I'd be riding the wind of his glory. Instead, I found a lost and angry fool. And Warwind's ambition is driving Aeron to recklessness and self-punishment." His gaze flickered up and down her length. "You have grown since I last saw you. You look … different. Healthy."

"Does Mite know what's happening in Terren?"

"Aye, he knows everything. He's got spies, and letters arrive for him each day. But Duke Warwind will not surrender his army to Northwind's command until after the wedding."

"The wedding is tomorrow," she said, and something akin to regret pierced her chest.

Pebble stared at her intently. "Aye. So why are you here? What do you mean to do?"

She looked at the window and shrugged. "Never seen any other city save Terren. Always wanted to see what else was out there. Might be I'll have a look around."

"I can show you the city," he said too quickly, too eagerly, as if afraid she'd get lost.

"First, tell me why Shoran came to see you."

He was silent for a moment until she turned her gaze on him, then he rubbed the back of his thick neck. "He'll take flesh off my bones if I …"

"No, he won't. Tell me or I might be tempted to do it myself. What does he want with Northwind?"

Pebble sighed with the resignation of a doomed man. "He wasn't here about Northwind, but about you."

That took her aback. "Me?"

"Wanted to know whether you've been seeing Northwind, or perhaps merely lurking around him. Whether Aeron knows you're alive. What I've learned from him about you and your past. Whether my father's mages have been sent to speak with me about you …"

"Your father … Tsarin Draygan? Why would his mages come to you about me?"

He threw his arms into the air. "Do you think it's only Reval who's looking for you? Ilikan and Draygan are also trying to find you. Their mageguards are questioning every tane and Dae they come across."

"Why?"

"Because they think you are Arala, and thus you have the claim to the Seat of Life in Alafraysia. They are afraid of you. The tsaren are more than kings to the Laifae, they are their gods, their world shapers. Like Alafraysia, the Laifae have no true shape or substance of their own, save one that is forged by dreams. But unlike the tsaren, Arala is the true demigoddess, and she can destroy all that they have built for themselves since the merging of the worlds. They believe she has the power to sunder the realms, for there are whispers that she was the one who joined them."

"Do you think I'm her?"

"I … I do not know," he replied sounding boyish and lost.

Elika sighed. "Come, show me the city."

Though her experiences of such things were few, having never been outside of Terren, she could not imagine a more dramatic city than Windhay.

It was perched high on a steep hillock and encircled by a thick stone wall. An ancient fortress crowned the top of the city, and from its vantage, it overlooked the surrounding lands. Every street in Windhay was a steep road, and every alley was made of stairs. The houses were small and crowded together, with tiny gardens. Amongst human homes, she saw mages' shops, which were now abandoned and plundered. Pebble had told her that when Duke Warwind returned with Northwind and an army in tow, the mageguard overlord of the city fled to Terren, taking the majren with him.

Despite its prominence, Windhay was no larger than the Daetown district of Terren, confined as it was by a sharp cliff edge around three sides. Streets ran up to the sheer drop and stopped at the low stone wall. No doubt it stopped many a drunk tumbling over the side to their death.

Elika halted at one such wall and gazed down at the fast-flowing river encircling the base of the hillock. One bridge crossed it to the main gate, and there was only one road in and out of the city.

There must have been a deluge of summer rains, for far in the distance the river spilled at its banks onto outlining farms. When she looked closer at the land, her whole being jolted with recognition and dawning horror. For there, plain before her lay the terror she thought they had left behind when they crossed the bridge into this world.

"The fields … they are wilted," she said on a breath, for there was no mistaking the signs.

Pebble leant his hands on the wall and followed her gaze. "Everywhere we go, we come across patches of death; crops, orchards, animals and sometimes men caught unawares."

"The Blight," she said. The unmistakable signs were engraved into her memory. Save that it was not like the Blight she knew. Death was contained to sections and did not expand beyond a patch of wilt.

"It comes without warning, destroys everything, then vanishes again. Within days, fresh shoots emerge where the old have wilted. No one can make sense of it."

An image of the web afire flashed in her mind. "This is happening across the realm?" she asked.

"Everywhere we've been to, we've seen this. Trouble is, too many farmers have lost this summer's harvest and animal stock. Come winter, the cities will grow hungry."

Elika turned away, for she could no longer look at the horror they were weaving. The war in Terren was being felt across the land in more ways than anyone realized.

They resumed walking, and it did not take them long to circle the city until they reached the outlook to the southern and western lands. There she saw the river race to the coastline, and in the distance, the edge of the sea merged with the sky. But her gaze did not linger, for it was ripped from the beautiful vista to another sea, fashioned from thousands of tents and wavering columns of campfire smoke. And when she beheld the great army gathered to Northwind's cause, all thoughts of the Blight fled, and her heart swelled with a certainty that Terren would be saved. For surely no power of gods or magic could stand against such a great sea of men ready to die for their realm.

"'Tis more than I imagined," she said breathlessly and a smile stretched across her face.

Oh, Mite, you've done it.

"He deserves your songs, Pebble," she said in a choked voice. "It's our salvation that he brings with him."

The minstrel leant on the railing above the sheer drop below and pointed. "Those are Warwind's banners, beside Northwind's blue ones. Aeronmite has called upon old vassals loyal to his bloodline to join him here. Many answered. Many more did not. His own army is but a third of Warwind's. Not enough to take Terren. Northwind's strength is tied to the duke and his daughter. Do you understand what I am showing you?"

"Aye. No wedding, no victory," Elika replied dryly.

She turned away to face the courtyard of the Temple of Neka. Priestesses dressed in green robes walked in and out of its doors, so reminiscent of another temple she had known long ago. This was where Mite would be wedded to his bride come sunrise. All around, the streets were decorated with strings of flowers and silken ribbons. The air was festive, and excitement gripped the folk of the city. Through the day, city criers announced the wedding between Prince Aeronmite Northwind and their Lady Mirana Warwind. And in taverns, men raised their cups to their new king and queen.

It was not the wedding, but the bedding the army waited for, before marching. There would be no war until Northwind seeded a legitimate heir in Lady Mirana's belly. Those were Warwind's terms. Though if rowdy rumors and laughter were to be believed, the duke's daughter was already carrying Northwind's child. The midwives had been seen at her side. Men called him a stud and a stallion, and come the day after tomorrow, the army would march on Terren, with Northwind at its head.

"Come," said Pebble as he began to walk again, somber and thoughtful, heading down the steps towards the river. "Let me show you the stone gardens of ancient heroes."

~

Cry ho! Behold the sword of ice,
Brought forth upon the wind from north,
Hail sacred justice of the one
Who wields it for the man and realm.
Cry not good women, but rejoice
The king of old returns,
And tyrants tremble in their beds
As northern wind blows forth.

Elika drank her ale until her eyes were blurry and listened to Pebble's songs until she was singing along with the rest of the patrons crowding the tavern.

Only once she had needed to pull her knife and cut a drunk with overly familiar hands that wandered to places they should not. When the fool drew his own knife, Pebble put down his lute, dragged the drunk outside, broke his nose for good measure, and threw him to the ground, before returning to his songs.

After that, she was left alone to drink in peace.

"Come, princess, let's take you to bed," came a gravelly voice from above her as a large arm came around her. Elika lifted her drowsy, spinning head from the table. "Don't stop singing, Pebble," she muttered.

He helped her up, took her to his room upstairs and deposited her on his bed. After taking off her shoes, he spread his cloak on the floor and lay on it.

"Pebble?" she said drunkenly, fighting the pull of her eyes to drift closed.

"Aye, princess," he said, whilst staring up at the ceiling.

"Is Mite happy?" she slurred.

There was a long silence before he replied. "'Tis a hard thing to be happy when carrying great burdens and lives of men upon your shoulders."

Elika lost the fight with her eyes and heard nothing more.

In her dreams, a crow cawed. Then voices spoke in the darkness.

"She followed you here."

"Northwind or me?" asked the other who sent her heart racing.

"He grieves, as does she …"

"'Tis not their fate," said the dark voice. "The union was never meant to be."

"'Tis unresolved."

"Then Fates will demand a reckoning."

The crow added its voice to theirs.

A warm hand brushed her hair. Lips pressed to her cheek. "*Isa shamorg deiri fia si, Aleyala.* 'Tis the shadow's heart you seek."

The dream faded and that night, she dreamt no more.

~

The bells rang and rang. Flowers rained from balconies and windows. Trumpets sounded above the din of cheer. Every man, woman and child of Windhay and the surrounding lands was gathered around the temple, where Prince Northwind and Lady Warwind were swearing a blood oath to each other before the statue of Goddess Neka.

Elika sat with her back against the chimney, watching the crowds below, waiting for the ceremony to end, whilst thinking back to the Hide, to Mite and his loyalty to them, his fierce protectiveness, his smiles, and the way the other boys always straightened and stood taller when he was around. She thought back to his outstretched hand at the bridge and imagined herself taking it. Then she indulged an image of herself beside him, kneeling in front of Goddess Neka's statue, and the priestess dressed in green joining them for life.

She smiled, for beneath those wisps of regret, lurked acceptance and peace. Mite had made his choice, and she had made hers. This is where it led them. Around her, a group of youths who had followed her up to the roofs were watching the proceedings. Thousands waited before the temple doors for the king of men to emerge with his new bride.

Pebble was down there also, a guest of honor inside the temple, alongside local nobles and the lords who had travelled far to witness the occasion. Overhead the white-tipped crow cawed as it circled and landed on the chimney behind Elika. She did not turn to look at it. Nor was she surprised to see it. Surely the messenger of the gods would wish to witness this glorious occasion, as Northwind was once against restored to the world, with a queen beside him and a babe to follow.

The doors of the temple opened and the crowd roared in joy.

"Northwind! Northwind!" The youths on the roof joined the chanting.

The procession came out, led by a proud king dressed in an ice-blue vest, leading on his arm the bride, clad in a dress of the same color. Elika's throat clenched. Mite looked magnificent, and his wife was radiant and striking beneath the crown of flowers and lace. Yet, a hint of sadness seeped from behind that dazzling smile.

Elika's gaze returned to Mite. And it was with deep regret that she realized there was no trace of the boy who had crossed the bridge two summers back. A man she barely recognized stood in his place. But then, she was not the same girl who had watched him walk away. If there was little joy in his bride's face, there was none in his. There was a stiffness about him, an acceptance and determination, but no happiness.

Suddenly, he raised his face to the roofs, and his gaze fell on their group and snagged. His feet slowed. Aye, that was Mite, always checking for watchers and threats. Might be he had not changed as much as she had imagined.

They were too far away, and her face was half-covered with the hood of the cloak that Shoran had given her. Mite would not recognize her. *She* did not recognize herself from the time they had parted. Yet he kept staring and staring, until his bride whispered something in his ear, and his gaze returned to her, and they strode arm in arm beneath the shower of flowers and seeds, towards the waiting carriage. He helped his bride to her seat and took his own beside her. Then Elika watched them ride away, and she knew beyond doubt that Mite was forever lost to her. That he was forever lost to her the moment he had crossed the bridge.

A sad, bittersweet smile touched her lips, for he was never hers to lose.

"Be happy, Mite," she whispered and released him from her heart.

CHAPTER TWENTY-SIX

Archmage Tridamor

"Archmage Tridamor began his life as the arch and captain of Arala's court in Alafraysia. Unlike the other mageguards, who are melded with human bodies and souls, she shaped the archmage with her magic into his own humanoid form and bound him through that magic to herself. No one was more fiercely devoted to her than he. No one was said to have loved her more, save Reval. She took Tridamor to Seramight on all her travels and always sought his council. Reval was always jealous of their closeness, murderously so. But Arala had threatened to leave him if he ever harmed Tridamor. To this day, Reval dare not harm him, as he awaits her return. Tridamor knows his fate is tied to Arala's. For were she to return, she would destroy him. Were she to fail to return, Reval would kill him instead."

The History of Alafraysia and Seramight,
By Mageguard Bluelight

The day after the wedding, Elika watched the camp followers pack the sea of tents, as Northwind's army began its slow march towards Terren. It was a joyous occasion indeed, for that meant that Queen Mirana was indeed with child and Northwind's precious heir. The soldiers marched out at dawn with King Aeronmite Northwind on his armored horse leading at the head. Duke Warwind rode beside him. Other lords of note rode behind them, bearing the banners of their noble houses. It was hard to turn away from the magnificent sight and the terror it promised to bring upon Terren.

The sight ignited afresh the purpose in her. Mite was coming to save Terren, and she had little time left to kill Tridamor. That would be her gift to Mite, and to the long line of men marching to take their world back from the Laifae. For them, she would see it through to whatever end.

A silent shadow appeared at her side and her heart skipped and danced, and it became hard to breathe, to think, to speak. So, she did not. Together, they watched the long line of horses and men snake away into the distance, heading north to the crossing of River Rockfoe that marked the boundary of Duke Warwind's lands.

As she watched them, Shoran's nearness grew stifling, and the silence stretched and pulled her into that dark garden where he had seen her kiss Duke Orland. Aye, he saw everything she and Rory wanted the nobles to see, and it cut her to know it.

Then he spoke, his voice deep and hard. "What game are you playing, kitten? Pining for one man, seeking a conquest in another, whilst demanding kisses from a third."

She'd rather he used his sword to slice through her than those brutal words, for she bled inside regardless. And she wanted nothing more than to confess and tell him everything. Only the sight of the army marching to the aid of Terren held her back; as a single moment of her weakness might turn the tide of war.

It hurt not to trust Shoran. But then, he had refused to help men, hated Northwind, and kept his own secrets from her. He served Syn'Moreg, and she must never forget that, no matter that her heart bled at the thought of allowing him to believe what he saw.

It made her angry, for those in pain always seek to wound. She wanted to hurt him back, to remind him that he was not one to cast aspersions. "Do you judge me, Shoran?" she asked coolly. "Yet were you not the one to place me in the room of your former lover? Do you think one kiss, reluctantly surrendered by you, grants you authority over me?"

He lowered his face to hers. "My duty to the gods grants me authority over you."

And his words just kept slicing and shredding her heart. She was a duty to him, nothing more. She knew that, of course, so why did it matter?

"Spare me your accusations. I do not pine for Mite," she snapped back. "I miss him. He is a friend and always will be, and much more besides. He is a brother to me. And I owe him more than I could ever repay." She all but shouted it at him, unable to bear his cold gaze any longer, nor the dispassionate disdain in it.

Shoran's eyes darkened and his jaw twitched. "Then what do you want from Orland? And do not tell me he is a friend. What seek you from him? Coin, mansions, jewels and servants? A duchy in your name? Whisper what it is you want and it shall be yours. No need to sell your body for it. I would never ask such a price to fulfil your heart's desires."

She threw a punch at his jaw. "Damn you, Shoran. Get out of my sight."

He took the punch, turned his head back slowly. Then even slower, raised his hand and cupped her cheek, so gently, tears clouded her eyes. He leant in and pressed his lips to her temple. "Tell me what it is you seek, what you need. Why him?"

And his tenderness, his softly spoken words laced with repressed anguish, nearly ripped the truth from her. She shook her head in denial, refusing to release it. His scent filled her head and she recalled those lips on hers.

"Why are you truly here?" she whispered, still not looking at him, ashamed to show her feelings, afraid of what she wanted from him.

"Trust me." And she heard it in his voice, the matching rawness of her own heart.

"I cannot." And those were the hardest words she ever had to say.

He leant his forehead against hers. "I cannot save you unless you trust me and show me the pattern of your folly. Name what you wish and I shall grant it."

Tridamor's death.

But she said it not, for she could not trust him to grant it.

"Another kiss," whispered the voice of her heart instead.

Abruptly he stepped away, aloof and cold, and her foolishness rushed in on her. One kiss he had given her, which she had demanded, and now she imagined his heart beat to the same song as hers.

She turned away again, towards the dark snake waving its way through the lowlands towards Terren. "The ugly rumors ... they are not true," she said after a few aching heartbeats.

Silence.

She turned around.

He was gone.

~

Elika had heard of heartbreak, had seen girls in their pack pine for men who did not want them. She had imagined she understood the ache of rejection they spoke of, for she too had lost loved ones. She had lost her parents, understood grief, yet she was wrong. Until now, she could not have imagined the soul-crushing pain of grief for someone who was still living. Aye, it was grief and longing and soul-deep regret combined into a force that made it hard to breathe and think and even stand. Her appetite was gone, and the days were grey and lifeless.

She leant on the bookshelf of Rory's study. It held her up. For in truth, she wanted to curl up and weep for the absence of Shoran's voice, his warmth, his touch, his lips. Even now his touch lingered on her skin, warm, firm and always gentle. She wanted him back, wanted his black eyes on her, his steadiness, that soothing stillness in the world spinning and churning with madness. But it was the loss of his regard she mourned the most.

"Northwind is five days' march from the city," Captain Trian's voice cut through her thoughts.

"He's been five day's march from the city these last ten days," Rory replied. "They haven't moved from the banks of Foxgrave River, whilst the Harvest Ball is three days away. If Lady Fair does her duty and does not fail us, the archmage will be dead long before Northwind arrives."

"I've sent three messengers to him," Trian replied. "They have not returned, and I've heard nothing from Aeronmite. Something is wrong."

"We have no choice but to proceed with our plan," Rory said.

"Aye. Though I fear unless Aeronmite hurries, Southfire will claim the crown of Terren once Tridamor is dead. It will turn the city against us."

"No, it won't," Elika said, pushing aside those relentless thoughts of Shoran, and thinking instead of the army she had seen outside Windhay. "Southfire will use Tridamor's mages to restore order on the streets. He will send them against Northwind. Mite is marching with men, for mankind. He is offering them freedom from the Laifae rule and the fickle powers that rule their world, from Reval's raving moods and Ilikan's vindictive tantrums. Remind men of this and they will wait for Northwind. They will not side with Southfire."

"Aye, there may be truth in that," said the captain thoughtfully. "The prince is not popular in the city, save that he is an Alterrian by birth. His pandering to the tsaren and the mages is well known. Men seek change in Northwind. Terren is his ancestral seat of power. The city is his by right."

"Are you ready then, El?" Rory asked her. "Are you ready to do your part?"

She nodded. "'Tis time."

"Then we leave for the palace tonight. Your maid has packed your things and the chest of our possessions is on its way to the palace. So, go and get ready."

Elika was glad to leave them. They have been watching her too closely. Both had noted her subdued mood and were worried she was having doubts about their plan, that she would fail. More than once she had to reassure them that she would kill the archmage even if the price was her life. A part of her felt as if she had already paid that price.

Upstairs in her room, she stood by the darkened window, watching the glow over the city. Daetown was afire. Mageguards had intensified their attacks against the rebels.

Earlier, she had watched an army of Prince Southfire's vassals march through the city gate to join the city's defenses. Many more made camp outside the city walls. Southfire and the archmage had called every vassal from the lands around to defend Terren. Folk on the street barricaded windows and doors. More and more battles were breaking out on the streets between Daes and Alterrians. Between magic-haters and magic-lovers. Between Northwind's and Southfire's subjects. Shops and workhouses were raided by gangs claiming allegiance to one faction or another.

Elika walked through it in a haze, waiting for her moment to be presented at court, waiting for the first sightings of Northwind's army from the roofs of Terren, waiting for the day when Terren and Seramight would be restored to men.

"I'm to get you ready for travel to court," Liffy said as she came in. "Lord Nightkill has ordered you're to wear this dress." She laid it neatly on the bed. Beside it, she placed a box of matching jewels. "Shall I call for the servants to fill your bath?"

She did not wait for the reply but gave instructions to the footmen outside.

Elika turned back to the window, feeling hollow and strangely unafraid.

~

The throne room was brightly lit. It was obscenely decorated with the wealth of all the ages past. A place built by the demigods of old who gazed down on the race of man and demanded nothing less than awe and worship. The room was vast and airy, and overlooked much of the city from the balconies along it. The view encompassed the sea and the mountains and the ever-present chasm sundering their world. But it was the red smoke rising from the harbor and Daetown that reminded her of the looming war and what she was here to do. So Elika turned her attention back to the long procession of dukes and lords shuffling past an equally long line of mageguard sentries, to pay homage to Prince Southfire.

As she drew closer, she finally glimpsed the dais ahead and the man reclining in the throne. She had known him as a foe, a traitor to mankind, an enemy to Mite, and upon arrival in the palace, she was ready to hate him at first sight. Yet when she finally saw him, she was taken aback by the man before her.

She had imagined him as sickly, weak and spindly in body, who was afraid to stand up to the mages. Else in her mind's eye, she saw him as an overfed tyrant, with hard eyes and a cruel twist to his lips. From the talk in the *Eagle's Feather*, she thought he might be spoilt and ill-tempered, a child wearing a man's body.

He was none of those.

Instead, he was everything a king might be; broad, strong, with a solid, square jaw and authority seeping from his skin, even in his leisurely reclined posture on his throne. There was no cruel, hard glint in his eyes, merely polite curiosity tinged with boredom. He wore a silver circlet over his rich red hair, its color matched by his neatly trimmed beard. There was a resigned air about him, of one who was used to watching the world dance around him. If the coming war troubled him, he gave no sign of it, save for the hard determination in his face that matched Mite's.

The prince she saw before her was not a traitor to mankind, was not a spoilt or frightened child, but a shadow of a true king, stripped of his crown, weary and determined not to war, but to find a way for men and Laifae to co-exist. There was wisdom in his gaze that robbed her of all inclination to hate and detest him. Worse still, the longer she watched him, the harder it was to see him as an enemy.

The line of lords and ladies moved forward, and more of the dais came into view. On a smaller throne beside the prince sat a regal woman, clad in a deep-red dress that matched the lush tint of her lips. She was possessed of the dark Sachi features and silvery eyes …

Recognition struck Elika. This was the woman whom Shoran had met in *The Thirsty Dagger* tavern. He had called her Meyara. The same woman who was asking questions about Lady Fair. There was disturbing intelligence and shrewdness in her face that matched the much older prince beside her. A quickness to her eyes, as she passed her gaze over the crowds, betrayed cunning. Aye, she was seeking someone, and every survival instinct screamed at Elika that this was a trap.

The line moved forward.

She thought quickly. It was too late to retreat. The woman had been seeking Arala. She was here beside Southfire, and she wanted to meet Lady Fair. It suddenly occurred to her that the invitation for her and Rory to attend court had arrived far too soon after her encounter with Duke Orland in the gardens.

"My lord," she whispered urgently to Rory.

He lowered his head so she could speak closer to his ear. "My love, is the air too hot for you?"

That was the code they had for asking whether something was amiss.

"'Tis far too stifling. I feel as if I might faint," said Elika as they moved closer to the dais.

Rory's eye sharpened as he glanced towards the mageguards. "'Tis far too late to leave, my dear."

"But of course, my lord, I know this. I would not want to disappoint the lady beside the prince, for I strongly suspect she penned our invitation."

His head snapped up towards the woman. "I must admit I have never met her."

"Nor I. But I have seen her from afar," Elika said, wary of other ears listening to them. "Though I did not realize who she was."

Rory's nod was barely perceptible. He understood and knew to be cautious.

The line moved again, and no one now stood between them and the dais.

"Lord Nightkill and Lady Fair," announced the royal herald.

The woman's strange eyes fixed and sharpened on Elika, and a small, knowing smile touched those luscious lips. There was no subtlety about her, and her intent interest in them was clear for everyone to see.

"Lady Fair," the prince said in a booming, yet oddly kindly voice, and waved them forward. "Many speak of your beauty and freshness, and now that I see you, I find myself equally intrigued."

Elika curtsied in a way that would have made Lady Rosalina weep with pride. "My prince, I am humbled to be allowed to stand before you. My father spoke often of your majesty and your unrivalled wisdom."

He chuckled. "Your father was a sly man with a poisoned honey tongue, if what I remember of him is true."

The woman's lips curled into a cynical smile and her eyes flashed with secret amusement.

Elika remained in her curtsy. "I beg forgiveness for any offence he might have caused. It shames me deeply."

"Rise, Lady Fair. I dare say both of us have been freed from his tyranny. I hear he held you locked in your room for many years."

"I was not so badly mistreated. But I must say, Lord Nightkill has been far more generous than my father ever was," she said with a glance of adoration at Rory beside her. In the crowd, she spied Duke Orland gazing at her with greedy expectation.

"Lord Nightkill," said the prince. "I must admit, each time we find someone from Dae-Terren claiming to be an heir of an extinct noble bloodline, more often than not, they are eventually discovered to be charlatans."

"I know it myself far too well, your majesty," Rory replied easily. "I have been plagued by imposters claiming distant relations, both in Dae-Terren and here, too. None were as bothersome as the one marching against you, of course. Some even tried to kill me a time or two to gain my titles and wealth."

"Indeed," said Prince Southfire. "I can see you are a man of great resilience. And your efforts to bring the rebels in Daetown to heel have reached my ears."

Rory bowed. "Were I to have but a few more guards, I am certain I could crush the rebels. My men are few, but they are ready to defend the city. They stand beside your troops along the city wall."

"Dae men?"

"Dae and Alterrians both, my lord. Those who would see you crowned as our king one day. Those who know that the one claiming himself to be Northwind is nothing more than an orphaned street thug with a penchant for elaborate ruses."

The hall fell silent and Elika heard an intake of breath.

The prince leant forward. "To speak of kings is treason."

"If it is treason to name you my liege, then so be it. I shall surrender my head to your sword." And Rory fell to one knee before the prince and bowed his head.

Southfire sat back thoughtfully. "I respect a man who is not afraid to speak of such ... illicit things. A man who voices aloud what others merely whisper." He waved his hand dully. "Rise, rise. I bore of constant bowing and stooping."

Rory rose and stood tall.

"But tell me," the prince continued. "Why is it that men now want a *king* to speak for them? Is a *prince* no longer a palatable title for them?"

"Ahem, a prince is surely a lesser man, implying an unseasoned youth who bows to his elders."

"I bow to no one."

"It is not what men say on the street," said Rory, and as the prince's face darkened, he rushed to add, "No matter how many tongues I cut out for speaking thus against our king—ahem, pardon, our *prince*—they will not be silenced."

"You have a dangerous tongue, Lord Nightkill. Dangerous to yourself and ..."

The woman leant to whisper something in the prince's ear, her gaze on Elika. The prince fell silent, and his gaze, too, drifted to her. And she knew a moment of weightlessness and hopelessness as she watched the delicate thread of their plan unravel.

Southfire showed no reaction to what it was the woman had whispered, and when he spoke again, it was in a composed, cool tone, addressing Rory. "Your thoughts intrigue me, Lord Nightkill. I would hear more of them. You and *your cousin* will join me for a private dinner this evening."

If Rory noted the change of tone in the prince's voice, he made no sign of it. "It will be our pleasure, your highness. 'Tis indeed a great honor." He bowed and Elika curtsied, and they moved aside as another lord and lady stepped forward to be presented to the prince.

Rory did not linger, but strode outside into the corridor, marching towards their chambers. "What are you keeping from me, Spit?" he asked, when no one was around to overhear. "What transpired in there?"

"He suspects I am not Lady Fair. The woman with him believes I'm Arala. I overheard her speaking with a mage some nights ago near the harbor."

Rory pulled her into an alcove in the corridor and turned on her. "Why would she think that?"

"I don't know, and I'm not, before you get it into your head to doubt it. You know me, Rory. Might be I've got a bit of magic, but that doesn't make me a goddess."

"Who is the woman?"

"I don't know, other than her name is Meyara."

"Meyara …" Rory repeated, his jaw tightening. "Blood Dog spoke of her to me not long ago. She comes from Reval's court. Some say she is Southfire's mistress. She is … not human, but one of the Elders, with the blood of the gods in her. If she believes you to be Arala, then so will Southfire and the archmage."

"Yet she hasn't raised the alarm."

"Then she wants something from you."

"Not from me, from *Arala*," she said.

"Something's afoot, Spit. We cannot go to that dinner before we know what the prince knows and what he wants."

Elika ran her hands through her hair, and a pin fell out of it. "They *know*, Rory. They know I am the Rogue. They suspect I am Arala, and they suspect I am here to kill Tridamor. Yet they do not apprehend me. They have not alerted the mageguard, nor sought to bring Reval upon us."

Rory was thoughtfully silent. "Then you must speak with her," he said at length.

She thought back to what she had overhead when Meyara spoke with Shoran. "'Tis not Lady Fair she wants to speak with," she said, whilst searching for any thread, no matter how fragile, to keep their plan from unravelling.

"We cannot retreat," said Rory harshly, seeing something of her panic in her face.

Elika took a slow, deep breath, for there was only one path left to them now. "I must go to them as Arala. They must believe me to be the demigoddess returned."

Rory considered it. "Then be her."

If they suspected she was not Lady Fair, they would know Rory was not who he claimed to be either.

"You need to leave the palace, Rory. Do not delay. The guise of Arala will protect me, at least for a time, but Lord Nightkill won't be shown the same courtesy. They will be coming for me … and for you. There is nothing more you can do here."

A tightness set in his jaw. She could see he was torn between the truth of what she said and fear that without him, she'd fail.

"I will not fail," she said before he had a chance to voice it. "And if I do, then you need to be on the other side of these walls."

"Very well, Spit. Do what you need to do." And with those coolly spoken words, he strode away down the hall.

After he was gone, Elika marched to the wall, and through it into the Tower of the Abyss and into the chamber that was once Arala's.

~

For long moments she stood in the center of the room, imagining the woman whose vanity was said to match her beauty. Elika had played many different characters on the street to gain food or coin, to trick a fool or steal a secret from the lips of the unwary. They all had in the Hide. The trick was to wholeheartedly believe yourself to be who you pretended to be. Yet never had she been more daunted by the farce she was embarking on. Every shred of her soul rebelled at pretending to be Arala.

Might be she feared that were she to pretend, she would forever be lost to the mad lie. Slowly, Elika approached the discarded gold dress. She ran her hand over the silk and adorning gems. The gown was made for a goddess.

Elika stepped out of her dress and after taking a deep breath, pulled on the golden gown. It was too long on her, but fitted well enough around the chest and waist.

You are Arala. You must be Arala.

She went to the dressing table, sat in another woman's chair and stared into the mirror a goddess had once gazed into.

I am Arala. I am she, the demigoddess returned. She repeated the truth in her head, for truth it must become.

She picked up the elegant, silver brush with another woman's hair still clinging to it, and ran it through her hair.

A man appeared in the mirror behind her.

"How did she wear her hair?" she asked him, her voice dull.

"No. You are not her," he said fiercely.

"'Tis not what I asked you."

He marched towards her, pulled her up by her shoulders, spun her round and glared at her. "What madness are you falling into?" His eyes searched hers. "You are not her." He shook her slightly, as if to make her see sense. There was anguish in his face that wrenched pity from her. "Take off this dress," he demanded.

She gently pushed him away. "You told me I could make use of anything in this room. You put me here with her lingering spirit. What madness made you do it? Might be you, too, sometimes believe I'm her. Do you want me to be her?"

"No," he growled through gritted teeth.

She picked up the necklace from the dressing table and put it on. Then she put on the earrings and rings, whilst he watched her, fury brewing and building in his face. When she took the small scent bottle, something snapped in him. He took a step forward, snatched the bottle from her hand, threw it at the wall and smashed it. And the winds of the Abyss gave voice to his rage as they rose and circled, whipping her hair and gown, and spreading the scent of Arala's perfume around them.

Though he glared at her, Elika was not afraid. Somehow, she was hurting him, and she knew not how or why. Something in him was being tortured. Why had he put her in this room? Why was he looking at her with so much grief and anger and despair?

"Tell me how she wore her hair," she repeated, making herself cold against his secret demons.

"I would sooner destroy you than watch you become like her," he said darkly and the room shook with his unrestrained rage.

"'Tis the path you showed me with your mirror, Shoran," she said and put power into her voice to match his, as black strands flowed out of her to crawl over the walls and floor. "'Tis a goddess you named me, and a goddess I shall be."

He turned on his heel and stormed out, as the winds circled and spun around her.

And stilled.

~

Vanity craved adoration. Thus, everything touched by the gods and their descendants clearly demanded it. Elika's chamber in the palace was no less obscene in its splendor than anything else she had seen so far. It went beyond inimitable beauty and brazen opulence. A dusting of vulgarity coated everything. With quick work from her knife, she could peel precious gems out of ornate pillars and statues. A surreptitious flick, and the sapphire eye of the stone serpent would slip into her pocket. A barely perceptible sleight of hand, and the gold horse would be hidden in the folds of her cloak. And she doubted anyone would notice the missing mote of wealth.

When the knock came on the door, she knew who had come to claim his dues. Her stomach tightened, and for a moment she thought about not answering. Then she caught sight of herself in the mirror.

Arala. A goddess did not fear mere men. She would not hide in her room.

She straightened her back, threw back her shoulders and ripped apart her fear. Then she strode to the door and pulled it open.

Duke Orland strode in, uninvited. Arala closed the door behind him, for he would not deign to turn around and do it himself.

He was upon her in an instant, punning her to the wall, breathing and grunting like a dog in heat. "You do not know how long I have waited to be alone with you." His lips attached to her neck.

But it was a frightened Elika who tried to push him away. "Your grace …" she began as his hands gripped her dress and pulled it up above her knees. Then she remembered who she was and sent her magic to wrap around him.

His cry was brief before the black strands lifted him off the ground, pinned him against the wall and wound around him like a spider's web around its prey. He grunted and groaned in outrage and fear against the black tendril covering his mouth.

Arala straightened her dress, stood tall, and gave him the most imperious look she could muster. "I am afraid I cannot accommodate your demands, Orland," she said in a voice that belonged to a demigoddess.

His eyes widened with confusion and fright. He made a noise that sounded like words of outrage combined with a question.

"You know who I am. Let us not play games any longer," said Arala as she strode to her desk, where she found pieces of parchment, ink and a gold feather quill.

She sat down and wrote a brief note, whilst the duke groaned and squirmed in his restraints. Then she pulled a bell rope hanging next to the table. Barely a few heartbeats passed before a servant knocked on the door. Arala opened it and handed him the note. "Deliver this to Lady Meyara without delay and tell her I wish to see her in my room."

The servant bowed.

She closed the door, and ignoring the duke, went to sit before a mirror. She picked up her old brush which she had taken from her room in the dark tower and ran it down the length of her hair.

When another knock came on the door, she did not rise as it opened without prompting. In the mirror, she watched Meyara stride into the room, past the nervous-looking servant.

"Leave us," Arala said to the servant without looking around, and adding power to her voice worthy of the daughter of Goddess Neka.

He bowed and closed the door.

Arala turned her gaze on the woman. "Meyara," she said coolly, watching her in the mirror. The name hung between them as they assessed each other.

"*Lady Fair*," she replied with a sly smile.

"Grauhn, uhm ahnmm," the duke grunted.

Meyara tilted her head towards him. There was no surprise in her face. "Duke Orland," she said with a note of amusement. "I am intrigued to find you so incapacitated. Dare I ask how you came to be there?"

"Hgnm kgh khm," he replied.

Meyara turned back to her. "Would you perhaps release him, so we may speak in private?"

Elika's mind broke through the guise and noted that it was not a demand. The woman was speaking in measured tones as if addressing her mistress, the one with whom she was close.

She still knows her place, thought Arala, and withdrew her magic strands. The duke fell to the floor. He was red in the face, with fear and impotent anger warring for expression. "I'll ..."

Lady Meyara raised her hand and he fell abruptly silent. "Return to your room and speak to no one of this if you wish to see sunrise tomorrow."

Without another word, he scrambled to his feet and stalked out, slamming the door behind him.

After he was gone, Arala held out her silver brush. "I want to look my best for the prince. My maid cannot do the hair the way I prefer it."

The woman approached with prowling caution, her gaze on the brush, recognition flickering in her eyes. The brush, like everything else about the gods, was a product of vanity and majesty combined. And like the gods, it was unique.

Tentatively, Meyara took it and began to brush Arala's hair with the ease of having done this countless times before. "So, he has been keeping you hidden, Arala."

"He did what I asked."

"You do not look like yourself," Meyara said mildly. Though there was neither surprise nor suspicion in her voice.

"I do not feel like myself," she replied and the pain of that truth seeped into her voice.

Meyara's face softened. "Then let us return to Reval's court. I will look after you," she said and her strokes grew more certain.

"Not yet. I have unfinished business here."

Meyara put aside the brush and picked up the hair pins from the table. "You are here for Tridamor," she said as she pinned up strands of Arala's hair.

"He has betrayed me. I must end him."

"Reval will end him for you."

"He is mine to end," Arala said coolly.

"But of course, tsarina."

"What did you tell Southfire of me?"

"I warned him to heed a goddess in disguise."

"I would rather you had not betrayed me. I had hoped you understood this in the look I gave you."

"Southfire can be trusted," Meyara said and stepped away to allow Arala to inspect her hair.

She rose to her feet. "I trusted Tridamor once."

"The dress is a little long for you," Meyara noted with a sly curl of her lips. "It was always your favorite."

"Was it Shoran's favorite?" Elika emerged to ask before she could stop herself. Nor could she fathom why she was tormenting herself with questions to which she did not want to know the answers.

Meyara circled her. "You forget much, then? It can happen on reawakening."

Elika slinked away.

"I recall enough," Arala said imperiously.

"This dress was Northwind's favorite," Meyara replied. "It is the dress you wore to seduce King Airling."

"The king who raped me?"

"Raped?" Meyara lifted her brow. "My, you have forgotten much. You made him a slave to your every whim. You seduced him and used him. And invited me to do the same. Do you not remember?"

"I do not," Arala replied, pushing Elika and her emerging, irrelevant questions into a dark cage deep in her mind.

"He hated us for it—when he was lucid enough to hate. It was indeed a great shame Tridamor gave him the antidote to my potions. Oh, but you did not know that it was him who betrayed us and gave Northwind power to imprison you." She smiled, and there was cunning in it. Her eyes, however, had the watchfulness of a predator under threat. "I bore King Airling's child, you know. But then … I am not half Laifae." There was something cruel in her voice when she said that.

Arala considered her. "You bore Northwind's child … his heir."

Her grin was sly. "A boy. Reval does not know, of course, else he'd have cut my son out of my stomach. He hunted down every Northwind's heir but two: Lord Silvering, the first of his line, and my son."

Arala quickly pieced everything together. "Southfire … He is your son. King Airling's son. He is Northwind, in truth."

No, it could not be, Elika's mind intruded, breaking out of its cage. *Mite was the rightful heir.*

Meyara smiled. "I crossed the bridge you gave us, Arala, and returned to Elder Valley, and back to the Asari. Effina was going to turn me away, unforgiving as ever, but I told her I carried a child. So she allowed me to stay, and helped birth and raise Adren."

"He has aged worse than you," Arala said dismissively. "Clearly, there is too much of a human in him."

Annoyance flashed in Meyara's face. "I am the fifth and thus the last generation of the Elders, unaffected by Moreg's curse. My son, though long-lived is not blessed with eternal life. Had Shoran …" She clamped her lips abruptly.

Elika emerged again to recall Meyara's sensuous hands on his chest and his dismissal of her. "Had Shoran fathered him, your son would be an eternal," she finished for her.

"It matters not what my son is, save that he is mine," Meyara said, as she strode around the room. "After three hundred years in exile, I returned to Terren with him and told Reval that Southfire was his father. Adren's hair gave credence to my claim, for it comes from his paternal grandmother who was, as the fates would have it, a distant descendant of their line."

"And the true Southfire's heir?"

"All dead. The sacred bloodline of Demigod Verin Firestorm is extinguished. So you see, Adren is the true heir of Terren. The city is rightfully his."

"He is a bastard son. Aeronmite is the true heir." Elika took the bait, despite herself, for she could not help but come to Mite's defense.

It was a careless blunder, for Meyara's gaze grew more feral in its intensity, and more cunning yet. She would protect her child and his claim to Terren, against the gods if need be.

"My dear," she said, and her eyes glowed like silversap. "You know better than anyone the way of the Sacred Crown succession. Founded by the Silver Blood, and by the Silver Blood shall it be determined. There are no bastard children amongst the gods. Each one is pure and sacred. Aeronmite is the seventh generation Northwind from King Airling's loin. Twenty-fifth of his line. But my son is the *nineteenth* king. He is the child of King Ailing himself and an *elir* mother."

Meyara was an *elir*. Elika snatched that morsel of information about her and devoured it. She recalled that the *elirs* were the fifth-generation descendants of the gods, gifted with the long life of the Elders yet held no powers of the demigods. They were, in truth, mostly human and could not tap into the wells of power. Which meant that Meyara had no magic to draw upon.

"Blood of the gods is strong in his veins," she went on. "He is Airling's true son and not a distant grandchild born of human wombs with not a drop of silver blood."

These were dangerous revelations, dangerous to Mite. If what Meyara was saying was true, Southfire held the true claim to Terren. Meyara had hidden her son from Reval's wrath by lying about his true father, and Elika was certain they would both continue to hide the truth. But whether or not Southfire was the true heir to the seat of Terren mattered not. He had failed men. His allegiance lay with the gods and the Laifae. Men needed Mite.

"If he is the true heir, which well of power does he draw upon?" she asked, recalling the question Shoran had once asked of her.

Meyara stiffened, and her silence betrayed her son. He had no magic, not like Mite.

Elika retreated, and it was Arala who brushed her fingers along the length of the gold serpent with sapphire eyes. "You said it yourself, Meyara, by the Silver Blood it shall be determined. Strange that, I always thought, how the blood of gods can strengthen and wane through generations. 'Tis indeed the Fates who decide where power should lie."

"You speak as one who cannot possibly know what it is to bear a child in your body, to watch new life emerge, which you have fashioned, and to hold it in your arms. A true child of your flesh, Arala, and not an empty dream born of tears and despair. All you have ever borne were *tanes*." Her lips twisted with disgust. "You cannot understand the need that drives a mother to do anything and everything for her child. Adren will be the king of Seramight, this I swear."

Meyara's agitation grew feral in her fear and need to protect her cub. It was a weakness that could be exploited.

Arala prowled towards her. There was challenge in those silvery eyes that needed subduing. "Do not test my patience, Meyara. Do not forget who I am, lest I remind you. Your petty squabbles over the rule of the human domain concern me not. At least as long as your loyalty to me remains true, and you hinder not my rightful vengeance."

Meyara bowed, but there was no sincerity in her acquiescence. "I remain your friend and servant, always."

"Then prove it. I want Tridamor. He is the only one who stands between your son and his coveted crown. If you mean to do anything for him, then do this. Take me to Tridamor."

"And is that all you wish for, tsarina? For if it is, then it's a trifling request, and I will grant it."

"It is all I wish from you."

"Then let us speak with my son, the future *king* of Seramight."

~

Arala strode into the prince's private chambers. Before her, stood a prince. No, not a prince, but a lesser being with no magic to draw upon. One not worthy of her contempt, only pity.

The prince smiled without artifice. "No more pretense then, tsarina."

"No more pretense, Adren," Arala said imperiously and strode forward. "I am told you are not an enemy to me."

Adren's gaze darted to his mother. The look he gave her was brief, and had Arala not been watching him closely, she might have missed the flicker of uncertainty in it. He was deferring to Meyara, seeking her guidance, her approval. He was a boy who had been sheltered and protected by his mother his whole life. And if nothing else told Arala that he was not fit to be king of their broken, bleeding world, it was that.

"You almost fooled me, you know," he said, turning back to her. "Now here you are, the perfect image of power and grace, a true vision of a goddess. Your whole body is dripping with magic. I feel it on my skin, on my soul. And I shudder to think what you are hiding deeper in you, what you are holding back."

"Then you will know to tread carefully when speaking with me."

"Why the ruse, tsarina? I dare say I am looking at the Rogue herself. Why the carnage? Why not come to my palace doors? I would have welcomed you."

"Welcomed me? As you welcomed the mage who had betrayed me. I was told you and Tridamor are close."

"Betrayed you? I thought that was only a malicious rumor," the prince lied, and once again his eyes darted to Meyara.

They both knew. Arala heard it in the delicately fearful timbre of his voice. They knew and yet they allied with the man who had betrayed a goddess, one who gave him life.

Something of her thought must have shown on her face, for he rushed to add, "He denies it vehemently. And in your absence, he speaks with your voice, as per your decree. Would you have us deny him, and thus deny your authority?"

"Now that I have returned, I expect you to heed my authority and deny me nothing I desire."

"But of course, tsarina," the prince said with a bow.

"Then I wish to see Tridamor."

"You mean to kill him?"

"Does that trouble you?"

There was caution in his face, masking the glimmer of ambition. Once again, his gaze sought his mother. "If he betrayed you, then it troubles me not. Only, what do you plan to do after that?"

"I will leave."

It was for Aeronmite Northwind to wrest the throne from Southfire and claim his city. Her task was only to destroy the archmage.

"And return to Reval?" the prince asked carefully.

"That is not your concern."

"No, of course not. Except … you have been attacking the mageguards and siding with the Dae rebels against us."

"The archmage wishes me dead. I sought allies where they were to be had."

"You have been slaying the Laifae in their beds, tsarina," he said far too mildly.

"Obscenities he created in my name," she snapped back. "Whilst *you* have failed to protect your people against Tridamor the traitor. You watch and do nothing, as he snatches men out of their beds. If you are indeed Airling's heir, you are a weak one."

"Arala!" Meyara stepped forward in her fury. "You promised …"

The prince put up his hand to stop her saying anymore. "I was born into the world still reeling from the chaos of Syn'Moreg's sundering. Though I was sheltered in my early years, Mother once brought me as a child to Terren, to show me what my legacy was to be. I saw it all, the early days of darkness, cruelty and terror …"

"Cruelty of the mages."

"Cruelty of men! They were wild, base, murderous ..." He stopped himself and took a calming breath. "Tridamor restored order to the streets ..."

"By enslaving men."

"Men have always been enslaved by their hatred. Had Tridamor not done what he did, there would be nothing left of this half of the world either. They would have burned it to ash, just as they have done on the other side. The Blight would have swept through this half of Seramight and Alafraysia ..."

"Alafraysia ...?"

He smiled ironically. "The two worlds are merged, as per your will, tsarina. Both have been sundered. The Blight tore through Alafraysia as it did through Seramight. Were you to go home, you would see for yourself. They, too, lost half their world. Except, it was not the doing of the Laifae, but of men. The Laifae watched helplessly and died as half their realm grew barren, where dreams no longer lived, and the Black River could not flow. And so many of its streams and brooks perished as the Blight advanced. Every aeon and majren you slew has fled the Blight into this world. They fled into Seramight to escape death. Tridamor is not seeking to destroy men but to save his own kind. *Your* kind, tsarina, your subjects who look to you for protection."

Arala wanted to scream in fury and grief. Only Elika's numb, horror-stricken mind held her back. Like the Daes, the Laifae were fleeing a dying realm, caused by the destructive blood-salt fires started by men. Who then was the true monster in this war?

'Tis you, whispered a voice in her head.

Southfire must have seen her horror for he went on speaking fervently. "Tridamor has found a way for our two kinds to coexist. A way to stop men from destroying themselves, the Laifae, and everything around them. Alafraysia and Seramight are safe ... for now. And they will remain safe as long as you do not destroy the fragile truce."

And with each of his damning words, he pushed her closer to that moment the wise Sachi priests would warn you about. When you are faced with a choice so profound it irrevocably reshapes the very soul and heart of you. The gods called it the *Fate Slayer's Curse*. For there was no choice the Fate Slayer could make that would not scar their soul. Where every choice led to destruction.

Walk away, allow Tridamor to live, and watch men being dragged off the streets to forge more majren, watch Mite's army slaughtered by the combined force of Southfire and the archmage. Spare the archmage, and watch men continue being enslaved by the Laifae. Do nothing and watch Penny's red-haired babe, Eli, grow up wearing the collar of ownership around her throat.

Then she saw the alternate fate she was setting them upon. Tridamor's death, the Laifae vanquished and once again hunted. Blood-salt fires and the war spreading to encompass the last of their realm. The purge of magic. The return of the Blight. She saw the web of light and life and magic engulfed by the red flames, and the dark strands beyond the rift lifelessly flailing in the dark winds of the Abyss.

A fissure of despair cracked inside her soul. There was no walking away. There was no path she could take that would not damn her.

For a moment she was frozen. Surely, these were not the only two futures before them. Perhaps there was another, one in which Mite was the king, who made peace with the Laifae. Where the world once again belonged to men who co-existed with the mages as equals. Such was the time of peace under the fifth King Northwind, when their realms were joined for nigh on a century, before drifting apart.

Southfire smiled, and it was a sad, sage smile. Wisdom shone in his eyes as he read her thoughts and doubts. For he himself must have spent centuries pondering that which she had been pondering mere moments. "So, Fate Slayer, what choice will you make? Name it and the curse shall be yours to bear until your soul is bleak and life tastes of ashes on your tongue."

Meyara looked aside then, her lips pressed tight with anguish. Elika knew why. Whatever choice she made, it would haunt Meyara's son as well.

But there was no time to ponder the Fates. She had not the centuries to think upon it, whilst sitting on the glorious throne of the demigods, nor to dwell upon the cruelties of times gone past. Men were dying now. Mite was marching towards them. Six hundred years they had, to find a better way. And might be Rory was right, better to die than be enslaved for eternity. She need not ponder, but merely listen to her heart.

"Take me to Tridamor," Arala said imperiously, meeting the prince's gaze. "I will have vengeance that is rightfully mine. And I shall leave it to the kings of men to forge peace with the Laifae."

"So be it," said the prince. "I will take you to Tridamor. I do this, Arala, because I need you to know that I am not your enemy, nor am I the enemy of man. Aeronmite will burn the world. He will bring the Blight upon us. Of this, I am certain, for I saw it in his face when he stood before me and threatened to do just that."

Everything in Elika rebelled at his words. Lies, she thought. She *knew* Mite. He would never destroy that which he was entrusted to protect.

She kept her expression steady. "Lead the way, Adren."

~

The prince threw open the doors. None of the mageguards stopped him. "I bring a gift to you, your eminence," he announced to the solitary figure in the room. "Arala, daughter of Neka."

Arala strode forward, whilst keeping Elika's trembling heart from taking over her body.

The archmage turned and his eyes widened. He was long and frail of body. His gaze fixed on her and she might have imagined him paling, were he not already so wan. His bizarrely long fingers moved, as if trying to grasp something that was not there.

"No ... it cannot be," he gasped.

"Leave us," she commanded and threw out tendrils from herself. "All of you. As your tsarina, I command you to leave this room," she ordered the mageguards standing around the walls, and as one they marched outside, following Prince Adren Southfire.

"Stay! For I am your master," the archmage cried, but they heeded him not.

Elika reached out to Tridamor with her senses. He radiated power so potent it smothered the air out of the room, power that Arala had given him long ago. A strong barrier guarded his essence, which she had failed to break through twice before.

For long moments, he seemed too stunned to utter a word. She took advantage of his shock to probe his protective wall of magic, whilst looking around the room as if curious.

"Why do you tremble, Tridamor?" she asked of her betrayer. "Are you not pleased to see me? I always thought us to be … close."

The archmage pierced her with his gaze. "I have missed you greatly, my goddess."

The air shimmered around the archmage as she drew closer, seeking a way past the invisible barrier. She probed it with her mind, and found it to be solid, yet fluid and trembling slightly as if under great strain.

There was a cup and jug beside his chair. He lifted the cup to his lips and took a sip. Silversap. He was feeding his magic, which meant he was using it now. And she wondered where his source of silversap came from, for surely it was not from Gods' Wood.

She continued to stroll around the room, gently probing his magic, trying hard not to alert him to it. "Tell me, why did you betray me?"

"Betray you, my tsarina? I would never …"

"Spare me the lies, Tridamor. I know what passed."

Anger twisted his features and the magic in the room grew thick, restrained only by his fear. "Always you expected me to grovel at your feet. Always you asked for and ignored my sage advice. Yet always have I stood by your side, even when Reval would not. I warned you to steer clear of Airling Northwind. I warned you that no babe would ever grace your sterile womb, for the black river runs through you far more strongly than Neka's grace. Yet you spread your legs for him, anyway. So look and see where it brought us."

Arala toyed with a strange statue of a wave swirling around a tree. "You were jealous," she said mildly, without looking at him.

"Everything that has come to pass is upon your soul to bear. All your conniving plans. The merging of the worlds … all for nothing in the end. There was no babe, Arala, for there could never be one."

She looked at him then. "I had many babes, Tridamor."

He laughed. "Oh, come, Arala, you have never claimed those abominations as your babes before." He moved, his motion mirroring hers, his body tense.

"No, of course not," she ceded quickly before suspicion grew wings in his mind. "Still, you have not yet answered my question. Why did you betray me when I asked for your strength in forging the bridge?"

"You were draining my strength and pleading with me to sacrifice the only thing I could not give up for your folly. You wanted me to surrender my life to save yours. Had you asked me anything but that, I would have given it gladly." He spread his hands. "Yet here we are, and despite everything, I am still your most loyal and faithful servant, my light."

She did not believe him, for she saw the stark fear in his eyes, saw him gathering magic into himself, and she knew she was out of time.

"But you are not my faithful servant," she said. "For I am not Arala." That stumbled him long enough for her to draw her own magic towards her. "I am Eli Spider, of Bad Penny's pack."

And with that, she pushed an explosive wave of magic outwards, adding flame and wind and black strands of her magic to encircle the archmage.

He staggered back, pushed aside her magic and threw out his own. Tendrils wrapped around her throat. "I will not submit to your wiles again. I will not be ended."

Elika's knife was quickly in her hand and she sliced through the black strand holding her, grabbed him and pushed a wave of fire into him. But it did not reach him, for there was no heat in her illusion. With little time for thought, she pulled on the essence of the Great Web and drew upon its light to help her conjure the wind. It swept through the room, pushing the archmage to the ground. Then it picked him up.

He shook his head in horror. "No, it cannot be … your power … 'tis true, you are not Arala. Stop, mistress!" he cried, as she peeled layer after layer of magic from him, until the protective barrier around him was gone. She grabbed his essence and …

Do not harm the web.

She closed her eyes and gently tried to push the archmage's essence out of this world. "Return to Alafraysia," she said, with a pang of pity for this creature who feared death more than he loved life. "'Tis mercy I grant you."

"No!" he cried and threw his magic outwards.

It struck her hard. Knocked all air out of her. She fell to her knees but kept the wind flowing and flowing, then grabbed again for the archmage's essence. But there was too much of him to push away. He was too large … too deep.

One of the strands came at her with a knife. She rolled out of the way and recalled Shoran's magic. Light … she needed the light of the web.

She felt for the web that permeated the world, and it was a living thing. She drew on the light and it gathered inside her, and she pushed it out towards Tridamor. The webbing of light raced through the floor and engulfed the creature. As she watched him struggle against its hold, she realized that his body was but a thin shell, encompassing a Laifae inside it. It never belonged to a human. Arala, like Neka, could fashion life in whatever image she desired.

Once Elika realized that, some deep innate knowledge came to her of how to peel away the shell. It was but a fragile cloak made of glass. She struck it and it shattered into pieces.

Tridamor cried out and his true form emerged; a shapeless creature made of shifting black magic strands. The creature was ugly, and yet fluid and graceful as it moved and churned. It tried to take on the shape of man, stretching and standing tall, reminiscent of those statues mages crafted, of twisted shapes that resembled their earthly form.

Elika looked closer at the world, and the veil between their realms thinned. And she saw faint mountains hanging upside down above fields of purple grass. She pushed the creature towards it, as it fought and grasped at everything in sight as if to anchor itself to this world, whilst fading from it all the while. The creature cried out with the voices of many. Then it was gone and where the archmage had stood, lay a pile of his robes.

The wind died. The fire stopped. The room was charred and broken, the furniture upturned.

The door opened. Prince Southfire stood behind three mageguards.

"Tsarina," one said and knelt before her.

The others followed.

"What now, tsarina?" Southfire asked. "Will you take his place?"

"'Tis not my place to take," said Eli Spider of Bad Penny's pack, and walked past him. Past the human guards who did not stop her, past the mageguards still kneeling on the ground, and past the lords who came to see what the commotion was about. And like a god of old, she strode through the wall and into the Tower of the Abyss, and from there into Elder Valley, where she drank deeply of the silversap to purge her body of Arala's invading presence.

Shortly, a strange sense of calm and detachment from the world settled over her. Her task was done. And Arala was gone.

Tis up to you now, Mite, thought Elika and closed her eyes as power surged through her veins, renewed again by the sap of the silvery trees.

CHAPTER TWENTY-SEVEN

The Betrayal

"No being is more highly protected and coveted in the three realms than Aleyala, the daughter of the gods. They are few and possess powers over life the sons of gods are oft denied. To harm an Aleyala, is to bring the wrath of the gods upon you. To disobey one, is to bring her wrath upon you. To love one, is to bring forth the wrath of every man and god who craves her."

The History of Alafraysia and Seramight,
By Mageguard Bluelight

Elika scraped the mud off her boots on the wire rack outside Rory's mansion.

Toad was holding the door open. He grinned. "Tridamor's dead and buried and we haven't seen a mage in the streets since."

If only that gave them respite from battles raging across the city. They were just as fierce, though they were no longer between men and mages, but those loyal to Southfire and those to Northwind. Tridamor's death sent a shudder of shock and fear through the mages as now only the tsaren had the power to fashion them.

"Is Rory in good spirits, then?" Elika asked.

She hadn't seen him in three days since they parted in the palace. She had spent that time replenishing her strength in the orchard of Gods' Wood by night and helping Daetown defenders during the day. Southfire had continued to send wave after wave of attacks against the rebels. But so far, only human guards assaulted their defenses. She had not the stomach for warring against men, however. So, she embraced chores that did not involve using her magic or killing men. She helped tip arrows in blood-salt ready for when the mageguards returned to attack them. Helped women cook on the streets for the fighters. Helped to bandage their wounds and apply healing salves.

Toad's grin fell away. He scratched his head. "Been broody, somewhat. Since Southfire proclaimed himself king, no one's been sending invitations to Lord Nightkill. And we haven't seen Blood Dog around to fix it for 'im. One Eye's expecting you though."

"I'll go see him soon, after I get my bag and the things I left behind."

"Then you'll not be staying?" he said, almost regretfully.

She shook her head. "Done what I promised to do. Now I'll be doing my own things."

"And what might that be, Lady Fair?" He winked at her and gave her a wide grin.

Elika didn't know. She thought of Shoran, of his anger the last time she saw him. Might be she'd speak with him one more time and tell him the truth.

To Toad, she said, "Got battles to fight and help Northwind take the city. Might be I'll help him from the parapets."

She strode inside past him, feeling light, as if her soul had been unburdened. Their farce was over and that brought its own peace. And Mite was only ten leagues away. She entertained no illusions about the difficulty he would have in taking the city. The self-proclaimed King Southfire had gathered the mageguard under his command. He had sworn to protect the majren, and to restore peace between the Laifae and the humans. He had also sworn to end slavery and to remove every collar from the throats of mankind. Many things had he sworn, but had not yet done, to turn the nobles of Terren from Northwind.

Trouble was, it was Arala who had ended Tridamor, and having lost his protector, Southfire was rapidly losing his allies, too. It seemed the nobles were slow to forgive his long years of pandering to the archmage. More importantly, it was Northwind who promised to restore their lands and titles. It was the king riding from the west, who swore to restore the world to how it was in those golden days before Reval destroyed the houses of the Sacred Crowns. And it was Northwind who had a god-anointed right to Terren.

Upstairs in her room, Elika changed into a clean shirt and skirt, then threw spare clothes into the bag. Liffy was nowhere to be seen. She would have to speak with Rory about the girl. Elika had done her part, and he had no cause to keep the maid, unless he meant to look after the girl.

A servant led her to a dining room, where his lordship was awaiting her. He was dressed smartly for dinner.

"Hey, Spit," he said coolly.

"Rory," she countered, noting his dark mood.

"Wasn't sure you were coming back."

"Came to get a few things and to speak to you about my maid."

"You are leaving." There was no surprise in his voice.

"Got my own things to do now."

"Then let us have dinner before you go, like old friends." There was nothing friendly in his voice. Still, she had to speak with him about Liffy, and she was hungry besides. She put down her bag and joined him at the table. Around the room, his guards watched on.

She had noted the lack of invitations in the bowl by the entry. Now that their ruse had been exposed, there would be no return to court or the noble circles for him. At least not until Northwind took power and made him a lord, in truth.

After the archmage's death, Southfire sent his guards to the real Lady Fair's country mansion, where they found her locked in a room, alive and well looked after. She was promptly and hurriedly left there, once they saw her disfigurement wrought upon the family by a curse from a vengeful god.

As Elika pondered that, servants placed pieces of roast chicken on her plate.

For a time, Rory was silent, merely eating his food. She suspected he was carefully weighing his next words, and she knew what they would be.

The tension in the room grew into its own awareness.

"I've heard we gained Captain Smokeheart's battalion two days ago," she said, if only to fill the silence. "They fight for Northwind now."

She thought Rory's mood would lighten at being reminded of that, but he turned his head, his dark eye pinning her to her seat.

The look sent a shiver up her spine.

"Always wanted you to be one of us, Spit. You're a smart one. Always liked that about you. I don't suppose you'd like to stay."

Once, the offer might have been tempting. But she had left that girl behind on the other side of the bridge. She wanted a different life. She had cast aside every collar that had anchored her to Rory and the street and was lighter for it. Ahead, the future was a wide vista. And she wanted to explore it.

What shape that life would take, she knew not, only that it was not on the streets, running with gangs, killing men and women on command. She remembered what Rory had done in the past when he was Peter Pocket's man. And he'd expect no less from her. Inside, she was shriveling and decaying with every life she took, human or Laifae. She wanted peace. Might be she'd spent her days walking and sleeping under the silvery trees of the God's Wood.

"I can't," she said. "This is where we part ways. I've done what you asked. Our debt is settled. The archmage is dead. Chelik stays with Penny until he's of age. Mite will keep his word when he's king and you'll be a lord, in truth. I was hoping to take my maid with me, too. I'll pay you any money she owes you, and more besides."

"Indeed," he said coolly. There was a thoughtful look in his eyes, one that chilled her blood. It was the same look he'd give you before he cut the flesh off your bones.

"You will keep your side of the bargain … about Chelik," she said, making certain it did not come out as a question.

"I'm a man of my word." Again, his voice was cool, his gaze steady. "Before we part ways, Spit, I want to show you something."

She almost refused him. But magic pulsed powerfully in her veins, and she feared no man or mage any longer. "What do you want to show me?"

He rose to his feet. "Come, you'll want to see this."

He led her into a cellar, and Elika fought against the painful, prickling sensation on her skin from the surrounding blood-salt. There was always blood-salt under Rory's house. Stores and stores of it.

A group of his toughs were below. They moved aside to allow them entry into a storeroom. Instantly, a sense of incredible weight crushed her body from all around. The room was painted in blood-salt, and barrels of it lined the walls. A mage was strapped to the table in the center of the room. A thug was doing something to him. When he saw them enter, he wiped the blood off his hands on an already stained cloth and threw it aside. "My lord," he greeted Rory with a nod and stood aside.

Elika hated being here, hated what he did to the mages. It sickened her to the very core of her being. "There's no need to torment them! They are ... they are like us."

"Us?" He raised an eyebrow at her. "Or like you?"

His question chilled her to the bone, for she saw in his eyes something she did not want to see before. But before fear had a chance to work its way into her, a whimper drew her gaze to the corner of the room. And there she saw a pitiful, dirt-stained creature, huddling in terror, shivering and weeping. Liffy.

Shock froze Elika's mind. She turned her head to look closely at the mage and felt the blood drain from her face, for there was Mage Blackfly, the one Liffy believed was her brother Sam. Elika should have unraveled him long ago, should have spared Liffy this torment of watching her brother butchered alive.

"Why is she here?" Elika asked, and her voice trembled.

Rory was not one to miss another's blunder. Aye, he saw her horror and her fear. He tilted his head at Liffy. "Bring her here," he said to one of his toughs, and Elika knew that calm, steely tone and what it meant.

"Liffy ..." the mage moaned from the table to which he was strapped. "Liffy, our sister."

Elika stepped closer to her. "Whatever she's done, do not do this."

"Please, my lord," Liffy sobbed and whimpered. A bruise stained her jaw.

"This flower here," said Rory. "Has claimed a mage for her own. She's a magic-lover."

"Rory, don't … I know her. She hates magic, but she loves her brother. She doesn't know it's not him. Doesn't understand."

"But you do," he said and handed her a red dagger.

Elika could not take it. Pain racked her body just from being this close to it.

Rory smiled. "But of course. You can't take it, for you can't touch the blood-salt. Matters not, though, does it? Kill him whatever way the Rogue does it."

"No!" Liffy screamed.

"Liffy," the mage moaned and fought his restraints.

"Please don't," Liffy wept and grabbed Elika's arm. "Don't kill Sam. Please, don't kill him."

Rory gave a barely perceptible nod and two ruffians instantly pushed Liffy to her knees.

Panic and shock seized Elika. He was testing her. Rory was a cruel bastard when he wanted to be. Deep inside, he always feared and hated those he could not trust. Now he was testing her loyalty. To prove it, she'd have to destroy the mage and Liffy both.

"Rory … please. I'll kill the mage. Just take her out of here."

Liffy screamed. "No! Not Sam."

One of the thugs holding her down drew his knife.

"Rory, don't do this," Elika pleaded and reached for her magic, but the weight of all the blood-salt crushed her efforts to draw upon it. "I'll kill him. I'll do anything … just leave her be. She is no threat to you."

"Spit, you know me better than that. You know I hate betrayal. You never rightly understood this fight. Every one of them, including this pitiful girl, is a threat to us. For six hundred years, magic-lovers like her have allowed mages to take over our world and imprison our kind. Even now, magic-lovers attack us. There are only two sides to this war. There is no third enemy."

As he spoke, Elika used all her strength to fight the restraint of blood-salt. She groaned with the effort of it and threw out a single black strand at the thug with the knife holding Liffy.

But it was Rory who stepped forward, and with a flick of his knife, cut the girl's throat.

Elika's legs almost gave way from under her as she watched Liffy gurgle and choke and die, her eyes wild and fixed on her brother.

"Liiiiiffy," the mage cried and screamed and thrashed.

"Take her next door. Do not waste her blood," said Rory impassively.

Two big thugs dragged the dead girl with sandy-colored hair braided with flowers out of the room. Elika heard a rattle of chains, the clank of a bucket placed on stone, then *drip-drip-drip*.

"You've always been a callous bastard," she said hoarsely.

But his attention was on the whimpering mage. "Come closer, Spit."

Elika moved, only because she was too numb to do anything else. From the corner of her eye, she saw six more bulky toughs come in and stand around the edges of the room. Her every sense and fighting instinct sharpened.

"Release us," hissed a voice from the table, pitiful and pleading.

"End him," Rory said blandly.

Gently, she pushed the Laifae out of the body and back into his realm, leaving behind a man's corpse.

"Can you do the same with men?"

The quietly spoken question struck her with such force, she was rendered speechless. She had never considered it, had never questioned her power or its limits. And the question terrified her. "I … don't know. I've never tried. I would not try …" But words failed her, for the answer clawed at the edges of her mind, like a beast ready to pounce and devour her from the inside. She had tried it with Shoran and might have ended him but for his power to fight off her attack. "No," she shook her head vehemently. It was a lie. She knew it. "Only with them … the mages."

Rory slowly walked around the dead man, watching him as if he might come back to life. "The priests say Arala had Neka's magic of life. She had power *over* life. That she could destroy it at will, reshape it, and bring it forth in whatever form she wished.

You see, the magic of the Laifae is not the same as that of the gods. Though both are deadly to us mortals. Arala could wield them both, for she had the blood of both races. And that made her more dangerous than the gods themselves. Did you know it was she who joined our two realms?" he said the last so quietly, Elika barely heard him.

"I'm not Arala."

But Rory's gaze was still on the mangled corpse before them. "Arala wielded that power whenever a whim took her, heedless of the lives she destroyed. And she destroyed many before Northwind finally captured her. He tried to end her, you know. Save that he didn't know how." Something in Rory's dark eye told her that *he* knew how you ended a demigoddess.

"I am not her," she repeated, her voice rising. "I was born on the other side, remember?"

"So what are you? For you are not one of us," he said softly, and her blood turned to ice.

I'm human, was on her lips to say. But no denial came out, for it was a lie and might be she had spoken too many lies in her life. And she could no longer bring herself to believe this one.

Shapes moved around her, whilst the blood-salt painting the walls restrained and encaged her magic. The longer she spent here, the more weight pushed upon her. She had to distract Rory and his men for long enough to flee.

Elika crossed her arms, trying to make light of this threat. "I'm one of you. Always have been. Just 'cause magic polluted me, doesn't make me one of them, any more than a title deed makes you a lord."

He gave her a mocking smile. "But I'm human, and you are not."

She opened her mouth to deny it, but no sound came out. Instead, her ears tuned into the slow treacle and *drip-drip* of Liffy's blood into the metal bucket in the other room.

"You're one of them, Spit. Aye, you may think you're one of us, but one day you'll see that we are not the same."

A door shut behind her. She readied her magic to fight back, but it recoiled and shrank away. She pulled out her knife, turning her body so she could keep an eye on as many of these bastards as she could. "Don't do this, Rory. You need me. We can help each other."

He gave her a small, sad smile, and for a single hopeful moment, she thought he would try to convince her again to join his men.

Pain exploded in her back, and her shocked mind saw her terrible mistake. She gasped, tried to move, but her limbs would not obey. She reached for her magic, but it slipped away, like water flowing through her fingers. Blood-salt, she realized as her head was jerked back by her hair and the knife found her back again. A cold blade sliced against her throat and shadows surrounded her. Pain exploded everywhere—her chest, her stomach, her back. Then she could feel no more, save the jolting strikes of hate and cold blades butchering her flesh.

"Enough," said a calm voice.

And it was over.

She staggered, slipped on her blood, and fell to her knees. Blood filled her mouth. She crawled towards the wall, her vision dimming. Her hands were shaking, but she still clutched her knife. She waved it blindly, warning them off, but they just stood there, watching her die. Blood gurgled in her throat, mingling with what breath she could rasp into her broken chest.

"I'm sorry, Spit," said Rory, and there was honest regret in his voice. "But you are one of them. You are one of the monsters hunting our kind. And we cannot allow another one of them to invade our world. If you are not ours, you are theirs. And they must never have you, for you are far too dangerous to us. 'Tis monsters that we slay, El, so that our children need not fear the dark."

She coughed up blood.

"She's like them," someone said. "She ain't dying."

A hot burning blade pierced her between her shoulders and the pain was nothing like it was before. Light exploded in front of her eyes, and in that light, she saw Shoran and safety and his calm, solid strength. She touched the wall, grasped for a thread and fell towards it.

The long dark hall closed in around her ... a door ... too far away to reach. She opened her mouth to call out and choked on her blood.

She clung to the wall, pulled herself up to her feet and tried to move one foot, then the other, heading towards the light. A shape appeared in front of it. She slipped on something wet at her feet and sank to her knees.

Strong arms were there to catch her, and she groaned at the pain of their embrace.

"Oh, kitten. Shh, I've got you."

She could not reply, could only gasp for air. Her body trembled and burned as if afire.

Then something was yanked out of her back. With a foul curse, he threw it aside. The blood-salt dagger skidded along the stone.

Gently, he lowered her to the floor. "Heal yourself," he commanded.

She gripped his hand in hers. Her body was broken beyond any healer's care. "Don't want to die ... alone," she choked out and coughed up blood. "The duke ..." she rasped. "... not real. Had to kill ..." She wanted him to know the truth before she died. Somehow, it seemed more important than life itself. She needed him to know that she was not the woman she pretended to be.

"Shh. I know, kitten. I know everything. It is done. Do not speak. Just heal yourself."

"Shoran ..." She touched his face, for in it she saw anguish, raw and unfettered. Surely, he must know, not even the gods could save her from drowning in her own blood.

"Heal yourself!" he shouted, his face looming over her.

"Can't ..." She shook her head, the movement sent shards of pain through her.

He pressed his palm against her cheek. "You are mortal unless you choose not to be. You need not die unless you choose it. Heal yourself. It is your gift." His words were spoken softly, yet there was such power and certainty in them that she believed him.

Only, she did not know how. She sought her magic, but it was distant and dying like her. A tear streaked down her cheek. She wanted to do what he asked and live, but there was no strength left in her.

Again, he cursed, looked up in despair and returned his gaze to her, hard and determined. He closed his eyes tightly, took a breath and opened them, and there was light in his irises. He tore her shirt, placed his hands on her bare skin over the wounds and shut his eyes again, mumbling in the language of the gods.

Fire spread through her, but it did not burn. Instead, it seared her pain, and violently ripped it out of her body. She gasped, arched and felt her body infuse with another essence and then knit. Shoran groaned, and she watched his shirt grow red and slick with blood as strains of pain appeared in his face. Red drops formed in the corners of his eyes and dripped onto her, mingling with her blood. Blood filled his mouth, and he spat it aside.

"Stop," she pleaded and weakly pushed on his shoulders.

His blood ran in rivulets along his arms towards his hands he held against her skin, as if every cut he healed he took upon himself.

"Please, stop." Her voice was stronger, the pain subsiding. One by one, each knife wound was ripped from her body. She could breathe again. But his breath was now ragged and choked.

He fell back against the wall, breathing harshly. His head rolled back. He was bleeding. Elika crawled towards him, her body still raw, unwieldy.

"What have you done?" She reached for his shirt.

He grabbed her hands, spun her around and clasped her against him. "Leave me be," he said breathlessly, and she heard restrained agony in his voice. "Leave me be," he said more faintly.

Her strength gave out. She leant back against him and waited, listening to him struggle to breathe, fearing each breath would be his last. But his arm held her tightly against him, and she took comfort from feeling the strength of his grip. For surely it meant that he was not dying. Gradually, his ragged breathing grew even, and the tension in his body dissolved. She thought he might have lost consciousness, but his grip on her was still firm and strong.

He did not move and they sat there, for how long she could not say. There was so much blood, her blood, and his.

"Shoran?" she whispered.

"*Morna frya deari*," he said weakly. *Still the fire in your heart.*

And those words, his weak but steady voice, finally broke her.

It all came crashing in on her. Liffy with her throat cut. The mage who cried for his sister. The face of each majren she had murdered, each Laifae's plea for mercy she had not granted. The cold gazes of the men who slew her for the monster that she was.

You are not one of us.

She was not one of them. *Them* who she had fought for. They had murdered her.

You're one of the monsters.

She was their enemy.

A sob escaped her as the image of the knives in the hands of men came at her again and again. Her body trembled as the memory of every one of those strikes pierced her body, her heart and her soul. She relived their anger, their rage, felt every blow.

I'm human, and you are not.

She was not human.

She was not one of them.

Elika curled in on herself as arms tightened around her, and she turned and wept into Shoran's chest. She could not stop those tears. For she understood their hatred of everything she was and was not, the same hatred that drove her hand when she destroyed the Laifae. The same hatred that burned in her blood also drove them to do what they did to her.

"Shed not your tears, my love," whispered the darkness embracing her. "Upon your blood and mine, I will avenge you."

She wept until her tears were spent, and then she stilled, and listened to the strong, steady beat of Shoran's heart. He had not moved, had not spoken again. Only the gentle pressure of his arms around her told her he was conscious and silent. She closed her eyes and slipped away into the welcoming Abyss, where she was a small spider clinging to the strands of the shimmering web. The giant spider watched her from afar but came not near.

CHAPTER TWENTY-EIGHT

Shadow's Vengeance

"It is a secret known only to the tsaren and the Laifae; the dark river of our race is drying. Unlike men and gods, it is not in our nature to grow and multiply. We have no young, no old, only us of the river who arose on the tide of creation. And it is drying, for men are destroying us drop by drop, when they burn our kind in the blood-salt fires, and when they slay us with blood-salt weapons. The magic of our world is fading, and soon, there will be no more dreams. Maybe men will rejoice, but we grieve for that which is destined to die. And ever we plead with the gods to take pity on our kind and shelter us from savage destruction by Man."

The History of Alafraysia and Seramight,

By Mageguard Bluelight

B rief waking moments came and went. Vague flashes of raw awareness and glimpses of light assailed her before she retreated again into uncounted hours of darkness. When consciousness returned, she was back in Arala's room. She wore a light shift and nothing else. A blanket covered her. Behind the curtains was eternal darkness, where the winds never ceased. There was no way to know whether it was night or day in the world of man. Bland indifference followed that thought.

You are not one of us.

Her body was stiff and sore and her head throbbed. She stared sightlessly into the candle-lit chamber, her mind imprisoned inside the dank cellar, where knives came out of the dark to kill her. *Drip ... drip ... drip*, came the echoes of Liffy's blood, as Rory watched on with merciless regret.

You are not one of us.

No, she was not. For that, she was butchered like a beast. Men saw her as a beast, and she could not blame them.

She recalled weeping like a child into Shoran's chest and grew deeply ashamed. She sought a reason to rise and found none. Distantly, she pondered whether Northwind had reached the city, and found emptiness where an emotion should have stirred. He did not need her. Men did not need her. It was their world.

At that thought, those wretched tears came unbidden. What world did she belong to, if not to Seramight?

A door opened silently. A woman Elika had never seen before slipped into her room with a tray of food. The woman was a young tane, dressed in a servant's plain frock. She started when she saw Elika watching her.

"I'm sorry, mistress, I did not realize you were awake." She placed the tray of food on the small table, curtsied and rushed out.

Elika closed her eyes. Soon after, she heard the door open again, and close with a firm click. Solid, steady steps approached her bed. She felt the heat of the man beside her.

Her shame deepened.

"Give me a name," said the voice darker than the Abyss and deeper than the endless night.

Its rumble spread through her chest, shook her and filled her with an even deeper craving of an alien nature. Elika opened her eyes and focused on the soft velvet of his cloak, on the gloves covering his hands. Cold air clung to him and brushed against the skin of her face.

He crouched down and his eyes filled her vision. "A name. Give me a name," he repeated.

Hot, barely contained power pulsed from him with every savage heartbeat, and Elika held strong against his demand that drew the name to her lips.

She sat up with effort and winced at the remnants of pain. She looked down at the clean shift, touched her chest and her stomach where the knives had gone in. Nothing hurt on her skin. Only a deep ache warned her that her body was still healing.

She then looked at his shirt. "You were bleeding."

"I am unhurt."

She knew that was not true. Whatever he did to save her, hurt him. He took on her pain, her wounds. "*Morta neda veria la fia*," she said the words he once said to her. *Blood does not lie for you.*

For the briefest moment, something eased in the tense lines of his face before vanishing again. "Do not distract me with playful words, Aleyala. They will not stop me."

She met his gaze. "I'll not have vengeance in my name."

She felt neither pity for herself, nor anger towards Rory or his men. Might be a part of her was truly dead, but she could not bring herself to hate them. She couldn't bring herself to hate at all. In the place where it once lived, nothing remained save the emptiness of the Abyss.

"They butchered you," he said with restrained ferocity. "They left a blood-salt dagger in your back." Righteous vengeance dripped from every one of his calmly spoken words.

"They did no less than I expected them to do. I'm not one of them," she said, and the words cracked in her throat. "I cannot seek vengeance for their hatred of that which I hated myself."

His gloved hand cupped her cheek. "I cannot allow it to pass. 'Tis the blood of gods that drives me now. I will destroy the whole city if I must, but vengeance will be done." He rose to his feet in a fluid motion.

Elika grabbed his gloved hand. "Please, Shoran. You are his servant, but do not be your master. Do not destroy mindlessly. This is not your fight. You owe me nothing."

"'Tis not so. As your guardian, I failed you. The price of that failure we are yet to pay, and it is higher than you yet realize, for blood is binding. As your protector, 'tis to me the vengeance falls upon. The gods would demand nothing less."

She released his hand. "Last I recall, you wished to kill me yourself."

His eyes flashed in annoyance, his jaw clenched. "I would not have tormented you in death."

A smile tickled her lips. "And that's why we are such good friends," she mocked gently.

Again, his jaw clenched, and without another word, he stormed out.

"Shoran, wait." She leapt to her feet to run after him, but when she reached the door, the dark hall beyond was empty.

Outside, the Abyss was dark and lonely, and she craved the solitude and peace it offered her.

Then his words came back to her. *Upon your blood and mine, I will avenge you.*

Dread filled her gut. A blood oath made by a demigod was unbreakable. He had bound himself to the deed.

She dashed for her clothes. Every movement was a difficult chore. She ached everywhere. Her body shook. Merely pulling on her trousers left her breathless and dizzy. She sat on the edge of her bed, caught her breath, and pulled on her shirt and boots. Even her knife sat heavy in her hand.

On the table, beside her food, was a jug of silversap. She drank deeply of it and darted for the door. She turned around in the hall, seeking his thread, but found the essence of his rage instead. He seemed far closer than he had ever been, as if the link between them had solidified and strengthened. There was no door in sight … she reached for him, walked to the nearest wall and walked through.

As soon as she did, she staggered back in horror. She was back in that cellar. Blood was everywhere. Her body trembled uncontrollably. Pieces of men were strewn across the floor, knives still clasped in severed hands. She tried to understand what she was seeing. Tried to see beyond her private nightmare of the moment when those same men with severed limbs had stabbed her with those blood-salt knives.

She briefly closed her eyes and forced herself to detach from the macabre sight, to retreat into a place deep inside her where horrors could not reach her. Shoran stood amongst the dead, his sword stained with blood. A barely perceptible tilt of his head towards her told her he knew that she was there, but his attention was taken with another.

Rory was on the floor, nursing a stab wound to his stomach. His sword arm was severed at the elbow. The rest of his arm lay beside him, still holding a red-bladed sword. His wild yet mocking eye rose to his assailant.

"Who are ye? What do you want?"

"You hurt what was mine. You hurt she who belongs to the gods."

"What? Speak sense, I don't understand ye. I don't bloody know who you are."

The memory of Liffy's pleas echoed in her ears, followed by the sound of dripping blood filling the empty metal bucket. Elika took a step forward to look at the man who had butchered and slain without pity or remorse.

He saw her. "Spit?" he said and laughed loud and bitter, before coughing up blood. "So 'tis you who brought him here. What powerful friends you have. Why, you never told me you had a demigod lover. Might be things would have gone differently between us, had I known." He laughed and coughed again.

Elika tried, but even now she could not rouse any hatred towards him. Emptiness was all she felt. His life did not matter to her, but for now, the city needed this bastard. And she needed him alive to help Mite.

"Might be best if you stay silent, Rory," she warned him and turned to Shoran. "Not him ... you've killed the men who stabbed me. He wasn't one of them, 'cause he's a rotten coward. Let him go. I can kill him myself when I'm ready."

"'Tis mighty kind of you, Spit. Always knew I liked ye," said Rory, cocky to the end.

"The pledge is made upon your blood and mine. In torment, both of us will live until it is fulfilled." Shoran moved forward.

She blocked him again. "Don't. Men need him, just for a little longer."

"No, they do not. 'Tis the sacred law of gods that I uphold. To spare him would be a crime."

She blocked him again with a hand to his chest. "In Seramight we live by laws of ..." she began.

"Hey, Spit?"

She turned. "Silence, Rory."

He shook his head. "'Tis no good. The bastard's killed me already. Let him finish what he started. Always liked ye, you know. Didn't want to do what I did to ye. Only wanted to set the world to right and slay the monsters."

Elika briefly closed her eyes. Aye, for them she had become the monster. "I understand, Rory. I do."

"Hate me if you will, and I don't blame ye for it. But I've got a favor to ask of ye again. 'Tis not for me, but for another. My son ..." He coughed, then spat out the blood. "He's not tainted with my deeds. And I know you'll do right by him. I need you to keep Mitey honest, El. The lordship he promised me must go to Chelik."

She nodded. "I'll make sure he's given it. He'll be a lord in truth, just as you wanted."

Rory grinned weakly, his head lolled to the side. "And, El ... if it's in ye heart to speak of me to him ... tell him of what I tried to do for the city, for men, and for him. How I wanted to make Terren a better place for him and for the rest of us wretched bastards. Tell him about the good parts of me."

"I'll tell him. He'll be proud of how you fought for men and Northwind."

"Always knew I liked ye, Spit," he slurred as life drained out of his one good eye.

Faster than she could see, Shoran's sword moved and Rory's head rolled off his shoulders.

Elika knelt beside his body. "I didn't wish for his death. I am tired of it, in truth."

"'Tis the burden we bear when we weed the Garden of Fates."

Then she felt the essence of the world bend and flow towards him. The house shook, and stone walls cracked and crumbled. A web made of light emerged from the floor, the ceiling. And everywhere she looked, strands of bright light wrote the same words on the stone:

Upon the wrath of light, thou shall neither harm nor torment the daughter of the gods. Upon the sacred blood, thou shall protect an Aleyala.

She looked around, reread the message again and again, then met his gaze. "Am I ... one of you?" she asked him uncertainly. She wanted to be one of someone.

"Aye, you are one of us, Aleyala." And he extended his hand to her. She looked at it and remembered another hand she had not taken so long ago, belonging to another man.

Tentatively, she reached up and placed her hand in Shoran's and he pulled her up to her feet.

The door to the cellar burst open and Blood Dog charged in, followed by more toughs, Toad amongst them. They stopped abruptly.

Shoran raised his sword, took two steps forward ...

"No," Elika put herself between him and Blood Dog. "He wasn't there. He's innocent of this ... they all are."

But Shoran was looking past her, and when she turned, his gaze was locked with Blood Dog's. Recognition, and so much more, passed between them.

"Elrik Westwater, so you live still," said Shoran, and her mind seized.

Surely that could not be the fifth King Westwater, but a distant relative named after the last king of their bloodline.

"It's been a long time, ye bloody, ill-tempered bastard," Blood Dog replied, and there was no enmity in his voice. Then his gaze moved to her, and moved again to take in the scene, the dead men, the blood and the severed limbs. They lingered on Rory. Slowly, those eyes moved to the glowing writing on the wall. Then ever so slowly his gaze returned to her, and he stared and stared and stared.

"Aleyala ..." he uttered, and there was shocked denial in it.

"Has ale finally clouded your eyes to that which is as clear as sacred light that once shone in your crown, Westwater?" said Shoran.

Slowly, Blood Dog lowered his sword. His face paled. "It cannot be ... she was on the other side ... a half-breed runt, but not Aleyala. The gods had left. Only Arala ..." Again, he shook his head in rough denial. "It is impossible ... she cannot be ... Northwind could not ..."

"Northwind?" Shoran said quietly. "Look closer Elrik, for surely centuries of vice have not blunted your ageless wisdom. Whose face do you see when you look at her?"

The sword fell out of Blood Dog's hand, and his breath caught in his throat. All the while, his horror-filled eyes never left her. "No …" he choked out. Until now, she had never seen that moment in a man's eyes when something strong breaks inside him. Helplessness washed over his face. And it was hard not to pity the ruffian who mocked the world and all in it. "Amelina," he said brokenly.

"Why are you looking at me like that, Dog?" she asked, unsettled, and took a step towards him. "Who's Amelina? Name's Eli …"

An arm came around her shoulders and chest and gently pulled her back towards a warm, solid body. "Tell me, Elrik," a deep voice rumbled against her back, soft and threatening at once. "Did you know she was drinking blood-salt? Were you there to witness it?"

Horror deepened on Blood Dog's face, and an anguished roar escaped him. He fell to his knees. "I didn't know … ye shouldn't even be here," he cried, his eyes never leaving her.

Ever more confused, Elika tried to turn and face Shoran, but he held her firmly in place, as if determined to torment Blood Dog with the sight of her.

"Stop it," she said, turning her head to look up at Shoran. "'Tis not his fault for my choices. Never even met him till the temple. And I didn't want to talk to him either. He's a foul ruffian, no matter what kingly blood flows in him."

Blood Dog flinched at her words and looked aside as if shamed by them. It was not what Elika had intended. Once again, he looked at the writing on the wall.

"Indulge my curiosity, Elrik," Shoran spoke mockingly. "Why *were* you in that temple, drinking blood-salt?"

Blood Dog did not turn as he spoke, his gaze fixed on the writing. "Orolan led me there. I knew not why. He had no voice left in him. And 'tis not for me to question the path shown by the gods. So I went inside, drank the blood-salt and the priestesses took me away to join the others who could not be purged. Orolan watched us through the window, and I knew that I was there for one of them in the group. All a miserable, worthless-looking lot, they were. Nothing about any of them drew my eye. Save a young boy of noble blood. He was a quiet lad. Thought maybe he was an heir of some blasted house, and it was him I was there for." His face turned back to her, and again he stared and stared. Then he raised his gaze to Shoran. "Upon the blood of gods," he said and pushed aside the greasy hair from his neck. "Make it quick, old friend. 'Tis right that you should do it." And he hung his head, exposing his neck to Shoran's sword.

Elika stiffened, tried to take a step towards him, but the arm around her clamped her tighter and refused to release her.

"I have never been one to slay fools, Elrik Westwater. And fool you have become." And with those words, Shoran turned, taking her with him, and the chamber of blood and death was replaced by a long dark corridor.

CHAPTER TWENTY-NINE

Shadow's heart

"For most of the existence of the three realms, no one but the five ruling gods of El'Sandria knew of the existence of the Stone of Chaos. No one even suspected such a terrible weapon could be fashioned from mere blood and salt, both of which are plentiful in the realm of man. Yet not long after the end of Elriad's war against the gods, knowledge of the blood stone found its way into the hands of men. The fifth Northwind king of the Sacred Crown, Areshan, was the first to wield it against my kind. History does not record how he had learned of this terrible weapon. But much of the speculation and blame falls to Elriad, for he hated the ruling gods and had much to gain in using their secret weapon against them."

The History of Alafraysia and Seramight,
By Mageguard Bluelight

In the days that followed, Elika had stopped nursing the wounds from Rory's betrayal, for they went far deeper than her flesh. Instead, she gave in to them. She allowed herself to hurt, to feel what pain she would. To hold it back was useless. Yet in the dark tower, she had discovered peace in the silence, and healing in the solitude.

For want of anything to do, she spent her days in the library, reading or watching the green fire. It was the fire from the gods' realm of El'Sandria, Shoran had told her one day when he joined her beside it. He spoke little and rarely. But in those days, when she sought not the light of the world, but the emptiness of the Abyss, he spoke more.

He told her of El'Sandria, of the gods, of Neka's love of strawberries and her contempt of god Moreg, who loved her despite it. He spoke of the demigods who lived in the realm of light, his sister Inika amongst them. It was the only thing she knew of him. Shoran had a sister. Such a small thing, but Elika buried it away and cherished that piece of knowledge like a treasure.

Often, she would listen to him in silence, allowing his rumbling voice to guide her away from the loneliness of her own thoughts. Once, in just such a moment, his warm hand wrapped around hers, drawing her back to the present.

"'Tis the fire we burn the world with that burns us in turn, Aleyala. Be careful where and why you cast your powers."

Alone in the silence, she had pondered those words for many long hours. Men did not need her to fight their battles. It was a hard truth to accept. For so long, it had been her driving purpose. She had been both arrogant and naïve to think that she alone could save them. Men were saving themselves. They did not need the Rogue Mage or the gods. They did not even need Rory. They only needed hope and the will to fight.

Aye, Rory had killed her. Eli of Bad Penny's gang was dead. In her place sat a shell, a being with no home, no belonging, save the one Shoran had given her.

You are one of us, whispered his voice in her mind, and an answering ache grew in her chest.

There was peace here, in the Abyss. The winds howled beyond, but here, in the tower, there was silence. And each day she spent here, the Abyss wrapped itself tighter and tighter around her, until she was certain it would never release her. The thought troubled her. More so in the long hours when Shoran left her alone, for she knew she could not hide away from life forever. In those listless hours of solitude, she thought of him often and missed him acutely.

Something had happened between them the day he had healed her. Some deeper, darker bond that was not there before had forged itself into her flesh and soul. And she suspected into his, as well. As yet, she had not found the courage to speak to him of it.

Across the three realms, blood held great power. The magic tied to it was said to be more dangerous than any other. She sought books about it in Shoran's library, needing to understand what had transpired between them, why she felt him so acutely since he had healed her. Nor was she blind to his own fight against that link; sensed him wrestle against its hold on him. She sensed his dismay, his torment and bitterness. Book after book she sought on the magic of blood. She had climbed the many stairs and ladders and flicked through many pages writ in the tongue of men and the Laifae.

It was during one of those searches that Shoran came upon her.

He stopped abruptly.

"You seek books on blood magic," he said and she saw the same haunting in his face as she felt in her soul.

"'Tis answers I seek," she replied and glanced at the book she was holding, written in the language of flourished and elegant runes.

He strode towards her and turned the book around in her hand.

She flushed. "'Tis the language of El'Sandria. Might be you could teach it to me one day," she said without raising her face from the pages, keenly aware of his nearness.

She replaced the book on the shelf, then reached for another. Before she could take it, he took hold of her hand. The gesture made her heart start and ache with longing.

He turned her hand palm up and she saw a flash of silver.

She snatched back her hand. "What are you doing?"

"'Tis time you learned how to heal yourself. I cannot teach you without cutting you."

"Oh." She stared at the knife, as from the dark recess of her mind, red-edged blades came at her.

He must have seen her fear, for he passed the knife over his palm, drawing blood. "No mortal blade will ever frighten you again once you learn it cannot harm you."

As she watched, his skin knitted together, and within three heartbeats, the cut vanished.

"Give me your hand," he said gently.

Haltingly, she extended it towards him. Despite her reservation, she barely saw the quick slice across her palm, and hardly felt the shallow cut.

"Do I just wish it gone?" she asked and did just that. Nothing happened.

"'Tis not the magic of the Laifae that heals. To wish for it, is useless. 'Tis the power of life's essence, and that is the well you must tap into. Find your essence, as you find another's. Your true power is not meant to be used to destroy, but to heal."

She reached deeper, seeking her magic. It uncurled, excitedly, eager for freedom, and rushed out in a tangle of black strands surrounding her and Shoran. They wrapped around his legs.

"Pull in the waters of your dark river, Aleyala," he said with mild impatience, sending out his web of light and gently repelling her strands. "Seek instead the light that's yours to wield and fear not its burn."

She focused on herself, on her own essence. It fluttered like a lost butterfly in her hand.

"When you have it," he continued, "guide it towards the wound, for your body is merely a manifestation of that essence. Draw upon your light."

Elika reached for the warmth of her own body and channeled it towards the cut. The skin slowly knitted together. A moment later, she touched where the cut had been. Nothing remained but unblemished skin and tenderness.

"The discomfort will linger a little longer. The memory of the pain is not as quick to subside."

"How long have I been here, since …?"

Since they killed me.

"Time has no dominion here. But ten days have passed in the earthly realm."

Elika could not tear her gaze from his strange eyes, from the darkness that swathed him, from every compelling line of his face. He looked so much like a man, it was hard to remember he was anything more. And it grew harder to hold her yearnings for another kiss at bay. Always, his fleeting presence left her breathless.

Abruptly, he turned away and walked aside.

Would that she could heal the cut to her heart from his sharp rejection of the question unasked. Aye, the question hung between them, burrowing its way to the surface, though neither of them spoke or made any motion to acknowledge it.

"Shoran …" she began uncertainly, not knowing what to say or ask.

It seemed he heard her question regardless, for he stiffened and she saw a battle in him. "Do not tangle us, kitten. You are lost, but I am not your path."

And his harshly given answer finally made her hear the question brewing in her heart. *Can you love me?*

A bitter smile touched her lips at his unspoken answer. *I cannot.*

She was a fool. His heart was taken. "Arala … she meant something to you."

Silence.

"I am not as beautiful as she," Elika said a little sorrowfully and wished to be the woman who had claimed so many hearts.

His eyes slanted towards her—inscrutable, searching … tormented. "You are more beautiful than she ever was, for there is depth to your beauty she never had." He ran his hands through his hair, and without another word, marched out.

She stared at the lonely door through which he had vanished, wondering how such generous words could hurt so deeply.

Soon after, she returned to her room … to Arala's room, and deeply resented the woman who had once lived here.

Elika was tired, but restlessness besieged her, and those yearnings that kept her awake at night. Her mind whirled and spun with thoughts of Shoran, of his kisses, of his arms around her, of the raw anguish in his eyes when she was dying.

She glanced at the bed and saw Shoran there, wrapped in the arms of another woman wearing the gold dress. Elika had been that woman briefly, and Shoran hated her for it.

But she could not stop her fingers from caressing the shimmering gown strewn on the chair, feeling what Shoran must have felt when he touched it …

She snatched back her hand.

You're a fool, Eli, tormenting yourself thus.

Might be it was time to leave this place and never return.

Shed not your tears, my love.

The memory of his voice came from the dark. Her breath caught. Aye, he had spoken those words. *My love.* And it grew impossible to deny her own heart. He was driving her mad … Arala's shadow was driving her mad with images of them together—of her own inadequacy. For she was nothing like the goddess who crushed men's hearts, who still held his heart in the cold grasp of her dead hand.

Elika fled the room. Outside, the hall was dark and forlorn. She could not return to that room, could not bear to be there any longer. Aye, it was time to leave, to find another life for herself. But her mind was treacherous, for a door appeared in the distance to the only place she wanted to go.

Her feet moved.

She pushed on the door. Beyond, the bedchamber was empty.

His bed was neatly made. The room was ordered, forlorn, and aching of lonely centuries he must have spent here.

Her fingers brushed the silk of his bed. She remembered him lying there, naked, asleep, fierce yet vulnerable in slumber.

The compulsion was too strong to resist. She lay down and was immediately surrounded by his scent. So achingly close. She closed her eyes and wished for his kiss, his touch upon her skin. She grew drowsy, sleepy, and all the while, her soul demanded his return.

Fool, she thought harshly and threw out that craving for the Abyss to swallow …

She wrapped her arms around his pillow and felt at peace, for he was close and the ache in her heart was soothed. And she allowed herself to fall asleep.

Slowly, her eyes fluttered open. She was still holding onto his pillow; his scent was everywhere. A fire crackled in the hearth.

Before it stood a shape, his back to her, his hands gripping the lintel as if they might crush the stone. She sat up and put the pillow aside. The muscles in his shoulders twitched.

"In saving you, I have doomed us both." His voice was raw. "You must leave and draw not upon the power of my blood. Demand not what cannot happen."

She did not move. "I … I did not want to be alone in that room. Can I sleep here?"

"You are not a child to sleep chastely in my bed. Leave. Get out."

The deep anger in his voice, the blunt rejection, spurred her to jump from his bed and head for the open door.

Damn you, Shoran. She would leave and never return.

At the door, she glanced at him, for it was impossible not to, and froze. For in that glimpse, she saw not anger but torment. She saw his inner battle and soul-deep pain. *She* was hurting him somehow.

Images flashed in her mind, memories of his arms holding her tight, of dark whispers and brushed kisses, of secret caresses and aching tenderness. *My love.* With his arms he pulled her closer, with his whispers he held her there, with rough denials he pushed her away. Aye, there was a battle inside him. Just as there was one inside her, and might be, she was just tired of fighting.

She closed the door and rested her head against it, gathering her thoughts, wanting to understand what secret anguish he was hiding. He was watching her now over his shoulder with a heated gaze and that sense of inevitability and doom.

His head drooped between his shoulders. "No. Get out." He growled like a wounded bear.

"I can't," she whispered. "Though you are hurting me." She approached him, carefully, as if he was indeed a wounded beast. "Your angry denials belie your deeds."

Silence. But in that silence, she heard him wrestling for words.

"I want another kiss," she pleaded softly.

She brushed his back, and his muscles twitched under her fingers. His hands gripped the lintel harder, and the stone cracked under his fingers. Elika snatched her hand from him. The stone was thick. No ordinary man could crush it.

"The gods would laugh were they to see you here, pleading with me for that which I have no right to offer. Don't do this, kitten. You will regret it."

"I regret many things, one more matters not."

"You do not understand. For my deeds, I have been banished by the gods, despised by them and cursed to live in the eternal darkness, cursed until the harm I have done is once again undone." With those words, his emotions turned into a vortex of invisible power that surrounded them and threatened to strip the stone from the walls.

Elika took a small step back, stunned by his revelation. To be banished from El'Sandria meant he must have committed a terrible sin against the gods. "What did you do, Shoran? What was your crime?"

Silence.

"Tell me," she demanded as fear grew in her heart. "Please … I need to know."

She could see he did not want to tell her, saw the mix of anger and self-loathing flitting across his face. "Like you, I lived as a human once and believed myself to be more human than god. And like you, I abused my power, to intervene between men and the Laifae …" His face grew haunted and hard at once.

Elika suddenly understood why he lived in this forsaken tower. His life was a prison. Serving Syn'Moreg was a punishment. She had suspected as much, had seen the weariness, the loneliness. She saw it now, in his features, the despondent bleakness of a caged man. Only the most grievous crime against the gods would cause banishment from the celestial realm.

"What have you done?" she asked on a breath.

His face turned towards her, and his voice was quiet as he spoke his damming confession. "It was I who gave mankind the secret of blood-salt."

Her world shifted, spun and blurred. Outside, the Abyss was dark, his punishment eternal. He gave men the weapon that brought on the Blight, the weapon that ravaged half of Seramight and Alafraysia, the weapon that shredded the Great Web.

"Aye, I took pity on them in their fight against the Laifae. They knew not how to battle the ethereal magic, for the magic of the gods grew weak in the blood of the Sacred Crowns. So I whispered to them the most guarded secret entrusted to me by the gods. I betrayed them to help the people who had raised me. But the gods kept the true nature of the Stone of Chaos, as they called it, hidden even from their children, lest someone like Elriad used it against them. Thus, I knew not the damage it would do to the Great Web when combined with fire."

He had warned her once; interfere in the world of men, and the consequences will be etched into your soul for eternity. She saw it now, felt it on the emotional vortex encompassing him— regret, anguish, helplessness and above all, unebbing anger. The mistake of his youth, one that reshaped the world of man and the realms beyond it. The Blight was the price of his gift to mankind. So much destruction, so many lives lost. She thought of everyone who had been killed by the Blight. Yet instead of hatred, she felt like weeping for him, for the tragedy of his misguided gift, for his endless punishment.

He was doomed and bound by the laws of gods, and she finally saw the chains that held him. She recalled the helpless rage in Shoran's face when he spoke of human and Laifae age-long warring. It was why he looked away from it, for each day he watched his dreadful mistake grow and bear poisonous fruit.

She stuck her hand in her pocket and withdrew the stone spider. She gazed at it and smiled sadly. "'Tis strange how we stop fearing the inevitable. Were I to kill the spider, would you be free?"

There was no anger in his gaze, only regret. "For an eternal, death is the most coveted freedom," he replied and looked away. "Leave, Aleyala. There is nothing for you here. Were you to give yourself to me, you would be tainted by my crime also. The gods would not look kindly at any union between us. They would punish you and me."

She hated that this being of such power and strength feared the gods. Hated that he was at their mercy, banished, unforgiven and yet loyal to them still. "Damn the gods. Damn then to the Abyss. You have suffered enough. How long is their punishment to last?"

"Until the crime can be undone. An eternity, for it cannot be undone."

His words stoked her anger. Once released, knowledge could not be recaptured and hidden away. He could never atone in the eyes of the gods.

"Damn the gods!" she cried out in frustration. "Nor do I see fear in your face. Why do you hide from me behind their wrath? Why do you fight me so, yet hold me in your grip? What is between us, Shoran?"

"There is nothing between us. Nothing that can ever be." He closed his eyes as if in pain. "I have taken you into my heart, now I must purge you."

"Then purge mine, too, whilst at it."

"Foolish whims of a naïve girl. What know you of heart's pain?"

"Only what you've been teaching me," she bit back.

"Your heart is split in two. 'Tis another whom you want."

"My heart is whole, and it beats for you," she confessed before she could hold back those words and instantly felt foolish and raw and exposed. She bared her heart to his blade and deep would his rejection strike her. "'Tis your heart I ponder. When you look at me, do you wish I was another? Do you wish I was … her?"

He raked his hands through his hair. "No. It would destroy me were you to become like her."

She let out a sigh. She wanted to believe him, more than anything. "Then why do you keep pushing me away?"

Instead of answering, he only shook his head. "Three thousand years, and I'm still a damned fool who craves that which will never be his."

"What did you crave?" she asked softly.

He turned his face to look at her. "A different fate for myself. One I could never have."

"We make our own fates."

"Mortals make their own fates, for their lives are fleeting. Beings like you and me are given ours by the gods."

"What fate did you yearn for?" she asked.

"One where I was just a man," he said and looked towards the window.

After all that had happened, she understood that longing as never before. "To me, that's what you are," she said with a shrug.

"Long have you tangled me with your thread, yet I have not the heart to tear it. Take it away, little spider, and free me. You have not seen the other gods. Your eyes are fixed upon that which is broken, and yet you do not see the ugly cracks. I cannot undo the blood-bonding, but it will grow weaker with time if you do not give in to its draw. Leave," he said harshly.

"I can't." She closed her eyes and leant her forehead on his shoulder, allowing his scent to fill her head until she grew drowsy with need. "One night. Just one. Give me that and I will leave and never trouble you again. One night is all I ask."

He threw back his head and laughed, but there was no mirth in it. "You have bound my heart. There can never be just one night between us. Anything less than an eternity would not be enough. Give yourself to me and you will be forever mine."

His words should have frightened her. Instead, they surged through her, washed away years of loneliness and promised her a home, a place to return to.

"And that frightens you." She moved around him and placed both her hands on his chest. Again, he twitched under her touch.

"You do not understand what it is you stir here," he said roughly.

"Then tell me," she said without meeting his gaze. Beneath her palms, she felt his rapid heartbeat, his heat, his promises. She wanted him to take away the yearning, the need that raged inside her.

His hands knitted in her hair and he raised her face to his. His look was raw and savage. "If you do this," he spoke slowly urging her to understand. "We will destroy each other. 'Tis the irrevocable fate of a union between us, Eli Spider. It is inevitable.

You give yourself to me and you will bind us forever. Bind us and we will break against each other." There was intent belief in his eyes that would not be denied.

"I'm not afraid," she said breathlessly. "Shoran ... kiss me."

"Think well and hard upon it, for I am not the man you think me. I am not a boy in love with life, nor one to give you more than what you see here. Yet you are young and free. I am bound to this tower, and here I will spend eternity to come." He began to push her away by her shoulders.

She gripped him harder, her hands fisting in his shirt. "I'm yours." The truth resounded through her heart. Aye, she was his, for she could not imagine being anyone else's, could not imagine the world where she belonged to anyone else. Could not even imagine wanting anything more than she wanted him now.

His hands tightened on her. His gaze grew searching, his jaw clenched as he wrestled with the denial and need born of loneliness that surely rivalled her own. And she saw the moment he gave in to his heart and hers. Despair and inevitability eased his features. And he looked at her in the way no one had ever looked at her before. It was not love, but raw need, a craving that had to be sated. He looked at her as if she was his silversap and he a man starved of magic.

"And you shall drink upon her lips, her tears, your tears intermixed," he muttered, and his lips were suddenly on hers, hungry, urgent.

When he crushed her against him, she felt such deep relief she almost wept with it. He wanted her. His body trembled with it. *How long has he been alone?*

She flung her arms around him and dug her fingers into his hair as she strained against him. His heat, his scent surrounded her and drowned all thought and emotion but one—*closer.*

His hands roamed over her body.

With equal clumsiness and desperation, she pulled on his tunic.

He stopped and stilled her hands. "Time will not end tonight, Aleyala."

He took a breath, composed himself, cupped her face and kissed her cheek, her lips, then trailed kisses along her jaw down to her neck, her collarbone. He pulled away and taking her hands, tangled his fingers with hers. His palms were callused, the skin rough, which made no sense to her for it was at odds with his lordly bearing. As he raised her hands to his lips, she could not help but notice how thick his fingers were for all their tenderness, and she wondered what it was he did with his hands to wear them so. The thought faded as he wrapped his arms around her and kissed her again, languidly this time.

"*Isa shamorg deiri fia si,*" he whispered as he kissed her neck. And those alien, sensual words caressed the depths of her soul. "*Fia mana. Afaya te mia.*"

She knew not what those words meant, but they filled her with lethargy and drowsiness and the need to merge with him, to meld into his skin and become part of him. His arms tightened around her, and she was not sure whether she was standing or floating. Everything faded into vague shadows and shapes of the room, the fire, and his eyes as he raised his head to look into hers.

"*Ima lesa mana nera elesa, Aleyala,*" he said and his voice was impassioned, his gaze intent.

The words rumbled through her, seared her with some secret promise, imprinted on her. "I ... I do not understand," she said breathlessly, sensing that whatever he had said was too important not to understand.

In reply he kissed her deeply, and slowly peeled aside her shirt. And she forgot those words, for nothing else existed but the feel and taste of him. He broke away briefly to pull off his tunic and throw it aside on the floor, before embracing her in a deep, sensuous kiss. His bare, hot skin against hers sent ripples of forbidden pleasure through her. The silkiness of his skin, contrasted starkly with the hardness of him. A part of her became aware of his raw strength, of how much larger he was than her, of her own insignificance in his embrace ...

"*Fenri nada mana elesa. Ledan nada mana deari.*" His voice was intoxicating. "Fear not my soul. Shy not from my heart."

And his words washed away the tension she did not realize had wrapped her body; softening and melding her body to his. Tentatively, her fingers explored his shoulders, arms and chest, trailing down to his stomach. Of their own accord her lips touched his chest needing to taste his skin, and the intense sensation that coursed through her was at once too much and not enough.

"Shoran …" she groaned, not knowing what it was she asked for.

Again, his lips were over hers, and for a moment they soothed her need. Vaguely, she was aware of his fingers on the buttons of her skirt, of it falling away and his hands drawing her closer and closer.

"*Ima lesa mana nera elesa, Aleyala,*" he whispered again, those words that seared her with some dark power.

Then she was floating and falling, as he lowered her onto his bed. He kissed her neck, her shoulder, her breasts, and she arched beneath him. His hands moved reverently down her body and his kisses followed. Her body moved of its own accord, meeting his caresses. She strained against him, her blood afire …

Fire exploded around them. Elika gasped and sat up. Shoran chuckled against her thigh, where his lips had wandered. "Still the fire in your mind, before you burn us both. Think not of the flame."

"I … I did not mean to …"

He sent his own magic to quench hers and cold air washed over her hot skin. Then the demigod was once again above her, his eyes aglow. He suddenly stilled, his body tensed. "Are you a maiden?"

"What?" Her befuddled mind could not understand him as her gaze drifted down between them, raked his stomach and fixed on his manhood pressed hard against her thigh. She regarded it with not a small amount of trepidation and keen anticipation.

"Have you known a man before?" he repeated slowly, drawing her gaze up.

She shook her head and blushed fiercely. "Does it matter … now? I'm not ignorant. I know what goes on between a man and woman. I grew up on the streets. 'Tis hardly rare to see."

He exhaled, tensed, leant his head against hers and closed his eyes. "'Tis not what I speak of," he said and fell silent.

"Shoran …?" she prompted him in confusion.

In reply, his hand ran down her body, the roughness of his palm strangely pleasant against her silken skin. His hand roamed lower, towards her legs, urging them to part for him. His fingers caressed her, all the while she felt the tension in him.

She grabbed his hand to still him. "Shoran, what is it?"

He opened his eyes and stared into hers. His breathing grew labored, troubled, but he spoke not. Then he did, as if compelled to do so. "There will be no path back, Aleyala. In the eyes of the gods, you will seal that which cannot be unwrit."

"I care not for what is writ or unwrit," she said breathlessly and kissed him again.

He relaxed against her. "*Ima lesa mana nera elesa, Aleyala*," he whispered and made her legs widen more, settling between them.

A web of light ran over his arms, his chest, and jumped the distance between them to flow over her and into her. It was warmth and life and a river of pleasure. She arched from the wonder of it, from the sensation of being one with him. Suddenly nothing made sense, only the need to have him closer.

"*Ima lesa mana nera elesa.*"

His scent filled her head and drowned out those searing words. His skin was silk under her fingers. She wrapped her arms around him. The taste of him made her tremble with want.

He kissed her back fiercely and still she wanted him closer. He slipped between her legs and … pain. She bit his shoulder and moaned. She knew of such things, had heard girls talk of it, still the shock of it took her aback and doused her ardor.

He buried his face in her neck and stilled. "*Fia mana*," he whispered. And the words coated her with warmth, melting away the sting of him. "*Fia mana*," he said again as if he expected her to answer. "You are mine," he said more gently.

"Aye, I'm yours," she replied and nipped his neck to force him to move.

He raised his eyes. His tender hand cupped her face. "Remember that always … no matter what comes between us."

She kissed him. He moved, and she was lost in the softly glowing golden hue of his eyes. And with each kiss, she fell deeper and deeper into the Abyss of their black depths. When a wave of pleasure shook her, she gripped him, afraid to let go lest she fall and fall for eternity. But the wave faded and she breathed in his musky scent. Their clammy bodies went limp, still wrapped in each other.

Slowly, his breathing grew steady under her cheek, whilst his arm cradled her to him. And she fell asleep wrapped in his arms, thinking she had never been safer, and knowing she was finally home.

CHAPTER THIRTY

The Asari of Elder Valley

"Long ago, four demigod brothers raised in the lands of Elder Valley grew curious about the cursed human realm beyond the Sea of Fire. They crossed the perilous sea and found a realm divided into a hundred kingdoms. With the power of the gods, they deposed the human kings and divided man's domain between them, forming the houses of the Sacred Crowns. They took she-human wives, one after another, for the first kings were eternal and their queens were not. They bred a plague of children, the oldest of which they kept as heirs. The rest were cast aside to roam the lands. But ambition festered in the hearts of the discarded sons who craved the crowns of their fathers. Wars were fought, and the first kings were slain one by one by their own children. And their children became kings and birthed more sons with hearts stained by hate and ambition. And so it went, until the blood of gods had thinned and Elder Valley was lost to the heirs of Sacred Crowns, and magic faded from the world. But everything changed when Arala arrived with a gift for mankind that would reshape their world, bring about terrible wars, and cause untold suffering and death. Has there ever been a more foolish gift given to mankind than the sacred, silver-leaved trees?"

The History of Alafraysia and Seramight,
By Mageguard Bluelight

A strange thing it was not to dream and to awake with no feelings save one of complete peace. There was no past, no future, no world beyond the embracing arms, the silken kin, and the warmth of the man beside her. Never had she slept so deeply that no nightmare could reach her. Never had she known such depths of tranquility and gently humming thoughts. And never had she felt so safe as now, cocooned in strength and love, as tender fingers caressed the scars on her back, tracing the lines of old cruelties.

So she lay there without stirring, lest the dreamy moment slip away. She kept her eyes closed, lest the world beyond the musky scent of man invaded the floating clouds of her awareness.

Nor was she yet ready to extricate herself from her rather ungracious sprawl. She was lying on her front, the silk sheet covering only the lower half of her body. Her head was turned away from Shoran ... from her demigod lover. The thought flowed to her lips and tickled a smile out of them.

For long moments, she savored the brush of his fingers along her back, whilst her mind drifted to the night before, to what they had done. She had fallen asleep wrapped in the man she had made love with. She had learned then that no pillow was more comfortable than the shoulder of a man, and no armor more shielding than the drape of protective arms.

He pressed his lips to her scars. "Your breathing changes when you wake," he said over his kiss.

Her smile widened and her body buzzed with awareness and pleasant achiness, and she grew restless for more.

"I was drifting in the clouds," she mumbled dreamily.

"Aye, I've been watching them overhead."

She raised her head and true indeed, clouds were floating above them. She sighed with mild bewilderment, rubbed her eyes and stared at the window. Somehow, she had expected to see sunlight there, for that was what filled her heart. Instead, an oppressive darkness greeted her and dimmed the light inside her.

She turned her head to face Shoran, and instantly felt shy and awkward to look at the eyes that had seen the most intimate parts of her, and at the lips that kissed those intimate parts. Shoran reflected none of those doubts, relaxed as he was in his repose, one arm behind his head, as if he had woken up naked next to her a thousand times. He looked almost bored by it.

She sat up and became aware of her nakedness and embarrassment heated her cheeks, which was ridiculous after what they had done. She pulled up the blanket to cover herself and returned her gaze to the Abyss beyond the window.

"I always wondered what it was about bedding that turned decent men into letches and sensible women into giggling fools," she said, thinking that a part of her did indeed want to giggle.

He chuckled, a soothing sound from deep in his throat. She dared a glance at him and it snagged on his smile. Aye, he was right, there could never be just one night between them. Countless nights would never be enough.

His smile faded. "Tell me how you got those scars." It was a mildly spoken command, and she caught a flash of savagery beneath it.

For the first time, the ugliness of those scars bothered her. She wrapped the sheet tighter around herself. "It was nothing but my own foolishness," she said and told him about the different trials she had endured in the Temple of Arala to purge magic from inside her. "The trial of Syn'Moreg gave me those scars. A reminder of the destructive force of magic. Death, pain, fear, is what it brings, and the whip taught us that lesson."

There was a terrible, dark stillness about him as he listened in silence. When she finished, he was silent for a moment before speaking. "'Tis a grave perversion of their order. Arala would have punished them for such a vile thing, as I would have done."

It stung that in this moment he would think of Arala again.

Elika smiled faintly. "Brood not on vengeance, Shoran, for there is no one left to kill. The priestesses are dead. Though I would not have wished it on them. They sought only to help us." She turned to the window again. "'Tis the darkness that brings on such dark thoughts. I wish it was not so bleak here always. Is it day or night in the world of man? It would be nice to wake up to sunshine now and then."

"If that is what you wish, my love, then so it shall be," he said and the world reordered.

Daylight flooded his chamber. Sunlight poured through the window, warm on her bare skin. Blue skies and bright fields of many colors lay beyond.

She frowned. "Am I dreaming?"

His finger traced an old scar on her back. "You are awake."

She rose out of bed and taking the sheet with her, strode to the window.

Fields of bright wildflowers stretched to the distant white-capped mountains. There was a woodland nearby and orchards surrounded the tower. Two men were weeding a garden below, and a youth was cleaning out the stables. Another was brushing the shining coat of a black stallion. Amongst the horses, there was a striking white mare with a silver mane that seemed half-ethereal in grace and sheen. She broke free from the man leading her out the stables and raced towards the meadow.

It must be a dream, for surely no land was this beautiful.

"Where is this?" she asked.

"Do you not recognize those mountains?"

Aye, she did. She had gazed upon them often when she came for silversap. "Elder Valley. I can see the silver woodland far in the distance."

She looked at him over her shoulder. He lay there, naked and frightening in his glory, deprived as he was of his sheet. And completely unashamed. Sunlight streaked across his body. In daylight, he looked far too human in his indolent repose with his hand propping up his head, his lips upturned in amusement.

"Somehow I thought you might die were sunlight to touch you."

His smile widened.

Her eyes feasted on his chest, his broad shoulders, his face, and the black hair her fingers had tangled in. "How is it that the tower is suddenly here?"

"The tower exists between the worlds. This is the place it can be reached in this realm."

"Whenever I come here, the tower is in the Abyss."

"Not the tower, but you. 'Tis where you chose to visit it," he explained, as if it made perfect sense. "'Tis also where I often chose to be."

She gazed out the window again. "May I go outside?"

Suddenly, arms wrapped around her. "You may go anywhere your heart desires," he whispered into her ear and kissed her neck.

Her thoughts scattered like startled butterflies.

The stones in the wall beside the window pulled apart, and an opening appeared beside the window.

His kisses trailed along her neck, and it grew hard to speak. "You are … making it impossible to leave …"

He pulled away, gathered and swept her hair over her shoulder, and bared her back. "A crime has been committed against you, one I must correct."

Before she realized what he meant to do, he placed his hand on her back and fire radiated from it. She gasped and tried to pull away.

"Stay still. I will not harm you."

"You're burning me."

"It hurts to heal," he said and moved his hand lower.

Warmth radiated from his fingers as he pulled the old wounds from her skin, and she shuddered and tensed as her skin reordered beneath his touch. The sensation of breaking and mending was almost too much to bear.

Then it stopped, and his fingers and soft kisses caressed the fresh skin.

Her body felt as if it was born anew, cleansed of the past, of the worries of the world, and of those scars of pain and loneliness. She turned in his arms and met his lips. Then she was back in bed, bathed in sunshine and his kisses, and surely there was no greater happiness than she found in his gentle ministrations. Never had she felt more loved.

For a long time afterwards, she lay wrapped in his arms, languid and drowsy, listening to his strong heartbeat. And it took great effort to tear herself away. "If I lie here any longer, I'll miss the day completely."

He released her easily, silently.

She dressed under his oddly tender gaze, trying not to feel self-conscious. For it was clear he did not, lying there as he did, shameless in his nakedness, thinking thoughts that stirred him anew.

"Cease your lecherous gazes towards me," he said with a sparkle of amusement. "Else I will be forced to return you to bed."

And damn her, but her chuckle came out as a giggle. She quickly stifled it, and before she was tempted to jump back into bed, raced outside through the newly formed opening beside the window. There were steep stairs beyond, leading down to the garden. She was high up, and the stair hugged the tower as she descended. Once she did, it vanished as if it had never been there at all.

From below, the black tower belied any reality she had known of it. Black as the Abyss itself, it rose high above the trees. It was as magnificent as it was frightening and so very alien in this pristine landscape in the world of man. It was thick at the base, but it was not endless like the hall inside it. The corridor could not have been as long as she had known it. Nor could it have been so endlessly straight. There were many windows, belonging to many empty rooms, and Shoran's life seemed even more stark and bare inside it. He watched her now, from the balcony of his room, a dark, lone figure.

She walked around the tower. A dirt road led away from it towards the woodland and the mountains to the west. Workers smiled and bowed as she passed, calling her mistress, tsarina or princess. Every one of them was a tane. She saw a cook carrying eggs, a maid picking peaches from the orchard, washerwomen in the walled courtyard beside a well.

Elika kept walking around until she came to an enormous set of doors. They were unguarded, but when she approached them, a young man stepped across her path. "Are you lost, princess?" he asked with a slight bow.

"This tower … does it vanish?" she asked and ran her gaze up it to its sharp crown of spires.

"The tower is always here," he replied with a confused frown. "I have been tending to it all my life."

"'Tis bewildering magic this tower possesses," she said distractedly before turning back to the youth. "Who are you, then?"

He beamed. "I'm Trily, Son of Reval."

"Name's Eli," she said in reply and walked past him through the doors into a wide, circular hallway.

Shoran appeared at the top of the black staircase, dressed and descending towards her.

"Master, I found your lady wandering about," said Trily with a bow.

Shoran stopped in front of her. "Come, I will show you the land. We will ride."

"Surely you can traverse it faster through …" she waved her hand. "The walls and the veil."

"We could, but it would not be near as enjoyable," he replied. "I dare say you fancy the white mare."

"How did you know?"

"It was Arala's favorite, too."

The day dimmed, and a sharp knife of jealousy slashed at her joy. She hated that he spoke of the beautiful demigoddess so casually, so easily, as if she was still here. Hated more that the dead goddess was never far from his thoughts.

But he noticed not her abrupt silence as he took her hand and pulled her towards the stables. "No rider was her equal," he continued. "She loved to gallop through the meadows with carefree abandon." He turned to the youth following them. "Trily, bring the white mare and saddle her."

Elika cleared her throat. "Might be I'll try the grey one instead."

"As you wish," he replied, and the boy rushed to his task.

Shoran let go of her hand and approached a restless black stallion. It was a giant horse that did not seem too friendly. Although he allowed Shoran to stroke his neck without fuss whilst another tane saddled him.

"These horses must be very old indeed, if one of them was Arala's favorite," Elika said into the silence.

"They are eternal," Shoran replied as he stroked his stallion. "For they are Neka's creation, a gift for her daughter. This one is Theas. He was Neka's gift to me. Long before I lost her favor," he added a little gruffly.

Trily returned, leading a silver mare, and Elika mounted it with perfect grace, feeling foolishly pleased that Tane Rosalina had taught her to ride. But Shoran paid her no mind as he adjusted the straps of her seat, then checked the saddle of his own steed and leapt gracefully into it.

Elika shook her head at herself. There she was, craving his attention like a love-starved child. Worse still, she allowed it to sting when he didn't notice her efforts. With an inward sigh, she spurred her horse onward.

Shoran, atop his stallion, fell in step beside her as they quickly put the distance between themselves and the tower. A sense of freedom surged through her. She wanted to enjoy the day and the fresh, unfamiliar landscape, but her wretched heart would not release those restless stirrings of envy.

"You speak of Arala often," she blurted out despite her better sense, and she could not hide the note of resentment.

She suspected he heard it, too. Only a deaf man would not. He gave her an intent, sidelong glance. "I speak of her so you might know her better."

"I know enough," she replied blandly, her eyes straining on the lazy path ahead. "Beautiful, graceful, loving and kind. Everyone loved her."

"I see the priestesses have been teaching you legends. Arala was many things, but kind was not one of them, for it was smothered by her vanity."

"She healed the sick and loved children."

"Aye, she did her duty as Neka's daughter."

"And she was your lover," Elika said bluntly and everything inside her tensed in anticipation of his reply.

Yet again, he regarded her in that thoughtful way of his. "Arala was never my lover," he said, and there was an edge to his voice.

She stared at him, searching his face for the truth of it. "She lived in your tower. And they say she was … passionate. Besides, I heard what Meyara said to you. Reval is convinced of it."

"'Tis a common fallacy that Arala was my lover, for no one can believe that a man might not want her, nor that he would be able to resist her advances."

"You loved her, nonetheless," she said and probed his face for a replying emotion.

No emotion, only silence, but in it, she heard his reply.

Elika pulled on her reins to bring the horse to a stop. "I need to know what passed between you and her. You loved her, I can see that it is so. Shoran, tell me, for it will torment me without end. Do not let me drown in my own suspicions."

He pulled up beside her, a faint yellow glow in his eyes. "You delve deeper than you know, into a place best left buried. Aye, I loved her. Arala was made to be loved. She was beautiful beyond compare. So much so, it would shred your heart just to gaze upon her. Her spirit was wild and free. She was bright and alive and everything that is life and air."

The fires of jealousy grew into a searing, wild flame inside her chest, threatening to burn her from within. And damn if she could hide it.

He must have seen it, for his anger receded and he looked away as if pained. "We grew up together and I thought her a sister. I loved her as such."

"Did you … not want her?" Elika asked carefully.

"No," he said abruptly and spurred his horse onward, rigidly staring ahead. "Though she made it hard for me not to."

She rode beside him. "How could you not want her?" she asked doubtfully, despite her good sense telling her to let it be. She could see the memories were hurting him. But she needed to know, for she would drive herself mad, imagining all that never was but could have been.

"With that kind of beauty, there is always arrogance. Her heart was unbound and fickle. I knew were I to give her mine, she would crush it."

"Can you choose who you love?"

A cynical smile touched his lips and his gaze darted to her. "No. But she was not the woman I could ever love as others did. I watched her grow and take lover after lover. At first, she did it to spite me. Then she did it because she loved nothing more than to be worshipped. I watched her shred countless hearts and laugh at the folly of men. Were it any other woman, I might have despised her. But one could not hate a joyous spirit like hers. So I looked aside, and she laughed at my prudish nature. Many a time she sought to seduce me, to show me she could. I did not give in, though she was … tempting. Cruelly so. My rejection of her drove her into rages. She tried everything to break me, even potions to fill me with unwanted lust."

"She tormented you," Elika said with a pang of protective anger.

"In many more ways than merely trying to seduce me. We were kin, and my loyalty to the gods meant I was bound by duty to protect her. Trouble was, no one could stop her when some whim took hold of her. Not even my fervent council. She used the laws of gods to punish those who wronged her, and I was her punisher when she had not the heart to do it herself."

"You loved and hated her," Elika said, understanding. "You would not be the first man to be thus tormented by a woman."

"Perhaps not." He smiled wryly. "I was glad when Arrain Northwind came to these lands, for her attention turned to him. I did not see her for centuries after that, until long after Arrain died and Reval had claimed her. He bound her and all but imprisoned her with his affections. He was jealous of every man who gazed upon her and sought to crush her wild spirit. But it was not to be crushed. Many times she fled from him and came to me … to the tower, to escape him. It was the one place Reval could not reach her. By then, bitterness had reshaped her."

"You cared for her even then."

"Always. No matter her deeds or moods. Though my love was not the type she wanted. And despite everything that came to pass, she was not without a heart. Then one day, she finally came to me asking for the one thing no one could give her. But she had hoped that my banishment from El'Sandria embittered me enough to spit at the laws of the gods."

"What did she ask for?"

"A child." He slanted her a look. "Always, she wanted a child. Though she was Neka's daughter, there was too much of a Laifae in her. Reval could not give her a babe. Neither could any human."

"But you could?"

He stared ahead. "Aye, for I am more god than human. Even were I willing to indulge her desire, a child between us would have been forbidden. There was a chance it could have been the foretold trika, a child carrying the blood of humans, Laifae and the gods. They would have punished me and her for conceiving such a creature."

"Why so?"

"A trika is foretold to be more powerful than any other being across the three realms, for they can drink deeply out of all three wells of power, the Ethereal Essence, Celestial Spirit and Elemental of the Earthly. Fates demand that every power must be balanced and countervailed. A trika would unbalance the carefully guarded natural order, and lead to the destruction of the spheres."

"You say that with certainty."

"'Tis the Fates. The crows have sung it. That which is possible is always doomed to pass."

"Then it seems to me that the realms are always doomed to die."

"Aye," he said slowly, as if it was obvious and needed no stating. "And 'tis our task to forestall that inevitable end."

They rode in silence for a time through a wild orchard of apples and apricots, as she pondered what he had told her. "Tane Igla was Arala's daughter," she said after a while. "Arala had many children by humans."

"Aye, all her children were tanes," he replied whilst ducking under a low-hanging branch.

"'Tis a baffling thing why the tsaren and Arala reject their children, why they are so hateful of them. You say the tsaren cannot have them, yet what of the tanes?"

He cast her an odd glance. "Do you not see what they are, Aleyala?"

"They are … strange, but harmless," she said with a frown. "Their nature is not one to be despised. Though Lady Rosalina is a trial, I find," she added.

Silence. One of those thoughtful ones, as if he was seeking the right words. When he spoke again, it was softly, as if afraid to startle her. "They are not children of their bodies, Aleyala. Nor of their soul. A tane is a dream that dreams itself. It is a dream that wants to live and be believed. It lives as long as it wants to live and fades when time to die is nigh. Tanes exist in both worlds but cannot live in either. When the spheres of the Ethereal and the Earthly part, and the realm of dreams drifts away, they cease to be."

Everything in her recoiled at his words. She shook her head furiously. "They are real. They speak and touch and breathe."

And feel no pain or cold or heat.

He stopped his horse and sidled close to hers. Then took her hand and opened her palm. "Imagine an apple."

She frowned. "Can you not do it?"

"'Tis a well of power I do not drink from."

Frowning still, she did what he asked. An apple appeared in her hand.

"Touch it."

She did, with her other hand, then lifted it to show him. "It feels like an apple."

"Taste it."

She bit into it and spat it out. "It tastes of … nothing."

"It is a wish you brought to life. It feels and looks real, but it tastes hollow, for it is hollow. Its existence is tied to your wish."

The apple fell out of her hand and hit the ground with a dull thud. She stared at it for long moments, recalling Bill and his odd tales, and Igla and Pebble and even Lady Rosalina. Shadows of somebody's dream, all of them.

Not even the gods can kill a dream.

The apple vanished.

"Pebble is … not real," she said dully, and could not fight a strange swell of grief.

"'Tis a hard thing to ponder. Many a scholar has tried, and not even the gods are certain of that answer. You need only ask yourself, is he real to you?"

Elika stared at the place on the trampled path where the apple had vanished. She thought of his songs, his anger when she was killing the majren, his kindness and fear for her. Then she recalled his fear that she would turn against him were she to discover what he was. "He is real to me," she said at length. "Be he a dream or phantom, he is a friend to me."

Shoran's lips curved, clearly pleased with her answer. "I always thought that anything that wants to live should be allowed life and peace." He spurred his horse to ride on.

"How do the mages kill a dream?" she asked as she joined him.

"As you destroy any dream. You make it believe it is impossible for it to exist. If you reshape a dream to be what it cannot bear to be, it fades away. They die because they know the time for them to die has come."

A sickening suspicion entered her mind, something Bill had said long ago. "They are tortured," she said with a wince.

"'Tis a brutal and slow death they suffer, whether pain touches them or not."

"When Bill and Igla died, they did not fade."

"In the joint realms, they leave a shell behind, an imprint of their body."

She recalled that Bill and Igla had not decayed in many days since their passing. They looked frozen in time, as if sleeping. She had not pondered it then, thinking the distance played tricks with her mind.

"'Tis a terrible thing magic," she said. "How does one conceive a dream into a child?"

"The tsaren, though shaped by the gods, are barren beings, for they were forged from the Black River. Yet they crave the children of the flesh. It is their one weakness. And here, in the earthly realm, the deepest desires of their heart merge with the elemental magic of the earthly and take true form."

"Arala was half Laifae … then her father was a Laifae."

"It was not his seed that gave Neka her daughter, but a piece of his black water. Goddess Neka took his essence and combined it with her own soul and body. 'Tis the magic of the gods. One that Arala could never fully master."

They rode in silence again, and after a while, despite her grim thoughts, her foolish heart grew light. Arala was not his lover.

~

They rode into the fields of wild flowers and Elika had never felt so alive, so wildly delirious. Aye, foolish indeed was her heart and mood, as she laughed and spurred her horse on into a gallop. Shoran gave chase before overtaking her. Afterwards, they slowed to a leisurely pace, riding with no obvious direction. It was a perfect day. And it was hard not to stare at him every moment as they rode. There was such power and beauty about him, it hurt her chest to gaze upon him, at those lips that did such wonderous things to her body …

"If you do not stop gazing at me with such salacious intent, I fear I might have to give in to the temptation."

She chuckled. "'Tis hard to do when the air is so balmy and the scent of wildflowers so heady."

Without a word, Shoran stopped his horse, jumped off and reached up to pull her down from her mare. He kissed her deeply before setting her on her feet. But her arms were around his neck and she did not want to release him. His kisses grew more demanding. And before long, they were lying naked in the grass, whilst their horses grazed upon the flowers nearby.

Elika had never been so giddily happy as she lay beside him, staring up at the cloudless sky. There was no past, no Eli Spider, only the present.

Yet her mind was treacherous. Ever it steered her thoughts towards darkness, for it was hard not to grow suspicious of such joy. So rare were such moments in her life that she had learned to grow suspicious of them. The weight of happiness, Penny would say. The fear of joy, they called it. Ever such times would come to an end, and ever more bitter and dark the following days would seem.

"It seems like a dream. I fear it will end," she spoke her thoughts aloud. "I'll awake and you will be gone."

"Stay true to me and I will be yours forever," he replied languidly.

"I am not the one who's likely to stray. 'Tis the fickleness of men," she teased.

"'Tis the fickleness of fickle hearts, my love," he teased back and brushed his lips against her temple.

Elika rolled to gaze into his face. "You are half Sachi," she said a little wistfully, running her fingers along his jaw and cheek. Then she smiled wryly. "I have their look, but they always told me I was not one of them."

"You are not."

She took her hand away, feeling oddly rejected again. "How can you know that? How can they?"

His lips turned up. "Your eyes are not black."

She frowned. "All Sachi … even half-breeds have black eyes?"

"'Tis an indelible mark of their kind."

"Then why do I look like them? Why do I feel a vague kinship with them?"

He brushed her cheek. "'Tis not the Sachi, but the gods you feel a kinship with. The Sachi have served the gods since the beginning of time. For that, the gods have gifted them with features that resemble their own."

She could not help but shake her head. "The gods are vain indeed. Still, I'd rather be one of the Sachi than the gods."

"If that is your wish, then 'tis an easy thing for me to grant it." He rolled onto her, kissed her deeply, then abruptly rose.

Feeling lethargic, she questioned not his assertion. Instead, she watched him dress, such a mundane task that made him seem like any other man. And it was strange how much pleasure there was to be had in watching the simple movements of his body, the gentle ripple of muscle and the sheen of skin as he dressed. When he was fully covered, and pulling on his boots, she sat up with a sigh and reached for her tunic.

He crouched in front of her, his glistening eyes level with hers. "'Tis time I took you to a place where you will know no strife, only acceptance." He rose and pulled her up by her hand. "We will visit my mother's tribe. They will accept you as one of their own, for you are now mine."

His words washed her with warmth and some deeper fear she could not quite grasp. But then his lips were on hers and she forgot that stirring fear.

They rode towards the western mountains as the sun began its slow descent towards their icy peaks. The land was bright and rich with life. There was a sense of agelessness about this valley. That comforting unchangeability, as if the world was frozen in a perfect moment of some distant time. How easy it would be to spend the ages here, to forget there was another world beyond this sleepy valley, shielded as it was by mountains of ice and fire.

It was close to dusk when they reached the silver trees of Gods' Wood. Shoran dismounted and helped her down. She suspected his chivalry was merely an excuse to kiss her some more.

"We do not ride but walk the rest of the way," he said after he placed her on her feet. "'Tis tradition for guests to arrive on foot. The lands of the Asari tribe start at the edge of this wood."

They pressed ahead, leading the horses, pushing aside fruit-laden branches. He led her deeper into the wood than she had ever dared venture, where the trees grew thick and unruly, before becoming tame again. He plucked a fruit from a thick branch and offered it to her, then picked his own. They ate in silence and they strolled through the trees, and once again that sense of giddy joy warred with her fear of its inevitable end.

The silvery trees fell away abruptly, and they walked into a wide, grassy clearing. A village of tents was nestled here, around a slender tower of green stone and a webbing of silver veins. The tower was reminiscent of Shoran's black one, save that it was not as tall or imposing.

Throughout the village, Sachi men worked and crafted beside their tents, whilst women tended communal fires. A small group of barefoot children played with sticks in the distance.

A cry went up and faces turned towards them. The villagers stilled. A hush fell over them.

An old man came forward and bowed. "Welcome home, Shoran."

"Spare your old back the bowing, Joran, and do recall that you once bounced me on your knee."

The image of this stooping man bouncing Shoran on his knee tickled a smile out of her.

"There is no harm in courtesy, even at my frail age," Joran replied. His old eyes shifted and found her. An alarmed expression crossed his face, as if he could not believe what he was seeing. Catching himself, he bowed abruptly. "Aleyala, you are unknown to us."

"I have not been here before," she replied.

His distress seemed to grow. He turned to Shoran. "The tower has not lit up in over a thousand years ..." he stuttered. "Is she ... yours? You know the laws ..."

"She is mine, but she is not of my blood. Though our bloods are now bound," he replied and stepped forward, shielding her from Joran's sharp gaze.

At that moment, a group of young women ran towards her, went to their knees and placed flowers at her feet. "Aleyala," they said as they did so.

Elika stepped back. "'Tis no need for that," she said awkwardly.

Shoran paid them no mind as he continued to address the old man. "I wish to speak with Effina. Is she in the village?"

"She returned not long ago from Kaycove," the old man replied. "She will be glad to see you. It has been a long time since you graced us with a visit."

They followed old Joran into the heart of the village, towards the largest tent. All the while, women ran ahead and threw flowers at her feet as she walked.

"Welcome, Aleyala."

"You honor us."

"With your light you grace us."

Elika could take no more. "Ladies, do not grovel at my feet. 'Tis foolishness of the highest order. Nor do I gain pleasure in trampling your flowers. Though kind you are to throw them at me. Just let us pass in peace."

The women halted with their mouths ajar, their hands frozen on flowers they carried in their baskets. Then they bowed. "As Aleyala wishes," they said uncertainly and followed at a respectable distance.

Elika glanced at Shoran, who looked like he was trying to hide a smile.

"Having flowers thrown at your feet sounds much nicer than it is," she mumbled and his lips did twitch then.

It seemed news of visitors travelled faster than they walked. As they approached a dark green tent, decorated with silver thread, a tall woman waited for them beside it. She was clad in a brown robe adorned with leaves, reminiscent of those worn by the priestesses.

"Shoran." She said his name with disapproval. "Rare is it now that you return to us."

"It could not have been so long, Effina, since you look not a day older than when I last saw you."

"It has been six hundred years," she said pointedly, her tone chastising. "Little do I care for your flattery when you avoid us for so long. And now you bring a stranger to us." Like the old man, she looked unsettled as her eyes roamed over Elika's face. "Aleyala … how is that possible?"

"Name's Eli," she replied if only to hide her discomfort. "Eli Spider …"

"Spider!" The priestess blanched and her gaze flew to Shoran.

Something must have passed between them for he wrapped a protective arm around Elika's waist, drawing her closer.

"Is she for the tower?" asked the woman. "There are no signs of the gods, no warming of the tower stones. If she traverses …"

"No," he said and his voice grew dark. The arm around her tightened. "She's not to step foot into that tower, Effina."

A cold wind blew past and died.

The priestess was clearly taken aback. She looked hard at Elika and her hand flew to her mouth. "Her eyes … I know them. It cannot be …" Her distress grew.

"Let us speak," Shoran said abruptly, stopping her, it seemed, before she said anymore. He turned to Elika. "Stay here. I wish a word in private."

"If you would speak of me …" she objected, wanting to know why they looked at her as if she was the goddess Neka herself come to earth.

"Wait here," he said more firmly, and it was his restrained agitation that held her from arguing back. Then, as if he could not help himself, he cupped her face and brushed his lips against hers.

"Shoran!" The priestess boomed

Elika started and broke their kiss.

"Release her! What mean you by this outrage?" the priestess demanded.

Slowly, Shoran turned his face to the horrified priestess. "'Tis a daughter I bring you, Effina," he said quietly. "*Ima lesi mana elesa.*"

She put her hand to her chest and shook her head in sharp denial. "No. If my dire suspicions are correct ... you cannot. Neka will destroy you. You hold no more favor with them." ·

Fear seeped into Elika. He had warned her their union would be frowned upon by the gods. She thought nothing of it then, but somehow, here in this place, that warning became stark reality.

"'Tis too late to deny it," he replied gravely.

Effina's face hardened. She spun on her heel and marched into her tent.

Shoran followed her inside, and the day seemed to grow darker. He was keeping secrets from her, thought Elika, secrets to do with her and her birth. She should have heard voices from the tent, for barely a piece of fabric was between them, but a wave of magic passed over it and she heard only silence.

Whilst she waited, the Sachi folk approached her one by one, placing flowers at her feet and murmuring reverent greetings. A woman offered her an unfamiliar fruit from a basket she carried. "Aleyala, for you."

For fear of offending her, Elika took it and thanked the woman somewhat gruffly.

Shortly, Effina strode out of her tent, tense and clearly unhappy. "Come inside, child," she said, looking intently at her.

Elika did as she was bid, glad to get away from the attentions of the villagers.

The tent was deceptively spacious inside, with a pile of sleeping furs in one corner and an audience chair in the center. A thick rug covered the ground. Dried branches and flowers made sparse decoration. It was the way of the Sachi to choose simplicity over lavishness, and small comforts over opulence.

Shoran stood to the side, his hands behind his back, his face solemn.

In the center of the tent, Effina lowered herself into what looked like a throne woven of silvery branches. "Come forward, Aleyala."

"Name's Eli," she repeated, if only to remind herself of that and dispel her growing unease.

"Eli *Spider*," the priestess said pointedly.

Elika glanced at Shoran, seeking to understand what was happening.

"Answer my questions, girl. He is not to interfere in our business. Merely to observe."

She turned her attention back to Effina, and ire rose in her chest at the priestess' abrupt demands. "You did not ask a question."

"You are known as Elika Spider. Is this correct?"

"Aye," she replied uncertainly.

"Tell me who gave you that animal's title."

She scrutinized the priestess. Not a moment ago her people were laying flowers at her feet. Now the priestess addressed her as a subject. "If you believe that I'm Aleyala, what authority do you have to demand answers from the daughter of the gods?" The question was one of curiosity, nothing more. She needed to understand the hierarchy of this place to know how to deal with this woman.

The priestess, however, stiffened with affront and sat straighter in her chair. "I have god-ordained authority to ask you these questions, Aleyala. In this place, the children answer to me and I answer only to Goddess Neka. So tell me who named you *Spider*."

Elika shrugged. "Always had it, at least since I joined Bad Penny's pack." Her Dae accent grew thick as her mind went back to a time so far from here. "It's 'cause I could climb roofs and walls like one." A wistful smile touched her lips. "No one in my pack was faster than me at climbing. See?"

"I see. And who are your parents?" Effina asked, and there was now a note of kindness in her voice.

Again, Elika looked at Shoran's impassive face. She had human parents who had abandoned her, but they were not her true parents.

"Do not seek answers from him," said the priestess. "'Tis your answer I require."

Again, the woman's tone grated. Elika crossed her arms. "Don't know why you are asking me these questions, but I have no parents. They're dead. Been dead too long for me to remember them."

Effina's face did not change. "Then who has guided you to adulthood?"

Elika's anger grew. "'Tis not your need to know this. But if you must pry, then I'll tell you who I am." She made a mock bow, dramatically spreading her arms as Pebble might have done. "A thief, a Dae, the one they call the Rogue Mage. Lived on the street most of m'life. Killed men and mages and stabbed more than a few of them as well. You and your Sachi priests and them damned nosy tanes got it into their heads that I am a tsarina, Aleyala, Arala, or a daughter of the gods. Been called human, magic-lover and magic-hater, and Laifae too. See, everyone's got their own thoughts as to what I am. Might be I'm all of them or might be I'm none. I care not what power or woman bore me. Nor whether I'm a child of the godly womb or that of a poxed whore. 'Tis all the same to me, you see. 'Cause there was no one there to claim me, save Penny. And thus, first and last until I die, I'm Eli Spider of Bad Penny's pack."

A taut moment of silence followed her outburst. Then Effina's face softened. "Still the fire in your heart, child. 'Tis a terrible thing to befall you, one which I cannot correct, save that I might welcome you into our ... *pack*. And offer you a safe place to return to, where you will be loved."

Elika's anger fled, replaced instead with bitter resentment. "The Sachi always chased me away when I sought a place amongst them."

Effina did not seem pleased to hear that. "Our distant cousins forgot much and saw little when it came to you. Though they had no right to claim you, sanctuary should have been offered to you. You can only become part of a Sachi tribe if you are born to it or bonded to one who is born to it." She glanced at Shoran, then turned back to her. "I am told you gave yourself to this man. You were a maiden at the time."

Elika flushed but remained silent.

"You must answer me, for I cannot accept you into our tribe until I know the truth of what has transpired."

Elika sighed and nodded. "Aye."

"You gave yourself freely to him."

"Aye," she said slowly and again flushed at the impertinent questions.

"And has your blood mingled?"

Elika blinked, about to deny it, when an image flashed in her head of Shoran covered in her blood and his, healing her wounds whilst his blood dripped onto her. She nodded, again looking to him, uncertain what the questions signified.

Effina kept her face steady, though tension bracketed her mouth. "Then by our laws and those of the gods, you carry the blood of a Sachi, and you have accepted his gift. Just as you granted him the gift of your blood and purity." She rose from her chair. "This cannot be undone. You are a part of this tribe, whether you will it or not. We will mark the ceremony of the cleaved souls with the feast tonight in honor of our new daughter."

As she strode past, she halted and placed her hand on Elika's cheek. A small, sad smile touched her lips. "I welcome you with joy, my daughter. The two of us will speak again. Take not to heart my abruptness. 'Tis a grave and callous shock Shoran has dealt me. Nor is this the manner in which he should have brought you to us. From what he tells me, he knew of you for some years and kept you from us. I am ... deeply aggrieved with him. Nevertheless, I am happy for you both." With those words, Effina left the tent without glancing at Shoran. Once outside, she called out to the village to prepare for the soul-joining feast.

Elika watched the priestess stride away and doubts ate at her.

Shoran strode to stand in front of her. He lifted her face with his finger under her chin. "Cleaved Souls ceremony is an ancient tradition, given to the Sachi by the gods. It recognizes you as the daughter of this tribe. This will always be the place where you will find sanctuary. Do you wish for this? If not, speak now, for the acceptance is irreversible. You will belong to this tribe and no other. You will no longer belong to Penny's pack."

"Effina said I was already part of this tribe whether I wish it or not."

"Aye, they have accepted you as their own. This is now about you accepting them, about you breaking bonds with your past allegiances and eschewing any new ones."

A crow cawed above them and her head snapped up.

The white-tipped crow sat on the beam above the door, his head tilted, his yellow eye trained on her, as if he too had come to witness her decision.

"How did *you* get here, you damned creature?" Elika muttered.

Ignoring the bird, Shoran turned her face back towards him, waiting for the answer.

Three women came into the tent. He raised his hand, and they halted. "Eli?" His deep voice was a caress upon her soul, compelling in its power. "Are you ready to leave your past behind, to leave Bad Penny's pack?"

Everyone always left their pack. It was a way of things. She always knew her time to leave would also come one day. Still, her heart turned over painfully in her chest at the thought. She thought of Penny and Mite. They had their own family, they had their new pack. Mite was wedded. Penny belonged to Anten. Then she thought of Rory and the knives in the dark. She need not be alone. She had Shoran now, and he was giving her a family, a Sachi family. She would belong at last. A gift from a demigod. A wish fulfilled. And yet …

Yet everything was spinning too fast for her to truly understand it, a blur of rough, ill-thought decisions that would reshape her life. "I feel like I'm trapped in a dream," she whispered. "One I never want to wake from. None of this feels real. And yet, sometimes it feels far too real and … frightening."

His lips brushed hers and she was sinking again into his dark eyes.

"'Tis not a dream, but real and binding. The ceremony and your acceptance will seal our fates, a joining of souls neither gods nor time can break. Do you wish for this?" he asked again. "Do you wish to become the daughter of this tribe?"

Her head swam. He was offering her an eternity of love and acceptance. She nodded, for she could not walk away from so beautiful a dream.

The women were suddenly upon her. They took her away before she could say more to him. Pulling her along by both hands, they led her to a river, where they washed her and dressed her in the Sachi robes. They brushed her hair and sang to her. Through it all, Elika was near delirious with a strange sense of floating outside her own life. A dream. This was a dream and she would live it and take every moment of it for her own. Even if it ended come dawn, she would cherish and savor it forever.

Dusk had fallen when she was returned to the village, and her heart jumped and skipped in her chest when she saw Shoran waiting for her. He was dressed in Sachi clothes, sitting on a carpet on a dais in front of the large fire, around which every villager had gathered. Effina sat beside him.

Elika walked towards him. When he saw her, he rose, and his eyes lit up in the way no man's ever had when they gazed upon her. Her heart danced and sang and did a silly flip.

"Is this real?" she whispered when he took her hands and softly brushed her lips with his.

"This is real, my love," he whispered back.

The feast began with drums and songs and music from long pipes. There was dancing and platters of fruit, sweet breads and cheeses. Poles were erected around the dais and decorated with flowers, vine leaves and branches from the silver trees. Villagers came forward to offer her gifts made all the more special for having been fashioned by their hands. There were rugs and light summer dresses, a Sachi blanket of many colors, and woven baskets filled with small things she might need in her new life— soap, hair brush, washcloths and cushions, and many such little things. A lump rose to her throat and tears threatened. These people were her pack now and as they were introduced to her one by one, she made certain to remember each of their names.

Afterwards, Shoran pulled her to the fire, into a Sachi dance the others knew by heart. She was clumsy, but she had drunk enough fruit wine to drown out her shame in stumbling and tripping through the steps. With a rumbling chuckle, Shoran was always there to catch her and stop her from falling.

Then he led her to the priestess, knelt before her and pulled Elika down beside him. Effina spoke words in the tongue of the gods and produced a slender crystal with sharp edges. "Both of you must grip it tight until blood flows into this stone."

The crystal was just long enough for two hands to hold on to it side by side. Their blood flowed and mingled in the crystal and it turned red and glowed. Then the priestess took it away, placed it on a stone pedestal and hit it with a hammer. The crystal stayed whole. The priestess nodded and held it up for everyone to see, upon which a cheer went up.

Elika remembered to heal her palm, as Shoran had taught her.

"Rise daughter of the Asari tribe," Effina said and there were tears of joy in her eyes. "Rise my daughter," she added with a smile and her eyes glistened. Then she kissed Elika's cheek. "'Tis happiness you bring me," she said before bestowing a kiss to Shoran's cheek. "Long had I hoped for this, my son," she whispered to him and walked aside to dab the corners of her eyes.

From atop a nearby tent, the white-tipped crow watched them. It cawed and cackled and took to wing, circling above them, as if it too partook in the feast.

Elika's head swam as Shoran's lips found hers … else she found his. He tasted delicious and warm, sweet wine upon his tongue. And she forgot where they were … until he gently pushed her away. "Do not still that fire, my love," he whispered seductively into her ear as he took her hand and led her to the edges of their grassy clearing illuminated now by moonlight.

The music and laughter grew distant. He pulled her into a tent at the outskirts of the village. It was his tent. She knew so instantly. Clothes to fit him were laid out, though their style was unfamiliar to her. There was lonely simplicity about the lack of everything beyond the necessary. Six hundred years since he's been here, she thought, and yet, everything looked freshly laid out and clean. Nothing was faded. The scents were of fresh flowers scattered over bright rugs on the floor. Brushed furs were laid out on a low bed for two people. Amongst the simplicity, there were many little comforts: plush cushions beside a low table, baskets with folded clothes, a mesh around the bed to keep the insects from you whilst you slept. A beautiful Sachi blanket stitched from pieces of many different fabrics was folded neatly beside the bed.

"This will be your tent whenever you stay with the tribe," he said. "'Tis a simple life we prefer, to keep our spirit light and uncluttered of needless burdens. But nothing you wish for will be denied you."

"Why have you kept away from here for so long?" she asked.

He cupped her face and moved his lips close to hers. "There was nothing for me here to return for, save dusty memories, grief and longings for things that could never be," he said and kissed her before she could say anything more. His arms encircled her, wrapped her and crushed her to his body as he drank from her lips.

He undressed her slowly, and whispered things to her in a language of the gods. Words she did not understand, yet they flowed like warm kisses through her, caressed her soul, heated her body, and dizzied her with bliss. And she craved more of them. She repeated the words back to him as he kissed her body, and she knew they did something to him as well, for he shuddered and grew more ravenous.

Then he made love to her, whilst the dancing and music continued into the night. Once, when she opened her eyes, she thought she saw Priestess Effina watching them from the tent flap, with a crow perched on her shoulder. It could not have been, however, for she blinked and there was nothing but dark shadows where she thought they had stood.

CHAPTER THIRTY-ONE

Orolan

*"In Alafraysia and Seramight, there are two towers that belong to
the gods. The Tower of the Abyss and The Tower of Light. One
was built by God Moreg, the other by Goddess Neka. Each has a
different purpose. The Tower of Light is used by the gods as a portal
into our realm when the celestial sphere brushes past our own. Eagerly
do we await their return. Three branches of our river guard and
watch the Tower of Light for signs of their arrival. It is through this
portal that Arala arrived into our world. The first time she had fled
Reval through that tower, he had sought to destroy it so that she
would never leave him again. He might have succeeded, had the deed
not caught Syn'Moreg's notice. His wrath was swift, the punishment
long-lasting. He imprisoned Reval in a cage fashioned of silk and
light. So mockingly flimsy and yet so strong was his prison, that not
even Arala could break it when she eventually learned of Reval's
plight. She went to Syn'Moreg and pleaded for him to release her
beloved. Syn'Moreg heeded her pleas and released Reval. By then, our
glorious tsarin had spent fifty-three years in the cage, and the
imprisonment affected him deeply. He became withdrawn and sullen.
Arala blamed herself for his suffering, and in her regret, she offered
to be imprisoned by him in a gilded cage until he saw fit to release
her. He agreed, and for fifty-three years, her cage hung from the ceiling
of his chamber. Reval watched her and fed her, but he spoke not to
her, nor allowed any other to look upon her."*

The History of Alafraysia and Seramight,
By Mageguard Bluelight

It was not a dream, thought Elika as she stretched and looked over the comfortingly plain Sachi tent that was to be her home. The bareness of it spoke of a simple life, free of the clutter of worries. Aye, she now belonged to a Sachi tribe.

Upon her cheek lingered the imprint of a recent kiss. She turned her head and found herself disappointingly alone. She brushed the place where Shoran had slept beside her. Still warm. A trace of his scent still lingered in the air like a phantom. She smiled, feeling foolishly giddy. Restless energy buzzed through her, and she jumped out of their roll of furs and blankets and found her clothes from yesterday gone. A light Sachi dress was neatly folded on a stool. She threw it on and went outside.

There was no sign of the revelry from the night before.

Though the sun was high, there was a sleepy feel to the village. The men were mending, and working, or packing small trading wagons drawn by ponies. The women carried baskets of washing to the river, hung strings of fruit to dry in the sun, or wove all manner of items from thin branches and wicker. Everyone moved at a leisurely, unhurried pace Elika was not used to. Her eyes skipped over the scene until they latched on to Shoran. And just like that, nothing else existed in the world.

He was speaking with a young, and far too attractive woman. Cutting jealousy hit Elika before she could stop it, and no amount of chiding herself could abate it. Never mind that nothing about his manner suggested he was wooing the girl. But he was smiling, and the woman laughed and touched his arm. And Elika wanted to singe that hand …

A spark of light burst on the woman's hand and vanished. She cried out and snatched her hand from Shoran. He turned his head towards Elika, his eyes dancing with amusement, though his smile was gone. The woman followed his gaze and abruptly strode off, rubbing her hand.

Elika hugged herself, feeling a hundred types of wretched. She had to find a way to control her erring magic and stop it from acting out her every errant thought.

"I didn't mean to do that," she said glumly as Shoran approached.

"I am flattered by your jealousy, my love, but it is misplaced," he said dryly.

"I'm not jealous," she lied, and her blushing face betrayed her. "Magic just escapes me sometimes."

A smile tickled his lips. "Shara is deeply in love with the man she is speaking with now, and always has been."

The woman was indeed gazing at a young Sachi man with love-stricken eyes, whilst he examined her singed hand.

Elika felt a hundred types of fool.

Shoran twined his fingers through hers and pulled her along. "Come. We are to have breakfast with Effina. She wishes to know you better."

When they entered Effina's tent, she was not alone. A white-tipped crow was perched at the low table set for them. She was feeding the bird a small berry from her hand.

The crow cawed at Elika when she entered.

"You know this girl?" the priestess asked the crow.

A loud caw was her reply, then a rattle, which sounded like a laugh.

Elika narrowed her eyes at the crow. "'Tis a pestilent bird that follows me. I'm yet to catch it and eat it." She made an abrupt movement with her hands as if to do that.

The bird took to wing in a panic and rattled again. From the corner of her eye, she saw Shoran trying hard not to laugh.

Only Effina remained unamused. "Orolan is not for eating. He is an ancient. A demigod who has chosen to live as a bird and bear witness to the history of Seramight."

"He is a pest," Elika grumbled. Then his name sank in. "Orolan … the demigod who foretells the will of Fates?"

"'Tis him," Shoran said from beside her, with a downturn of his lips.

The bird circled above her, then landed at her feet and grew and grew and grew into a creature that was half man, half bird. Or rather, it was a man, but his hands and face and bare feet were covered in fine feathers. He was tall and of a height with Shoran, and beneath his feathers, she could discern Sachi features.

He bowed to her, somewhat mockingly. "My fair maiden …" He glanced at Shoran. "Or rather maiden no more." He had a croaking voice, much like a crow might were it to speak in a man's tongue.

"Careful, Oro," Shoran warned him. "It would be a shame to lose your feathers to my wrath again."

"I recall now why I miss you, brother. Always so prickly when it comes to women of your heart." He turned back to her. "Though none I dare say have claimed it as firmly as you, my dear."

She crossed her arms and shook her head. "Bloody, cursed magic. I thought it was just one of Bill Fisher's tales that the gods could change into animals. No one ever believed him. I dare say no one will believe me either when I tell them."

Orolan flapped the remnants of his wings at her. "Some can change better than others. Too rarely I now take the human form. It never comes back as it should anymore."

Elika took another step back. "Why do you follow me?"

He titled his head at her like a crow, with those beady yellow eyes. "Why would I not? You are worth following. So full of surprises and adventure. But we did have fun in the old city, did we not?" There was secret amusement behind his eyes. "Tell me, brother, does she know?" he asked Shoran without looking at him.

Shoran stiffened beside her, his jaw tense as he glared at the man-crow. She was certain he was contemplating singeing those feathers.

"Know what?" she asked.

"Oh, this and that about our kind." He waved his feathered hand as if it was of no consequence. "Pay no mind to me, little spider," he chuckled.

"Orolan," Effina snapped. "I will not have fighting in my home. Today is a joyous occasion. You may join us if you wish but put aside your brotherly strife."

Orolan turned back to her. "We put aside that long ago, Mother Effina. Have we not, brother?"

Shoran strode to the low table without answering and lowered himself on the cushions next to Effina.

Elika did the same, keeping a close eye on Orolan. She did not trust him, not least seeing as he rattled Shoran with his secretive smiles.

"'Tis a special day indeed for my brother. Who am I to ruin it?" Orolan sat across from him.

Shoran did not look too pleased, but he held his tongue.

The table was set out with trays of fruit and cheese and berries amid the freshly picked flowers. Elika followed their example and filled her plate.

It was strange to realize herself in the presence of Elders, the race of first humans, untouched by Moreg's curse. Effina was indeed ageless looking, though there were signs of frailty about her, as if her body was wasting away rather than growing old.

"I forgot the jug of silvering," said Effina and made to rise.

Shoran halted her with a hand. "Sit, Mother. I will fetch it." And he bounded to his feet, to fetch a jug from the tray on the side table.

"Mother ...?" Elika echoed, looking from him to Effina.

The three of them turned to look at her as if she spoke in an alien tongue.

Effina turned her questioning gaze on Shoran. "Did you not think to mention it to her, son?"

"I thought it was clear," he said with a frown, as he returned with the jug and lowered himself beside the priestess. "I told her the Asari were my mother's tribe."

Elika heated and looked down at her plate. "Aye, he did. I ... misunderstood. It's just that ... he's so ancient and you're human."

Effina placed her hand over Elika's. "It is hard for us to remember you come from a different world. What is natural to us, is very alien to you. Shoran is indeed my son. But not Orolan, though he likes to call me Mother."

"You are more of a mother to me than mine ever was," Orolan said.

Effina poured them each a wooden cup of silversap. The bird-man drank deeply and shuddered. His feathers flew around them in all directions.

"Can you change into a crow?" Elika asked Shoran curiously.

Orolan laughed, a cackling sound.

"No," Shoran replied, casting Orolan a warning look.

The bird-man leant towards her across the table. "You see, what my brother will not say is that the animal inside you is chosen by the Fates. The gods do not know what you are until the signs are clear. Many forms there are amongst our kind. The rarest of which is a spider."

"Enough," Shoran growled, low and hard.

"I want to hear him," Elika cut in as something frightening flitted through the back of her mind.

"Of course you do, my dear," Effina said and gave Shoran a stern look. "You cannot shield her from the truth her whole life. Shiara made that mistake with Elriad."

"What signs do you speak of?" Elika asked the crow-man.

"In dreams, we walk as who we are. In dreams, we find our true nature. What do you dream about, Aleyala?"

She chilled as she recalled those many dreams of being a small spider in the web …

"Enough!" Shoran boomed. "'Tis not her time to know."

"When is?" Effina asked him mildly. "Son, what is happening to you? You cannot hide the truth from her, for it will never grow easier to learn it."

"She was abandoned. She had no keepers, no one to guide her and teach her. A careless, ill-timed truth can break a person. As it broke Elriad. So judge me not, Mother, for when I found her, she believed herself to be human."

Orolan chuckled. "Aye. I recall how she drank the blood-salt. I thought she would stop after the first time. But no, she would not stop. She would retch and squirm in agony and get whipped for her efforts. But still she drank and wept." His voice turned contemptuous, angry. "Her stubbornness is a match for yours brother. As is her self-punishment."

Elika's appetite fled. She was back there, in the city on the brink of destruction, watching the Blight turn the lands fallow and grey, the men lying dead on the streets …

Shoran kicked out and Orolan flew backward onto the floor. She saw but a flash of movement, and he was on top of Orolan, a sword pressed to the feathered throat. "You watched, you saw, and you did nothing to help Aleyala. You stalked her but came not to her aid. You *knew* and let harm befall her?"

"Shoran! No!" Effina cried. "'Tis not his purpose."

"'Tis the law of gods!" he roared.

Elika was on her feet. She grabbed his arm and tried to wrest it from killing Orolan. But his arm would not budge, as if it was a tree she was trying to move.

"'Tis not my task to interfere, brother. I watch and I witness and I bear what I see to the gods. You know the price of interference better than anyone, do you not? Even if I wanted to reveal myself to her, there were no silversap trees left in that world, and after six hundred years, my magic was spent. Even now my form has grown to be more bird than man."

"I would make you suffer for your disregard of her suffering, but I will kill you for your mockery of it. By my hand, vengeance will be done …" He pressed the tip of his sword into Orolan's throat …

"No!" Elika tried and failed to push him away from the hapless bird-man. "He saved my life! I forbid any harm to be done to him."

Shoran turned his dark gaze on her.

"It's true. I owe him my life. The Blight would have got me, too, if not for him."

Orolan's feathers grew longer and thicker. In a puff of them, he changed into a bird and flapped his wings hoping to flee, but Shoran still had him pinned to the floor.

"Aleyala has spoken, and thus is her command," said Effina calmly, though Elika could see that she, too, was shaken. "Release him, Shoran. Or will you defy her will?"

He opened his hand and with a loud caw, the crow flew out through the tent flap.

"Do not glare after your brother thus," said Effina. "He has his purpose and keeps true to it. Which is more than I can say for you."

Shoran rose to his feet and his sword vanished. He was still gazing at where the crow had fled, as if he thought to follow him. In his hand he gripped a clutch of black feathers, strangling them instead of the crow. Then he threw them aside. "Warn him, Mother, the next time I catch him, I will break his wings. 'Tis the only mercy I will show him."

Elika shook her head. "It's not his fault what befell me and all the people left behind. Blame Syn'Moreg for that and everything that I endured, for it was he who had sundered the world and men knew not what lay on the other side. 'Tis him you should threaten with your sword."

Shoran's head snapped towards her.

Effina gasped and put a hand to her chest. "Shoran ..." she uttered, and there was a question in her faint voice. Tears gathered in her eyes and try as she might, Elika could not explain them. "What have you done?" the priestess whispered.

Something passed between them and a chill raced over Elika's skin.

"We will speak later, Mother. Now, I wish to show Elika the lands that are to be her home."

He marched out and she turned to follow. Effina grabbed her hand to halt her, and there was deep sorrow in her face. "No matter what, Aleyala, you are now our daughter, *my* daughter, and you must always return to us."

Elika nodded and followed Shoran out.

He ran his hand through his hair.

"What passed in there?" she asked him.

"Centuries of mistakes and grief are converging. I cannot forestall the winds much longer. Our time is brief, for everything will soon unravel. Let us enjoy the moments we have left together."

His words plunged her heart into a pit of dread and fear, for he spoke as if they were soon to be parted. "Shoran ..."

He silenced her words with his lips. "There will be time to speak, and grieve, but now, we will seek that which is truly rare in this forsaken world. Let troubles rest awhile and enjoy the time we have together."

And she felt as if she was standing on a slowly cracking glass suspended above a precipice. It was hard, but she gave him a wavering smile and nodded. For he was right, true joy and happiness were rare and not to be cast aside when gifted.

~

Aye, blissful were the days that followed. Shoran took her riding across the lands. The Asari tribe of his mother was not the only tribe in the land of Elders. There were many others, though the Asari was by far the largest, and only they were tasked with raising the children of the gods.

There were other human villages in Elder Valley, scattered around the valley, along river banks and small lakes. These humans, though not Sachi, were also long-lived. Untouched, as they were, by the curse that aged humanity before its time.

There was a sleepiness about Elder Valley, and peace so profound it was hard to imagine any battles and wars touching this land. Though Shoran had told her that they were not unscarred by the violent nature of man or the cruel vanity of the demigods.

As they rode from village to village, Elika saw that folk here did not live too differently from those in Terren. There were trades of every kind to be found; blacksmiths, chandlers, spinners, weavers and scribes. There was nothing these people appeared to lack. The markets were vibrant and the goods of ageless quality and beauty.

From the talk she heard in the streets and eateries they had stopped in, there was little to trouble the folk of these lands. Save the timing of the next harvest, and whether cider would be as sweet this year as the last. Others pondered when Neka's tower would once again light up and the gods return. For when they did, they would bring another brood of sacred babes with them for the raising in these lands. The last brood of young demigods had departed for El'Sandria when the spheres once again moved apart. And that was over a thousand years ago.

By the time evening came, she wanted nothing more than to make love to Shoran, and afterwards curl up beside him and whisper of past and present. But never the future. For his face grew haunted when she touched upon it, and his silences grew stark and dark.

Elika had not seen Orolan since Shoran had chased him off. Nor did she want to be the cause of trouble between them. Shoran refused to speak of him, and his menacing silence made her worried he would indeed break Orolan's wings the next time he caught him.

"It is always the same with them," Effina told her one day. "Orolan watches the Fates. Shoran confronts them. And ever their natures clash."

The silver-veined, green tower was the only place she was forbidden from going near. Effina and Shoran were the only ones who were allowed inside. Neither of them, however, approached it.

Or so she thought. Until one morning she awoke to dawn light peering into the tent. Shoran was deeply asleep beside her, his chest rising slowly and deeply. When she brushed away his hair from his eyes, he stirred not. Last night they sat late by the communal fire, drinking fermented berry juice and watching the village maidens dance. They had retired late and made love even later into the night. And though Shoran had been quick to fall asleep, she remained awake for long hours afterward as her mind refused to release a sense of foreboding.

With an inward sigh, she rolled onto her back and found Orolan, the crow, sitting on the beam overhead. As soon as she saw him, he took to wing and silently flew out of the tent.

Being careful not to disturb Shoran, she crept out of bed, and after throwing on her dress, tiptoed out of the tent. Cool air tickled all her senses awake. The village was still sleeping, and Elika felt as if the world belonged to her.

She looked for Orolan and found him circling the tower. She strode towards it but halted abruptly when she saw Effina slip inside the door and close it.

Curiosity propelled her onward.

She reached the giant tower door and was about to push on it when a voice spoke from behind her. "I wouldn't do that if I were you."

She spun and faced Orolan in his human form, though feathers stuck out all over his skin, and his wings had not fully morphed into arms.

"That brute forbade you near it," he reminded her. "And Effina will not go against his will in this matter."

"What is she doing in there?" Elika asked.

"Praying to the gods, of course."

"And they hear her?"

He smiled. "Come, let us walk. I want to show you something."

She glanced at the village. "Just be careful not to let Shoran catch you. He's still angry with you."

The crow-man chuckled. "He always takes everything so seriously. He was much better humored in his younger days. But grief does that to you."

"Grief?" she echoed, remembering Shoran had mentioned it, too.

"Never mind. 'Tis not important. Come, follow me."

Orolan led her around the base of the tower. It was far wider than it seemed, though it was not overly tall or imposing. Like the black tower, it had a crown of elegant, twisting spires.

"I wanted you to be the first to feel this," he said and placed a hand on the wall. "Come, do not be frightened. It will not hurt you."

Tentatively, she touched the green stone. "It's warm."

He cocked his head at her. "Look closer. What else do you see?"

She regarded the wall. The silver veins in it were ever so gently glowing where the stone was warm.

"I saw the glow last night as I huddled in the rain in a tree over there. Didn't want to be caught in a tent with that damned brute skulking about with an eye out for me." He laughed lightly and it sounded like a cackle. "Do you know what this means, Elika Spider?"

She took away her hand. "The realm of the gods is close," she said with an ever-deepening sense of foreboding.

"Aye, they are coming." His beady yellow eyes fixed on her. "They are coming for you."

"For me?"

"Well, not for *you*. They do not know about you, since I have not told them as yet. But Reval has sent a crow to them claiming Arala has returned and Shoran is keeping her prisoner."

"'Tis lies," she said with outrage.

He pointed up. "The windows in those spires are for the crows to fly through. The messenger birds come to this tower, and they go through the portal inside it into El'Sandria. It is a one-way journey until the spheres brush past each other. The gods have heard and Neka will come for you and Shoran both." He said that in a menacing way, as if it was the direst of things to befall them, and a wicked smile danced on his lips.

"Then why haven't you flown to them with your tales?" she asked.

He cackled. "I am watching a tale unfold as we speak, and I dare not miss a moment of it." Then his face grew belligerent. "A warning I bring you from the Fates, little spider. 'Tis foretold that there can never be two spiders in one web. 'Tis their fate that one will destroy the other. And the one that is left will take on the curse of the other."

Elika shook her head. "You make no sense, Orolan. 'Tis the problem with prophecies and trying to foretell the fates. Used to know this old witch, or so she claimed herself to be. Old Nina Nine-Toes, they called her. Used to love to come out with all manner of useless fortune telling. Once I gave her a penny to tell me mine, only 'cause I wanted to know whether there was anything good in my future. It was a wasted penny I should've spent on food, for all she said was ..."

"Fate Slayers have no future," Orolan finished for her.

She frowned. "How did you know what she said?"

"'Cause she was one of the best fate readers around. She was an Elder, born in Dreamwell village not far from here. And it was a wise warning she gave you. Fate Salyers make their own future, and the price is that they never find peace and always destroy that which they love. So you need to …" His gaze darted past her. "Damn that brute." He shifted into a bird and, with a loud caw, took to wing. A blast of wind threw him off balance and spun him through the air. He righted himself and flew into the trees, out of sight.

Elika turned and crossed her arms as Shoran marched towards her. "There was no need for that," she said. "We were only talking. And I don't want you hurting him."

"'Tis an easy thing, if he keeps away from me," he replied.

Elika sighed. There was no reasoning with him when it came to Orolan. Effina had said as much.

He seemed about to say more when his gaze snapped to the stone and he stared intently at the glowing silvery veins. His jaw hardened.

"Orolan said he saw it last night."

Shoran looked down at the ground, deep in thought. After a long moment, he spoke. "There is a stream nearby, with a warm pool for bathing. It is reserved for the children of the gods, for its waters have a strange, soporific effect on humans. Come, I will show it to you."

And that was that. Without a word about the tower or Orolan or that the celestial sphere and its realm of El'Sandria was drawing closer, he took her hand and showed her the way to the sacred pool where the water was always warm.

The next morning Elika awoke to find Shoran missing. Fear gripped her, for the night before, he had been sullen, troubled and silent in his own thoughts.

She dressed quickly and rushed outside to find him speaking with Effina. Both were grim. They glanced her way, then he quickly looked aside. Effina walked away, whilst Shoran stared at the ground, waiting for Elika to approach.

"I must leave," he said.

She knew what his words would be before he spoke them. It did not lessen their impact.

"I will go with you."

His face shuttered. "You cannot. To be with you, I have neglected my duty to the gods I serve. A purpose that cannot be forestalled. I must go. But you must stay here and learn the ways of the tribe, their laws and customs, and wait for my return."

"Syn'Moreg calls you away," she said, and it was jarring to recall that he was the monster's servant, punished by the gods, banished, and forced to repay a debt which could never be repaid. Those invisible chains he wore would always take him away from her, she now realized.

"Duty and need call me away."

"What does he ask of you?"

It must have been a terrible question indeed, for in reply, she felt him withdraw, grow cold and distant, once again a stranger to her. A shadow fell over his face.

He did not want to speak of it. She understood that.

"Might be it's time we went ..." *Home*, she almost said. "... back to the Abyss. I'll wait for you in the tower ..."

"No. I do not wish it. This is your home now, not Nerasky. You are safe here. As safe as you can be. To do what I must, I cannot be torn in two as I am when you are near. Stay here, Elika, I beg of you. I will return. Soon."

His words were so impassioned, she could not refuse him. Though every fear and doubt she held back reared inside her. It felt like another rejection.

He kissed her tenderly, then marched towards the trees and vanished.

CHAPTER THIRTY-TWO

Syn'Moreg

"It would not be wrong to say that Syn'Moreg is the one overseeing power of the three realms. Reval despises him, Ilikan fears him, and Draygan is cautiously weary of him, whilst the Sacred Crowns revere him. No one can dispute, however, that everyone bows to him, for he is the only Spider-child born to the gods since God Moreg himself, and the only one with the power to guard the web. Were he to march from the Abyss and claim the seat of power granted him over the three realms, no one would dare oppose him, save the gods themselves. Yet rare is it for him to wield the power and authority he holds. The last time was when he marched to Northwind and demanded Arala's release. History might record that Reval saved her with an army. But those who were there know that it was Syn'Moreg who saved her with one quietly spoken command."

The History of Alafraysia and Seramight,
By Mageguard Bluelight

"Aleyala, your fingers are lithe and clever," said Shara, whilst watching her weave a basket from straw.

"'Tis easy," Elika replied absently, her thoughts drifting away from the chatter of the women in the circle.

Today, they were weaving baskets, bowls and platters from straw, which they would then trade with the local villages for grain and meat.

Shara had never given her anything less than a kind smile and gentle words, and she waved aside Elika's apology for burning her hand. "It was naught but a small blister, Aleyala," she had said. "Young gods often struggle to contain their growing powers. Shoran himself once accidentally cast a fog over the land which he could not remove. Effina had to deprive him of silversap until he weakened enough so that the fog dissipated of its own accord."

They spoke of Shoran whenever an opportunity arose. Elika might have enjoyed it more, save that whenever talk turned to him, her heart grew heavy, and her mood turned dark.

She placed aside the basket she was weaving, wearied by his absence. "I'll go for a walk."

Instantly, they were on their feet. "We will come with you."

She was rarely left alone. Always one of them asked to walk with her lest she wanted company. At night, one of the daughters of the tribe would offer to sleep close to her, lest loneliness or fear found her.

"I prefer to be alone right now," Elika said.

"As you wish, Aleyala," Shara replied.

Outside their communal tent, Elika searched the sky and trees for Orolan, but he too had vanished after Shoran had left, with no one the wiser where he went.

It was a small mercy that there was always much to do in the tribe. Little things, that in a quiet life such as this, always took on higher importance than they might have in Terren. The Sachi taught her how to weave with straw and branches. How to braid hair their unique way. How to ferment god's fruit, and where to plant flower seeds to bring the birds and butterflies into their orchards. They had been delighted she knew how to weave with a cotton thread and the more delicate silk thread of silkworms, and promptly made her join them in weaving bright rolls of silks using simple handlooms.

When they worked, they told her stories of the gods and the sacred children they had raised. They spoke of their own warriors who had sided with the gods against Elriad in the war of the three realms. The tribe lost many sons then. In return for their loyalty, Goddess Neka protected them against Moreg's curse he cast upon the rest of humanity. They told tales of notable Sachi priests and priestesses who had visited the celestial realm when the worlds were joined, and of the Sachi women who had given themselves to the gods as lovers. Effina was one of the few who had crossed into the sacred realm of light and returned decades later. Though she spoke not of what she had seen there.

Might be if her heart did not ache with longing, Elika would have paid closer attention to their tales. As it was, she only half listened to them, for her thoughts were always taken with Shoran.

'Tis an unhealthy obsession, she scalded herself as she strode from the village to wash in the warm pool Shoran had shown her. It was the only place where she knew she would not be disturbed by well-meaning companions.

She missed him, painfully. And as days went by, she felt like an abandoned bride. Especially when the night fell. Night after night, she lay awake, restless and troubled, waiting for him. Now and then, when the village was asleep, she would traverse the veil into the Tower of the Abyss. But his bed was cold and unslept in and all doors led to empty rooms. Surely, a man who could traverse the world in an instant might find a moment to come to her.

Fears roiled in her mind. Syn'Moreg was keeping him prisoner … or else he had been punished for being with her. Had he not said as much himself? The gods would punish him and her for their union.

Since Neka's tower had started to warm and glow, his mother, the priestess, spent most of her time inside it. When Effina was not in the tower, she would ride out to visit other tribes, or host council meetings with other Sachi priests and tribal chieftains. One by one, they had come to greet Elika, as if she was a long-lost princess of the land.

The Sachi bowed to her in passing. The women brought her food and flowers and helped her dress. Whilst she slept, freshly picked flowers were placed around the tent. Nothing was denied her, save Shoran himself.

What need pulled him from her and kept him away? Might be she imagined all that had passed between them. Else she was just another woman, another conquest for him. Surely, he could find the briefest moment to be there with her. On and on, those doubts poisoned her mind.

Another day had come and gone. And then another.

Today, the women went to gather fruit from their orchards. It was more play than work, in truth. They ate as they gathered, told silly tales, and laughed without much cause to laugh. The women ran ahead and threw fruit at each other, like children with no cares. But Elika had not the heart to join them.

"Aleyala," Shara called out and ran over to grab her hand. "'Tis a wonder you must see. There is a meadow sparrow come to sing for you."

She pulled Elika towards a peach tree, where a bird with wonderous plumage was singing its glorious song. It was a rare bird fashioned by the gods, and its brazen feathers and long glorious tale reminded Elika of Rosy Rose. She had a bird akin to this one …

The thought of Rosy Rose shattered the dream around her. It was as if she had awoken inside a perfect dream and knew that it was a lie, and she was still sleeping. Shoran had placed her here, far from the troubles of the realm, distracting her from the war that surely must now grip Terren. What else could keep him away but war and blood and Terren burning, and the Great Web aflame with the fires of the blood-salt?

The bird spread its tail and hopped about in a mating dance, and the women of the tribe laughed and clapped their hands.

Aye, there was war beyond the Mountains of Fire. By now, Mite must have reached the city with his army …

Shoran. He had been a part of what had been transpiring so far. He had interfered, despite telling her it was forbidden to do so. And he had kept her from it. What part was he playing in that war? For she was certain he was playing some part. Shoran confronts the Fates, Effina had told her.

Do not harm the Great Web.

The image of Rory's head rolling off his shoulders came to her. It morphed and it was Mite's head lying on the floor.

She thought of Penny, Anten and the children. Of Bobquick, Blood Dog and countless others whose faces and lives and voices she knew. None of them had held the knife that had cut her link with humanity. None of them had betrayed her. Yet here she was, hiding in a place beyond the reach of war, whilst they fought and died for their survival.

Suspicion festered in her mind. Shoran had brought her here, left her here. He had never wanted her interference. Had she been a fool … a love-stricken fool? *He left you here and did not return.*

Surely, he must miss her as she missed him and could spare a moment for her.

Pieces fell together, whilst the bird sang and sang, and Shara laughed and pointed at it.

Shoran believed Mite would be a bad king. He knew Southfire's mother, Meyara. There was a past between them. Past and secrets he had never revealed. With the archmage gone, Shoran would be the one to help Southfire if it was in his power to do so. Her mind churned, and those suspicions became poison. He had left her here to stop her from interfering with his plans.

Mite needed her. Aye, he had an army, but his army was made of men, not mages.

Shoran is keeping you away.

Sickness settled in her stomach. Was everything between them a lie, a ruse to bring her here far from Terren, far from where she could help Mite?

I must contain you. Echoed his threat from the past.

"Aleyala? You look angry." It was Shara's tentative voice breaking through.

"I … I must leave," Elika replied and her own voice seemed to come from far away.

"Oh no, Aleyala." One of the women grabbed her hand. "He bade us you stay here."

The sickness in her stomach intensified. Aye, he did, she thought darkly. Trust me, he had said. Yet what did she know of him? He had never trusted her enough to confide in her what it was he did for Syn'Moreg.

Elika removed her hand from the woman's grip. "Thank you for being so kind, Mari. And thank Effina for me."

Shara grabbed her hand next. "No, please don't leave. He will return."

Six hundred years he had been away the last time, before he had returned with her in tow.

"When?" Elika asked faintly, as the suspicion that she had indeed been a fool grew deep roots into her soul.

"Soon," Shara said, far too eagerly. "A few days perhaps ..."

Elika pulled her hand from Shara's grip. "It's not for him that I must leave."

The other women were staring at her with frightened eyes, and if nothing else told her that something was wrong, it was that. They were tasked with keeping her here.

"You must see Effina," said Mari and ran off through the trees to fetch her.

"Thank her for me, Shara." And with those words, Elika strode towards the tree and through the veil into the Tower of the Abyss.

Darkness engulfed her, pressed in on her.

She was back in the endless long corridor, back home ...

Home. Another lie? Another worthless hope for that which never could be.

'Tis naught but your fears, Eli, a small frightened part of reason chided her. *Speak with him. Do not judge too soon.*

She reached for the thread that linked them, desperate to speak with him before her suspicions irreparably poisoned her soul.

The thread that bound them led her to the door of the library, but the room was empty. She had never questioned why the link guided her to where he was not.

She had always thought she merely got lost. Else he had been there recently. She gazed along the long, dark corridor and again sought that thread. Another door appeared. It led her to an empty bedroom. The bed was unslept in. The windows were as ever fathomless pitch black. She reached for him again and the thread led to another forlorn room, and then another and another. The study was empty, as was her chamber ... Arala's old chamber, with lonely echoes of her past.

Elika stopped and listened, and there it was, a faint but certain pull upon the thread she followed. Another power was guiding her, leading her astray, trying to confuse her. She stared at the dark hall and her heart became afraid. He was keeping her away. She closed her treacherous eyes, for they deceived her, grabbed the thread and followed it blindly towards him.

Aye, she was a fool. He did not want to see her. And here she was, running about, seeking him like a love-stricken child. She stumbled on that thought … She *was* love-stricken, and she was a fool. Penny had warned her long ago to be careful what man she opened her heart to, for the wrong man would seize it and use it as a weapon against her.

Slowly, she placed one foot in front of the other, drawing closer to Shoran with each step, his essence growing stronger. She had given him her heart, had bedded him and followed him blindly. He had called her naïve, and now she knew herself to be just that.

What did he do for his master? Did he murder, did he destroy, was he killing Northwind even now? *Mite* …

She opened her eyes, walking faster and faster along the endless corridor, and yet it grew longer and longer, and no more doors appeared. But he was close, his power potent …

A doorway formed at the end of the corridor.

Her feet slowed. She knew that gaping hole. Had been through it once when Shoran had dangled her over the Abyss. Knew that the Great Web lay beyond it.

Walk away, Eli, her mind whispered. But it was too late for that.

There was no walking away from her fears. If Shoran was there, she would find him, save him, demand answers and love him …

Aye, she would do that.

She stopped in front of the opening, took a breath, and walked through.

The Abyss rushed at her. Her ears filled with the screech of the winds, and she fought the sensation of falling as they screamed and pulled and pushed, at once warning her away and demanding she join them.

She looked past the darkness, her gaze traversing the distance to the silvery web spreading far and wide. But it was not how she had seen it last. It was afire. Everywhere she looked, dark red spot fires erupted and vanished, leaving behind tears and flailing strands. And as she watched, more and more fires burst into life, only to quickly vanish, leaving dark holes in the web.

She turned her head slowly, absorbing its enormity ... Sudden terror gripped her. For there, in the web, sat the spider from her nightmares.

Syn'Moreg.

Strands emerged from his giant feet, silvery strands which he fastened to the web. He was facing away from her, doing something to the web, but she could not see what. His size belied reality, for surely, he was bigger than a city ... bigger than the realm of Seramight ... Impossible, of course. But in this strange place, where reality and distance held no sway, and time was but a breath upon eternity, there was no way to know, to judge his size.

The spider stilled and turned its head. Its giant yellow eyes found her, fixed on her and held her. Surely, she was too small to see. Each one of his eight eyes were larger than she, larger than any ship that sailed the seas. And yet it looked at her and looked at her. Then the spider released an awful sound that pierced the Abyss. The winds replied and grew ever fiercer.

The spider spun and darted towards her on giant, hairy legs. Its fangs, bigger than a horse, moved and clacked as he charged. Elika stumbled back from the vile creature, back through the door, too small for him to come through. The spider only grew larger and larger as it neared, and she was certain that it would break the tower apart to reach her ... eat her ... drag her into the Abyss ...

The winds intensified and the tower walls around her broke apart and flew around her. Only the stone floor remained between her and the nothingness of Nerasky.

The spider loomed above her, his black claws holding onto the silvery strands of light.

Elika raised her arm to ward him off, but instead of the arm, a hairy spider leg rose from her body. She screamed.

A nightmare. It was a nightmare she was trapped in. She would soon awake in Elder Valley ...

Another deep screech came from the spider, shattering that thought, and bringing the stark and terrible reality of it back to her.

She retreated until she reached the edge of the stone platform suspended in the Abyss.

'Tis the end, she thought and pulled out her knife with her other hand.

"Stay away from me, Syn'Moreg," she screamed. "Why do you haunt my dreams? What do you want from me?"

He moved from his web, his awful legs finding a perch on the platform she was on, and his form began to change. The six legs shrank back and were replaced by two human legs. His body morphed, the abdomen retreated into a human stomach. And for a brief moment, she saw not Syn'Moreg, but the god with spider legs from the temple—God Moreg himself. The last of his hairy spider legs retracted into him and a man strode towards her. But the man she saw was more terrible to behold than the spider.

A scream of anguish tore from her throat. A scream of loathing, of self-disgust, of betrayal deeper than the Abyss around her. She stumbled away from him. Denying the horror of what she had done, of what she had been too blind to see.

"You should not be here, kitten."

And a cry of rage burst from her.

You will forever be mine.

I'm yours.

Self-loathing filled her chest, her stupidity, and hatred of this creature. Hatred of him.

"You lied to me!" she screamed.

"Lied?" said the darkness, and his eyes flashed. "'Tis you who named me. You who saw two beings where there was one."

"You are a beast, a monster."

"As much as you are one, *my love*," he replied and his gaze fell on her spider limb at her side. "And yet I do not recoil."

"I'm not a monster! I'm not like you." She drew the magic back inside her and the spider limb was replaced by a human arm.

"Aye, you are like me. And long have you haunted my web, little spider. Long have you tormented me."

She shook her head in denial. "No … it was but a dream."

"In dreams, we travel. In dreams do we traverse the veil between the realms until we learn to master it in waking." He was suddenly before her, holding her arms in a tight grip. "Aye, you are a spider, for you are a half-breed child of the gods, and the Fates have shaped you. 'Tis your true form, for it is written in your purpose, Eli *Spider*." He said the last mockingly. "'Tis your purpose to guard and protect the web."

"No!" She stabbed him in the shoulder with her knife and he released her.

He pulled out her knife from his shoulder and threw it aside.

She backed away from him as white light exploded in her mind. She pushed it out at him, wanting to hurt him. But instead of light, fire exploded around them. And in that fire, she saw her parents turn to dust on the bridge, saw countless souls die trying to cross the chasm this creature had created. So many had fallen into it. She saw a river of blood and uncounted dead, and the Blight pushing them over the edge of their world.

Hatred burned through her. "Damn your gods. Damn you. Let them burn and let the web burn. I will deliver men from magic, and then I will turn on the gods. I will burn them in the blood-salt fires!" she screamed and recoiled from her own dreadful words of madness, for there was no saving men without the Web. Yet in that moment, she wanted to hurt Syn'Moreg, the gods, the world and everything and everyone in it. "I will be your monster!" she swore, and the fire intensified.

"The gods will not be threatened," he growled and a burst of flame flew towards her, hit her in the arm ... *burned* her.

She cried out in pain and took a step away from the fire as it advanced on her. The wall of flame parted around him.

"Your flames do not scare me." She gasped as the heat grew fierce, and the flames moved towards her again.

"I'm not the master of these flames." He took a step towards her. "Still the fire in your heart, for you have turned your rage against yourself. You have drawn the fires of hate towards you."

The fire rose higher and grew hotter until there was nowhere to escape it. Yet he was unaffected by it and that alone told her they were his to command.

"Stay away from me, Syn'Moreg!"

But he would not stop. He kept advancing on her, herding her towards a corner. "Put aside your hate, kitten, else I must contain you."

A ball of light formed between his hands, and he stretched it into a web that grew and grew, and she knew what he meant to do with it. He meant to catch her and imprison her.

Elika reached for his essence, for the link between them. Damn him and damn her. She would burn them both. Might be they were both monsters the world would do better without. And with every shred of power inside her, she pushed the flame along the link connecting them.

Fire raced through his veins under his skin. He staggered back in surprise and shock, and suddenly he became man and flame as one. She gaped in horror as his flesh began to burn and melt. He gasped in pain and … and laughed as his flesh turned to fire. "Oh kitten, I was a fool to love you."

He spread his arms, groaned, then roared and turned to ash.

Elika screamed and called on water to douse the flame that was no longer there. The heat was gone and so was Shoran.

Her rage fled and her hatred with it. She fell to her knees and dug her hands into hot ash. "Shoran …" Grief choked her as ash fell through her fingers to be carried away by the winds. "No … No. Shoran … please …" she sobbed.

She was his monster. She had killed him …

Pain pierced her chest as her heart shattered into countless pieces. And her screams drowned out the winds of the Abyss.

Around her, the web was empty as more and more blood-red fires erupted in it. A small part of the web fell away. And she suddenly understood what it was he did, what the spider's purpose was. He was weaving the light strands and mending the web. It was his curse, his punishment for giving men the weapon to fight magic.

The dark walls of the tower rose around her, encased her, enslaved her. The endless corridor stretched on and on. She sought Shoran's thread and found nothing but the empty void beyond.

CHAPTER THIRTY-THREE

The Fall of Terren

"Scholars have long debated the legend of the Silvery Web and its guardian spider. The story has its roots in the Sachi old lore of the celestial gods. It is said God Moreg seduced a human princess and seeded a child inside her. She gave birth to a spider. In disgust of the creature, a human king threw the child into the Abyss through a well inside Moreg's Temple. Soon after, the king was found beheaded in his room, amongst the bodies of his guards, who tried to protect him. They were wrapped in the sticky, thick shroud of a spider's web. The king's daughter, the princess, was never seen again. Centuries later, Moreg's son returned to the world of man as heir and rightful king of the Kingdom of Wavestar. His name was Shoran Syn'Moreg."
The History of Alafraysia and Seramight,
By Mageguard Bluelight

Her feet moved, though she knew not where they took her. She staggered through the streets, holding herself tight. Her tears were spent. Where her heart once beat was a mangled rag of flesh and pain. Red smoke rose above the roofs. She turned a corner and saw a mage burning on a pyre, whilst men threw blood-salt into the flames. Guards and soldiers raced along the streets towards the sound of battle. Blood was everywhere. Death was everywhere.

Windows and doors were broken. Homes had been burned. On the ground lay a charred, crumpled figure. The vision dissolved and instead of the black corpse, she saw Shoran burning and turning to ash.

More soldiers raced past the dead, headed for the city walls, ignoring the band of men setting fire to mages' homes.

Everything moved around her, and yet she was not a part of it. She gazed at the dead and the living with a sense of empty detachment, feeling nothing, caring not.

You are not one of us.

You are like me, whispered a dark voice, and hot shards of grief burned through her.

She wanted to scream all over again. And it was all she could do to hold herself together, whilst her heart bled for the one she wanted to forget. Her heart bled ... she might have laughed. Would that the pain was so paltry. Her very soul had been ripped out, shredded, and the rags shoved back into her miserable body. She did not recognize herself, knew not what she had become. She had killed Shoran, the man she loved, the shadow she hated.

No, she was not one of them, these humans running through the streets, burning the magic from this world, burning the web. A web now without a spider. What punishment would the gods bestow on her when they learned of what she had done? She was certain God Moreg would slay her for killing his son. He would torment her before he did it, too. And aye, she'd welcome the pain of the flesh, if only to mask the pain in her soul.

Without Shoran, she now existed between worlds, like his dark tower. Belonging nowhere, alone, moving yet not feeling, here yet elsewhere. She could not return to the Asari tribe. How could she face Effina having killed her son with the fires of hatred? Might be she'd lock herself away in the tower for eternity once this war was done.

Overhead, Reval's island menaced the city and hatred swelled in her chest. She wanted to push it back into Alafraysia. She wanted to destroy. A churning heat of power made her believe she could do just that, as Reval had done long ago ...

The thought brought her up short. Then she laughed, bitter and broken, for she suddenly understood the rage that sent him to destroy the world when Arala had perished, understood the grief that drove him to madness. Aye, she wanted to destroy, for rage was a balm to grief.

Save that she was not like him. She was not the monster Rory feared her to be. She was Eli Spider of Bad Penny's pack ... No, she was not. Not anymore. She had given that up. She had accepted the Asari as her tribe, her pack, and she could not go back to them. Not after what she had done.

As she passed a washing line, Elika snatched a pair of boy's trousers and a tunic. She changed into them behind a cart loaded with hay. Then she sheared her hair with her knife. Shoran's blood still stained it.

She found her way to the roofs and gazed over the city wall to the surrounding land where Northwind's and Warwind's combined armies had gathered to reclaim their realm. Tens of thousands of soldiers lay siege to Terren.

A fierce battle was being fought beyond the city wall. In the churning sea of mud and blood, flesh and sword and trampling horses, there was no way to tell who was fighting who, or who was dying.

A cloud of arrows flew from the city wall, where human guards of the newly anointed King Southfire fought side by side with Reval's personal mages. She recognized them from the robes they wore and the fire they sent at the assailants.

The outer wall of the besieged city was charred. Many lay dead in the trampled ground beneath it. A line of Southfire's cavalry, their armor glowing red in the dusk light, charged the flanks of the attackers.

Horses and men fell, as the clash of steel and battle cries rang out over the roofs. Another cloud of arrows rose into the sky, but this one was flying towards the city wall.

Then she saw another king in pale-blue armor on top of a great steed, leading a charge of fresh soldiers towards the battle at the city gates. A sword of ice shone in the dying red sun.

Arrows filled the sky. Shields were raised. The newly arrived soldiers fought their way to the center of the battle and formed a protective wall around the wounded. Slowly, step by step, they fought and retreated to the sea of tents in the distance.

It was a mercy for Southfire's men, for they, too, fled back into the city, dragging their wounded with them.

A fireball flew overhead from Reval's island and struck the heart of Northwind's camp. The camp exploded into activity. Men threw wooden barrels into it and flames turned red and fierce … then abruptly died away.

Elika gazed up at Reval's island and felt a stirring in her chest, a spark of flame and life. An emotion she thought she would never feel again. Hope. Hope for a better world, without magic. He was powerful, but they had defeated him once before.

Nearby sounds of a battle within the city drew her gaze. Another army of blue-clad guards loyal to Northwind charged the city gate from the inside. She turned and saw more such battles throughout the city. Magic against sword. Sword against sword. Blood-salt against magic.

Blood-salt coated swords slashed the black strands of the Laifae and slew the mages. Large stones flew at the human assailants as a building was ripped apart by dark strands. The mages retreated and fled before they were overrun by human pursuers.

Elika spied a line of carts stacked with barrels of silvery liquid making its way towards the palace gates. Beyond those gates, she saw mages weakened and wounded waiting for their silversap. It was their weakness, as it was hers. Their magic needed feeding. They needed time to recover for the next battle ahead. You need not destroy them with fire and blood-salt, but starve them of power.

Her feet moved. She raced ahead, close enough to cast her magic, and sent thin tendrils towards those carts. Along those strands, she sent flames, which she fed with the wind she conjured, until the carts were ablaze. Their drivers jumped to the ground and ran to the wells for water. The mages raced to put out the flames, but it was too late to save the food source of their power. Elika watched them grimly for a moment longer, then retreated.

Night was falling. The battles had broken up. The wounded were fleeing, the dead lay where they had fallen. Elika made her way into Daetown, where she spied a group of Dae youths throwing dice by the fire.

She sat down beside them.

They blinked at her.

"What's the game?" she asked conversationally.

They relaxed once they heard her Dae accent. "Who are you?" they asked in reply.

"Name's Eli." Her voice was hoarse and oddly dead-sounding to her ears. It was an effort to speak at all. "My pa's off fighting with Lord Trustar's men, trying to take the walls, so I came along to cook for 'im when I can find some food."

"You look like a girl," said the fat one.

She shrugged. "So what if I do?"

"It's better than sounding like a Dae," grumbled one of them with a soft Alterrian accent, who too looked like a girl.

"Know how to play dice?" asked the one with the head of wiry red hair. He was the largest of them, and thus, by the unspoken laws of the street urchins, their leader.

"I know how to win, not so good at losing."

They laughed. "A cocky one, ain't ye. There you go then, you can throw first. We're playing for chores, not pebbles or coins. This round is for laundry. You lose, you'll be doing it tomorrow."

Elika settled into the game and proceeded to lose that round to earn herself the unpleasant chore of washing blood, piss and shit off soldiers' clothes. She had learned from living on the streets that even the bravest were not above soiling themselves when faced with death. She'd done it herself, too, when she was younger, to her eternal shame.

As they played, she learned their names. There was Red Clay with red hair, who the others looked up to. Hairy Berry was the fat one with a soft growth of hair on his chin and jaw. There was Winy Ginny, the girl among them who also dressed in boy's clothes.

Then there was Fast Fox with restless fingers, which always tapped or toyed with a stone, a button, or else anything to hand. He rolled the dice. "Damn, looks like I'll be cleaning swords again. I hate the blood. There's always bits of flesh to scrape off, too."

One Eye's men staggered past, drunk and laughing, wearing all manner of wounds, some of which were bandaged with rag strips.

"Who's taken over One Eye's gang now that he's dead?" Elika asked. "Who's running Daetown?"

"Where have *you* been?" said Hairy Berry.

"Blood Dog's in charge now," said Red Clay as he threw his dice.

Elika raised her head at that. "Blood Dog," she echoed. That did not sit right with her. She could not see him as a gang leader, or a leader of any type. Their last meeting also left her deeply troubled. She put aside those thoughts for now and threw the dice.

They played until late and settled to sleep around the fire. But there was no sleep for her. Shoran's eyes haunted her nights and there was no holding back the tears.

An unstoppable river of grief flowed out from her until blessed darkness drowned her. And when she slept, she dreamt of his kisses, the gentle touch of his strong hands, his body afire above her ... and his bitter, broken laugh as he turned to ash. And she dreamt of the spider aflame, burning and burning, and she was burning with him.

Ima lesa mana nera elesa, Aleyala. Those inexplicable, power-laced words seared her soul and she wanted to scream from the pain they now caused her.

Then the spider turned into a man, brushing her hot skin with his hand, drawing away the heat and the pain of a hundred blood-salt fires lit around the city. She opened her eyes to her dream and her fingers caressed the burned, scarred face above her. "Shoran," she mumbled sleepily and her heart broke into a million pieces all over again. "I'm sorry I killed you."

His scarred, raw lips brushed hers. She closed her eyes and lost the dream to darkness.

She awoke shivering, both hot and cold at once.

Red Clay stood above her. "You look sick," he said. "Been sweating all night and mumbling something about the spider and killing someone. Tried to wake you twice."

She had been there before, lost to feverish dreams when men lit blood-salt fires close to her, and she burned inside them in her dreams. She pushed herself up. Her body felt raw, her mind unrested.

"We got to wash the clothes since we lost the dice for that chore," said Hairy Berry. He was carrying a basket with blood-stained shirts and soiled trousers. Elika joined him at the well and they began to scrub.

Around them, newly arrived wounded limped along the streets, some lay in roughly sewn tents where women tended to their wounds. Haunted-looking soldiers and city guards rested by the fire.

Elika washed and hung the clothes on a line, then joined the others at the communal stew pot. She did not allow her mind to think or ponder beyond the motions of getting through another day. She forced herself to eat, to listen to the soothing hum of humanity, and to speak when others turned to her. She forced herself to pretend that grief was not devouring her inside.

As she ate, she learned that King Southfire had decreed that there was only one heir of the Scared Crowns. Terren's seat of power was his. Duke Firewind of Wavestar, sent an ambassador to offer his full support to King Southfire, declaring Northwind an imposter.

"Southfire would rather the duke send him his army," said Red Clay over his watery stew.

"Thought he might, if only to avenge Lady Kristina's death," said Fast Fox as he toyed with the belt of his tunic.

Elika looked up from her stew. "Lady Kristina is dead?"

"Haven't ye heard? Had her throat cut, they say. No one saw the assassin. But everyone knows it must be Northwind or Warwind, or both. He can't have bastards running around, claiming the right to his throne." Fast Fox said it with an indifferent shrug, as if killing women with babes in their bellies was just a way of things and not to be dwelt upon.

She knew Mite would never do that, not to the woman or his babe.

"Why would a man kill his own babe, bastard or not?" Red Clay echoed her thought. "Makes sense that Reval would kill Northwind's child. He hates Northwind."

And so they argued about who'd want to kill Lady Kristina and why her father had not sent his army to Southfire's aid.

Elika ate in silence after that, a suspicion niggling at the back of her mind, to do with Blood Dog.

She finished her meal and the rest of her morning chores. Afterwards, she went to *Eagle's Feather*. It was bustling with men, both wounded and merely battle-worn, drinking their ale and snatching some rest.

She saw Bobquick with his head wrapped in a bandage, sitting alone in the corner. She strode straight for him and slipped into the seat in front of him.

His jaw hung open. "You're alive … they said you were dead." Blood seeped through the dirty bandage. "They said One Eye killed ye 'cause you were a traitor."

"I'm not. And as you can see, no one's killed me."

"Someone killed One Eye," he said gloomily. "They say it was a god who done it."

Shed not your tears, my love.

Elika felt a sensation akin to a knife twisting in her chest. "Why would a god kill One Eye?" she asked dismissively, if only to stop Bobquick dwelling on such horrors.

"'Tis true. He and a dozen of his men were found dead in a cellar with blood all over it. A dark mark was burned into the flesh of their chests. The mark of a spider. They say gods can rip a man's life out of him."

"What happened to you?" she asked with a nod to his head.

"Wasn't fast enough, that's what. Got cut by a magic-lover. But Sally Pickaxe knocked him out dead in one hit. We've been trying to take the city gates that are keeping Northwind out. If he can get into the city, it'll be his. But mages are guarding it, and there's no sign of the Rogue. They say he's dead, or she. Some say it's Arala returned. Don't know what to believe anymore."

"Don't go fighting anymore, Quick," she said. "Let grown men fight their own battles."

He shook his head. "Got to help them. They killed Tom. Northwind will avenge him. They say he means to kill every mage in the city. Half of 'em already fled just thinking of it."

"I'll set this right, Quick," she said and rose.

"Don't know what you can do. You're just a girl."

She ruffled his hair and left him there looking miserable.

At another table, she found a group of men she recognized as once being loyal to Rory. "Need to find Blood Dog. Do you know where he is?"

They turned. "Not seen you around here for a while."

She knew these men were not close enough to Rory to know what went on between her and him. She also knew they were decent enough, with families and children of their own.

She shrugged. "Been busy with the war. Doing laundry."

"Blood Dog's taken over Lord Nightkill's residence, now that One Eye's dead," said one of them.

"See him over there?" She nodded to Bobquick. "See if you can take pity on him and keep him away from the fighting."

"Do we look like nursemaids to you?" another growled.

"No, just men who might want to protect a kid, one of their own kind, no less, who's got no one else to look after him."

They swore under their breaths, and one of them rose and strode to the boy, sitting at the table. As she left the tavern, she gave Bobquick one last glance and saw his face light up with that wide-eyed expectation of a lost pup who had found a new master.

~

Blood Dog did not rise from the seat where Rory once sat. He barely raised his eyes to her as she entered, before dropping them again to a ring he was turning and tapping on the table. He said not a word as she approached the table where his feet rested. Nor did he lift his gaze when she sat in front of him and threw her own feet on the desk, pushing aside a stack of thick tombs on royal and noble lineages.

Worse still, she was not even certain she was looking at the same man. His clothes were clean, his hair washed, and there was no stench about him. Even his beard was trimmed. His clothes, though, were as beggarly as they had ever been, despite him inheriting the mansion and Rory's wealth.

"You cleaned up, Dog. Almost didn't recognize ye," Elika said as lightly as she could into the suffocating silence.

But he just kept flicking the damned ring, saying nothing.

"Look, Dog. Don't know what passed between you and Shoran …" Her voice choked on speaking his name aloud. "Nor why you were acting all upset and falling to your knees, but I need to talk to you."

At her words, he finally lifted his gaze to look at her, and there was nothing sly in it, none of his usual mockery, no filthy insinuations. He simply looked at her.

"Surprised to see ye back here. Heard what them bastards had done to ye," he said, with no more feeling to it than one who's relaying the price of cheap meat at the market. Again, the silence stretched, as if he knew not how to speak to her, his gaze again on his ring. A dark blue stone flashed past as he flicked it, and an emblem on it she could not quite grasp.

"Look, Dog. Did you kill Lady Kristina?"

The ring stilled. Again, he lifted his gaze to hers. "And what if I have, mousy?"

Another turn of the dagger to her chest as she saw Shoran burn. "I just want to know why. I know it was you. I can see it in your eyes."

He lifted a glass filled with amber liquid, downed it as if bored, then dropped his head back against his chair. "Spare me the fools in all their guises. Look 'ere, queeny. There's a saying among the gods. Fate is like a garden. It must be tended and nurtured, else weeds will overrun it. So I'm weeding, see? There's a time and place for bastards, for jilted lovers and scorned women. This is not one of them. If Northwind had not felt the need to drop his pants and seed the poor lady, I'd never need to do what I did."

"The babe would not be a threat to anyone for decades."

"That's where you be wrong, little queeny. Think on it. Southfire's got his crown. But he has no heir, bastard or not. The thing about Sacred Crowns is that if you look back far enough, they're all intermixed. No line is pure anymore, save one." He paused and his gaze grew intent on her. "Now, Southfire or Northwind will kill one another. Though if my suspicions about

Prince Adren Southfire are correct, it's between Northwind and Northwind, hey mousy? Don't know who will kill the other, and don't care either. But if either of them dies, Firewind has a bastard grandchild who'll be the next heir to the Sacred Crown. Now he can twist it whichever way he wants. The heir is not just Northwind's. The bastard child is the heir to all the crowns. 'Cause Northwind is the heir to all of them. Long ago, his ancestor wed the daughter of Eastrise. Before that, Westwater. And Northwind had a daughter who went on to wed Southfire's heir. See what I am saying?"

"Then why would it matter? Let the bastard child take the throne. There's four crowns anyway."

"Have you looked out the window, mousy? Do you see what the two heirs to the Sacred Crowns do? Now imagine centuries of this, city after city besieged and raised as they battle for lands and dominion. The four demigods divided the world between them, and not amicably either. It was a truce and never a true peace. Each of them wanted to be the sole king of the entire realm. This is what they and their heirs seek. To have peace in Seramight, you can only have one king, or queen if Fates deem it so. The wars must end. Fates will choose who will be the victor, but only one crown was ever destined to be worn."

And it was as if the veil parted from her eyes, and she suddenly saw Blood Dog for who and what he was. Aye, he was the heir of the Sacred Crown, but he was also serving the gods. They called men like him the Dark Gardeners of Fate, for it was their task to shape fate to the vision of the higher gods.

"Which god set you on this path?"

He poured himself another drink from the bottle and raised a toast to her. "Now you finally see me, queeny. The same god who claimed you, the one who slays men for you in vengeance." He downed the drink.

"You are Syn'Moreg's servant," she uttered, and again the knife twisted in her chest.

"I am no one's servant. Shoran and I go a way back."

Shoran. A turn of the blade in her chest. Blood Dog knew him as Shoran.

"I wouldn't call us friends," he continued. "But he ruffled my hair a time or two when I was a lad growing up in Elder Valley. And later we were united in common purpose. The fourth king of Westwater, with the power to traverse the veil and visit the orchards, seeded me in my ma. She was of the Asari tribe. Her name was Liassa. But I've not enough god's blood in me to tap into the wells of magic. And only one fate is ever afforded the fifth descendant of the demigods."

"The Gardener of Fates."

"Aye, and the garden has grown very weedy since Arala joined the two realms. Syn'Moreg's been striving to fix it, but it takes centuries for seeds of our deeds to grow and bloom, and no doubt he thought he had it all arranged. Until you came along." He threw back his head and laughed. "Oh, what must he have thought? I'm surprised he didn't kill you the moment he saw you. Guess your prunny is sweeter than I thought."

"You're a foul dog," she said.

He laughed again, without humor, and it was a self-deprecating laugh. "Been alive too long to care about such things. Know how many prunnies I've tasted in my life? More than that overgrown prude, who's claimed ye, I dare say."

Elika studied him. She thought of Meyara, of Orolan the crow, of Southfire and aye, Shoran. So many of these beings were tending to the Garden of Fate, shaping the world, molding it into their vision. And she had become one of them the moment she discovered her powers. Magic. It was at the heart of everything wrong with their world, for it made power a being in its own right. It sought life and wanted to be avowed and hailed.

Long ago, Shoran had told her that her power, her magic, would not be contained. It would always seek its own voice. The need to change and shape the world was a part of her, born of the power magic gave her. And that need would never ebb. With startling clarity, she understood that now.

"What is your name, Dog?" she asked him softly. "Shoran called you Elrik Westwater. Are you him … the fifth and last king of the Sea Kingdom, slain by Reval, leaving behind no heir?"

His mirth died, and his gaze fell away from her, and again he turned the blasted ring in his fingers, tapping it on the table as he did. "Aye, he slew me. And I was looking forward to death. To peace and release from this endless existence. But then Shoran came upon me and took me for healing to the Sachi priests. I cursed the bastard for his interference. By the time I came to, he had sundered the web and the world." Blood Dog pushed aside the empty glass, grabbed the bottle and drank out of it. Then he threw his head back on the chair. "Always I was careful to never seed an heir or a bastard. Never took a wife. Never even left a whore with a babe inside her. Westwater line was meant to end with me, queeny." He drank out of the bottle again. "But even I was no match for her wiles."

"Elrik," she said mildly. "What passed in that cellar? Why did ye go falling to your knees and looking at me all funny?"

He closed his eyes. "Ah, mousy. You'd not want to know. 'Tis best if you just let me be and never lay your eyes on me again." She had never heard him sound so forlorn and broken.

"Please, Blood Dog. Shoran ... he kept things from me. And now he's gone."

"Gone?" His head snapped up. "What have ye done, mousy?"

Tears filled her eyes. "I killed him," she choked out hoarsely. And it was a relief to confess it, to speak it aloud, to hear herself say it.

He just stared at her. And stared and stared. Then he closed his eyes and rubbed his face. "Oh, mousy, what a fool you are. Just like me. If what you say is true, then we are all doomed. And you are our doom. And I was the bastard who helped to make you happen." He buried his head in his hands, heavily running his fingers through his hair. "Go, live, and die. For I cannot undo what you have done. No one can, save perhaps the gods if they get here in time. Nothing we do now matters." Then he laughed. "I should have cut off my cock, save that I knew it couldn't happen." He laughed again without humor and raised his glass mockingly to her. "I underestimated you, Fate Slayer, for you are not what I thought you to be. Go, plant those weeds in the

Garden of Fate, and we'll watch how they grow. And here is your other weed to tend to." He slid the ring towards her.

She looked at it, but did not touch it. A stone as deep blue as the ocean was set in the ring. It bore the emblem of a watery crown.

"'Tis the ring of the Sacred Crown of Westwater. It's yours now, by right," he said bluntly. "Do with it as you will. March to Ilikan, if you wish, and take the ocean and the islands from him."

Elika stared at the ring. "What are you telling me, Blood Dog?"

"What do you think I'm telling ye, queeny?"

She raised her eyes to him. He was looking at her steadily. She stood up, knocking the chair over, and ignoring the ring, strode out.

~

Days went by where she knew nothing but the cries of the wounded, the stench of rotting flesh, the tending of festering wounds and washing clothes of blood. Days of cooking, laundry, oiling weapons, whilst waiting for Northwind's next assault on the city. And when the night arrived, and the Abyss loomed high above her, yellow eyes haunted her wretched dreams, churning and ripping her soul apart.

Might be she was cursed, in truth, for too often his whisper soothed her nightmares. Whilst the gentle touch of his rough hand upon her face and the soft lips upon her cheek would ease her grief. Too often she reached for his hand and cherished its warmth, afraid to open her eyes lest she awake. Then it would fade and she would want to weep all over again. And sometimes when she awoke, she imagined there was an echo of warmth on her skin, the lingering memory of his lips on her cheek, the faint scent that made her ache with longing. Just a dream, she would tell herself as tears returned to her eyes. She dreamt such dreams often in those days of war and endless hours of battles as Captain Trian's soldiers fought their way towards the main gate.

But as days passed, Mite's army remained encamped. Yesterday, they had fallen back after another defeat. Many lay dead between the city walls. Priests went out to retrieve the bodies and pile them on the pyres. Thrice now, Northwind himself had charged those gates with his men, and each time he failed to reach them. She had watched from afar the line of mageguards on the outer city wall, sending black tendrils to wind around the legs of galloping horses. Mageguards conjured a wall of fire to block their advance, and water to turn fields into impassable mud. They summoned the winds to rip men from the horses and throw them from the sky. The magic attacks were brief but destructive. The mageguards tired quickly and had to be carried away.

Sometimes Elika joined those fights, sending her magic against the mages. But like them, she tired quickly, and her attacks were never enough to break the long line of defenders along the wall and beyond the city gates.

Today was no different. The skies were grim and dark with red-tinged clouds. Rain weighed the spirits of the battle-worn. She climbed to roofs, as she did each day, to take in the defenses and the strength of the attackers.

She watched as Captain Trian's men were pushed back from the main gate until the wounded turned and ran. Today, once again, Trian had lost more of the streets, which they had gained with the blood of his men. The united battalion of men and mages pushed back his forces. Each day, Daetown lit more pyres for the fallen, and hope gave way to the growing certainty that the sword was no match for magic. They were losing this war.

A strange calm descended on her, as everything slowed around her, and instead of the roofs, she saw a garden, with trees made of chimneys and smoke. The mages were the weeds in the flower beds of humanity. And she was the gardener who had to remove the weeds. Fate Slayer. Might be she was, for she suddenly knew what she had to do—her one task in this war, the one that would restore order to their world. She had to open the gates for Mite.

Captain Trian Truestar fought hard to give him just that, but the gates were protected with magic and mageguards. And only magic would break them apart. But Mite needed to believe that they would be opened for him, so that he would charge at them with the full army of his men. If she failed, they would be slaughtered.

The day was waning. She had to act soon, for each day, Mite lost more and more men. It did not take long to find an abandoned house to sneak into, one that belonged to a rich pouch. In his study, she found a parchment next to a silver-feathered quill and a small jar of ink.

She sat down at the desk, chose her words and wrote,

Northwind,

Tomorrow at dawn, your time to rule will come. The gates will open. Upon the blood of gods, I swear this. Do not delay. The streets are drowning in blood and red fires are burning life from our realm. The web is dying. Ride with all your men at your side. Those loyal to you await in the streets to rise. Fear not the unknown, for there is nothing behind you.

Your friend,
The Rogue Mage.

With her blood, she signed and sealed it.

Now, she only needed to get inside his camp to deliver this note.

The city was sealed and surrounded. Not even Captain Trian could send a messenger out. Yet so many times she had thoughtlessly followed Shoran when he traversed the world. Always, he had set the path for her to follow. But he was not here now, and she had to find her own path.

She strode to the wall, closed her eyes and opened them again in the dark corridor. It was empty, silent. No doors marked the walls. On instinct, she reached for Shoran and found only emptiness where his essence once breathed. A void where a link once existed between them. And that emptiness engulfed her soul and choked her.

She turned and fled back into the world of man.

The night was upon them, for it was late autumn and days were short. Many retired to their pallets and beds. She stood at the wall, in a shadowed alley where she would not be observed. The stone was solid beneath her hand. She reached out with her mind, seeking, though she knew not what. Before, she would seek Shoran, and his essence would lead her to him through the veil.

She imagined the camp beyond the city, thought of Mite and his essence, and probed for the path to that place beyond the walls of Terren. The stone beneath her hand grew faint and vanished. She stepped forward and through.

A woody scent of cooking fires hit her nose, and she opened her eyes to a city of tents. Men were asleep around the fires. The sentries at the edges of the camp strained their gazes towards the night and the walls of Terren aglow in the light of the torches. Elika moved and merged into the life of the camp. She threw a log on the fire and picked up discarded bowls to wash in a trough nearby. Then she settled beside a group of sleeping camp followers and waited for dawn.

She slept only briefly and jerked awake to the hum of activity. Before anyone paid her any attention, she joined the camp followers in their chores. Some looked at her questioningly and nudged each other to look her way. She was careful not to meet any eyes as she handed out bowls of stew to newly risen soldiers. Then she sat on a wooden stool and began to oil the armor outside one of the tents.

After a moment, as she expected, no one was looking her way, not even the soldier emerging from the tent she sat beside. Inside, she glimpsed a camp whore still asleep in his rolls. He went about his ablutions, wiping himself with a damp cloth beside the barrel of water, before pulling on his shirt and joining the other soldiers by the cooking fire, where he was given a bowl of hot milk and grain.

There was talk, but it was not of the battle, but of the things that awaited them back home, of the lands they were promised, and the lack of ale and wine in the camp. They spoke longingly of the whores who made rounds through the camp and recounted cherished tales of their loved ones who were waiting for them to return.

Her own thoughts drifted to Blood Dog. She did not want to think about their last meeting, had avoided doing so these last days. She dared not entertain the possibility that the ring he pushed towards her, was hers by right of blood. He was wrong, else he was mistaken. For if there was any blood shared between them, she would surely hate him. Might be she hated him already for the detached way he regarded her, as a man might an unwanted bastard. For the casual way he pushed his damned ring at her as if it was a belated, worthless gift of a forgetful father, to wipe away years of neglect and abandonment. Her parents were dead, it was all she needed to know. It was enough for her.

It was late morning when there was a shout of cheer, and she looked up to see Mite riding through the camp. Beside him, on a fine horse, rode his beautiful bride, Lady Mirana. She looked downcast, though she tried to smile at the soldiers, who were surely half in love with her themselves. But it was Mite who pulled her gaze. His face had grown harder, harsher. And there was a cynical twist to his lips Elika had never seen before. Though his lady wife said things to him, he not once glanced at her, and his replies were brief.

Elika put aside the leather armor she had finished repairing, and slipped into the curious crowd before Mite's eyes found her by chance. As she did, she saw him start and turn to look where she had sat not a moment ago.

"My love, what is it?" asked his lady.

He did not reply as his gaze searched the crowd. His eyes had always been sharp, and his senses alert. Elika knew he would spy her shortly, so she slipped away and hid behind the soldiers hailing their king and queen.

Lady Mirana drew level with him, looking concerned. "My love?"

Without a word, he spurred his horse onward, looking agitated, his jawline tight and harsh.

Elika followed the others who were eager to see where their king was headed. They did not ride far before Mite dismounted, and without interest helped his bride down from her horse. They were outside a large tent flying Warwind's banner. The queen went inside, leaving Mite alone with Duke Warwind who'd come out to greet them. He looked like a king himself. There was a strong, regal quality to his features and bearing, despite his late years. He had shrewd eyes, that were not unkind. But as they gazed on Mite, it was not hard to see that there was tension between the two men.

They walked aside from the soldiers.

Elika crept closer, circled and hid behind one of the tents until she could just make out what they were saying.

"My spies tell me they are certain it was Southfire who killed Lady Kristina," said the duke.

"We need proof to give to Firewind. Without it, he will not listen. He claims to have proof that your agents were the ones to blame."

Elika knew that could not be true. Firewind only had suspicions … unless Blood Dog wanted him to think Warwind was responsible.

"Forget Firewind, we do not need him," said the duke. "His army is not his to command. I warned you of this, Aeronmite, yet you would not listen. Her death, no matter by whose hand, is on your conscience. We should never have gone there, and you should have …"

"Enough! I will not be berated like an unruly child. Firewind can still cause us problems by turning others against us. The death of his daughter will gain us new enemies. I have also received word from another of my spies. It appears Trian has been less than honest with me. One Eye's death was by Syn'Moreg's sword. His mark of a spider was burned upon the bodies and a warning written in fire upon the walls. And from what I can gather, One Eye was in league with the Rogue Mage. There is no doubt about it anymore, it was a woman with noble bearing who killed the archmage."

"It can only be Arala, then. I've had my own spies seeking the truth of this. There's a rumor the Rogue is a Dae girl."

"A Dae girl?" Mite echoed, and she heard a strange note of tension in his voice.

"I don't believe it either," the duke said thoughtfully. "Just as many of my spies told me it was a man dressed as a woman. Others claim it to be the Goddess Neka herself, avenging Arala's death."

"We will get to the bottom of this matter once we take the city." He began to walk away, his steps long and harsh.

"Aeronmite," the duke said carefully, and there was an abrupt halt in Mite's steps. "I am not one to pry into the affairs between a man and his wife, but Mirana is my daughter, and I wish to remind you that she is your wife. You need an heir, especially now that the only other Northwind in existence has been murdered with his mother."

"I have not neglected my duty, Warwind," Mite snapped. "I seeded her once, and I will do it again. Perhaps if you did not feel the need to drag her with us across the lands to battle, she would not have lost the babe."

"I had no choice, Aeron. Would you see her and my grandson she carried murdered like Lady Kristina?"

"She was better guarded in Windhay than here on the road."

"She might have still lost the child. Her own mother lost five."

"A fact which you did not mention when you pushed her into my bed," Mite replied cruelly.

"Damn it, Northwind. My daughter tells me you have not visited her bed in many days."

"I am not your stud, Warwind," Mite roared. "And I will speak with her about carrying her complaints to her father rather than her husband."

"You gave me your word when I gave you my army."

"And I wedded her, did I not? You'll get your heir when her womb is ready for another."

"*Your* heir, Northwind."

"Aye, my heir, and Mirana is my wife and you will stay clear of what happens between us."

"I must …"

"You must do nothing! Am I your king or some damned whore you tell when and who to bed?"

There was silence. Then, "Forgive me, my king. I overstep myself. You are right, of course. The queen must rest."

Mite stormed off.

Elika watched him charge back to his horse and ride away, and she could not help thinking how much he had changed. She followed him and watched from a distance for the rest of the day. Men and camp followers alike gravitated to him. There was always someone who sought an audience. Most of his day, he spent in council with various captains and soldiers.

Elika waited until nightfall. Mite was outside his tent speaking with his commanders, all looked grave and worn.

Under the cover of darkness, she crept behind his tent. No one was inside. Lady Mirana was in her own tent, no doubt awaiting the nightly visit from her husband.

Elika kept out of sight as she released a fine wisp of her magic strand, gave it the letter, and sent it through the gap into Mite's tent. She placed it on the table, pulled in her magic and waited hidden outside.

Shortly, Mite returned with another lord trailing in his wake.

"Must you two always argue," the man was saying as he followed Mite into the tent. "Warwind is as angry as a bear in a trap."

"I'm sick to death of him, Rex," Mite said.

"You are here because of him, Aeron. You have enough enemies. Do not make an enemy of him. You'll find no man more loyal."

Mite breathed out harshly. "Let us speak no more of him. He said his peace, and I said mine."

"Yet your queen sleeps alone again tonight."

A drink was poured. "I'll visit her later."

"She is beautiful, Aeron. Why do you dislike her so?"

"I don't dislike her. She's a fine lady."

"She is madly in love with you. Let go of the past and see what is before you."

"I tried, but the past is haunting me still." There was despair in his voice. "I've been seeing phantoms, Rex. In the camp today, in Windhay ... in Terren also, in the harbor ... Might be the world has truly turned and the dead are walking among us. Or might be I'm going mad, seeing what's not there to see."

"That's possible, seeing as Alafraysia is all around us. One moment you think you are in Seramight, the next Alafraysia intrudes and shows us things that are not there. I've been here ten years and I've had many visions, especially after a few drinks. But Luce always sets me right. You should have crossed with me when I asked you. You were like a brother to me, you and Trian both. Never understood why you stayed behind. Our fathers were dead, either in the rebellion or by the knives of assassins. Had you come with me when I followed Trian across the bridge, you wouldn't be so broken now."

"I wish you stayed behind. After you left, it was never again easy for me to sneak into the priests' temple," Mite replied with a note of humor, and Elika heard his old self in his voice.

"I fear I was never made for a life as a priest. Reading and scribing day and night and chanting their damned prayers that do nothing but give me sore knees. I was never so happy as when I crossed the bridge. Except when I saw your damned hide emerge from that mist eight years later. Almost didn't recognize you. Trian and I have given you up for dead. Thought maybe you had turned to dust like others."

"It was not so simple for me. I left too soon, in truth." He sighed, frustrated. "I've made many mistakes, Rex. Lady Kristina among them."

"She must have been special, seeing as all the whorehouses and fine ladies couldn't make you forget the damned girl."

Elika frowned. Forget who, Lady Kristina? He loved her?

"What's this?" mumbled Mite, and there was a sound of paper being opened.

"Rex, who's been in my tent?" he asked mildly, yet steel laced his words.

"No one. The guards are posted outside, and I've been facing the entrance all evening."

"There is a note from the Rogue Mage." Mite's voice was dangerously calm.

Footsteps. Silence. Then, "It must be a trap. Southfire wants you to attack. They must have a plan to break your army."

"I know these words," Mite said in that calm, deadly voice that would have sent the boys in the Hide scattering in all directions. "Fear not the unknown, for there is nothing behind you."

"What do they mean? A secret code?"

"It cannot be …" Mite mumbled and Elika held her breath. "I spoke them once to another … a friend."

Long ago, Elika had overheard him whispering those words to Penny. She was too young to remember why Penny was weeping, why she clung to Mite's shirt wishing to die. She knew now, though. It was after he rescued her from the city guards. Penny said things Elika did not understand, yet made her terrified, for she had never seen Penny so broken.

Neither of them knew they had been overheard, and Mite would trust Penny with his life and the lives of all his men if he thought the note was from her.

"Wake Warwind and get the men ready," he barked. "We march on the city at dawn."

"You cannot believe this note, Aeron."

"Rex, if you disobey your king's order again, I will have you in chains. Wake the commanders and wake Warwind."

"As my king commands," he replied stiffly and marched out of the tent.

Elika sighed in relief, whilst chilling with that haunting finality. *What have you done? What if you fail?*

But those thoughts did not stir the dread they once might have. *If I fail, we all die.*

Shoran's burning skin and bitter, pained laughter flashed through her mind, and she realized that she was not afraid to die. Nor did she fear the inevitable end he had spoken to her about. Come what may, she would open those gates or die trying.

With those thoughts, she strode into the night and returned to Terren the same way she had come.

~

At dawn, trumpets sounded from afar. Answering bells rang through the city. Everyone who could, grabbed their weapons and raced to the walls they held in Northwind's name. Elika joined them at a distance. She raced along the roofs and came to a stop above the broken part of the inner-city wall where magic had severed it from the rest of the city's defenses.

It was one of Captain Trian's favorite haunts and he had defended it fiercely. From here, his archers could shoot arrows at Southfire's men along the outer wall. Trian's men were there now, sending a volley of them at the guards on the main city wall. Elika ducked as they fired back, then rose again and peered at the land beyond. An army of ten thousand men was charging towards them, with Mite at the head. The king of old rode to reclaim his crown, to reclaim the lands lost to the tsaren and the Laifae. It was a glorious sight, beyond any she thought she'd ever see, one from which songs and tales were made. It was the sight mankind would never forget, and she allowed herself a moment to bask in it, hoping that Pebble was also watching.

She could almost hear his ballad now, of the blinding dawn light shining off Northwind's armor, of the cry on his lips and the sword of ice raised high. Of the thick rain of arrows flying from the city wall towards him. Of magic strands rising from the ground in their path, tripping horses and grabbing men out of saddles …

Through cloud and deadly rain, they rode,
Undaunted by the strike of arrows.
And many fell upon the dirt,
Beneath the hoofs of charging army …

She was living that song now, in which Aeronmite Northwind cut through the black strands with the swipe of his glistening blue sword. He charged on his horse, drawing his men onward, slaying magic and men in his path. The ground churned beneath the storming army, and around her, men cheered and were spurred on to fight with the ferocity of the last battle. And flaming arrows flew at the mages on the wall who were sending their magic against Northwind …

> *A vengeful rain of flame and blood,*
> *Fell hard upon the warring traitors,*
> *And mages burned where they had stood,*
> *As the dark river dried and faded …*

Aye, she was inside a song, or one of Bill Fisher's old tales, watching the magnificent terror and splendor of war for the freedom of man. And might be she belonged in that song, too, for she turned her attention on the mages, felt for their essence and pushed them back into their own realm, to merge with the Black River of their kind. The ground beneath Northwind stilled as the black snakes of magic vanished.

"Fight for Terren!" someone shouted, and she recognized Pebble's rumbling voice coming from one of the city's inner walls. "Fight for your freedom mankind! Fight for Northwind!"

And she was glad that he was watching, for now, she knew that this moment would forever be sung of in the taverns and by storytellers at firesides.

> *Sing of the Rogue, for all she's done,*
> *Sing fondly of her love for mankind,*
> *For though her part was only slight,*
> *Forget not that she fought beside you …*

Mite charged on and on, his horse a fierce, unstoppable beast, his sword of ice flashing in the sun, a cry of fury on his lips. Blood of his foes streamed down his face and his armor.

Elika's heart swelled, and she rushed to help him, unravelling mage after mage until no magic remained beneath the feet of the charging army.

The army reached the walls and soldiers threw themselves against the waiting force of the defenders.

Elika found another mage and …

She staggered back from the impact to her stomach.

She looked down. An arrow shaft stuck out from her gut. *No. Not now. Not yet.*

Panicked, she yanked it out with a groan.

She leant on the chimney, breathing and bleeding and dying.

"Shoran," she uttered his name as a prayer and recalled his teachings.

She focused on the essence of her soul, drew on it, closed her eyes and healed her wound. The effort drained her.

She took the flask she had strapped over her shoulder, and drank deeply of the silversap inside it, leaving nothing behind.

Power surged through her, restoring her spent magic, and she turned her attention towards the gate. Beneath it, mages kept it locked and protected. She sent her magic towards the giant doors in the distance but was repelled by another force. And the glorious song in her ears began to fade, for there was no victory, and no glory for mankind.

No, she could not fail. There was no going back. She would be part of that song—nameless, but not forgotten. Elika focused on the mageguards beneath the gate. As she had done with the archmage, she peeled back layers of consciousness, and one by one, sent them back to Alafraysia.

Then she knelt and touched the tiles of the roof and sent a wave of power towards the gates. "Destroy them," she whispered. "Blow them apart."

She pushed that command outwards, drawing upon the essence of the world, putting all her strength and force into that swelling pulse of magic, driving it onward to break through the shield guarding the gates.

A deafening blast ripped them apart and a terrible wave rolled through the city. It shook the ground and air and the sea as the gates and the wall that held them blew apart, sending rock into the air.

Silence fell.

Northwind and his army came to an abrupt halt, reining in their horses as the stones from the city wall rained down on the defenders and attackers alike.

Elika's legs gave way. She sank to her knees, feeling as if her body, too, was blown apart by the same magic. It hurt everywhere, and the stones crashing to the ground seemed like pieces of her flesh. She lay down, beneath the spinning sky, pulling in her magic, trying to reform herself.

There was another blast … no, it was a roar akin to one … a cheer that shook the stones she lay upon, and the chants filled her ears.

"Northwind! Northwind!"

"For Northwind!"

"Fight for your king!"

Elika pushed herself to her knees again, to witness the last verse of the song, in which Northwind charged and led his army through the gap in the wall where the gates had been. A great battle cry resounded as Southfire's men rushed to meet them. And in the last verse, there was a clash of two kings, as both Southfire and Northwind fought towards each other, slaying man after man in their way.

> *Blood dripped from the faces of two kings,*
> *Their swords clashed in an age-long battle,*
> *And sparks of ice came from the steel,*
> *As Northwind's wrath sliced through false king …*

A magic strand wound around Mite's throat. He cut through it with his sword. Southfire took a moment of his distraction to stare at his chest in surprise, where Mite's sword sliced through armor and leather and skin. Mite regained his balance on his horse and charged again at Southfire.

Elika saw Captain Trian, another hero of the song, charge the mage who had sent his magic against Northwind. He attacked the mage with a blood-salt sword, whilst the mage fought back with more tendrils. Trian leapt aside, slashed through them, reached the mage and cut off his head. But more and more mageguards sent their magic against Mite, as he battled the wounded and bleeding Southfire.

She reached for her magic to help him, but it was faint and slippery, like her essence. Soldiers leapt to Mite's defense instead, fighting magic with red-tipped metal swords. Then she saw Mite yanked off his horse by a black strand. He landed heavily and lay motionless on the ground.

"Mite!" she cried and pulled herself to her feet. Southfire was still seated on his horse, looking down at his opponent. He jumped down and strode towards Mite with sword in hand.

His comrades ran to surround him, putting themselves between their king and Southfire. And they fell where they stood as he advanced on Mite. Southfire lifted his sword ...

Mite shook his head and looked up at the sword above him. Using what strength she had left, Elika pushed out the black tendrils of her magic. They wound around Southfire and he stumbled back, unbalanced. It was enough for Mite to roll, grab his sword and rise again to his feet.

Elika's vision began to dim. She fell to her knees, and breathed, just breathed. When she looked down again, Mite was pulling his sword out of Southfire as his guards rushed to surround their fallen king and carry him away. Mite paid them no mind as he turned to fight the mages still casting their magic whilst Southfire's soldiers fled. When the mages around Mite were dead, he limped towards his horse and mounted it with the effort of a gravely wounded man.

Despite that, he sat tall and straight, as he raised his sword. "The city is ours!" he cried.

"Northwind! Northwind!" The city roared in reply.

And she watched him ride towards the palace and the seat of power, where his men were ramming the gates. Elika tried to move, wanting to break them apart also, but her legs would not obey. Everything was spinning. She pulled out the flask with the last of the silversap and sucked the few remaining drops from it. They were enough to steady her, nothing more.

"Open the gates, you fools, 'tis Northwind come to save you," shouted someone at the defenders of the fort.

"Open the gates or be traitors to mankind," yelled another.

"Northwind! Northwind!" shouted the soldiers below.

The defenders hesitated, then lowered their bows and swords, as King Northwind rode towards them, holding his sword of ice high. The sun flashed on his blade, like a beacon of hope, and the defenders of Terren's Seat of Power rushed towards the gates and pulled them open for their king.

> *Six hundred years of blood and mourning,*
> *Of sleeping vengeance of the dead,*
> *Does he of the old kings of glory,*
> *Rides back to claim the kingdom's fate.*

Thus, the ballad ended, and Elika laughed through tears as King Northwind rode through those open gates to claim his Sacred Crown.

But the unsung battle was not over. Up and down the streets men were fighting the last of the mages. Fighting and dying, for magic was too strong for many of them. She gathered the last of her strength granted to her by the few drops of silversap.

For men I die, she thought, and Shoran's face flashed before her eyes. For surely there was no life without him. And she pulled upon the strands of that wonderous essence, found and undid all the archmage's creations within her reach, and sent the Laifae back to their realm.

"Northwind! Northwind!" She heard their cheers.

She lay back and felt at peace. Might be she was ready to leave the world behind. Or maybe she just needed to rest …

"ARALA!" A terrible roar pierced the sky and shook the wall beneath her.

Above her, Reval's island city spun in the sky. It cast a shadow over her. And from it, upon a cloud, descended a figure of a man with fire where his hair should be, his red eyes and burning gaze fixed on her.

CHAPTER THIRTY-FOUR

Reval's Madness

"It is said that long ago, when Arala fled Reval, he had found her in Seramight and brought her back to Alafraysia as a prisoner. Before then, we, the Laifae, never understood the power of blood binding. For she was not imprisoned by any magic he possessed, but by the magic of her blood and the oath she gave him. No power is greater amongst the gods. Centuries passed before she was able to break free and once again flee to Seramight, where she might conceive a child. Although we searched everywhere for the details of Reval's magic that held her for so long, there is no record of it. Our tsarin himself says nothing, save that the chains that held her were the ones she gave him as a gift of her eternal love."

The History of Alafraysia and Seramight,
By Mageguard Bluelight

"ARALA!" The roar ripped the air, and the flames emerging from the apparition's head burned brighter.

Elika rolled, struggled to her feet and limped away from the approaching nightmare.

The being floated towards her, his arms spread wide. "MY LOVE!"

She tried to run and stumbled as vortex winds appeared out of nowhere. They surrounded her like the bars of a cage, imprisoning her in their restless dance around her. She staggered to the edge of the roof, but a wall of mageguards rose on clouds and blocked her escape. Desperately, she reached for the magic in her, but found only a weary and spent ball of power refusing to heed her.

The tower ... she put her hand to the chimney, focusing, seeking the path ...

The chimney burst into flame, its heat pushing her back, as Reval advanced on her. She turned and another wall of fire appeared in front of her. The wall of flame closed her in, its heat burning her.

It's not real, she chanted, for fear fed their magic.

A being walked through the flame, a man with hair afire and eyes of molten embers. His fingers were smooth, bizarrely long appendages that flexed as he walked, and had no fingernails.

Elika gathered what magic she could and threw black tendrils at the tsarin. He grinned, his eyes alight. "My love, 'tis indeed you." Effortlessly, he caught her magic strands with his hand, wrapped them around his arm like silk and yanked.

Elika fell forward. Tried to pull back her magic, but he held her firmly. She tried to crawl, but his hold on her magic was absolute. He walked forward, whilst wrapping her magic around his arm.

Elika pulled out her last weapon, the knife she never went without.

He stopped above her, his gaze merciless and mad in equal measure. His hair was fire, but she felt no heat from it. He tilted his head and smiled like a delirious youth. "Arala, why do you run from me? Do you not remember who I am?" There was anguish in that question, and madness churning in his eyes that terrified her.

Elika's throat closed up. She wanted to tell him she was not Arala, but her lips remained sealed. Her tongue would not move to deny him. This was the tsarin who had started the Sundering War and slaughtered the houses of the Sacred Crown when he had learned of Arala's suffering. The tsarin who had burned their world when he had learned of his beloved's death. He had convinced himself that she had once again returned. What would he do to Terren and to Seramight if he lost that hope? What would he do to her if he came to suspect that she was not Arala he so desperately searched for?

"Arala, my love," he said and knelt in front of her. He touched her face gently, his hands soft as silk, and far too warm, his fingers strange and fluid.

Elika recoiled from his touch. She wanted Shoran. Wanted him now more desperately than ever.

Reval pulled back his hand as if burned. "Long have I grieved you, and when they told me you were dead, I did not believe them." He studied her with a frown. "This face you wear bears your old likeness, but it is … plain. Never mind, Arala, in time we will restore your beauty. I am here now. You need not run and hide. I will protect you, my love."

Elika shook her head, a denial she could not contain any longer.

Suspicion crossed his eyes. "Why do you look at me as at a stranger?" And in his eyes, she saw doubt seed its roots, and close in its wake was monstrous fury.

"I am but wearied," she managed to say with a wavering smile, trying to keep that hot fury at bay.

"Blood will tell," he uttered and out of nowhere, pulled out a silver bracelet with a red stone. Before she could stop him, he snapped it closed around her wrist. On his wrist, he wore a matching one. Both their stones glowed red. His fury vanished and a wide smile broke out on his face. "Blood does not lie, my love. The bracelet knows you. Our bloods are mixed. My blood flows through your veins and yours through mine. 'Tis was your gift to me."

Elika could only stare wordlessly at the glowing blood-stones on her bracelet and his. The bracelets must be mistaken. She was not Arala … she could not be.

"Why have you been killing my mageguards, my love?" He tilted his head quizzically. "Do you still blame me for Syn'Moreg's deed? It was not my fault. I told you so before. You were angry with me, but I was not to blame for what men did to you and then to our people. But never mind that now. You have returned as I always knew you would. They called me mad. But now that you are here, I will show them they were wrong. Come, we will go home. I have restored our palace to what it was. You will remember it in time. I, too, came as a babe to this world … it confuses your mind. Come, my heart. I wish to make love to you."

"No!" Elika slashed at him with her knife and tried to crawl away.

He gripped her arm, took her knife and cast it aside. It bounced and rolled off the roof to the street below.

Then, with the strength beyond that of a normal man, he lifted her to her feet, and pulled her to his chest, smiling benignly like a love-stricken fool. "My love, must you always fight me, before drowning me in your passion? You are so fickle in your love."

And then they were flying up and up, upon a cloud.

The ground raced away beneath her feet. The roofs grew small, and it was all she could do not to give voice to her terror. She gripped him tightly as Terren grew distant below, before vanishing completely. And there was no land, no sky, no clouds, no sun or stars, only the white and churning emptiness. And up above, his island spun and spun in the sky, which was no longer blue but colorless and shapeless.

Elika closed her eyes and once again sought the path to Shoran's dark tower. Once again, an invisible wall blocked her path, and the bracelet on her wrist burned hot.

"Oh, no, my love," he said in a sultry voice. "No more running. You are back where you belong. We are going home to Alafraysia. The gift you gave me will keep you close to me forever. Never again will I let you go, my love. Never again will we be parted."

Author's Note

Dear Reader

Thank you so much for reading Book 2 of the Sundered Web series, *The Rogue Mage*. If you liked Elika's story, and wish to know what happens to her next, know that I am working hard on the third and final book of the Sundered Web Series, *The Fate Salyer*.

In the meantime, please get in touch, leave a review or merely a rating to let me know your thoughts on my book.

If you would like to be updated on my new releases, please subscribe to my newsletter here:

www.alexthornbury.com/subscribe

I will not spam you, and you can unsubscribe anytime.
For now, know that you are never far from my thoughts.

Alex Thornbury

ACKNOWLEDGEMENTS

Being an author is a lonely thing. We toil away until our hopes feel like a dusty landscape of our dreams unrealized. We tread the minefield of endless edits and reworkings. Yet in the end we are not alone on our journey.

I would like to thank the wonderful folk who have helped me along the way and made this book what it is today—Barbara Unkovic and Rob Bignell for their expertly edits, Alejandro Colucci for his artwork and cover design.

A thank you also to Simon Ward at Simon Says Web Design, Albert Griesmayr at Scribando for his marketing talents, and everyone at Smith Publicity who worked to promote my first book, with a special thanks to Andrea Kiliany, Olivia McCoy and Kellie Rendina for bringing this series to the attention of the readers, bloggers, reviewers and editors out there.

And most of all, a special thank you to Brian Keaney who guided me through the dusty landscape of my hopes towards the meadows of my dreams fulfilled. His tireless insights, edits and comments have morphed me from a struggling writer into an author I am today. I would not be where I am today without his help and guidance and brutally honest feedback. I am forever in your debt, Brian.

About the Author

Alex Thornbury is an award-winning author. She grew up in Cheshire, UK, and developed deep love of history and fantasy thanks to the many castles she visited as a child. Though she grew up to be an Alchemist by trade, she never stopped fantasizing about other worlds, dragons and epic battles. She has abandoned her Alchemy and potion making career and is now a full-time author of high fantasy.

www.alexthornbury.com

Facebook:
https://www.facebook.com/author.alexthornbury/

Instagram:
https://www.instagram.com/alexthornbury.author/

TikTok:
https://www.tiktok.com/@alexthornbury.author

Goodreads:
https://www.goodreads.com/author/show/22845843.Alex_Th
ornbury

Newsletter:
https://alexthornbury.com/subscribe-to-my-newsletter/

Bookbub:
https://www.bookbub.com/authors/alex-thornbury